CW00447146

THE
MOUNTAIN
WHISPERER
JIA PINGWA
Translated by
Christopher Payne
SINOIST

ACA Publishing Ltd
University House
11-13 Lower Grosvenor Place
London SW1W 0EX, UK
Tel: +44 (0)20 3289 3885
E-mail: info@alaincharlesasia.com
www.alaincharlesasia.com
www.sinoistbooks.com

Beijing Office
Tel: +86 (0)10 8472 1250

Author: Jia Pingwa
Translator: Christopher Payne

Published by Sinoist Books (an imprint of ACA Publishing Ltd) in arrangement with People's Literature Publishing House

Hardback ISBN: 978-1-83890-525-5
Paperback ISBN: 978-1-910760-69-7
eBook ISBN: 978-1-910760-70-3

A catalogue record for *The Mountain Whisperer* is available from the National Bibliographic Service of the British Library.

THE MOUNTAIN WHISPERER

JIA PINGWA

Translated by
CHRISTOPHER PAYNE

SINOIST BOOKS

A Note from the Publisher

Jia Pingwa is one of my favourite contemporary writers. He was already famous during my school years in 1970s China, and so his writings accompanied my classmates and me as we came of age, giving a voice to those of us who grew up under the reforms.

Jia chose to set the action of *The Mountain Whisperer* in the rural backwaters of Shaanxi Province, on the Loess Plateau: his native land. Across the novel he casts in stark light both the simple goodness and the backward superstitions of the ordinary folk who inhabited it during an era of massive national upheaval, starting with the bandit uprisings and civil wars of the early 20th century then traversing revolution and its grim excesses all the way through to 'reform and opening'. Those who find themselves at this bottom tier of society are capable of both kindness and evil, honesty and treachery, devotion and abjection, tenderness and brutality. Under his pen, minor village officials, kidnapped women and funeral singers all become vivid, deeply human characters.

Thanks to the hard work of the rights managers at People's Literature Publishing House, we have been able to bring this fantastic author's works into English; first with *Broken Wings* in 2019, now with *The Mountain Whisperer*, and if all goes well through many more works across the coming years.

For those less familiar with Chinese literature and culture, we recommend that Jia's afterword be read first. He attaches these thoughtful pieces to each and every one of his works, and they always provide enlightening (and often deeply personal) background information, as well as all-important historical context.

May you enjoy this book as much as we did.

Ying Mathieson
Chief Publisher
Alain Charles Asia Publishing

TRANSLATOR'S NOTE

Jia Pingwa has included nine excerpts from *Pathways Through the Mountains and Seas* in his novel *The Mountain Whisperer*. They serve to link his own tale with tales of the strange and marvellous from ancient China. In rendering these translations, I have consulted Anne Birrell's complete translation of *Shanhaijing*, or *The Classic of Mountains and Seas* (Penguin, 1999). I have also used Richard E Strassberg's more scholarly *A Chinese Bestiary: Strange Creatures from the Guideways Through Mountains and Seas* (University of California Press, 2002). Strassberg's work is not a complete translation of the Chinese language original, but rather a wondrously detailed examination of the images that have accompanied *Shanhaijing* through its many iterations, and the commentaries many Chinese scholars have written about the work. In places, I have added information from these commentaries, via Strassberg's study, which provides a more complete picture of what the anonymously written *Shanhaijing* was describing about the ancient past and the mythical and fantastic creatures that dwelled in it. In some instances, I have continued to use Birrell's proper names; in other places, I have used Strassberg's, while a few of the proper names are my own. Any errors are of course my responsibility.

A BEGINNING

A RIVER WINDS its way uphill through the Qinling Mountains.

Each and every year, on the twenty-third of the twelfth lunar month, the first day of the New Year festivities, it was custom for the people who lived in the mountains to take to walking back the years. To do this, they'd follow the river. There, along its banks, they'd toddle, stepping over stones, thistles and thorns, trudging east to west. Some would amble on, while others would find themselves becoming muddleheaded. In that haze, the more they'd walk, the younger they'd become. Even their frames would seem to shrink, causing one to wonder what would happen if they kept at it. If they continued to mosey right along, would they wind up right back to where they began, nestled safely in their mother's womb?

Nearly forty miles away along the same mountain range sat Shangyuan, a small village known for the towering mountain that stood behind it, thrust erect like some angry wooden club into the clouds far above. Despite its great height, it was an empty mountain, topped with a giant, yawning maw – a cave so high up in the sky that men and birds alike were unable to reach it. For the most part, the mountaintop remained dry and, on the face of it, inhospitable. At least until a man of, shall we say, certain rank paid the area a visit. On such occasions, it was said that running water would trickle forth. To the mountain whisperer, who was wont to stab his finger into the air as though checking the wind for the stories it told, the water served to announce the arrival in the north of troops under the warlord Feng Yuxiang (1882-1948). Feng was a man known for his dedication to Christianity, as well as his penchant for betrayal (although that was a reputation he'd earn later). Under his command, his forces had marched across much of China. They traversed mountain valleys, straddled gaping gorges of more than seven *li* and passed through the Dayu Mountains that rose up between Guangdong and Jiangxi. They tramped across the Central Plains and marched from Sichuan to Zhejiang. Inevitably, the troops made their way to the capital, Beijing, to have a direct hand in the ousting of the last Manchu emperor, poor Puyi, holed up in his Forbidden City.

Then there was Li Xiannian (1909-1992). On his way to Yan'an, he'd travelled across Hubei and then Henan, following the Yancao Ravine and then up and over the red cliffs that bordered the area. There on the high pass, he came upon a plain of walnut trees, and finally the village of Shangyuan. He stayed for three days, during which time the water on top of the mountain started flowing. In later life, he served a number of years as chairman of the Communist Party.

Mei Lanfang (1894-1961), the most famous Peking Opera star of his time, also visited the area. He arrived in a sedan chair, as was his habit, to see the golden snub-nosed monkey, also known as the Sichuan snub-nosed, and during his stay the water again trickled down from the mountain. When the Chan Buddhist master Xuyun (1840-1959) visited, the same thing happened. According to the mountain whisperer, however, the villagers knew nothing of these past events; for them, they weren't all that important. All they did recall was that, when Kuang San had made up his mind to join the Northwest Army as a company commander, the mountain stirred. But not in the manner expected. During that first winter when Kuang San's convoy passed through the village, the water started gushing. However, it froze almost immediately, creating a great white sheet across the land much like a curtain hangs from the ceiling, obscuring the wall behind it. Strange indeed.

Interestingly, seven years prior to this, when the provincial governor inspected the area due to the drought that had ravaged the land, the entire village erupted in furious gossip, wondering if water would again make its way out from the recesses of the mountain to welcome the important visitor. Alas, on this occasion, the mountain whisperer, who'd heralded previous visitors, never left the cave he called home. Instead, he remained inside, tapping his belly and chanting instead:

A bamboo stem grows soft and smooth,
Voices carry on the mountain wind a family in mourning beckons me,
Beseeching me to sing for their departed;
They ask why I've not gone to see the water spew forth;
A provincial governor has come.
But I shan't sing, no, my hands are busy tapping this tune.
I know in my heart, too, the governor is no one of import,
The water won't come.

Strange indeed, for his words rang true: despite the governor's presence, the mountaintop remained dry.

Naturally, the mountain whisperer's premonition got the villagers talking, with many of the discussions veering off into matters of bewitchment and devilry. They believed the mountain whisperer must be a demon, a goblin, a monster, manifest in his appearance. He was tall, but with a small head perched precariously on his frame. His eyes had a glazed, porcelain appearance, his face was smooth with no trace of stubble. The younger adults in the village spoke of how, when they were small children, his appearance was the same. The older people echoed this assessment. The caves he resided in had been home to an uncountable number of poor families, and yet he'd seemingly been there for innumerable years himself. But he wasn't always there, or rather, there'd be times when he'd suddenly disappear and no one would see him for what felt like years. In his absence, his millstone roller seemed to stand guard at the mouth of his home, eventually taking on a bluish-green hue like the Azure Dragon from Chinese cosmology. The stone itself turned a whitish colour that brought to mind the White Tiger. Unsurprisingly, most villagers believed the old man was dead.

But then, suddenly and out of nowhere, he'd return, walking in his usual manner, a bamboo staff supporting his steps. When he'd left, it was deep in winter, and all he had been wearing on his feet was a pair of flimsy straw shoes, a bit of cotton stuffed into each for padding and warmth. The cotton, he was heard to say, was like the clouds, meaning he wasn't really walking on the ground at all. When he returned, it was summer, so it wasn't a shock to see him carrying a makeshift parasol. His explanation for it was similar to the one he gave for the cotton: the parasol was sunshine itself.

For what seemed like forever, the old man never ate lunch, choosing to drink only a little water instead. Of course, people would ask how it was possible for him to sustain himself on just water, to which he'd respond with a question: Don't trees only need water? Doesn't rainwater bring about new growth from the leftover husks in an abandoned mortar? He then changed topic and spoke of the funeral he'd attended, of the strange thing that'd happened when he sang for the deceased. It went like this:

As he sang and mourned the departed, he began to hear a muffled cackling sound coming from within the coffin. Then, as if in response to the sound inside, a rat scurried its way on top of the closed casket and began to busily trace its steps back and forth across the wooden surface. He watched it perform this ritual, and then, deftly and quickly, he snatched the vermin in a handkerchief and flung it to one side, shouting: "Be gone! To be dead is dead, so take those worries and pain, and go!" The bundled rat crashed to the ground, but then, before his very eyes, it grew wings and took to the sky. The scratching from inside the coffin ceased. Strange indeed.

The excitement over, his ceremony complete, the mountain whisperer decided to stay in the village as a guest, at least for a spell, but when he went to find lodgings, he discovered the place had been emptied of people. Therefore, he had little choice but to return to his cave. Before doing so, however, he made sure to declare to whoever was in earshot: "This won't be forgotten!"

Such were the mountain whisperer's tall tales, shared and enjoyed by those who listened, but believed by few. In truth, some tales seemed to be out-and-out fabrications. Regardless of the veracity of his stories, however, there was a mystical quality to the man. He'd spent his life in between this world and the next, an intermediary for the living and the dead. This is not to say he'd treat you well when you spoke to him, that he'd smile and show a dimpled face. He wasn't that sort of man. He wasn't looking for friends. Indeed, whenever his own time in this world was due to end, it was said he'd rather plunge his failing form into a freezing lake or into a burning inferno and suffer the torment that this would entail. This is not to say he wished to forget. He had no desire to drink the waters of oblivion; his lot was, he believed, to persevere in this world. This was what destiny had bequeathed him.

He wasn't the kind of man to say death was just a passage to some other place, either, like walking over a bridge to some new home. His reasoning was unique. He believed that, since men were made of earth and water, this meant there were other places in the recesses of what we could see, locations buried deep in the crevasses of the world around us. As a result of this intermingling of the living and the dead, of the dead continuing on, communication was possible, either through ceremony or through dreams. Or so believed the mountain whisperer.

It was through his stories of the mundane, mortal world that the mountain whisperer was able to tell of Qinling's past. He knew of the ancient relay stations once used for postal horses. The old stamps were often a source of great comfort; he would gaze at them and remember places he'd been. He could recite clamorous stories of bandits. He recalled, too, the many stories of marriage, of tales that spoke of the union and even sometimes love. Of course, he was also familiar with the desolation of funerals. As for matters more mundane, the mountain whisperer remembered what clothes people wore and what they put in their tummies, of who lived where and who had left. He could even tell you of the particular way they spoke. He knew, too, of the birds and animals that populated the area, the trees and the flowers, their habits and characteristics, their sounds and colours. His knowledge of Qinling was so complete, in fact, that he could tell in great detail the family history of the most important figure of all: Kuang San.

Kuang San had got his start with the local militia before working his way up the ranks, first becoming a district chief, then a political commissar in the army and finally commander of the main force in the northwest. In short, he'd gone from being a young vagabond to prince of the whole region. And not just Kuang San; his extended family also did very well for themselves. One cousin served as mayor before being promoted to deputy governor of a neighbouring province. That cousin's secretary ended up being county chief for Shanyin. Another cousin sat at the top of the provincial judiciary offices, and his daughter-in-law was in charge of the provincial women's federation. Kuang San's sister's son was a chief of police and another nephew served as chief of the armed forces for Santai County. An uncle was in charge of a provincial department of civil affairs, while his secretary held the top post in the transportation department for Qinning County. His wife was deputy secretary. The three secretaries who worked directly under Kuang San all had chair positions as well. One was in charge of the municipal administration, another ran the agricultural offices and the third one was responsible for the forestry department. Kuang San's oldest daughter had held the offices of chairperson for the municipal women's association and deputy director of the city council. His oldest son had first served as chairman of the labour union before becoming a deputy mayor. He was now deputy head of the provincial branch of the Chinese People's Political Consultative Committee. Kuang San's younger son became a bureau chief for the municipal offices in charge of foreign trade, and later on chairman of the board for the provincial electricity supplier; his wife was president of the committee for the advancement and promotion of foreign cultural exchanges. Kuang San's youngest daughter also held an important post, running the provincial education department, and her husband was head teacher for… such and such a unit. One of his daughter's sons was a manager for some company in Beijing, the other a mayor down south. In total, his family held more than twenty senior positions across the country, especially in and around the many counties in Qinling. In fact, out of 143 county and municipal positions, seventy-six had some connection to his family.

Whenever he related this information, the mountain whisperer displayed a familiarity that surprised most of his audience. Not once did he require a family chart to keep things straight, never did he draw a family tree. And when his recitation was complete, he'd simply reach for some wine, take a big swig and end by asking his audience if they wished to know more. Of course, his wine pot was never empty; whenever he lifted it to his mouth, the wine always sloshed out. And no one dared ask if it'd gone dry, fearful that such a question might actually chance fate.

On the surface, he appeared a gregarious fellow, never taking offence to what others asked, or what they said. He seemed happy to talk about the comings and goings in Qinling for the last two centuries, the ins and outs of the people and what they got up to. All anyone needed to do, it seemed, was ask! But despite this appearance, he was generally uncomfortable with fielding further questions. In truth, he'd much prefer to simply head off into the mountains, find a quiet field with just a shepherd and his sheep, and there he'd sit to enjoy the sun, whiling away the time under its warmth, watching the sheep graze, their hearts content to just be.

It was often a father and son who tended the sheep. And as expected of people of their station, life was hard. This pair were both widowers, their days limited to time spent with their flock. The only consolation for such a life was that the son's child, the third generation, had displayed some prowess for learning and was now in the city studying. Neither father nor son could read or write, nor could they tell you how many sheep they actually looked after. All they'd do at the end of every day was round them up, gesturing and pointing at each of them as they were led into the enclosure, shouting this one, that one, this one, that one. Despite their lack of learning, they knew which sheep had returned and which hadn't, even if they couldn't explain how.

But they were good people. If someone paid them a visit, it didn't matter who, they'd end up being offered something to eat, or at least something to smoke. And it often didn't matter what answer was given; they'd simply lay out some food, and then a tobacco pouch. Of course, no one would take them up on their offer; instead they'd ask them about their sheep, about conditions on the hill and about their neighbour across the ravine. The mountain whisperer's cave could easily be seen, its gate drawing one in to a blanketing darkness. The visitors would ask the shepherds if they knew the age of the mountain whisperer. The father would reply that all he could remember was when he was young, on those occasions when the mountain whisperer had lifted him up onto his shoulders to play about, his hair was already white. The visitors would follow up this information by asking for the old shepherd's age, to which he'd reply with a question: How old do you think my son is? About fifty. You're right. He's fifty, which makes me seventy. Then they'd turn to the son and ask for confirmation; the son would nod in affirmation.

When spring came to Shangyuan, it brought a blanket of clouds with it, transforming the sky into a sheet of billowing whiteness that swallowed the village. It was at this time that the mountain whisperer reappeared, standing on the riverbank at the eastern edge of the village. It wasn't much of a river, however, having been nearly dry for more than fourteen months; nearly all the water had drained away, leaving mostly sand in its wake. He crossed it by means of a bamboo pole, and as he did so, the people working nearby watched.

No one asked where he'd been or where he'd come from. Instead, their questions were about the clouds that were blocking out the sun. He ignored them, however, his attention instead focused on the sheen of gold that lay underneath. Amazing! The river had dried and hardened and left large clusters of gold strewn across the riverbed, each worth at least six yuan. As the knowledge dawned on the people who heard his words, they soon regretted not having collected the sand before now.

The mountain whisperer collected none. He spent the remainder of the summer and autumn, aside from his travel and assistance to houses beset by tragedy, picking the wild berries and other fruits that grew on the mountainside. On occasion, he'd even have company as the villagers would also scour the hills for the same wild berries and fruits, their favourites being the schisandra berry, wild and sour dates, cherry tomatoes and august melons, and even the occasional kiwi. As he picked, he would shift back and forth from shooing away crows to depositing berries into his mouth. And when the sound of a woodpecker carried on the wind, he'd click his teeth in concert with it.

Autumn was often a time when many of the villagers would be stricken with illness. They'd be feverish and cold all over, their flesh spongy and wet, even if they happened to be buried under multiple quilts due to the cold weather. All except those who had eaten the berries and wild fruits like the mountain whisperer – they remained unafflicted.

The mountain whisperer greatly enjoyed bathing in the sun, much like the musk deer who resided in the forest on the other side of the mountain. He'd stretch out like the deer, basking his body under the sun, keeping warm in spite of the cold weather. His appearance on the mountainside would often serve as a signal for the villagers to hunt the deer. They believed that if he was out there sunbathing, the animal's glands, particularly the musk pod, were properly mature and full of prized musk, which they would extract for great profit.

The following year, the plains beyond Qinling were wracked by an earthquake, the tremors and aftershocks even reaching Qinling itself. The doors to the homes across the region shook and rattled on their hinges, forcing the villagers out of doors to sleep upon the grass. They did this for seven days, fully expecting further reverberations to follow. But they never did, much to the villagers' consternation as they'd been hoping the quakes would come quickly. Then, finally, on the eighth day an aftershock did rumble through, a single one, which caused no loss of life, nor property damage of any kind.

Freed from worry about an imminent geological disaster, they suddenly realised there'd been no sign of the mountain whisperer since the initial quake. Had he known already there'd been nothing to worry about? The father and son shepherds went to check on him, noticing the dove tree blossoms that had bloomed around the entrance to his cave were white like snow. Inside, lying quietly upon his raised bed, the mountain whisperer was motionless. His straw sandals lay beside the bed, a hill squirrel nestled safely within. When it saw them enter, however, the squirrel washed its small paws across its face, and then moved off in somewhat nonchalant fashion. The mountain whisperer was ill. He'd never been sick before, but the affliction that had befallen him now was serious. His legs were swollen, his skin coarse and inflamed. His lips, so accustomed to telling tales, were pinched together tightly like a baby's arse. And even though he tried to open them, no words emerged.

The shepherds, leading one of their animals into town, went to see the local physician. After they described the condition of the old mountain whisperer, the doctor replied there was nothing he could do. He was adamant: he treated illness, he couldn't bring back the dead, or the near-dead. The father and son protested, stressing the importance of the man, that he shared his spirit with that of the mountain, but the physician's reply was again blunt: even gods must die. He then ushered them out, making sure they took the sheep with them.

Exasperated and dejected, the two shepherds returned to the mountain whisperer's cave. They decided to sit beside him and wait for the end. After which, they would handle the burial arrangements. For twenty days and nights the mountain whisper ate nothing, drank nothing, but death still did not come. A small, flat drum that was hanging on the wall seemed to gently tap out a rhythm in the evenings all by itself. His bamboo pole stood perched behind the door to the cave. It was dark in there, a sickness hung in the air. But still, when morning came, streaks of light would reach inside.

With the end of winter approaching, the village children would start returning for their spring holidays. The elder shepherd's grandson would now be able to attend to the old man, stand vigil over him. The young boy's presence would allow the shepherds to return to their flock. They instructed him to be watchful, attentive, but should the old mountain whisperer breathe his last, he wasn't supposed to cry out nor let tears roll down his face, for the old man would finally be free of the pain of this life. And besides, great explosions of grief would only serve to distract the spirit of the dead, it could easily lose its way. After all, the path to what came next was not hard to miss. And if that were to happen, then he'd be a lost spirit, adrift, left to roam as a wild phantom, a ghoul. They all agreed they didn't want this. The boy had to be sure to make an offering too, if he died. He had to be sure to burn the hell money the old mountain whisperer would need. Only when this was all complete was he to leave the cave and call out to them. They'd wait for such a call and come immediately, of course.

And so, after he returned, the boy stood vigil. At first, he stayed away from the prone figure in the bed, but after some time passed and he became more comfortable, he went to look at the mountain whisperer more closely. The old man's eyes were shut tight, and the boy believed perhaps he'd already died. He stretched out his hand to feel for breath under the man's nose, and was surprised to discover he was still alive. Over the next few days, this became his routine, his ritual, constantly checking to see if the mountain whisperer was hanging on.

But young boys become distracted easily, and soon he grew bored with the monotony, deciding to look for something else to do instead. Strangely, perhaps, his mind turned to his studies, particularly classical Chinese, especially since he was disappointed with his grade. The time he spent in the mountain whisperer's cave thus became the time for him to study. To this end, he begged his father to find him a tutor so he could get the academic help he needed. His father agreed, and negotiated a suitable fee: for his effort and time, the tutor would be given five *jin* of wool, equivalent to about half a kilogram.

As for the tutor, he was learned and erudite, his knowledge encompassing diverse fields, especially those of the ancients. The text he brought with him was *Pathways Through the Mountains and Seas*. Their schedule was set: he would come once each day, and they would study two passages each time.

Despite being bedridden, the mountain whisperer's ears were alive and trained on what was happening around him; his mind was clear and attentive, too. He therefore listened carefully to the lessons the boy received. As he did so, the wind would occasionally force its way into the cave, bringing with it the blanket of white clouds, enshrouding the place in an eerie mist. There was also a strange scent carried on the air. Butterflies would flutter about. It was a very odd scene indeed.

Now, the mountain whisperer had sung songs all his life, his words had told the tales of past and future dynasties, but he'd never read *Pathways Through the Mountains and Seas*, he'd never even heard of it before. But here, as he lay in bed, this teacher was speaking of the mountains, the seas and the stories they held. He'd never seen the ocean and had no idea of its size, but this didn't stop the folk of Qinling from talking about the seas, even if they were more inclined to believe they were not much bigger than a reasonably large bowl. But mountains, well, he'd been to all the local ones, had traversed every valley and stream. In truth, was there any cliff he did not know?

The old man so wanted to join their conversation, but his body was failing him. He didn't even have the strength to twist his tongue, let alone form words. All he could do was keep on breathing, sometimes hurriedly, sometimes more slowly. The only feeling he experienced was that the hair upon his head continued to grow, as did the hair on his arms and legs, akin to wild grass. Although he couldn't move, he could hear the room alive with sounds. The ants were mustering at the foot of his bed, preparing for their advance. The wings of butterflies flapped rapidly, uninterrupted, then whooshed away. At times, the young boy would be lost in the swirl of butterflies, longing to reach up and catch some, but each and every time he thought of doing so, the teacher would rap his pen over the boy's head and scold him: Concentrate! Once the butterflies left the cave, they'd perch on the underbrush outside and soon transform into flowers.

THE FIRST TALE

Question:

Does every mountain possess spirits?
Should we offer sacrifices to them?

Answer:

There's a saying: the heavens created the myriad things
and sent spirits to accompany them.

Question:

Why must the sacrifice be in white?
Why not some other colour?

Answer:

White is a clean colour. It demonstrates sincerity.

THE FIRST TALE

To begin, let me tell you a little about *Pathways Through the Mountains and Seas*. In short, it's a compendium of the strange and fantastic. It includes tales that cover the ancient geography of China, its heavenly texts, history and myths. It touches on meteorology and describes the various flora and fauna that inhabit the land. There's information on minerals and medicines, religion and so much more. In total, there are eighteen chapters. *Pathways Through the Mountains* contains five chapters and *Pathways Through the Seas* has eight. *Wasteland Pathways* contains four, and finally *Pathways Through the Inner Sea* has one. The compendium contains the names of more than 5,300 mountain ranges, 250 names of seas and other bodies of water, 120-plus references to animals, and more than fifty kinds of plants and plant life. We'll study the first chapter today, *Pathways Through the Southern Mountains,* which begins with the Magpie mountain range.

I'll read the first sentence, you read the following one.

The first mountains in *Pathways Through the Southern Mountains* make up what is called the Magpie Range. Its first peak is Shaking Mountain, which overlooks the Western Sea. There are numerous cinnamon trees on these mountains and a great abundance of gold and jade. There are plants here that look like onions, but with greenish flowers; they are known as the Prayer-for-More. Eating them will save you from starvation. There are also trees on this slope that look similar to the mulberry, but their bark is riddled with black markings. Their blossoms, however, possess a brightness that illuminates the ground around them. The tree is known as the confusion mulberry since it is purported to stave off mental confusion should you wear it around your belt. There is an animal that calls this mountain home. It bears resemblance to a long-tailed ape, but it has white ears. It crouches as it walks but runs like a human. Its name is the xingxing. Eating its flesh improves one's running ability. The Lithe-Deer River emerges here and flows towards the west to empty into the sea. Along its banks grow many yupei herbs. When cut and worn about your belt, you'll be free of stomach worms.

Three hundred leagues farther east is Mount Hall-Court. There are numerous fruit-bearing shrubs on its slopes and many white gibbons. There are also great quantities of rock crystal and yellow gold.

Three hundred and eighty leagues farther east is Gibbon-Wings Peak. A great number of creatures live on the mountain, while curious-looking fish swim in the streams that run down its face. White jade is plentiful. There are also many fearsome serpents and reddish-coloured vipers that have needles sprouting from their nose. Both congregate around oddly-shaped trees. The mountain is not to be climbed.

Three hundred and seventy leagues farther east is Mount Sunny-Cherry. Quantities of scarlet gold can be found on its south face, white gold on its north face. A unique-looking creature resides on this mountain. Resembling a horse, its head is white, and its body is striped like that of a tiger; its tail is a rich crimson. It sings like a human and is called the shu stag. Wearing strips of its flesh on your belt is said to ensure you will sire a great many descendants. The River Strange rises here to flow east, emptying into the River Joyous-Wing. Dark-shelled turtles can be found in abundance in these waterways, but they have the head of a bird and the tail of a snake. They are known as the twirling-turtles. They make a strange noise that sounds like wood being split. Wearing a piece of their shell about your belt wards off deafness; it's also good for treating calluses.

Three hundred leagues farther east is Mount Root. There are a great number of streams and rivers, but no plants or trees. In the hillier parts, the waterways are full of fish that resemble oxen, but they have tails that resemble a snake's. They also have wings and feathers that grow beneath their flanks. They make noises that remind one of brindled oxen. They are known as the winged-bluefish. They are believed to die in the cold of winter but come to life again in summer. Devouring their flesh is said to save one from swellings.

Four hundred leagues farther east is Mount Chanyuan. Many rivers and streams start here, but the mountain is bereft of vegetation. It is regarded as unclimbable. Upon its slopes lives a beast that looks like a wild cat, but its mane is much longer. It has no name and is said to be hermaphroditic. Eating its meat can cure one of jealousy.

Three hundred leagues farther east is Founding Mount. On its south face are quantities of jade, and on its north are many malformed trees. A creature lives on this mountain that resembles a goat or a ram. It has nine tails and what seem to be four ears. Stranger still is the presence of eyes on its back. Its name is the boyi. Wearing a piece of its flesh on your belt will remove any fear. There is also a strange bird-like creature that lives on this mountain. Some have said it looks like a chicken, but the creature possesses three heads, six eyes and six matching feet, but only three wings. It's called the changfu. Eating its flesh will keep one awake.

Three hundred leagues farther east is Mount Green-Hills. Much jade can be found on its southern face, while fine, dark cinnabar litters the north face. A nine-tailed beast that resembles a fox makes its home here. When it howls, it sounds like a human baby, but it is said to be a man-eater. Anyone eating it is protected from insect stings and certain toxins. A dove-like bird also lives on this mountain. When it makes a noise, it sounds like an angry man shouting. It is called the guan. Wearing its feathers and flesh about your belt wards off delusions. The River Brave starts high up on Mount Green-Hills and flows south to empty into Carp-Wings Marsh. Scarlet fish inhabit the River Brave. They are said to have human faces and call out like mandarin ducks. Eating them can prevent scabies.

Three hundred and fifty leagues farther east is a mountain called Winnow-Tail; it slopes down into the East Sea and its face is covered with sandy gravel. The River Spate emerges here to flow south into the River Breed. There is much white jade to be found in the River Spate.

The ten peaks of the Magpie Range cover a distance of 2,950 leagues. The deities of these mountains, from Shaking Mountain to Winnow-Tail, all possess the bodily shape of a bird and the head of a dragon. The proper sacrifice to these gods is an animal that is uniform in colour. The ritual calls for a jade blade being buried with the corpse of the animal. Glutinous rice is to be the offering of grain, served on a jade disc and mixed with husked rice. Blanched reeds are to be used for the seating mats.

Do you have any questions?

Question: The title of this book includes the word 'ching', which is the same word that is used in the titles for the *I Ching* and the *Tao Te Ching*. But we don't call it a 'classic' like we do those texts. Why's that?

Answer: Ah, yes… well, there is debate about this, but the book we're studying references history and experience and has little to do with the philosophical reflections of these other works, hence the difference in its name.

Question: So… do you mean to say it's just about the names and places of mountains, the rocks you can find there, as well as the plants, birds and animals? That's a bit strange, isn't it?

Answer: Why, the nerve! This book's about ancient China, boy. The names given here are important! When this book was written, people were just beginning to understand their place in the world and in nature. They didn't have names for the mountains that surrounded them, they didn't know what to call the seas, nor did they know what to call the vegetation, nor the rocks, the birds and animals, as you say.

To these people, the world they found themselves in couldn't help but be strange, frightening even. Now Qinling, this place we call home, well, it was rife with chaos in ancient times, without form. It was the rat that used its teeth to tear open the day and let in the sun, the ox then tamped down the earth and settled the land... have you not heard these stories? This was how ancient people understood the world they lived in. It was also how they came to know the rat and the ox. You could say *Pathways Through the Mountains and Seas* is the record of man's growth, it tells the story of how humanity learnt of the strangeness he found himself in and how he, in turn, overcame his inherent fear of the unknown.

Question: Why are there so many instances of phrases where they say things like: if you eat it you won't starve, if you eat it you'll have a good stride, if you eat it you won't itch and if you eat it you'll not need to lie down?

Answer: Ah, this in an interesting question. Let's start by noting that tigers, leopards, hawks and falcons are all predators, that is, they eat meat. Cows, horses, pigs and sheep, on the other hand, eat grass. When the heavens made man, however, it was never decided what food they should eat. Consequently, man has forever experienced hunger, we've constantly had to search for what is actually edible in the environment around us, and while we can eat pretty much anything we find, we do have to continually figure out ways to prepare the things we gather, the things we catch. In a manner of speaking, we could say humanity has broken the natural food chain and established its own path, our history is one written according to the food we eat.

Question: How's it that there's a ram-like creature that has nine tails and four ears, its eyes on its back, and, as the book says words to the effect that, if we respect it, we won't feel fear? Earlier on it talks about a stag-like animal and if we were to wear it, it'll 'help us in having children', and what about the animal that's both male and female and that if we eat it we won't fall victim to 'jealousy'?

Answer: Good questions again. Hmm. Let's consider. Perhaps respecting the boyi will allow us to 'feel no fear' inasmuch as knowing the existence of this animal would dispel any fear should we encounter it on our travels. That's to say, such an animal, with its nine tails and four ears would no doubt be able to hear everything around it, yes? Its eyes, too, would permit it to see in all eight directions. Surely such a beast would never know confusion, it would always know where it is and what was around it. Well, such knowledge would prevent it from ever being afraid, no? So this is what we can learn from it, be alert and aware of one's surroundings; knowledge of the world cannot help but dispel our fear of it. Now, as for wearing a piece of shu stag as a means to increase one's virility and ensure one's line continues, let's first consider where it lives. I mean, discovering that it inhabits "a mountain that's littered with pure gold on its south side and white jade on its north", well then, such a mountain in such perfect balance, with such resources, wouldn't it surely furnish man with the ideal conditions to procreate and thrive? Alright, your last question. With regard to the animal that's both male and female and the question about its flesh freeing us from 'jealousy', well, we might postulate that jealousy actually emanates from the differences between the sexes. Now, wouldn't the union of these differences in this animal's flesh set the stage for harmony between men and women? In the ancient past, humanity existed in much greater intimacy with the natural environment than we do today. They understood nature, they adapted to it instead of the other way round. Step by step, this knowledge has served as the foundation for how the Chinese people think, and, do you know what, it continues to do so in the present day.

Question: Does every mountain possess spirits, then? Should we offer sacrifices to them?

Answer: There's a saying: the heavens created the myriad things and sent spirits to accompany them.

Question: During sacrificial ceremonies, the text says blanched reeds should be used as seating mats, but why must it be whitish and not some other colour?

Answer: Well, that's fairly straightforward. White looks much cleaner and better displays the devoutness of the ceremony. To trace this custom to the present day, funerary rites also prescribe the use of white, the clothes worn by the family in mourning are white, the corpse is wrapped in white, the attire they're dressed in is also white, the canopy, too, and even the paper that's used for the funeral couplets is white.

No, no, this can't be right. The reason why white is seen at funerals is because simple white cotton is used as paper, and black symbolises a certain virility, strength, liveliness even. When people die, Death comes to collect their souls. If it showed up at a house in which everyone was dressed in black and full of piss and vinegar, well then, Death wouldn't be able to do his job, now would he? And that'd mean the spirit of the deceased would be left to roam as a wandering ghost, and so that's why white cloth is used to wrap the body of their loved one. And how the hell is a magpie a mountain… it's a person, don't you know… Lao Hei's mum is called Magpie. When she died, you know I went off to sing the mourning song for her. Well, they were still stuffing her in the coffin as I got there. Lao Hei's father was trembling and twitching all over, rolled up on the ground like a great big lump. I sorted things out, got him to put on a white hat that helped him gather his wits.

Lao Hei's dad was a fool. He'd been in service to Wang Shizhen's household for ages, never once thinking beyond his position. One day, while weeding the corn fields, locusts suddenly appeared in the sky, blotting out the sun and covering the land. Lao Hei's pa kept looking up at the sky as the locusts descended onto the corn. In a matter of seconds, the verdancy of the vegetation was gone, enveloped by the swarming insects. A few minutes later, nearly half the field was devoured. The locusts left nothing behind but half-eaten stumps. The whole scene terrified Lao Hei's dad, ultimately causing him to flee.

At about the same time, Lao Hei was coming into this world. He arrived backwards, feet first, a stocky baby his terrified dad had to help pull out. Blood gushed everywhere as he did so, covering half the bed and more. After his father had pulled him out, the first words he said were not words of love.

"Shit, he's a dark one isn't he!"

Xique, his poor mum, turned over and died not long after her son was born. Her eyes simply rolled back into her head, exposing a deathly whiteness that contrasted with the colour of her son. Lao Hei grew up dark, his skin like burnt clay left in the kiln too long. People reached out their hands to touch his face, curious to see if the blackness would rub off onto their own hands.

After his mother died, Lao Hei lived with his father on Wang Shizhen's estate. He grew like a weed right before their eyes. By the time he was fifteen, he was taller than most door frames. His shoulders were broad, and instead of two eyebrows he had one long, thick one that extended across his face. A strapping young lad, he would soon accompany his old man out to the southern gully to tend the fields and sow poppies. At around the same time, Wang Shizhen was dispatched to Zhengyang to serve as secretary in the administrative offices. He relocated there with his concubine, leaving his first wife to handle the estate and all his holdings. The lady of the house had fond feelings for Lao Hei, and each time he went to work the fields with his dad, she'd prepare steamed loaves of bread for them, wrapped in a cloth pouch along with several garlic cloves. Lao Hei's dad couldn't help but remark that she'd given them too much, but she would only say that a growing boy needed it. She'd then take hold of Lao Hei's hand and thrust into his palm a small wooden sword made from the branches of a peach tree. This, she told him, would ward off evil.

The administrative region encompassing the town of Zhengyang was gifted with a great expanse of forested area. The trees, mostly camphorwood and pine, grew tall and strong, some reaching forty to fifty feet high. Around the massive trunks, cattle and wild pigs roamed, bears too, as well as some even larger animals. The bears especially enjoyed wandering through the poppies, which meant that each and every time Lao Hei's father tended to the poppy fields, he was sure to strap sturdy bamboo rods over his arms for protection. Once his son began tagging along, he told him to do the same. And should they ever come upon a bear unexpectedly, his father told him, the bamboo would save his life, for while the animal would smile in an almost mischievous manner and try and clamp its jaws round the bamboo, they'd be able to slip their arms right out and flee. His father added that they also had to be quiet when out in the woods, since causing a racket would bring trouble for sure.

On one particular jaunt into the woods, however, Lao Hei couldn't control the excitement he felt at seeing the poppy plants flower. They were simply too gorgeous to behold, especially as the sun shone across their gentle petals and inflamed their reddish hue, casting a multicoloured image across the landscape. He was so overcome with pleasure that he let loose a shout loud enough to shake the heavens and cause the dark clouds to spill a shower. His father cursed his impulsiveness, warning him that shouting would bring out the bears. Sure enough, this being mid-autumn when the bears were most plentiful, his fears were justified: father and son soon came face to face with a growling bear.

In movements much swifter than they could imagine, the bear chomped down hard on Lao Hei's arm, while all he could do by way of response was to try to kick at its flank. In a voice filled with panic, Lao Hei's dad yelled at him to play dead, which he did but not because of his father's words. And then it happened. The bear began to laugh, a deep guttural, boisterous cackle. Lao Hei's eyes strained wide open, astonished at what he was seeing. He waited, unmoving, as the bear laughed itself to near unconsciousness, and then he withdrew his arm, spitting a stinging rebuke at the animal: stupid bear! He thought about drawing out a blade to lop off a paw, but his father pulled him away and together they fled.

Unfortunately for Lao Hei, this was the last day he spent with his father. As they were fleeing from the bear, his father lost his footing and fell over a cliff, dropping thirty feet into the remains of a recently cut grove of trees. The older man fell headfirst into them, and by the time Lao Hei descended the mountainside after his dad, he was shocked by what he saw: a headless corpse covered in blood. Then, upon closer inspection, the gruesomeness of his father's death became clear. He'd impacted the ground with such force that his head had been driven straight down into his chest, a rather painful way to go.

His dad now dead, Lao Hei was an orphan, ostensibly under the care of Wang Shizhen, who assisted with the burial. But beyond this show of consideration, Wang's means to comfort the boy were not what one might expect. He referred to him as an unlucky lad, and then on the same day his father was buried, he took Lao Hei out for something to eat. The young boy could hardly anticipate that getting a little something to eat meant being given a rifle and conscripted into the army. Apparently, in those days, boys like him were known colloquially as 'grain' for the military. This was how Lao Hei found himself to be an enlisted man, swallowed up as provisions for the armed forces.

But despite any reservations he may have felt, he now had a gun, which seemed to suit him so naturally that it became like an extension of his arm. He didn't need to keep his rifle wiped clean either, he simply had to feed it. If he spied an eagle, he'd shoot it dead, the same for a swallow. If he came upon a mangy dog lying about on the road, he'd curse and chase it away. And if it didn't run, he'd feed it too, to his gun. After all, the gun was always hungry. The air would echo with a clap, a bullet would pierce into flesh and blood, and if it were a dog he shot, the top of the animal's head would explode and its tongue loll to one side. Another meal for his weapon.

At this time, the Communist Party had occupied Yan'an in the northern province of Shaanxi and was busily sending out cadres and troops to make revolution, implement some degree of land reform, attack warlords and resist the repeated attempts by the Kuomintang to encircle them. Although Qinling had yet to be fully touched by the turmoil and chaos of war, there were attempts to prevent such initiatives from reaching them, as well as calls to be on guard in case trouble should find its way into the area. Wang Shizhen busily toured every town and village, instructing the people on how they should respond and what they should do.

On 24 April, he was dispatched to the area of Panyu that lay along the Mang mountain range in southern Hunan, near the border with Guangdong Province. The route was a well-known passage for pack animals carrying agricultural produce between the interior and the more coastal regions. Caravans were frequent, which meant there were also many bandits, especially as they would often transport wheat and barley, crops of great value. Some of these bandits were armed, while others would wrap shafts of wood in red fabric in the hope of passing them off as rifles. Quite a few were mountain farmers who would normally be busy tending to their own crops, often spending the better part of their days digging potatoes from the ground.

On one such occasion, when one of these farmers turned bandits fell upon an unsuspecting caravan, the porter in charge couldn't help but challenge him: "Just what the devil are you doing? You look the part of a farmer like me. Aren't we in the same boat? Surely you're not here to rob me..."

The bandit replied with a question of his own: "You're not from Qinling, are you?"

"What! How could you think I was from anywhere else?"

"But," said the bandit, "men from Qinling have square jaws, their voices echo like the clanging of gongs... you're far too frail and weak... your voice carries a foreign accent, too."

The porter laughed by way of a rebuttal, and then claimed to be dying of thirst.

"I've water in my calabash," the other man replied. "Here..."

The porter's eyes shifted towards the ground where the calabash lay. "Thank you, thank you... you don't know how thirsty I am."

Before stooping to pick it up, however, he reached into the basket he carried upon his back and drew forth a small money pouch, intending to pay back the apparent kindness he'd been shown. Then, as he bent to retrieve the water, the bandit's mattock dug deep into the back of his head, killing him dead. A mattock was an essential tool for digging up potatoes. It also served well in digging shallow graves, which the bandit now did, rolling the dead porter into it. As he did so, he wondered how easily the other man's head had cracked, almost as fragile as an eggshell. The deed done, and an ill-gotten profit made, the bandit now returned to digging up potatoes.

Mount Mang was not a safe place, and Wang Shizhen made this clear to Lao Hei as they passed through: "Keep your wits about you."

Lao Hei straightened his neck, which was rough to the touch, and replied: "Who'd try anything with me? It'll be the other round, heh, heh!"

As night came and they settled down for the evening in a hamlet perched precariously on the mountainside, Wang Shizhen was feted by the headmen of the area, invited to enjoy some drinks while Lao Hei remained on guard outside, his rifle clutched tightly in his hands. As the night grew dark around him, Lao Hei was feeling as though he'd gone blind when his eyes were drawn by a flash of light that swept across the headman's encampment wall. Believing it to be a cat or some other animal out hunting, he fired his weapon without hesitation. To his surprise the sound of bullet eating into flesh came with a yelp: "I'm shot!" Realisation came quickly: he'd murdered someone… but he didn't really seem to mind.

The village layabouts all knew Wang Shizhen was visiting the headman's compound. They'd heard, too, he was grossly overweight, his waist being much greater than his inside leg measurement. Upon hearing the commotion outside, Wang emerged to see what had happened, a cigarette perched lazily on his lip. And there he saw a man, slumped against the encampment wall. The bullet from Lao Hei's gun had entered through his mouth and blown the back of his head clean off. He looked at Lao Hei, and simply nodded.

Three months later, the headman arrived at the town's militia offices and told them the grass upon the dead man's burial mound had grown wild and fast. It was luxuriant even, the colour of greenish flame.

Wang Shizhen asked Lao Hei: "Have you ever had nightmares?"

"No."

"You ought to go and make an offering to the man you killed, burn some hell money for him… that'll sort things out."

Lao Hei went, but he didn't make the offering. Instead, he pissed over the man's grave, and on top of the burial mound he buried the root of a small peach tree – this was his offering for the man's soul.

I shall tell you of three strange events that befell Zhengyang in the second half of the year…

The first happened in the village of Chagu and concerned an old lady. One day, her son and his wife were up on the mountain picking ragweed, where they were ambushed and killed by a mottled lynx, leaving the old woman to care for her grandson alone. When the child wailed, well, she'd pull out her withered old breast and jam her nipple into his mouth, but whatever milk she had had long since dried up and no matter how hard her grandson sucked, nothing would come out. Naturally, the child would soon resume crying uncontrollably. The old woman could do nothing but try to console the child, urging him to listen to his granny, to be a good baby. But the child could not understand.

The old lady's cat, however, seemed to listen well and soon began to meow the word 'granny' over and over. On one such occasion, while the old lady was out in the alleyway near her house talking with other villagers about the weather, the cat came bounding up meowing repeatedly 'granny, granny'. The other villagers were astounded and more than a little afraid. They thought disaster was just around the corner, and urged the old lady to strangle the beast.

Soon afterwards, I found myself in the very same village. I'd been asked over to sing, and I happened to come across this old lady. While I didn't speak much to her, she appeared to be still quite sensitive about the cat, and any mention of it would bring her to tears. I wasn't there long, but as I left Chagu and headed for Santai County, the old woman, her grandson bundled up on her back, asked me if she could tag along... evidently, she had relatives in Santai whom she was going to ask for help in rearing the child.

I remember the day we set out. The sky was dark and the rain pelted down on us. The fields were filled with maize that stood about half as tall as a man. Together we walked, more or less side by side, with the baby strapped to her back. His two little feet were nestled firmly in her hands near her waist. And as we walked, she wouldn't stop prattling on: Hold on tight little one, you wouldn't want a wolf to come and steal you away!

As it was just the two of us, well three, I couldn't help but ask about her cat again. Her response was intriguing: If men could grow to look like pigs, while others resembled monkeys, then why can't a cat learn to speak? I could only laugh in reply, and then I noticed her grandson bore a striking similarity to a cat. His ears were pointed and stood erect on the side of his face, his eyes were somewhat bulbous, and as I looked at him then, his two hands rubbed at his nose as a cat would do when cleaning its face. The little boy would never return to Chagu, but instead settled in Santai County in the town of Guofenglou. His name was, is, Liu Xueren, and he became a cadre in their local commune I believe…

The second strange event happened near the end of spring, when falling stars are common. On such evenings when the night sky is lit up by these celestial candles, some folk fear they'll hurtle down into their midst and destroy them. These are the people who tend to cower under stone awnings, hoping to avoid disaster. Others, equally afraid, dive into the furrows that stretch across their fields, covering their heads with their hands as a desperate form of protection. It's funny, really, since all the falling stars only ever ended up crashing into Mount Zhu.

Then, out of the blue, I remember word came that the falling stars weren't stars at all, but meteorites from space, rocks, stones, and that the provincial capital was keen to collect any that actually made it to the ground. Unsurprisingly, people began heading off to Mount Zhu to gather what they could, and they made quite a bit of money out of it, too. The story goes that a man with the surname of Lei went in search of these meteorites coveted by the authorities. And wanting to get a head start on the competition, he set off early in the morning to collect what he could. But when he reached Mount Zhu, the sun still hadn't risen, and so there was nothing to do but sit and wait. He found what he thought was an old felled tree and crouched down to smoke away the last hours of the night. He smoked and he smoked. And when his pipe grew hot with ash, he tipped it over on the tree he was sitting on. He never expected that very same tree to move, and he soon discovered he'd been sitting on a large python and not a tree at all. The snake, however, did him no harm, but rather slithered away, leaving him untouched. Small favour, perhaps, for the man still fainted with fear and collapsed to the ground. That's where he was found hours later by the other villagers who'd come in search of meteor fragments. They picked him up, returned him home, and there he remains, unwaking, a human vegetable.

Now… once word spread about the large python, the people who lived on the mountainside set off to trap it, and before long they'd killed their quarry. I heard that after they finished the kill, the grass and trees all across the mountain withered and died, and forever after, when the wind blew, a mournful whistle could be heard. The air was said to have a whiff of ammonia about it as well.

The third strange event involved Kuang San. By now, everyone in Qinling was aware of Commander Kuang's revolutionary exploits, but who knew much about his youth? Well, as a boy it was said that Kuang San had a rather large mouth, one so big in fact it could accommodate his entire fist. Now, there was an old saying in Qinling that went something along the lines of 'a big mouth eats everything in its path', and so it was to no one's surprise that Kuang San's dad had been heard repeatedly moaning and complaining about his son eating them all into the poor house. And in truth, he did eat a lot. Where most other children had maybe two bowls of rice for their meal, Kuang San would have four at least and still refuse to lay down his chopsticks. On these occasions, you could hear his old man call out: "Enough, enough!" And then he'd forcibly pull the bowl and chopsticks out of his son's hands. It actually got so bad, they ended up selling most of everything they owned, all to keep the boy fed. Of course, they couldn't keep on like this and so one evening, Kuang San's dad stole into his room, ostensibly to strangle the boy. He never did, no one knows why, but thereafter, father and son would go out begging for food together.

Kuang San knew his father didn't think much of him, and he was quite fond of opposing him… sometimes just for the sake of it. I mean, if his father said white, he'd say black, his father said the moon was round, he'd say it was flat… that sort of thing. And so it was when they went begging. At each and every intersection, his father would gesture in one direction and say let's go to the village that lies this way. Kuang San would say let's try the other direction. Their views were forever divergent, each wanting something different than the other.

In those days, it was quite usual for most village households to keep a dog or two, and it wasn't long before Kuang San's father realised he'd better take steps to protect himself. Thereafter, he'd always carry a heavy stick with him whenever they went begging. Kuang San, however, didn't fear dogs. If one charged at him, teeth bared, he'd simply reciprocate and charge at the dog, baring his own teeth in return. Stunned, the animal would generally stop in its tracks, sit and begin wagging its tail instead. When he did beg, Kuang San felt no qualms about nicking whatever food he stumbled upon, such as the dried persimmon a villager might have left out unsuspectingly. They were a particular favourite. He'd even sneak into the fields he walked by to pinch a radish or two that was still in the ground. And if he was found out and chased by those he was stealing from, he'd simply toss away the basket he'd stolen and run off. It was said he had little trouble scrambling over the elevated mounds of earth that divided and protected the fields from the elements, even those that were thirty feet or more high. And compound walls, well, apparently they posed no impediment to him either.

When Kuang San was thirteen, his old father died. In the time leading up to his death, he grew increasingly fearful his son would simply dig a shallow grave near the river to save him the trouble of properly burying him up in the mountains. To prevent this from happening, and appreciating the fact they were always adversaries, Kuang San's father attempted to use reverse psychology to ensure he spent the afterlife in the mountains and not next to the river. Son, he had told him, after I breathe my last, don't bury me up here, it's not necessary. Just wrap me in my death shroud and bury me next to the river. Now, for the better part of his whole life, Kuang San had never listened to his father, never did as he was told. But upon his death, he followed the old man's wishes to the letter and buried him as he was instructed, in a shallow grave next to the river. That spring, the riverbanks nearly burst with water. The old man's grave, such as it was, was washed away, leaving not a single trace.

I remember hearing that after Wang Shizhen had heard these tales, especially the last one, he had roared with laughter and spat out words to the effect that raising a pig might've been preferable to having a son.

Interestingly, Wang Shizhen himself had no son, which is why he took a concubine. His second wife used to work in a theatre troupe, and she had a distinct look about her. She was also quite skilled with string instruments, including the *huqin*. Despite having been married for a good number of years, she still bore him no child. Her saving grace was that each and every time Wang Shizhen encountered some trouble or other, she'd soothe his worries by pulling out her *huqin* and performing some old piece from Qinqiang Opera.

Once, Wang Shizhen and his concubine spent an afternoon under the grape vines that grew just beyond his compound wall, eating, drinking and relaxing the day away with music. As the afternoon turned to evening and the weather chilled, Wang instructed Lao Hei to go to his office to fetch his Sun Yat-sen-style jacket, and the younger man promptly complied. Wang's jacket was his most formal item of clothing. In all of Zhengyang, he, the secretary, was the only person to wear one.

Entering his superior's office, Lao Hei decided to pick up the jacket and try it on before bringing it to Wang Shizhen. He just couldn't resist its allure. As he stood modelling it in front of a mirror, he began to feel a pair of eyes trained on him, and when he turned around, he was surprised to find Wang's concubine staring at him. He removed the jacket as quickly as he'd put it on, and then started to walk off to where his master was seated, a distinct look of anger on his face. The concubine's eyes followed him all the way back to where Wang Shizhen sat. Then, as he moved to drape it over his master's shoulders, the music stopped.

"Be sure to brush off the dirt!" came the shrill voice of Wang's concubine.

"There's nothing on it, I'm sure of that," Lao Hei replied.

Wang's wife wouldn't let it go: "But there's dirt on you!"

Wang Shizhen did not understand the exchange, but Lao Hei knew what she was getting at and immediately removed the jacket from Wang's shoulders and brushed it down. Once done, he placed it once more over his superior's shoulders, staring at the man's concubine as he did so. Then he relayed to him the incident with the snake on Mount Zhu.

Wang Shizhen was astonished: "Such a large snake?"

"Yes," said Lao Hei, "I bet it would be good to use its skin to cover a *huqin* for your ladyship, you know..."

"Yes, yes, what an excellent idea!"

On the following day, Wang Shizhen and Lao Hei travelled to Mount Zhu. Before they departed, however, Lao Hei had a few words for his superior's concubine: "I wouldn't be surprised if that python lived the better part of a millennium!"

The woman did not reply, but her husband did: "Tell me, Lao Hei, doesn't she look like the beautiful fameflower, the very Jewels of Opar!"

After arriving at Mount Zhu, they soon learnt the man primarily responsible for capturing and slaughtering the snake was called Lei Bu, the son of the poor fool who'd been rendered a vegetable due to shock. Lao Hei wasted no time in trying to obtain the snake skin. He walked brazenly into the home of Lei Bu and announced: "The local administrative secretary's here. Where's the snake skin?"

Lei Bu, however, was not at home. Only his mother and father were to be seen, the old lady tenderly caring for her incapacitated husband who simply wouldn't wake up. His body was slowly wasting away, small now, more akin to a child than a man. The two visitors paid no heed to them and walked out behind the house. There, on an escarpment barely thirty feet from the back door, the snake skin was nailed up to dry. Below the cliff's edge ran a mountain stream, so far below, in fact, that it would take quite some time before one would hear the boom of a rock thrown from the edge.

The old lady now appeared behind them: "That snake skin's ours. We're not giving it away… my son's put it out there to call his father's spirit home."

Lao Hei was quick to respond: "How the hell did he hang it up way out there?"

"There used to be a suspension bridge, but after my son pinned the skin out there, he feared someone would try to steal it so he cut the bridge down."

Lao Hei ventured towards where the skin hung and discovered near the mountain stream the carcass of a solitary tree, covered with moss and grass and with bracken growing up about it. The tree must have been split apart some time ago by a lightning storm. The look on Lao Hei's face was clear: he was going to climb the dead old tree to reach the snake skin. As he moved to do so, however, Wang Shizhen shouted after him: "You can't. It's too dangerous!"

"But you need the skin!" Lao Hei's answer was brusque, forceful. Without another word, he clambered up the trunk of the tree. As he did so, the stream far below seemed to rush towards him, yearning to swallow him whole. His body swayed and he cursed: "Fuck!" His grip loosened and he fell back towards the ground. A minute later he tried again, but this time he used his rifle as a balancing pole. Inch by inch, slowly, slowly, he reached the snake skin, grabbed it, and then returned. An instant later the tree cracked with a loud, echoing groan, before splitting into three pieces and tumbling into the stream below.

There was no question he was brave, felt Wang, and after they returned he intended to recommend to his own superiors that Lao Hei be promoted to platoon leader. His second wife disagreed, however.

"The men'll be scared of him like I am," she argued. "He has no scruples, no concern for his own life. How can he be put in charge of other men's lives?"

Wang Shizhen was adamant: "He's done everything I've asked him to… and with great aplomb. He deserves the promotion."

And thus he was given it. Along with the rank of sergeant, Lao Hei was also given a Mauser semiautomatic, a much more powerful weapon than he'd had previously. But despite the adulation, all he could think of was the tree. If it had broken apart while he strode across it… life was hard… he thought to himself, he'd have more to fear in the future than merely being platoon leader.

Another year was drawing to a close, and as was often the case, Wang Shizhen complained about his lower back. Lao Hei, as was his habit, offered advice and said the pain had to do with his kidneys. In Chinese medicine, the kidney is the source of many ailments. By way of treatment, he accompanied Wang Shizhen to Qingfengyi to eat what was colloquially known as 'money-meat'.

Qingfengyi was in the far western reaches of Zhengyang Township, and although it was really only a hamlet, its layout was far more expansive than that of Zhengyang itself. Its streets, for instance, were much wider, and it had everything and more than might be expected in a much larger place.

Qingfengyi also had a great number of donkeys. There were so many, in fact, the business of selling donkey meat, especially the penises, was quite lucrative. Most popular were the rashers of flesh marinated for a month in a sauce containing more than forty-eight different seasonings. The meat, once cut, would be left to pickle and then after the month was up it would be taken out, sliced into smaller pieces, often lightly fried, and eaten that way. It could also be enjoyed cold, a type of jerky. Even the way it was cut was suggestive of the money that could be made since the strips bore a striking resemblance to coins strung along a piece of rope as in olden times. Hence it soon acquired the name 'money-meat'.

There were six shops selling it across Qingfengyi, and each did its best to attract the most customers they could. They'd shout out the benefits of eating money-meat, how it was particularly helpful in increasing a man's virility. On each wooden shopfront they'd place an earthen jar, usually reserved for wine. It would sit there, lidless and filled to overflowing with strips of donkey meat that stood erect, suggestively poking into the air.

As the two men strolled in search of a suitable shop, Wang Shizhen suddenly recalled a favourite, a purveyor of money-meat by the name of Mr Yan. Unfortunately, however, once they reached his shopfront they learnt he'd died the day before, and the family were busily making preparations for the funeral. They were forced to settle on another shop, ultimately choosing one nearby called Defadian, a name that was suggestive of a certain high quality product.

As soon as the shopkeeper spied Wang Shizhen approaching, he reached purposefully for a particular portion of money-meat and hung it in front, easy to see for the customer heading towards him. Then, he deftly pulled out a strip that'd come from a female donkey and wrapped it round the male piece already suspended in the air. The image it created was clear. As if on cue, the butcher responsible for cutting the meat used his blade to slice into the rashers on the table behind. What was being demonstrated was plain: they used live meat to make the rashers. There was a saying, or something along the lines of a saying, that went: what was fit for a man to eat was hated by a woman, and what was fit for a woman was hated by a man, but the act done in bed, well, that was often something unbearable for both. Of course, such a saying only made Mr Yan curl up his lip in disgust; his money-meat was the best around.

At the same time as Wang Shizhen visited, I'd been asked to come to sing at Mr Yan's funeral… I recalled what his younger brother had told me: Mountain whisperer, he said, you must do your utmost to sing the mourning song for my brother, to send him on his way… and if you do, Wang Shizhen will surely come and see.

Singing and performing such a spectacle was all part of the

ceremony when someone passed. To begin, I piled up some wood and set it alight at the main crossroads in the village in order to pay my respects to heaven and Earth. I was then transformed... I was no longer myself, but the mountain whisperer. I could now see into the other world, have knowledge of it. I felt a limitless power engulf me, and when I looked at the people around, I saw glowing auras circling above their heads.

I grabbed my drum and pounded out a beat to call for the lightning and the rain, and then finally I closed my eyes, drumming and singing at the same time as I made my way to the family's funeral hall. I walked smoothly, erectly, without stumbling or knocking against anything. The dead man's family, so pious and filial, followed behind. They rolled together the hemp paper they were carrying and let it trail on the ground behind them, where they set it on fire.

The song I sang first called out to the heavens to open their doors, the Earth, too, as well as the Confucianists, the Daoists and the Buddhists. My song then shifted to the family. I sang of how being filial meant taking great care to select the burial mound location. The coffin, too, must be made of the stoutest wood and the burial clothes of the finest fabric. My song continued and I beseeched the gods of the Three Realms, along with the family's ancestors, to be sure to sit in the central family hall so that they might welcome the recently deceased in the greatest of splendour. In the second to last refrain, I sang of how life and death are but two sides to our presence on Earth. And then, at last, I offered praise to the dead in order to honour those left behind and ensure the family's pride was satisfied.

By the time I arrived at the funeral hall, my back was drenched with sweat, my eyes wide, possessed. The family immediately took to prepare the ceremonial wine. They lit incense and burnt more hell money, then prostrated themselves on the ground, their heads touching the earth as they wailed mournfully. A wisp of smoke curled up from the burning paper, and I saw the spirits and ghosts riding along with it, milling about before finding their seats. It was quite the spectacle, if I do say so myself...

Wang Shizhen, however, didn't come to see it. The afternoon stretched into the night and I continued to sing songs of worship, of flattery and remorse, songs to entreat the heavens for grace and more. Family friends and acquaintances, the whole neighbourhood from up and down Qingfengyi… they all came to pay their respects, carrying incense sticks and hell money, as well as rice and dried meat, all to commiserate with the family of Mr Yan. But not Wang Shizhen, he never came to offer his respects. I remember that clearly. Kuang San did, though…

Kuang San felt he had to offer his condolences to the Yan family. He also brought his bowl with him, and before long was in front of the food prepared for the attendees, busily scooping up noodles into it, not bothering whether he might be taking too much. I remember him struggling a little, unable to manoeuvre the noodles back onto the tray. He used his hand to stuff them into his mouth, shouting: "Where's the salt? Where's the vinegar? Is there any hot chilli oil to splash on them?"

A man next to him replied: "You know why we're all here, don't you? Eat what you've got. What the hell are you shouting for?"

Kuang San did not reply. He stood there, holding his bowl, and then kicked at the wall before murmuring to himself that they probably didn't have any garlic either.

I had met Kuang San three days earlier.

I'd spent a full month in Qingfengyi, residing in the temple dedicated to Guan Yu on the easterly part of the main road. I soon got to know the shop assistants who worked at Defadian, but out of everyone I met there, I became best acquainted with a man whose head was as bare as could be, a man known simply as Baldy.

Besides money-meat, Defadian sold roast donkey as well. Those shop assistants not responsible for the money-meat would be sent to go up and down the streets every day selling other cuts of meat. They'd do this until nightfall, after which they'd return their vending boxes to the store front, and then, under the light of a lantern, they'd place them behind the counter. At these times, no one would direct their attention towards his hairless skull.

One evening, as I finished singing at another house in mourning, I bumped into Baldy on the street. We were both heading for the temple. I remember him speaking first.

"So, how many houses have you sung for?"

I replied that I'd been to five different households.

"If I were a family head, I wouldn't let you come," he continued. "When you do, so many people die!"

"But if I don't," I offered by way of a rejoinder, "the deceased won't be able to stride upon the Six Paths and thus will never be reborn. What's more, Qingfengyi is rife with ghosts, many who gave their lives for the nation..."

Baldy looked all around, apparently fearful of what phantoms might be lurking. And so I taught him a technique to deal with them: when walking at night, I told him, take both thumbs and press them hard into the base of your ring finger and then make a fist in order to prevent any evil or nasty apparition from getting in. Baldy made a fist, firm and strong, and together we strode across a cleared area where mounds of wheat had been piled up.

As we walked, a wolf, seemingly out of nowhere, leapt out in front, frightening us both. In near panic, we flung the roasted donkey meat and noodles we'd been carrying and started to flee. As the wolf plunged its teeth into the meat, another figure emerged from the pile of grain and snatched it away. It was then we noticed the first animal that'd jumped out was no wolf at all, its tail was too curly. No, it was only a dog, and the second creature, which now stood up, was in fact a man.

Baldy was first to speak: "Kuang San, what in heaven's name are you doing hiding in a pile of hay with some dog?"

"Shit," he started, "he's cold isn't he... if I didn't hold on to the mangy beast throughout the night, he'd freeze, wouldn't he!"

Baldy and I regretted throwing away the meat in haste. But Kuang San, apparently without shame, asked for more: "Grandad, give us a little more and I promise to repay you in the future!"

"What might you have to repay me with?" I asked.

Before replying, he did something quite unexpected. First, he scrounged around for an earthen tile that he then buried, stamping on it steadfastly with his feet. Once finished, he pissed over the very same spot before finally speaking: "Remember this place... in the future... yeah... that tile'll be transformed into nuggets of gold! Guaranteed!"

We didn't give him any more food, but held on tightly to what we had left and began to walk away, soon finding a suitable spot to sit down and enjoy our meal. Kuang San, as though living up to how we first perceived him, wolfed down the food he'd first got from us. When he spied me doing the same, in less ravenous fashion, he came over to speak with me.

"You're eating, too, huh?"

"Well," I replied, "I also have a stomach to fill... we all have to eat, and then eat some more... even in death, I'll wager, a man thinks of eating. It's just that he can't, right!"

Kuang San then asked me about the funeral: "This guy, he's really dead, yes?"

"That depends on whether you think death really means to die," I told him.

"Whaddya mean, if death isn't death, then what the hell is it?"

"When some men die," I explained, "they're forgotten, and that really means they're gone, but for others, yes, they die, but people remember them, so their death is not really the end, they're not really dead."

"Ah... Well then, in the future, I'll be sure not to die and end up being forgotten."

I assured him that that was unlikely. As I finished speaking, I looked at him with a sense of wonder, then thought of the tile he'd buried and his promise it'd transform into gold. He was certainly a unique young man.

"You've got quite a way with words, Kuang San," I said with a chuckle.

I didn't expect a response, but he immediately broke into curses: "They hate me, you know, hate me for being here, for eating like I do... because of this mouth, shit, they ought to let me prepare the food for funerals... I'd do a far sight better! And another thing, Defadian, well, that place can't hold a candle to old Mr Yan's! Whew!"

I laughed once more: "Some vehemence... did the proprietors of Defadian not let you dine there or something?"

His reply was quick: "Ha, fuck them I say, the bastards!"

Before Kuang San had come to eat at Mr Yan's, he'd been at Defadian.

Wang Shizhen had also been there, busily eating the money-meat he'd ordered. The shopkeeper had warmed his best wine and deep-fried some peanuts to go along with the meat. He'd even prepared some fried tofu. As he was bringing the snacks to Wang Shizhen's table, Kuang San burst in, first eyeing the people sitting down before roaring loudly: "Look at the rats up in the rafters kicking up a fuss!"

While everyone's eyes turned to the ceiling, Kuang San stole a plateful of tofu and left. The shopkeeper, however, saw what he'd done and gave chase. Kuang San was too slow to get away, so he spat over the tofu, covering it with a film of thick, greenish mucus. Wang Shizhen stepped in to tell the shopkeeper not to bother, to let him eat it, and then he asked whose child he was.

Seething, the shopkeeper replied: "Begging for food is one thing, but nobody knows where that wild animal's come from. He's been roaming the streets for more than six months now... the wretch."

"How come he's got no family?" Wang asked. "Strange... and my word, his mouth takes up fully half his face!"

Wang Shizhen continued to drink and devour the money-meat he'd purchased. The clouds above were busily weaving themselves together like soft cotton. There were streaks of crimson red and gold mixed in among the black and white. Suddenly, he spied from beyond the shop door a woman squat down in a nearby doorway selling beansprouts. She looked about eighteen or nineteen years old. She had no proper measuring device, so she'd weigh the beansprouts for buyers with one hand, while in the other she'd hold onto the extra ones. She'd positioned herself at a slight incline, a long leg extended to prevent the chicks milling about underneath from getting at her beansprouts. The chicks, in response, pecked at the embroidered flowers on her shoes.

Wang Shizhen thought the scene was garish and yet beautiful, like something out of a dream. He coughed slightly to clear his throat and said: "Quite the sight, eh!"

Mistaking his master's meaning, Lao Hei responded: "These clouds are quite common for Qingfengyi."

Wang Shizhen paid him no mind. He stopped eating and drinking, and then shifted his stool so he could get a better look at the scene outside. The young woman had put the beansprouts to one side and began to adjust her hair. Holding a clip between her teeth, she tried with both hands to remove the hair hanging down in front of her face. As she did so, she realised someone was looking at her. It felt as though the eyes were devouring her flesh, like a tongue is used to taste a morsel before it is swallowed. She blushed and shouted in the direction of Wang Shizhen. Her voice caused the chicks around her to halt. Grabbing the basket that was next to her, she stood up abruptly and turned, and then stormed back to the door whence she'd come, locking it behind her. The beansprouts were left spread out across the ground. Above the frame, Wang noticed the images of Qin Qiong, a door god used to ward off evil spirits.

The girl now gone, Wang Shizhen returned his attention to the food once more, mumbling that he'd seen a work of art. Lao Hei, thinking Wang was still speaking to him, replied: "A work of art?"

A roar of laughter echoed throughout the shop.

On the following day, the local headman from Qingfengyi knocked on that particular door with fifty silver yuan in his hand. He was there to propose marriage on behalf of Wang Shizhen. The betrothal gift was also rather heavy, causing the parents of the girl who'd been selling beansprouts the previous day to pause out of confusion; they had no idea what was really going on.

"What're you talking about… who's this from… what're we supposed to do with this?"

The headman was frank with his answer: "You consent, that's what you do! Consent."

But what happened the following day would never have occurred to the young woman's parents, for at dusk, after they had put the chicks up for sale, Lao Hei arrived with an entourage of men carrying a palanquin for their daughter, all ready to bring her back to Zhengyang. They felt a small wave of panic wash over them, reluctant to let their daughter be taken away so suddenly, but Lao Hei insisted. Acquiescing, the young woman's mum prepared two bowls of the finest blue-and-white porcelain and filled each with rice and noodles. These were for her daughter to take with her as a token of good fortune. According to custom, the two bowls would ensure her child would always have food and drink. When the palanquin departed, however, a strong gale rushed through the street, distracting the wedding party and the girl's parents. The two bowls were forgotten.

That night, once they'd returned to Zhengyang, Wang Shizhen lit charcoal fires in each of the four corners of one wing of his compound and prepared a bath for the girl. Plum blossoms were mixed in with the hot water to create a sweet fragrance. She was to bathe for him. Afterwards, he had a stout wooden bed moved into his room and red candles placed all around it. The candles were coarse and of all shapes, and were placed somewhat haphazardly, but the room was nevertheless illuminated in a fiery glow. The young girl was ushered into the bed, while Wang Shizhen sat beside it in his smoking chair, sucking intensely on his hookah.

The girl wanted to cover herself with the quilt that was spread across the bed, but Wang Shizhen forbade it. She suggested getting dressed, but again he wouldn't allow it. The girl twisted and buried her face between her arms, embarrassed by the situation. She asked him to finish his hookah and come to bed, but he made no effort to hurry up, slowly kneading more tobacco and stuffing it in his pipe, then blowing on the ash to ensure the new tobacco burnt. He smoked, inhaling deeply until the tobacco was gone, and then he repeated the entire process once more. Over and over again he drew on his hookah until thick clouds of smoke enveloped the room.

During the course of the night, Wang Shizhen spoke only a few words, commenting almost to himself that she reminded him of beautiful jade and tender snow. He continued to smoke throughout the night until morning came, his eyes never leaving her naked form. Finally, Wang Shizhen put down the hookah and stood up. Stretching out the cramps that had claimed his body during the night, he called out to Lao Hei: "She didn't stop me from staring at her... I did... the whole night... my eyes devoured her... but I've had enough now, send her home."

Lao Hei tested his ears: "Send her back?"

Wang Shizhen was clear: "I'm done, I need to rest."

Lao Hei entered the room and told the young girl what his master had said. She broke into tears and threw her head at the bed frame. A bloody welt formed immediately across her brow. Lao Hei reached out and took hold of the young woman, stopping her from further hurting herself. Crying would serve no purpose. He urged her to collect her things quickly so that he might bring her home. But she refused to get out of bed. Lao Hei tried to use the quilt to wrap her up, but she flung it to one side. It was then he saw her bare skin, the first time he had seen a woman without clothes. He grabbed the quilt again and once more she struggled against him. He relented and left.

Lao Hei went to speak to Wang Shizhen, unable to hide the redness of his face: "She's gone and cracked her head against the bed, she's looking to kill herself I'll wager... but if you don't want her, then give her to me, alright?"

Wang Shizhen was taken aback by Lao Hei's words. His eyes widened. "I don't want her simply means I don't want her, so what the hell are you driving at, eh... are you trying to say we should be brothers or something?"

Lao Hei spun around and went back into the room. He gave the girl a quick punch to the jaw and knocked her cold, then bundled her in the quilt, tossed her in a basket and flung it over his back. He was returning to Qingfengyi.

The girl's name was Si Feng. She had an older brother by the name of San Hai. San Hai was skilled in the art of castrating animals and would spend most of his time assisting people across the region with neutering their pigs and dogs. Naturally this meant he wasn't often at home, but on this day, he was returning just as Lao Hei was bringing back his sister. The two men, evenly matched, came to blows over the treatment of Si Feng.

Lao Hei, feeling he'd met a man equal to him in strength, shouted wildly: "I'm armed, you know. I could shoot you down, but I won't, not in front of your sister!"

San Hai's parents rushed out to pull their oldest away, telling him Lao Hei was not the one responsible for the outrage. He collapsed to the ground and kowtowed to the heavens before slapping his own face, wailing as he did: "Oh what evil is this, what sin has befallen us!"

The two men exchanged no further blows. Instead, San Hai continued his lament, pointing at the sky to curse that one day he would have his revenge, that that bastard Wang Shizhen will lose his... "I swear, I'll lop his prick clean off!"

Lao Hei was saved from becoming the object of San Hai's vengeance. In fact, he felt a certain form of respect towards the other man's anger and ill-temper. He thought they could be friends, and a few days later, he found himself once again at San Hai's door. Because he carried his rifle with him at all times, no matter whose house he visited, he was always able to bring food along with him, sure in the knowledge that no one would try to rob an armed man. This he did, showing up at San Hai's home with a chicken in hand and a request to stew it... and to provide the necessary wine as drink.

They repeated this ritual more than once, soon becoming fast friends. On one such occasion, they indulged in quite a large quantity of wine, after which Lao Hei stated his desire to wed Si Feng. San Hai answered with a challenge, telling Lao Hei that, should he be able to polish off the entire jar of wine, he'd raise the issue with his sister. Challenged accepted, within minutes the jar was dry.

While the two men enjoyed their evening, San Hai's father was out in the courtyard busily arguing with a stranger. Now it must be said, San Hai's family dog was male, and as male dogs are wont, it was constantly out roaming the streets in search of female dogs to mount. Of course, it was forever being chased away, only to keep returning over and over again.

On this evening, quite unexpectedly, two dogs had clambered up on the roof of their neighbour's home, and were making noises that seemed as though they were crying. San Hai's father remarked that if it was dogs that they heard crying, then surely it was the female making the racket and not their animal. The neighbour offered a rebuttal, saying that in all likelihood it was their dog that was crying for having failed to seduce his bitch. The argument, of course, grew louder and louder until it reached the ears of Lao Hei and San Hai.

"A dog's crying?" asked Lao Hei. "That I've got to see."

Together they walked over to the neighbour's house and as they drew close they could see and hear, just as the man described, two dogs on his roof wailing into the night. Lao Hei asked the man: "Which one's yours?"

"The one on the left."

In no time, Lao Hei pulled out his pistol and shot the animal dead. It tumbled to the ground and as it fell, Lao Hei turned and levelled the barrel of the gun towards the man's forehead: "Do you know who I am? If you ever come looking for trouble with my in-laws again, you'll eat the next bullet."

Terrified, the man stumbled backwards and fell to the ground. Lao Hei collapsed too, completely inebriated.

He spent the night where he was, and as he slept off the booze, San Hai's father asked his son: "Why'd he refer to us as his in-laws?"

"He's drunk," began his son, "he just wanted to frighten the man, that's all."

On the following morning, once he'd recovered sufficiently, Lao

Hei stated his intention to leave, but before departing, he wished to see Si Feng. The girl, however, remained in her inner chambers, refusing to come out.

On 15 April, Lao Hei was dispatched to the county capital to take up an official position. On his way to assume the post, he unexpectedly ran into someone at the temple built in honour of the deity that protected the city: a cousin on his mother's side.

There was nothing out of the ordinary about the temple itself, but the gingko tree planted near the gate was a sight to behold. Its girth was so great it'd take four men, hands clasped together, to fully encircle it. It stood at least 300 feet tall and normally, when its leaves turned a golden colour, the city would be bathed in a soft glow at sunset. But for more than two months now, a dark expanse of what the inhabitants seemed to see as smoke had settled on the city. It wasn't the case that the gingko tree had met its demise due to some conflagration. This was much stranger, for the blackness that had engulfed the city was nothing other than a swarming mass of mosquitoes that had seemingly emerged from out of the sky just above the tree. This cloud of insects grew into the shape of a large straw hat which then appeared to grow great tendrils that stretched out over the city like some ominous, dark mist. Each day the mosquitoes would form this dome of darkness, and each time it would take great effort to disperse it. Upon entering the city, Lao Hei heard of the strange occurrence and simply had to see it for himself. As he strode towards the temple, however, he felt someone poke him in the side, causing him to spin around and pull out his gun. That was when his eyes fell on his cousin.

His cousin's family were very well-off and therefore able to send their son to study in the county capital. It had been more than ten years since he'd been home. To see him now as such a handsome and learned young man, bespectacled and possessing an air of erudition was, to say the least, a surprise. Apparently, he was a county middle school teacher, had been for three months. He'd also changed his name and was now known as Li Desheng.

Lao Hei told him of his own position in the militia in Zhengyang and that he was a platoon leader, a sergeant. They'd both made something of themselves, one in education, the other in martial arts. Finding a small bar, they enjoyed each other's company, and when it was time to depart, Lao Hei made sure to tell his cousin that, should he ever need him, to just ask and he'd settle whatever it may be.

Over the coming weeks, Li Desheng sought out his cousin frequently, but not because he had problems. Rather, they simply enjoyed drinking together. Once, he gave Lao Hei a book, despite the fact his cousin couldn't read and had little use for printed paper. It was then that Lao Hei noticed the size of his cousin's stomach, cinched in by a leather belt that was far too wide to be sure. Lao Hei's appearance was much different: his belt was only loosely tied around his shirt, his pistol holster hung at the hip, his gait betraying a slight forward tilt.

Lao Hei was hungry for information about life in the county capital, and Li Desheng was happy to oblige. He told Lao Hei the country had fragmented and that military cliques and factions were busily dividing up the land. In short, the nation was falling apart, and chaos was the new order of things. Lao Hei acknowledged that he'd heard a little about such matters, and uttered an axiom to sum it up: whosoever holds a gun can become a prince.

Li Desheng also told him about the marches that frequently took place in the provincial capital, how young students were taking to the streets in force to oppose these dark times and show their support for progressive movements. Of course, this brought the students into constant conflict with the warlord forces that ran the city, much of it bloody. Many had, in turn, fled to Yan'an.

At this point, Lao Hei interrupted his cousin: "This Yan'an you mention, it's held by the Communists, yes?"

Li Desheng confirmed it was the same Yan'an he spoke of, but before giving any more details, aside from telling him the Party had set up a soviet-style government there, he told him he could say no more for such information was prohibited around here. In fact, those in charge forbade any discussion of Communist activities, and instead exhorted the people to guard against it. Their discussion of Yan'an at an end, they lifted glasses and continued to drink. Lao Hei shifted his attention and started to speak about Si Feng.

Sometime later, the two men found themselves on the road to Qingliwu, and Li Desheng fancied having some sticky rice cakes. They hadn't quite reached their destination when Lao Hei spied a solitary house built deep in a valley. Deciding to pay the house a visit, they found out the lonely structure was once home to a family of four, but now the only person left was a crippled man of sixty. Evidently, his son had gone off to make a living by offering his services as a carpenter, and his daughter-in-law, along with his grandson, had departed soon afterwards, returning to her maternal home. The old man, despite his circumstances, was affable in the extreme, inviting the two of them into his home; he'd just boiled some potatoes that he was about to mash and make sticky cakes from, and they were welcome to join him.

They accepted, and Li Desheng even assisted in mashing the potatoes, asking at the same time how things were for the old man. His reply made clear what he thought of the times: there's really nothing good to say, we've got today but probably not tomorrow. Once the potatoes were pulverised into a sticky paste, the old man took out a steamer basket and lumped the mash into it. At the same time, he took out his pipe tobacco and offered it to them.

"You're hungry, I'll wager. The sticky cakes'll be done soon."

Li Desheng and Lao Hei took the time to sit under a tree near the door and chatted freely. A small flock of birds that'd been perched on an adjacent beam now took to the air. In spite of their impressive wingspan, their wings actually seemed rather thin, like pairs of sticks churning up the air. Li Desheng sounded out his cousin. He wanted to know what things were like in Zhengyang.

"I've heard of Wang Shizhen, but his reputation isn't the best," Li Desheng began, "and yet he promoted you… gave you the pistol you carry. What gives?"

Lao Hei's response was pointed: "Well, if you eat a family's food, it isn't long before you become part of the family, too."

"I suppose a tadpole starts off much like a fish, but after the waves come, it loses even its tail, hmm."

"Ah, who cares about all that. The road ahead is dark whatever we do."

Li Desheng laughed, and then added: "Hey, the side you're on is not exactly weak, nor are the weapons you carry…"

"Yes, it might be as you say," Lao Hei countered, "or maybe it's just about the gun a person carries, that's what determines his fate." He pulled out his pistol and took aim at a cluster of calabash trees. "Do you think I can hit them?"

Li Desheng didn't hesitate: "How about letting me try?"

Lao Hei handed the weapon to his cousin and said: "Careful you don't misfire!"

He squeezed the trigger and the gun echoed. His shot missed the mark, but claimed the life of one of the birds flying above.

"So," began Lao Hei, "you can shoot a gun?"

From inside his jacket Li Desheng pulled out his own firearm, a much more impressive one than Lao Hei's, leaving his cousin speechless. Li explained that he'd brought the weapon back with him from Yan'an.

"You… you've been given arms by the Communist Party?" Lao Hei asked, the question betraying his shock.

"I am a communist, cousin!"

Lao Hei stood up in disbelief, and grabbed his pistol out of his cousin's hand. Li Desheng didn't react, but simply told him to put it away. He reached out his hand and passed his own gun to Lao Hei: "You won't report me, will you?"

For a moment, Lao Hei held two weapons. Then he returned the one his cousin had given him and sat back down. "Well," he said, "you've not tried to kill me, what's there to report? Besides, we're both armed, that means there's a balance! And whatever we might say about who's arming whom, shit, it's all just a mess, isn't it!"

"True, but there's often method to madness. Let me ask you, do you consider yourself a bandit?"

The question had never occurred to Lao Hei. His eyes widened and his voiced rang out like the clang of a bronze bell: "A bandit!"

Li Desheng continued: "If you are one… then why don't we do it together!"

At this point in their discussion, the door rattled and the two men turned their heads. The old cripple staggered and stumbled outside before running towards the back of the building.

Li Desheng's face blanched: "Did he hear us?"

"So what if he did?"

"No, no, that's not good!" Li stood up and chased after the old man.

Crippled though he was, the old man had already reached a grove of Sichuan pepper trees further down the slope. Li Desheng raised his pistol and fired. The old man tumbled over. When Lao Hei caught up, he could see the man had already lost consciousness, the embrasure where the bullet ate into his flesh was oozing blood. In his hand, he was clutching leaves from the pepper tree.

Lao Hei crouched low and said: "That was a mistake… a mistake… the old man had only come out here to get seasoning for the sticky cakes."

Li Desheng remained quiet for a while before offering a defence: "But how could I know that? He didn't say anything, he just left."

Lao Hei understood what his cousin was saying. He stood up, pointed his gun at the man's head and pulled the trigger. Brain spattered over the ground and the body went still. Lao Hei fired again: "Well, we're bandits, aren't we… this old bastard was in the way!"

The valley deep in the spine of Mount Qingliwu was essentially a stone pit, and the bottom of the pit was filled with water many fathoms deep. A temple once sat at the edge of the pool of water, dedicated to the Dragon King. When the days were dry and the ground thirsted for water, people would visit the temple and pray for rain. But praying for rain didn't involve burning incense sticks and kowtowing to the sky. Instead, one would stand in front of the temple and lash the air with a whip, about forty-eight times. Once this was complete, the statue of the Dragon King also had to be whipped. If these actions were properly completed, rain would fall in three days.

When news spread of the murder of the old man, Wang Shizhen sent the local militia to arrest the culprit. Naturally, Lao Hei was there. Standing in front of the Dragon King Temple, he couldn't help but feel the statue of the Dragon King was staring at him, so much so in fact he wondered if the murderer might not be hiding within it. To confirm his suspicions, he pushed the statue over and proceeded to smash it to bits. Afterwards, the temple no longer had a statue to the deity it was dedicated to, but it did have an old man who took up residence inside. No one knew if he was some Daoist recluse or if he was on the run. However as time passed, he began to resemble the crippled old man more and more, with his short stature and one leg longer than the other. Many years later, this old man relocated and settled down in

Lingning County. He sired a son who ultimately served as head of the county's People's Congress. His grandson too would hold a position of influence in the municipal government in Guofenglou.

After the murder, Lao Hei believed there was no way he could continue as platoon leader, so he decided he ought to head towards Tiger Mountain, which was about eighty *li* from Zhengyang. The mountain, he knew, boasted an old, dilapidated fort, and Lao Hei fancied he could use it to make himself king. Li Desheng, however, advocated he return to Zhengyang, for the authorities would never suspect he was responsible for the murder. If a turtledove borrowed a magpie's nest to lay its eggs, essentially using the work of the magpie for its own benefit, then the same might be true of the town militia. That is, if Lao Hei could sway others to his side, his own power would increase, and then later on they could declare their secession. After listening to his cousin's advice, Lao Hei returned to Zhengyang, and within three months he incited several to rebel, one by the name of Yan, another called Guo. Lei Bu and San Hai were also being groomed.

Lei Bu had remained on Mount Zhu hunting musk deer and wild boars. While the musk obtained from the deer was valuable, the animal itself seemed to have fantastic powers. On far too many occasions, just as he was about to pull the trigger, the damn beast would transform itself into a man and cause him to hesitate. It would, just as suddenly, transform back and disappear. At other times, his gun would strangely misfire, and again the deer would escape.

Hunting wild boar, on the other hand, was something he mastered quickly. First, he worked out that the beast had the habit of charging straight at its attacker. It would actually run into the bullet, and so he would lure the animals to the edge of a cliff, and then hide behind some shrubbery before firing at it. The boar, as its habit dictated, would then charge towards where the bullet had come from, realise the danger too late, and then topple off the cliff. The other boars in the area easily met the same fate.

Once successful, Lei Bu would often enlist the help of the townspeople to scale down the side of the mountain to collect the dead carcasses, out of which he'd want just one for himself; the rest they could take back with them. The people would agree heartily, even on the condition that they would have to carry the sole beast he wanted all the way to his place, then skin it, and properly smoke and cure it.

Lei Bu got on well with other people, and no matter which house he visited, he would always be welcomed with food and drink. The households that were a little better off would often ask questions about things such as how much he smoked. With regard to smoking, he'd simply say that, up in the deep recesses of the mountains, poppies were quite plentiful and he often picked them, boiled them up to make a paste, and when important guests came, he'd take some out for them to enjoy. As for himself, he never touched the dark paste he made, but simply packaged up the poppies to await for visitors. All year round he carried just two items in his pockets. One was the carapace of poppy seeds, which, should he encounter someone suffering from a headache or a toothache, he'd quickly mash with a little water and get them to drink it down, and afterwards the pain would disappear. The other item was deer musk, which he had specially prepared to use against anyone he held a grudge against, most especially Wang Shizhen.

In fact, it wasn't long after Wang had stolen the snake skin that he learnt the older man's concubine had become pregnant. On many occasions, Lei Bu visited Zhengyang in order to wait for the chance to run into Wang's wife. His purpose was clear: he wanted her to breathe in the deer musk to provoke a miscarriage. Unfortunately for him, her appearances in Zhengyang were rare, and when she did come to town, she was always escorted by armed soldiers. The only recourse left to Lei Bu was to pay a visit to Wang Shizhen's compound itself, naturally bringing the deer musk with him. And this he did, walking in circles around Wang's muskmelon field, which promptly resulted in all of the flowers and young fruit to fall to the ground, wounded and inedible due to the pungent deer musk.

It was after this that Lao Hei went in search of Lei Bu, inviting him to participate in the current disturbances he and his comrades were responsible for. Lei Bu, however, didn't initially believe him.

"Disturbances!" he said. "I just want to kill that bastard Wang Shizhen!"

Lao Hei only egged him on: "Kill him then!"

Lei Bu's reply betrayed his suspicion: "But aren't you always tagging along with him, his loyal soldier… now you say murder him!"

"If the blade says someone has to die, then the blade I'll listen to," and he gestured to the weapon Lei Bu carried.

"Well, here," Lei Bu replied as he handed the knife to Lao Hei, "take it and plunge it through my leg, show me you mean what you say."

Grasping the hilt, he held it close to his face: "You're thirsty for blood, aren't you, you long to taste it, right?" And soon it did, as Lao Hei thrust it into the other man's leg. Afterwards, they were like brothers, despite the fact Lei Bu could never really walk the same way again, his right leg permanently wounded by the knife Lao Hei had stuck into it.

As for San Hai, he still castrated pigs and dogs. According to Qinling custom, upon castration, the removed organs belonged to the person who actually cut them off, and so San Hai frequently carried the soft meat into town in search of Lao Hei to have a good old fashioned fry-up with some wine. But after the encounter with Li Desheng, it was now the other way around: Lao Hei had gone to Qingfengyi in search of San Hai. So, when he came out with the meat in his hand, he couldn't help but be somewhat surprised by his friend already standing in front of him.

"Well I must say, you've got a knack for chancing upon fine food!"

Unexpectedly, however, Lao Hei grabbed the spongy organs and flung them over the courtyard wall before raising his voice to question his friend: "Is this all we have to eat in this damned life?" Weapon in hand, he marched off down the main street in the direction of Mabao Village where a moneyed shop owner lived. Lao Hei never told San Hai what he had said or done, but he returned with a sheep in tow.

As the freshly acquired mutton was prepared to be stewed, Lao Hei did his best to recruit San Hai to his growing number of bandits. In truth, he didn't take much convincing. San Hai was more than willing, opening a fresh jar of wine to consummate the new arrangement and encouraging Lao Hei to go and check on the meat to see if it was ready.

When he did, he came upon Si Feng who was in the kitchen attempting to light the stove fire, pumping the bellows over and over. When she saw Lao Hei enter, she stopped what she was doing, stood and made to leave the room. Lao Hei intercepted her exit, extending his arms and taking hold of her, trying to plant his lips on hers. Deftly, Si Feng threw off his arms and moved to leave. As she did so, Lao Hei mumbled longingly after her, telling her he had a mind to marry her, that he'd already discussed it with her brother. He turned his head and his eyes fell on an apricot that lay on the table. To him, its form looked like Si Feng's mouth and so he pried it apart into two halves, eating it ravenously.

Wang Shizhen would be sixty on 23 September, but about two weeks before, he was already thinking much about his birthday: when the year of a man's birth comes upon him, he told his second wife, when one's fate and health reach such a critical juncture, it's quite easy for that man to fly into a rage, to be irascible and generally ill-tempered; be careful, he told her, don't provoke him.

On the morning of 15 September, as Wang Shizhen was busily practising taichi on the veranda towards the rear of his estate, near where the grape vines grew, a snake appeared out of nowhere, as though it had fallen from the sky. Startled, Wang yelled for his servants to come and deal with it, but the snake itself barely moved. In fact, the reptile's belly was bloated and round so that all it could do was squirm and twist, finally regurgitating what it had swallowed, which, as one might expect, was a large rat.

Shortly afterwards, the servants arrived and summarily beat the snake to death, but not before its appearance had planted a seed of concern in Wang's heart, particularly because of the significance of the rat for it was the animal under which he was born. His concubine understood his concern and worry, and so not only did she take care of all the arrangements for the guests, she also invited a theatre troupe to perform for the duration of the celebration, at least three days.

To Lao Hei's mind, this seemed like the perfect opportunity to bring his plans to fruition, and so he consulted with Li Desheng to get a sense of how best to proceed when Wang's birthday finally arrived. Together, they planned every detail, but a mere three days before the old man's birthday, trouble befell them. One of their co-conspirators, Mr Yan, along with a number of other militiamen, had been out drinking and gossiping with little concern. When another patron of the same establishment pulled out a pack of Hatamen cigarettes – from where he had got them no one could say – he shared them with everyone except for Mr Yan.

Taking offence to the slight, Yan began to curse loudly: "You just wait. In three days' time, all your arse-kissing won't be worth a hill a beans!"

Naturally, the man informed Wang Shizhen of what he had heard, who, in turn, summoned Yan to his compound almost immediately. As things turned out, Lao Hei was also in attendance when Yan was questioned.

"So," began Wang Shizhen, "what're you intending to get up to in three days' time, hmm?"

"Well… aren't we celebrating you, sir, wishing you a long life? I'm planning to kowtow at least three times, sir."

"Look me in the eyes and say that!" Wang's voice was quick and harsh and filled with suspicion. Most of the time, Wang's eyes were narrow, almost half asleep, but now they were opened incredibly wide. Great white globes with small, dark pupils bore into Yan, the force of which seemed to make him kneel to the ground, to confess everything.

Lao Hei felt a wave of anxiety wash over him, fearful his role in the plot would be discovered. He interjected: "Just what the hell are you planning, huh?" His rage was overt, although for reasons unlike his master's.

Wang Shizhen, pretending to be much calmer, tried to deescalate the situation: "Let him speak. Whatever he's planned, he can't have organised it all by himself… who else is involved, eh, Yan?"

Yan started to divulge everything, giving up the name of Guo without hesitation. Then his eyes shifted to Lao Hei, who lifted his foot to kick at the now prostrated Yan. Lao Hei's foot made contact with Yan's face, his nose, cursing all the while: "You dirty fucker, how dare you try to rebel!"

Again trying to calm things down, Wang Shizhen stopped Lao Hei's assault in an attempt to mine more information from Yan: "Continue, I want to hear everything. Just what were you planning?"

This time, Yan held his tongue, offering up no other names or details. Wang turned his eyes now to Lao Hei, who shifted a little and then feigned to pour more tea for his master. Unfortunately, the pot was dry.

"He seems unwilling to tell us more, doesn't he?" Wang Shizhen's voice was still apparently full of suspicion.

"Water! More water!" Lao Hei yelled out before turning to Wang. "He won't speak? Give 'im to me, I'll get it out of him, I'll get the fucker to sing!"

Wang Shizhen grunted in resignation and then laughed: "Betray me? Is there a man alive who'd dare!"

Shortly afterwards, Lao Hei had both Yan and Guo dragged to an empty room towards the rear of the estate. As soon as they stepped inside, Yan tried to appease Lao Hei: "Come on, let me go, we're brothers in arms, aren't we?"

Lao Hei's voice dripped with rage: "If I hadn't've been there, you'd've given me up, you prick. Tell me, do you wanna hang from the rafters, or shall I get out the tiger bench?"

Fear was evident in Yan's voice: "Please, spare me..."

"Spare you! You fuck! If I did that, I'd be guaranteeing my own death!" He grabbed the other man's collar and slammed his head into the wall, over and over until there was nothing left but a bloody stump and the stain of blood and flesh pulverised into the stone. Lao Hei turned and his eyes ate into Guo: "And what about you, huh?"

"Wang Shizhen can kill me, fine, I won't give you up."

"You'll swear to this?" Lao Hei asked.

"Yes, I'd bite my tongue off before I'd say a word." Guo tried to carry out his promise. His teeth bit into his tongue, but he couldn't manage it.

Lao Hei volunteered to help: "Here, let me." He pinned Guo to the ground and pressed his foot into the man's cheek. Harder and harder until blood spurted from Guo's mouth, along with his tongue. Lao Hei dragged it out further and sliced it clean off, leaving the man to bleed out.

With both Yan and Guo dead, Lao Hei detailed his report to Wang Shizhen, informing him Yan had taken his own life for fear of punishment. Guo's death needed little explanation, so he told him the man bit off his own tongue and bled to death.

"Oh," came Wang's reply, "surely there must be more accomplices. Pity we didn't get any other names..."

He gave orders for Lao Hei to round up some men to dispose of the bodies. Yan's body could be buried, Guo's too, but his tongue should be given to the cat to eat. Lao Hei needn't deal with it directly, for Wang Shizhen had another task for him: "My wife's been ill these past few days. I need you to go to Mawang and fetch the village doctor."

Acknowledging the instructions, Lao Hei turned to leave. As he did so, Wang gave him a few further words: "Leave your weapon, I don't want you scaring the doctor."

Lao Hei was momentarily stunned: "Quite the arrogant sod, this doctor, hmm. Without my gun, I mightn't be able to get him to come."

"In that case, take my pistol instead. If he doesn't trust you, he'll recognise my weapon and come for sure." They exchanged guns, Lao Hei taking his in place of his own.

It was about ten *li* to Mawang. On the way there, Lao Hei took a diversion so that he could speak to Li Desheng. As they discussed what had happened, Li came to the conclusion that Wang was beginning to suspect Lao Hei. He urged his cousin not to return, but Lao Hei couldn't help but feel annoyed by the whole situation. Yes, they'd run into some problems, he'd lost two hands, but did they have to give up on the whole thing?

"I've been with him for so many years," he continued. "I can't believe he suspects me of anything, and besides, I'm carrying his pistol, that's gotta count for something!"

Once he'd finished, he told Li Desheng to get Lei Bu and San Hai together. Before night fell, they had to lie low near the mouth of the river that stretched through the gully. If he showed up later with more men willing to join them, then they'd take what arms they had and squirrel themselves away into the mountain, waiting for the moment to put their plan into motion.

Lao Hei soon returned to Wang's estate with the doctor, where he relayed to Wang Shizhen a wholly fabricated report of how, when he was in Mawang, he received news of a group of bandits hiding out in the nearby ditch busily waylaying travellers as they passed by. It was said, so the false report went, that they were relieving those unlucky enough to encounter them of any goods they carried. One businessman in particular, who was returning from Hankou, had had several chests of fine satin stolen by the rascals. It was clear, Lao Hei argued, he ought to take a contingent of men to apprehend them, preferably armed men, say five or so.

As he spoke, Lao Hei's face remained stoical, betraying nothing of his true intent. There was no way for him to know, however, that Wang Shizhen's nephew lived in the very same region, and, moreover, that he'd come to celebrate his uncle's birthday on this very day, bringing with him some delicious jerky for the occasion – he'd mentioned nothing of bandits. As he listened to Lao Hei's report, he continued to hold the hookah steady, smoking the tobacco, waiting for his moment to speak: "Is that so?"

Lao Hei reiterated the false details: "Yes, very fine satin. It was actually meant as a gift for you!"

Wang Shizhen, who by now had finished smoking his tobacco, blew out the remainder and spoke: "Excellent, excellent, yes, go at once. Your name's Lao Hei, after all. It should be you who goes to such a dark place, the Black Gully, I say, its name honours you. How many men and weapons did you say you needed? Five, six, that'd be plenty. Are you sure you need so many armed men to deal with country bandits? I mean, who among the men would you trust arming! Ah... just a second, I'd like to introduce you to my nephew... he comes from that area... You Tian, You Tian!"

Wang Shizhen called for his nephew, who now emerged from the inner rooms. He was a broad-shouldered young man, his face fierce and serious. In his hand, he carried Lao Hei's pistol. Wang continued: "Return Lao Hei's weapon to him, and you take mine. He'll need it to round up that ragtag band of criminals!"

You Tian walked up to Lao Hei holding the gun, then, as he reached him, he lifted the pistol and pointed it straight at his forehead. Lao Hei gasped and shifted quickly out of the way. He drew the gun he was carrying and pulled the trigger. It was empty... a thought raced through his mind: Wang Shizhen must've cleaned out the chamber before they'd exchanged weapons.

Then, in hurried movements, he threw himself at You Tian, wrestling his own gun out of the other man's hands. Unprepared for the assault, You Tian lost the weapon to his attacker and felt a bullet drive into his chest, knocking him down dead. As the gun echoed, Wang Shizhen pulled on a rope he'd strung up behind him, depositing a basket of lime dust he'd tied to the rafters above. The dust landed over Lao Hei, turning his dark skin white. By now, Lao Hei fully understood how much Wang Shizhen had grown suspicious of him. He'd tricked him into giving up his gun, exchanging it for one that wasn't loaded. He'd strung up this basket of lime dust so as to impede his vision and make him easier to catch. He was in quite the pickle, or so it seemed.

Lao Hei spun and fired in the direction of Wang Shizhen. His master had been standing, watching the scene unfold, but now he slumped back in his chair: "Men! Men! Me..." He fell from the chair onto the floor. His last breath gurgled in his throat: "…n."

From out in the courtyard other voices could be heard: "Arrest Lao Hei, arrest him!"

Lao Hei jumped from the window and ran towards the rear of the compound. He scrambled up the ladder standing next to the wall and up onto the roof of the building. His left eye was bleeding due to the lime dust, so he paused a moment, rooted into his trousers and wet his hands with some piss, then pulled his eyelids apart to wash them, at least a little. Like a cat, he bounded from roof to roof, heading west across the estate and to freedom.

In one sustained burst of energy, Lao Hei ran straight to the gully where his comrades were supposed to wait for him. By the time he arrived, the sun was already setting, but Li Desheng and the others had yet to show up. He didn't dare wait for them, but instead kept on running, finally reaching the home of San Hai in Qingfengyi before night fell. Si Feng was in the main room at her needlework when Lao Hei burst in.

"I've killed him, I've shot dead Wang Shizhen. Come quick, we must flee!"

Si Feng did not respond. She put down her needlework, walked off to her room and closed the door behind her.

From the other side of the door, Lao Hei beseeched her: "I've seen you, all of you. You should be mine!"

The door remained shut. Voices carried on the air from outside and Lao Hei believed it must be the authorities come to arrest him. He fled again as fast as he could. As he scurried through Qingfengyi, however, he noticed something unexpected. There, under the lantern of a money-meat stand, he spied a group of men busily beating Kuang San.

I remember that evening being fairly dark, most of the light from the moon was obscured by the clouds that hung heavy in the night sky… there was a whiff of piss in the air… I don't know, perhaps someone had the penchant to mess around with cow dung in the wee hours of the night… hmm… Anyway, Baldy had asked me to accompany him out onto the street, and it was there we bumped into Kuang San. He'd just pinched some sweet potato that'd been hanging to dry from the eaves of one of the houses, and the owner and his family were furiously chasing after him. When they saw us with Kuang San, they yelled for us to grab him. I reached out my hand as though to latch onto him, but deliberately let him slip through. Still pretending that I was trying to catch him, I grabbed a broom that was next to the store front and slammed it down onto his shadow. Strangely enough, Kuang San felt the pain, despite the fact I never actually hit him… I remember he jumped… I repeated the action and so did he. Unfortunately for him, this was how he was caught…

The angry mob flung him to the ground and began to drive their feet into him. Kuang San's face received most of the blows, but still he tried to stuff the dried sweet potato into his mouth. They shouted at him to spit it out! Over and over again… He appeared to acquiesce… finally… and vomited up the sweet potato… but a second after, he tried to swallow it once more. That was when Lao Hei arrived.

At first we didn't see him, only his pistol echoed upwards into the night sky. The sound of it caused the crowd to scatter, while Kuang San remained crumpled on the ground. I recall Lao Hei spoke to him… asked him if he'd had his fill. No, was the answer. Then Lao Hei told him to eat it up and come with him. Pointing down the street with his weapon, Kuang San got up and followed after him.

—

Let's take a look at another mountain range from *Pathways Through the Southern Mountains*, shall we? I'll read the first sentence, you the second...

The first peak of *Pathways Through the Southern Mountains, Part II*, is called Tea Willow Mountain. To the west stretch flowing yellow sands, home to both the Xin and Feng tribes. To the north rises Mount Zhubi and to the east is Changyou Mountain. The Eminent River emerges from these slopes and flows towards the south and west before merging with the River Scarlet. White jade can be found in the Eminent River, as well as large amounts of fine-grained cinnabar. An animal resides on Tea Willow Mountain that bears a striking resemblance to a boar. It is said to have sharp spurs on its feet and has a bark like a dog. It is often mistakenly called a mangut or a tanuki, although it is neither. It is said to be an omen of impending earthworks in the area in which it is seen. An owl-like bird nests upon Tea Willow Mountain. It is said to have human hands instead of feet. When it hoots, it sounds like a hen quail, a long 'joo, joo', after which it is named. It, too, is said to be an omen, signalling the imminent banishment of government officials from the area.

Four hundred and fifty leagues to the southeast of Tea Willow Mountain is the above-mentioned Changyou Mountain. Its slopes lack vegetation, but there are several rivers and streams. A beast that resembles a long-tailed ape claims this mountain as its home. It is reputed to have four ears, and to sing like a human. It shares its name with the mountain. Its appearance is said to prophesy major floods in the commandery.

Three hundred and forty leagues farther east is Mount Lofty-Glare. It bears this name due to the great quantity of sparkling jade on its south face, and to the abundance of gold on its north face. A creature said to resemble a human dwells on this mountain, but its back is covered with hog bristles. It finds shelter in the many caves on this mountain and is said to hibernate in winter. It is called the huahuai. It makes a sound like wood being chopped. It is, by all accounts, an omen that military conscription will soon be carried out in the district.

Mount Feather rises three hundred and fifty leagues farther east. At its base stretch many rivers and streams. The summit is said to experience constant rain showers. There is little by way of vegetation on the mountain, but there are many huge vipers.

Wary-Father Mountain is situated three hundred and seventy leagues to the east. Like Mount Feather, it is devoid of vegetation, but there is said to be enormous amounts of gold and jade across its slopes.

An additional four hundred leagues east is Mount Bendy, but little is known about it.

Five hundred leagues farther east is Fuyu Mountain, which overlooks the great Lake Juqu to the north and the River Zhubi to the east. A beast that looks like a tiger inhabits this mountain. Known to eat humans, it is said to have the tail of an ox, and to bark like a dog. It is called the zhi. On the northern face of Fuyu Mountain rises the River Reed. It continues north to empty into Lake Juqu. The River Reed is said to be full to the brim with knife-fish.

Success Mountain rises five hundred leagues farther east. It is almost rectangular in shape, with four jutting sides and three natural dips that resemble altars. At its peak are gold and jade, while at its base much dark cinnabar can be found. The Zha River gurgles forth here and flows in a southerly direction into the River Houbi. Great amounts of yellow gold can be found just below the surface of the Zha.

Five hundred leagues farther east lies Mount Gather-Hill. It, too, has four faces and considerable gold and jade on its summit. At its base, white jade with streaks of red can be found on the surface. The River Bi begins here and flows south to merge with the River Jing.

Five hundred leagues farther east is Mount Pacified. It is mostly covered in sand and thus there is no vegetation, not even small shrubs. The River Jing starts here and flows south into the River Ni.

Another five hundred leagues east and one arrives at Mount Helper-Hook. It, too, is topped with a great amount of gold and jade. At the foot of this mountain there is an enormous amount of vegetation, but it is devoid of birds and beasts. There are seemingly no streams or rivers either.

Five hundred leagues farther east is a mountain that is nearly always covered in shade, so its name has been lost. Nothing grows upon it, nor is there any water.

Another five hundred leagues east is Mount Xun. Great quantities of gold and other metals can be found on its southern face while jade is present on the north face. A creature that looks like a ram lives on this mountain. It is said to have no mouth, and thus to be immortal for it doesn't need to eat. People call it the huan. This is where the River Weep rises to flow south into Gengsi Marsh. Purple molluscs are plentiful in the River Weep.

Four hundred leagues farther east is Mount Houbi. Catalpa and wild plum trees flourish on this peak, especially the summit, while thorn and willow trees cover its foot. The Surging River begins here and flows east towards the sea.

Five hundred leagues to the east is Hoard-Cry Mountain. Like Mount Pacified, the surface of this mountain is mostly sand and consequently there is no vegetation. The Stag River rises here before emptying into the Surging River to the south.

Five hundred leagues farther east is Mount Luwu. Its summit is bare of vegetation, but gold and minerals are plentiful. The River Zegeng rises here and flows south into the Surging River. A great beast resides on this mountain, a bird-like venomous creature. A single horn juts out from its head, and when it makes a noise it sounds eerily similar to a human baby's cooing. It is a man-eater.

Five hundred leagues east again is Mount Qiwu. Like other mountains in this range, it has no vegetation. There are, however, plentiful precious metals and minerals upon its slopes. But strangely no jade. This final peak lies in the East Sea facing Mount Mound. When the sun rises, it reflects off Mount Qiwu and bathes everything below in a glaring light; when the sun sets, all is returned to darkness.

Altogether, seventeen peaks are described in *Pathways Through the Southern Mountains, Part II*. Beginning with Tea Willow Mountain and ending with Mount Qiwu, more than 7,200 leagues are traversed.

The gods that call these mountains home possess dragon bodies and bird heads. The ritual sacrifice to these deities involves an animal of uniform colour, along with a jade disc that is to be buried with the animal. The offering of grain is glutinous rice.

So, anything to ask?

Question: What's this animal… the joo?

Answer: It's a bird, similar to a quail.

Question: And this primate-looking creature thing?

Answer: Hmm, sort of a long-tailed ape.

Question: Now… these seventeen mountains… how's it that nine of them are barren?

Answer: You weren't paying attention. Yes, they might be barren, but didn't you notice how they're littered with gold and jade? So they're not wholly barren, just no vegetation. Once ancient people discovered this phenomenon, they were soon able to conclude how Fu Xi created the world and how the elements of metal, wood, water, fire and earth engendered one another, what we now call the five phases.

Question: Much is recorded about the sounds of many strange animals. There's the animal that's sort of a cross between a racoon and a dog, and it barks like a dog, the owlish creature with human hands that calls 'joo, joo', a long-tailed ape that croons like a man… then there's that man-like creature with hog bristles that, when it groans, sounds like someone chopping wood… well, are all of those sounds important?

Answer: We often say that the world around us is a world of sounds and colour. The 'sounds' mentioned here are those very same sounds mentioned in *Pathways Through the Mountains and Seas*, the colours refer to the shapes of the myriad things. Every animal, of every species, uses whatever voice it's been gifted by the heavens to demonstrate its existence. Its 'sound' calls out its presence in the cosmos. Later on we have time, time shows that us humans are here, it creates the loudest sound of all across the emptiness of space. We also have the bodhisattva of mercy and compassion, Guanyin, who according to Buddhism, rescues us from pain and hardship.

Question: Man has language. Are these animals really all that different, do we have nothing in common?

Answer: Yes, it's true man has language, there's English, German, French, Arabic, and here in Qinling, in Shanyin, Santai, Qingning, Qinghua, all these counties, aren't there also many different dialects? Have you heard of The Bible... it's an important book in the West. Well, The Bible speaks of how their god, in order to prevent mankind from uniting, shattered any unity by making people speak in different tongues, thus preventing easy communication. And then on top of that, their god further scattered them across the land... that's what they believe, in the Western world. Well, I'm telling you that it's much the same here in the East. In ancient times, there were so many animals, the world was full of them, but man's power wasn't what it is today. Now, if all the animals spoke in the same manner, made the same sounds, what of man... hmm... that's why the heavens gifted them all with different calls, different sounds, different voices.

Question: Why does the book say that, whenever a man spies that owl-like creature, officials are sure to be banished, that when a long-tailed ape is seen there'll be floods, and that should a... a... hog-human, you know, the man-like animal that has hog bristles, well, anyway, why's it say that, should it appear, people will end up being conscripted into work or the military... I don't get it.

Answer: Have such animals been discovered? Man is part of nature, we exist together with the animals and plants, but man's never been afraid of animals and plants. We've only ever feared other men, we're the root of all disasters, we cause catastrophe.

Question: What about the beast that looks like a ram but has no mouth and can't be killed. Is it really impossible to kill?

Answer: Saying that it can't be killed actually means it's still alive.

Question: It lives without a mouth?

Answer: That just means it's not permitted to speak, the sound won't come out, or it can't.

Not much can be said about Kuang San's youth and what he got up to while he was young. At the gates of nearly every wealthy home in Qinling stood rather imposing stone lions, there, ostensibly, to protect the homes they stood guard over. But at other doorways on streets behind the main one, a much more common sight were stone statues of Wang Wenchang's companions. Usually they were children, one carved with its hand over its mouth, the other with hands over its ears. Wang Wenchang was a figure from Daoist myth, known as the god of culture and literature, and the two young companions were there to represent the proper education of children; they were to be seen but not heard.

In practice, however, at least since Liberation, this sort of attitude towards children was no longer evident, partly because those who had used it most in the past had all died. As a result, there weren't many who really witnessed it, saw it, heard it… it was almost as though treating children in such a manner had never really been that way, despite what the statues might suggest. But whatever the case might've been, it's true beyond doubt the glories Kuang San ultimately won, the pride he felt in his accomplishments, the curvature of his life, all of it, started with his decision to follow Lao Hei into the mountains.

Lao Hei stuck to his original plan, and together with Kuang San they retreated into Tiger Mountain and the ancient fort that rested on its slope. That same month, Tiger Mountain was visited by a rather strange occurrence, one might even call it a supernatural event. A man had let his cattle out to pasture when thunder and lightning reverberated throughout the sky with little advance warning. Clouds billowed and rolled seemingly intent on swallowing the mountain whole. It was as though lustful dragons had descended from the heavens to mate with the unsuspecting bovines, or at least that's the way it looked to some of the peasants who lived on the side of the mountain.

Li Desheng and the other rebels arrived on Tiger Mountain soon after and heard almost straight away of this extraordinary affair. For Li, who took a special interest in it, such 'copulation' was particularly auspicious and sure to result in the birth of a *qilin*, a sort of Chinese unicorn. These beasts were exceptionally rare, of course, usually only appearing on the eve of the arrival or death of an eminent ruler or sage.

Once Li Desheng relayed the tale to the cattle owner, the man was overjoyed. He immediately set off for the village at the foot of the mountain to spread the news, remarking to whoever would listen that while a scholar expecting to pass the provincial-level exams is looking to get ahead, dragons dropping from the sky to mate with his cows told him that true heroes had arrived... and whaddya know, Qinling had its very own band of guerrilla fighters! When the calendar rolled over, the guerrilla band left Tiger Mountain for Mount Bear Ear. As for the dragon-impregnated cow, it gave birth to a pig that didn't really look like a pig, its mouth was elongated and its ears much too short.

Unsurprisingly, Li Desheng had assumed leadership of the guerrilla soldiers; Lao Hei was his second in command. In the span of a year and a half, they'd been able to recruit an additional thirteen stout men and carry out three raids on the militia headquarters in Zhengyang. Out of their men, four had been killed and nine had been maimed, but they had come away with two more firearms, which, when added to Lei Bu's hunting rifle, gave them a total of five guns.

They carried out additional raids as well, looking for money and valuables. Whenever they encountered a walled compound, a solid gate, they'd simply bound over the walls and take whatever wasn't nailed down, or at least as much as they could carry. If there were people at home, their lives would be spared, so long as they readily turned over everything they had. For those who resisted, death would invariably follow. But not, interestingly, at the end of a gun; bullets were far too important, and the guerrilla band hated to part with them. Knives became their weapon of choice in matters such as these, and besides, it was much easier to lop off a head with a blade than with the butt of a rifle.

Of course, they only attacked the wealthy. They were like a band of merry men, for whatever they expropriated, they redistributed to the region's poorest residents. As a result of their actions, more and more people sought them out for refuge, so many in fact they soon numbered nearly two hundred. They came wearing all manner of clothes, but each one had a red bandana tied around their waist and an axe or a sickle tucked underneath it. A band of merry men indeed, ready to work whatever fields lay before them.

The guerrillas' main aim was revolution, but Kuang San didn't really understand what that truly meant. All he got out of the rhetoric and the sloganeering was that revolution would fill his belly. He was constantly underfoot, and no matter what the leaders might be discussing, it never prevented him from interrupting them. After breakfast, he'd pester everyone to see if there was any steamed bread left. At lunch, he'd nag about what they were going to have. And he ate like a horse. One steamed bun was never enough, and so you'd often see him wielding a bamboo stick like a skewer, five buns or more impaled upon it. When they had scalding hot rice porridge, everyone else would blow on their bowl to cool it down, but not Kuang San. He'd open his mouth and slurp it down in a single great gulp.

On one occasion, when there wasn't much cornmeal to actually make porridge, Kuang San abandoned the use of a bowl altogether. He simply grabbed a stick, thrust it into the pot, scraped out what he could, and proceeded to lick the stick clean. Despite acting in this way, Kuang San didn't seem to possess a great deal of courage. One evening, as they were preparing to raid a wealthy shop owner's estate, the men hid near the edge of a small ravine and instructed Kuang San to steal up close to the compound to see if anyone was at home. This he did readily enough, but as he drew near, he was startled by the wealthy owner who had at the very same moment decided to empty the family's night soil basket in the ditch just outside the main gate. Kuang San crouched almost instantly, and pulled his trousers down round his ankles.

The homeowner called out: "Who's there?"

"Just me," was all Kuang San said by way of reply.

"What the devil are you up to?"

"Shitting."

"You're doing what?" the man asked. "You'd better clean that up."

As if on cue, Kuang San stood and lifted his trousers, shifted his feet, and then squashed his faeces under a boulder. His bowels emptied, he returned to his comrades hiding near the ravine and informed them there was no grain to speak of, let alone anything else to steal.

"What!" the other men responded, surprised at this bit of information. "But he's such a rich bastard... how's it that he has nothing?"

"Well," said Kuang San, "if he's so well-off, how come he's emptying his own night soil?"

"You little shit," cursed the men, "you're happy to take the food we give you, but you aren't prepared to work for it, are you?"

As evening dragged into night, the men sneaked into the wealthy man's estate. There they found three large storage containers filled with wheat and corn, as well as vats containing salt and oil. Furious, they scolded Kuang San again for claiming the man had nothing. Unfortunately for the guerrillas, however, things did not go to plan. Just as they were about to carry off the grain, the salt and oil, the owner appeared along with four other men, all bearing knives. A melee ensued and one of the comrades shouted at Kuang San to stuff however much wheat he could into the bags they'd brought with them and flee. This he did, and with one bag over his shoulder, he ran.

The fight ended with the wealthy landowner and his men dead at the feet of the guerrillas. Two of their own number were also seriously injured. One of the wounded men reported afterwards to Lao Hei that Kuang San never lifted a finger to help them fight.

Surprised by this information, Lao Hei immediately questioned Kuang San: "What the hell's wrong with you, huh?"

Kuang San's response was quick: "I haven't got a gun, have I?"

"You've a knife, though. Didn't you bring it?"

Kuang San again replied without hesitation: "I've never even killed a chicken before. How am I supposed to..."

Lao Hei cursed and slapped the young boy's face: "No, I suppose not... all you do is fucken eat!"

Consequently, Lao Hei took to training Kuang San. The first lesson involved capturing locusts and explaining how best to remove their legs, one at a time. Next, he had to learn how to eat scorpions, how to place the living creature in vinegar, let it soak for a while and then swallow it whole. They then moved on to trapping snakes, and Lao Hei showed Kuang San how to behead a viper and slurp out its blood. These were all vital lessons to make Kuang San a suitable solider.

As winter arrived, so too did the county militia, who took up positions around their encampment in an effort to drive them out and hopefully destroy them. The guerrillas had few options, so they fled Mount Bear Ear in the direction of the Hubei border region and the ravines that lay there. Upon learning of their impending arrival, most of the residents in the area fled, which resulted in the guerrillas going without food for several days. As a result, they ended up devouring whatever they could find, even the dogs and cats that were left behind when the people ran, as well as the rats they found in the many traps put out by the villagers.

Kuang San soon took to setting his own rat traps morning to night, which he'd check each time the sun rose. On one such morning, he discovered a snared rat with only a single leg on its tiny torso, the other three had apparently been gnawed away by the creature itself, leaving only bloody stumps instead of feet. At first, Kuang San wasn't sure what had happened, but Lao Hei informed him that the rodent must have chewed off the other three limbs in a vain attempt to free itself.

Kuang San's rejoinder was unexpected: "So, rats can feel hunger too, huh?"

"It was trying to save its life, you fool," responded Lao Hei.

Again, Kuang San's reply was unexpected: "It was that determined… wow."

"Well," Lao Hei added, "in times like these, only the strong survive and the weak'll end up being their food!"

For a moment, a quiet pall fell on Kuang San, before his eyes brightened yet again. He grabbed at the trap and pulled the rodent free, tore its remaining leg from its body and sunk his teeth into the creature. It squeaked once, twice more, and then it was gone. Kuang San had devoured it.

The border region was not a long-term option for the guerrilla band, and before long they were on the march again, heading further and further north. Hot on their tails were the militia, so close in fact that actual skirmishes broke out between them, the first near a rocky ravine named Huajiala. It was a fierce battle, and this time Kuang San participated directly. Brandishing a butcher's blade, he killed two militiamen on his own, and then lopped off their four ears as a trophy. After the fighting ended, Kuang San made a point of showing off his martial prowess to Lao Hei, boasting he killed not two but four enemies.

Huangfujie is situated in a basin about a dozen miles, or forty *li*, north of Qingfengyi. The area produced rice and lotus roots and was home to many wealthy residents. Li Desheng's guerrilla band had raided Qingfengyi more than a few times. They'd scorched numerous store fronts, killed tens of people, and so naturally the wealthier inhabitants of Huangfujie had become quite fearful, terrified even of the guerrilla band's proximity. As a result of this fear, they actually hollowed out caves in the rock face of a precipice that was located just a little distance past the village. Some of the caves were large, some were small, some for single occupancy, others for whole groups of people; some even had rudimentary kitchens and water cellars. In front of the caves, a number of deep ridges were carved into the stone, making easy passage impossible. This was all by design, for the people of Huangfujie had also constructed stone pillars that were in turn placed at the entrances to the caves, with large wooden planks placed on top. Like drawbridges, the pillars could be removed should the need arise, essentially cutting the caves off from the outside world. And should the guerrillas decide to pay them a visit to raise funds, as it were, the wealthy residents would simply pack up their food stores, their money, whatever else of value, and retreat into the caves, sealing themselves inside and keeping the bandits out. Even firearms would be useless if the guerrillas tried to mount an attack. The fortresses constructed by the affluent citizens of Huangfujie were impenetrable. To add insult to injury, the guerrillas even had to endure the ignominy of having faeces wrapped in lotus leaves flung at them.

As expected, the whole situation infuriated Li Desheng, so much so that he resolved not to leave. Instead, he decided on a new course of action, something to drive them out of their cave hideaways. He ordered his men to pile high in front of the caves the firewood left abandoned by the wealthy residents of Huangfujie. He set the wood ablaze, and within a day, not only had all the grass in the entire region burnt, but even the chickens' feet were left charred and ruined. Unfortunately for the guerrillas, however, no movement was detected from within the caves, nor could a sound be heard. This only served to further enrage Li, so he dispatched San Hai and a few other men into the forest to fell trees. These, too, he would burn at the entrance to the caves. It was while out performing this task that San Hai received news of his sister.

After San Hai had found common cause with Li Desheng and accompanied him into the mountains, the militia spent the better part of ten to fifteen days searching and rummaging through his home in Qingfengyi. Of course, they weren't really expecting to find anything, their main aim being to threaten and frighten San Hai's remaining family. Now, since his mother and father had died, it was his sister Si Feng who bore the brunt of their intimidation. Of course, she hadn't really helped her own cause.

She was unmarried, and had no parents to actually arrange anything. She therefore took matters into her own hands and snipped off her girlish pigtails, darkened her face and came in search of me, the mountain whisperer. Why? That's easy to answer: she wanted me to take her under my wing, so to speak, and learn to sing the mourning songs, to travel, basically, from village to village, sending the dead on their way. Unfortunately for her, she didn't possess the mind needed to remember the lyrics, the music; the roots of the songs just wouldn't take and so, inevitably, she could never quite recall the songs when needed. What was even more annoying was that, after I taught her four or five lines from *The Song of Remorse*, all she did was break out into tears.

That's when I told her: "Sweetie, since your parents are gone, you won't be able to sing this song… I'm sure of that."

Her reply was plaintive: "If you're not willing to take me on, I've nowhere else to go. I'll simply die right here in front of you."

It was then that she pulled out the shears she used to cut her hair and held them to her throat, ready to pierce her supple flesh. I'd never seen this side of her before, never realised she had such passion, and so I left her there to cry for her dead mother. This was as it should be, funeral arrangements required tears, and since there was no filial son to speak of, someone had to mourn, to cry for the deceased.

Since then, whenever devout families called on me to sing the mourning song, I'd ask if they needed a young lady to cry as well. If they did, I told them to call Si Feng. She was quite good at it, I must say. She didn't fake it, she really wept. Not only would her eyes grow red and puffy, her voice would even crack. There was one instance, a man had died in the village of Wangwu, and Si Feng and I went together to perform the rites.

I sang throughout the first evening, and on the following day, the deceased's relatives came to pay their condolences. As they arrived, I remember a gale suddenly buffeting the house, toppling two poplar trees that'd stood by their front gate. The wind was so strong it whipped up the water in the reservoir, partially flooding the estate. Surprisingly, the wind left a single fish in its wake.

I began to sing:

Where is the goodness in life on this earth,
When a blade of grass clinging to the wall cannot help but perish in
the wintry frost?
Where is the goodness of life on this earth,
When an old walnut tree stands bare, its leaves long since fallen to the
ground?
Where is the goodness of life on this earth,
When a poor mandarin duck meets its doom in the talons of an eagle?
Where is the goodness of life on this earth,
When mention of death quickly brings it knocking on your door?
Friends and relatives don't know.
Friends and relatives don't know.
The deceased stands all ready on Narakade Bridge,
Perched between this world and the next.

Si Feng wept as I sang. Her eyes swelled red; she sobbed for her father, her mother, for the deep, profound sorrow that plagued her heart. A bystander called out, I recall, something along the lines of a grandfather has died, weep for him! And Si Feng continued to cry...

for her parents, for everyone. I maintained my rhythm, beating the drum without pause. My eyes were closed as I circled the coffin, drumming and singing all the while. I was lost in the ritual, absorbed in singing. Like an ox destined to keep walking round a grinding stone, my eyes were trapped in the routine.

But then, from the fringes of my trance, I heard the family excoriate Si Feng… accuse her of crying for the wrong person. Without forewarning, the thumping of feet echoed and was followed by a clap. The crying stopped and a wail of fear emanated from out of the room. I thought for a moment they'd come to blows, that the family was physically abusing poor Si Feng, but when I opened my eyes wide to see what was happening, I was shocked to see San Hai. Not only had he arrived without notice, he'd picked up his sister and thrown her over his shoulder, intent on taking her away.

When San Hai had gone to chop trees, as instructed by Li Desheng, a poor woman of the area had recognised him and told him of what she'd seen. On the previous day, while she was in her mother's hometown of Wangwu, she'd seen San Hai's sister weeping for families in mourning. San Hai listened to the tale, then lifted his head and cursed into the sky: Father! Mother! He swore. Silence hung in the air for a moment afterwards, a melancholy that seemed heavy and oppressive. Finally, he'd grabbed a donkey and set off for Wangwu. It hadn't taken him long to find his sister, and once he did, he tried to drag her away. The family in mourning, however, refused to let her go, and so San Hai brandished his weapon and fired into the crowd. By good fortune, the bullet tore through an incense burner instead of flesh, defusing the prospect of further conflict. Shortly afterwards, San Hai left the village, Si Feng seated on top of the donkey he'd come with.

On its passage through the incense burner, the bullet grazed the coffin, nicking the lid and leaving a small crack. The cover had been made out of pinewood and did not deserve the wound it endured. I knew, too, that it had woken the spirit of the deceased, and now it would be unable to enter the next realm. As expected, a neighbour's pig became pregnant, and six years later gave birth to eight suckling piglets, one of which had the face of a man.

—

San Hai returned to Huangfujie with his sister in tow, explaining to Li Desheng, in no uncertain terms, that he couldn't just leave her out in the wide world to endure the hardships she had already experienced. Li, however, was not immediately welcoming. After all, no conditions had been discussed or established for the acceptance of family into their merry band. His initial inclination was to simply find her a family in some faraway village, but before he settled on this solution, he solicited Lao Hei's opinion.

"What do you think, hmm... would she make a suitable wife for you?"

Lao Hei agreed almost instantly, and this time, so did Si Feng.

Out of the corner of his eye, Lao Hei spied Kuang San walking towards them carrying a clay pot. Seemingly overwhelmed by the turn of events, Lao Hei slapped the boy's shoulder excitedly, causing him to start and drop the pot. It smashed on the ground, scattering the fried mixed vegetables along with it.

Lao Hei, still overjoyed, despite what he'd done to poor Kuang San, grabbed his firearm and set off to march through the village; he was going to find a new family home. Prying open doors to the vacant estates left by the moneybags who once inhabited the street, he came across one filled with all manner of decorative furniture and a bed, too, made of the finest Chinese cedar with a canopy hanging down around it. The quilt that lay atop the bed was of the most exquisite material, dyed red and embroidered with flowers. On a stand next to the bed sat an enamel wash basin and a bronze-framed mirror that looked like something from the Tang dynasty. The former owner, he later found out, had several stores in the county capital; here in his home, his wealth was on clear display.

Lao Hei believed he was already married, that all he'd needed was his cousin's word, and so now he simply had to show Si Feng their new home, to settle on it, and then they'd get right at consummating their relationship as husband and wife. However, Si Feng had other ideas. She wouldn't let him touch her, they had to have a proper ceremony three days hence... that was the only way.

During the two days prior to the ceremony, Lao Hei used the time to wash in the river, even using honey locust to scrub away the grime and filth he'd worn for so long. No matter how much he scrubbed, however, he never washed himself clean. Dark he was and dark he remained.

In another wealthy shop owner's former home, Kuang San discovered a jar of corn whiskey tucked away in the family cellar. This would be used for the wedding. Lei Bu wished to contribute to the festivities, too, and set upon slaughtering a pig to go along with the booze. As he was busy at work, however, something unexpected occurred. He'd stabbed the pig to drain its blood, placed it in the roaster to cook, but as he was about to shave the skin clean of hair, the beast leapt up and ran off through the town. It actually made it some distance, jumping across one of the sewers that ran along the main street before it finally collapsed, dead. The slight delay behind them, in an adjacent courtyard the meat was boiled in a savoury and spicy broth. The remaining bones, and what meat was still stuck to them, was collected and divided between Lei Bu and Kuang San. Two other married women were also called to accompany Si Feng, to get her ready for the ceremony and to talk to her about the new expectations she would soon have to meet. The two women also enjoyed the bones, gnawing at them as they talked.

As the evening turned to morning, a wisp of fog could be seen billowing out of one of the caves that dotted the mountainside. And hanging down from the mist that sheltered the entrance was a rope. When those below discovered it, they couldn't help but be a little bewildered – just what was going on? Then, a little to the west, another rope dangled down from a cave entrance, this one with a man shimmying down it. Lei Bu immediately fired at the man, catching the rope and splitting it in two. The man who'd been climbing fell to his death, landing on the inferno still burning below. (The guerrillas had kept the flames alight, taking care not to be too distracted by the wedding celebration.)

Once the fires burnt a little lower, they went to inspect the man's remains only to find just the scorched aftermath of their bonfire. Nearby they also spotted a streak of blood and a footless shoe but no corpse. They began to suspect that perhaps others from the cave highest up had similarly descended and that they'd already fled. Lei Bu, however, didn't inform Li Desheng, nor did he speak to Lao Hei about it. Instead, he sat down with the few other men who'd been watching the fires with him, and together they roasted potatoes, intent of wasting away the rest of the day.

At noon on the third day of the wedding festivities, Lao Hei moved into his new home, bringing along with him thirty-two candles, twenty-six oil lanterns and quite a few twigs and branches from a pine tree that were to be burnt to add a pleasant fragrance to the air. Si Feng, however, opposed his plans and permitted him to keep just a single oil lantern.

Out in the courtyard, the food was prepared, the tables set. San Hai was in the kitchen preparing the meat, slicing it into even portions. Another attendee was pouring the corn whiskey into smaller, more suitable decanters for placing on the tables. The whole courtyard was busy with activity and the bustling sounds of the impending feast. On the other side of the estate wall, an owl sat perched in an elm tree, watching the spectacle unfold. Its head was overly large, its eyes a glistening yellow. It had wedged itself between branches, unmoving. San Hai spied the bird and shouted at it, trying to frighten it away. The owl remained, its eyes intent on the scene. Exasperated, San Hai flung a small reed broom at the owl to shoo it away. This time the bird shifted its position, took to the air and left. As if on cue, Lao Hei appeared, dressed in new clothes that seemed a little too tight for comfort.

"What's going on with the tree, huh?" he asked his soon-to-be brother-in-law.

"There was a magpie there," answered San Hai. At the same time as he spoke these words, a flock of magpies covered the sky.

"That's a good sign, now isn't it!" Lao Hei exclaimed. Then he called out to Kuang San: "Go an' fetch Lei Bu and the others, it's time to feast!"

Kuang San, however, was nowhere to be found, nor heard. In fact, he'd taken advantage of all the hubbub to crawl in under the great cedar bed in order to wait for Lao Hei and Si Feng to arrive later that evening; Lei Bu had told him to frighten them as part of the wedding celebrations.

While he was hiding beneath the bed, the two married women, along with Si Feng, came in and sat on top of it. Positioned on either side of the soon-to-be-married woman, they were busy getting Si Feng ready. The woman on the left was using silken thread to braid Si

Feng's hair. It hurt plenty and Si Feng couldn't help but wish she didn't have to go through the experience.

The older lady assured her, however, that she did: "These were the rules, my dear, old rules. A wedding required you to bare your face. You can't have it hidden behind your hair, now can you? After all, you wouldn't eat pork if it hadn't been shaved, now would you? Does it hurt? Just wait… tonight you'll experience real pain, ha ha, that's for sure!"

The lady on the right ran a comb through Si Feng's hair, grumbling all the while that she had no osmanthus oil to work into Si Feng's scalp. Resigning herself to doing without, the older woman finally spat into her palm and used it to comb Si Feng's hair.

Just as they were making her up, two other guerrilla fighters came into the room, each carrying an embroidered pillow. They didn't explain where they'd come from, but both pillows were finely stitched with mandarin ducks, a symbol for a happy marriage. They placed the pillows on the bed and joked at her expense: "Hey, she'll soon be in bed. Why does she need to make herself up?"

The other man offered an answer: "You ought to know why, you damn fool. I reckon they won't be doing much sleeping tonight, ha ha."

And just as the words fell from the man's mouth, the whole structure was engulfed in a great explosion.

The blast was the consequence of one of the wealthy residents of Huangfujie fleeing the caves and making it all the way to Zhengyang. From there he reported to the county militia that the bandits were holed up in his hometown. The militia naturally dispatched troops to reclaim the town and hopefully destroy the bandits. They were the ones who'd fired the ordnance and shattered the celebratory atmosphere. This was their first volley before they marched down from the mountain ridge that lay to the east of the town.

They hadn't targeted Lao Hei's wedding as such, this was just how it turned out. But the missile struck the very same marital bed Si Feng and the other two women were seated on. Miraculously, Si Feng was unharmed; the same, however, could not be said for the other women. The one on her right had her breast torn open and the organs beneath exposed. She died without uttering a sound. The one seated on her left had a gaping hole in her abdomen. She moaned and cried out in pain, before all sounds ceased and she was quiet, too, the life having passed from her body.

In the courtyard, bricks and tiles from the house were smashed and scattered everywhere; wood frames, too, lay in ruin. Mixed in among the debris were body parts, an arm, a leg, a torso. A great cry sounded: The militia have come! Li Desheng and Lei Bu, who'd just run up to the small alley that wound its way into the courtyard, were yelling to rally the troops out onto the main street.

When the shell first landed, San Hai was in the kitchen. He'd just picked up two bowls to fill with cornmeal porridge, thinking how necessary this simple ritual was, and how Si Feng had been denied it on her first inauspicious marriage to Wang Shizhen, when the detonation rang out. Thoughts had been swirling through his mind. His sister was getting married, which meant they had to prepare the *wuliang*, or five-grain congee, for her new home. On that evening when Wang had come for his sister, the rascal hadn't even followed this basic custom, or so he'd been told. Nor had he tried to make it up to her when she arrived at his estate. In fact, he'd done nothing for his sister at all. He was her brother, he had been thinking, her only family… it was the least he could do. And then, just as he noticed there were only two out of the five grains prepared, just as he asked the woman watching over the cooking fires where the other grains were, and just as she replied by asking him what he had in his hand, the explosion echoed in the air.

He put the bowls down immediately and rushed out, shouting: "What the hell's going on. What's happened?"

When the blast echoed, Lao Hei had been in the toilet, emptying his bowels. A shower of glass had struck the toilet walls and he'd recognised it almost immediately: the glass had come from the Tang dynasty mirror that'd been in his new home. He yanked up his trousers, fastened his belt and took off to see what had happened.

At the gate to his prospective marital home, he saw two prone bodies, comrades shredded by the blast. He raced into the bedroom and saw the two dead women. And Si Feng, too, still sitting on the bed, shell-shocked by what she had experienced. It was then that Kuang San crawled out from his hiding place.

Lao Hei took Si Feng in his arms and said: "You're not hurt, are you, you're not dead?"

His embrace seemed to wake her from a trance. She shifted as life returned to her body, then buried her head in his chest and cried uncontrollably, like a small child. Lao Hei wanted to console her, but he knew now was not the time: the militia had come and he had to make her safe; she had to hide! Releasing her, he drew his gun and headed outside.

Released from his grasp, Si Feng scrambled through the rubble looking for her shoes. She was intent on following him out, but at first she couldn't find her footwear. By the time she did, Lao Hei was already through what remained of the door.

"I'm coming with you," she shouted after him. "I'm your woman now, which means I go where you go!"

Lao Hei rebuked her: "It's too dangerous. There's no way you're coming with me."

Her response was just as quick: "But you've married me, haven't you? If you are to die, then we die together!"

Lao Hei was already running out into the courtyard. "It's not me who'll be dying!" He then yelled to Kuang San: "You take care of her, she's your sister-in-law now. It's up to you to hide her well."

Taking hold of her hand, Kuang San pulled Si Feng towards the back of the courtyard where he found a cellar used for storing potatoes. He suggested they hide inside it and use the nearby discarded cornstalks to cover the entrance. Si Feng, however, was unwilling to hide. Instead, she kept repeating her desire to be with Lao Hei.

Kuang San tried to persuade her: "Please, you must hide here for now. Once we've driven the enemy off, we'll come for you." But she wouldn't relent. Giving up, Kuang San changed tactics: "Alright, fine, if you won't hide in the cellar, then you'd best make sure the enemy doesn't find out about the wedding. Quick, run back and grab the bridal quilt and pillows, hide them in the cellar."

A few moments passed and she had returned with the quilt and pillows, and flung them into the cellar. Before she could do anything else, however, Kuang San's fist connected with her chin, knocking her out almost instantly. He dragged her unconscious body into the cellar, fixed planks over its entrance, then the cornstalks, cursing as he did so: "Women are such bloody trouble!" Once he thought she was safe, he ran off towards the battle that was raging in the town.

By the time Lao Hei reached the street, the militia were already swarming through it, and so he hurriedly dived behind a small stone wall for shelter. As he did so, he heard the enemy shout: "That was Lao Hei!"

And then a hail of bullets buffeted his hiding place. He returned fire and one of the men running at the front of the column fell. It never crossed his mind that he'd hit any more of the soldiers, but they fell too. He knew they would be well-armed, but he was equally brash. Loading his gun with more bullets, he spat on them as he did so and yelled towards the enemy: "I'll blow all you fuckers to kingdom come!"

The next bullet whistled through the air as if guided by some divine hand before exploding the head of yet another militiaman, one who'd been bringing up the rear.

Lao Hei yelled out once more: "Captain! Captain!"

But there was no sign of Li Desheng, or of any other comrades for that matter. Meanwhile, he spied out of the corner of his eye seven or eight more militiamen marching down a side alley. Their weapons crackled in the air, but they were firing wildly. Lao Hei turned and fled. His whole body felt like a leaf from some tree, fluttering from place to place, touching down on a wall that ran south down the street, then just as quickly arching back up into the sky to land on a wall running north. Before realising it, he'd exited the street.

A hand grenade tumbled through the air towards him, and he threw himself to the ground and dodged for cover into a nearby pig pen. The grenade exploded. He opened his eyes and blinked; he was still alive. He grabbed at his crotch, and all was intact.

"Motherfucker!" he cursed.

He lifted himself up and on all fours made his way across the mouth of the street. Once in relative safety, he stood and ran again, straight towards the river dyke and the willow tree grove that shielded it. There he discovered more than a dozen of his comrades, including Li Desheng, all hiding among the trees. Lao Hei noticed, too, that his commander had wounded his left hand somehow, for it was all bandaged up.

Li Desheng and Lei Bu had rallied the troops shortly after the ordnance blast and had engaged the militia that had come storming in from the west. They had actually managed to push them back a little, forcing them to withdraw to the temple grounds not far from the western edges of the village. But as they did so, they heard the crackle of firearms to the east.

That was when Li Desheng asked the men who it was they were fighting: "Who the devil has come? Are they county or town militia?"

"I saw both," Lei Bu replied. "There were men from the county militia, and I saw a platoon commander from Zhengyang. They must've joined forces."

"But we had sentries stationed at the eastern edge of the village. Why didn't they sound the alarm?"

"Er Kui, Er Kui!" Lei Bu cried out.

They had put an immediate subordinate in charge of sounding the alarm, but despite calling out his name, no reply was heard. Li Desheng's ire and exasperation grew.

"Someone bring me the bloody spyglass!"

Lei Bu handed it to Li Desheng. They'd obtained it in a previous engagement with the county militia; it was, as they say, one of the spoils of war. Li Desheng climbed on top of a pile of wood lying adjacent to one of the houses and directed the spyglass towards the east. Dozens of men were marching down the street and he knew they would soon be hopelessly outnumbered.

He turned back to his men and said: "Round up everyone you can and withdraw towards the outer edges of the village. Quick!"

As he spoke, a bullet whistled and struck his hand holding the spyglass, shattering flesh and bone. The shock propelled him from the wood pile to fall hard on the ground. Everyone was paralysed for a moment, and then panic began to overtake them. Lei Bu managed to keep his composure, and he knelt down near Li Desheng, picked him up and flung him over his shoulder. As he did so, Er Kui came running up to them and assumed Li Desheng must be dead.

"The commander's dead? Dead!" he cried out in fear.

Everything was happening so quickly. Their momentary hesitation gave the troops holed up in the temple the opportunity to advance once more.

Lei Bu tried to gather his wits: "He's not dead, just unconscious. So stop your fucken whimpering, will you?"

"He's not dead? Not dead!" Er Kui reached into his pocket and pulled out a bloodstained length of cloth that he now used to wipe Li Desheng's bruised and battered face.

Lei Bu rebuked him: "Shit, there's no time for that. Take him and go!"

"But he needs attention… help… otherwise…"

When the battle had started, Er Kui had shot dead the first militiaman he'd seen, but upon that man's heels came another dozen or more soldiers, and so all he could do was duck for cover in a nearby toilet. The toilet, however, wasn't empty. As he tumbled inside, he spied a woman crouching down, her trousers around her ankles. She was on her period. He didn't speak to the woman; he only grabbed her bloodstained cloth and scrambled back out of the toilet. Fortunately for him, the enemy troops had already passed by.

With one hand, Lei Bu pushed the other man away and said: "You were supposed to sound the alarm you fool, but now you show up with this? Go, get outta here, take the commander and retreat!"

They ran down a small alley, while the militia circled in from both directions. Bullets whizzed past them like swarming locusts.

Realising their situation to be dire, Lei Bu shouted to the men: "Make your way to the edge of the street, to the rear. If you can't, then head towards the trees by the riverbank."

With that, he climbed up over a compound wall and shimmied up onto a roof. Surefooted, he ran from building to building, firing rounds as he did so, hoping to lure the enemy into following him. Unexpectedly, Er Kui leapt up after him, and despite Lei Bu's repeated orders for him to retreat along with everyone else, Er Kui refused.

"It's my fault we're in this predicament. I didn't raise the alarm. Let me try and make it up to them!"

"Your legs are too short to run across rooftops. Are you trying to get yourself killed?"

"I've already got a blood-soaked rag!"

They ran together, the enemy taking the bait and chasing after them. Er Kui was hit, a bullet tearing into him. He crumpled across a central beam and more bullets hit him, pocketing him with so many holes he looked like a beehive, but red instead of yellow. Lei Bu seized advantage of the enemy's distraction – Er Kui's sacrifice – and leapt down into a side street, following after the rest of the men in the direction of the willow trees.

Seeing Li Desheng's injury, Lao Hei reproached Lei Bu: "You were supposed to observe the enemy's movements. What the hell were you looking at? Why'd you let the commander scale that wood pile, huh?"

"The spyglass was his, wasn't it? For the commander to use!"

Lao Hei, who'd been holding the spyglass, now threw it to the ground and crushed it beneath his boot. He counted the men to see how many had escaped. They'd lost about half of their number. San Hai was nowhere to be seen, nor were Kuang San and Si Feng. Lei Bu updated Lao Hei on what had transpired. The enemy had swarmed through the street, entering it from both directions. They were everywhere. Bullets had rained down on them, and he had no way of knowing if any other men had got out.

"Then I'm going to find out, damn it!" countered Lao Hei, and he turned to run back towards the street. Almost immediately he had to deal with enemy troops who were busy mopping up any rebel stragglers they could find. He spied the corpses of twenty or thirty of his comrades. But San Hai wasn't among them, nor were Kuang San or Si Feng. His mind wandered to earlier in the day. It was supposed to be his wedding, not the bloodbath it'd become. It had never crossed his mind the enemy would encircle them as they had, catch them so unaware, unprepared. Lei Bu had told him of the rich shop owner who had escaped from their mountain cave refuge. He knew who it had been, knew their home, too. And as soon as he found it, he set the home on fire, staying just long enough to make sure the blaze caught. Then, under cover from the smoke, he ran back towards the forest. The fire burnt into the night, lighting up Huangfujie. There was no way they would recapture the area, they'd lost this fight. There was nothing left to do but cross the river and head deeper into the mountains.

Kuang San left the courtyard and then realised he was unarmed. He turned and retrieved an axe to brandish as a weapon. As he did so, his eyes fell on the meat they'd prepared for the wedding. Cooked, sliced and ready to eat, he couldn't simply leave it. He picked up a handful and stuffed it in his mouth, then grabbed half the pig's face and tucked it under his arm. He ran off, navigating his way through twisting alleyways. A group of militiamen had surrounded a compound. High up on the roof were about seven or eight of his guerrilla comrades. They were without firearms, so they took to flinging roof tiles down at their attackers. Bullets sailed back in return, and soon they were out of sight. The enemy troops grabbed a ladder and scurried up after the guerrillas, only to be met by swords as the comrades fought on. In response, the remaining militiamen on the ground set the house ablaze, forcing the guerrilla bandits to jump down. One hit the ground and shattered his leg. The militiamen surrounded him, mercilessly impaling him with their bayonets. A comrade tried to rescue him, only to be wounded in the process. The militiamen then bound his hands and feet and tossed him into the burning inferno. The other five landed without incident and fled down a narrow lane, the enemy hot on their tails. The comrade bringing up the rear tumbled and fell. He died shortly afterwards, speared through his rectum with an enemy blade. So hard did the militiaman push, his blade became stuck. Kuang San leapt out, swinging his axe wildly, driving it into the enemy's shoulder. He was going to grab the man's gun.

That was when the remaining four comrades reappeared; they'd not run off. But they hadn't come to save him, either. Instead, they swore at him, clutched both his arms and shouted to the militiamen running forward: "Don't kill us. This scamp's important, he's ward to the deputy commander. We've caught him to give to you!"

Kuang San called out in outrage: "Wang Zhangli, you bastard, I won't forget this!" And he turned and swung his foot into the man's crotch. Wang Zhangli crumpled and released Kuang San, who fled. The militiamen opened fire and the remaining four comrades fell to the ground. Kuang San clambered up a broken wall that was still taller than a man, and leapt down the other side. He landed hard, winded, and for a moment did not move. Then, as he tried to stand, someone took hold of him again. This time, however, it was San Hai.

He'd been separated from Li Desheng and Lei Bu when they advanced west, and so he'd dived behind a millstone and busied himself sniping at the enemy. He aimed and took down one almost immediately, then another; in total he killed five enemy soldiers. When he had the sixth lined up, his gun jammed and he was forced to retreat into an alley. He'd been lying low ever since, that is until Kuang San literally fell down beside him.

Once he recognised the identity of the man who had grabbed him, Kuang San shouted: "A gun… I want one… I can't stand losing like this!"

San Hai didn't reply, but instead dragged him to his feet and together they ran. They soon came upon a compound whose main gate had been shut tight. They rushed at the door, forcing it open. Inside, an older woman, the master of the house apparently, tried to push them back, but San Hai persisted. The woman shouted, and Kuang San hurried to silence her. This proved to be more difficult than he expected, and when he could no longer hold her mouth shut, he punched the old woman, square in the chest. She dropped to the ground, her eyes rolling over white. They didn't know if she was still alive, but they couldn't leave her like that, and so they found a wide reed mat used for sitting and rolled her up in it. The two of them then looked for a suitable place to hide. Walking into one of the bedrooms, Kuang San found he was small enough to worm his way into the hollow of the *kang* bed-stove. San Hai, however, was much too big to fit, his broad shoulders preventing him from getting inside. That's when his eyes fell on a large earthen water jar, filled to half way. He climbed in, using the lid to hide his presence. When the militiamen burst in shortly afterwards, about six or seven of them, they at first found nothing. That was until they were about to leave, when one of them noticed the lid to the water jar shift, just a little. They marched over to it and discovered poor San Hai hiding inside.

The guerrilla band withdrew deeper into the mountains, finally making their way to Huangbocha, a remote, somewhat desolate hamlet nestled where the mountain range branched into two.

There were only three households in Huangbocha, and each was surrounded with walls towering about twenty feet. Built with pale limestone, the walls were clearly there to protect the people from the wild animals that roamed the area: the wolves, the jackals and wild boars and bovines. It was said these animals feared the dusty limestone. But not leopards, it seemed, for the hamlet's chickens and pigs often went missing.

It was the third night of the moon's cycle. It was dark, and the wind blew fiercely. And under the cover of darkness, the leopards came… again. At the edge of the village, on the road that led into it, one near-defenceless cow struggled with a leopard. Both animals possessed similar physical strength, and so in a contest of brute force against brute force, the natural result was that both were nearly exhausted. When dawn broke and the first few villagers went to work the fields, they discovered the two beasts locked together, dead. The leopard's foreclaws were still dug deep into the bovine's shoulder, while the cow had used its great neck muscles to drive its head into the leopard, evidently shattering its vertebrae. In a strange sort of way, they both seemed to be propping the other up, although it took only one kick to crumple them over onto the ground.

The cow belonged to a family by the name of Ran. But it wasn't just a beast of burden, it was more important than that, and so they didn't have the heart to eat it. The only other option, then, was to bury it, which is exactly what they did. The leopard was skinned and its fur hung up in their courtyard. At about the same time, an old man sporting an incredibly long white beard showed up at their door. They invited the man in, fed him and gave him a new pair of sturdy, straw sandals. Shortly before the man departed, he pulled out some rice paper and painted a written charm for the family. He also cut off his beard. He told them that a calamity was highly likely to visit the place, and that if it did, they were to burn the charm along with his beard, then add it to water and leave the hamlet. That was the only way they would avoid disaster. On the ninth day of the current month, it was to be the third anniversary of his mother's passing. As he made the offering at her grave and burnt the hell money and incense, he cried. Afterwards, his two neighbours were invited over for food and drink, and together they planned to leave the next morning. At around lunchtime, Lao Hei, Li Desheng and the rest of their guerrilla band arrived.

On the road to Huangbocha, Li Desheng's hand was treated with a salve of pumpkin pulp. The mixture would aid recovery, or so it was believed. It also helped reduce the pain and swelling. The only negative side effect was that it resulted in a sour, upset stomach, an ailment Li Desheng had been suffering from for some time. In fact, he couldn't get the taste of bile out of his mouth. While they'd been in Huangfujie, he'd drunk too much, he'd been neglectful, and now that lackadaisical manner had come back to haunt him. In his mind, he'd acted poorly. He'd made a strategic error, he'd let his guard down. And as a result, he was to blame for their defeat, for the great number of casualties they suffered. These thoughts plagued his mind, and did nothing to help his stomach.

Lao Hei, on the other hand, seemed to be free of troubles. Once they reached Huangbocha, he divided the men into groups and directed each group to call at one of the three village houses. Whether or not the three families understood who had come was unclear, but they were polite to the strangers nonetheless, each offering to feed the men who'd shown up at their door. The Ran family was not an exception; they treated their 'guests' with great deference and courtesy, immediately lighting the kitchen fires to prepare food and drink. But not all was at it seemed. Instead of actually serving the guerrilla band, the Ran family heeded the old man's advice and placed his written charm, as well as his white and frayed beard, into the flame, incinerating them both in flash. The ashes were then scooped up and deposited in the water that had just come to a boil. The ashen mixture was first offered to the head of the family, a rather old man with more years behind than in front. He declined, claiming that due to his great age and chronic pain, there was little point in him trying to flee. The concoction was therefore given to his son, who gulped it down. Whether or not the mixture gifted him with the necessary courage to try to escape is difficult to say, but he did make the attempt nonetheless. Thinking up an excuse in order to get outside – telling Lao Hei he needed to pick some hot peppers for the meal they were preparing – he tried to flee. The sentry that'd accompanied him, however, realised the man's intention, and so before he could take a few steps, the alarm was sounded and three or four fighters ran out to deal with the situation in whatever way necessary. The younger Ran was tackled to the ground quite easily.

"You dirty bastard," cursed the men. "You thought you could get away, head down the mountain and report on our whereabouts. Didn't you, you fucker!" And he was dragged back inside the walls and thrown at the feet of Lao Hei.

Lao Hei was irate: "Do you know what? I hate rats." Turning to his men, he ordered: "Take him outside and bury him!"

The younger Ran was paralysed by fear, his body unmoving. Except for his bowels, however, which released a small rivulet of shit that now trickled down his leg. The elder Ran hurried forward and knelt down beside his son, begging for mercy: "Please, please, don't make me have to see my son buried before me!"

Lao Hei stared at the man's son: "I see the look in your father's face... I guess I won't put you in the ground." He then picked up one of the family's sickles and slashed it hard down on the younger man's foot, nearly lopping it off. This was designed to prevent any further attempt to flee. It also served as a warning to the other households, who in turn were well-behaved, providing Lao Hei's band with all their food and drink; the guerrillas were welcome to stay a day or two, a week, a month, however long they needed. That settled, Li Desheng climbed up onto one of the *kangs*, and with his good hand, he wrote the following: 'The revolution has succeeded.' The note, he explained, was to be taken to his superiors in the Party soviet and cashed in for Party-printed money... for at least triple the standard rate!

No one in the mountain hamlet knew what a soviet was, and neither did Lao Hei for that matter. Once the two men chosen to deliver the message stepped outside, Lao Hei turned to Li Desheng and said: "The Party soviet?"

"It's our government."

"We've really got a government?"

"That's the whole aim of the revolution!"

They enjoyed a dinner of cornmeal congee with simmered potatoes and pumpkin, each eating his fill until their stomachs gurgled like croaking frogs. Soon after eating, Lao Hei found himself in the toilet, an outhouse constructed behind the main building, a short distance down the slope of the mountain, past a field flush with celery wormwood, their white tips blowing in the breeze.

One of the homeowners yelled out as he made his way across the field: "You need to stamp it down with your feet."

"What the hell does that mean?" came Lao Hei's reply.

"The whole field's haunted, and the ghosts love to eat shit. You need to hide out in the toilet."

"Ghosts... Ha, they don't scare me!"

But in the toilet Lao Hei did discover something unexpected. There, crumpled on the floor, was a used piece of paper, shit stained and filthy. And while Lao Hei couldn't read, he did recognise it: the very same piece of paper Li Desheng had used to write those words. After finishing his business, he marched back to the landlord and chided him for what he had seen: how could he have used Li's words to clean his arse?

"Well, I was hoping you wouldn't notice… and that you'd just leave and return to your men… so why don't you!"

Lao Hei glared at him. "You don't believe we've a government, do you? You don't even think our revolution's succeeded!"

Frightened, the landlord interjected: "No, no, it's succeeded, it's succeeded."

Li Desheng wrote out the phrase again, but this time it was securely affixed to the central beam of the house he was staying in.

Three days passed, but still Li Desheng's stomach problems persisted. In fact, they'd got worse as he was now vomiting blood along with the bile. He was also nearly completely bedridden. To Lao Hei and the men, it was clear their commander needed to see a doctor, needed some medicine. But at the same time, this would mean trekking back down the mountain, something they were reluctant to do. Besides, there was no guarantee a doctor would come, or if even medicine could be purchased. But Li Desheng required treatment, they needed a hash pipe at least and some opium to go with it. So someone had to go. There was really no alternative. But who? Lao Hei pre-empted any discussion: he would go, but before leaving, he had to make sure Lei Bu understood that the men's safety was his highest priority, nothing else mattered. He got the landlord to fry up some corn, and then he dressed like one of the mountain people. With a log of wood over one shoulder to complete the disguise, he headed off down the mountain.

While Lao Hei was away, Lei Bu made sure Huangbocha was secure. Besides tending to Li Desheng, he posted additional sentries and patrol routes, and did everything he could to rouse the men. As a result, nothing unexpected transpired. But this is not to say all remained quiet, particularly with one of the other households. Two brothers were effectively in charge of the house, but the elder one was a fool. He'd not married, and for as long as anyone could remember, he spent his nights in the cookhouse near a pile of wood used to feed the fires. His younger brother, who was married, spent his nights in the house proper along with his wife. This structure had five rooms in total, a large central one with smaller rooms on either side. Four of Li Desheng's guerrilla band had been sent to share this house, and after they moved in, the younger brother and his wife relocated to an easterly room. The four guests stayed in a westerly one.

Before their guests moved in, the married couple had always placed their chamber pot beside their bed, but now that it had to be shared, it was left in the central hall for everyone to use. This in and of itself wasn't an issue. Except for the fact the lady of the house had a perhaps unusual ritual: each and every night she would awake two or three times to use the chamber pot. Since she now had to actually leave her room to do this, the potential for problems was bound to arise. And they did, for the distinct sound of her urine sloshing into the chamber pot at night woke the sleeping comrades, to the extent that they would toss and turn for the remainder of the night, unable to go back to sleep. Then, when dawn broke, the previous night's story was soon shared among the rest of the men. As a result, when night came once more, nearly all of the men clamoured to spend the night in this particular house, even arguing and jostling with each other for the privilege.

Lei Bu understood the situation and planned to deal with it as he had done in the past when faced with something similar, namely, unconditional punishment. But he couldn't do that now, not here. Instead, his only course of action was to berate the men and call them out for being rude. They'd acted, or so he told them, as though they'd seen Diaochan, one of the four beauties from history, in place of a sow. After cursing the men, however, he had little choice but to allow them to take turns spending the night in this house. The sole condition was that they could listen but do nothing else; they had to bind their arms together, and should one need to piss, they all had to go together to ensure nothing untoward happened. The day after, he used ashen water to write slogans across the compound walls. The first was unambiguous: 'The guerrilla band must annihilate reactionaries.' So, too, was the second slogan: 'Work hard to establish the Qinling soviet.' The third, however, was less clear: 'We must march from Qinling and into the provincial capital. One man leads a female student, one man gets the girl!'

The mountains of Qinling reach high into the sky, its roads stretch long and meander across the terrain. The delivery of books and letters often took ten days or more, sometimes as long as a fortnight. If the missive was urgent, then a chicken feather would be pasted to the corner of the envelope, a mark to instruct the receiving station to take the letter by pony instead of simple human delivery. Such deliveries had to be completed in one or two days. As the march down the mountain was long and arduous, Lao Hei had wrapped his lower legs with puttees before departing. This would help ease the strain on his legs, especially with the log he carried over his shoulder further weighing him down. But he didn't return to Huangfujie; instead, he avoided it and made his way to Qingfengyi. The fried corn served to ward off hunger, and the mountains were replete with streams to drink from. He didn't stop either, walking through both day and night. By noon on the fifth day after leaving Huangbocha, he reached Qingfengyi, but rather than going straight to the station post, he decided to wait until night fell, holding up in a Buddhist temple that lay on the outer limits of town.

Out of the eight attractions in Qingfengyi, the temple was considered the most impressive. In reality, however, it was not much more than a mountain cave. According to legend, an elderly monk once spent an entire year meditating in the cave, during which time an old tiger was said to have guarded the entrance every night. Hence the name: the Protective Tiger Temple. Now, however, the monks had long since left and even the small structure that stood previously at the mouth of the cave had partially collapsed. When Lao Hei entered, he was welcomed by nothing but darkness. Even so, he could still make out the worn statues carved in honour of the Buddha, despite the cobwebs that clung hungrily to them. A small sacrificial table built out of stone stood in the centre of the room, but no incense burners could be seen. The soles of his feet began to feel warm and he carefully removed his shoes, stepping into the temple cave with bare feet. As he did so, he heard his stomach grumble; not once, but continuously, so much so that it began to sound as though it were singing a tune. He smiled and rubbed his tummy, then realised the tune was coming from beyond the cave. He quickly picked up his shoes and moved deeper inside, hiding in the darkness. A moment later he was surprised to see Kuang San enter, and was about to call out, but decided to hold his tongue. In his mind, he wondered about Kuang San's sudden appearance. After the guerrilla band had scattered, for him to now show up here, had he returned to Qingfengyi with Si Feng? He settled on teasing Kuang San instead.

Kuang San had entered the temple cave carrying a wicker basket, which he now placed on the ground. Once he'd done that, he turned and departed the cave, and Lao Hei crept out from his hiding place. Overturning the basket Kuang San had left behind, he discovered it was filled with dried persimmon, sweet potato and pancakes made with okara, as well as a single radish and a bundle of something wrapped in Mongolian oak leaves. Lao Hei opened the bundle straight away and was startled by the sight of a cooked pig's nose. He picked it up and squirrelled back into the deep recesses of the temple cave. A moment later, Kuang San returned with his hands filled again, this time with dried reeds and grass. He threw them down on the ground and collapsed on top of it to sleep. Lying outstretched, he used the basket as support for his head, but an instant later, he jumped up.

"Thief!" he yelled. "Come out, now! If you've dared eat my pig's nose, then I'll eat you in kind!"

"You'll eat who!" Lao Hei boomed from behind the Buddhist statue before leaping down.

Kuang San wept at the sight of Lao Hei and told him everything that had happened. He'd hidden under the *kang* until night fell before crawling out. None of their band could be found, so he set about looking for something to eat. While he ate, he overheard some people talking and learnt of San Hai's demise. He'd been decapitated not long after he was apprehended. The authorities also tore him limb from limb, but they didn't use their bayonets. Instead, in a twisted sort of homage to San Hai's own profession, they found a small blade, much like the one he used to castrate pigs and dogs, and slowly cut flesh and bone. Once done, they announced their encircling campaign had succeeded, and they'd cut off one rebel strand. With regard to Si Feng, he'd only learnt snippets of information. She'd been found unconscious in the cellar, but she hadn't been executed along with her brother. Rather, they bound her and escorted her back to the county capital, along with her brother's head. He hadn't been able to learn anything more after that.

After relating all of these events, Kuang San added: "I survived because of that pig's face, although all that's left now is a nose. Go ahead, take a bite."

Lao Hei flung the snout back at Kuang San and cursed: "You little shit. I told you to take care of her, didn't I, but here you sit, free, and she's heaven only knows where!"

"But I told you, I'd hidden her. She was safe in the cellar. How was I supposed to know they'd find her?" He waited for Lao Hei's fists to pummel him, willing to let the other man beat him to death. But Lao Hei's fists never landed. He merely stood up, moved back into the darkness and remained there for the rest of the day, silent except for the grinding of his teeth. Fear crept over Kuang San and his eyes stayed on Lao Hei. The sound of him grating his teeth hung in the air.

Finally, Kuang San broke the silence: "Spit it out, spit."

Lao Hei swallowed hard.

Kuang San swore he would make it up to him, that he'd atone for his crime. He told Lao Hei to remain in the cave, he would go and fetch the medicine for Li Desheng. A moment after leaving, however, he returned to say more to Lao Hei. If he was not back by dawn, then it must mean the enemy had captured him and most likely taken his head, too. If that was the case, he hoped Lao Hei would bury whatever was left of him in the back of the cave. And then, when the time came to honour the dead, steamed buns – black or white, it didn't matter – could be offered in his memory. He didn't want to end up a hungry, starving ghost.

But Kuang San never went to Huangfujie. He came looking for me, instead.

Once I'd finished singing in Wangwu, I received a request to travel to Jianzi, on the road between Qingfengyi and Huangfujie. There wasn't much in this village, but they did have a chemist's shop run by a man named Xu. And while this chemist was technically a subsidiary of the shop in Qingfengyi that was known as Guangrentang, in reality, the smaller store was the key supplier of medicinal ingredients for its much larger counterpart. There was also a family connection between the two pharmacies: Xu was the nephew of a Mr Wang, the man who owned Guangrentang. It was said the pair had been in the medicine business for more than ten years.

Now, Wang had the somewhat strange habit of burying money under a persimmon tree that stood within his courtyard, and every time he did so, Xu was aware the money was there. Then, some years later, when Wang went to dig up the money, there was nothing to be found, and so, quite naturally, he questioned Xu. The response he received was as strange as Wang's habit: Xu told him, with great certainty, that money was known to run away once it was buried underground. A truth he could attest to, moreover, since none of Wang's money remained. Perhaps surprisingly, given their close working relationship, I'm not sure, but Wang was a little suspicious of his nephew. Despite these misgivings, or perhaps because of them, Wang continued to bury money underground, but from this point on he chose a pear tree just outside his courtyard walls. He still believed his nephew. Xu, however, decided he no longer wished to work at Guangrentang, and instead relocated to Jianzi where he set up his own chemist business. Presumably, he wanted to be his own boss. We can perhaps wonder where he got the money for such a move, but...

Xu had only one son, and to ensure his future influence, he sent him to enlist in the county militia. Of course, he never once thought that his son would eat a bullet during the assault of Huangfujie, which was the reason I was called there in the first place; he wanted me to sing. It was only after I showed up that I learnt his son's age... he was just twenty-three when he died. He hadn't married, and so Xu had already made arrangements with a family in a neighbouring village. This family apparently had had a daughter, also unmarried, who died due to illness. Together, the two families agreed their children would wed; a posthumous marriage so that each would have some company in the afterlife. Once I learnt what they'd planned, I told them straight away that I sang mourning songs and that a wedding, even one such as this, wasn't for me, and that they ought to contact someone who sang songs more suited. Xu replied emphatically that this wasn't the case, and besides, he didn't want to bother anyone else. This marriage, after all, could hardly be seen as a joyous occasion. I acquiesced and stayed.

The houses in Jianzi were quite dispersed, scattered, one could say. And the pharmacy was perched high up the slope of the mountain, so that it looked down on the other households. On the day of the death marriage, red banners rather than white ones were hung on the main door; a red canopy was used too. As the bells tolled out the start of the wedding ceremony, the two coffins were placed alongside each other. It was soon time for me to sing, so I cleared my throat and began. The words went something like this:

With the beating of this drum I begin my song.
Let's welcome the marriage parties to this gate.
For those of you who stand beyond,
Please raise your heads to see this sight,
A pair of white chickens has perched on this arch.

As I reached the final line, a house servant interrupted me to explain the pair of white chickens were in fact a brace of phoenixes. Naturally, I had to adjust my tune, and soon sang of the dazzling display, hoping the phoenixes would quickly let me in to the main hall. We moved forward well enough, but as we approached the wedding chamber, two black dogs lay across the gateway. Again the servant offered advice, saying in fact these were not dogs at all, but rather a pair of unicorns. Once more I incorporated this into my song, asking for the beasts to make way so we could step inside to properly start the wedding. In the main hall, I strode around the coffins singing *The Eighteen Tears* from Kunqu Opera. You know the tune, it's rather silly, first talking about the sun and the moon and the stars in the sky, about the evil subterranean monsters that lurk beneath, of the commander-in-chief, the monarch that watches over the world between heaven and hell, and the pair of ideal lovers. There's more, too. The song references pigs, dogs, cattle and sheep, and the basic necessities of life. All you need is a good memory, you know, and a way with words, then there's nothing you can't sing about.

Anyway, I continued and sang these words:

Hey, listen, my asthmatic brother,
You spent your previous life mumbling to yourself,
And now you're trapped by a wheezy chest.
My pockmarked brother,
You used your last life to fight with pigs for nothing more than chaff,
And now your face is forever scarred.

And you, my crippled brother,
you spent your life so far stealing pears,
And now all you can do is saunter down the street on uneven legs.

Then, as I was singing, do you know what happened? There was an actual cripple standing next to me holding a long tobacco pipe, which he now used to rap me over the head and interrupt my song with his own ditty:

Hey brother,
In a previous life your mouth was filled with maggots,
And now look at you, you're resigned to be a mountain whisperer!

The assembled crowd all burst out into laughter and so did I, it was rather funny. And as we were laughing, the village head arrived. Someone announced his visit, shouting he'd come to offer his salutations, but this wasn't why he'd appeared. In his hand, he held a gong, which he struck three times before declaring: "The militia, I'm happy to report, has just apprehended another guerrilla bandit and a thief, too. He was on his way to the county capital when he was caught passing through Jianzi. The authorities have instructed all villagers from across the region to accompany the militia on their march to the city. We must attend the sentencing of this criminal and his co-conspirators!"

Upon hearing the announcement, I saw Xu weep, his eyes rolling over in grief at the disruption. The guests all rushed to ladle up what broth they could, swallowing hard, before they straightened out their clothes and tried to regain some composure. The village head, however, wouldn't permit Old Xu to attend.

That's when I spoke up: "I'm not from around here, I'll stay with Xu."

"You're here, which means you're under my command... Now go, you're going to march with the rest of us!"

I had little choice but to join the villagers.

It was in among the incarcerated that I spotted Si Feng. She was wearing new clothes, but they were stained through and through with blood. Her hands held firm to a heavy pole with a basket tied to one end. Stones filled the basket. On the opposite end hung her brother's head, its mouth open and stuffed with dirt. She didn't look at the crowd. Instead, her eyes were fixed on her brother's head as she told it what had happened to their parents.

They'd been taken away not long after he joined Li Desheng's guerrilla band, tortured and humiliated. When released, they decided they couldn't live with the shame and torment and so they'd hanged themselves with a length of rope; they'd strung it over a window frame so that one dangled on the inside, the other one outside. Si Feng then told her brother how a young woman called Liu from the eastern part of Qingfengyi fancied him. That was until he became a rebel. She ended up marrying someone called Zhang, the fourth son of a noodle shop owner who lived on the outskirts of the village. Why the hell had he hidden in a water container, and why wriggle about once safely hidden? She had a dream, she told him, about a month before. It was a strange dream... she was at home, and in the courtyard a pack of dogs, along with a sounder of swine, were busily talking to each other, saying they were going to castrate you, she told him. She cried... then laughed... then stopped moving... perhaps she had to pee, I'm not sure, but whatever it was, the militiamen guarding her took to whipping her with the sticks they carried.

Suddenly, I heard them shout: "Piss then, bitch, right in your trousers!" And she did, as if on cue... I saw her trouser leg become moist and then reddish, bloody urine running down over her shoes.

A tired-looking donkey was walking behind her. It carried five seriously wounded guerrillas on its back, one on top of the other. The beast marched in tandem with us, and when the militiamen came upon an elm tree, they decided to rest, the donkey stopping first, before it bent its legs and squatted on the ground. By the look of it, it wasn't going to make it any further.

That's when I heard someone else call out: "It's too heavy. The weight'll kill the poor thing, and what's the good in that? Why don't we just bury the bastards right here?"

Within seconds, one of the militiamen marched up to the wounded rebels, a determined look on his face, a stick in his hand. He rapped one of the men with his stick, but he didn't budge. Then he struck the next two and heard a single groan. Finally, he hit the last two, neither of whom moved. The order was given to bury them. To do that, of course, a pit had to be dug, so the militiamen enlisted the villagers to do it. They complied, naturally enough, but I noticed that none of them would actually lift the corpses into it… no, they simply grabbed a limb – a leg, an arm, it didn't seem to matter – and flung the bodies into the yawning hole in the ground.

That was when I yelled out: "Hey, lay them flat at least!"

"Do it yourself!" was the response I got.

So I climbed down among the four dead men, repositioning their bodies so that their heads faced west and their legs faced east. I noticed that one of the men had lost a shoe, so I yelled out once more, asking if anyone had seen it. Not surprisingly, it had fallen off near the donkey. Now I don't know who kicked it, but it was next to me soon enough, along with another body they'd just thrown in. But when I tried to set this one right, the corpse spoke to me: "Turn me over, I want my face in the ground."

That's when I realised he was still alive. I called out to the commander: "This one's not dead."

The response was not what I expected: "You looking for more trouble? Get the hell out of there now. We're filling it in!"

The not-yet-dead man called out to me again, but I couldn't hear his voice as clearly this time. I bent low and he told me once more to turn him over; he didn't want the earth to crush his face when they buried him. I understood, and did what he asked. With his last breath, he told me his name, Wang Lang. He asked me to tell people he was buried here. I'd just turned him over when they started to replace the earth. There was nothing left to do, so I scrambled up out of the pit as quickly as I could. It didn't take them long to level the ground, leaving little sign of the men who'd died.

It must've been four or five days later, I was in the pharmacy again. The wind was wailing, and I had the distinct feeling that Wang Lang was whispering in my ear. One night, I was already asleep, when I heard a noise at the door, a soft rustling sound… I grumbled, as you would, about whoever it might be knocking at my door so late… but I got up, dressed, and cracked the door open ever so slightly to see who it was. I was surprised let me tell you… for there at my door was a wolf! Its fur was a charcoal-grey colour, its eyes were green… it scratched at my door, crouched and growled in a low voice… then it raised itself again, turned, and with its hind legs it kicked at the dirt, sending it flying at the door… it growled some more… I had the keen impression it wanted me to open it.

There're a lot of wolves around Jianzi, this I knew, and of course I wasn't about to open the door. In fact, I thought it best to barricade it, just in case. Once the animal realised the door would remain shut, at least I guess that's what it realised, it walked once more up onto the steps and deposited something it'd been carrying in its mouth… afterwards, it lay down and continued its howling… but not for too long… perhaps three howls… then it stood once more and left. I didn't dare leave the house for the rest of the night, not even to pee. I stayed inside until the sun was high up in the sky, when finally Old Xu came and opened the door… he had a silver necklace in his hand. At first, I figured the wolf from the previous night must've either eaten some child, or at least carried it off, and that that necklace had been round its neck… but then I thought some more and wondered why the hell had the wolf given the necklace to me? I remained puzzled for most of the day, then sometime in the afternoon it all became clear to me… the man I'd turned over, the guerrilla fighter who didn't want his face to be crushed by the earth as it fell on top of him, well, I'd heard wrong, his given name couldn't have been Lang, meaning 'bright', it must've been Lang, meaning 'wolf'… that's the beast that had come the night before… it had come to say thanks! I could then make lunch, and not just for myself, no, I returned to where the fighters had been buried to offer the meal to them… and that's when I bumped into Kuang San.

He looked filthy. You could even say half his arse was hanging out of his trousers. A straw hat sat upon his head, and he walked as though he'd gone lame. He looked nothing like he did before, but I knew it was him, it was Kuang San. I gestured for him to come closer, and together we went over behind a solitary tree that stood to one side.

"Why the hell have you walked down this road?" I asked.

"Why the hell not!"

"Didn't you march off with Lao Hei? Aren't you part of his guerrilla band? There're wanted posters up everywhere for him."

"Who said I went with him? I might've left Qingfengyi at the same time, but that doesn't mean I'm with him."

He offered no further explanation, but reached down and picked up the food I'd brought for the dead men. As he stuffed it into his mouth, he asked me why I was there, and I told him I was staying at the place of Old Xu, the chemist. He asked to go there immediately, but I refused, lying that I had some other things to take care of in the village. I turned and left quickly.

He called out after me: "Hmph, rather small bowls… you couldn't prepare more, could you?"

When I was staying in Jianzi, Old Xu would often leave me in the pharmacy at night to look after things, while he would spend his evenings a little way down the mountainside. He spent this time in the company of a widow, the two having become very close. He told only me about her, about their relationship, and to be honest, I encouraged him, told him not to worry about the shop. And he didn't. After all, he said, who'd dare provoke a man such as me, a man, you know, in communion with both yin and yang, a man between this world and the next. Besides, it wasn't as though I could eat the stock he carried! So he trusted me, and I spent the nights in the pharmacy just drinking tea, minding the shop… generally very quiet. Until that evening, however, when Kuang San came, saying he wanted to buy… supposedly… some medicine.

That, in and of itself, wasn't a problem. But he only knew the name of the drug, not what it looked like. To make matters worse, I didn't know what it looked like either, and so he nagged me to go and fetch Old Xu. I resisted, naturally. But Kuang San's response… well, I suppose it wasn't wholly unexpected… he said fine, in fact, and then wondered what there was to eat in the shop. Of course, there was nothing, which he soon discovered, and so, quite brashly I must say, he plopped down on my bed, intent to settle in for the night. He didn't even remove his shoes or change his clothing, the rascal. Apparently, it was too dark outside for him to leave. He went on to say that he wouldn't even go when the sun came up, no, he was going to stick to me the same way sticky rice cake sticks to your teeth. What was I to do? I had to take him to see Old Xu, there was really no other option.

And so we strolled down the mountain to the widow's house and I knocked, perhaps a couple of times. While we could hear noise beyond the door, it didn't open, so I called out to Old Xu and told him it was me. Finally, the door opened and I could see Xu's face. It was flushed and sweaty, his clothes were on backwards. He cursed at me for calling so late at night, swearing it must've been a ghost that'd driven me out! I replied there was a matter of some urgency, and he swore some more. If it was urgent, why hadn't I yelled out, why just come and knock on the door? I knew what he meant by that, of course. When I'd knocked first, not knowing who it was, he'd squirrelled himself away behind the widow's firewood, only coming out after he heard my voice. I guess it must've been a great... annoyance... interruption? Whatever, he then asked what it was that couldn't wait till morning. That's when Kuang San pushed his way in and told him he needed to buy some medicine. Naturally, Old Xu asked him who he was, and Kuang San replied with his usual sharp tongue, asking if a shopkeeper was more concerned with making money or getting to know people. Without waiting for a response, he simply blurted out the name of the drug he wanted. I could see Xu disliked Kuang San almost immediately, and that he wasn't keen to sell him the medicine. If the actual sick person wasn't here, Old Xu told him, then he couldn't buy the drug.

Kuang San's face changed suddenly, taking on an odd look. He announced he was wanting to buy the medicine for Qinling's guerrilla band. He blurted out further details about how the guerrillas, hundreds of them, were holed up in a hamlet high up on the southern mountains. Then he added they were planning to march on Qingfengyi in three days' time. Xu didn't believe him, said it was all bullshit; in fact, the guerrillas had been destroyed, scattered to the winds. Those who hadn't been killed... they couldn't possibly have that many men. I remember Kuang San retorted that it was up to him to believe what he said or not, he didn't care, but the medicine was for Li Desheng, the guerrilla commander. Old Xu responded in kind, wondering if the younger man thought he didn't know who Li Desheng was, because he did, he'd seen him before in Qingfengyi, although they'd not exchanged pleasantries. Kuang San seemed to relent, resigning himself to the fact Old Xu wouldn't sell him the medicine, so he changed tactics and said the older man ought to go and see the commander for himself. I remember he actually yelled something along the lines of "I'll take you with me now", or words to that effect. Old Xu was growing irate, I remember, and rebuked Kuang San, saying he was tossing around a lot of horseshit, that he shouldn't presume to tell Old Xu what to do or where to go, that he wondered if Kuang San had taken him for a blind fool.

Now I should say that since he was little, Xu *did* have a bad eye, the right one, so perhaps Kuang San's words were sort of on the mark, but whatever, it was now this eye that he directed Kuang San to look at. Kuang San, naturally enough, exclaimed in surprise, but then he drew a blade he'd kept concealed under his jacket, brandishing it menacingly… frightened me half to death, I don't mind saying. Xu trembled too… but Kuang San used the knife to snip the straps that held his sandals to his feet, and then he threw them to one side, strode over to the bed and slipped on the new shoes he saw there. There was another pair of shoes beside the bed, too. Embroidered with flowers, I remember. Kuang San looked up at the bed. Moonlight was creeping in through the window, and he could see another person sleeping under the covers, unmoving, peaceful-like. Kuang San turned back towards Old Xu and teased him: by the looks of it, he said, the old man *did* like groping around in the dark, and even when the sun was up, that dead right eye would still see only black! Old Xu had no rejoinder this time. He got dressed and together we returned to the pharmacy. There, Xu collected his medicines and other paraphernalia of his trade, and left with Kuang San. I remained in the shop.

Kuang San guided Xu to the temple where Lao Hei had been hiding. He'd tied a length of rope to one of Old Xu's hands, the other end fastened to his own. The three then departed the Protective Tiger Temple and headed for the mountains, despite the sun having not yet risen. After three days imbibing the concoction Old Xu had prepared, Li Desheng's stomach pains subsided. Xu left shortly afterwards, but before he did, Li Desheng instructed Lao Hei to swear an oath of brotherhood with the older man.

Later, Lao Hei wondered to his commander why he'd made such a request: "So, I'm a sworn brother to a one-eyed dragon… what the hell for?"

"To be frank," came Li Desheng's reply, "I'm worried he'll inform on us."

"Do you think he'd dare?"

Old Xu kept to his word, he didn't say anything to anyone about where the guerrilla band was hiding. In truth, he viewed the connection to them as in his best interests. After all, collecting medicinal ingredients up in the mountain made sense. And if it meant delivering medicines to Li Desheng's camp, which he did on several occasions, then so be it.

Unbeknownst to Xu, however, his changed routine did not go unnoticed by the Jianzi militia, and they soon grew suspicious of his frequent trips into the mountain, especially since he never seemed to bring back all that many ingredients and in the past he'd only ever remained at the store, preparing drugs and selling them. As a result, several of the militiamen took to paying regular visits to Old Xu's shop, ostensibly to enjoy some tea, to smoke. But they rarely spoke much, they just sat there. The only really noticeable thing they did was to put up wanted posters for Li Desheng and Lao Hei on both the walls and the door of the store. Afterwards, when Kuang San paid Old Xu a visit and saw the posters for the first time, they couldn't help but make him feel a little uncomfortable, perturbed even.

"Do you know, I'm important too, a lieutenant. Why isn't my name up there?"

Later that same evening, under cover of darkness, Kuang San crept back into Jianzi and scaled the walls of the village head's compound. As it happened, the man, carrying a small oil lantern, had just come outside to relieve himself when the first thing he saw was Kuang San sitting astride a cupboard in the main hall.

Startled, he blurted out: "Who the devil are you?"

"The rebel fighter Kuang San, that's who I am."

"I don't recognise the name."

"You will now you bastard!" Kuang San pulled out his firearm, as well as one of the wanted posters, which he threw in the direction of the village head. "Eat it!"

"I can't, I'll never be able to swallow it."

"Then burn it to ash and eat the remains."

The village head did as he was told, and once the poster was burnt, he mixed it with water and drank the mixture down.

"If you dare go to the pharmacy again to put up these posters, I'll murder the whole fucken village!"

The older man kowtowed several times, assuring Kuang San that no further posters would be put up. And then he pulled out a wad of twenty silver yuan as though offering compensation.

Not long after this incident, the mountain whisperer was called to sing for someone else. He never set foot in Jianzi again.

Jianzi was located on the main administrative road that linked the county capital with Huangfujie, and so it was a convenient place to rest. What's more, the village pharmacy had become a secret relay station for Qinling's band of rebels. And Jianzi's village head? He worked for both sides. He was also a man of the arts, quite a skilled painter. His son lived in the capital and owned a small gallery. When the area's militia marched through Jianzi, they of course paid the village head a visit, had a drink or two at his home, and, to show his hospitality, he would often paint for them. Soaring eagles, falcons or other birds of prey were a common subject matter, and to finish the image, he would usually inscribe the characters for 'hero' at the top. When, on the other hand, the guerrillas paid him a visit, they wouldn't go to his home. Rather, he'd receive a missive to meet them, making sure he brought wine with him. He'd also paint. Again, birds of prey were his choice, the characters for 'hero', too. The rebels, however, would often drink their fill and then forget to take the painting with them. This had happened so many times that the walls of the pharmacy were lined with numerous paintings, each one a bird.

In April of the following year, the peach blossoms bloomed a wonderful white. Li Desheng's hand had healed by this time, but it hadn't healed well; his right hand appeared more like a chicken's claw than a human appendage. He couldn't even use it to pick up chopsticks, let alone fire a gun, and so all he could do was practise his aim with his left hand. To make matters worse, his stomach illness returned, as painful as the first time, and no amount of herbal tea could settle it. Whatever he ate, he vomited back up again. As a result, he became frailer and frailer, a shell of his former self.

It was because of this that Li Desheng, along with his ever-loyal comrade Lao Hei, spent more and more time at the pharmacy, eventually moving in and bedding down there most nights. A few weeks after they started doing so, word came from the village that a woman was soon to give birth. Upon hearing the news, Old Xu sent his widowed paramour to request the woman's placenta. This, he told them, could be dried, powdered and mixed up with water for Li Desheng to drink; it might be just the thing to treat his recurring stomach ailment.

Dutifully, the widow did as she was told, but the family of the new mother refused, saying the placenta had to be buried under the tallest tree they could find to ensure their new baby would grow as tall and strong as the tree. Hearing this response, Lao Hei picked up his gun and went to see the family himself. A short while later, he returned with the placenta.

"How the hell did you get them to give it to you?" asked Old Xu.

"It's to treat illness, isn't it? So I told them, as the child's not yet born… well... I'll just tear its mother's belly open and take it that way!"

Xu asked no further questions, but simply took the placenta, washed it free of blood and cut it into pieces. He placed the pieces next to the charcoal stove and allowed them to dry by the heat of the fire.

It was at the same time that he was preparing this treatment that the county militia arrived in Jianzi. The village head immediately sent word that Li Desheng and Lao Hei needed to flee. Unfortunately, Li was in no shape to go anywhere, certainly not up the mountain, so Lao Hei hoisted him onto his back and together they made their way into the nearby ravine.

Li Desheng mumbled as they left: "Strange… this is… a place that was once very dangerous and has now become safe."

When they showed up at the village head's compound, his shock was hard to disguise, and for a moment, he was unsure what to do. Finally, he told them the only option was to hide between the walls of the main hall. Lao Hei was dubious at first; it never occurred to him that the walls might actually have a space in between, but once they saw inside, they noticed foreign currency, reams of silk, smoking paraphernalia and other valuables.

Lao Hei turned towards the village head: "When I asked you for money before, you cried poor, but look here at all these valuables, huh?"

A look of embarrassment spread over the man's face. "Er… um… take what you want, then."

Li Desheng assured the village head they were interested in none of it. "If you don't believe us, then send your old mother in here with us."

The village head understood what Li was getting at: "Are you trying to say you don't really trust me?" He called out to his mum, and told her to hide inside with the two men.

Once they were safely between the walls, the village head left to properly greet the militiamen. Wine and food were enjoyed, and as before, he took out his painting brushes. His easel was in the main hall, just a few feet from where Lao Hei and Li Desheng were hiding. He painted the same subject matter, a bird of prey. The weather was fine, not hot at all, yet the village head's face dripped with sweat.

"What's wrong with you? You're sweating like a pig," came the commander's voice.

"Oh, it's nothing, I'm just wearing heavy clothes, that's all." He removed his outer garment, leaving him with just an undershirt that seemed much too tight. "Ha ha," he laughed uneasily, "don't they say something about poor sweat and rich oil? Let me tell you, if I had your robust complexion, then I'd be a happy man for sure!"

Li Desheng's ability to avoid calamity, to turn defeat into victory, certainly suggested he lived a charmed life. But who could predict he'd be felled by his stomach, that for twenty-two days he'd vomit only blood, then collapse and not wake again?

Then, in the dead of night, from far off in the distance, piercing calls sounded.

"Do you suppose it's an owl?" wondered Old Xu.

"I imagine so. Sounds like an owl to me," came the widow's reply.

"Not good, not good, a bad omen for sure."

"Shut it, both of you!" Lao Hei cried out.

Li Desheng coughed his last ragged breath and died. Lao Hei, overcome with rage, seized Old Xu and began pummelling him with his fists.

"Control your rage. Ow! Stop beating me. I'm the only one who can make the final arrangements!"

Lao Hei let go of the man, reached for a ladleful of gruel and slowly regained his composure.

There was no coffin for Li Desheng, no memorial tablet. He couldn't even be buried during the day. By cover of darkness, Lao Hei buried his commander, his cousin, his friend under a castor-oil bush that grew near the widow's home. No burial mound marked his grave. They even had to turn the earth over once he'd been put in the ground, fearful it might be discovered; there had to be no traces. It took all night to turn over the soil, and when the sun rose, a neighbour, who'd come out to empty his chamber pot, noticed Lao Hei just finishing his work.

"Why've you rooted up all of the castor bean?"

"I'm going to plant some alfalfa," came the widow's reply. "You're up early to empty your chamber pot, aren't you?"

"I mightn't always be the one who dumps out this shit, literally speaking, but when I do, I'm sure to do it early! That castor bean had grown so nice, you know. Why would you uproot it to plant alfalfa?"

"I like alfalfa, what of it? I say, if you're the one to take out the shit, you ought to be a county magistrate!"

The neighbour smiled and laughed. "You've turned the earth over by yourselves… you don't have a cow to do the work?"

Lao Hei lost his patience: "Go on, fuck off, enough of your shit. You do blather on, don't you."

Undeterred, the man continued: "I know Old Xu. It'd make sense if he was here to help her, but who're you?"

"Go! Fuck off!" The vehemence in his voice finally did the trick. The man turned and beat a hasty retreat.

The tone of Lao Hei's voice, however, would give rise to greater trouble. The man he'd spoken to so roughly was a lifelong bachelor, a bare stick as they say, and so whenever he bumped into the widow who lived nearby, deliberately or not, he delighted in the opportunity to strike up a conversation, to shoot the breeze, to have some female companionship, even if it was only idle chitchat. But when he heard she'd become Old Xu's lover, he soured immediately on the older man and grew to hate him quite vociferously. Later, when he learnt of the guerrilla leader Li Desheng frequenting the pharmacy, that he was ill, he hoped that the militia would appear before long and drag Old Xu away for collaborating with the enemy. He didn't know Lao Hei, but now to receive such a dressing down by a stranger, well, it raised the bile in his throat.

Later, when he found himself in the village, he noticed straight away bulletins pasted on the arch that welcomed visitors. They were quite unmissable, and so he took some time to look at them a little more closely. He couldn't read the characters written at the top, but the picture was clear enough. The man the authorities were searching for was the very same man who'd scolded him so viciously outside the widow's house. Naturally, he shared his experience, particularly with one of the village moneybags.

As it happened, this shop owner had only the day before returned from Qingfengyi, where he'd witnessed first-hand the authority's treatment of these rebels. They'd torn down San Hai's home... dug up the burial site of his parents... their ferocity towards the guerrilla band was unparalleled. Fearing possible retribution if they said nothing, the shop owner ran off to inform the militia leaders of what he had learnt, and before he could return himself, soldiers had already been dispatched to question the informant and to get him to guide them to the widow's house.

After they showed up at her door, it didn't take long for them to hear the whole story, the widow had the backbone of a jellyfish, and so they marched off without delay, straight to the pharmacy.

Having buried Li Desheng, Lao Hei and Xu returned to the pharmacy and packed up the dead man's belongings. Once that was done, they began to prepare a meal before departing, but just as the table was set, Lao Hei paused and spoke to his now deceased commander: "You eat, comrade. When you're done, I'll have what's left."

At the same time as Lao Hei was going through this ritual, a platoon of soldiers were taking up positions on an embankment just beyond the front gate to the pharmacy. And once set, the only warning they gave was the clap of their guns being fired before bullets rained down on the shop. Instinctively, Lao Hei grabbed Old Xu and the two men fled out of the back door. Xu's eyes were poor, however, and he staggered and tripped over the stones and rocks that littered the mountainside.

"Lao Hei, you're killing me!"

Lao Hei turned to see the older man huffing and puffing. He ran back and began pulling him along, and as he did so, a bullet struck him in the left leg, boring into muscle.

"You've killed *me*, you damn fool!"

Wounded and burdened by his companion, Lao Hei still managed to flee with Xu, ultimately stumbling upon an old kiln to the north of Qingfengyi that had once been used for firing tiles and bricks.

By the looks of it, the kiln had collapsed a long time ago, the remnants of its structure overgrown with potato sprouts. Here, the two men hid for two days. Hunger and thirst tormented them over the course of the two days, but they had few alternatives, despite being surrounded by potatoes. Unfortunately, the ash from the former kiln, along with something that seemed suspiciously like chicken shit, had grown into and corrupted the potatoes themselves, leaving the new sprouts on top sickly, wilted and deformed. Even after the two men wiped away what ash and chicken shit they could, the potatoes were still barely edible. They had other concerns, too. Lao Hei's leg had got worse, due in no small part to the effort he'd spent digging into the ground. The exertion tore the wound open even more, so that the bone was now clearly visible. Old Xu tried to help. First, he ripped his clothes into strips to use as a bandage, and then he wrapped them tight around Lao Hei's leg, who sat enduring the pain by chewing on a small piece of wood. All of a sudden, he bit hard into the wood, snapping it in half.

"What village are we near?"

"Woheigou," was Xu's reply.

"What an awful name. How the hell did it come by it?"

"Oh this is bad, very bad. Your name's Lao Hei, the same 'hei' that's in the village name… black, blackness, this's a bad omen for you."

"Bah, you're talking rubbish."

Old Xu offered no reply this time, but sighed despairingly.

The day darkened once more, and Xu warned Lao Hei not to move. His leg was broken badly and in desperate need of a splint. Xu told him to remain hidden; he would try to find some suitable wood. Unfortunately for Lao Hei, the older man never returned.

But Lao Hei waited. What else was he to do? Then, when day broke and there was still no sign of the older man, he manoeuvred his frame as best he could to peer out from their hiding place. Pressing his face up against the tiles, practically grinding off his eyebrows, the only thing he could see was the occasional soldier marching back and forth. When night came again, Lao Hei steeled himself, gritted through the pain and crawled out from the kiln. With great difficulty, he made it into the village, whereupon he discovered a rather large fire blazing brightly in the night sky with four of five militiamen guarding it. There was little chance of him making it by them unseen, so he retreated behind a large pile of wheat and waited for an opportunity.

While he waited for his chance, the village chickens began to cluck, loud and excited. It seemed as though a wolf or some other predator had found its way into the coop. Curious as to what was happening, Lao Hei drove his hands into the pile of wheat to clear a line of sight, and his eyes fell on a soldier engaged in the interrogation of a woman. She looked a mess, her hair dishevelled and her belly large with child. She was busy shouting at the man who was supposed to be questioning her.

"Let me pass, now. I live on Station Street. I need to get home."

The soldier refused. She wasn't going to get by him.

As they jostled, another militiaman walked up: "She's mad. I saw her just a month ago in Jiwa. Let her pass."

"A madman," said the other soldier. "Well, a madwoman… pregnant… what man would want to plant that seed?"

"Lao Hei, one of the guerrilla bandits you're all searching for. He's the father!"

"What's your relationship to Lao Hei, huh?" asked one of the militiamen, now much more interested in the crazy-looking woman.

"Whaddya mean what kind of relationship, he's my man!"

Hearing her speak, Lao Hei's heart jumped… could she be Si Feng? He looked more intently at the woman… it *was* her, his Si Feng. But was it really? He still couldn't believe it, so he rubbed his eyes furiously, wondering if he had become delirious… but it really, truly was her, Si Feng! She'd gone mad, she looked almost inhuman. It'd been two years since he last saw her, how was she still alive, and whose child was she carrying? These thoughts burnt through his mind, and he buried his head in the wheat, tears gushing forth. He couldn't look at her any longer, he didn't want to, but then she cried out once more.

"Lao Hei is my man! And he's got a gun!"

The soldiers smiled and laughed; she was crazy, talking nonsense. One turned to look at the others: "This mad old bird's been raped, that's for sure."

"Well then, if someone else's done the deed, so can I!"

The other man walked up to Si Feng: "That's right, hmm. Now let me see that bastard Lao Hei's seed, hmm!" And in one swift motion he tore her jacket apart.

At that moment Lao Hei burst out from behind the hay, steadied himself on his one good leg, and fired. The first shot pierced the man who'd ripped off her jacket, the second drove through the man who'd planned to rape her, and the third bore into Si Feng's heart. He couldn't bear to see her like this, to have her live such a life. His fourth shot was intended for the tall, skinny soldier standing watch over the fire. But this man shot first and Lao Hei hit the ground.

The militia's inability to capture Lao Hei at the pharmacy had been a source of great embarrassment that led to rage, so much so that their initial reaction was to return to the widow's house and force her to dig up the remains of Li Desheng. The widow, unsurprisingly, had had her nerves rattled after the first time they marched upon her house, that she could no longer think straight, let alone identify the spot where he had been buried, especially since they'd turned the earth over so thoroughly. In response, the militia commander ordered his troops to round up all of the villagers; they were to be forced to dig from east to west until they found Li's corpse. Once that was accomplished, the body was dragged before the commander, who summarily fired a shot through the already dead man's head, in through one temple, out through the other. To further prove that Li Desheng had died by their hands instead of as a result of some illness, the commander ordered the widow to find a chicken and bring it to him. She complied, and once the chicken had been brought, it was slaughtered and its blood used to stain the barrel of the commander's gun; they had to have proof. The widow watched the scene in horror and begged for them not to hate her. Then the sound of a firing gun rang out, and her head slumped. She exhaled her last breath.

Li Desheng's already defiled corpse was returned to the county capital where its head was lopped off and put on display at the city gates. For the next two days a great wind blew, whipping up dust and sand, blackening the sky. On the third day, Li Desheng's head was gone. Word spread quickly throughout the city: the defeated remnants of Qinling's guerrilla band must have sneaked into town and stolen the head back. Others said they'd seen two eagles swoop in and carry it off, each holding an ear. Whether any of these tales were true or not, no one could say for sure, but what was clear enough was this: there were damaged sections of the main gate and each of these broken pieces was stained with eagle dung, white, almost ashen in colour, stretching a good three feet long.

Not long after, the Zhengyang militia marched into the county capital, towing along a bound and defeated Lao Hei. Both his legs had been mangled, and he was unable to walk. He'd been trussed up with a rope that'd been soaked in water so as to allow it to better bite into the skin, and then strung up over a pole so that he could be paraded into town. As they marched by each and every village on the way to the county seat, the militiamen beat a gong to mark their passage and to ensure every villager witnessed the scene. The wealthier shop owners popped firecrackers in enthusiastic response, then spat at Lao Hei's face. Before long, the mucus and saliva crusted his eyes, preventing him from really seeing what was happening. One bystander was especially pleased with Lao Hei's capture. His son, the younger Mr Yan, had died in service to the militia. They were natives of Qingfengyi, and when the older man learnt they'd be parading Lao Hei through the town, he made sure to arrive early, carrying the memorial tablet of his son with him. When the militia marched through, he shouted loudly for all to hear.

"There he is, son, look, that bastard Lao Hei is getting his comeuppance!" He gave a deep, hearty chortle, before collapsing onto the ground, quiet, unconscious. Blood could be seen dripping from his ears.

Wang Shizhen's concubine showed up, too. She'd already remarried, this time to a wealthy shopkeeper who lived in the city. She'd had a child, a boy, and no longer went by the name of Wang. Her family name was now Lu, and what's more, she was connected to the city leadership, her husband being cousin to the county head commissioner. She'd come to request that Lao Hei's black heart be gouged out so that she could offer it as sacrifice to Wang Shizhen's spirit.

The authorities agreed: a memorial ceremony would be prepared to honour Wang Shizhen. When the day arrived, his spirit tablet was put front and centre, flanked by sacrificial offerings that included heads from both a boar and a bull. His former concubine burnt hell money and offered wine, and as she did so, Lao Hei was brought forward. The sky had a crimson hue, the sun blazing above them like a swirling mass of hot oil. Lao Hei lifted his head, the day felt hot.

"Oh, a bit of rain'd be nice," he lamented.

And then, on cue, the sky opened and a raindrop fell. But only one. The size of a soybean, it splashed square down onto his forehead. The new town secretary had the family name of Lin. Before assuming the post, he'd studied in the provincial capital, had perhaps even known Li Desheng personally. The figure he cut was in contrast to the previous secretary. Wang Shizhen enjoyed the leisure possibilities afforded by his position; he was always ready to sit, relax and smoke. Secretary Lin, however, never indulged in tobacco. His figure was more akin to an opera star, refined and effeminate, one more comfortable toying with a folding fan than anything else. As he moved to question Lao Hei, the fan he carried snapped open and closed repeatedly, smoothly. This was the first time he'd seen the rebel.

"Well now, you really are quite black, aren't you!"

"Locusts filled the sky and blacked out the sun on the day I was born."

"I've heard stories that say you're capable of leaping up into heaven and burrowing down into hell. How's it they captured you, hmm?"

"Ill fortune. I was trapped on cursed ground. I should never have gone close to Woheigou."

"Do you know why you weren't executed right there and then when they captured you?"

"I reckon it's because you wanted to thank me in person."

"I offer thanks to you?"

"Well, if I hadn't killed Wang Shizhen, you'd never've become Party secretary."

Secretary Lin snapped his fan closed and put it away. "Hmm... why don't you tell me why you killed Wang Shizhen?"

"I needed a gun."

"Do you mean to say you live for a gun!"

"I am one!"

Wang Shizhen's former concubine interrupted the exchange: "Lao

Hei, you dirty, heartless traitor. Wasn't the man you murdered your only benefactor?"

"Well, I'm repaying that debt now with my life."

"Yes, your life is suitable repayment, but not just yours alone. Your son's life is needed, too."

At that moment, on cue, the authorities dragged Si Feng into the open. She was already dead, pulled in by her hands and feet, and then left sprawled on the ground. The men who'd carried her drew a blade and cut open her stomach.

"Cover her face at least," came Lao Hei's voice.

Her eyes were still open, orbs staring at nothing. The militiaman who'd plunged his blade into her belly withdrew it upon hearing Lao Hei's voice, cut off a piece off her tunic and threw it over her face, covering it from sight. He then continued his work, pushing his hands into her torn stomach and pulling out a baby boy. The baby was dead, of course, but this didn't stop them from cutting it into pieces.

Lao Hei shouted at the man wielding the knife: "It's not my son, you know. Give it your all!"

Secretary Lin slapped his fan on the table, startled by the words he had heard: "Who'll repay your debt if not your son?"

"I shot Wang Shizhen right between the eyes, you'll do the same. But let me tell you, if you're off by even just a bit, I'll laugh all the way to hell!"

Secretary Lin laughed at this, too: "But I can't fire a gun, you know."

Several militiamen marched forward carrying what looked like a great wooden door. Lao Hei was heaved on top of it, and his hands and feet were nailed into the wood. He didn't cry out once in pain, his eyes merely bore into the men responsible for nailing him to the door. It took two strikes of the hammer to pierce the nail through his left hand and into the wood underneath. On the fourth attempt with his right hand, Lao Hei finally broke his silence: "Get on with it man!"

The work complete, Lao Hei's eyes bulged, the only sign of pain he betrayed. The punishment, however, was not finished. The men brought forward smooth fragments of a millstone. One was hammered in his behind, piercing the flesh of his buttocks. The other was placed over his midriff, before the iron nails mulched his testicles. With the final strike of the hammer, Lao Hei's eyes popped out of their sockets altogether. Long tendrils of sinew, however, kept them attached to his face. Lao Hei had lost consciousness.

"Continue," came the instructions from the secretary. "A man such as this must be properly punished."

Cold water was brought and thrown on Lao Hei's face in order to wake him up. Once he stirred, they continued with their hammering. Lao Hei's crotch area and midsection were a bloody pulp, the flesh mangled and torn. But still the men kept at it, only stopping when he'd been ripped in two. At exactly the same moment, the pig's head that sat on the offering table moved and an enormous housefly emerged from it; the eggs must've been laid some time before.

Wang Shizhen's former concubine tried to get out of the way, but she couldn't. She broke into tears: "Shizhen, oh Shizhen, I know you've come!" And then in a voice loud enough to scrape one's throat raw, she roared: "Gouge out his heart! His heart!"

The men complied, cleaving it from Lao Hei's chest. At first, it seemed a heart like any other, a bloody red mound, but shortly after they placed it next to Wang Shizhen's memorial tablet it dissolved, turning into a pulpy mess not unlike okara gruel.

San Hai, Li Desheng and Lao Hei had all died in quick succession, and so leadership of the guerrilla band now fell to Lei Bu. His first order was to temporarily disband the unit, but he, along with three other men, swore to kill the new Party secretary in Zhengyang, along with the bastard Wang Shizhen's former concubine. Dressed as simple spectators, the four of them walked into Zhengyang and headed straight to the Guandi Temple to light incense sticks for their fallen comrades. Their respects paid, they headed towards the central offices in Zhengyang.

The municipal compound once had poplar trees all in a row in front of the main gate, but now these had been hewn down. The word on the street was the trees were haunted, that the ghosts residing there were constantly causing a racket, and people were increasingly afraid to go anywhere near the central offices. According to the stories, on a few occasions people were said to have heard a noise that sounded like hands clapping. At other times, especially when the wind blew, it was said the trees seemed to moan, a plaintive sort of wail echoing across the city. Hence, the poplars were cut down.

The entrance to the compound had changed in another way as well, for now there was an extra sentry station that prevented anyone from just walking up and entering the government offices. Even the local street vendors selling nothing more than food had to register and submit to being searched upon entering and leaving. As a result of these changes, there was simply no way for Lei Bu and the other men to launch a sneak attack, and so they had to think of an alternative plan. This came to them easy enough, for they figured the best way to exact their revenge was to find suitable accommodation near the municipal offices and then dig a tunnel under the sentry station and the exterior wall. Once inside, they could attack and satisfy their thirst for vengeance. Unfortunately, however, none of the homeowners in the area were willing to rent them rooms, and what's more, one of them actually recognised Lei Bu, which, in turn, forced the men to abandon their plans altogether. In fact, they felt impelled to look for the quickest means to leave the town.

Shortly after they departed, the authorities implemented additional security measures, some designed to prevent the very plan Lei Bu and his men had devised, namely digging a tunnel under the walls of the government complex. To stop this, the authorities ordered several pits to be dug in the central courtyard, and then earthen jars were placed inside. The jars were filled with water and men were sent periodically to check on them, day and night. They would look for any sign of ripples across the surface; if the water moved, even slightly, they would know someone was digging a tunnel underneath.

As for Lei Bu and his three comrades, they retreated into the southern mountains, to the small village of Goushuwa. There they stayed for three days, distraught, disappointed and literally weeping over their failure to exact revenge. Their torment was so great in fact, their hair soon turned the whitest of white. The militia, too, continued to scour the mountainside, looking for any trace of them. Whenever they discovered anyone with white hair, they'd apprehend them, just in case.

While all this was happening, I was in Siping, a village situated on an old mule path up in the mountains. As usual, I'd been asked to come and sing for a recently departed family member. During my time there, on a day much like any other, I bumped into someone I hadn't expected to see. I had just finished my lunch and decided to browse through the street market, and as I looked from side to side at the usual activity – a man kneading dough, a street vendor pushing snacks – I spied another man walking in my direction carrying baskets of fine fabrics on a pole he'd slung over his shoulder. The baskets dangling in front of him were of many different sizes, the ones behind more bundles of fabric tied together with strips of bamboo. I immediately gave way. After all, I was just browsing, but as he passed, I felt a foot come down hard on my own, the pain shooting up my leg.

"What the hell," I said, greatly annoyed, "have you worn out the soles of your shoes or something!"

The reply I received was most unexpected: "Follow me… to the trees just in front… I've something to speak to you about."

My eyes fixed on the man, and after a moment I recognised who it was: Lei Bu. I didn't dare say anything more. Nor did I utter a sound. I simply followed him, making sure to keep a discreet distance, and then, when we finally reached the trees, I decided it was safe enough to break my silence: "Why the hell have you shown up here?"

"I've got men to bury," was his reply, and then he related to me all that had happened. Once he'd finished, I did the same, telling him what I'd seen and heard, everything I knew. A quiet moment passed between us. Lei Bu broke the silence by asking if I could sing a mourning song for San Hai, Li Desheng and Lao Hei. Then he told me how each of them had died, how their bodies were mangled and mutilated, how they were… incomplete… and how they hadn't been put into the ground yet. He paused for another brief moment, then wondered aloud if this was the reason why his comrades had not been reincarnated, the treatment they'd received, the lack of a proper burial, this all meant they'd been forced into becoming lonely spirits, wandering between this world and the next, never knowing peace. He asked me again if I would sing. I told him, on the basis of the loyalty he displayed, there was really no way I could refuse. But there was a problem. Where was I to sing since there were no graves to speak of? His reply tried to take this very real problem into account. His solution was unique. He planned to make wooden carvings of his fallen comrades, San Hai, Li Desheng and Lao Hei, and then afterwards dig a proper grave for them to be lowered into. His idea was to see them buried on the slopes of Mount Zhu, near his own home, and it would be here that I would sing. After listening to his plan, I suggested one more detail: if he was going to engrave likenesses of his dead comrades, then perhaps he ought to do one for Si Feng as well. He didn't say any more, we simply agreed that once his work was done, I would be there to sing. And so we left each other's company and I continued to Qingfengyi, intending to call on my old acquaintance, the bald proprietor of Defadian, who somehow always seemed to know my whereabouts, seemed to read whatever signs there might've been and to know when I was due to pass by.

Lei Bu, however, never came to find me again. I even asked Baldy if he'd seen him, but he hadn't. It was as though he'd disappeared without a trace. Then, some three months later, I was on the road again, it was dusk and the moon and stars were just visible in the sky. There was no one around. I'd just walked into a narrow ravine and found four stones neatly arranged, each inscribed with a name. I looked closely and discovered the names were for none other than San Hai, Li Desheng, Lao Hei and Si Feng. Lei Bu had followed through on his promise, and so would I. I buried the stones, and then sat down on the freshly dug earth and sang. I first sang a song to praise the four compass points, the gates to the east, west, south and north, then a tune to honour the treasures of the Buddha, the five elements of metal, wood, water, fire and earth. I did this to aid their spirits, to help guide them on the path between heaven and hell. Then I sang a song of remorse:

Pity the young woman sent off to be wed,
A year of toil was what she was fed,
Dozens and dozens of steamed buns made,
A pound of sugar waiting to be weighed,
Enjoy your meal the only refrain.
Pity the young mother, a baby clinging tight,
A visit to home but only sad news to blight,
There in the doorway, peering inside,
A painted coffin, a call to dad, a weeping mum and feelings of regret,
Longing to see them but now that time had passed.

As I was singing, I began to feel the approach of something, as though, out in the grass, a leopard was stalking nearby, quiet, slowly moving closer, ready to pounce. The pigs had noticed, too, for they'd stopped moving. Then a log-tailed fox emerged, followed by a snake with brightly mottled skin. They hadn't come to hurt me, and so I saw no reason to stop singing, or to run away. Once I finished my song, I stood up and the fox did the same. The snake too raised its head. We all departed. The wind picked up again and blew hard. The fields nearby were soon blanketed in white as flower after flower bloomed, and in the next moment, the blossoms were lifted by the wind and blown into the air like a flock of doves.

Sometime later, I can't remember when, I learnt the flowers I'd seen that'd taken to the sky so well were in fact called doves.

Since Lei Bu and his men were unable to launch their attack, they resigned themselves to an alternative target. This proved to be the grave of the town secretary's father, which they exhumed in order to defile. To their surprise, however, when they opened the dead man's casket all they found were snakes wriggling about, a supposed sign the deceased's descendants would hold office. Determined to have their revenge, Lei Bu and his men beheaded the snakes, slicing them into pieces, before removing the skeletal remains and stomping them to dust. As a coup de grace, they splattered the dust with dog's blood.

News of their sacrilege spread, and once it reached the ears of Wang Shizhen's former concubine, it was days before anyone saw her out in the streets again. Not until 8 April, when she was called to visit the temple fair, did she leave her home, and then only reluctantly. Her concerns turned out to be warranted. While on her way to the fair, as she stopped to buy incense sticks, she heard someone call out from behind her.

"Mrs Lu!"

But before she could turn round to see who it was, Lei Bu and his men threw a hemp sack over her head, picked her up and fled all the way to the nearby riverbank where they debated the best way to kill her. Shooting her, unfortunately, was out of the question, since they had no bullets left. They discussed whether to beat her to a pulp using whatever heavy sticks they could find, or if they should weigh down the sack and throw her into the river. But before they could decide, their own curiosity to discover just what kind of woman she was overwhelmed them. How was it she was able to not only worm her way into Wang Shizhen's bed, but also shopkeeper Lu's as well? So they opened the sack.

"Shit, she's a looker, isn't she!"

"Aye, she's got a face on her, for sure, and a poisonous heart to go with it!"

She knew she'd been abducted by the guerrilla band, or what was left of it, but she didn't personally know the men who now stared at her. She didn't ask for mercy either, nor did she cry.

"Boys… let me pretty myself up before you kill me, alright?"

This was not what they were expecting to hear, but neither did it move them. Lei Bu laughed, and drew out a blade. On the bridge of her nose he carved the first character for Lao Hei, and right below it he carved the second one. Her face split open and blood poured out. Lei Bu turned to his men and instructed them to leave.

"We're not going to kill her?" was their surprised response.

"No, we're not. Let her live… live with a face like that!"

Their thirst for revenge sated, Lei Bu and the three other comrades were unsure what to do next. They did decide to bury their weapons and change their names, but after that, what should they do, perhaps head into the deep mountains and look for work? That might be an option, but none of them truly wanted it. It had been so long since they'd been farmers, was that all that was left for them? They dug up their rifles and wept. One of the men, through his tears, lamented he'd simply become too used to carrying his gun, he didn't want to do anything else, he might as well ask Zhou Baihua for asylum rather than return to a life in the dirt.

Zhou was a wealthy landowner in Lingning County, based in the village of Zhulin. He'd done battle with his uncle who was a brigade commander for the provincial forces in the northwest. He had his own private army, which was increasingly well armed and growing in numbers. So large, in fact, that the official militia in Lingning had no way of bringing him to heel, essentially acquiescing and letting him be de facto ruler over his immediate area. Zhou was the second of two boys, so he was often called Mr Two. He'd managed his growing power and influence well. After all, a rabbit won't eat the grass nearest its burrow, and Zhou's initial efforts meant he surrounded himself with friends and locals, he repaired roads and bridges, made sure food relief was brought in, and even built a school that was free for the townspeople's children. In short, his region was autonomous and he was in control. The villagers had no pictures of Chiang Kai-shek hanging on the walls; they only had portraits of Zhou Baihua. Many years earlier, Li Desheng had actually travelled to Zhulin to enlist Zhou into his guerrilla band, promising him that, once they'd successfully extended their reach, he would be made a commanding officer and a political commissar. Zhou declined, however, and from that time onwards, there'd been no contact, only a mutually nonaggressive approach to each other's activities. The suggestion by one of them to seek shelter under Zhou's banner caused the other two to dissent; they'd made overtures to Zhou Baihua years ago, was their point of view, how could they now wish to join him?

But what alternatives did they have? Not retreating into the mountains and requesting Zhou's protection would end up hastening their own demise. Had this not crossed their minds?

"Let's let heaven decide," Lei Bu said, as he pulled out a coin. Heads they'd march for Zhulin, tails they'd return to the dirt to take up their previous lives. And at those words, he tossed the coin into the sky. It landed heads. "So, off to Zhulin? Or shall we say best of three?" He flipped the coin again, and once more it landed heads up. For the hell of it, he flicked it up once more. Heads. The four left for Zhulin.

They weren't sure, however, if Zhou Baihua would offer them a welcome, and so preparations had to be made, especially if Zhou had mind to kill them, in which case they'd need to seize whatever opportunity presented itself to fight. But once the town guards relayed news of their arrival to Zhou, he appeared wearing white round his head, a look they had not been expecting.

"Mr Two... we've arrived at perhaps a bad time. You're dressed in mourning, are you not?" asked Lei Bu.

"I'm dressed like this to pay my respects to Li Desheng and Lao Hei!"

At these words, tears welled up in Lei Bu's eyes before rolling down his cheeks. He handed his weapon to Zhou, and the other three men followed suit.

"How can soldiers be true to themselves if they've don't have their guns? Keep them, please!" Zhou Baihua gestured to Lei Bu and his men to follow him down the streets of the town. Upon arriving at the main intersection of Zhulin, the four men saw an impressive stele standing at the centre. It had four sides and was about thirty feet tall, with characters carved into its surface.

Zhou Baihua stopped in front of the stele, then proceeded to read aloud: "Ensconced with this eternal Peach Blossom Grove, my only desire is to scale this wooden pillar into heaven." The words, Zhou told them, were once spoken by Yang Changji (1871-1920), a scholar of some renown.

"I may have many weapons at my disposal," he continued, "but I can't bear to see the death they inflict… ruling a town is like taking care of one's family, benevolence and virtue are paramount… if you're willing, then take charge of the forestry station… what do you say?"

Kuang San had not accompanied Lei Bu, but he had heard of how they had defiled the grave belonging to the Lin family, how they'd cut up the face of Wang Shizhen's widow. He'd gone in search of him, but had been unsuccessful, and so he resigned himself to enacting his own revenge, first on that landlord he'd seen emptying his own chamber pot, and second on the moneybags whose son served in the local militia. The county authorities had rewarded both of them ten *dayangs* for their service to the community, while the latter's son had been handsomely rewarded by being promoted. It was on his way home, while crossing the bridge leading into Qingfengyi, that he'd encountered a bandit intent on relieving him of his money. Naturally there was a struggle, clothes were torn, and ultimately the man ended up being thrown over the bridge, falling to his death below. Kuang San left no traces on the corpse, but set about finding information about his second target. After learning what he could, he made his move, circling the moneybags' compound for nearly half the night before climbing over the walls in search of blood. Fortunately, the man's wife was at that very moment crouched down over her toilet, making it easy for him to plunge his blade into her heart, ending her life instantly. Kuang San entered the main house and soon found the wealthy owner fast asleep in one of the side rooms. He walked over to the slumbering fool and drove his weapon into the man's abdomen. He thrust hard, the knife piercing deep. So deep in fact, he couldn't withdraw it. In the side room opposite the one Kuang San was now in, the man's daughter-in-law heard the rustling sound and decided to investigate. She carried with her an iron lantern, which Kuang San was quick to take from her. He used it to bash her head in, pulverising flesh and bone. His revenge complete, Kuang San fled and resumed his previous profession, a homeless wanderer always begging for food.

Two years later, on 15 July, Mount Zhu was hit by another meteorite. This time it wasn't a falling star, but a hard rock the size of a shallow basket used to dry peppers in the sun. Its impact left a crater about five feet deep, and before long people began talking, insisting this was an omen from heaven, that heaven itself had cracked open and disaster was coming. This time, no one dared to go and collect the meteorite fragments. Even if they had, they wouldn't have found anything since great rains fell in the aftermath of the celestial visit, filling the crater with water. What's more, the watery hole soon gave birth to turtles and snakes, and then served as the resting place for two daughters-in-law, both of whom flung themselves into it, never to be seen again. In October of the same year, the Twenty-Fifth Regiment of the Chinese Red Army marched from Hubei and into Qinling; they were on their way north to Yan'an. Hot on their heels were forces from the Kuomintang's Northwest Army, which soon set up camp around Qinling in order to encircle their enemy. Their intentions were clear: they would cut off supplies and wait for them to surrender, or die. The result was a stalemate: three years of bloody combat back and forth.

Upon learning of the arrival of the Twenty-Fifth Regiment, Lei Bu and his men felt the time was right to re-establish their guerrilla band, and so they took their leave of Zhou Baihua and went in search of Kuang San and whoever else they could find. At around the same time as Lei Bu and his men left Zhulin, the Twenty-Fifth were cornered by the Northwest Army in a gorge that stretched about ten *li* in length. Lei Bu's guerrilla soldiers saved them, partly due to their intimate knowledge of the terrain and their guile in combat. Their reward: more guns and ammunition. This increased strength, in turn, allowed

Lei Bu to recruit better, eventually surpassing the number of men Li Desheng had by half.

But relations between the Red Army and Lei Bu's forces weren't always amicable. Once, when the Red Army was engaged in battle, they sent word for Lei Bu's men to attack from the rear to disrupt the enemy's lines. But Lei Bu refused, choosing instead to maintain his position and current level of strength. On another occasion, after Lei Bu had managed to collect more than a thousand pecks of grain to feed his men, more than what he actually needed, he dispatched only three hundred to the Twenty-Fifth Regiment. The remaining seven hundred pecks were hidden away high in a mountain cave, only to be discovered by the local militia, who incinerated it. Naturally, the commander of the Twenty-Fifth was irate at this turn of events, and so ordered one of his own men to assume the position of political commissar for Lei Bu's guerrilla band. He went by the name of Deng. His first act once he'd joined up with Lei Bu's men was to purge the guerrilla band of dissident and troublesome elements, executing eight men in total, including the three who'd been with Lei Bu from the beginning. Needless to say, Lei Bu and Deng did not get along entirely well and were constantly at each other's throats.

During another battle between the Red Army and the Kuomintang forces, the guerrilla band was ordered to cut off the enemy's reinforcements as they marched through a strip of land bordered on both sides by hills. The reinforcements comprised three platoons from the local militias, a considerable number of men, and over the course of three days and three nights of fierce fighting, Lei Bu's men were nearly wiped out; only Deng and five other men managed to retreat. Lei Bu was not among them; he died on the battlefield with so many of his comrades.

On the third morning of the battle before Lei Bu's demise, Kuang San finally arrived, and after a brief greeting, Lei Bu ordered him to courier a message to the Twenty-Fifth Regiment, before returning to join in the fight. He never made it back in time, but heard afterwards from the few remaining survivors of how Lei Bu had sacrificed himself near a lacebark pine tree that stood on its own at the edge of a gully. Apparently, as he moved forward, a bullet pierced him from behind, dropping him to the ground almost immediately. Kuang San wept at the news, before retreating himself. He had no other option but to return to the Twenty-Fifth. Once Deng made his way back to the regiment, he was questioned about Lei Bu's death, particularly with regard to how the bullet evidently hit him from behind. Unsurprisingly, they asked who had fired it. Deng said he was unsure. In the chaos of battle, who could say who shot whom? Bullets, after all, seemed to have hungry eyes for human flesh. Sometime after, it was difficult to say when, Kuang San became an official member of the Twenty-Fifth. A year later, the entire regiment finally reached Yan'an.

After Liberation, Zhengyang constructed a martyr's cemetery to honour Qinling's guerrilla forces. Each grave contained a wooden statue and the name of the martyr who'd died. (Their actual corpses had long since decomposed, most where they'd fallen.) Kuang San had actually come to oversee the work, ensuring that each wooden statue was made in the likeness of the named man. It was something only he could be responsible for, as he was really the only person left who had first-hand knowledge of the martyrs, how many there'd been and how their faces looked. By this time, Kuang San was living in the central administrative city that oversaw Qinling; he was commander of the military forces that were responsible for the whole area. Serving alongside Kuang San were two people in charge of governmental affairs. One was Zhou Baihua, who now held the post of deputy county commissioner for Lingning, and the other was Old Xu, who was deputy commissioner for the county of Shanyin. He still had his dead right eye, but had taken to wearing an eye patch over it, earning him the nickname The One-Eyed Commissioner.

Old Xu lived until he was seventy-seven. It was rare to see him not wearing his four-pocketed Mao suit. In summer, that was all he wore, and in winter he'd simply put a dark lambswool overcoat on top. Whenever he was asked to make reports to local primary and middle schools, he'd always talk about the heroic fighters of Qinling's guerrilla band.

THE SECOND TALE

QUESTION:

Why have all the chimeric creatures vanished from sight?

ANSWER:

Because man has come to dominate this world. The great majority of animals are extinct already, or on their way there, and the other ones... well, they've become men.

THE SECOND TALE

TODAY WE'LL LOOK at the third mountain range in the south. I'll read the first sentence and you follow.

Part three of *Pathways Through the Southern Mountains* begins at Tianyu Mountain. Many rivers flow from its base, making it a mountain that should not be climbed.

Five hundred leagues to the east stands Mount Pray-Pass. Atop this mountain is much gold and jade. On its lower slopes, great herds of three-horned rhinoceros graze, as do one-horned rhinos. Parades of elephants and small birds can also be seen. The birds resemble small waterfowl, but their heads are white, they have three feet near their tails, and instead of duckbills they have human faces. They are called juru due to how they cluck. The River Yin emerges here to flow south into the sea. Along its banks live many tiger-dragons, crocodile-like creatures that have fish bodies and snake-like tails; small legs protrude from under their bellies. Its call sounds strangely like that of the mandarin duck. Eating its flesh will reduce and prevent swelling and haemorrhoids.

Five hundred leagues to the east rises Mount Cinnabar. Great amounts of gold and jade can be found near the summit. The River Cinnabar emanates from here to flow southwards before emptying into the Gulf Sea. A small bird that resembles a chicken proliferates upon its slopes. Its plumage is fantastically coloured, which gives rise to its name: celestial squall. There are markings on its head that form the character for 'virtue'. Markings on its wings form the character for 'justice'. On its back one can see the character for 'ritual', on its chest the character for 'humanity' and on its belly the character for 'faith'. This bird draws its sustenance from itself, and it sings and dances for itself, too. Its appearance symbolises that all under heaven will be peaceful and orderly.

Four hundred leagues farther to the east is Mount Lively. There is no vegetation on its slopes, but there are numerous rivers and streams and a great number of white gibbons. The River Piao begins here before turning south to fall into the Gulf Sea.

Another four hundred leagues to the east brings you to the foot of Tail-Banner Mountain. To the south is the Valley of Zhongchu. Many strange birds can be found here. It is also from here that the gentle south wind originates.

Four hundred leagues beyond Tail-Banner Mountain rises Mount Wrong. The summit of this mountain lacks water, but there are rich reserves of gold and jade. The foot of the mountain is inhabited by numerous vipers that all grow to an enormous size.

Five hundred leagues farther east is Mount Sunny-Tight. It is devoid of vegetation but water is plentiful.

Five hundred leagues farther east is Mount Daoyou. Its zenith is nearly overgrown with trees, but there are no smaller shrubs or plants. A great number of strange birds nest in among the trees, but they are the only creatures here.

Another five hundred leagues towards the east is Chicken Mountain. Gold is plentiful on its summit, while its base is covered in granular cinnabar. The River Black originates here to flow south before emptying into the sea. Freshwater fish are numerous in the River Black. They bear a likeness to carp but have hog bristles and make noises not unlike a squealing pig. Their presence is an ill omen, signalling severe drought for all under heaven.

Four hundred leagues farther east is Mount Command-Excellence. Its slopes lack vegetation, but from a distance it often appears as a fiery brilliance. Facing south, one can see the Middle Valley. It is from here that the northeast wind blows. An owl-like bird that has a human face with four eyes and ears calls Mount Command-Excellence home. It is known as the yu because it can be heard to 'yuhoo'. Like the freshwater fish in the River Black, its appearance bodes ill, again signalling an imminent and desperate drought for all under heaven.

Thinker Mountain lies three hundred and seventy leagues farther east. Large deposits of gold are visible on the summit, while its base contains much dark cinnabar. The trees that grow on this mountain resemble the mulberry, but their roots and bark possess crimson-coloured veins that ooze a sweetish sap similar to lacquer. Eating the sap staves off hunger and replenishes one's spirit and energy, especially after a long day of work. It is known as the white perilla despite its scarlet hue, which can be applied to jade to make it the colour of blood.

Five hundred and eighty leagues farther east is Mount Yucao. Residing upon its slopes are numerous bizarre beasts and exceptionally long vipers.

Another five hundred and eighty leagues to the east is Mount Yu-Ape. Various precious metals and jade litter its peak. Many streams and rivers flow from its base. Water spouts forth from near the summit, which then welcomes it back in like a geyser. This only happens in the summer, however, for in winter the geyser lies dormant. The River Aid originates on Mount Yu-Ape, then flows southeast to disappear into the sea. The celestial squall with its beautiful plumage lives here alongside the diving-speed bird.

Fourteen peaks make up *Part III* of *Pathways Through the Southern Mountains*, starting with Tianyu Mountain before ending at Mount Yu-Ape, covering a distance of more than 6,350 leagues. The gods that live upon these mountains have dragon bodies and human faces. The ritual sacrifice for all of them requires a white dog to be offered in prayer; glutinous rice is the grain offering.

This concludes *Pathways Through the Southern Mountains*. Altogether, forty mountains have been noted, some small, others quite large. The total distance is some 16,380 leagues.

Do you have any questions?

Question: So what kind of wind goes by the name of *kai*?

Answer: A wind from the south.

Question: So what's a *tiao* wind?

Answer: That's one that blows from the northeast.

Question: What's blood jade?

Answer: Ah… it's not that the jade is made of blood, but rather it's been stained so that it resembles the colour of blood. So 'blood' isn't a noun here, it's a verb, as in 'to bloody'.

Question: What about this… this… what is it… a dragon that looks like a tiger, or is it more a striped crocodile… the one shaped like a fish but with a snake-like tail… the book says it makes a sound like a mandarin duck… why does eating it prevent swollen carbuncles and treat piles at the same time?

Answer: Let's change our perspective for a moment, that is, when people in the past ate this creature they… supposedly or not, I can't say, but… well… the text says they no longer suffered from swollen boils or haemorrhoids, that we can agree on. Now, ancient people were often keen to draw all sorts of conclusions from the natural phenomena they saw around them, so this tiger crocodile beast, it sounded like a pair of mandarin ducks, and that pair, well, it was one male and one female, a pair of lovers, which is to say, two becoming one, and if anything can get the blood pumping, the *qi* aligned, well, it's two lovers, isn't it! Hence, ancient people slowly began to view the world around them as a combination of opposites: the moon has the sun; black, white; man, woman; water, fire; soft, hard; up, down; before, after… you get the idea. To extend this, Chinese medicine also has the same principle: if one eats red-coloured food it's supposed to increase blood production, darker foods are good for your kidneys, walnuts… they look like brains you know, and are supposed to be good for your brain, and donkey penis is, well, it's good for your virility.

Question: Usually, names are given by other people. So how's it there're so many birds and beasts in these mountains that call out their own names?

Answer: Ah, that might just be people using the sound of their calls to give them names, or, on the other hand, it's a case of people mistaking their calls as their names. I've mentioned this before: an animal call is a way for them to announce themselves, right? Now, if these calls are simply their names, well, aren't they showing instead some form of complaint, denouncement, a venting of their feelings of being wronged, their misfortune... aren't people the same?

Question: Virtue, righteousness, ritual, benevolence and faith, these are all feudalistic values. How's it that this multicoloured bird, the celestial squall, can be described as bearing these five characteristics as part of its plumage?

Answer: There're two possibilities here. One, this is just a case of the pictographic qualities of certain Chinese characters. If in those times these words were written upon the celestial squall, then the appearance of this bird would represent the peace of heaven and the rules by which humanity should order its society. Two, people, when copying *Pathways Through the Mountains and Seas* years later simply added these details... we Chinese are quite skilled at doing that, you know. I mean, aren't there stories about the former bandit Liu Bang, about how his father had seen a dragon hovering over his wife one evening and that, soon after, she'd become pregnant with Liu Bang? Didn't they also say that, after becoming the first emperor of the Han dynasty, Liu Bang would take on the form of a dragon while asleep? And what about Chen Sheng and his uprising against the Qin dynasty, the first true peasant revolt against an elitist court... didn't they say he carved the word for 'prince' on the belly of a fish?

Question: This mountain range... the book records that it was littered with gold, silver, copper and iron, heavily populated by oxen, horses, sheep and chickens. There was rice and wine freely available, even war and corvée labour. Doesn't this prove that, during those times, people had already mastered agriculture, spinning and weaving, raising animals, smelting metals and treating illnesses? If that's the case, then where did these skills come from and how did people learn them?

Answer: The gods, they imparted the knowledge.

Question: Do the gods really exist then?

Answer: *Records of the Grand Historian* teaches us that the Yellow Emperor taught man about the transformations of the birds, beasts, insects and moths. Fu Xi is said to have remarked on the number of wild beasts under heaven and of the need to teach man how to hunt. Qinling has its own stories of the mouse that broke open the sky and the ox that tamped down the earth. The Yellow Emperor is a god, so's Fu Xi, and the mouse and the ox, too. You might say the gods – those beings with the gift of foresight – are able to stand on top of the tallest mountains and at the same time wander into the deepest of valleys. They belong both to the heavens and the Earth, they're sensitive to man's needs and understand the importance of educating us in myriad things. Perhaps that's what it's all about, the interrelationship between fire and water, the balance between yin and yang. It's only natural, I suppose, for the unseen world of the gods to hold dominance over this mortal plane.

Question: But are there still gods today?

Answer: Yes, the gods are still with us. Or perhaps it's our innate fear of empty space, of the void and how our hearts need to bring forth images to explain it. Well, those images are the gods, they give us strength. You don't believe science and technology were heaven sent, do you? Take, for instance, how people in the past looked at meteorological phenomena: they thought the wind and rain were carried by spirits, that a talent like clairvoyance was a gift from the gods, and that someone with preternaturally good hearing must've been touched by heaven. But nowadays, haven't science and technology disproven all of that?

Question: Ah... then... do I have the ability to be... a god?

Answer: Gods are to be revered, and that reverence starts here, with your head, then in here, your body, this is where your concentration must lie. Do you know what the three energies of Chinese medicine are? Well, they can't exist without each other. If you lack essence, *jing*, then your *qi* is not aligned, and if you've no *jing* and no *qi*, then your spirit will leave your body... the three have to exist together; if not, there is none.

The town of Lingning had lost its *qi*, and as a result its spirit had left. That's how it ended up a shambolic mess.

No one knew what the planners had intended, but as the seat of government for the county, Lingning had been constructed on the northern side of the river that ran uphill through Qinling. What's more, there were only three gates into the town: an eastern one, a western one and one to the north. It lacked a south gate. The distance between the east and west gates wasn't all that great either. In fact, they were quite close, so much so that should a person passing through the eastern entrance lose his hat to the wind, there was really no need to rush after it for it would only end up blowing as far as the western gateway.

In the thirty-third year of the Republic, 1945 by the Western calendar, the head commissioner was standing in the southern reaches of the town, watching both the river as it flowed underfoot and three cypress trees as they reached into the sky. Standing there, he sighed with regret. It'd been a hundred years at least since the county he led had sent a student to the provincial capital to study, something, he thought, that might have been due to the lack of a southern gate for the town.

As a consequence of these thoughts, he organised a group of men to cross the river and in the gap between the mountain ridges that looked down over the town, he told them to construct a southern gateway, although it would lack any practical purpose. Three years on, however, not only had the county still failed to send a student to the capital, but the head commissioner had lost his head as well.

Qinling's guerrilla band had perpetrated the deed. On the day it happened, snow had been floating down from early in the morning, covering the ground to the depth of nearly a chicken's foot. Despite the weather, or perhaps because of it, Lao Hei had ordered his men to attack Lingning. They'd scaled the northeastern corner of the town wall, and as they climbed, wisps of white smoke mixed in with the snow billowed up in the direction of the Niang Niang Temple, like a large mushroom cloud marching into the sky. It was said afterwards that the guerrillas had been responsible for setting the temple afire, but in fact, they hadn't. Their target had been the eighteen militiamen defending the temple, or rather, defending the twenty-three rifles they'd stored there. Once Lao Hei's raid was complete and they'd succeeded in getting what they wanted, the guerrilla band retreated, and that's when the smoke first appeared, followed immediately by the clanging of the town bell and calls for the well to be used to fetch water. After the guerrillas departed, a number of residents decided to seek out the county commissioner to learn what had happened, and that's when they discovered he'd lost his head, apparently while sitting at his office desk. At the same time, it ceased snowing and hailstones fell instead.

The mountain topography of Qinling is varied, so naturally each area had different flora and fauna, and different people, too. Deep in the mountains of Shanyin County, the trees grew exceptionally tall and there were many leopards, bears and takins. The people were sturdy and broad. Chuandao was in Lingning County. Here, the trees were small and there weren't many wild animals, except for the occasional dhole or wolf that one might encounter. There were, however, a great number of birds, especially sparrows, which were often seen perched on walls and buildings across the town. In truth, there were far too many of them. Their incessant chirping echoed throughout the day, annoying the residents no end. What's more, for the food vendors selling dishes such as spicy soup and pig intestines, or for the men who enjoyed drinking and eating outside, they often had to be more concerned about bird droppings than actually taking pleasure in what they were doing. The birds had the smallest of beaks, and their eyes, too, were tiny. They loved to eat pig intestines. Many people do as well, so do dholes, but when these sparrows showed up in the town, there were soon stories of them burrowing into the arses of cows, donkeys and sheep and literally dragging the intestines straight out of them. As a result, people would often wake in the morning to find dead livestock scattered about their land. They'd curse, then swear at heaven for allowing some creature to steal the intestines meant for them!

The hailstones fell throughout the day, ruining lunch and dinner. Some were the size of chicken eggs, others as large as a fist. They pummelled the town, smashing roof tiles and stripping the leaves of elm and locust trees that ran from the east gate to the west gate. The hailstones killed the sparrows, too, so many that the streets were soon filled with their tiny carcasses. Just beyond the north entrance, a dhole had died as a result of being struck. Further up in the nearby mountains, a labourer in the employ of the landowner Wang Caidong was busy sending his sheep out to pasture when the hailstone onslaught began. Hesitating instead of searching for shelter, he squirrelled underneath a sheep to cover his own body. The sheep ended up with a bashed-in skull.

It was on this day, too, that Bai He hit the road. He'd eaten three bowls of hot pig intestine soup, and in his cloth pouch he carried the string of coins his young wife had prepared for him, as well as a wok the depth of three fingers. He'd also passed by his father's grave, but he didn't stop to pay his respects. He hated his father, an opium addict who'd smoked his family to ruin. They'd been left just three *mu* of land to till, equivalent to half an acre, and a widowed mother to look after him and his younger brother. Bai He had departed to find fortune and glory, or at least something better than what he had.

"I'll never kowtow!" were the words he uttered in setting off, but just as he said them, the hailstones fell, hard and fast. He pulled out the wok from his pouch to use as a helmet, and scrambled to find somewhere to shelter.

The beheading of the county commissioner was a unique event, unheard in Qinling's five hundred years of recorded history. The provincial authorities had always felt Lingning was just a small county town, far removed from civilisation, but now, once news of the beheading reached them, it also earned the reputation of being dangerous. Consequently, a decision was made to revoke its status as the main county town and instead the village of Fang was nominated in its place. But a few years after this decision was taken, the new county town ended up losing nearly all of its stores, and the people soon scattered. The walls that had been constructed when it was first awarded its county town status fell into disrepair, abandoned to the elements. The village that became a town was once more a village, its fall from grace complete. Its new name reflected this past, for Laocheng meant 'old city'.

There were no vendors of pig intestine soup in Laocheng, but the remaining villagers did enjoy eating it and so most cooked it at home. It seemed as though there were still quite a few sparrows in the village as they would often be seen hopping about and across any buildings left standing. If someone drew near them, they'd cheep and take to the air like a grey mass of ash covering the sky. When the person had passed, the birds would return to their perches, the grey ashen mass descending once more.

After Bai He left, his young wife departed shortly afterwards, taking her two children more than twenty *li* away to stay with her parents. That left only Bai He's younger brother, Bai Tu, and his days became increasingly busy, as well as restless. Three years he lived like that, but still his older brother had not returned, nor had his sister-in-law and her children. His father had already died, so when his frail old mother passed, there was no way he could arrange the funeral on his own. His asked his neighbours, a family by the name of Hong, if he could borrow money to buy bricks to mark her grave, then he went to Wang Caidong to see if he would lend him money for a coffin. Wang immediately saw Bai Tu for the simpleton he was and felt pity for the young man. He decided to help with the funeral arrangements by inviting a mountain whisperer and hiring men to attend to the coffin when it came time to lower it into the ground. He would also prepare twelve tables covered with food for the wake. The mountain whisperer he invited was me, of course.

Now, my invitation didn't mean Laocheng had no mountain whisperers of its own. There was an old grey one who worked in the village, along with two apprentices, but their skills could not compare to mine. When it came time to sing a mourning song, he'd be more interested in eating and drinking the hot soup. On top of that, when it was time to leave, not only would he ask for payment, he'd also ask for a small box of tobacco. It was quite expected, then, for Wang to invite an outsider, to invite me. Of course, the other local mountain whisperers didn't take this lying down; they were quite angry in fact. But I sang as requested, right up until midnight when we all returned to Bai Tu's home. That's when the local mountain whisperer asked to sing a duet. I'd sung duets previously, more than once, but it always felt as though singing with another mountain whisperer transformed the evening into something more sombre. But on this occasion, I'm not sure what had happened – the idle chatter of the evening, the boasting that accompanied it – well, it was as though neither of us wished to give an inch, each more concerned with outdoing the other, and before long it came to shoving and pushing, until finally Bai Tu prostrated himself on the floor and kowtowed to all of us. Seizing the moment, Wang jumped in and agreed to pay the local mountain whisperer for his troubles, and that was the end of it.

Because I'd had this experience in Laocheng, Wang allowed me to stay in the Niang Niang Temple for several days. The monk who lived in the temple was a deaf mute, and he wasn't exactly welcoming. When dusk fell, I'd hear him rattling about in one of the side rooms, drawing water from the well and mumbling at the same time. Of course I didn't understand what he was saying, if he was actually using words, but I got his meaning: there were eighteen ghosts standing about the well, the ghosts of the men killed when the guerrilla band attacked. I told the monk, as best as I could, that I didn't fear ghosts, so he deliberately placed my bedding in the same small room. The monk, however, didn't drive me away. Each and every day he would head out to beg for alms, sitting squarely on his prayer mat and beating his Chinese temple block. When he beat the drum, my backbone would ache as though I were the temple block itself, enduring the rhythmic tap, tap of his movements as he relayed the story of what had befallen Laocheng.

His mother in the ground, Bai Tu offered sincere thanks to Wang Caidong, kowtowing in front of him until the skin on his forehead broke and blood trickled down. In lieu of payment, he volunteered to go into service for Wang, to do whatever work was needed. His family's remaining three *mu* of land he turned over to his neighbours, the Hongs, saying they could use it for themselves until his brother returned. He would then give them back the money they'd lent him. However, if his brother didn't return within another three years, the land would be theirs to keep. The Hongs were willing to agree, but they wanted everything in writing. Unfortunately, Bai Tu was illiterate.

"Believe me," he said, "I'll cut off one of my ears to prove what I say", and he reached for a blade and sliced off the lobe of his right ear. Bai Tu had grown up evil, his eyes like those of a mangy dog, his mouth just as big. Now with half his right ear missing, his gait became unsteady and he listed as he walked.

While in Wang's employ, Bai Tu spared no energy in completing the work he was assigned, nor was he fussy about what he was given to eat. A visitor once commented on Bai Tu's diligence, as well as his voracious appetite: "He certainly gets the job done, but he eats like a pig. Heavens, what a racket he makes!"

After hearing comments like this, Bai Tu took to eating his meals in the kitchen, out of sight, and hopefully out of earshot too. But he didn't eat any less. At each meal, he had three bowls of whatever was given him. The old lady who did most of the cooking often asked if he'd want the scorched rice that usually stuck to the sides of the pot, to which he'd reply 'yes'. On some occasions, after he polished off his usual three bowls, the old lady would tap her ladle on the cooking pot and ask if he was full.

His response would always be the same: "Is there anything left?"

"No!" she would often say, teasingly, and so Bai Tu would head back to work.

As winter came, Wang ordered new rooms to be constructed in preparation for a wedding. In total, three rooms were built and Bai Tu lugged each and every brick needed for them. From kiln to site, he bore the weight on his back, the bricks eating into his flesh, causing bloody blisters to form up and down his spine.

Watching him trudge back and forth, a curious villager felt compelled to ask: "So what're you building, more rooms I guess?"

"Yes, yes indeed," was his reply.

"Is there to be a wedding?"

"Yes, a wedding... Oh, but not mine."

The villager smiled and playfully pulled his ear, the one missing its lower half: "Did you think I thought it might be yours!"

A sour look cast across Bai Tu's face. He wouldn't let anyone touch his ear again.

Wang's new wife came from Shiweng, over thirty *li* away. The village was a mountain stronghold, reachable only by a winding path that stretched along the mountain ridge like a rope snaking across the land. The path was so difficult, in fact, that the use of a wheeled palanquin was impossible. The bride had to be transported by sedan chair instead, and naturally this task fell to Bai Tu. On the wedding day, Bai Tu made sure his clothes were washed and his hair was cut. He also decided to wear a cover over his disfigured appendage, choosing to hide his mangled right ear from sight. The object he had to carry resembled a chair, of course, but its back was incredibly high and was wrapped with fabric, which in turn was tied around his torso. The young wife would sit upon the frame so that she was staring at her home as she left it behind.

While on the road, Bai Tu's breath became increasingly ragged due to the burden he was carrying, and so he stopped to rest, placing the bride and her chair on top of a boulder. A member of the wedding party encouraged him to have a little smoke in order to relieve his tiredness, but Bai Tu retorted that all tobacco did was choke one's breath. And he certainly didn't want to do that to his master's prospective wife.

"Such thoughtfulness!"

Bai Tu rubbed at the cover over his ear and smiled to himself. In truth, he was less concerned about her health than the likelihood of the tobacco overpowering the sweet smell of the young woman he carried on his back. He didn't know what type of perfume she was wearing, but the scent was intoxicating. And not just to him, if the butterflies and bees that buzzed around them were any indication.

Wang's new, young wife was called Yu Zhuo. It wasn't long after she moved to Laocheng that the bitter lives of many of the residents brightened up. On one occasion, while Bai Tu was preparing the feed for the pigs, she saw him accidentally slice his finger, and she immediately chased after the chickens that milled about the courtyard, desperate to pluck some feathers to help him staunch the bleeding. On a cold winter day during the twelfth lunar month, she noticed Bai Tu's heel was cracked and sore, and she set about preparing a balm. To do this, she took a helping of pig's lard and roasted it near the cooking fires until it was suitable to use.

"You needn't use an ear cover, you know." Her words were kind and heartfelt.

Bai Tu didn't remove it, however, so she made a new one for him. She then exchanged it for the old one so it could be washed.

When Bai Tu took the sheep out to pasture, he already knew the hills behind the village were bereft of grass, and so he had to go higher. On reaching a gully high up in the mountains, he let the sheep feed as best they could, while he climbed further, returning only when the sun set. But on this occasion as he tried to round up the sheep to return, many did not follow, instead climbing higher up on the steep precipices in order to eat their fill. No matter how he called out to them, they simply would not descend.

At the same time, Yu Zhuo was also in the fields, picking radishes, their leaves green and lush, a stark contrast to the whiteness of her face. When she saw Bai Tu unable to bring the sheep in, she called out, doing her best to help him. Surprisingly, the sheep responded to her voice immediately. This happened more than once. And on those occasions when Bai Tu did not return at dusk, Yu Zhuo would step outside. If it was apparent that Bai Tu was having trouble getting the sheep down, she would call out, and they would return.

"How's it that you only need to shout once and they respond?"

"Well, I'm their owner, aren't I?"

"Eh, I guess you are."

After the first couple of times, Bai Tu began to wish for the sheep to ignore his calls, since that way he was sure to see Yu Zhuo, sure to hear the crispness of her sweet voice.

"Bai Tu, did you hear?" said Wang from the other end of the compound. It was an ordinary day like any other, but his words lingered in the air. "The Kuomintang and the Communists were engaged in fierce fighting the other day in Santai County. Several refugees ended up here, one a young woman who'd come begging for food. Why don't you go and have a look? If you're up for it, perhaps she can be your wife."

"I can't, no... I can't... would you go and speak to her and her family for me?"

Wang showed no sign of agreeing to carry out his servant's request, but instead shouted back: "Do you mean to say I've got to teach you about being with a woman, too!"

Yu Zhuo rescued him once again, and together they went to see the woman Wang had talked about. But when they arrived at the eastern gate, she was nowhere to be found. Apparently, another villager by the name of Old Geng had invited her to eat some melon. Naturally, the two of them marched off in the direction of Geng's small plot of land where he grew the crispiest and whitest of white melons. At the edge of the melon field stood an old hut that Geng had constructed to serve as a guard station for his land. He was inside now with the woman who'd come in search of food. He was holding her down underneath him.

"Pretty, isn't it?"

"Oh... yes... very sweet," was the woman's reply, her mouth full of melon.

Yu Zhuo pulled Bai Tu away, saying: "No good, no good. She wouldn't be a good match, that much is clear!"

Bai Tu, however, escaped from her grasp and ran towards the small hut. Yu Zhuo cursed him, calling him a scoundrel, but she was surprised by his actions for he took his foot to the frame of the small structure and kicked it down, reducing it to a heap.

Another three years had passed and still Bai He had not come back. The Hongs harvested their autumn crops and then ploughed the fields. "There's no sign of your older brother," they said, "which means I'll be using this land to sow my wheat."

It never occurred to the Hongs that Bai He would return, but just as they were about to sow the seeds, he did. He brought his wife with him as well, and took possession of the three *mu* of land once again. As for the debt owed by his younger brother, he told them he'd arranged for a large batch of fabric to be sold in the nearby county, in Huangfujie, and within two weeks, he'd have everything his brother owed them. The village soon took to spreading rumours about Bai He's reappearance, most saying that while he'd been away for so long, he'd become a wealthy clothes merchant. His silk robes and gold teeth were testament to this, or so people said. It was his gold teeth the Hongs put their faith in, they'd happily wait. Bai He, it should be noted, didn't have just one gold tooth – which was hardly a sign of wealth since many other villagers had at least one as well – but an entire set.

As for the fields, Bai He planted wheat and barley, the same crops the Hongs had intended to sow, and each stalk grew big and strong. But he never repaid Bai Tu's debt, despite the Hongs coming several times to ask for it. This got the village into gossiping even more about Bai He, most saying that, while he had money and that business beyond the confines of Laocheng had been good, Bai He, like his father before him, suffered from the same sickness: he'd smoked his fortune away, hence his return. Needless to say, such hearsay resulted in the two families having a falling out, and the Hongs subsequently demanded repayment.

"It's like this," Bai He argued with all seriousness. "We owe you money, not land, so we'll not be giving you our three *mu*! Shit, you're quite the cold-hearted family now, aren't you!"

The Hong family had a son who was already married, so there was an element of strength about them, but Bai He's two boys were still only young rascals, reckless and potentially very rash. Even though this conflict had arisen between the two families, primarily due to Bai He's irascibility, the Hongs dared not provoke anything more. But that didn't stop the Hongs' daughter-in-law from actively slandering Bai He and his family. And when she did, her parents-in-law would yell curses over the adjacent courtyard walls, saying it was their son's wife who had spread the vicious lies. The Hongs' tactic of letting their daughter-in-law attack for them had the desired effect: the Bai family's faces would blush with shame, but they could do little about it.

This daughter came originally from the village of Wanggou. The story was that one of the old ladies there simply couldn't get on with her daughter-in-law, mostly because she suspected her son's wife came from a poor family, and all she'd given them in return was three daughters and no boys. Finally, when a boy was welcomed into the family, the daughter-in-law's only response was: "You can burn more incense. Let me tell you, I've had enough!" And then she summarily hanged herself. Needless to say, with his wife dead, the father of four found himself in difficult circumstances, which is how he came to be giving away his youngest daughter. She was first given to a childless couple, but a month or so later, the oldest member of the family fell ill and a dhole killed the family pig, causing them to believe the child was ill-fated and unlucky. Consequently, they sent her back. The third daughter was then given to another family, but she spouted such foul language at having been sent there that she refused to stay. The family, for their part, felt the child to be too wilful, and so again she was returned home.

As it happened, the Hong family's daughter-in-law had yet to have a child of her own, so the decision was made to take this young girl in. Quite unexpectedly, however, within a year of welcoming the young girl into the family, the daughter-in-law became pregnant. As a result, the expectant mother soon took to persecuting and abusing her adopted child, instructing her to do this and that, and generally making life unpleasant. If, moreover, she failed to meet expectations, she'd end up having her ears boxed or her thighs pinched so hard that bruises would form almost immediately.

The villagers all suspected the daughter-in-law of being cruel and malicious, but no one wanted to outwardly provoke her, so instead they took to speaking behind her back about how they wished the ghosts of the river would pull her in and drown her when she was busy washing clothes, or how they hoped sparrows would shit in her hot pig intestine soup, curses of this type. While ghosts never did appear to drag her to a watery death, on one occasion, rather surprisingly, when the daughter-in-law was out enjoying some soup, the sparrows did succumb in this manner. Apparently, the expectant mother had forgotten to lock the door, and so when she put her bowl down to race home to shut it properly, she returned to find three sparrows perched on the rim of her bowl and using it as a toilet. Outraged, she cursed heaven in language unbecoming of an expectant mother, but the three sparrows, having flown off to sit in the trees, fell to the ground and were quickly scooped up by a hungry cat.

During the same year that the Hong's grandson was born, Bai He's wife also gave birth for the first time. Unfortunately, however, she soon afterwards developed chronic dizziness, a condition that made the world around her spin, so badly in fact that she had to place her hands on the nearest wall in order to walk anywhere. Bai He's life was naturally very busy, but he was far from being an expert farmer. In the summer when all other families were busy milling their grain and storing it for the winter, Bai He's three *mu* of land still had wheat and barley growing tall on it without anyone making the effort to harvest it. When he did finally get round to the task, he'd complain vociferously about the pain it caused, how he was going to break his back if he didn't stop. On one such occasion, he flung his sickle to the ground and shouted to no one in particular: "My back, what about my back!" At the same time, he spotted a persimmon tree and squatted down to rest.

Ma Sheng was the local orphan. His face was flat and broad, but his eyes, nose, ears and mouth were tight and close together. Behind his back, almost everyone called him a mule, which had a great deal to do with his name, the first character 'ma' meaning horse, and 'sheng' meaning to give birth. So why not call him a horse? Well, that was due to the fact that Ma Sheng never spoke much about his parents and so no one knew who they were, nor what they looked like, which is exactly what a mule is, neither a horse nor a donkey, but something in between. People noticed, too, that he never once burnt hell money on the tomb-sweeping holiday, nor on the lunar new year's eve. Some took to calling him out for his blatant lack of filial piety.

"You devil, you, you don't even burn hell money and make the proper offerings at your family's grave!" was a familiar refrain.

Ma Sheng's reply was usually a question: "Surely you're not talking about how poor I am? Let me tell you, I've no complaints at all."

He'd often be seen reclining bare-chested on his summer sleeping mat, a bamboo basket clutched tight to his breast. Known as a bamboo beauty, the basket shared a similar shape to that of a woman. Its aerated design meant it was especially good at alleviating the oppressiveness of the hot summer nights.

Walking with a donkey in tow, Bai He came upon Ma Sheng stretched out as he was and couldn't help but stir him: "If you help your uncle here now with this beast and the burden it's carrying, there'll be a bowl of noodles in it for you."

Ma Sheng stuck his big toe up in the air, then spied a soft, red, oval-shaped persimmon hanging in the tree overhead: "Uncle, shake the tree will you? Knock that persimmon down as I quite fancy one."

Annoyed at the young man's response, Bai He yanked on his donkey's rope, egging it on without stopping. Ma Sheng stared at the animal's backside and thought if he were a dhole, he'd have that arsehole.

Bai He still schemed, thinking of all manner of business possibilities. After all, once Liberation had been achieved, there'd be no more fighting and no more war. With these thoughts in mind, he decided to travel to the county capital, which was at that moment in the midst of violently suppressing anti-revolutionary forces. On the banks of the river to the south of the village, the local Kuomintang secretary, the county commissioner, as well as the chief of public security and the militia commander, were all executed by firing squad. They'd even lined up a dozen or more local bandits, owners of the local brothels and the opium dens, and shot them dead as well. Most stores were shut, too, causing Bai He a degree of consternation; perhaps this hadn't been the best time to arrive. Despite these reservations and the closed shops, he did find open a small drinking establishment where he met a great uncle on his father's side who told him what had happened.

Apparently, Kuang San, leading a Red Army detachment, had liberated Lingning and once his troops had moved on, installed himself as military governor for the region. What's more, Kuang San was actually a distant relative of Bai He's great uncle. Learning of this family connection, weak though it may be, Bai He pleaded with the older man to speak to Kuang San on his behalf, requesting he be allowed to carry out business in the town. After all, he told his uncle, he had no desire to remain in Laocheng tending a measly three *mu* of land. Rather unexpectedly, Bai He's uncle did in fact speak to Kuang San about his distant nephew, but the newly installed governor was somewhat suspicious about Bai He's age and his potential usefulness. So he proceeded to ask the older man if his nephew had any children. Yes, was the reply, and Kuang San at once telephoned the local county government, who, in turn, sent word for Bai He's son to travel to the county capital. Not long after arriving in the city, Bai He's son was appointed errand boy for the main government offices.

Bai Shi was the name of the younger Bai. After about a month in the capital, he returned to visit Laocheng wearing a Lenin suit.

"Bai Shi, I heard you left to be a eunuch's servant, hmm?" Ma Sheng's words had a barely disguised bite to them.

"A eunuch's servant… what the devil are you talking about?"

"You know, you follow the official around, going wherever they go, a lackey."

"I'm no secretary."

"Alright, then answer me this – if so and so calls out to you, you come running, right?"

"I'm a messenger boy!"

That night, the exchange with Bai Shi weighed on Ma Sheng's heart, causing it to sour. And as he dreamed, he turned the conversation over and over in his mind. Soon it felt as though he were chewing a mouthful of pomegranate seeds in his dream. He spat a seed out only to discover it was a tooth. Then he spat again and another tooth fell into his palm; again and again until he had no teeth left. The following morning, he bumped into Bai He and instantly asked him to interpret the dream.

"Losing your teeth like that means your father and mother have died."

"They've been ghosts for more than twenty years, don't you know!"

"Ghosts can die too, you damn fool."

At the same moment, Wang Caidong passed by and announced he was on his way out of the village. He was doing his uncle's duty by gifting his sister's son with *guokui*, a Shaanxi delicacy expected at times like these. The massive round flour pancake was elaborately decorated, with a silk bow tied around it and knotted at the centre. Wang Caidong was literate and cultured and simply had to interject his own opinion on Ma Sheng's dream.

"You're both fools," he said. "It means they've been reborn!"

Bai He responded first: "Your nephew certainly has a wealthy uncle to fawn on him, doesn't he? Look at the size of the *guokui*!"

Ma Sheng was more to the point: "What the hell does it mean, they're reborn?"

"The teeth symbolise bones, don't they?" Wang Caidong answered.

"So… are you trying to say I've changed my teeth… got rid of the milk ones and have permanent teeth now… is there any meat to eat!" Ma Sheng paused for a moment and then continued: "If you're saying I ought to eat some meat, when're you going to slaughter that pig… and if you won't give me the head, will you give me the tail at least?"

Wang Caidong didn't answer straight away, but pulled out some cash that was still used by the Kuomintang, and tossed it to Ma Sheng: "Here, go get yourself some of that hot pig intestine soup."

Ma Sheng didn't use the money he'd been given to buy anything to eat, but rather went to the market to purchase some fabric to make some clothes. Unfortunately for Ma Sheng, he was told by the market vendors that fresh directives had come from the new government and they were no longer accepting Kuomintang currency, only paper money issued by the Northwest Peasant's Bank. The money he'd been given by Wang Caidong was useless. Furious, Ma Sheng set off for home, cursing his rotten luck and at the same time tearing the worthless money to shreds. After returning to the village, he went in search of Wang.

"Do you know that money you gave me isn't worth shit?" were his first words when he found him.

"I've just learnt that myself!"

Ma Sheng threw the shredded bits of money in Wang's face: "Here, I'm returning it... I want nothing more to do with you!"

Suddenly, a brood of chickens scurried towards them, clucking madly. It sounded as though they were laughing. Then, just as quickly as they'd come, they scampered away again. Soon, everyone in Laocheng heard the news: the Kuomintang's money was worth less than the paper used to wipe their arse.

The richest man in Laocheng was Wang Caidong, the poorest was Ma Sheng. This was clear to everyone in the village, just as head lice are easy to spot on a bald man, so there was no need to draw attention to it. Bai He, however, loved all the attention he could get. Despite his financial straits – he was, after all, still in debt to the Hong family – he'd always try to make a show of what meagre wealth he possessed. For instance, whenever he had lo mein noodles to eat, he'd make sure anyone and everyone noticed. He'd sit outside in his courtyard atop a millstone, or on some other raised surface, and hold his bowl aloft, pulling the lo mein out with his chopsticks and high into the air for all to see.

"Enjoying your lo mein, I see!" became a common refrain as people would pass by.

"Yes indeed, every day," was his reply.

On those occasions when all he had to eat was rice gruel, however, he'd leave the gates closed, making sure no one else could see.

In the autumn, he'd dig up mushrooms in the mountains and then sell them in the market for a pittance. But he was easily parted from his money, all for the sake of appearances. On one occasion, a fellow villager by the name of Liu Shuanzi was due to marry his son and came to Bai He to borrow money to buy the wine for the ceremony. Despite having little to spare, he gave it all to Liu, only to receive a harsh scolding from his wife. The defence of his actions only further enraged his wife: "The Hongs curse me for being a poor, cheap bastard, a deadbeat who won't repay his debts... my reputation is not much better than dirt around here, but Liu came to me for money. How could I not lend him what I had? In his eyes, I'm rich!"

Bai He was the exception. Every other villager did their best to conceal their real standing and wealth, should they have any, which most did not, not really. But should a villager have a new item of clothing to wear, for example, they'd just as likely cover it with something old. If there was drought and crop failure… they'd more likely eat air and shit nothing but wind! Of course, they'd still ask each other how things were, if they'd eaten or not, but the answer was always 'nothing'. Naturally, not eating meant they'd be hungry, but politeness only went so far; they'd never invite anyone over for a meal. A stiff upper lip was the most common trait among the residents, this was true, but once the Kuomintang's currency became worthless, they lamented out loud. They cursed the heavens for making the only money they had useless, and then they burnt it, roll after roll, bundle after bundle… what else were they to do?

At last, Liu Shuanzi arranged the wedding for his son. On the day, he slaughtered a chicken, giving the animal's intestines to Ma Sheng to enjoy. He left with the entrails in his hand, and then spied the canisters outside the villagers' doors, burning money.

"Wow, you must have a lot of money to be out burning it like this!"

No one paid him any mind, so he kept on walking, a cloud of flies hot on his trail, attracted by the chicken guts he carried with him. The Hong family used their useless currency as toilet roll, at least this was what their son intended. The head of the family disagreed, however; he'd rather burn the lot instead of be reminded of how much he'd lost whenever he went for a shit. So they burnt it in the courtyard. First, the younger Hong dumped the whole lot into the fire, but fearful it wouldn't burn all the way through, his father picked it out and began burning smaller clumps of the paper money. Watching the cash incinerate, Hong's son couldn't help but betray his hot temper to everyone around.

"Land was expensive. Always, wait, wait, save a little more money, and for what? Wait so long and you'd never be able to buy any, and the money saved, worthless!"

"That might be true, but tell me, who can see the future, huh? I wish someone had told me you'd end up a thankless wretch, an ingrate. I'd have drowned you in the chamber pot had I known!"

Father and son then set about grappling with each other, until the son's wife flung a small wooden statue made in the likeness of the god of wealth at the two of them, cursing as she did so: "And I've spent all my days showing the both of you the proper respect, and for what? You've done this to me, wounded me, that's what!"

Not really sensing the moment, her adopted daughter interrupted the exchange, asking in a soft voice what they planned to have for lunch.

The son's wife now directed her anger at the young girl: "Eat your bones, you little wretch!" She threw the nearby incense burner, which struck her adopted daughter on the shoulder, but the ash exploded over her own face.

In an even louder voice she wailed: "I'm cursed. By what law am I meant to endure this torture? I'm surrounded by greedy exploiters, rapacious mouths everywhere I turn, all of them trying to eat me whole! Don't you spit out the bones once you've eaten the meat?"

As she uttered these words, Ma Sheng had just walked up and couldn't help but add his own two cents: "Shit, you're making quite a racket. Who're you cursing, hmm, the government? They've been rounding people up nearly every day, you know, taking them all down to the river to feed them a bullet!"

She paused for a moment on hearing Ma Sheng's words, before coming up with a reply: "I don't know who gave the government the idea, but it took decades for us to be rich, and now we're poorer than the poorest ghost... does that make any sense?"

Her words dripped with resentment towards Ma Sheng, he knew this, but he didn't let it get to him. Shaking his head, he turned to leave and said: "We're all the same. People are people, you know. Who's without a nose, who's without eyes, who's poor, who's rich, huh?"

Unlike most others, Wang Caidong didn't burn his Kuomintang currency. Instead, he wrapped it in greased paper, stuffed it in an earthen jar and hid it in his cellar. He'd also taken a roll of two out to bake in the sun in his courtyard. It was warm. A flock of sparrows perched on his compound wall, chirping incessantly as though they were planning some mischief or other.

Looking at his wife and then at the money baking in the sun, he wondered out loud: "Do you think you could bludgeon someone to death with this roll of money?"

"Yes, you said so yourself, the year before last. You said money couldn't help but kill people."

"I said that? Really?" Surprised at these words, his mind suddenly went to mush. He stood up to use the toilet, but he couldn't recall if it was in the northeast corner or the northwest... that wasn't the gable to the main hall... he stumbled, struck his head and then slumped against the compound wall.

"What's wrong? What's the matter?" came his wife's plaintive cry.

Her voice actually stirred him awake, and then he noticed the blood on the wall. Stunned and confused, he spoke once more about the money: "How could so much be so useless? How'd this happen?"

Yu Zhuo escorted him to his bed, and once he was lying down safely, she returned to the courtyard and collected the rolls of cash. She didn't put them back in the earthen jar, however, but placed them in a hemp sack and hid them away in a corner under the raised bed. That night the hustle and bustle of chickens clucking sounded twice, waking Yu Zhuo from her slumber. Wang Caidong was already awake and sitting on the bed.

"You've not slept?"

"I've been keeping watch over our money. I don't want the mice to take it."

"But it's nothing but worthless paper. So what if the mice get at it... let them."

"Are you saying this isn't real money?"

"Yes, it's worthless... for everyone... we're all in the same boat."

"Nonsense, money is money."

"Alright, it's money, money, but please put it down, right here, on the mattress." Together they spread it out, a layer the size of the bed itself, but still there was more. Wang Caidong cried out again and grabbed at the money, stuffing it now into a basket that sat on the floor. He told his wife they should take it to where his ancestors were buried.

Yu Zhuo agreed: "Yes, let's make an offering at their grave... perhaps they'll be able to use it in the afterlife."

But when they left, Wang Caidong carried a hoe for digging.

Yu Zhuo stood at the main gate to their compound, but as she opened it to step out into the street, she got the feeling there was someone else there and quickly shut it once more. She waited a little while, but heard no footsteps outside. Opening the door again, she accompanied her husband through the north entrance to the village and headed off towards the foot of the mountain where the graves of her husband's family lay. Wang never burnt the money in offering to his ancestors, but instead dug a hole near where they were buried. Then he wrapped the money in greased paper as he had done before, removed his coat and bundled it all up together.

"Father, mother, grandparents, family... please look after this for me. In the future, this money will grow new cash!"

Yu Zhuo couldn't help but feel her husband had become stricken with some illness of the mind, but at the same time, she wouldn't call him out on it. Besides, there was something more important to worry about: he couldn't use his own clothes to wrap the money; that would only bring them misfortune. Burying a person's clothes, after all, was a common way of putting a curse on someone.

"Stop! What're you doing? You're burying yourself if you bury your own clothes!" She unbundled the money and returned the garment to her husband's shoulders, and then placed the money in the ground.

Yu Zhuo was at the gate to their compound once more, and again had a feeling that someone was outside. This time, the feeling proved to be true: a man was walking through the alleyway. It was Ma Sheng. He suffered from insomnia and had taken to strolling about the streets at night. His feet padded softly on the ground, much like a cat's. When the opportunity arose, he was also not averse to eavesdropping. There was always a husband and wife talking about something or other, even if he could seldom quite make out what they were talking about. This night he'd heard Wang Caidong and Yu Zhuo, but then there was a crashing sound farther up the alley, so he returned home, bitching about women in general before groping at his own manhood. He'd walked from south to north, east to west, thinking all the while about this woman and that woman. He gripped his penis again, hard, and soon shot his filth over the bed. The wall next to where he slept was spotted with stains, and he looked at them now. Each stain could've been a child, he thought. By his calculation, he would've had more than a thousand kids by now. The whole village would've been his.

On this particular night he'd planned to eavesdrop on Wu Changgui's home. Wu's wife had stayed at her mother's place for just over a month. She'd come back wearing a pretty flower-printed blouse, and as she walked, the gentle curve of her buttocks, tight and firm, pinched together. It just seemed so... But he hadn't made it to Wu's house. He'd been surprised by Yu Zhuo opening the gate and his own curiosity got the better of him. He'd wormed his way behind a tree and watched the scene unfold, following them to the foot of the mountain and right up to when they sat down near the Wang family graves. He'd stopped following then. He had no idea what Wang was up to in the middle of the night, but on the following day at around lunchtime, he had to go and see. Strangely enough, nothing seemed to be out of place, except the ditch just behind the grave was flowing full with water. Evidently, someone had irrigated the land a little higher up the mountain. Using his hands, Ma Sheng pried the ditch open, releasing the water and inundating Wang Caidong's family grave.

"Drown you bastard!"

Later, when he heard his family grave had been swamped by water, Wang Caidong went to inspect the scene, discovering the water had seeped into the ground, transforming the land into an oozy mess. To the right of the burial site he also spied a small mouse hole. There was a good chance the water had drowned the mouse hole, too, opening up another hole under the ground. Of course, he had to speak to the other household that had irrigated the area to figure out what to do next. They didn't offer compensation as such, but they did assist in filling in the hole opened up by the water. Once the other family departed, Wang Caidong directed his concern to what really mattered: had the water ruined the money he'd buried? Uncovering it, he found to his dismay that it had. The entire lot had become a pasty mess, even more useless than before. He wept, banging his head against the grave.

Yu Zhuo had been with him the entire time. She tried to console him: "This means your ancestors have taken the money. They've taken it to the world beyond this one."

A month later, a fresh sapling sprouted on the grave, assuming a shape no one had ever seen before. As time passed, the tree grew rapidly and within three months, it had become half the height of a man. It had blue flowers and roundish petals. Wang Caidong was sure it was the fabled money tree that had grown on his family grave. All they needed to do was shake it and money would drop down.

"Don't tell a soul," he told Yu Zhuo. "We'll be rich yet!"

Wang Caidong's face began to take on a sallow, melon-like shape. He became withdrawn and isolated, often sitting alone, mumbling to himself. He had lost interest in domestic affairs and what was happening around him, despite the fact his family owned a great deal of land and livestock that needed to be tended to regularly. These tasks fell to Bai Tu. First, he brought in outside help to harvest the fields and thresh the grain. Then he made arrangements for the land to be fertilised. He would plough it himself. This was a difficult job, and by midday the ox he'd been using was worn out and in need of a rest. He roped in another beast for the afternoon's work, but Bai Tu himself took no breaks, working straight through the day and into the night. When the moon was high above him, he finally stopped. His legs were caked in dirt. He sat on the embankment that marked the Wang's fields and smoked to relieve as much of the day's toil as possible.

By this time, Bai Shi had been promoted and was no longer errand boy for the county offices. He now held the post of deputy mayor for the town, and on this night, he returned on his bicycle to visit his family. Upon seeing Bai Tu, he shouted his greetings: "Uncle! Uncle!"

Bai Tu had seen a deputy mayor on a bicycle before, but certainly not his nephew. The sight made him happy: "Bai Shi, look at you! You've got your own steel donkey, hey?"

"Actually, it's the mayor's."

"It suits you. So young and already deputy mayor! That's much better than town head, isn't it!"

"Well, the new government polices need able cadres to do the work."

As the two chatted back and forth, they were distracted by a wild duck that splashed down in the paddy field nearby, before taking off once again and soaring over their heads. Bai Shi asked his uncle why he was out tilling the fields so late at night, criticising Wang Caidong for working his men so harshly. Bai Tu responded by saying there was simply too much land and that if he left the work for too long, he'd never be able to sow the seeds in time. Quite unexpectedly, he then berated his nephew for riding his bicycle in the dark, since nobody would see him coming and that could lead to disaster. Bai Shi informed his uncle of the reason he'd come: the village needed to nominate a representative, someone to attend the local committee meetings and give the views of the residents.

"Ah, you mean a *baojia* neighbourhood meeting."

"That system's been abolished," Bai Shi retorted. "I'm talking about a peasants' committee."

"Why's everything being abolished? Our money is worthless, the *baojia* is finished... is that all it takes, to say something's abolished and then that's it?"

"You don't understand," shouted Bai Shi. The conversation ended, he picked up his bicycle and left.

Bai Shi wanted the villagers to nominate their own representative, but they wouldn't convene a meeting to actually do so. Resigned to their intransigence, he asked his father for suggestions. Bai He proposed several men, but they were so busy tilling their land they simply didn't have time to play at politics.

"I don't have any land to tend," said Ma Sheng. "I can go." But he followed this statement with a question: "Are meals included?"

"Is that all you think about, stuffing your mouth and filling your gut?"

"Shit, isn't everything for a thousand *li* around us all about eating and having clothes on one's back? Do you mean to say they're not thinking about their mouths!"

Bai Shi refused to engage Ma Sheng further, but his problem remained: there was no one else able to attend the meeting. Reluctantly, Ma Sheng was named as village representative.

The primary aim of the meeting was to establish a peasant cooperative, so reps from every town, village and hamlet were expected to attend. The second order of business was the implementation of the land reform policies issued by the central government. Those who attended the meeting would be on the standing committee for the peasant cooperative and responsible for getting things done. But Laocheng's representative was Ma Sheng, far from being the ideal candidate. Bai Shi reported as much to his superiors.

"Is there anyone else from Laocheng who's qualified to take up the post?" the mayor asked. "They must be poor, destitute even... and young."

"There's Hong's son, Hong Shuanlao."

"Then put him in charge... but keep Ma Sheng, too. You've said he's a bit of a hooligan, a rogue. The land reform initiative needs people like him, too. Make him Hong's deputy."

Learning of the mayor's orders, Ma Sheng couldn't help but remark: "I've no land to my name, I'm poorer than poor, doesn't that make me more qualified than Hong Shuanlao? How's it that I'm supposed to be *his* deputy?"

"Take it or leave it. We can always find someone else."

Ma Sheng didn't protest further. But he'd lost none of his gall. He looked at Bai Shi and told him to return to Laocheng with him, on his bicycle, so that a proper announcement could be made. They were about halfway back when Ma Sheng spoke up again. He wanted to try the bicycle. Bai Shi relented, and before too long, both Ma Sheng and the bicycle ended up tumbling down a mountain slope, cracking his head open in the process and warping the bicycle's wheel. Bai Shi was furious and made Ma Sheng carry the bike over his shoulder for the remaining eight *li*. On reaching the village, they went straight to the Hong family residence.

In the courtyard, Shuanlao's wife was sobbing. She was sitting on the stone used for washing clothes, holding tight to a length of leather.

The Hongs had a dozen or so *mu* to till. They'd already worked themselves to the bone, but no dinner fires had been lit. About three days earlier, Shuanlao had set off with a pack animal to walk the forty *li* to the Renchuan coal mine. On his way back, carrying more than a thousand *jin* of coal, he walked through Jinshui Valley. For the first five *li* or so the slope of the valley walls was shallow and his pack animal was able to keep its balance. But afterwards, the terrain changed and the beast's steps became uneven; it started to resist going further. Shuanlao persisted by gathering up stones from alongside the trail to try to cushion the wheels. He also used his whip to urge the ox on. It moved, but the incline was so great the animal was soon sweating profusely. The sky was overcast, the clouds hanging so low they seemed to be wrapped around the trees that dotted the path. Shuanlao cursed his luck, figuring it would rain soon. He egged the beast on, trying to get it to walk faster. He used the whip again, not realising the ox had one foot stuck in a pothole in the road. White spittle bubbled from its mouth. Shuanlao relented, allowing the beast to rest. He used the time to have a smoke, going through three pipes before finally trying to get the animal to move once more. But it wouldn't raise itself from the ground. Shuanlao realised it was dead.

He began to panic, stranded in the middle of nowhere. His only option was to head for the nearby walled hamlet known as Jinjia, about five *li* away. He might be able to get help there, or perhaps find another ox to carry his coal and dead animal back to Laocheng. Unfortunately, the animals in Jinjia were all busy ploughing their own fields, and there was no ox available. As despair was about to overtake him, the local butcher offered him a donkey. The only problem was he wanted five *dou* of grain as payment. The price he was asking was worth more than the coal he'd left strapped to the back of his own dead ox, so naturally Shuanlao declined the offer and instead tried to bargain with the man. After some back and forth, they hit on a price that involved his own dead beast serving as currency: the meat would be the butcher's, while he would take the hide home with him.

A consummate businessman, the butcher still tried to make a profit: "I've heard the people in Laocheng love their pork, beef, lamb intestines, right? How about I give you some?"

Angrily, Shuanlao refused, and the butcher resigned himself to taking the ox at least. Accompanying him back to where the animal fell, the butcher sliced up the animal on the slope of the mountain. He asked Shuanlao for a little help, but none was forthcoming. Shuanlao didn't even want to see the butcher's blade cut into the flesh of what was once his trusty ox. The rain poured down as the butcher worked. Shuanlao found a small covering and sat down to brood, smoking as he did so. He returned home on the following day as the sun was coming up. A donkey was carrying the coal, the hide from his ox slung over the shaft of the cart. His wife knew immediately that the ox had perished on the way. She didn't ask if he was hungry, or if he wished to change out of his sweaty clothes. She simply grabbed hold of the leather hide and wept.

Bai Shi asked if Shuanlao was at home, but his wife only cried in response. Ma Sheng wrested the leather hide from her hands and tossed it to one side, saying: "Dead's dead, you can always get another!"

Through tears, Shuanlao's wife finally spoke to them: "Will you give us one?"

"Fine, yes, whatever."

"And what about the remains of our old one, will you bring me those, too?" And she cried again.

Bai Shi and Ma Sheng ignored her weeping and went into the main hall. Shuanlao was inside, smoking. His face had an odd, almost aubergine colour to it. Bai Shi told him of the decisions that'd been made: he was to lead the peasant cooperative and implement the directives given from the central government. Shuanlao accepted the position without debate, then looked at Ma Sheng and asked him to fetch back the hide he'd thrown to one side. Ma Sheng complied, but after he stepped inside the main hall with the leather in hand, he made a great show of draping it over Shuanlao's shoulders. There was a violent fierceness in his voice: "You've just been named head of the peasant cooperative and this is the first order you give your deputy!"

No one expected what happened next. The hide wrapped itself tightly around Shuanlao as though it were trying to seal him off from the world. Bai Shi rushed forward and tried to pull it loose. As he did so, they could hear Shuanlao shout: "This'll make me an ox!"

The strangeness of what happened to Shuanlao never happened again, even on those occasions when a villager might drape leather over his shoulders. Bai He, with his usual acerbic wit, summed it up by reference to the Buddhist belief in reincarnation: "Once livestock, always livestock, eh!"

With the establishment of the peasant cooperative, Laocheng embarked on land reform. The first order of business was the recording of land deeds and then house sizes. This was followed by a counting of the number of servants and labourers, both long term and short term, employed by wealthier families. For those on short-term arrangements, the intensity of the work was also measured. Normally, short-term workers were employed for two seasons, spring for planting and autumn for harvesting. But they could also be involved in the laying of bricks for extensions, the upkeep of courtyards, the work associated with weddings and funerals, and even for helping in the kitchens. Inventories were also made of the number of trees on family properties, as well as the number and type of animals kept: every cow, horse, donkey, pig, sheep, chicken and even dog had to be counted. Farm tools were catalogued, too. How many carts did a family own, how many ploughs, drills and tillers? Lists were also made for household furniture items such as wardrobes, chests, tables, looms and spinning wheels, storage jars, baskets, tofu millstones, noodle-making machines, everything. Of course, cataloguing land, mountainous areas and trees was straightforward – they didn't go anywhere and they didn't really change. So it made sense, to Ma Sheng at least, to first register household items and farm tools. And to do this, he had to look the part, which meant procuring the smoking pipe once owned by Wang Caidong's father when he was still alive.

He carried it like a walking stick, and when he wanted to smoke, he'd place the tip of it between his lips and wait expectantly for someone to rush up to light the tobacco for him. Then he'd survey the particular home he happened to be in, using the pipe to stab the air and calling out at the same time: "Three main rooms, two side rooms, one kitchen, one storage shed for firewood, one cattle enclosure, one for donkeys as well. My, oh my!"

Shuanlao would be sat in the courtyard with a notebook on his lap busily transcribing Ma Sheng's every word. His records weren't always complete since there were many characters he simply didn't know. His writing was also slow, which resulted quite often in the ink soaking through the paper, tearing hole after hole in the notebook.

As the work continued, the homeowner tried to correct Ma Sheng's reckoning of possessions: "The cattle and donkeys are housed together, that's only a single enclosure. I've just divided it down the middle."

"Not to my eyes it isn't," replied Ma Sheng. "I see one for cattle and one for donkeys!"

"Slower, dammit," Shuanlao yelled. "I can't keep track!"

"Can these grass enclosures actually be considered rooms?" asked the owner.

Ma Sheng's response was quick: "They're in better condition than the shithole I live in. What else are they if they aren't rooms?"

The owner used his foot against one of the grass pillars of the enclosure wall. The whole structure wobbled and then collapsed. The cow remained where it was, unmoving. The ass, however, kicked in fright, landing its rear hooves against Ma Sheng's backside.

"Ow! You motherfucker, you… but hey, I guess you no longer have two animal pens!"

Shuanlao crossed out the previous line with his brush, and then saw the donkey race by, braying loudly as it ran into the alleyway beyond the courtyard.

Ma Sheng continued to boom out his list: "I count a single cow, one donkey, one pig and one dog… a cart, a plough, a drill, a tiller, a hoe..."

A great clang and clatter rang out as the homeowner flung his hoe, shovel, sickle, flail, spade, water pole, baskets, rope and whatever else was to hand all out into the courtyard.

"This stuff," began Shuanlao, "we don't record this stuff."

Ma Sheng bellowed out a list of furniture: "A three-drawer cabinet, two smaller cabinets with two drawers each, a pair of wooden chests, four earthen jars, a table and four chairs, a flat-basket tray, one loom, a pair of birdcages – hey!"

"Aren't you only supposed to make record of larger household items… surely two birdcages hardly qualify… hmm?"

"Delete the pair of birdcages," Ma Sheng yelled, "but that inlaid and decorated coffin – hey, that counts for sure!"

"We're not recording the coffin," Shuanlao yelled back in response. "It's not furniture."

Tapping on the ornate coffin with his pipe, Ma Sheng marvelled at its quality: "Other houses have nothing like this, some only slabs of timber stuck together… but this, shit, we count this. Look at the craftsmanship… yup, this's gotta be recorded!"

Shuanlao complied, noting the exquisiteness of the item, the excellence of the wood.

Once it was written down, Ma Sheng spoke directly to Shuanlao: "Alright, read out what you've written. Let him hear."

Shuanlao did as he was told and, when completed, he turned to the homeowner: "Any mistakes?"

"No, you've got it all." He paused, before asking a question of his own: "So what's the point of this list?"

Ma Sheng gestured towards Shuanlao: "You tell him."

"We'll use the list to determine your status, your social standing."

"What the devil are you talking about?"

"Your class."

"My class… then what is it?"

"We won't know that until we've made records for everyone in the village. Once that's done, we'll make our determinations."

Ma Sheng instructed the man to mark his thumbprint on the paper in order to verify that the items listed actually belonged to him. It also served as the man's pledge that no item listed would be damaged or removed from the household. Such a guarantee was necessary, for failure to comply would result in the man violating the new, recently promulgated land reform laws, and that meant punishment.

The homeowner wondered out loud: "Punishment? What're you talking about?"

"Well," started Ma Sheng, "if, later on, anything fails to match the list you've just verified, then you'll face punishment. You might be paraded through the streets as a class enemy, or you might even be sent to prison, or worse… for example, nearer the county capital, in the village of Dongbali, one wealthy family poisoned their own cattle, eight heads in total, in an effort to make it seem like they owned much less than they actually did… and do you know what happened? The family head was arrested and shot… the authorities even made the family pay for the bullets used. I trust this makes things clear, huh?"

The homeowner didn't respond to Ma Sheng's question. Instead he kicked at the wall, lamenting his fate: "The heavens have changed! Everything's gone to shit."

Despite the sun blazing hot above, the wind was chilly as it whipped around them. It carried a cold that seeped into their bones, and by the time they were finished, both Shuanlao and Ma Sheng had runny noses. Ma Sheng was without socks, too, his feet protected by nothing more than the flimsy straw sandals he'd always worn.

"You see that?" he said, pointing at the nearby windowsill. "The corn husks there… grab them for me so's I can wrap my feet."

Betraying his anger at Ma Sheng's impertinence, Shuanlao spat back: "Am I the boss here or you? Do you presume to give me orders!"

Using his hand to clean his nose, Ma Sheng chortled: "Alright, alright… it's just I don't have any fucken socks, OK… you're the boss, alright, you're the boss!"

He slapped Shuanlao on the back, wiping his hand free of mucus at the same time.

Wang Caidong's house was last. The rice fields owned by Wang constituted about a third of the shoreline of the river that flowed through the region, all the way down to the western basin where the water emptied. A stone marker stood bravely to supposedly ward off evil spirits. When Shuanlao and Ma Sheng paid their visit, Bai Tu was still out in the fields, tilling the land.

Originally, Wang's land measured twenty-five *mu*, but it was now thirty in total. The additional five *mu* used to belong to Xing Gulu, but not any more. After the elder Xing died, his son caught the gambling bug and soon frittered away what little the family had owned. Indeed, they once used to live in a large home comprising five rooms, but he ended up selling it to feed his gambling addiction. As a result, the family now lived in a much smaller structure, only three rooms in total. The five *mu* in question had been sold to Wang Caidong, again because of his gambling. Distraught and angry with her husband's actions, Xing's first wife hanged herself. Xing, however, kept on living the same way, even marrying another young woman from the village. And still, every few days at least, he'd be off to the militia barracks in Huangfujie to play cards, mah-jong or whatever else he could wager money on.

As Shuanlao and Ma Sheng arrived, Bai Tu had only completed tilling about three *qi* of land. The ox he'd been driving had refused to move any more, so Bai Tu took to whipping the beast, trying to egg it on. The ox responded by slipping out of its harness. It wasn't resisting Bai Tu as such, nor did it run away; it just stood there enduring Bai Tu's ire.

Realising the intransigence of the creature, Bai Tu changed tactics and spoke to it in soothing tones: "Come on now, my sweet old ox. You're on this earth to plough fields. Why won't you do it?"

The animal snorted in the dirt, its ears flapping against its side.

"Come here, come on. We'll plough it together, and tonight I'll give you something good to eat, honest. I'm not joking."

At that moment, a curious Xing Gulu appeared. "Just who're you talking to?" he asked.

"This old ox is refusing to work…"

"Don't you know the peasant reps are here. They're itemising everything in Wang's home. Why the hell are you still out here ploughing the fields?"

"Well, sure, they'll be measuring Wang's land, but doesn't that mean they'll still need it for planting? Have you been off gambling again? You need to be careful, brother. It'll be the end of you!"

"I'm only gambling my own money. You'd do the same… if you had any money to gamble!"

Bai Tu reached into his inner pocket, pulled out a wad of cash and shook it in front of Xing: "And you say I've no money!"

"What! Ha ha, you're still calling that Kuomintang crap money? It's only good for wiping your arse!"

Bai Tu was indeed holding onto the currency once used by the Kuomintang. Wang Caidong had given it to him just over a month ago. Xing Gulu laughed again and turned to leave.

Bai Tu shouted after him: "Whatever you say, it's still money to me. But I'm not planning to use it, I'm just keeping it on me. That way I can say I'm a wealthy man!"

Bai Tu directed his attention once more to the ox, trying to urge it on to work. As he did so, Shuanlao and Ma Sheng arrived to calculate Wang Caidong's holdings. For the most part, Bai Tu wasn't all that concerned with the accounting they were here to carry out. In truth, he was more worried about them stamping on the freshly ploughed ground, which is exactly what they did, ruining nearly all his work.

"You two've never tilled land, have you?"

"What's there to know?" came Ma Sheng's biting rebuke. "You simply start where the land is soft and go from there!"

"You're a bit touchy aren't you. What's burning in your gullet, hmm?"

"Who're you addressing?"

"You."

"And who the hell are you, Wang Jiafang?"

"I'm Wang Caidong, actually."

"In that case, you call me Director Ma!" Ma Sheng paused for a moment and glanced in the direction of Shuanlao. "I mean Deputy Director Ma!"

Bai Tu refrained from saying more, and he certainly didn't call him deputy director anything. He stopped talking altogether, and instead swatted at a gnat that was buzzing round his ox.

Once they reached the stone marker identifying the land as belonging to Wang Caidong, the illiterate Ma Sheng turned to Shuanlao and asked: "What does this say?"

"It's a Taishan charm to ward off evil spirits."

"To ward off who now? Oh my, as a member of the peasant cooperative, do we deserve such respect, heh, heh!" He put his foot to the marker, kicking it over. Then, with an iron mallet he'd been carrying with him the whole time, he smashed the stone marker to pieces, stomping down the earth in the process.

"Do you know how much that cost? It came all the way from the north, from Mount Taishan!" Bai Tu's complaint was ignored.

"Is this land yours?"

"It belongs to Wang Caidong."

"Would you like to have your own land?" Ma Sheng continued.

"In my dreams, sure."

"Then shut your hole!"

When evening fell, Bai Tu related the day's events to Wang Caidong, who was eating his dinner in the courtyard. He didn't react to the news, but simply put down his bowl and chopsticks and went to bed.

Yu Zhuo emerged from the kitchen and tried to explain her husband's actions: "You don't need to tell him anything, he knows already."

Wang had known since earlier in the afternoon that the peasant cooperative had come to make an inventory of his land and belongings. He heard, too, how they destroyed the marker he had brought all the way from Mount Taishan. But he didn't care about it; he was more concerned about the outcome of the land measurements Ma Sheng and Shuanlao had taken, and what this in turn would mean for him. He needed information, or at least other people's opinions. He recalled what his wife had told him about Bai He's wife, that'd she fallen ill yet again and was in need of medicine. Perhaps he could prepare some kind of herbal remedy, then pay Bai He a visit and learn what he could.

According to custom in Laocheng, it was considered bad luck to bring a herbal concoction to someone who was ill, for it was tantamount to bringing the illness with you. Instead, one had to borrow the herbs and tools from the person who was ill. As a result,

Wang couldn't simply knock on Bai He's gate and present him with the remedy he'd made, so he placed it at the foot of the tree that stood just outside Bai He's compound, and then went to see if the other man was in. Unfortunately, he wasn't. As a matter of fact, according to Bai He's wife, he'd gone to visit his great uncle in their hometown out in the country.

Disappointed by the news, Wang still needed information, so he shifted tactics and inquired about the time when she had taken her two children to stay with her mother.

Bai He's wife, however, was not exactly forthcoming: "What business is it of yours?"

Wang decided to come clean, at least to a degree: "I'm here to determine your family's class credentials. Tell me, how many years were you in service to the woman you call your mother?"

"I *really* am their daughter, by blood," she retorted, angered by his impertinence. "Now do you really think that when I went home I went to work!"

An argument ensued, until finally Wang Caidong caved in and changed the subject: "I've heard you're sick again. Is that true?"

On cue, the woman rubbed her chest and coughed, her breathing ragged.

"I've brought a herbal remedy. I've placed it outside, at the foot of the tree. Go and get it. I'll leave."

That evening, Wang was unable to sleep yet again. He sat up in bed, mumbling to himself. Yu Zhuo was sound asleep beside him, but this didn't matter. He pushed at her until finally she awoke: "Make me something to eat."

"It's the middle of the night. What am I to make at this hour?"

"My parents, you know, are out there sitting down in the main hall."

Yu Zhuo went back to sleep, but Wang Caidong was unrelenting. He woke her again, this time telling her he'd heard men outside. They'd dug a hole under the rear wall to their compound. Yu Zhuo dragged herself out of bed to go and see. Returning a few minutes later, unable to find the hole he mentioned, she intended to berate her husband. But when she stepped into their room, she discovered him fast asleep. As for her, she was now wide awake and spent the rest of the night listening to the mice scurry about, nibbling at the furniture.

The records collected on the entire village showed clearly which class the residents fell into. Notes were made according to the newly promulgated policies, identifying families as landlords, rich peasants, middle-class peasants and poor farmers. Most people in Laocheng fell into the middle-class category, with only a few earning the status of rich peasant or poor farmer. Wang Caidong was, of course, classified as a landlord, and besides him, the other well-off families included those headed by Zhang Gaogui, Li Changxia and Liu Sanchuan. The deeds and measurements taken of the lands controlled by each of these families showed Wang with the greatest amount, a total of sixty-six *mu* belonging to his family. Zhang was next, owning fifty *mu*, while Li had thirty-three and Liu had twenty-seven. There was a clear difference even between these better-off families, with Wang holding double the acreage compared with Li and Liu. Zhang Gaogui, on the other hand, owned just twenty per cent less land. It was clear, then, to Ma Sheng: Zhang would be classified as a landlord, just like Wang Caidong.

Once this was decided, attention turned to Li and Liu. To Ma Sheng's mind, both ought to be confirmed as rich peasants, but Shuanlao was unsure, or at least unwilling to make an immediate decision. According to the higher-ups, he argued, it wasn't just a case of how much land a family owned; consideration also had to be given to the expenditures of these families. The cut-off point was twenty-five per cent, namely, if a family spent more than a quarter of its annual income on hired help, then they'd be classified as rich peasants. Consequently, the information recorded about Li Changxia and Liu Sanchuan had to be examined and questions asked: how many indentured servants did they command? How many short-term and itinerant workers did they employ? These numbers all had to be tabulated.

With respect to Li, that was straightforward. He clearly spent more than twenty-five per cent of income on hired help and thus he was identified as a rich peasant. That meant in Laocheng, there were two landlords and one rich peasant. However, this didn't sit right with Shuanlao and Ma Sheng. Their base was two, meaning that was the minimum number necessary for each class. Since things didn't line up,

Li Sanchuan's information was calculated again. This time they determined he spent more than twenty-five per cent, so he too would be classed as a rich peasant.

As for the poor farmers, this was more straightforward. According to the records they'd made, Zhang Deming had only four *mu* to tend; Bai He and Liu Bazi had three each. Gong Yunshan had one *mu* and Gong Renyou had four-fifths of a *mu*. Xing Gulu and Ma Sheng had none at all. Bai Tu was an indentured worker, so he had no land of his own, either. Everyone possessing less than five *mu* was to be classified as poor farmer. The remaining villagers then all fell into the category of middle-class peasants.

"So," Ma Sheng began, "the middle class are farmers holding anywhere from five *mu* to twenty *mu*. Now, your family has twenty-one *mu*, so you fall into the middle class, too, hmm."

Shuanlao's face grew dark, but he didn't respond immediately. When he did, it was to ask a question: "So what're you getting at?"

"I just mean to protect my immediate superior… you're the director of the cooperative, after all, so if anyone starts to gossip or wag their tongue a little too much, I'll be sure to say something!"

"I'm the director. I don't need anyone's help. I'll nip this in the bud before it has a chance to do any damage!" Taking his brush, he amended the regulations: a middle-class peasant was any family possessing between five and twenty-two *mu*.

With the villagers divided into their respective classes, those listed as landlords and rich peasants were further identified as reactionaries. In plain language, they were the enemy, and thus to be subjected to the proper punishment. On the whole, the villagers were encouraged to call them out and criticise them. For the landlords, their property was to be expropriated and then redistributed to the poorest. As for the rich peasants, they were perhaps let off a little: their lands, according to an additional directive sent by the township government, would not be seized. Consequently, only Wang Caidong and Zhang Gaogui were stripped of their lands, while Li and Liu weren't. For their part, the poorest of the poor regretted the calculations that had been made. Three *mu* and below should have been the cut-off point, five *mu* was too high.

In the past, whenever Bai He had a large bowl of food, he'd always eat it outside, so that everyone could see. When he didn't, he'd eat inside. His behaviour now changed. Even with nothing more than a bowl of congee, he decided to eat it outside in plain view, and to do that, he strolled off in the direction of the large locust tree that stood near the main gates to Laocheng. It didn't have a great number of branches, but its roots were strong, many having thrust up through the ground to lie on top of it. More than a few villagers enjoyed bringing their meals to the bottom of the tree, to sit, eat and talk together. Bai He's congee wasn't all that thick, but it did contain boiled potatoes, uncut. Bai He popped them into his mouth whole.

"Bai He," a passer-by called out. "You've only got a bowl of congee to eat and yet here you are, outside in the open. Isn't that something, hmm?"

"Well, it's better to be poor nowadays."

"Isn't this the time of year when you usually head to the market to peddle what you've grown?"

"Not this year."

"Then how're you keeping busy?"

"I'm waiting."

"Waiting? For what?"

"For lands to be redistributed."

The other person, a so-called middle-class peasant, did not respond. For those who earned the label of poor farmer, however, they saw the potential opportunity of redistribution and so were paying very close attention to what was happening. There was much talk about Wang Caidong's land, about Zhang Gaogui's too. Which land was the most fertile, which the most able to provide a stable crop, even when conditions were not ideal? If they should be given land to till, what would they plant? Wheat they could later grind into flour so they'd have flatbread in the morning. Or would they plant rice so they could have it for lunch?

That same evening, Shuanlao's father had also come to the tree to eat. He carried a bowl of cornmeal congee mixed with braised noodles, a dish common for most folks in the village. He walked and ate at the same time, often lifting the bowl close to his lips to lick off the spillage. As he drew near to the tree and spotted Bai He squatting down eating his own food, he turned and walked in the opposite direction. They'd not spoken in years, and Shuanlao's father was still bitter over the three *mu* of land Bai He refused to pay in compensation for the help given to Bai Tu to bury their mother.

When he saw the older man turn away, Bai He called out after him: "Uncle Hong, uncle!"

Shuanlao's father ignored him, so Bai He stood up and chased after him. "I'm trying to show respect here. I'd like to talk to you, but you're still holding a grudge?"

"There's nothing to say between us."

"You ought to thank me, you know."

"Am I a sucker for punishment! Just what the hell are you getting at?"

"Haven't I been good to you? If I'd handed over that three *mu*, you'd be classified now as a rich peasant, not much better than a landlord, and then you'd be in the same boat as Zhang Gaogui, crying over something you can't do anything about!"

Zhang Gaogui was indeed holed up in his compound weeping profusely, like Liu Bei at the fall of the Han dynasty.

Zhang Gaogui owned fifty *mu*, but he hadn't always had such a large amount of land. In fact, he'd accumulated it over a long period of time, some years purchasing only one or two *mu*, other years purchasing a little more, say three or four. But despite the amount of land he owned, he'd never been able to build a larger home. Instead, he and his family resided in an old, rather small structure with only three rooms in total. Small though it was, it did come with a large rear courtyard, which Zhang had filled over the years with all manner of odds and ends, most of it not much better than junk. There were old willow and bamboo baskets, long and short lengths of rope, wooden staffs, chunks of firewood, iron basins with their bottoms worn out, fragments of roof tiles, iron wire for animal pens, rusty screw clamps, door bolts, sickle blades that had long since lost their shafts, chipped and dull axes, as well as strips of bamboo, cotton and sheaths for all manner of tools. In Zhang's eyes, all of this rubbish had some value, could be used for something, which was why he never returned home empty-handed. There were even times he came home carrying nothing but broken bricks, which he piled on top of one another.

When the peasant cooperative representatives arrived to calculate the amount of land he owned, Zhang went with them out into the fields. He didn't know at the time that his land would be forcibly redistributed. He had watched Ma Sheng count the feet and then the yards. He'd also seen him overlook a foot here, a foot there, and he'd reminded Ma Sheng to count them all. After all, he wanted things to be accurate. Once he understood his land was to be expropriated, he ended up spending far too much time out walking his fields that were soon to be gone. He'd traverse the eighteen *mu* to the river, and then sit down on its banks and weep. These eighteen *mu*, in fact, had formerly resembled a rocky beach, some boulders as big as a small room, and even the small ones as big as a dog. The work to clear the boulders had begun while his father was still alive. It had taken two years to blast through all of the rock.

His father had been a smart man, but not when it came to clearing the land. He'd been careless with the explosives he'd obtained, packing far too many in among the stones, and then, when he lit the fuse only for no explosion to result, he'd gone to see what was wrong. The blast tore him to shreds. After his dad died, no further work was done in clearing the beach for another two years. A full three years passed before work resumed, and the reason caused the other villagers to laugh and ridicule him. Apparently, his father had been visiting him in his dreams, cursing him for not getting on with it. It had got to be so much for Zhang that he felt there was no other choice but to remove the remaining boulders. The work took more than three years to complete, and aside from bringing in outside helpers now and then, all through the winters and into the summers he was busy on the beach, lifting the blasted stones away, and replacing them with earth suitable for farming. The work was backbreaking and there were times he could do little more than crawl, but he endured. The lumps and calluses that formed permanently on his knees were testament to his persistence. But all he could do now was weep. He'd lost everything.

On such occasions, his family would have to come and get him, often carrying him on their backs as they took him home. He'd see his straw sandals, worn and nearly falling apart and he'd start to cry once more. The sandals, of course, would go on the rubbish pile behind his house. Then he would find some small space to crawl into and weep some more. The tears stained his face, and no matter how his family might try to get him to stop, he didn't. Ultimately, they had little else to do but cry, too. And before long, the animals they shared the compound with, the donkey, pig, dog and cat, joined the chorus.

The cat's cries were particularly distinctive, sounding like the wailing of a small baby. What's more, it provoked the other cats in the village to join in, a veritable orchestra of howling felines. Throughout the day one couldn't really get a feel for it, but when night fell, they sounded particularly mournful, sending cold shivers down the spine. Unsurprisingly, Ma Sheng grew quite perturbed at the racket the animals were making and so, using the authority of the peasant cooperative, he rounded up Xing Gulu and Gong Yunshan to slaughter every cat in town. The two men were only too happy to comply, and with slingshots loaded with stones, they scoured the streets, searching along the walls and the eaves, looking for those two glowing green orbs in the night. And when they spotted one, they let loose their projectiles. Of course, cats have nine lives, and being struck with a stone didn't necessarily end all nine of them. The injured cats were brought to Ma Sheng who took them out into the courtyard that surrounded the offices of the peasant cooperative. There he strung up rope and choked whatever lives they had remaining. In total, eighty-seven cats met their end.

After his most serious bout of crying, Zhang Gaogui wouldn't leave home. He wouldn't eat or drink anything either. All he did was stay in bed. Hearing of his condition, Wang Caidong chose to call on him, but he was conflicted on how best to proceed. He understood Zhang's disposition, he knew he wouldn't necessarily be pleased to see a visitor, not in his current state, and so Wang decided to offer an excuse as to why he'd come: his grindstone wasn't working, something had gone wrong with its teeth, and he'd like to borrow a chisel to see if he could repair it, or clean out whatever was stuck in it. Zhang had a chisel, naturally, but he refused to lend it to Wang Caidong. He did, however, get out of bed and guide Wang towards the rear of the house; instead of a new one, he'd search through the rubbish pile and find an old chisel he could lend.

Zhang was correct, too, despite the fact that the chisel he found was far too blunt. "It's usable, yes. You can still make use of it."

"Brother, look at you... you need to eat." There was a plaintive tone to Wang Caidong's voice.

"I can't, I just can't stomach anything right now... Was it easy for me to get this land, all fifty *mu*? I just..."

"Yu Zhuo consoled me, you know, advised me really," Wang

explained. "She said if I let things get to me so badly, if I got so angry about it and I ended up killing myself, well then, what then? Would the land ever be mine again? I realised then, when she told me this… I was only torturing myself… acting as though I'd died!"

"I am dead… dead and buried… out there, in my field. I swear, I'll make sure nothing ever grows in it again!"

After returning home, Wang Caidong related to Yu Zhuo what Zhang had told him. She listened quietly, then went outside to capture five chickens and slaughtered each one. She boiled the chickens in a large pot, and made four large *guokui* to go along with them. That evening, Wang ate well. But not only him; Yu Zhuo invited Bai Tu and three other members of his staff to join him. The chickens were rather fatty, which resulted in the broth being overly greasy, a layer of oil floating on the surface. Bai Tu didn't want to risk ruining the mood of the evening, so he drank the soup in one gulp. It was so hot it ended up scalding his throat, preventing him from enjoying the *guokui*.

"Is it Wang Caidong's birthday?" Bai Tu asked.

"What difference does that make?" Yu Zhuo replied. "Eat and drink as much as you like, and then, before it's too late, mill some flour so that tomorrow I can make some dumplings."

The night hadn't yet become wholly dark, but Bai Tu and the other men were already stuffed, their stomachs gurgling loudly to show their contentment. In fact, they were so bloated their bellies couldn't help but bump up against the millstone as they pushed it round. As they pushed, it came to them that perhaps this was a good way to help digest the great amount of food they'd eaten, and so they started to push the millstone harder, breaking into a jog, huffing and puffing. Gradually, their stomachs loosened until finally they felt more like themselves again.

The day when the fields required watering was the same day the peasant cooperative came to take away Wang Caidong's ox, his farming tools and household furniture. Once that was done, they went to Zhang Gaogui's place to do the same. It had been a while since Zhang had got out of bed, so only his wife was able to greet them, albeit unwillingly. She watched as they removed item after item, but she was more concerned with the noise they were making.

"Quiet, quiet... don't make such a racket. Don't let my husband hear."

To her surprise, however, her husband did not call out. Nor did he cry. No sound at all came from their bedroom. Then, after everything had been removed, she went to check on him, only to discover he was dead. She turned away almost immediately, but no tears fell. Instead, she raced outside after the men who'd removed their belongings and threw her arms around the cedar coffin.

"You're not taking this!"

"Yes we are!" Ma Sheng's reply was quick and harsh. "We're confiscating everything from the enemies of the people, and that means especially landlords!"

"But you didn't give us advance warning you were coming today, and you won't move him, I'm sure. He... he... he needs this now." And she broke into tears.

"He what? Do you mean to tell me he's dead!"

"Yes... just now..."

Ma Sheng marched back into the house and straight to their bedroom. Zhang's corpse was on the bed, just as his wife had seen only a moment ago.

"What the hell happened? Why'd he have to go and die now? The bastard!"

But Ma Sheng wasn't completely heartless. He decided to let her keep the coffin. At the funeral, once the hell money had been burnt, Zhang's wife called out to her dead husband, wondering why he'd left her as he did, without saying a word. Then she cried pitifully, mournfully.

There was a rule in Laocheng which stipulated that once a man passed the age of fifty, then it was up to him to arrange for a coffin to be built, for funeral clothes to be stitched and for a burial spot to be chosen. During the tomb-sweeping festival, not only was such a man required to pay the proper respects to his ancestors, he was also expected to tend to the plot of land earmarked as his future resting place. Then on 6 June, he needed to place his burial clothes out to bask in the sun. Finally, his future coffin needed to be given a fresh coat of paint. Zhang Gaogui, however, had only managed to get his coffin built, and that was simply because another villager, a man by the name of Liu Wuyi, owed him money he couldn't pay; the dark cedar wood and the labour it took to cut the trees down served as Liu's repayment. In fact, the debt had been quite large, so Liu felled three cedar trees on his property and built a double-sized coffin with space for both Zhang and his wife.

But a gravesite had not been chosen, let alone dug. Nor had burial clothes been sewn. Zhang had kept saying he had lots of time, that he was going to live to the ripe old age of ninety-nine at least. And now, at fifty-four... he was dead. His wife, having no last words to go by, decided to bury him in the eighteen *mu* that stretched from their home to the riverside, the same place where his father before him had blown himself to bits. The men who'd come to help tried to tell her the earth was too wet, that burying her husband higher up the mountain would be better, but she insisted on having him buried there, nowhere else. She wanted him to rest in the eighteen *mu* of land that had cost so much to clear, that had meant so much to him. As they were about to drive their shovels into the earth, however, Ma Sheng appeared and halted their work. The land they were standing on was to be redistributed. And besides, it no longer belonged to Zhang Gaogui. He'd just have to be buried elsewhere.

While Ma Sheng was delivering these directives, Zhang Gaogui's wife was still at home, washing her husband's corpse. A neighbour had come to help and wondered why she was busy washing her dead husband from head to toe. Zhang's widow did not reply, but continued to prepare her husband for the next world. She marked his forehead, his cheeks, his stomach and finally the balls of his feet. Then, just as she was going to turn him over to mark his back, the men responsible for digging Zhang Gaogui's grave returned and told her of Ma Sheng's intervention. Her reaction betrayed her anger. She coughed and spat phlegm onto the floor, before marching off to find Ma Sheng.

Ma Sheng and Xing Gulu had already returned to what was once the county government building. Now, however, it served as the main offices for the peasant cooperative.

"Do you have any tea at home?" Ma Sheng asked the other man.

"Well, I may have got nothing to my name, but do you suppose I still don't have tea!" And he sauntered off in the direction of his home.

In truth, however, he didn't have any tea, so he wandered out past the western gate to where there was a small bamboo grove. He picked some soft leaves and returned.

"Let's drink a little of this, it'll help calm our nerves." Just as he lit a fire to boil the water, Zhang's widow turned up.

"Why've you stopped me from burying my husband, huh?"

"The land's to be redistributed, that's why."

They nattered back and forth, but no resolution was forthcoming. Finally, Ma Sheng grew angry: "You needn't spit at me, you cow. Cry, go on, cry, why don't you? Keep it up... your tears might create a river but it still won't matter. You can't use the land, and that's final!"

"I won't cry, not any more. My tears have all dried up. If you won't allow my husband to be buried where I want, if you won't allow him peace in the next life, then I'll just hang myself and curse you when I die!"

"Are you threatening me? Go ahead, hang yourself, here... I'll get you some rope." And he reached into an office desk and pulled some out.

The widow grabbed the rope and stomped outside. She tried to throw it over a branch of one of the trees in the office courtyard, but couldn't get it positioned properly. She threw it again, but was unsuccessful once more. Then, as she was preparing to try for a third time, Shuanlao appeared and snatched the rope away from her.

The older woman collapsed onto the ground and grasped at his leg: "Shuanlao! Do you remember when you were little... when you fell into the outhouse... it was your uncle who pulled you out... do you remember... will you not allow him to be buried in peace?"

"You can't use that land."

"But it's ours. Why can't we?"

"It's waterlogged for one. I bet if you were to dig down just a foot you'd find nothing but mud... Are you trying to tell me that's the best place for uncle?"

"Whether there's water there or not, that's got nothing to do with you."

"You're right... but it doesn't matter, that land's to be redistributed. And that, auntie, is my business."

"But it's not been divided up yet. If it were, then I'd let the wild dogs in the gully gobble up your uncle's corpse. But since it's not... I just want to bury him in land that's ours."

"Ah! There's just no way of getting through to you, is there! Alright, alright, go home, now. I promise we'll reconsider the matter. We'll do that now, and I'll come round tonight to let you know our decision."

He yelled out to Xing Gulu and instructed him to escort the old woman home.

As he pulled the widow along, Xing couldn't help but ask: "How'd you get to be so fierce, huh? Quite the set of balls on you."

"Fierce, angry, you've taken everything from me. Isn't that cause enough?"

As they strode away, Shuanlao waved and called out to them: "Bring her straight home and then return, no detours!"

Zhang Gaogui's family and relatives were milling about his compound, tears staining their faces and sad cries oscillating between high and low notes.

Xing leaned close to Zhang's widow: "I've brought you home. Everything's alright, I'll leave."

"You're not going to show your respect and kowtow to your uncle?" Her reply dripped with disbelief.

"You're a landlord family... the enemy. I won't kowtow. You don't deserve it."

Zhang Gaogui's younger brother-in-law, who'd been crying in front of the older man's memorial tablet, stopped abruptly. There was anger in his voice, and he spat a curse in Xing Gulu's direction: "It wasn't so long ago that he wasn't an enemy, but now he is, huh? Tell me, what did he ever do to you? Why's he your enemy? Did he steal from you, take your money, treat your sister like a prostitute... did he do any of these things?"

"The gall! " Xing struck the other man hard.

Zhang's younger brother-in-law didn't back down however, and returned the favour, landing a blow square on his jaw. Xing Gulu, quite unexpectedly, dropped to the ground like a ton of bricks. He was unconscious, his eyes shut tight. White spittle foamed at his mouth and he trembled all over.

"He's having a seizure," someone shouted. "Does he have epilepsy?"

"Hold him down. Quick, hold him down!"

Before anyone could react, Xing Gulu shouted: "Motherfucker! Mother- motherfucker!"

But it didn't sound like him, despite the fact the words came from his mouth. Rather, he sounded just like Zhang Gaogui. No one moved, no one opened their mouths. Xing, still in Zhang Gaogui's voice, shouted again: "Motherfucker! Can't you hear me? Are your ears clogged up with arse hair!"

He sounded even more like Zhang Gaogui, and what's more, the words he used were the same as those Zhang used to scold his wife; the very same. Everyone knew they were witnessing a profound event, just as the Great Dao outlined, that the spirit of the dead will inhabit the body closest to it in order to say its last words.

Zhang's widow broke into tears, muttering almost inconsolably: "Oh, my husband, when he died he said nothing before death came to take him!" She moved carefully towards Xing Gulu. "What is it... what do you want to tell me? I know you want to be buried in those eighteen *mu*. Oh I know it! Tell me the rest... please."

"I don't think there's anything we can do about that eighteen *mu*," Xing Gulu continued, in Zhang Gaogui's voice. "On the day I died, when they came to take my land, I went to each corner and dug a small hole, and in every one I placed a *pixiu*. You need to go and get them!"

"You buried what? Stone *pixiu*?"

"They guard against evil, don't they?"

"I'll go and get them... is there anything else?"

The unconscious Xing Gulu didn't reply to her final question. It seemed as though the spirit of Zhang Gaogui had left him. Then, as suddenly as he'd fallen to the ground, he opened his eyes and sat back up. Staring at the man who'd struck him, he spoke in his own voice again: "So you knocked me out, huh?" Zhang had gone, but he left Xing Gulu groggy and weak, his face dripping with sweat.

Before any more time was wasted, Zhang's younger brother-in-law raced off to the eighteen *mu* of land, digging into the ground as quickly as he could to unearth the four *pixiu* the spirit spoke about. Contrary to expectations, the villagers laughed and snorted at what'd been found: "An ox lets a man lead, but it begrudges reins!"

Shuanlao and Ma Sheng were still at the offices of the peasant cooperative discussing how best to resolve the situation, such as it was. Shuanlao was in favour of letting Zhang's widow bury him in the swampy ground. After all, he was already dead. If there was an afterlife, or rebirth, or whatever, how then would the land be divided? Ma Sheng was less inclined to let the old woman proceed. In his mind, Zhang hadn't been murdered, strangled or whatever, but burying him in those eighteen *mu*... what would happen if Wang Caidong tried something similar, choosing his own burial site on his land? The authorities emphasised the importance of struggle against contradictions. Wasn't acquiescing to her demands a reneging on that command? They were at loggerheads, with seemingly no way out.

"So," Shuanlao asked, "whose word shall we go on?"

Just as he was speaking, Xing Gulu appeared and deflected Ma Sheng's attention. He laid into the other man: "Where the hell did you escort her? All the way to the provincial capital? Is that why you're only just back now!"

Xing told the other two men of what had happened, how he'd been supposedly possessed by Zhang Gaogui's spirit. Neither man replied. They simply stared at Xing, their faces going pale.

Shuanlao finally broke the tension that hung in the air: "What the hell... what now?"

"Well," began Ma Sheng, "you're the director."

"So... was Zhang Gaogui some kinda hero... a martyr?"

"Shit, let's let him be buried where she wants," said Ma Sheng before pausing for a moment. "I need to say this – we can't let Wang Caidong follow suit."

A decision reached, Shuanlao and Xing Gulu set off to inform Zhang's widow.

Ma Sheng remained behind, cursing: "Balls to that. Fucken balls!"

As though heeding his words, a wind whipped up in the square just outside. It swirled, collecting up the dust that lay on the ground, and then took on the shape of a snake, erect and formidable. It moved towards the office. For a moment, Ma Sheng stared at the snake-like wind, his mind blank. Then he regained his composure and yelled: "I've let them bury you there, haven't I? Damn it, bloody well get on with it and lie down!"

The mass of dust softened and lost its snake-like form. A second later and it was gone. But the square was not vacant, for out of the once churning sand walked a young woman, wife to the Yao family, an embroidered handkerchief wrapped round her head.

Her name was Bai Cai and her face was long and slender. But to the villagers, it was not attractive, mottled by far too many freckles. Nevertheless, Ma Sheng had taken notice of her on the day she married into Laocheng. Or rather, he'd taken notice of her breasts, so much so in fact, that whenever he saw her, he couldn't help but feel the urge to fall upon her and tear her chemise loose to have a look at her. Ma Sheng had been eavesdropping on the Yao family home, of course, more than once in truth, and he'd even been discovered by Bai Cai, again more than once. On the first such occasion, she'd merely shut the window tight, bolting it in the process. The second time, she drew the curtains. When she discovered him a third time, she deliberately spoke loud enough for him to hear, yelling, presumably at her husband, for him to eat the scolding, steamed bread! The scene stoked Ma Sheng's emotions, forcing him to grind his teeth noisily. His hatred for Yao started to burn from this moment. But now, upset and out of sorts as he was because of his argument with Shuanlao, to see Bai Cai strolling towards him, he decided he was unwilling to let Shuanlao's anger hang in the air, loath to let it bring him down. And so he thought he might ask Bai Cai if she'd like to accompany him to the Iron Buddha Temple... would she be open to something like that?

The temple was located just beyond Laocheng, out towards the small valley that ran behind the village. To reach it, one needed to pass through the pasture area used by the local shepherds, and then cross over a loess bridge; it couldn't be missed. It was a rather large temple for Qinling, but after Liberation, four monks had fled, leaving only a single one to tend to the structure, a monk by the name of Xuan Jing. He looked a trustworthy man, still young, and he worked the temple fields, twenty *mu*, as diligently as he could. And when there was more work than he could handle, he'd call upon nearby devout Buddhists and get them to help. Bai Cai was one of them.

Ma Sheng had paid close attention to the comings and goings of Bai Cai, and seeing her like this now, wearing a floral handkerchief over her head, he knew she was going to the temple. He left the office and saw her as she walked through the small alleyways, heading north.

"So," he said in a piercing voice that carried to Bai Cai, "are you wearing that handkerchief for the monk?"

No response came, but this did not stop Ma Sheng from following her. The only problem was, by the time he walked out through the north gate and to the loess bridge, there was no longer any sign of Bai Cai. He cursed Shuanlao again in frustration, and began to scan the ground for any sign of her. After some time, he was finally able to make out some footprints, a set of prints, in fact, which presumably had come from a new pair of shoes. He pulled out his penis and proceeded to urinate all over the prints, speaking clearly as he did so: "Ha ha, Bai Cai, I'm pissing on you! I'm washing away any trace."

Bai Cai was not the only young woman at the temple. Several had come, and all of them were engaged in scooping up the fish that lived in the small pool near the front gates of the temple. In relay fashion, one woman caught the fish and then passed it down the line, finally reaching Bai Cai, who was farthest away from the pool. She, in turn, would pass it to the woman at the main gates, who would shout "Amitabha!" and then deposit the fish in the basin next to her. Ma Sheng had heard about these women. The story was that before finding their faith, they would come here to fish. But instead of giving them freely to the temple, they would charge pilgrims a fee to have them released, which most were only too happy to pay. It was, of course, good business, especially since the fish they had pilgrims pay to release, would only end up being sold again and again, turning quite a handsome profit for the temple.

Ma Sheng never expected to see Bai Cai labouring as hard as the other women around her, but labour she did, racing back and forth between the pool and the temple gates, her breasts bounding up and down as though she was holding a rabbit tight to her chest.

Ma Sheng, brazen as ever, strolled up to Bai Cai, intent on speaking to her: "Bai Cai, how much money do you make off a single fish?"

Bai Cai turned her head and her eyes fell immediately on the man who'd called out to her. She pretended neither to have seen nor heard him, despite the fact she'd turned round. She remained silent. A sparrow, perched on a nearby bamboo fence, cheeped once and then took to the air. Ma Sheng looked for a means to extract himself from the awkward situation he created, so he directed his attention towards Xuan Jing, who was busily packing up a chest that represented the different aspects of Buddhist virtues and achievements.

"Hey, monk... do you have any of that Kuomintang currency in that chest?"

"Yes... who's this man who seeks to disturb the Buddha?"

"Doesn't the Buddha also disturb man?"

"It's not wise to spread falsehoods in the temple grounds."

"I'm right, then, the Buddha does disturb man... don't you know... I've given the temple a *jin* of lantern oil, perhaps more, but I'm still a bare stick... now whaddya think of that! I know Bai Cai often comes here... burning incense, hmm... working... do you mean to say you've not suspected anything! What do you say Bai Cai?"

Bai Cai stood up at the mention of her name and walked off towards the pool.

Ma Sheng yelled after her: "Are you ignoring me? Fine, go ahead. You just wait until I get round to dividing up your family's land. You'll probably end up thinking you'd rather be anywhere else!"

"She's married to a middle-class peasant," interrupted Xuan Jing. "You won't be dividing her family's fields, so she won't be sent off to someone else."

"What do you know?" retorted Ma Sheng. "You spend your whole time holed up here in this temple, don't you?"

For a moment the monk seemed about to fly into a rage, the words were ready on his lips, but he held his tongue. Instead, he picked up a hoe lying nearby and went to till the twenty *mu* of land that belonged to the temple. Golden needles had been planted across the strip of land and they had just flowered, basking the area in a lustrous yellow glow.

It had been a horrible day for Ma Sheng, and the weight of it caused him to cough. Phlegm rushed up into his mouth, and he spat it out at the temple door.

The actual confiscation and redistribution of land eventually took place. Wang Caidong's plot of sixty-six *mu* was reduced to a mere ten, with the remaining fifty-six given over to poor farmers. Zhang Gaogui's family were also left with only ten *mu* out of the fifty they once owned. The ninety-six *mu* in total that the peasant cooperative claimed was distributed among fourteen poor households, each receiving an equal share of 6.8 *mu* per family. There were issues, however, that were a cause for concern. The first was the different individual circumstances facing each of these fourteen deprived families, as some were noticeably poorer than others. Second, the ninety-six *mu* of redistributed land wasn't all of the same quality, as some plots were more productive and fertile than others. There was also the issue of distance, with certain families assigned plots close to home, while others were given land much farther away. These issues resulted in furious arguments between the fourteen households, turning the whole situation into a mess. So much so, in fact, that when one of the more elderly ladies cursed the others, the response she received came in the form of a kick. Needless to say, a melee between the offending households ensued.

Ultimately, the peasant cooperative had to step in to resolve things, and after some discussion, they decided the previous status of each individual household made no difference; seven *mu* of land would be the standard. If one particular house received a better plot, then perhaps some proportion of the seven *mu* would be re-appropriated for a different family. If, however, a household received a less desirable piece of land, then naturally they would receive a little more. This proposed approach seemed to settle the arguments between the fourteen families, and each was invited to send a single representative to the cooperative offices to take their chances in choosing the best piece of land.

On the day in question, it didn't matter if a family sent a male or female representative; only one was to be admitted. The other family members had to wait outside behind closed doors. Notes were written up, rolled into balls and placed in a small earthen bowl. Once everything was ready, each family head was called forward to make their selection. Some had washed their hands for luck, others fabricated stories to delay the process. They tried to persuade Shuanlao they needed to return home, that they'd forgotten their pipe and had to smoke before making their choice; that was the only way they could keep calm. These were excuses, of course. It was more likely they wanted to pray at the nearby Niang Niang Temple. With this in mind, Shuanlao prohibited anyone from leaving, and so none of them did. Confined as they were, they soon took to kowtowing beneath a crape myrtle tree that stood in the corner of the courtyard. One after another they bowed and touched their heads to the ground, beseeching whatever power they could to give them the strength to choose the best plot of land.

"My son is already past thirty," wailed one poor peasant, "but he has little chance of finding a wife. Every potential one sees only his poverty… if I can give him and my family ten *mu* of fertile land, rice paddies lush and full, then for sure he'll find himself a mate!"

"Do you think the tree cares?" a bystander asked.

"Well, with such a tree here… in the cooperative's courtyard… it's got to have a power to it… let me tell you, when I scratched at its roots, the whole tree swayed… that proves a spirit resides in it." The peasant extended his fingers again and scratched at the tree once more. As if on cue, its branches shook in response.

At the same moment, a rat scurried along the eaves of the courtyard wall, lost its footing and fell. It tumbled onto Bai He's shoulder as he was about to draw a straw, and then hit the ground. Another peasant went to grab it, but it raced off through a small hole in the wall.

Bai He hadn't bothered with stroking the tree, but he couldn't help but shout at the sight of the rat: "That's a sign of good luck!"

"It's a bat not a rat that's a symbol of luck," retorted Xing Gulu.

"Shit… aren't they the same?" Bai He replied, and then he reached out to grab one of the scrunched-up pieces of paper.

As the scene unfolded, Bai Tu stood watching from the office doorway, trembling slightly. The palms of his hands were wet with sweat, forcing him to repeatedly dry them on his trousers.

"Why've you not chosen a ball of paper, hmm?" Shuanlao asked him.

"The last'll be mine, I needn't pick it myself."

When that time came, he unrolled the paper and asked Shuanlao to read it to him: "Three *mu* just beyond the foot of the bridge… that's a good piece of land… and 3.8 *mu* just up the slope of the mountain, shaped like an ox with a persimmon tree on it…"

"So… that land's mine?"

"Yup."

Bai Tu brought the rolled-up paper to his nose and sniffed deeply. He then put it into his mouth and chewed. "It won't be taken away from me?"

"Nope."

"Aiya… I ought to kowtow to you!"

Shuanlao grabbed him tightly before he could fall to his knees: "Kowtow to me? I'm not the one who's given you this land. The Party has given it to you."

"But where is it, where's the Party?"

"The Party is the sun in the sky."

Bai Tu tilted his head, looked up… and accidentally swallowed the piece of paper. He lowered his head again and Shuanlao could see the changed complexion on his face: "Shuanlao, Shuanlao… what've I done… I've eaten it!"

"What does it matter," Shuanlao replied. "I remember what was on it." Bai Tu let a smile cross his face.

Wang Caidong's family used to own eight head of cattle, but seven had been expropriated. Of these seven, Bai Tu was due to be given one, but he declined, claiming he had no need since the land he'd been given was fairly close-by and he was quite able to till the soil himself.

Ma Sheng jumped at the opportunity: "Well, if you don't want the bullock, I'll take it off your hands."

Once the land had been redistributed, it came time to parcel out the furniture. Bai He initially received a sturdy square table, but argued that a table needed at least two chairs, and so he was given these as well.

Ma Sheng was also to be given items of furniture, and he had long coveted an ornate chair that used to belong to Zhang Gaogui: "That three-drawer cabinet… give it to someone else. I'd like to have that chair… I've never sat on anything like it."

Ma Sheng was also given some floral bedding and a copper brazier, which he brought home along with the cow. He didn't keep the animal, however. Instead, he led it to Shuanlao's house, knocked on the door and waited for an answer. Shuanlao's wife opened the door, and when she did, Ma Sheng explained why he'd come: "Your ox died. I said I'd give you a new one, so here it is!"

While Shuanlao's family had already been given one head of cattle, his wife still fancied another. However, when Ma Sheng told her he wished to exchange the animal for more than a few pecks of grain, she refused to accept the deal. Ma Sheng departed, but he didn't return home. Instead, he paid a visit to Liu Laomao's home and proposed exchanging the animal for a cabinet with five drawers, a wooden ladder and a loom for weaving fabric.

Liu agreed to the deal, but wondered at the specifics: "What's a man like you to do with a loom?"

"Do you think I'll be a bare stick for the rest of my life?" he said as he took the loom and stormed off.

But that evening, each of the seven cattle returned to Wang Caidong's compound. He greeted them all, feeding each with a mix of cornmeal and straw. Ma Sheng and the new owners arrived not long after.

"These animals are not yours," shouted Ma Sheng. "What gives you the right to feed them?"

Wang offered no words in defence of his actions. He simply wrapped his arms around one of the cows and cried profusely.

Ma Sheng pushed him away, excoriating him as he did so: "So you're Liu Bei, too, huh, crying at the end of the Han... do you think your tears'll make any difference!" Covering the eyes of every cow, the new owners led them away.

Bai He received 6.6 *mu* of riverbank land once held by Zhang Gaogui, as well as the dead man's bones. He measured the burial site first and found it was about a third of a *mu* in area, so he asked the peasant cooperative to allocate him a separate piece of land equal in size to the grave. The cooperative refused outright, but once Zhang's widow heard the news, she offered her remaining bit of land to exchange for ownership of her husband's grave. Ma Sheng disagreed, however, arguing that the land given to the widow was on an incline and of lesser quality than that on which her husband was buried; an exchange was impossible. There was logic in Ma Sheng's words, but even so, the whole situation only served to create a new headache for Shuanlao, if for no other reason than that he had given her permission to use the land in the first place.

Bai He, for his part, wouldn't let the matter go, and he began to pester Shuanlao for a resolution. In a nutshell, his argument was that he ought to be given an additional three *mu* since the burial site was unusable. This made sense. The problem for Shuanlao, however, was they'd already finished redistributing everything they could; there was simply no land left.

But Bai He was unrelenting, using his own son's name to curse Shuanlao: "Shit, why the hell did Bai Shi make you deputy mayor, huh? How's it that your own father's land wasn't touched!"

The best and perhaps only course of action was to give in, to allow Zhang's widow to exchange the land. But still he hesitated. Zhang's wife didn't necessarily help her cause, either. Seeing an opportunity to criticise the whole project, she added her own tuppence worth: "My entire family's holdings are gone, divided up and given to strangers. You wouldn't even let me hold on to my own husband's grave. Tell me, how's that worked out?"

Shuanlao's reply dripped with anger: "I told you already, didn't I. You shouldn't have buried him there. But would you listen? No… the land belongs to someone else now. How can we accept it as your husband's grave!"

"Then give Bai He a third of what I have," pleaded the old woman. "Even if it's on a slope."

This was not acceptable to Bai He, however: "My land's of good quality. I don't want to exchange it for something worse."

"Gaogui! Oh my dear husband, Gaogui! Why'd you go and die? A bird in the sky casts its shadow on the land. Are you to have no grave to mark your passage in this world?"

"What are you, huh?" said Ma Sheng, interjecting himself into the argument. "You're a landlord, that's what you are! We'll just have to plough over Zhang's grave and flatten the land. We'll give you a stone to serve as marker. That's how you'll be able to find it the next tomb-sweeping day."

Once their work was complete, the land reform finished, both Shuanlao and Ma Sheng slept for three days. Upon waking up, Ma Sheng strolled out into the alleyway that ran adjacent to his home and called to the first person he saw: "Shit, this work, the peasant cooperative, shit, it'll be the death of me! Tell me, do you reckon anyone's made some hot pig intestine soup?"

As it happened, Bai He had only recently returned from the market. He'd gone to buy some pig intestines, but unlike in the past when he'd leave his gates open to show everyone what it was he was eating, now he kept the doors closed.

There was a knock on Ma Sheng's door. Liu Bazi had come looking for him: "Ma Sheng, Xing Gulu and Xu Shun are brawling in the streets!"

"That's got nothing to do with me. Go get Shuanlao, he's the boss!"

"He's there already, but he hasn't been able to stop them. He told me to come and get you."

"What? He can't handle it himself?" Reluctantly, he let Bazi guide him to where the men were fighting.

The conflict had to do with land, what else. Xing Gulu had been given four *mu* of land on the riverbank, as well as three *mu* further up the mountain slope. Xu Shun, on the other hand, had received five *mu* on the riverbank, and only half a *mu* up the mountain. They'd come to blows over what Xu Shun had suggested, that is, since he'd been given only half a *mu* of inclined land, this ought to be given to Xing Gulu in exchange for about a third of his flat riverbank land. Shuanlao had obtained Xing Gulu's permission to make the exchange, and they'd discussed the revisions, but once all had been said, a single tree and who it belonged to set off the argument.

The tree in question bore walnuts, which had just ripened sufficiently for picking. Naturally, both men intended to collect them. Xu Shun arrived first at the base of the tree, filling his basket half full. Xing Gulu intended to do the same, but the other man argued against it, claiming the tree was now on his land and thus his to pick. Xing Gulu fired back, saying the tree was his. It then fell to Shuanlao to try to mediate.

"For heaven's sake," shouted Shuanlao in exasperation, the tone of his voice betraying his rising anger, "you're men not animals, aren't you?"

"I've got this skin draped over me, that's true," Xing Gulu replied, "but does it make me a man?"

"So," began Shuanlao, "you reckon your hide is of good quality, do you? Then why the hell are you arguing and fighting over some blasted walnuts!"

"Shuanlao," interjected Xu Shun, "I'm just a poor farmer, but you... your position means you have to protect my best interests!"

"I'm a poor bloody farmer too!" shouted Xing Gulu.

"But I've been poor for generations. Your poverty is the result of your whoring and gambling."

And that's when they came to blows, Xing Gulu landing a solid fist on Xu Shun's cheek. Shuanlao didn't really try to stop them. Instead, he squatted down nearby and egged them on: "Go on, fight, kill each other!"

The two men were still brawling when Ma Sheng arrived: "Shuanlao, why haven't you stopped them? What's caused the fight?"

"How the hell am I to stop them?"

"Just wait, I'll show you!" And he returned home to collect his axe. Coming back a few moments later, he marched over to the tree and plunged his blade into its trunk. Crack, crack, the axe tore into the wood. Before long, the tree toppled over, and there was no getting around that. Xing Gulu was quiet, and so was Xu Shun. Their argument, their fight, was over. The tree lay in ruins, but out of its torn stump water spewed, flowing down towards the river. It was reddish in colour and resembled blood.

Bai He enjoyed three helpings of soup, one after the other, before he headed out to his fields to scatter his barley seeds. After the first major rain of the season, sprouts could be seen nearly everywhere, with the exception of one spot, the flattened grave of Zhang Gaogui. He tried seeding the area again, even pissing over the ground in the hope it might fertilise the spot, but nothing worked. The land remained fallow.

During the first few days of spring, Shuanlao and Ma Sheng adopted new attire: black trousers with white shirts and a belt around the waist. A light cotton overcoat with deep pockets finished off their new look. They were the first to sport such clothing, but before long, it became the attire of choice for nearly every peasant cooperative across the area. From the bigger towns to the smallest villages, this look became the accepted standard, a uniform even. In certain places, the heads of the cooperative were old men, many with poor sight, so they often wore spectacles of some form or other. This in turn meant their pockets were usually filled with cases for their glasses. Shuanlao and Ma Sheng, however, didn't need spectacles, and so their pockets held nothing but their official seals as director and deputy director of the peasant cooperative. Ma Sheng also carried the cooperative's ledger in his pocket. This was in spite of the fact he was illiterate and that whatever needed recording had to be done by Shuanlao. They each also carried keys to the cooperative offices.

On this day, as they stepped out into the courtyard, they were greeted with a crew of sparrows chirping loudly. The birds remained on the ground, refusing to take to the air despite the appearance of the two men. Their incessant cheeping sounded very much like a heated argument.

Why the hell, thought Shuanlao, does it seem as though every day there are more and more of these bloody sparrows about the place?

"The more the better," countered Ma Sheng. "I love a good racket!"

Shuanlao disregarded Ma Sheng and reached for a broom to scare the birds away. Looking at the sky as he did so, he wondered out loud: "Do you suppose spring's nearly here?"

Ma Sheng stuck a finger into the air: "The day after tomorrow, I reckon… oh, that happens to be my birthday!"

"I thought you were born on the fifth of the last lunar month… that's surely not spring?"

"Well, that's easy to explain. I've changed the date of my birthday. I now celebrate it on the same day as I was named deputy director and that was the beginning of spring. So there you have it. I mean, the beginning of spring is generally thought to be good, and being named deputy director has been good, so shouldn't we celebrate the start of spring? That's an old custom here in Laocheng, used to be Wang Caidong's old man, along with Bai He's, who arranged it all, but after they died, well, no one carried it on."

Shuanlao was momentarily stunned: "You want the whole bloody village to celebrate your birthday?"

"I never said that. Shit, how's that even possible," replied Ma Sheng. "But will you prepare my birthday noodles… you know, nice long ones to symbolise a long life?"

"Shit… you're really something, aren't you!"

"Yeah, I am… but still, we completed the land reform, everyone has their own patch… shouldn't we celebrate that? I mean, you're the director, why not take on the role in its fullest!"

Shuanlao thought it over for a spell and then agreed, but on one condition: "Fine, let's do it, but you keep your mouth shut. Don't say a word about it being your birthday."

They decided to use Ma Sheng's fields to hold the celebration; after all, it was the best piece of land in all of Laocheng, once used by Wang Caidong to grow rapeseed. After Ma Sheng came into possession of it, however, the soil hadn't been turned once. On the day before the festivities were to be held, Ma Sheng went through the village shouting that everyone had to attend. Unfortunately, no one could have predicted that disaster would befall Liu Bazi.

The day started with Liu Bazi feeling a sharp pain in his gullet, forcing him to race to the toilet to open his bowels. But out in his courtyard, he discovered a trail of blood smeared across the ground, leading back towards the cattle enclosure. He walked over to where the cow was kept and was greeted by a gory sight. He hadn't had the animal for long – it'd been one of Wang Caidong's – but now it lay sprawled on the straw, a gaping hole where its arse should be, its innards nowhere to be seen. Liu Bazi collapsed right there and then and cried.

Ma Sheng happened to be walking by when he heard the commotion inside, and immediately went to investigate. Seeing the dead animal, he admonished Liu Bazi: "What the hell've you done? Today's supposed to be about welcoming spring and you've gone and done this!"

"Do you really think I wanted this to happen? How'd I know a dhole would fall upon my only cow? There're so many other households in town, but it came to mine. What've I done to deserve this, why's my cow been offered up as sacrifice?" He fell over once more and continued to cry.

"Stop it. Crying like that is an ill omen for the beginning of spring."

"But I've no ox now," Liu Bazi said through tears. "Will the cooperative provide me with another one?"

"If it were you lying there dead, do you think I'd give my best to Lord Yama!"

"But what'll I do, hey, what'll I do?"

Irate, Ma Sheng stormed out of Liu Bazi's courtyard, slamming the gate behind him. He didn't go home, however, but went straight to Gong Yunshan's house, enlisting him to help with the day's festivities, as well as directing him to bring two head of cattle along with him.

Once back on the road, they bumped into Bai Tu, who was also en route to Ma Sheng's plot of land.

"Spring's upon us," Ma Sheng shouted. "How's about tilling my land for me?"

"Sure, sure," replied Bai Tu, seemingly enthusiastic. "I'll plough your entire field if you like!"

"Hey now, that sounds very much like what a poor old farmer would say!" Ma Sheng reached into his pockets and pulled out a pair of boiled eggs. "Would you like one?"

"Nah," Bai Tu answered, "I'm not hungry."

"But you'd still like to have one, wouldn't you?" He handed an egg to Bai Tu, who gulped it down without hesitation. "Do you know why I gave it to you?"

"Well, you had two of them."

"No," Ma Sheng began, "that's not the reason. I gave it you 'cause today's my birthday!"

"It's what!" exclaimed Bai Tu, and then he shouted out to Xing Gulu whose house they happened to be standing outside. "Say, Gulu, do you fancy a boiled egg? Today's Director Ma's birthday!"

"Shit!" Ma Sheng cursed. "Don't tell everyone. It's supposed to be a secret."

At that moment, Shuanlao appeared in the alleyway, a drum strapped over his shoulder. His adopted daughter trailed behind, carrying a pair of percussion mallets. As they walked, periodic 'booms' echoed out.

"Cui Cui," called Bai He, "you shouldn't strike those things, you know. It's just your dad looking to punish himself!"

Shuanlao's wife, who along with a number of other village women was already waiting near the eastern gate to the village, now spotted Cui Cui and her face darkened: "I told you to prepare the feed for the pig, but now I find you here, huh?" She grabbed at the mallet the young girl was holding.

Nearly every villager, every household had come to welcome in spring. Xing Gulu was busy pounding a drum, Gong Renyou clanging a gong and Bai Cai's husband, who was known for his strength, played the cymbals. This orchestra of noise greeted Shuanlao as he arrived, but he paid it little attention. Rather, he strode straight for the centre of Ma Sheng's fields and dug a small hole, about three feet deep. He rammed a bamboo rod into the hole, using the displaced earth to secure it in place.

At the same moment, Ma Sheng's voice could be heard over the din: "Bai Cai, come to the front!"

She appeared in minutes, holding a great white rooster. Ma Sheng gestured for her to hand him the bird, but she refused and instead pulled a bunch of feathers from the cock and handed them to Shuanlao, who in turn deposited them in the bamboo tube. He then turned to the crowd: "Silence now, silence!"

The drums and gongs ceased and the assembled villagers grew quiet. They waited with anticipation for the moment spring arrived. After waiting for what seemed like half a day, the villagers started to grow concerned, the cock's feather didn't move at all.

Finally, Ma Sheng could hold his tongue no longer: "Spring ought to be early this year. Put some more feathers in the tube!"

"Step back, come on," Shuanlao instructed. "You're making way too much noise. How the hell do you think the feather's supposed to come out!"

Ma Sheng, who'd been fighting with his bladder, stepped back alongside Xing Gulu and spoke as he did so: "Don't just stand there, play. Come on, play! What… you've not eaten breakfast? Ah… so what… come on, play… put your back into it! I've got to find some place to… damn… I'm dying for a piss!"

Alone by himself, he undid his trousers and peed over the grass, cursing Shuanlao and Bai Cai in the process, if only under his breath. As he did so, he heard a great popping sound, followed by Xing Gulu's voice: "Ah shit… the leather's ripped!"

He fastened his trousers and returned to the bustling crowd. Sure enough, the drum Xing Gulu had been using was torn, and so Ma Sheng proceeded to curse Gulu for not maintaining a proper rhythm and beating the drum evenly across its entire surface. After all, a mallet shouldn't be able to tear through a drum, should it! At almost the same instant, the rooster feather floated up from the bamboo tube. It was as though someone or something had suddenly blown on it, but whatever the reason, it didn't seem to matter. The feather just kept floating higher and higher.

Shuanlao shouted out: "Sound the whip!"

The whip in question was in Bai He's hands, a length of leather about twenty feet long. When it was pulled back and snapped, the crack it made would echo loudly across the area. At the tip of the whip, Bai He had attached an additional piece of hemp rope, which he'd dipped in water. Gripping tight onto the shaft of the whip, Bai He raised his voice and shouted: "Out of the way, out of the way!"

Before he snapped it, however, Bai Tu called to his brother: "Let Ma Sheng do it, it's his birthday after all!"

The assembled crowd gasped in surprise: "Today's Ma Sheng's birthday?"

"Whose birthday?" asked Shuanlao. "Surely you're talking nonsense. Ma Sheng was born on the fifth day of the last lunar month, certainly not at the beginning of spring… no, no, your minds are being poisoned by his ramblings, how can it be his birthday! The first day of spring's supposed to be a great day, an auspicious day. It marks the birthday of Laocheng, that's what it does… now crack the whip, crack it!"

Bai He did as he was instructed, snapping the whip ten times. Each time he did so, the crowd cheered. Bai Tu harnessed one of the oxen and began to plough the field.

As before, I'll start and then you follow.

Pathways Through the Western Mountains begins with Money-Come Mountain, the first peak of the Lotus Blossom range. The summit is covered in pine trees, while near its foot, there are numerous stones often used for washing clothes. Residing upon this mountain is an antelope-like creature called the xianyang. It has a horse's tail that is reddish in colour, and its fat can be used as a salve for chapped skin.

Forty-five leagues to the west is Mount Pinecone. The Huo River begins here before flowing north to merge with the River Wei. Beneath the surface of the Huo are large deposits of copper. Living on its banks is a bird that bears a striking resemblance to a pheasant. Its body is mostly black, while its feet are red. The bird, known as the tongqu, has a reputation for being able to smooth one's skin and flatten wrinkles. It is also believed that the creature can quell disasters.

Sixty leagues farther west is Larger Lotus Mountain. This peak has four sheer faces. It is said to be about 40,000 feet high, and ten leagues across. It is home to neither mountain fowl nor four-legged beasts, but there are serpents that live here. They are known as the feiyi because of their plumpness. It is said they grow to a length of more than six feet and have four wings to transport their great girth across the land. Its appearance is believed to herald terrible drought for all under heaven.

Eighty leagues farther west is Little Lotus Mountain. Two types of tree cling to the slopes, the thorn and the willow. Wild buffalo roam among the trees in great numbers. On the north face of the mountain, there are stones that seem to reverberate with the sound of music. On the south, tufu jade can be found. Birds nest in the trees, of which the scarlet mountain fowl is most common. It is said these birds ward off fire. Other vegetation found on the mountain tends to grow over the rocks and roots of the trees like a sort of moss. Rock fern, sometimes known as the dwarf fig tree, is also fairly common in among the rocks. Consuming it will alleviate chest pains.

Eighty leagues to the west is Mount Fuyu. Copper is plentiful on its south face, while iron is common on the north face. A tree with a striped pattern around its trunk can be found near the peak. It bears fruit that resembles jujubes. It's said that eating them will cure deafness. Other types of vegetation on the mountain include various allium plants that look more like mallow. In flower, they take on a crimson hue; later, the flowers turn into a yellowish fruit that has the shape of a small child's tongue. Consuming them will ward off hallucinations. A river bearing the same name as the mountain begins here and flows north before merging with the Wei River. The beasts that live on this mountain are called the conglong. They look like goats but have red manes. Min birds are thought to be common on this mountain as well. In shape, they resemble the kingfisher, but their beaks are crimson. Domestically-raised min are believed to protect against fire.

Sixty leagues farther west is Mount Stone-Brittle. Palm and wild plum trees share its slopes, as do varieties of allium that smell of garlic but have whitish flowers and black fruit. Consuming this fruit can prevent scabies and other skin complaints. On its southern face, one can find a great deal of tufu jade. On the northern side, copper is plentiful. The River Dao emanates from here to flow into the Yu waterways. The water is used to bathe oxen and horses to ward off illness.

Seventy leagues farther west is Mount Eminent. On top of this mountain can be found many holm oak and oak trees. Iron deposits are common on its north face, while copper is plentiful on the south face. The Yu River begins here before flowing northwards to join the Summoning River. Freshwater mussels are abundant in the Yu. They look like a turtle, but they sound like a mountain goat when they gurgle. Arrow-bamboo grows on the northern banks of the river, along with an edible white bamboo. Oxen and antelope range across this mountain in great number. The area is also home to the feiyi, a rather plump bird that resembles a quail; its body is yellow and its beak is red. Its flesh will cure skin infections, especially boils. The bird is also thought to be good at killing insects.

A further fifty-two leagues to the west is Bamboo Peak. The upper reaches of this mountain are littered with exceptionally tall trees. On its northern face, great amounts of iron can be found. A plant that has the form and shape of others in the ailanthus genus is also common. It has a yellowish hue, and its leaves resemble hemp. Its flowers are white and its fruit is a deep red, almost the colour of blood. Adding the fruit to your bath can relieve itching and reduce swellings. The River Bamboo originates here and flows northwards to merge into the Wei. Arrow-bamboo is plentiful on the northern banks of the river; so too is dark-green jade. Bamboo Peak is also the source of the River Cinnabar. It flows southeast into the River Luo. Rock crystal can easily be found, along with four-finned human-fish. The mountain is also home to a creature that appears to be a wild boar, but it has spikes along its back that resemble those of a porcupine. It is known as the haozhi.

A hundred leagues to the west is Floating Mountain. Many coniferous trees grow upon its slopes and they all have needles instead of leaves. The needles, however, are harmless and home to many tree insects. A smaller and highly fragrant plant also grows upon Floating Mountain. It smells like a mixture of herbs. Wearing clippings over your belt can treat skin sores.

Seventy leagues to the west is Ewe-Station Mountain. The River Lacquer begins on this mountain before flowing into the Wei. Holm oak can be found in great numbers on this mountain, as well as white-cherry trees. On the lower slopes of the mountain bamboo is plentiful, both arrow-bamboo and more common varieties. Copper deposits are common on the north side of Ewe-Station Mountain, while jade can be found on the south side. A creature that resembles a yu-ape ranges across this mountain. Its arms are much longer than normal, and it is adept at throwing things. Called the xiao, it is said to be rather noisy. An owl-like bird also resides on this mountain. It has a human face and only one leg. It is known as the tuofei. During the hotter summer months, the bird cannot be seen, but during the winter it is ever-present. Wearing its flesh or feathers around your belt will stave off fear of thunder and lightning.

A hundred and fifty leagues to the west towers Mount Shi. The mountain lacks any vegetation. The River Zhui rises here to flow into the Wei. Its bed is filled with rock crystal.

A hundred and seventy leagues farther west is Nan Mountain. Cinnabar is plentiful on its peak. The River Cinnabar originates here before flowing into the River Wei. The mountain is home to many ferocious leopards. A type of dove lives here too, although it looks more like a cuckoo.

One hundred and eighty leagues west is Mount Big-Shi. Holm oak and oak trees grow thick on its highest reaches. Silver deposits are common on its north face, while white jade is found on the south face. The Torrent River begins here before emptying into the Wei. The River Pure also originates on Mount Big-Shi, eventually flowing into the Han.

Three hundred and twenty leagues to the west is Boundary-Heap Mountain. This is the source of the Han River. It flows to the south and east to merge with the River Flood. The Raucous Rapids also begin here to flow north into the Boiling Springs. On the summit of Boundary-Heap, different varieties of bamboo grow like weeds, including the peach branch-bamboo. Xi and si rhinoceros herds range across its slopes, along with black and brown bears. White and gold pheasants are another common sight on Boundary-Heap. A flowering plant grows in places, its leaves resembling orchids. Its roots look like those of thorny shrubs and its petals are black. The plant bears no fruit whatsoever. It is often called the jungle-hibiscus. It is said that consuming any part of it will prevent humans from siring children.

Another three hundred and fifty leagues west is Sky-God Mountain. Both palm and wild plum trees are common on its heights, while reeds and orchids cover the lower reaches. A beast lives on this mountain that bears a striking resemblance to a dog. Its skin is said to make excellent material for matting since it wards off insects. In some quarters, it is referred to as the xibian. A quail-like bird also makes its home on Sky-God Mountain. Its feathers are streaked with black and its ruff is crimson. It is called the lixiang. Its flesh must not be eaten for it can cause haemorrhoids. A herb that looks like a mallow grows in places. It is often mistaken for wild ginger. Feeding it to horses encourages them to gallop; eating if yourself will cure goitres.

Three hundred and eighty leagues farther west is Mount Marsh-Mud. The River Rose emerges here to flow westwards into the River Zhuzi. The Muddy River also begins on Mount Marsh-Mud before flowing south into the Accumulation River. Grains of cinnabar can be found in great abundance on the south face of Mount Marsh-Mud, while gold and silver deposits are plentiful on the north face. Cinnamon trees grow thick near the top of the mountain. There is also a great deal of white stone on the slopes of Mount Marsh-Mud. Some say it is used to fatten silkworms, others say it is an effective poison against rats and other vermin. A parsley-like plant grows in abundance on this mountain. Its leaves resemble a mallow, but its underside is scarlet red. It, too, is an effective rat poison. A stag-like creature lives on Mount Marsh-Mud. Its tail is a bright white, its hooves resemble those of a horse, and its hands are human-like. Four horns crown its head. It is called the yingru. A bird that looks like an owl, but with human feet, nests upon this mountain. It's called the shusi. Eating its flesh is said to cure goitres.

The Yellow Mountain rises one hundred and eighty leagues farther west. Its slopes are nearly devoid of vegetation, except for arrow-bamboo which seems to flourish. The Watching River originates on this peak before flowing west and being swallowed by the River Crimson. Jade is plentiful in the riverbed and can be seen to sparkle beneath the water. An ox-like creature resides on this mountain. Its skin is a bluish-black. Its eyes are abnormally large. Its name is the min. A strange bird can be found here, too. It seems to be part owl, part parrot. Its wings are a vibrant green, its beak is scarlet. When it opens its mouth, a human tongue is visible; it is called the yingwu.

Some seven hundred and sixty leagues to the west is Verdant Mountain. Its higher reaches are covered with palm and wild plum trees. Arrow-bamboo is plentiful nearer its base. Jade and gold deposits are common on its south face. Its north face is inhabited by yaks, antelope and musk-deer. Numerous birds that resemble magpies nest in the wild plum trees. Red and black in colour, they are said to have two heads and four feet. There are also many birth-in-flight birds that look like magpies but are scarlet and black; they have two heads and four feet. It is said that these birds can ward off fire.

Two hundred and fifty leagues farther west is the final mountain in this range: Mount Blue-Horse. This mountain is believed to contain large iron deposits and stands as a wall to the Western Sea. It is devoid of vegetation, but much jade can be found. The Yun River starts here before falling into the sea. The riverbed is rich with coloured stones, gold and grains of cinnabar.

Nineteen peaks are described in the first part of *Pathways Through the Western Mountains*, covering a total distance of 2,957 leagues. Larger Lotus Mountain is said to be the most sacred. Ewe-Station Mountain is the central divinity. Ritual sacrifice requires torches, a period of purification that must last a hundred days and a hundred animals all of one colour that must be buried together. A hundred pieces of lapis lazuli are also required. The ritual wine is to be served in one hundred flagons. A hundred rectangular jade pieces are to be crafted into pendants. One hundred round, polished pieces of jade are also required.

The seventeen mountains remaining all require a sacrifice. The ritual must involve a goat of a single colour. Torches are needed to light the hundred bundles of plants. Their embers must be stoked for a time. White reeds are to be used for seating mats, each edged with vibrantly coloured silk.

Even I must say this was a long section! So, what would you like to ask?

Question: The wash stone mentioned in the passage, is that the same kind of stone we use to scald a pig's skin in order to remove the hair?

Answer: Yes, the same.

Question: In the text, that character, *yi*… it's used to talk about swelling and boils… what is it saying?

Answer: Ah… here it means to eliminate, to cure.

Question: These thorns that are harmless… is that true, I mean, can thorns really be harmless?

Answer: No, the book's referring to the points of the thorns, before they grow long. Those thorn tips can hurt, that's for sure.

Question: The passage talks about infants using a hundred rectangular jade pieces and a hundred pendant-shaped jade pieces… near the end… but is that possible, can an infant really use these to offer sacrifices to their ancestors?

Answer: Ah, you've misunderstood this sentence. The word you're reading as 'infant' has an older meaning, to revolve around, to spiral round. That's how it's being used here, which means it isn't talking about children at all; it's describing the shape of the jade pieces and how you use them in the ceremony.

Question: That word, *tang*, or soup… it should mean like hot or warm water here, yes, as in 'warmed wine in a hundred jars', but I don't really get it.

Answer: Yes, you're right. In this case *tang* is being used as a verb, it means hot or warm here… which is fine, isn't it… I mean, after all, don't we often use the word *tang* to say we need to boil up some peppers, you know, the leftover dregs in a bowl of soup? We're using it here as a verb, too... aren't we?

Question: Wow, I never really appreciated how much of our local dialect comes from ancient Chinese!

Answer: Well, over the course of so much history, it's only natural ancient Chinese became part of everyday local culture and that this culture has been preserved in local dialects. I mean, when we compare our way of speaking with what we see in popular books and in standard Putonghua, I guess we might feel that we're giving cause for city dwellers to laugh at the way we speak. But if we actually write down our localisms on paper, it's easy to see that what we're writing is reminiscent of classical, literary Chinese... high culture, even. Let's take the phrase 'carry your children in your arms', for example, which is what the city folk say using the verb *bao*. In Qinling, we say the same thing, but we don't use *bao*, which is a rather common verb. Instead we use *xie*, which is a much more articulate, more refined word. Or how about the instruction 'get out!'? City dwellers say *gunkai*, which has a somewhat vulgar sound to it. In Qinling, on the other hand, we say *biyuan*, which sounds much more polite, even though it means the same thing. Finally, in the city they say *beng shuohua* to tell someone to stop talking, which is alright, but we say it using much finer words... *beng yanchuan*... that sounds nicer, especially when we consider that *yanchuan* means to convey words, whereas *shuohua* simply means to talk.

Question: Ha ha, you're right... ha ha. I've another question... when the book mentions Mount Blossom, is that the Mount Blossom here in Qinling?

Answer: Yes, it is. So is the Raucous Rapids, the River Wei and the River Han.

Question: But... this chapter talks about nineteen mountains and their matching rivers and streams. How's it that there isn't more than this?

Answer: Ah… this is somewhat difficult to answer, if for no other reason perhaps than some of the names for the rivers and streams that line the landscape have changed over time, while others have had their paths altered, like the river that runs uphill through here. It's possible this is the result of some landslide or other… no doubt there're other waterways that've disappeared altogether.

Question: But… well… I mean… the China of the past must've had so many fantastic mountains, so many amazing rivers… I just don't understand why they weren't all written down and recorded… why didn't somebody do that?

Answer: That's easy. The ancients only wrote down what they saw themselves, or what they heard about… yes, they would add details when they needed to, but other than that, first-hand knowledge was key. Consider for a moment how the book describes this animal and that one, how they have the feet of an ox, the ears of a ram. You need to understand that this is because man had early on domesticated these animals, that's what was familiar to them… or how about when the text talks about what mountains have copper and gold, or metals like these… it's because these were the first metals man knew how to smelt, to mould into items they could use… the same's true when the book mentions the different grasses and trees and how eating such and such is good at reducing swelling or what have you. It's because these were the first sicknesses man knew how to remedy and treat.

Question: Do you think there were more sicknesses back then?

Answer: I don't know for sure, but I will say we're an animal that seems to carry illnesses with it.

Question: How's it possible that there were animals like that bird... what's-its-name... a tuofei... how does it have a man's face but only one leg... and the jue, a gibbon-like creature that has four horses' hooves but the hands of a man... and the shusi, it's got human feet... and the yingwu, a parrot-like bird... it's got a human tongue and can speak... I mean, how did creatures get like this?

Answer: Man and animals have lived together for eons, we still do... so let's flip things around... take the tuofei... couldn't we ask how we have its face? Or the shusi... perhaps it's us that ended up with its legs, hmm...

Question: But how's it that we can no longer see these kinds of creatures?

Answer: Because man has come to dominate this world, the great majority of animals are extinct already, or on their way there, and the other ones... well, they've become men.

Question: They've become men?

Answer: In the past, life was predicated on the relationship between man and beasts, now it's between man and man.

Liberation meant the transformation of this world, didn't it? Ma Sheng went from being small fry, a wee little chick, to a bird of enormous power. Wang Caidong, on the other hand, went from being a tiger to a diseased cat. And then there was me...

The next time I met Old Xu, the once-upon-a-time pharmacist, his bad eye was still bad, but he was now a deputy county commissioner. His first words to me weren't to say hello, but rather to ask me why I still lived on the road, singing at funerals for the recently deceased... wasn't I afraid of calling the ghosts to me... and then he said I ought to work for the revolution! So I did, I joined a county cultural work group and spent a good number of years in the service of the revolution and the people.

As chance would have it, that very same year I was asked by Wang Caidong to come to sing at the funeral for Bai Tu's mum. I ended up staying in Laocheng... and later on singing at the memorial services for another eight families, the last one for Zhang Gaogui. Of course, Zhang wasn't buried straight away. They couldn't decide where to put him, so he was kept interred in his coffin and left in his house. That's why his widow requested that I sing each and every day until the cock crowed for a second time, so until about one in the morning.

Because I didn't know when he was actually going to be buried, I sang about the wheel of life... you know, man comes from the earth, the earth ultimately welcomes us back. Zhang's widow wasn't happy about this song, though. She complained about me singing it, crying that they'd not yet found a place to bury him so it didn't seem right to sing that song. I acquiesced... why not... and sang about the path man should take into the next world. A lot of villagers would come to hear me sing, attracted by the hubbub I suppose... they'd nearly always participate in the singing, too. I'd start... the dead don't march towards the east, the sea is fierce and violent there... and then they'd be my chorus, singing in unison that life was hard to save once the fish got at your corpse! I'd continue... the dead don't march towards the west, there's only desert there, the Gobi stretching far and wide... and the villagers followed by singing that the sun would only roast your skin! The next stanzas followed the same pattern: 'the dead won't march south, they won't march north', and then finally came the last stanza about the deceased being allowed to walk to the centre. At this point, the dead person's family would take their cue and echo me, singing 'walk to the centre, walk to the centre', before ending with 'the spirits stand here waiting, ready to be guided by the divine cranes off to the heavens!'

I remember singing for five days... up until Zhang Gaogui's coffin began to ooze a yellowish liquid and give off a foul odour... he was finally buried not long after. It was at the same time as Laocheng was going through the land reform process, you know, when the land was being redistributed. With Zhang in the ground, I was preparing to leave, but I didn't... that's because, across the breadth of the county, in nearly all of the twenty-three towns, villages and hamlets people kept dying… and not just of natural causes, the number of former landlords who simply couldn't deal with their changed circumstances was far greater. There were also quite a few poor peasants who died, mostly due to brawling over what they thought was an unfair redistribution of land.

By this time, Ma Sheng wasn't all that fond of me… he called me an owl, claiming wherever I went death followed. I responded by saying it was the other way round… but I smiled to myself, I was like a bug, scurrying along to this place and that, yesterday here, tomorrow there, three or five days in some town or other, then back to Laocheng, but only for a day or two, then off to somewhere else. Finally, on the road, I bumped into Old Xu, the deputy county commissioner who was on his way to inspect the land reform initiative… and that's how I ended up back in the county capital of Shanyin.

On the day the inspection committee had organised for each town, village and hamlet to send their local director to the central county government to report on land reform efforts, Shuanlao came down with something and so Ma Sheng was sent in his place. During the meeting, the reps from the nearby villages updated the inspection committee on their progress, outlining in detail how most had completed the land reform. But an unforeseen problem had arisen almost as quickly as the land was redistributed. Namely, once the lands, livestock, tools and furniture of the landlords had been confiscated, the group that actually benefitted the most were the already well-off farmers. In fact, those classified as middle-class peasants were no worse off than the poorest of the poor. The question was therefore asked if these richer farmers ought not to have their lands and belongings expropriated also. And if not this, then mightn't it be better to confiscate everything and then redistribute equally among all villagers?

In response, Bai Shi reemphasised that there were rules to follow: that land reform had conditions and policy that must be adhered to, that what was written down and promulgated by the central authorities must be followed to the letter, and that deviations or creative interpretations were not permitted. Consequently, there were only two things they could adhere to, which they had already: the land and belongings of landlords were to be confiscated and reallocated to the poorest, while the land belonging to the richer peasants and the middle class should not be touched.

Ma Sheng was seated towards the rear of the meeting room, occupying a chair in the back row. His eyes never strayed from the deputy county commissioner, Old Xu, who sat up on the stage along with the other top cadres. He assumed that, since the old man's right eye had been blinded, there would be no way he could see to the left of him. So Ma Sheng nudged close to Liu Shan, who was the director of the cooperative in Laochi, another village near Laocheng.

"So," Ma Sheng asked the other man, "are you a Party member? A communist, I mean?"

"I joined the Party in forty-seven."

"Hey, let me ask you something... the Party stipulates the commonness of everything, right? I mean, that's what being a communist is supposed to be, yes? Then how's it that this doesn't sound all that equal?"

"What's wrong with you... you sound like you're repeating the same kind of slander the Kuomintang used... the Communist Party proposes free, open, common marriages. I suppose there's someone's wife you'd like the Party to give you, huh?"

Ma Sheng scoffed, despite the ounce of truth in what Liu Shan said. But as he laughed, Bai Shi heard and called him out, wondering what was so funny, before asking him to report on Laocheng.

Ma Sheng rose from his seat, preparing to give his report. As he did so, Liu Shan spoke to him in a low voice, urging him not to talk nonsense. Ma Sheng nodded his assent, and then shouted for all to hear: "I hate it all!"

Bai Shi jumped in astonishment, wholly unprepared for Ma Sheng's outburst. He turned and looked at Old Xu, ushering him with his eyes to respond.

"You hate," began Deputy Xu, "you hate who?"

"I hate Laocheng!"

Bai Shi now joined in: "Why... what's wrong with Laocheng?"

"It's poor. I've just heard all these other reports, right... Wangtian had four landlords, one of them had two hundred *mu* of land, another had a hundred and eighty, two more a hundred and forty-five each... And then... in Lijiazhai there're five landlords, Liangchabao has three, each with over a hundred *mu*... the landlord in Dongchuan had three hundred *mu*... and what about Laocheng? Only two... that's it, two landlords... and the richer one only had sixty-six *mu* of land."

"There's no point in comparing such things, it's irrelevant," said Bai Shi, interrupting his tirade. "You're supposed to report on the land reform."

"Alright, yeah... but... you said there're two directives that must be followed, right... but for Laocheng, well, there's a contradiction here... it is complicated... so... as a result... we've not completed the land reform."

"Not completed?" There was a note of growing displeasure in Bai Shi's voice, before he exclaimed: "Laocheng can't fall behind the efforts of everyone else in the county!"

"It's alright... leave it... leave it to me... I'll settle things quick."

"You'd better, as I'm sending the inspection committee directly to make sure you do."

Ma Sheng left the meeting as soon as it was called to a close, returning to Laocheng as fast as he could to inform Shuanlao of the impending inspection.

"But we've finished the work, you fool," began Shuanlao. "Why'd you tell them we haven't... are you deliberately trying to smear my face?"

"Did you know that most other landlords had more than two hundred to three hundred *mu* of land and that, once it was redistributed, the poorest villagers received fourteen to fifteen *mu* each... I only got seven, but we've got several of those well-off families holding thirty *mu*, twenty-five *mu*... I don't think we can say we brought down the two landlords that lived in Laocheng... or rather, we simply replaced them with two more, don't you think?"

"What do mean?"

"Land reform was supposed to be about change, about changing the fortunes of the poorest of us... emancipation... but all we've ended up with is the richest remaining peasants holding twice as much as everyone else... is that right?"

"But the orders were that wealthier families weren't supposed to have their lands confiscated."

"And I don't mean to... but I reckon we ought to reclassify them, make them landlords... then we can take their land, right?"

"You know... my family'd be classified as one of them."

"So... you can't cut the fat from your own limbs, huh, is that what you're saying?"

The two men discussed it some more, deciding initially to label Li Changxia and Liu Sanchuan as landlords. They then debated whether anyone else could fall into the category as well, but no other family seemed to fit. Finally, they settled on Li becoming a landlord, and thus subject to the land reform policy. They just had to be quick about it; after all, the inspection team was on its way and if they didn't get a move on, then there'd be no changing it.

Laocheng had a single carpenter, a single mason, too. In fact, they were one and the same man, Li Changxia. He was quite skilled at his work, but he had a foul temper, and things that would seldom cause offence coming from anyone else, when spoken by Li, couldn't help but make others feel uncomfortable. When the land reform was launched, he didn't really understand what it was all about. All he saw was that other tradesmen, craftsmen similar to himself, were classified as middle-class peasants, a designation he seemed disinclined towards and so he proclaimed he was a well-off peasant at least; that sounded better to his ears. Afterwards, when he realised what all the labelling was about, and that his family had been placed in the wealthier peasant category, he still wasn't entirely pleased; his family holdings were relatively large and so, naturally, they had to be exploited, there was really little else he could do. But once he heard Bai He had taken Wang Caidong's table, which according to him was the best table in the whole area, he couldn't help but pay Bai He a visit and drag him back to his place in order to explain to him some of the intricacies of woodwork. Namely, the differences between a walnut table, which was the wood Wang's was constructed of, and a cedar table, which he had himself.

Now that Ma Sheng and Shuanlao had determined to categorise Li as a landlord, Ma Sheng made the announcement, stating that Laocheng actually had three landlords and that only two had been dealt with, leaving one still to have his lands expropriated. As the poorer peasants listened to the new proclamation, they all assumed it would be Li Changxia, which, of course, meant they also began calculating how much of his thirty *mu* they might individually receive. That is, if Li was to hold onto ten *mu* for personal use, that meant each family would get about 1.5 *mu* of additional land, a not insignificant amount. Naturally, they all cheered at this new development, and shouted "Long live the Communist Party!"

Li Changxia was present while these deliberations took place, finally responding, as he stood in place, motionless: "My legs… my legs… I can't feel my legs!" His wife had to carry him home. The other villagers then remarked on Li's character, on his insolence, his brashness, his inability to react to unexpected situations in any other manner but to shout frantically and wildly.

Upon reaching home, Li Changxia fell asleep, and on the following day, he woke to find his face had turned green. Before, it'd been Zhang Gaogui who'd cried, now it was Li's turn. News of these developments didn't take long to reach Wang Caidong and Yu Zhuo, who were at home enjoying a meal, such as it was.

"Please," Yu Zhuo said to her husband, "have another bowl. I can't help but feel as Li does. I can't think of anything else… eat, please."

"You know, when I made renovations here… for us… Changxia helped enormously… you'd better go see him."

"How's it that they decided to classify him as a landlord, with that bit of land he had… do you suppose if I paid them a visit… well, mightn't his wife think I've come to laugh at them?"

"Hah, we're all locusts on the same piece of rope. Who'd be laughing at whom!"

Persuaded by her husband's words, Yu Zhuo called on Li's home, but she wasn't sure what to say. While she fumbled through her mind for the appropriate words, Li's wife embraced her, weeping and sniffling so profusely it didn't take long for Yu Zhuo's jacket to feel wet all the way through. Yu Zhuo couldn't keep her face dry either.

Shuanlao and Ma Sheng had wasted no time. Men were dispatched to parcel out the land, the family ox was hauled away, so too was their furniture. Li Changxia was bedridden throughout the entire time, his legs dead beneath him. All he could do was curse them.

Ma Sheng was ruthless in his reply: "What the hell are you swearing at me for, huh, landlord? Go on then, curse, come on, do it. I'll be sure to take an extra measure of grain for every foul word you throw our way!" And he stuffed more grain into the sack he'd brought with him, finally filling two whole bags. Li's wife then separated herself from Yu Zhuo and beseeched her husband to say no more.

They took nearly everything. Their two large wooden wardrobes, their three ornately decorated chairs, four chests, their loom, oxcart, five wooden rafters, as well as the cedar table and its four chairs. The ox wailed as they dragged it away.

Li turned to Yu Zhuo: "Can you bring her... my ox... bring her so's I might see her one last time."

Yu Zhuo complied, using her charm to convince the man who held the animal's reins to let her bring it into Li's room so that he might pet it a final time. Tapping it on the head, he spoke to the beast as though it understood his words: "Go... you belong to someone else now... or you soon will... but whoever it is, don't work for them like you did for me... don't give them your life like you would've for me."

Ma Sheng overheard Li's plea and burst into the room: "Whaddya saying, huh?"

"Ma Sheng," started Li Changxia, "do you know... the house you live in, your father asked me to build it. I didn't even charge him full price for the work. Now you're here with such hatred in your eyes... you've made me regret not having tricked your old man when I put up that roof... you fucken ingrate!"

Ma Sheng responded with a slap round the older man's ears. "You regret that, huh, you bastard? Well let me tell you, you did trick him, that's why my family's whole life has been such utter shite!" He slapped him hard again, knocking the cripple unconscious.

Yu Zhuo tried to subdue Ma Sheng's furore: "Please, Ma Sheng, he didn't say... he didn't do anything... he wouldn't, he's not that kind of man. Besides, to curse your family like that, he'd need to write it down, carve it into the wood... he's illiterate, so he couldn't've. I'm sure there's nothing wrong with the house he built for you, he wouldn't've gone that far..."

"What the hell are you doing here ... is this some pact you're playing at, a landlords gathering?" He went to kick her but missed the mark, and Yu Zhuo fled through the door.

Ma Sheng left Li a single chest, along with an arhat bed. Not much else remained. Before leaving, he even took the mirror that was hanging on the wall.

Ma Sheng hung the mirror alongside his front door, positioned exactly so that he could see the rear of the house immediately in front of his, the one belonging to Xing Gulu. Once the land redistribution had been completed, Xing returned to gambling straight away, ignoring the protestations of his wife. Resigning herself to the fact her husband wouldn't change, she took to playing cards with a group of local women, frittering away her own time as well. She didn't gamble money, however, but foodstuffs instead. Whoever lost ten hands had to turn over their foodstuffs to the winner. Xing's wife returned empty-handed.

It didn't matter if Xing came home early or late; his wife wasn't usually in. He'd see the pig groaning and snorting in its pen, the chickens laying eggs in the straw, and then he'd curse something fierce: "*Haalloo* – where the fuck have you got to… huh? The kitchen is cold, the flame's not lit… where the fuck is my dinner?"

A neighbour offered a reply: "Ha ha, your lazy wife's off with the other no-good women, wasting the days away."

"She's what now?" said Xing Gulu, laughing in response. "She's run off… ha, how'll she get by without me?"

"It's perhaps more worrisome that you won't leave her!"

This sort of exchange was in fact par for the course for Xing Gulu and his wife. Before long they'd be back in bed together, neither one able to leave the other.

Ma Sheng, of course, still kept up his habit of eavesdropping. On one particularly busy day, after returning home, he couldn't help but hear Xing and his wife going at each other. Gulu was cursing her up and down, using language of such coarseness that even Ma Sheng was impressed. He naturally had to listen, and so crept over to their home, positioning himself just below their bedroom window. But the shouting had stopped… all he could hear now was the slapping of flesh upon flesh. They were at it again… Xing was slapping his wife's arse, hard, forceful. The sounds were so arousing even a passing stray cat stopped to listen, first craning its neck to better hear the excitement and then meowing loudly almost in applause. Ma Sheng returned home, beset with a frantic feeling of not knowing what to do. He then remembered the mirror he'd hung and the scene it ought to be reflecting. Xing sat upon the bed, a shoe in his hand, slapping his wife's bare behind… her fleshy backside was white like a large, round stone.

From this time on, Ma Sheng always made sure to check his mirror whenever he returned home. Xing Gulu's rear window had no wooden shutters, only a large, wide frame. There was no dark paper hanging over it either, only a nearly transparent cotton curtain, which was usually left tied up on either side. Xing's wife slept on the bed, most often with her legs up. Perhaps they liked creating a scene, although there were times when the curtains were pulled. On those occasions, only the floral pattern of the curtains was reflected in Ma Sheng's mirror. He'd spit and curse on those nights, pacing back and forth in a sulk.

Once his mood got the better of him, and he marched off to knock on a neighbour's door, looking for a chance to shoot the shit and blather on about this and that. Eventually, the discussion would turn to the land reform initiative, and Ma Sheng would boast about the day he confiscated Li Changxia's belongings. Shuanlao, he'd tell anyone who'd listen, was scared of this and that, so naturally it fell to him to actually make things happen; after all, he claimed, once the land was to be divided, it was to be divided, right! He'd be given food and drink, and then keep on badmouthing Shuanlao: his boss was too soft, using words instead of the knife that was needed… the gristle had to be cut off and chewed up! Perhaps there was something going on at Shuanlao's house, he speculated, perhaps he was unwell. His ready audience would egg him on, remarking that if Shuanlao was indeed ill, then Ma Sheng ought to assume the leadership role. Ma Sheng would only laugh in response. He already had control, it didn't matter what title he held.

Since the beginning of spring, Shuanlao and his wife were going through a bit of trouble, and it was often the case that traces of blood were seen on his face, a clear sign of having been scratched. On some occasions, he'd come up with the excuse that he was scratched on a tree or something else, but there were times he'd clutch at his stomach and admit he was having difficulties. Despite these domestic problems, he was still director of the peasant cooperative, meaning he still had to deal with Ma Sheng. Sometime later, he called on the other man, looking for the records that'd been made concerning the land reform.

"I'm illiterate," said Ma Sheng in response to Shuanlao's query. "Surely you remember that… hmm… the ledger is with you, that I'm sure of… I can eat, I can run, sure thing… I can use my stamp to mark my name, too… you just tell me where, and stamp I will!"

"What the hell are you talking about?"

"You're unwell, aren't you… doesn't that mean I should be nice to you?"

"Don't bring that up… yes, yes, my stomach isn't the best and I've got to carry this medicine round with me… but I've got other tricks up my sleeve!"

On this day, as Ma Sheng strode down the alleyway, his belt hadn't been pulled tightly enough and before he knew it, one end of it was twisting down about his feet. It suddenly came to him that his belt was very much like his cock, swinging between his legs. He laughed and chortled to himself: "Wrapped thrice around my waist, dragging along the ground, now look… there in midair, an old crow in flight!" And he raised his face to the sky.

Xing Gulu's wife happened to be on her way to wash a coil of lamb's intestines in the river when she bumped into Ma Sheng as he strode along the alley.

"What're you looking at?" she asked.

"The sky."

"The sky?"

"Yeah, I wonder what it'd be like to soar like the crows!"

"Here, I'll throw this basket into the air to give you an idea!"

"You sure?" And he reached over and pinched her buttocks.

She ignored his physical advances and changed topic: "So, do you think you'll be giving us anything else, you know, after you divvy up the stuff?"

"Why? Do you think you'll be better off should you get more land, is that it?" Again he put his hand on her, this time on her breast.

She reacted now, swinging the coil of intestines and slapping Ma Sheng across the face before twisting around and stomping off without another word.

It took a stunned Ma Sheng some time to respond, but finally he did: "Do you think you're Bai Cai, hmm?"

A shadow of another person walking through the alleyway flashed by, but he only saw it out of the corner of his eye. He wondered for a moment if it could have been Bai Cai, but then he saw who it was, Zhang's widow.

"So… Bai Cai's off to the temple again, hmm?"

Zhang's former wife paid him no mind.

"A landlord's widow… and you dare ignore me?"

"As a landlord's widow I don't dare pay attention to you."

"So she's off to the temple then?"

"How the hell should I know?"

"I saw her wearing her floral handkerchief, didn't I?"

"Oh… in a couple of days there must be some meeting or other at the temple."

"Dear mother, I guess the monk's ship has come in again!"

Cursing the monk for his… good fortune, Ma Sheng suddenly realised the temple grounds constituted at least twenty *mu*, and then he wondered why they hadn't confiscated it. That same afternoon he went to inspect things for himself.

As he drew near to the temple, he spied Bai Cai and the other women cleaning the temple square in front of the main structure. He didn't speak to them, however, but waved them off with the back of his hand and then used his heel to begin marking off the land. The solitary monk still resident in the temple noticed his strange actions and ran quickly over to ask what he was up to.

"Ma Sheng! Ma Sheng!"

"I'm here as rep for the peasant cooperative!"

"Oh… Deputy Director Ma, my apologies… are you looking for something?"

"I'm measuring the size of your land."

"Measuring the land?"

"Yes, I'm determining how much to leave you."

"But… these are the temple grounds."

"All land, everywhere, falls under the jurisdiction of the cooperative. You've got twenty-two *mu* here in front, what about in the rear?"

"I need to speak to Shuanlao about this… he's the director of the cooperative. Have the policies changed yet again?"

"Don't you believe in the Buddha… ask him!"

Ma Sheng continued marking off the land with his foot, assuming the monk had returned to the temple proper to tell the women what he had said. He waited for them to come in turn to ask him about it, but none of them did. He finally reached the end of the plot of land, and then, for no reason, he measured it again. There was a small depression in the land near the front of the field; from the looks of it, it was a badger hole. This gave him something else to do: capture the animal. To do this, he needed some kindling to smoke it out, which he found nearer the temple. The day was coming to a close and the women who'd been working began to return to home. One by one they passed him, but none of them paid him any attention. Ma Sheng noticed Bai Cai was not among them.

The badger in hand, Ma Sheng returned to the village and headed straight towards Bai Cai's house. On arrival, he discovered her husband busy lifting weights in the courtyard. He was a simpleton, but impressively built and fond of using his rifle as a truncheon. From what Ma Sheng could see, he was lifting weights that were several tens of stones heavy, his arms pushing up and down. Ma Sheng stood at the gate and called out to the other man.

"I don't suppose there's a lady swaying back and forth around here, hmm?"

Ignoring the suggestion, he asked a question of his own: "Who're you looking for?"

"Do you eat badger?"

"Why would you give it to me?"

Ma Sheng tossed the badger corpse in his direction and asked: "Is Bai Cai around?"

"She went to her mother's this afternoon."

"Oh, did she now… how's it I saw her at the temple this afternoon?"

"Ah," he said in a low voice but offering nothing else by way of a response. Still making very little sound, he picked up his rifle and strode past Ma Sheng.

"You…"

"I'm going to the temple."

"Shit… quite the temper you've got, hey… little patience for this sort of thing, I'll wager, hmm? But don't go hurting anyone!"

Ma Sheng had exhorted Bai Cai's husband not to harm anyone, but he returned home to await such news.

Despite years of trying, Bai Cai and her husband had not been able to conceive a child. She had taken to visiting the Iron Buddha Temple to light incense and pray that she would. This is how she had first come to know the monk residing there, eventually calling on him every few days. The monk had even returned the favour more than once, visiting Bai Cai at home to encourage her and her husband to drink ashy water to pray for the conception of a child. But the village soon took to talking, wondering all the while why Bai Cai, when she called on the monk, always seemed to carry a bottle of wine close to her chest. Were monks allowed to imbibe such deleterious liquids? They also said the floral handkerchief Bai Cai wore about her head was a gift from the monk. Naturally, no one ever said these sorts of things when her husband was around, but whatever the case, they soon took to sleeping in separate beds, causing the seed of suspicion to grow in her husband's heart. Their subsequent conversations always seemed to revolve around the question of children.

"You'd like a child," her husband was often heard to say, "yet you won't sleep in the same bed as me. How're you going to get pregnant, then?"

"The Buddha will provide," was her usual response.

"The Buddha will do what now? Ha! Let me tell you something – if you dare try to make me some kinda cuckold, I'll arrange it so you never walk again!"

These exchanges became all too frequent, so when Ma Sheng deliberately let slip that he'd seen Bai Cai at the temple, her husband couldn't help but feel she'd lied to him. What made matters even worse was the mocking tone in Ma Sheng's voice, which further enflamed his suspicions and his ire. He grabbed his pole and stormed off to get to the bottom of things.

On arriving at the temple, he saw the gates were closed tight, which only served to stoke the fire burning in his heart. He pounded on the doors for what felt like hours before finally the monk arrived to unbolt them. He didn't wait for any word of greeting: "Bai Cai's here, isn't she?" The tone of his voice made clear his anger.

"No... she's not, no, no!"

"You're lying through your teeth I wager... huh?" And he pushed his way past the monk and into the temple.

"But she's not here!" wailed the monk from behind him in a high-pitched voice that was almost a squeal.

"What're you trying to do, huh, warn her I've come? Is that why you're talking so loudly!"

He strode into the main hall but it was empty, apart from the expected Buddhist accoutrements. The adjacent prayer room was also empty.

"Why don't you check the kitchen and the toilet?" the monk offered. "Perhaps someone is hiding there."

Bai Cai's husband did the opposite, seating himself down of the long bed that stood next to the prayer room wall. The bed was high, its legs long. But when he sat down on it, he noticed that the sheets and quilt were rumpled, half hanging down to the floor. Then his nose caught the scent of osmanthus oil, the same oil Bai Cai combed through her hair.

"She's here, I know it... where's she hiding?"

"She isn't, I tell you. She really isn't."

He stood up abruptly and, with great strength and anger, he flipped the bed over. What he saw underneath was most unexpected: another bed with his wife curled up on it. His fist flew through the air, caving in the bridge of the monk's nose and toppling him to the floor. He beat the fallen man several times with the pole he'd brought with him, and then grabbed his wife's hair and dragged her back to the village.

On reaching the village gates, they bumped into another husband whose wife often spent a great deal of time at the temple. Bai Cai's husband told him of what he'd learnt , and naturally the man shared it with as many other men as he could. That evening, several women endured their husband's fists as each demanded their wives come clean about what was going on at the temple. So violent were the beatings that each one confessed. As a result, the men, now better described as a mob, marched off to the temple in the dead of night, intent on teaching the monk a lesson.

And they did. The pummelling he endured was fierce, merciless, but before it went too far, a voice of reason in the mob cried out: "We've taught him a lesson now, enough is enough. I don't want to kill him. I don't want to take responsibility for that."

Bai Cai's husband, however, was unrelenting, his rage too great. He fell on the prostrate monk, tearing the trousers from about his legs, shouting as he did so: "Give it here, you prick, I'll show you what love is!" And he pulled out a pair of scissors, intent on castrating the poor man.

The monk squealed in terror, calling out to his mother and father to beg their forgiveness. He beseeched them not to cut it off, but to give him a bowl, allow him to bring forth at least some of his essence, his seed, give him until the sun rises and then spare him. They did. And while the monk was busy carrying out his promise, the men rummaged through the temple, taking whatever they could carry, smashing what they couldn't. When morning came and they checked on the monk, they discovered the bowl had but a small trace of his manhood. The man himself lay collapsed on the floor, his face turned away from them.

"Ha!" Bai Cai's husband laughed, "is this all you've got? Is this what you used to defile other men's wives!" And he kicked the man, turning him over. That's when they realised he was already dead.

With the death of the monk, the mob's furore waned and then disappeared. There was nothing left for them to do but disperse. Or so they thought. Before they left, Bai Cai's husband's voice halted them: "Whoever leaves now is the killer!"

They stopped in their tracks and discussed what to do. After much wrangling, they decided to bury the dead man in an unmarked grave in the temple grounds. Then they would report, more or less, what had happened to Shuanlao, outlining clearly the crimes the monk had committed, the adultery he'd engaged in. Bai Cai had been caught in the act, they would tell Shuanlao, and that's how they'd learnt of how many other wives the monk had been with. They'd decided to teach him a lesson, but when they reached the temple, so their story went, they'd discovered the monk had hung himself out of shame.

Listening to the tale, Shuanlao couldn't help but be startled: "He's dead?"

"Yes... dead," the men replied.

"You didn't lay a finger on him?"

"He was dead when we got there. What's the point of beating a dead horse, huh? He wouldn't've felt anything."

"Where's his body then?"

"We buried it. He had no family or friends to speak of. So we thought… well… it made sense to bury him in the temple grounds… right?"

Shuanlao had no further questions, but instead went to find Ma Sheng to tell him what had happened: "Brother… Laocheng's got more trouble to deal with!"

"Why, has there been a fight or something?" Ma Sheng asked.

"How… how'd you know?"

"By the look on your face, that's how. If it's not about someone getting into a fight, then…"

Shuanlao went on to tell him the whole story. Ma Sheng listened, dumbstruck for a moment. Then he chuckled: "That'll work… yes, that'll work fine. Nothing's stopping us now from confiscating the twenty *mu* of land belonging to the temple!"

"It's a man's life we're talking about! Shit… don't you have any sympathy?"

"Well… no. And if anyone asks, we can just say the monk decided to wander off, you know, to seek enlightenment or whatever… that'll work, won't it!"

"Work what?"

"Ah, it will! Don't worry."

"Fuck… I don't know what to think. Fine… whatever… go on… divvy it up."

The temple land was divided and parcelled out to the thirteen poorest families, each receiving 1.3 *mu*. When it came time to sow the crops, Ma Sheng decided that should anyone in possession of land near the river be willing to exchange it for the recently expropriated temple land, then one *mu* would equal two. After some further discussions, Ma Sheng ended up with twelve *mu* of temple land, Bai Cai's husband received three *mu* while Bai Tu got seven. What was even better for them was the fact that the land had already been ploughed by the monk before his untimely death, so all that remained for them to do was rake the soil and scatter their seeds. Ma Sheng carried out this work alongside Bai Cai and her husband. As he pulled the rake through the ground, he was unaware of the monk buried underneath. When his rake struck the coffin buried in a shallow grave, he yelled out to Bai Cai to come and see. She did, and collapsed onto the ground almost immediately. The shock caused her to lose her sanity and she never spoke again. Her mouth remained agape, saliva constantly drooling down her chin... except when she ate, of course.

Three days later, on the sixteenth of the month, at noon, the sun was high above Laocheng, its scorching heat bearing down on the men at work in the fields. Each of the men felt as though he'd been dumped into a pan of hot cooking oil, when suddenly and without apparent cause, smoke billowed up from the town square. It curled its way into the sky like a giant serpent dragon, twisting and turning as it went higher and higher. Then a wind came, flattening the dragon so that it covered half the sky in a blanket of smoke.

"What blind old lady has set her house on fire?" wondered Bai He aloud.

As if on cue, Shuanlao's wife came running up, crying madly that the village was a blazing inferno.

The story went that, earlier in the morning, she'd gone out to check her chickens to see if any eggs were soon to be laid. Expecting there to be some later in the day, she returned again at noon to the chicken coop only to discover there were none. Frustrated by her chickens' inability to deliver, she'd grabbed hold of one and started groping around its arse in search of eggs yet to be laid only to find that the ones she'd felt earlier in the morning had gone. Naturally, she ran out into the alleyway cursing whosoever it was that had nicked the eggs she'd been waiting for, and that's when she caught the whiff of smoke. Turning her head round to look for its source, she saw Xing Gulu's house engulfed in flames, the hot embers glowing most near the rear window of the house. She noticed, too, what looked to be an arm flailing back and forth as though it were waving to her, and so she called out to Xing Gulu, a frantic tone to her voice. There was no reply.

Shuanlao's wife, unsure of what to do and yet showing marked concern for a fellow villager, ran up to the burning house and called out. Still no reply. She tried the door, but it was locked. Her only recourse was to alert the village, which is how word spread to Bai He. Naturally, everyone came running, the fastest being Xing's closest neighbour, Gong Renyou. By the time he reached his neighbour's house, however, the fire had already risen to the roof and was soon to swallow the entire house. He grabbed what he could, a blanket, a quilt, and dumped them all in the nearby toilet, soaking them through with urine. Then he placed a ladder against his own house, climbed up to the roof and covered it as best he could with the soaked blankets and quilts. As the other men arrived to tackle the blaze, they realised they were too late, for the wooden frame, the roof tiles, the structure itself was collapsing in on itself, and no matter what buckets of water they tried to throw on it, the blaze only grew larger. A call went out for shovels, but it was in vain; the remaining beams collapsed.

His house destroyed by the fire, Xing Gulu was given an old, abandoned building to live in. Shuanlao gave him one of the sacks of grain they'd confiscated from Li Changxia so that he'd have something to eat, and then he launched an investigation into the cause of the blaze itself.

Ma Sheng was certain the fire was the result of class antagonism, that a class enemy had lit the match, so to speak. And for him, that could only mean the landlords were responsible. As a result, he set off to search the homes of these families, first visiting Li Changxia's. Li was still bedridden, unable to even get up to shit and piss, his wife constantly running back and forth between their home and the river to wash his soiled bedding and clothes. Gong Renyou's wife had seen her that morning at the river, too, as they both went there to do their laundry. The testimony from Gong's wife proved Li Changxia was not responsible for the fire.

Next, Ma Sheng paid a visit to Wang Caidong. Neither Wang nor his wife had been in the fields, giving them opportunity to start the conflagration. Yu Zhuo said she had been practising her embroidery and had not stepped outside the entire afternoon. Wang Caidong was ill, having caught a cold in the wind, so once she finished her embroidery, she'd made him some hot and sour soup to try to drive away the cold. He'd been wrapped in his quilt ever since, trying to sweat the fever out. There was no way they could have set Xing's house alight.

Finally, they had to question Zhang Gaogui's household. But when they arrived at Zhang's home, they discovered his widow had left the very same day to visit her mother's hometown. Ma Sheng was momentarily unsure what to do. But given his belief that class enemies were responsible, he thought things over some more and decided to return to Wang Caidong's house to question them again. At least, that was the plan.

"You did it," he shouted at Wang. "Tell me you did it, you started the fire!"

"How the hell did I manage to do that, huh?" said Wang Caidong.

"You're lying!"

"No I'm not."

"When I came here first, you said you'd caught a cold, right, that your nose was running, but that was already several hours ago and here I still see the snot above your mouth. You've left it there deliberately so's to make me believe you're sick. It's all just a ruse... hmph, the more you try to prove your innocence, the more you demonstrate your guilt!" Ma Sheng was incensed at Wang's supposed duplicity.

Bai Tu interrupted the exchange, supporting his former master: "But... he was in bed all day, with a cold. You can't argue against that."

"How the hell do you know?"

"I've been here all day shovelling pig shit. I know."

"You're still working for your former landlord?"

"He's sick... besides, the shit had got so deep it reached up to the pig's belly. I had to help."

"Go on, get the fuck out of here, you're giving the rest of us poor peasants a bad name."

Ever since Bai Tu had become indentured to Wang Caidong, he had lived in a small grass shed to the rear of the compound. Even after the initial land reform efforts had been finished and he had been given two rooms that once belonged to his master, Bai Tu had remained in the shed. His reasoning was straightforward: he felt uncomfortable living in the two rooms, especially since they weren't his. Yu Zhuo protested against his continued deference, assuring him the rooms were his, but her words fell on deaf ears. It wasn't until Wang had a rear door cut out of the back wall so that Bai Tu could come and go as he pleased that he finally relented and moved in. The first thing he did after moving in was tidy up the two rooms. He brushed off the dirt that'd become caked on his clothes, sprinkling mung bean shells across the floor. When the sun shone upon the shells and reflected up through the windows again, the room was bathed in light, giving the mistaken impression that it was filled with innumerable things. On that first day, Bai Tu felt as though he was dreaming.

Afterwards, without fail, he always paid Wang Caidong a visit, helping out with this and that, even without being asked to do so. If Wang told him to stop, he'd stop, but when he saw the state of the pig pen, this was some time ago, he knew he had to lend a helping hand. He'd done so three times already, but on this day, especially considering his former master was unwell, how could he not help? Ma Sheng, however, didn't seem to care, he'd come to investigate the fire, he'd cursed him and Wang, and finally he dragged the sick and infirm Wang down to the offices of the peasant cooperative for further questioning.

As night fell and Wang Caidong had not yet returned, Yu Zhuo was left to pace back and forth at home, anxious as to the fate of her husband, but unable to sit down and do nothing. Desperate to find something, anything to occupy her, she headed to the river to collect water, but only managed to fill half a bucket. It was heavy and difficult for her to carry, with most of it spilling onto the road as she walked. While straining to cart the water home, she bumped into Shuanlao's wife, who asked what she was doing out here fetching water. Yu Zhuo could hear the sneering tone of the woman's voice, but she didn't dare to make eye contact, instead keeping her head low and continuing on her way. But having taken a few paces past the other woman, she turned to speak.

"Sister, would you say everything'll be alright?"

"He started the fire. How's he not going to be in trouble?"

"But he didn't, he really didn't start the fire…"

"Well, if he didn't light it… tell me, why was he dragged off to the cooperative offices?"

Yu Zhuo didn't ask anything further, but returned home to collapse on her doorstep, feeling dejected and lost. The groans of cows could be heard on the air, along with the yapping of dogs. A few moments later, Bai He's son came running by, a radish in his hand. It was unwashed, but the boy didn't seem to care.

She called to the young boy: "I can peel that for you…"

"Do you have any dried persimmon?"

"Some, but not many. I can give you two pieces."

"I'd rather have three. If you give me three, I'll let you in on something."

She handed over the persimmon and waited for the boy to speak.

"Ma Sheng asked me to tell you something," he said. "You need to bring your husband some food."

She grabbed the boy's collar, pulling him close: "Do you mean to say he won't be home tonight?"

The boy stuffed his mouth with the dried persimmon she'd given him, making it impossible for him to reply, or even stick out his tongue. Before she knew it, he escaped from her clutches and disappeared.

Despite the worry that plagued her heart, Yu Zhuo did prepare her husband a meal, a tasty bowl of fresh ginger soup. And she decided to take it to him, as she had apparently been instructed. But as quick as she left, she was back again, carrying the food with her. She went inside and broke down in tears. She called out to Bai Tu, the only person she felt she could talk to, and told him how the men in the cooperative offices had beaten and abused her husband, how they punched him, how they'd hung him up from a tree branch and used pieces of wood to pummel his flesh. His skin was fresh with blood, and it was only her arrival that made them lower the rope so he could once more stand on the ground. She continued to pour her heart out, telling Bai Tu how her husband's mind wasn't fully there, how the abuse would no doubt make things worse. She'd seen that already, the glazed look in his eyes. He hadn't said a word to her, nor did he eat the food she brought him. Ma Sheng had instructed her to take it back with her, and to collect a quilt and return with it. His voice was dripping venom, coarse and cruel. Ma Sheng also told her that if they didn't receive an explanation, she shouldn't expect her husband to return. If this were to happen, in ten days, two weeks, he'd be dead. Bai Tu listened to her painful lament, but he couldn't tell her not to worry, there was no way he could console her. All he did was sigh and pace back and forth.

On the following morning, Old Xu and his investigation team arrived in Laocheng. Originally, the investigation was meant to examine the progress of the land reform, but since the village had endured such a conflagration, they decided to first hear the report offered by Shuanlao and Ma Sheng as to what had transpired. One member of the investigative team was a man called Wang Jiayou. He'd been a teacher in the past, before the revolution, and so he took it upon himself to interrogate Wang Caidong personally. His first impression of the case was that it was rather peculiar, which in turn stirred him to examine the actual site of the fire. He determined that the flames had started with the rear window, the curtains serving as a particularly useful fuel. But he also discovered something even stranger: the curtains hung directly opposite the mirror Ma Sheng had hung alongside his doorframe, and that it reflected the sun straight back onto the curtains.

Despite his supposed discovery, however, no one believed Wang Jiayou. He persisted, nonetheless, explaining he had studied this type of incident long ago in school. To persuade the investigative team that what he had learnt was true, he confiscated the mirror and returned with it, placing it just so, so that the sun would reflect off of it and onto a bundle of cotton. Just two hours later, the cotton was smouldering.

Convinced by what they had seen, and now convinced of Wang Caidong's innocence, Shuanlao decided to release the former landlord, ordering him to return home. Wang, however, refused to leave.

"You said I did it," Wang began. "You blamed me for the fire and then you beat me… and now… the real cause has been discovered and you tell me to just go home. What about the man who's really responsible for it, huh?"

"You're talking about me?" said Ma Sheng.

"It's your mirror, isn't it?"

"Yeah, maybe, but it came from a landlord's house!"

Deputy Director Xu interrupted: "Go… you've been given permission to leave, so do it. Your actions now betray your lingering animosity. You're upset your land's been taken from you, much of your furniture confiscated… am I right?"

Shuanlao stepped forward and pushed Wang Caidong out into the courtyard: "When you came here you were still suffering from your cold, right? It's gone now, hasn't it? Go, return home, now!"

He pushed the older man out through the gate and shut it behind him.

They'd established Wang was not responsible for the fire, but Deputy Xu didn't hesitate to use the disaster as an opportunity to teach Shuanlao and Ma Sheng a lesson. Yes, they'd confiscated the landlords' lands and their belongings, and they'd redistributed them, but they needed to be aware that such actions were bound to stoke resentment among the wounded parties; they had to realise the landlords would use each and every opportunity to overturn the land reforms. This wasn't only an issue in Laocheng, either. Xu told them about what had happened in Chengguanzhen, where a landlord had poisoned the local well. In Dongchuan, another landlord recorded those who had received his former land and belongings, etching the names into the main beam of his home as though it were a list of people he intended to avenge. There were examples from the countryside, too. In Taohuayu, a landlord had stolen the markers for his land and buried them in order to prevent a clear determination to be carried out of what belonged to him and what was to be divvied up. There were more gruesome examples, as well. In Wujiachuan, a landlord and his family hanged themselves from the main gate to their local cooperative offices and in Nanxi three landlords conspired together to assassinate the director of the peasant cooperative.

Listening to these tales, Shuanlao and Ma Sheng resolved to strengthen and reinforce the land reforms in Laocheng, and to guard against the reactionary landlords. It was decided there and then that the ringleaders, Wang Caidong, Zhang Gaogui's widow and Li Changxia, had to be struggled against; their plans, whatever they were, must be resisted.

Wang Caidong was to be their first target. The stage was the cooperative central courtyard. Lanterns were set up around the grounds, open wicks, rough and coarse stood erect like fingers poking up into the air. Bai He's young son was responsible for ensuring the lanterns were lit when the enemy of the people was brought before them. The scene set, Ma Sheng called on the first villager, Bai Tu, to speak of the landlord's offences.

"I've… I've nothing to say," said Bai Tu.

"If you've nothing to say, then you'd better be willing to box his ears!" said Ma Sheng, his tone dripping with vitriol.

"I can't hurt someone I know, that wouldn't be..."

"You're a rare kind of weakling, aren't you? You won't raise a finger... really? Go on then, fetch Wang Caidong. Let's get him up here."

Bai Tu did as he was told, leaving the cooperative offices to go and collect Wang Caidong. Unfortunately, having already received a beating at the hands of Ma Sheng, the former landlord's legs were so badly wounded he could no longer stand. Bai Tu had little choice but to return and inform Ma Sheng of Wang Caidong's condition.

"Should we change the day for the struggle session?" Bai Tu wondered.

"What!" said Ma Sheng, his rage growing. "Are we fêting him or something? If he can't walk on his own two legs, then drag him here by the scruff of his neck!"

Together with Bai Cai's muscular husband, Bai Tu returned to Wang's home, resigned to having to cart the infirm landlord to the struggle session. Holding a large wicker basket, the two men put Wang Caidong inside it, but not before his wife cushioned its bottom with a rolled-up quilt. Bai Tu positioned poles on either side to use as levers, and then grabbed the front end. He didn't speak, simply wanting the whole thing to be over with. He didn't want his eyes to fall on his former master, either; his own personal guilt weighed too heavily upon him.

With Wang now present in the cooperative courtyard, the struggle session began. The first person called, in place of Bai Tu, was a poor peasant woman who lived near the northern gate of the village. Her fury flowed easily.

"He's always got so much to eat, hasn't he... he and his family. They're forever stuffing their faces while we can go months without even lighting the cooking fires! And, and... there are always eggshells scattered about the front gates of his compound, like he's boasting or something, trying to make the rest of us envy his wealth. In the summer... I've seen him sitting around in silk garments... and then in the winter... well, he's got new clothes to wear against the cold weather... I've even seen him with a lambskin overcoat and a woollen hat! And do you know what, he actually hid money under that hat... right under it. Can you believe it? And quite a lot, too. But he never once thought to give us a little, to treat us to a meal or a drink, the swine..."

She paused for a moment, before shouting as loud as she could: "Down with landlords! Down with the old society!"

The crowd erupted in unison, echoing her slogans.

Watching the atmosphere grow to a fever pitch, Bai He's son couldn't help but join in excitedly, forgetting the lanterns he was supposed to watch over. They flickered and blinked, blanketing the courtyard in an unsteady light.

"You little shit," his father yelled at him. "What the hell are you doing... take care of the bloody lanterns!"

The second person called to the stage was a child. His father was a middle-class peasant, a man by the name of Wang Sanshui. He began his story: "I want to say... do you know... Wang Caidong's family compound... there's a peach tree there... but that old man never let me once go picking. I tried to get a peach once... I'd just climbed halfway up the tree, but Wang spotted me and cursed... he had a stick with him... tried to beat me... I was so frightened I fell right away... but later on, he let me pick some peaches... even told me that if I picked a lot, he'd give me some eggs... ones that were a little too far along... you know, the ones that have baby chicks in them."

At this point, Bai He's son interrupted the story: "Why didn't you share any of those peaches with me!"

"I was going to, honest... but when I was carrying what I'd picked... the peach skins... well... they were itchy... I decided to go home and peel them... but after I finished... well... I forgot all about you."

There was scattered laughter throughout the crowd. Even Wang Caidong smiled. But Ma Sheng was having none of it, excoriating the crowd instead to refrain from laughing. Everyone fell silent and Wang Sanshui's son continued his tale: "Later on... I understood why Wang had let me pick the peaches... he knew they were coming to take his land, to divvy it up. He wanted the tree to be bare when it was taken away from him... and he tricked me into helping him."

The third person invited to speak was Liu Bazi: "Wang... the old bastard... he once gave me one of his old coats... I guess it made me look a little better off than I was... but in return he forced me into helping his manservant harvest the grain in his fields… but, you know… it was May and June, when the weather is hottest… the sun, you know… it was baking me alive… and that coat… it was like a furnace, I was being cooked alive… and then… what food did he have Bai Tu bring me? Well… Bai Tu can attest to this… it was lo mein… leftovers… something whipped up using whatever bits were left in the kitchen… and only a single bowl… now how's that enough for a working man to eat, huh… shit, more got stuck between my teeth than what went into my belly!"

Bai Tu interrupted once again: "Ah… I should say… well… he'd prepared two bowls for you, but I ate one… I figured you were being lazy… in half a day you'd only managed to harvest a small patch… I didn't think you deserved two bowls…"

"What the hell are you talking about, Bai Tu?" said Ma Sheng. "If you've got nothing helpful to say, then shut it!"

"Well," Liu Bazi continued, "I was so hungry that day, I even peeled off the outer stalk of the wheat and ate the dried grain inside… it was hard, dry… shit… I thought I'd die of thirst from eating it… but there was no water to be had… that dirty fucken landlord never thought to give us water!"

At this point, a gust of wind blew through the courtyard, snuffing out the lanterns and throwing the struggle session into darkness.

Scattered murmurs rippled through the crowd: "Well… the river was right there… couldn't he go and fetch some water himself… lazy bastard…"

At intervals of between ten days and a fortnight, each of the three landlords was brought repeatedly in front of the peasant cooperative to be struggled against. Wang Caidong's injured legs only got worse, so bad in fact he could no longer be carried in the wicker basket. But his condition didn't seem to matter, he was still dragged up onto the stage, unloaded like so much rubbish to face the public's wrath. To those in attendance, he seemed increasingly like a simpleton, a dirty sow that could do little more than gurgle and snort. His words had left him, his body splayed on the stage, his eyes shut to the furore being hurled at him.

Ma Sheng interpreted Wang's actions as a form of defiance, but Yu Zhuo did what she could for her husband, bringing him cigars to smoke and small strips of bamboo to keep his eyes open. On one occasion, just as he learnt he was to be struggled against… again… Yu

Zhuo encouraged him to sleep. His period of rest was brief, but when he awoke he vividly recalled he had been dreaming of water, of the sea. Yu Zhuo listened to her husband's story and wondered. She'd heard dreams of water suggested good fortune in the future, but Wang Caidong would have nothing of it: "Good fortune! Ha! When we're so very much in the frying pan, you see good fortune? More like a coffin!"

Yu Zhuo raised her hand to her husband's lips and closed them shut; she had to stop him from jinxing the dream. She turned her head and spat several times out the window, vainly trying to dispel the bad luck he'd invited with his words. It seemed to work, if for no other reason than that Yu Zhuo's worries seemed to be less serious, her heart less encumbered by the troubles they found themselves in. She then took it upon herself to aid her husband, to try to do something, anything, to help him out. That's how she ended up at Ma Sheng's door.

"He's a landlord," Ma Sheng stated unsympathetically. "How can we not force him to attend... we're struggling against him, aren't we?"

"But he's sick, honestly, please show some mercy. I'd be ever so grateful if you would."

"Grateful?"

Yu Zhuo fell to her knees and kowtowed.

"What... what're you doing?" He lifted Yu Zhuo back to her feet, but as he did so his hands strayed purposefully to her breasts. She tried to resist, but Ma Sheng forced the issue, pulling at her belt, which was more a length of hemp than a proper one made of leather.

"Such a fine belt for a landlord's wife, hmm!" He yanked at it harder, but still he couldn't release it. Growing impatient, he grabbed frantically at her trousers, tearing at them as he pushed her to the floor. "Let me have it... and I'll see that he avoids being dragged out in public again."

The next morning, no one came to escort Wang Caidong to the struggle session. Yu Zhuo was thankful for that, but she couldn't forget what it cost. She boiled water and added mugwort leaves to it; she was going to bathe. Afterwards, she found herself sitting upon the pig pen wall, watching the animal wallow in its filth. Lost in a daze, she didn't hear her husband call out from his bed, not until he began pounding on the wooden frame, distracting her from her reverie. She rubbed her eyes and got down from the wall.

"Are you hungry? Perhaps I'll head to the market… pick up some pig intestines and make that soup you love?"

Wang Caidong's reprieve didn't last, however. In only five days he received a summons to present himself at the cooperative offices once again.

Yu Zhuo wouldn't leave things at that: "You go and tell Deputy Director Ma to come here… and quickly."

Ma Sheng heeded her call and turned up at Wang's door.

"Why's he been called again?" Yu Zhuo asked straight away.

"Well," Ma Sheng responded, "I've had my fill once… but I'm hungry again… you know. I never get tired of eating."

"Then," she paused, "let him off. I'll give you…"

"It's not enough," he cut her off. "I need at least… five times… that would be about enough for me to release him."

Wang Caidong propped himself up in bed, listening. In the adjacent room, Ma Sheng again forced himself onto Yu Zhuo, thrusting her up against the loom, tying her arms behind her with the cotton thread strewn over the machine. Wang tried to get down from his bed, but his legs betrayed him and he fell face first into the chamber pot. It'd not been emptied, and Wang Caidong drowned in his own piss.

When the investigation team departed Laocheng, Deputy Xu asked me to accompany them back to the government offices. He wanted to ensure I had some good food to eat; it was his way of repaying me for the work I'd done. I must say, the food wasn't half bad. Lunch consisted of cabbage and tofu soup, followed by a serving of braised meat, or eggs with garlic chives. Every two to three days, we even had hot pig intestine soup. All in all, I ate well.

But something strange did happen… and it had everything to do with Deputy Xu's blanket. On the whole, there was nothing really odd about it, except that it was yellow underneath with black spots on top. It reminded me very much of a leopard print. He told me the bedding was a gift from Kuang San, that a month before he had been dispatched into the field, he'd invited Xu out for a drink or two and that they'd consumed so much they ended up passing out in the same room together. That's when Xu first saw Kuang San wrapped up in the leopard-like blanket. Now… the quilt was more than big enough for Kuang San – he was rather thin after all – but still, on that night at least, he'd rolled himself up as tightly as he could. And that's when something strange happened. That is, when Xu awoke early the next morning, well, Kuang San looked very much like a real leopard and not a man at all! Needless to say, Xu was rather startled at first, but soon smiled about the whole thing, recognising the shape for what it was, Kuang San rolled up in a quilt. Then, before they departed, Kuang San surprised Xu by asking what it was he'd seen earlier that morning and that whatever it was, he'd give it to him… but all Xu could say was that he'd like to have the blanket… And that's what he was given… It's a strange story, for sure, but, you know what, that very first night, I deliberately didn't sleep, I stayed up instead to watch Old Xu… I wanted to see for myself what this blanket did… and, just like Kuang San, Xu wrapped himself up tightly in the bedding… he was quite fast asleep, too, but that didn't stop it… I mean the blanket… from conjuring an image of a leopard, augmented by the sounds emanating from Old Xu… I mean, he was the same man, still had the bad eye, but the other one opened and looked at me, and his snoring sounded more like the guttural roar of a beast than any sound a human would make… I tell you, it was really something…

Anyway, later on, Bai Tu showed up at the government offices. He'd come looking for me, to ask if I'd sing the mourning song for Wang Caidong. I'd promised to do it, but Old Xu wouldn't permit me to leave… he berated me, actually, wondering why I had no head for politics… I only responded by saying I didn't know what he meant… then he told me that all under heaven – yes, that was the phrase – he said all under heaven belonged to the Communist Party and that if I were to sing at the funeral for a dead landlord, it would be akin to paving the way for his reincarnation as a landlord once again… and then if that happened, what of the revolution? The only thing I could think of to say was that, if I did bring a landlord back as the same, well, that would at least mean there'd be a need for more struggle sessions… now am I right or what! Unfortunately, my quip only seemed to anger him and he accused me of being flippant… I took on a serious tone, tried to assure him I wasn't setting out to ridicule him… I even addressed him in the politest tones possible, you know, my respected deputy commissioner, words to that effect… and well, all was fine in the end. Finally, when the investigative team departed, I left too… with a note written by Old Xu and headed off to the County Cultural Arts Corp to take up the work of the revolution.

Wang Caidong was buried, rather unceremoniously, in a grassy field. After the requisite mourning period of seven days, Yu Zhuo had the oddest of feelings that a bee had bored its way into her skull and was buzzing around, day and night, forcing her to constantly rub at her temples to try to ease the incessant drone. If she bumped into someone, she'd fall into prattling on about nothing consequential, at times mentioning her dead husband's dream about the sea, how he'd drowned in piss and how piss started out as water. Her listeners feigned concern over her condition, but in truth the words didn't sink in, they didn't really care. As time passed, most took to avoiding her altogether, so she ended up blathering on to the livestock that occasionally wandered through the town; either the animals, or the trees. Strangely enough, the tree that stood just outside the main gate to her home turned yellow before long, and in six months it was dead.

When summer finally arrived, Yu Zhuo had become even more forgetful. There were days when she would be distracted by the most innocuous of things, such as the call of a sparrow causing her to forget she was supposed to collect her ration of grain to make the day's meal, or a pumpkin lying beside the road that would steal her attention and she'd end up lugging it home. Then there were the days when she wouldn't even step outside. Instead, she'd busy herself using talcum powder to colour her already white shoes, or the dust that lay upon the ground, or even the smattering of sparrow droppings… almost anything would do. And then she'd slip the shoes back on and wander into her bedchamber to ask if her husband thought they were pretty.

On one such occasion, Bai Tu, who had just returned to the compound from a day out in the fields, heard her speaking and thought she had guests over. Of course, he had no intention of intruding, but after he deposited the load of earth he'd been carrying in the pig pen, he went to see who it was who had come, only to discover Yu Zhuo by herself. When she spotted her husband's former servant, she left the room without uttering a word, and all that Bai Tu could think was how pitiable she looked. He decided then she needed companionship, and so he went to market and exchanged his own soybeans for a dark-haired mongrel... he believed it might be such a friend. Unfortunately, however, Yu Zhuo took to taking the dog down to the river every day, scrubbing its fur vigorously, trying to wash it white.

Bai Tu found himself at the market again, this time with a basket of sweet potatoes to sell. His buyer ended up being a restaurant, but after he returned home and checked his receipt, he felt he'd been short-changed and so marched off back to the restaurant to sort things out. On the way back to the market, he bumped into another villager on the same road who was pulling an oxcart behind him. Bai Tu wondered if he might hitch a ride, but the other man replied by saying this would require money. Bai Tu offered a trade instead: a lift for the string beans he had growing in his field. The other man agreed only too readily, and later on harvested the beans himself, a whole basket full. Once back at the restaurant, Bai Tu confirmed he'd been short-changed, one *jiao* in total, or a tenth of a yuan. Of course, the story couldn't help but make the other villagers laugh at poor Bai Tu: he'd given up one yuan of string beans for a single *jiao*. Bai Tu, however, remained obstinate; sure, he'd let the other man take a basketful of string beans, but if he was owed money, Bai Tu argued, he had to make sure he got it. The villagers likened Bai Tu and Yu Zhuo to two peas in a pod: neither was all that bright, so they ought to be together. Everyone needs someone, after all.

By the time winter arrived, Shuanlao had taken it upon himself to figure out what to do with Bai Tu and Yu Zhuo. The main point of the discussion was whether Bai Tu should welcome Yu Zhuo into his home, or if it should be the other way round, Bai Tu taking his pillow and moving in with Yu Zhuo. But when he mentioned this plan to Bai Tu, Bai Tu was adamant: "No, I won't consent to it."

"But why," countered Shuanlao, "why wouldn't you agree to us arranging a marriage?"

"Marriage... alright... I'll agree to that."

"Good, then from this day forward, consider yourself married to Yu Zhuo."

"Yu Zhuo's the wife of a landlord."

"Well," interjected Ma Sheng, who had been present during the exchange, "if you take the former wife of a landlord to bed, you'll be emancipating her for sure!"

Bai Tu, however, didn't welcome Yu Zhuo into his own, rather poor surroundings. Instead, he filled in the doorway Wang had first constructed for him at the rear of the main hall, and returned the house to its former layout. To Yu Zhuo, he said only the following: "You're my woman now, my wife."

"You're my woman now, my wife," Yu Zhuo parroted.

"No, that's not right, you've got it the wrong way round. I'm not your wife, you're mine."

Bai Tu combed her hair, picking clean the infestation of lice he found. "Do you have work to do?" he asked.

The only thing she fancied doing was smoking her hookah, a habit that had become an addiction. Bai Tu, however, didn't protest, and he lit the pipe so that she could smoke to her heart's content. Once she had finished smoking, but before heading to bed, Yu Zhuo wished to draw some water and wash. The basin filled, she told Bai Tu to leave the room and he complied immediately. Standing outside, he wondered why she needed to wash before going to bed. By the time he stepped back in their bedroom, Yu Zhuo was already fast asleep. Bai Tu hesitated, feeling around the bed before climbing in beside his new wife. But he didn't dare do anything. He stared at her plump, white flesh, but he feared he would hurt her. He sat like this until the wee hours, waiting patiently for sleep to claim him. When it finally did arrive, he slept like a log, wholly unmoving.

Bai Tu spent his days much as before, but during the evenings, for some unknown reason, he began to stir and find himself awake with the burning need to relieve himself. In a daze, half asleep and half awake, he'd climb out of bed and stumble through the dark to find the toilet. And then, once his bladder was emptied, he'd stumble back. But it was on his way back to bed that something strange would happen: he was sure an additional pair of shoes lay beside the bed. When it was time for him to rise and get ready for yet another day in the fields, however, the only shoes at the foot of the bed were his own, and Yu

Zhuo's of course. This made him suspicious of what he had seen, leaving him to assume it must've been nothing more than a dream, or possibly just a trick of the moonlight and the shadows it cast. But whatever it was, he experienced it more than once, three or four times perhaps. The latest occurrence had proven different, however.

This time when he woke, the night sky was clear and the moon was shining especially bright, blanketing the scene in a hazy, flickering glow. And it was in this glow that he could make out a pair of rubber-soled shoes lying next to the bed. To confirm what he saw, Bai Tu rummaged around for a small piece of firewood he could use as a torch. Then, as the flame he used to light the wood hissed and crackled, he swore he could see a dark shadow get down from his own bed and disappear. Unfortunately for Bai Tu, the small piece of wood hadn't really caught, so once there was nothing left but smouldering embers, the whole room was plunged back into a darkness that was even thicker than before. He pulled the window shutters open and knelt down to inspect the shoes – they were gone.

Bai Tu finally realised what was happening. In the dead of night, someone was creeping into his room, stealing into his bed, assuming he slept so soundly as not to notice. Bai Tu was overwhelmed with shame and humiliation, so much so that he began to smash his head against the edge of the bed. But he couldn't let on to anyone what was going on, he had to find out who it was, and to do that, he had to hold his tongue; he wanted revenge on this person, and he swore he would get it, but he had to keep things quiet, at least for now.

When the sun rose, Bai Tu examined the ground just outside the window, looking for signs of the intruder. As expected, he found the footprints of the rubber-soled shoes, and then began to wonder who in town wore such footwear. By his count, five people had this type of shoe, three men and two women. He excluded the women straight away, they wouldn't've been sneaking into his room at night. As for the men, one was the town's accountant, and it couldn't be him. Bai Tu knew this man, he had a lame leg which made him walk unevenly, the left foot always digging much deeper into the ground than the right one. That left two men, one of them being the son of the Mi family who lived near the western gate to the village. He was a smallish man with particularly small shoes. The prints he found couldn't be his. The last person was Ma Sheng. It had to be him.

This was a problem. Bai Tu had no idea how he could take his revenge, he didn't even know if he should dare. Perhaps the best he could do, for now, was to repair the compound wall and then place on top of it a row of thorns and spikes, to make it more difficult to climb over. He could also nail shut the window, leave it closed even on the hottest of days. Finally, he'd make sure to sleep lightly and close to Yu Zhuo, stuck to her even, his arms wrapped around her while she slept. The first time he tried this, she showed only indifference, neither welcoming his embrace nor pushing him away. This served to embolden him, so he kept her tight the whole night through. The dog he got for her had been kept tied up in the back, but now he tied it at the main gate so that it could warn him of anyone approaching. If he heard it howl, he'd get up immediately, grab the sturdy stick he kept next to his bed, and then shout to ask who it was. There was rarely an answer, but at least the dog stopped barking.

It wasn't long before Ma Sheng showed up at Bai Tu's house, his face looking long and perturbed. But he hadn't come to order Bai Tu to inspect the canal, or do some other menial task. He'd come to tell him another meeting had been called. Naturally, Bai Tu agreed to participate, he'd check on the waterways as well, make sure the canal was in good working order, but he did so with Yu Zhuo alongside. In fact, he tried his utmost to keep her as close to him as possible.

It wasn't long before people noticed the swell, Yu Zhuo was getting bigger. The villagers started gossiping, many seemingly desperate to ask her whose it was, but no one had the gumption to do so, and they weren't even sure if she would answer in any case. Afterwards, she barely stepped beyond the main gates to her home. Bai Tu was torn as to what to do. He couldn't take her everywhere with him. He had work to do that she couldn't be around, but at the same time he worried about leaving her at home. Then on a day much like any other, Bai Tu set off for the market, a rake and a pair of straw sandals slung over his back. Yu Zhuo walked with him. So, too, did the mangy black dog.

No one went in search of Bai Tu, not even his older brother, who only took the pig and chickens Bai Tu looked after as his own, as well as the potatoes and sweet potatoes he kept in the underground cellar. Bai He also discovered, quite accidentally, a jar of honey that he gave to his wife. He hoped it might do some good in helping her feel better; she'd been ill for so long, battling asthma and other ailments, spending most of the day in bed wheezing like a pair of tired bellows.

Bai He and his son spent most of their days in the fields, tilling the ground, sowing seeds, working a farmer's life. So it often fell to Bai Shi's wife to prepare the meals and tend to the older woman in bed. Bedridden though she was, Bai He's wife still wanted to see her son and so she often called for him to come and stay with her. The young boy would comply, but once he spied the honey his father had brought, he'd also use his visits to steal a spoonful or more and then leave, saying very little. He was so much like his father, concerned more with himself than with anyone else.

"Eh," his father remarked, "you know Mao Dan doesn't much like to spend time at his mother's side… but he should… she's not long for this world, you know."

A little less than a month later, she died, choking on her last breath, leaving her children in the care of their father and his sister-in-law. Unfortunately for them, Bai Shi's wife, who never much liked her brother-in-law's boys, decided to no longer bother much with them, especially with Mao Dan, the younger of the two. Her dislike became plain when Bai He was called away to the county capital to attend to some matter, leaving only his sister-in-law at home with his boys. It all began at dinner as she was ladling out the cornmeal porridge, which had noodles mixed in for extra substance.

Displeased with the food his auntie had prepared, Mao Dan leapt up onto the counter adjacent to the stove and shouted: "Give me more than this."

"What? Did I cook the entire lot for you!"

Her response sent the boy into a huff, but he didn't say anything more. He simply placed his bowl back on the table and dumped an entire side dish of fried onions into his porridge, saving nothing for anyone else.

"Those onions are salty, you know." Her tone dripped with anger.

Mao Dan offered no reply, but threw his bowl onto the floor. Watching the scene unfold, his brother walloped him over the head for misbehaving. He then dragged him out into the courtyard and forced him to kneel. Grabbing hold of the heavy wooden washboard that was nearby, he made Mao Dan hold it up over his head, his arms straight; it was to teach him a lesson. But at the same moment a neighbour strode into the courtyard looking to borrow a strainer, and the lesson was interrupted.

"Eh… Bai He's gone and whaddya do? Are you a pack of wild dogs or what!"

Taking advantage of the intrusion, Mao Dan flung the washboard to one side and ran out through the open gate. He ended up at the western entrance to the village, waiting for his father to return. When he did, Mao Dan immediately told him what had happened, but his father was unsympathetic: "What the hell… it was just the three of you at home… trying to have a meal together… why were you so greedy? Did you expect everyone else to have only the soup?"

His mood changed, however, once he returned home with Mao Dan. He realised it wasn't only Mao Dan that was at fault; in fact, he began to think that Mao Dan may be right, that he was being neglected. The only solution he could think of was to ask Bai Shi to take the boy in, to give him a home in the government offices.

"But what can the boy do?" Bai Shi asked.

"Well," his father began, "I was only eight years old when I started helping out at the local shop. I imagine you can give him pretty much anything to do."

Bai Shi relented, and made arrangements for Mao Dan to head to the elementary school. But not as a student; he was going there to be responsible for ringing the bell. Mao Dan didn't seem to mind; the job came with meals and even a monthly stipend of eight yuan.

As before, Shuanlao's wife still cursed and beat her adopted daughter, but unlike when she was younger, Cui Cui no longer talked back. In fact, she wouldn't say anything at all, but simply walked away, often meandering down to the riverbank to sit and while away the hours, or she would go shopping in the market, returning quietly only when the day was gone. Of course, her return was met with further abuse by her adoptive mother: "Why the hell did you come back? If you had any sense, you'd have stayed away!"

One day, as she worked the fields weeding the grass, she was expecting her younger brother to bring her lunch, but once midday passed and there was still no sign of him, her hunger made her dizzy and forced her to return home. As she walked into the compound however, the first sight she saw was her adoptive mother and brother sitting down enjoying their midday meal.

"Oh," Shuanlao's wife began, "I was letting your brother eat first before bringing food to you... how come you've returned?"

Cui Cui didn't acknowledge the question but walked straight into the kitchen. Picking up a small steamed bun, she turned and walked back out of the courtyard, shouting as she did so: "I'm off, back to my weeds!"

But she didn't return to the fields. Instead, she stormed off towards the county elementary school looking for Mao Dan. Unfortunately for her, Shuanlao's wife surmised she'd gone in search of Bai He's younger boy, and she followed shortly afterwards, grabbing her adopted daughter and dragging her home. Afterwards, she went to see Bai He to criticise him for being so unconcerned with educating his son and for letting him tempt poor Cui Cui. Bai He had not been expecting to receive such harsh criticism, and the shock of it affected him profoundly. Ever after, his mouth took on an unnatural slant and his gait became uneven, so much so that he had to start walking with a cane, even bracing himself against the town walls when necessary.

When Mao Dan returned to town to visit his father, the locals verbally pounced: "How'd you tempt Cui Cui to follow you to school?"

"She decided that on her own."

"So what'd you... hmm... get up to?"

"What?" he said, his face turning red. "Nothing... nothing at all."

The locals assumed he must be too young yet, that could be the only explanation, his cock still not able to look at the sky. Whatever the case, Mao Dan ignored any further questions and returned home. There, he told his auntie and his brother that he'd come to wish his father the best as a respectful son should do, and to advise them to do the same. "Make sure you give him a poached egg every day, alright," he added, "and don't worry, I'll give you the money for it."

On the day that Cui Cui had been dragged home, Shuanlao's wife beat her, going as far as to chop off nearly all her hair, giving her a look that was not exactly boyish or girlish.

Witnessing how they treated the girl, some people couldn't hold their tongues: "She's not a little girl any more. You can't treat her like that, you know!"

"Aye" was all Shuanlao would offer as a reply, his face showing the bitterness and pain he felt.

Everyone knew what kind of woman Shuanlao's wife was, but they didn't understand why she had gone to such extremes this time and why Shuanlao had done nothing about it.

Cui Cui's life was anything but peaceful, and so it was to be expected that she would run away again. This time, however, her adoptive mother didn't come to fetch her. In fact, she didn't seem to give a damn if Cui Cui lived or died, she only wanted to be rid of the bad seed, as she called her. Shuanlao disagreed, and the result was a fearsome argument that came to violence: Shuanlao's face was scarred with five bloody fingernail marks across his cheek. Afterwards, when he went out on cooperative business with Ma Sheng, his deputy couldn't resist teasing him. After hanging up his own hat on a peg, he'd look at Shuanlao and urge him to hang the mask he wore as a face up there as well.

Early on the morning of the winter solstice, Bai He was still in bed when his daughter-in-law brought him the poached eggs.

"You should choose a big one," Bai He told her, "and then you'd only need poach one."

"How can I poach just a single egg?"

"But… it'd save Mao Dan a little money."

Before they could say anything further, Xing Gulu burst into his room: "Get up, quick! Come on, Bai He, quickly!"

"I can't…"

"When I tell you what's happened, you will!"

He told him Shuanlao had been arrested, trussed up and taken away. This got Bai He out of bed, but he still couldn't walk, so Xing Gulu lifted him up on his back and carried him to the cooperative offices. Before they got there, however, they ran into Shuanlao being escorted out of the village, his arms bound behind his back. Ma Sheng was nearby, an officially stamped document in his hand. As they dragged Shuanlao away, Ma Sheng announced the charges: Cui Cui had reported to the main county offices that he'd raped her four years earlier. Not long after, under questioning, Shuanlao admitted to everything. He was never seen in Laocheng again, but immediately sent to prison in the county capital.

It was the fourth month of the New Year, and the cherry blossoms were in bloom and looking very much like a sheet of white snow. That was when Bai Shi showed up looking for me, a bag of mushrooms in his hand. I found out he'd been transferred to the county capital to take up the post of chief for the commerce bureau.

"Aiya! I've just realised I never congratulated you on your new position, and here you are bringing me a gift… whatever for?"

Bai Shi laughed, revealing his gold teeth. Now I must say, at that time, to have a mouthful of gold, well, it indicated a certain wealth, a certain status. I wasn't sure if they were just gold plated, or whether they were gold through and through, but it was definitely something to see.

"Well, I should say these mushrooms aren't from me, they're from Ma Sheng."

"Ma Sheng?" I asked.

"You don't remember do you, Ma Sheng, from Laocheng? The town's sent a request for you to come, they need you to sing."

"Ma Sheng's dead?"

"How's that now," Bai Shi laughed. "He's got something about him, you know, a special power, let me tell you, he's not dead, it's somebody else."

"Geez… I wonder how many have met their end at his hands… so who am I supposed to sing for?"

"Ma Sheng's getting married. It's not a mourning song they want, but a wedding song. Ma Sheng doesn't trust the troupe from Chengguanzhen, he reckons they're no good. He'd rather you sing, that is, if you can sing something happy. Hence the invite."

I remembered seeing the singing troupe from Chengguanzhen… it was at the recent Lantern Festival… there were more than a hundred singers, I remember… each wearing colourful costumes and holding red umbrellas. Some looked like civilians, others like soldiers, some like clowns singing all manner of songs, twisting and turning before spinning round and coming to a halt in myriad poses, each one different from the other. I saw plum blossoms, imperial cauldrons, rolled mats, eight-sided buildings and coiling snakes. But they weren't singing a song for the dead, they were singing it for the living as a way to bring good fortune and bounty. That's not what I sang; my songs were for the dead, to bring peace to their souls. How could I sing at Ma Sheng's wedding? I tried to convey these feelings to Bai Shi, to let him know I couldn't possibly accept the invitation, but that's not what I said: "Why bless me! That bare stick's been able to find himself a woman, has he… ha… where's she from?"

"Ha ha," Bai Shi chuckled. "She's no spring chicken though… more like used furniture!"

"She's been married before?" I asked.

"You must remember Shuanlao, right… but you mightn't know his wife all that well… anyway, it's her, that's who he's marrying."

How could I not know Shuanlao's wife? Of course I knew her… but I never would've expected she'd end up marrying Ma Sheng. The world really had been turned upside down. I found myself wondering more about what was happening in Laocheng so I asked Bai Shi about his dad, Bai He, about his uncle Bai Tu, as well… I asked after Bai Cai and Yu Zhuo, too… then finally about Li Changxia, Liu Bazi, Gong Renyou and Xing Gulu. It took most of the afternoon for Bai Shi to tell me everything, right up until the late afternoon wind began to blow, scattering the cherry blossoms across the ground like a blanket.

Just before departing, however, Bai Shi asked me, in hushed tones, if I knew the commanding officer in charge of the local regiment. Unfortunately, I didn't; the commander was a big shot, a man I'd never seen.

"You're pulling my leg," Bai Shi countered. "I'm sure you know him. I heard it said that you helped him out before the Liberation… I'm talking about Kuang San."

"Kuang San? He's the commanding officer! Kuang San? I wasn't aware of that… I suppose I could… introduce you… maybe… if that's what you're getting at… but I'm not sure if he'll recognise me."

Bai Shi never came to look for me again… I heard afterwards he'd met Kuang San… on the second day of the Dragon Boat Festival if I remember correctly… Old Xu had given him the introduction.

Once they'd left Laocheng, Bai Tu and Yu Zhuo continued walking east. Neither had been to Shanyin, they'd only heard tales about it, about Santai and Lingning counties and about Huangfujie that lay between them. They passed through Qingfengyi and kept on walking, following the main road. The farther they ended up from Laocheng, the better. After their food ran out – they hadn't brought much with them in the first place – they resorted to begging, eating what they could. On one road, they managed to obtain two steamed buns, food for each of them. The first one, Bai Tu gave to Yu Zhuo. Then he turned to the dog that still followed them and told it he was headed to the river to get a mouthful of water. After ten days of walking, they finally reached Shanyin.

The county capital was large, much larger than they were expecting. But begging for food was difficult, despite its size. Children became their teachers. They learnt to walk like they did, their feet turned in to make them hobble, or turned out to make them stumble. They ended up squatting down near a bridge covering a ravine below. Both of them were so hungry they could barely move.

"Come here," Bai Tu comforted Yu Zhuo, "lean up against me. Rest a little."

"Ah, this… damn thing… I want to throw it away, oh… how I feel like I'm sinking."

She had been holding a shoehorn and now flung it to one side. She then took out the pouch she'd been carrying and tossed it too. There happened to be two wooden bowls inside the pouch and they flew through the air. Bai Tu realised too late what she'd done and the bowls tumbled through the air. All he could do was roar in frustration.

Yu Zhuo's complaints continued: "Oh… my feet… they hurt so much… I wish I could be rid of them too!" She stood up abruptly and walked further along the bridge.

Terror swept through Bai Tu's heart and he reached out to take hold of his wife, pulling her close. He removed his shoes, thinking to give them to her, hoping they might soothe her tired feet. While doing this, he placed the shoehorn to the other side, worried Yu Zhuo might try to throw it away again. Something then occurred to him, and he wondered why he hadn't tried to sell his straw shoes, to exchange them for a little money so they could at least buy something to eat. With this thought in mind, he waited until dark and then sneaked into a family compound that lay on the outskirts of town. Creeping through the night, he came upon a mound of rice straw piled near the outer wall. He stole what he could carry and then fashioned sandals out of it. These he later sold in the market, one pair for one *jiao*.

Business was brisk and he soon thought he could perhaps sell the sandals he made for a little more, and so he scrounged around in the ditch that wormed its way around the town. There he found worn hemp and cloth, thrown away like so much refuse. There were dead infants in among the rubbish as well, wrapped in finer cloth. He stripped them of the cloth, thinking it would make for better shoes, more rugged and durable, more comfortable, too. He sold these newer shoes for 1.5 *jiao*, some even for two *jiao*.

Bai Tu grew quite pleased with his industriousness, and felt increasingly confident he could take care of Yu Zhuo. Finally, he managed to piece together a grass shed in the northern quarter of town, even furnishing it with a small cooking fire.

"Look," he said to Yu Zhuo once their house was complete, "we've now got a home of our own! We can be a proper family at last."

But when winter came, the grass shed did little to stop the cold wind from blowing in from all corners. All they could do was hold each other tight, wrapped together to conserve whatever warmth they could. They would even sleep top and tail from time to time, each grasping the other's legs so that they didn't freeze. On other occasions they lay face to face. Even when they weren't sleeping, they tried to stay as close together as possible, generating whatever heat they could. Then, when sleeping, if they happened to release each other, rolling to one side, they'd soon start to shiver with the cold and end up wide awake. Afterwards, they began taking the dog to bed with them, allowing it to squeeze between them. It was always warm and allowed them to pass the night in greater comfort. The only problem was that it farted, repeatedly and throughout the night.

Winter passed, and eventually 28 July arrived, Yu Zhuo's birthday. When she had still been married to Wang Caidong, her birthdays were a time for drinks and celebrations, and Bai Tu fully intended the same, or as close to it as he could. On the morning of the twenty-eighth, he decided to head into town and straight to the market, in order to buy some meat and vegetables. He thought, too, that he might even splurge a little and buy some pig and sheep intestines. It was her birthday, after all, and he had to give her a proper meal to celebrate. When he returned, he had three *jin* of flour and half a *jin* of pork.

"Yu Zhuo… do you know what today is?"

"Today… no… what day is it?"

"It's your birthday."

"It's your birthday," she parroted.

He didn't say anything further, but got to work preparing the stuffing for the dumplings he wanted to make. Once they were finished, he thought how great it would be if he had some hot peppers to fry, so he decided to return to the market to get some. Before doing so, however, he had to make sure Yu Zhuo would be all right, so he motioned for her to sit down and gave her a radish to nibble. Satisfied she was sufficiently occupied, he went to buy the oil for deep frying. He scooped up two bowls and asked how much it cost. The proprietor responded by saying it would be one yuan. Bai Tu replied all he had was three *jiao*. He couldn't afford it and so dumped it back in the larger basin. He settled on purchasing a dish of hot noodles, but soon realised he was just short of the necessary cash. He tried to bargain with the shopkeeper, a discussion that degenerated into argument nearly as soon as it had begun. In the end, he didn't buy the noodles either. With nothing but the traces of oil and spicy noodles in the bowls he had brought with him, Bai Tu resigned himself to returning home empty-handed.

As he left, the shopkeeper had some choice words for him: you filthy, dirty beggar, you're really something, you've not paid for anything and yet your bowl has traces of both hot oil and noodles!

Bai Tu just smiled and continued on his way. He didn't get very far however, as the shopkeeper ambushed him almost immediately, snatching the bowl from his hand and smashing it upon the ground.

With nothing in his hands, not even his bowl, Bai Tu returned to their poor grass shed only to find it empty. There was no sign of Yu Zhuo, except for the half-eaten radish.

Bai Tu searched all across the county for Yu Zhuo, but he didn't find her. He looked everywhere, even inspecting the numerous toilets as possible places where she might be. At this time, indoor plumbing had yet to arrive in the area, which meant toilet facilities were of the outdoor kind, usually two adjacent structures, one with a seat and the other simply a pit at the rear. These toilets were often fully exposed and offered little privacy. On many occasions, the filth would rise so high they'd be nearly impossible to use. The corn stalk that was placed alongside the toilet, ostensibly to help push the mix of faeces and urine back down, was of little use.

Bai Tu was worried about Yu Zhuo. When she hadn't returned straight away, he feared she had gone in search of him, had perhaps been careless and fallen into one of these foul wells. He therefore poked and prodded each one he came across, checking to see if she might be there, trapped. The fact that she wasn't was both a relief and cause for further concern. He called her name repeatedly, allowing it to echo through the alleyways, but there was no response. Finally, as night fell, Bai Tu grew hoarse from all of the shouting and retired to his dilapidated grass hut. Collapsing onto their bed, such as it was, he held on tight to the stone brick that served as her pillow and wept profusely. Through the tears, he vented his rage at her disappearance on their dog, beating and cursing it without remorse.

Nearly eight months later, the dog still in tow, Bai Tu found himself in Laocheng once again. But it was not the same place he'd left. The eastern gate had fallen into ruin; the cypress tree that'd watched over the southern wall had been cut. Ma Sheng was now married to Shuanlao's former wife, who'd become pregnant, her belly as large as an iron cauldron hanging below her breasts. She was, in fact, the first one to see him.

"You're a ghost. You must be, yes?"

"I'm Bai Tu."

"But we heard you'd left, had been eaten by a pack of wolves… how's it that you've returned?"

"I have… where's Shuanlao? I need to speak to him… I need to tell him I've returned."

She didn't answer him, but spat in his face before turning and storming off.

Bai Tu headed for his former home, soon discovering the grass had grown more than a foot around the structure. Spider webs hung about the eaves and windows, and there was dust everywhere, billowing up before settling back down like small storm clouds as he brushed past them. The stove was still there, the cooking pot covered in bird shit. He unpacked his bedding, placing it among the dirt and went to inspect his fields. They were lush and green, which he couldn't help but think was strange. Who'd sowed the seed in his absence?

By the afternoon, he'd learnt what happened to Shuanlao, how he'd been imprisoned and how his wife had married Ma Sheng. It naturally made sense to go and see the former deputy, who explained how his land had been tilled and seed planted.

Not long after Bai Tu had left, Ma Sheng's relatives had come from Shouyangshan, a town about ten *li* away. They'd come to seek his help, ultimately gaining permission to relocate their *hukou* to Laocheng. That's when they'd come to cultivate Bai Tu's fields, or rather, they'd done so once certain arrangements had been made. To be precise, Ma Sheng told him, his land had been taken over by Bai He, who was unwilling initially to let anyone else use it. But Ma Sheng's relatives had a young, unmarried daughter with them, and so, after discussing things with Bai He, it was decided she would marry Bai He's second son, who in turn would be given Bai Tu's land to till.

After listening to the story, Bai Tu had just one question: "So… I've no land?"

"Well… tell your nephew you need it back, that it's your land to cultivate."

"But can I do that to them… they're a family… it's just me…"

"My relatives… no, no, they're your relatives too… say… I know what you can do… the land they had in Shouyangshan… it's been left fallow. Why don't you go and claim it… yes, I know it's a little far from here, but it's only you, right, it'd be alright for you, wouldn't it?"

"It's not just me… I have Yu Zhuo to think of."

"Then… where is she?"

Bai Tu told Ma Sheng how he'd come to lose her, how he'd searched unsuccessfully for her. Ma Sheng's response was cold and unsympathetic: "She's dead, definitely. Shit… you didn't look after her you know… I mean, it sounds like you let someone come and just steal her away, doesn't it! She's dead for sure."

"No she isn't, she'll return, I know it." There was a certainty to Bai Tu's reply, and he stabbed at the sun as though to swear some curse at it.

"Fine, whatever, if she's not dead, then she's not dead… the land in Shouyangshan mightn't be the most fertile, but it is large, it'll produce enough, I'm sure, for you and Yu Zhuo to have a whole brood of children!"

Bai Tu didn't protest, he simply left Laocheng and headed for Shouyangshan. Two years passed. He had no ox and so he tilled the land himself, pushing his mattock through the unrelenting soil, clumped and filled with stones. The wheat he planted grew no more than a foot high before flowering. The grains he was able to harvest were no bigger than the head of a common housefly. The only consolation for working such infertile land was that Shouyangshan was home to a great deal of soft rush, which, once dried in the sun, was very good for making straw sandals, and much easier to sell; they were more profitable, too.

On one such occasion as he brought eighteen bushels of rush to the local market to sell, he gave the appearance, at least to the passers-by, of a bushel of hay moving across the landscape. Then, when he drew closer to them and they spotted his legs sticking out from underneath, they couldn't help but call out in jest: "Where's your head, eh?"

He never answered their calls, but kept walking on. When he finally reached the market and relieved himself of the burden he'd been carrying, his face was bright red, much like the colour of a ripe persimmon. But he had made it to the market and business was brisk. Afterwards, he had enough cash to purchase a little salt, some baking soda and oil for his lantern. He also chose to spend some of his money on a comb.

This last purchase would become a tradition of sorts, as each and every time he went to market he'd return with a new comb, some with large, coarse teeth, others much finer. He also took to speaking to the combs, telling each one they were for Yu Zhuo. His odd behaviour didn't stop there, either. In fact, it got worse. At mealtimes, Bai Tu would always serve a plate for his missing wife, encouraging her to eat up as though she were patiently waiting for him to come to the table too. When he had no cooking oil, he'd walk with purpose out to the fields and collect the seeds from the castor-oil plant that grew along the perimeter. He'd peel the seeds and fry them up, crushing them in the pan. Once ready, he'd add it to their meal for extra texture. The table set, he'd dig in, thinking, believing the chopsticks on the bowl he put out for Yu Zhuo moved along with his.

Shouyangshan, which literally means 'first to enjoy the sun', got its name because of its location, or rather because the sun, as it crested the mountains in the morning, always hit upon it first. As a result of its location, Bai Tu's mud house was bathed in a glowing red light every morning, which Bai Tu took to thinking of as Yu Zhuo. For him, the sun kissed his eyelids just as he imagined her doing, and on more than one occasion, the first word out of his mouth was her name. He'd do much the same in the evenings as he sat smoking under the light of his lantern, which, when it flickered off the wall, again appeared to him as his missing wife. Bai Tu became so obsessed with her, in fact, that even after he blew out the lantern, he'd get the feeling Yu Zhuo would be waiting for him in his bed, in their bed, tucked away under the covers.

Later, Bai Tu began putting ripe pomegranates out for Yu Zhuo to eat. On the following morning when he'd discover small bites in the fruit, as well as little footprints about, he believed Yu Zhuo had returned, never once thinking it could be mice. Soon, he began referring to the mice by her name; their dog, too. In fact, everything, whether in the sky above or on the ground below, soon earned the name Yu Zhuo.

One day, as he went out into the fields to tie up the red bean plants growing along the raised earth that served as boundary for his fields, he turned to see his dog missing and yelled out Yu Zhuo's name as loud as he could. One couldn't say if he expected an answer, but on this occasion he got one, a voice yelled out in reply; someone was walking towards him. Bai Tu stared at the approaching person, rubbing his eyes in disbelief, before smiling.

Yu Zhuo had returned.

Before arriving in Shouyangshan, Yu Zhuo had gone to Laocheng. She'd aged, looking like a woman well into her sixties, but her voice was clear, as was her mind. Unsurprisingly, the first question she was asked was where she'd been all this time. Apparently, she'd spent the past several years in Qijiazhen, a small town over 120 *li* away, famous for making limestone bricks; it was where nearly everyone in Qinling sourced their bricks. Quite a few villagers asked her how she'd ended up there, but she couldn't give them. a clear answer. All she remembered was that she'd been working there hauling carts of limestone. Then, on one occasion as she was pushing and pulling a cart along a mountain path, it tumbled and crashed, burying a great number of people in a cascade of limestone that stretched the better part of a hundred feet. No one died from the accident, but it did leave her unconscious for five days. On the sixth day, she awoke, her mind fresh, her memory restored. Returning to Laocheng seemed the right thing to do. It was a difficult journey, and she had to beg most of the way, but here she was. With her story more or less complete, Yu Zhuo was keen for news about Laocheng. First, the villagers told her Bai He had died. Then, they relayed the sordid tale of Shuanlao, who had been sent to a labour camp in Qinghai for re-education; both his parents were dead, too. She also learnt of Bai Tu's fate, how he'd moved to Shouyangshan, apparently to wait for her. Upon hearing this news, Yu Zhuo immediately went to the river to wash, especially her hair, which was still silky and dark. Then she set off for Shouyangshan. From here on, Bai Tu and Yu Zhuo were a couple in harmony. They never once returned to Laocheng, nor did anyone from the village ever come to visit them. But neither side seemed to care.

Not long after seeing his wife for the first time in many years, Bai Tu felt the urge to eat some tofu; it'd been so long since he'd last had any. He bought a roller to make the tofu, returning first with the top half, before a second trip saw him return with the bottom. Once the contraption was assembled, the soybeans were mashed into a pulp so that the liquid ran a brilliant white. They enjoyed a wonderful meal together, both eating until their bellies were about to burst. They spent the next three days bowled over with stomach pain.

Together, they sowed several different crops across their large piece of land. Cotton plants were placed on the side of the mountain; their yield would be ideal in making a thick, warm quilt for winter. They also planted sesame, which they'd watch almost daily to see if there was any growth. Bai Tu also considered planting a number of peach trees, but Yu Zhuo disagreed. The fur of the peach, she argued, only made people itch.

"How about some cherry trees instead?" she countered.

"Cherries it is, then. I'll plant a whole line of them!"

At the same time, Laocheng was going through its own changes: the villagers were organised into mutual-support teams and land was confiscated, yet again, so that it could be reallocated and brought under the leadership of the first social collectives that were then being established. For their part, Bai Tu and Yu Zhuo were completely oblivious of these changes.

They were also slowly growing older. Bai Tu felt this first in his teeth, which could no longer even mulch through a soybean, to say nothing of the pain he felt when he tried. To try to alleviate the pain, he'd taken to squeezing hot pepper seeds in between his teeth wherever they hurt, but this ended up doing very little, so he resigned himself to travelling to the market to have the offending tooth… teeth… removed. All told, Bai Tu lost ten teeth that day, causing him to cry out he'd lost part of his skull. Upset and feeling wounded, he buried his teeth as he would a loved one.

Yu Zhuo first felt her age in her neck, noticing the wrinkles there that now claimed her once smooth skin. Her feet, too, began to hurt, almost daily. Of course, large corns had developed on her heels before, but now the calluses were so big they'd take three to four days to cut back, and invariably she'd end up cutting so deep that blood would flow. On top of this, her toes would be almost equally painful and she could no longer walk without a cane for support. When this first happened to her feet, Bai Tu would help her down the mountain so that they could walk through the market together, but a year later, her feet hurt so badly she rarely went farther than the precipice that served as a boundary to their land. Whenever she had a craving for something they could only get at the market, like a serving of grass jelly, one of her favourites, all she could do was ask Bai Tu to bring her back some.

Realising how distressed she had become as a result of her inability to travel to the market, Bai Tu decided to build a halfway decent path that would lead out of the mountains so as to make the journey easier. Each day after tending the fields, he'd grab his hammer and chisel and soon the clang of metal on rock would ring out across the area. By the end of the summer, he had constructed nearly two dozen steps.

When winter arrived, their home would be buffeted by cold winds that'd freeze the small springs and rivulets that flowed nearby; they'd howl fiercely for days, sounding so much like someone whistling a tune. But after this particular summer and the hard work he'd put himself through, Bai Tu's age was becoming increasingly apparent on the top of his head. His hair had taken on the look of sallow, drought-stricken grass. Combined with his missing teeth, he appeared a very old man indeed. It didn't seem to matter, however, for he kept on chiselling steps out of the stone. By this time, Bai Tu's hands were cracked and dry, marked by bloody fissures in his skin. While he worked, Yu Zhuo was in the kitchen roasting potatoes. Once cooked, she took them out to Bai Tu, but he paid them no attention. Fearful they would get cold, she wrapped them again, and then held them close to her breast.

"Husband," she spoke softly, "tomorrow… I'd like you to go to the market to buy some lard. We can put it on your hands… they need it."

He heard her words but said nothing. In his mind, memories of what happened so many years ago rushed to the surface. He turned to look at her and smiled. His toothless grin looked very much like a baby's arsehole.

Over the next three years, Bai Tu carved 150 steps out of the rock face. When he finished the last one, he hurried off to tell Yu Zhuo who was asleep on their bed: "They're finished, the steps are done… tomorrow you can come with me… we can go down the mountain."

Yu Zhuo was quiet.

"Why haven't you made dinner?"

Still she said nothing.

Bai Tu reached out his hand to nudge her shoulder: "Are you angry at me?"

She didn't move. It then dawned on Bai Tu; she'd been cold to the touch. Dead. Bai Tu didn't cry, not this time. Nor did he yell. He went to the stove and made dinner, some noodles. After finishing his first bowl, he stood to get another, but toppled over before he could take even a single step. The bowl fell from his hands and smashed into pieces on the floor.

Bai Tu was dead, but he didn't feel it. Yes, his mind might've felt like a lantern had just been snuffed out, but in the moment before it happened, he could swear he saw Yu Zhuo sitting up in bed, enjoying the noodles, too. That's why he'd got up himself, to fetch his wife another bowl.

In truth, when a person dies, they never really feel it. Nearly every night I dream of dead people, they're all the people I sang for… after they died, of course… they always look the way they did when they died, too, not dressed up in funeral clothes, but in their everyday attire… they look and sound the same as when they were alive. Like Zhang Gaogui, when I saw him in my dreams, he still said the same things to me as he did before he died, you know, excoriating Ma Sheng and Shuanlao, calling them thieves and bandits for having taken everything, even his furniture… he complained about the quality of the wood used in the wardrobe and in the table… the fine, detailed work done, how it'd taken over a month to complete… the least they could've done was give the poor carpenter a bowl of spicy noodles, but they hadn't even done that… and on he went… of course, I'd talk to them, in the case of Zhang, I told him it didn't matter any more, he was dead, there was nothing anyone could do… and then, well, do you know what he said? He berated me for talking nonsense, said he wasn't dead at all… yes, his legs were bad and he was bedridden… but dead, no, not at all… so there you go, that's proof, dead men don't know they're dead… I guess it falls to me to help change that, you know, to tell them they are, that their bodies are in the ground, like an old house that's fallen into disrepair and is unliveable. That's what their bodies are like, sure, when they were alive they could love, they could hate, they could be poor or rich, healthy or sick… but all of that was gone now… they were dead… they were spirits… of course, I'd tell them that that meant they could go anywhere they pleased… which wasn't all that bad I suppose. But when Bai Tu died, well, no one asked me to go and sing for him, so he never visited me in my dream… he was a simpleton… so I guess his death was simple too.

It was Bai Tu's dog that told of its master's death. It had run all the way from Shouyangshan to Laocheng, and then sniffed out the whereabouts of Ma Sheng. Once it found him, it started nipping at his legs, something wholly unexpected. Ma Sheng was at first frightened, stooping down to clutch at his wounded leg, but still the dog yapped and snapped at him. He even grabbed a rock, preparing to cave in the animal's head, when he suddenly recognised the mangy mutt as belonging to Bai Tu and Yu Zhuo.

"Hey," he started, "has something happened to them… do you want me to come with you?" The animal stopped its assault, and not long after, Ma Sheng and several men returned with it to Shouyangshan. When they drew near Bai Tu's house, they were, to a man, surprised by the steps they discovered carved into the mountainside, one remarking they must be at the foot of some celestial stairway. A hundred-plus steps later, they found Bai Tu dead near the stove, unchewed noodles still in his mouth. Yu Zhuo was dead on her bed, although Ma Sheng wasn't sure at first if it was really her. He turned her face around and asked the men who'd come with him to confirm it was indeed Bai Tu's wife. It was, although her face had aged so much. He squeezed her cheek once, let a sigh fall from his lips as he remembered how he had had his way with her, and then he told the men to bury them both.

The land in Shouyangshan was rather desolate, so when it came time to collectivise, the leadership in Laocheng decided to simply assume responsibility for it; after all, no one lived there. Each following year, in spring, it was determined a number of villagers would be sent to plough the fields, plant some beans, or some other hardy crop, and then in autumn they'd be sent again to harvest what they could. Accordingly, a group was organised and dispatched to Shouyangshan. They left with cooking pots and pans, and sufficient flour to feed them for the planting season. Cui Cui, who was now team leader for the local Laocheng Women's Federation, as well as Mao Dan, whom she'd married some time ago, were part of the group sent to Bai Tu's former home. When they reached the mountain, the sky was high and bright above. The first thing they saw were the burial mounds for Bai Tu and Yu Zhuo, overgrown with weeds, as well as quite a bit of witches' butter that had grown in the shape of human ears.

"My word, will you look at that?" Cui Cui began. "That witches' butter'll be nice in steamed buns. Go… pick it." But before they could follow her instructions, something strange happened. The witches' butter, as though wary of the burning sunlight, curled up and retreated amid the grass; there was nothing for them to pick.

THE THIRD TALE

Question:

Oh... there's lots of jade on this mountain range. The passage says it can be planted and give birth to precious gemstones... can jade be planted in the ground?

Answer:

Everything comes from the earth,
so whatever is buried under the ground will sprout.

Question:

What about people?

Answer:

Well, after someone dies, we do bury them and yet their children and grandchildren live on... right?

THE THIRD TALE

Let's examine the second mountain range in *Pathways Through the Western Mountains*. As we've done before, I will start with the first sentence and you continue after me.

The first mountain in *Pathways Through the Western Mountains, Part II*, is Mount Qian. Its peak is covered in copper while the lower reaches abound in jade. Holm and other oak species thrive.

Two hundred leagues to the west is Taimao Mountain. Large deposits of gold can be found on its southern face, iron on its north face. The Luohe River begins here before flowing east into the Great River. Its bed is covered with dark-veined pieces of jade. Numerous white snakes live along its banks.

Mount Shuli rises a hundred and seventy leagues to the west. Within this peak is an abundance of gold. Silver can easily be found in the foothills. Holm oak trees are plentiful. Numerous parrots nest in them. The River Chu originates here before flowing into the Wei. Brilliant pearls can be found in the bed of the Chu.

One hundred and fifty leagues west is Mount Gao; it stands far into the sky. Silver is plentiful at the top of this mountain. Closer to its base there is much dark green jade and realgar. Palm trees grow on the slopes, as does bamboo. The Jinghe River originates in Mount Gao and flows east into the Wei. Chiming stones and dark green jade are easily found in the Jinghe.

Three hundred leagues to the southwest is Nüchuang Mountain. In appearance it resembles a lady's bed. Copper is abundant on its southern face, while alunite can be found in great amounts on its northern face. Tigers and leopards inhabit this mountain, preying on the herds of xi and si rhinoceroses. A bird that is similar to a pheasant also lives on Nüchuang Mountain. Known as the luan, its feathers are a rush of myriad colours. Its appearance is said to herald peace and order for all under heaven.

Two hundred leagues to the west is Dragonhead Mountain. Gold is common on its southern slopes, iron on its northern ones. The River Shao emerges here before flowing in a southeasterly direction to empty in the Jinghe; fine jade can be found in the Shao.

Two hundred leagues farther west is Deer-Terrace Mountain. White jade is found in abundance at the peak, while at the base there is a great amount of silver. The slopes are inhabited by yak, antelope and haozhi, a type of wild boar with porcupine quills on its back and which can be seen on other mountains. A rooster-like bird with a human face also inhabits Deer-Terrace Mountain. It is called the fu-xi because of the sound it makes. It is said to be a harbinger of war.

Two hundred leagues southwest is Mount Niaogui. Chiming stones can be found in great number on its south face. On its north face are numerous sandalwood and mulberry trees. The central track that runs down the mountain is fertile land for nüchuang plants. A river bearing the same name as the mountain begins here and flows westwards to empty into the River Crimson. Great quantities of cinnabar line its bed.

Small Station Mountain rises four hundred leagues to the west. Despite being much smaller than the other peaks in this range, it possesses great amounts of white jade near its summit. Veins of copper line its lower slopes. A small, gibbon-like creature known as the zhuyan lives on Small Station Mountain. Its head is white, and its paws are red. Like the fu-xi on Deer-Terrace Mountain, the zhuyan is a portent of war.

Three hundred leagues to the west is Large Station Mountain. A pale clay can be found in abundance on its southern face, while on its north face there is a lot of jade, all of it a deep green colour. Yak and antelope dominate the grazing areas.

Mount Xunwu rises four hundred leagues to the west. Nothing grows on its slopes, but there is much gold and jade.

Another four hundred leagues beyond Mount Xunwu is Whetstone Mountain. Thorny pine trees grow in great number on this peak. Wild plum and camphor trees can be found as well. The xi and si rhinoceroses call this mountain home, as do tigers, leopards and several small herds of yak.

Zhongshou Mountain stands high into the sky two hundred and fifty leagues farther west. There are large deposits of tufu jade near its summit. Sandalwood and mulberry trees grow thick nearer the base of the mountain. Gold is plentiful. Xi and si rhinoceros herds graze on its slopes.

Five hundred leagues to the west is Mount Emperor. Gold and jade can be found easily near the peak. Greenish realgar deposits are plentiful on the lower slopes. The River Huang begins here before flowing west to empty into the Crimson River. Grains of cinnabar line its bed.

Middle Emperor Mount stands three hundred leagues farther west. Gold is plentiful on its summit. On its lower reaches, marsh orchids grow in great numbers alongside birch-leaf pear trees.

Western Emperor Mount lies three hundred and fifty leagues to the west of Middle Mount Emperor. Gold deposits are common on its south face, iron on its north side. Elk, deer and yak graze its lower slopes.

Three hundred and fifty leagues farther west is Wild Weed Mountain. Sandalwood and mulberry trees are common. The luoluo bird nests in great number in these trees. It is said that they are man-eaters.

Altogether, seventeen mountains are described in the second part of *Pathways Through the Western Mountains*, beginning with Mount Qian, and ending with Wild Weed Mountain. The distance spans 4,140 leagues. Ten of the gods that live among these mountains have the face of a human and the body of a horse. The remaining seven gods also have human faces, but their torsos more closely resemble an ox than a horse. These seven each have just one arm which they use to grasp a walking staff, for they are gods more accustomed to flying than having their feet on the ground.

These seven deities require only a minor sacrifice. White reeds must be used for the seating mats. For the other ten gods, the ritual sacrifice requires a rooster to be slain, a prayer to be chanted, but no grain is needed.

So… do you have any questions?

Question: What's alunite?

Answer: It's a darkish mineral resin used in ancient times to colour eyebrows.

Question: Women coloured their eyebrows in the past?

Answer: Yes, just like now. Today they say that should you lose your eyebrows, you'd go blind. Without a proper brow, you've no eyes at all.

Question: So can greenish jade resin also be considered a dye?

Answer: Yes.

Question: Aiya… the text talks about gold and silver jade, copper and iron, a dark green one, realgar, some black resin called alunite, cinnabar… how's it there're so many ores on these seventeen mountains?

Answer: Well, my boy, it is, after all, where the Jinghe River runs! You know, it's the same area we Chinese are from, our birthplace. So it's quite natural it would have a favourable climate, abundant water and fertile land, and minerals and ores too.

Question: Isn't it more common to hear people say we were born out of the Yellow River?

Answer: The Jinghe River is a principal tributary, so when we speak of the Yellow River, it's the same as talking about the Jinghe River.

Question: Compared with earlier mountain ranges, it seems as though there are fewer strange trees and wild beasts, doesn't it?

Answer: Well, when there're more minerals and stones, there's bound to be less edible vegetation. Men discovered the properties of these minerals... they could be smelted and transformed into tools and that's how civilisation emerged. But with that development, well, naturally, wild animals were pushed further and further away, dislocated and marginalised.

Question: How's it there's no oil, nor any coal?

Answer: Both oil and coal are deep in the ground, they're not as easy to get at, but once man did so, they forever changed the way we live. Society was advanced enormously, but at the same time, opening up the land and bringing forth oil and coal has been like opening Pandora's box – you know what Pandora's box is, yes... yes, of course you do – well, since that time, we've lived a polluted life.

Question: Why does the book only talk about the land and say hardly anything about the heavens?

Answer: Didn't the earlier sections mention the gods? The Celestial Emperor is of heaven, after all – the heavens *are* above us, the earth below with its flora and fauna, like a mother and her children, and that means there's a father as well. Ancient people viewed heaven as a disinterested entity, akin to the sun and the moon and the stars. Heaven doesn't care if you're a man or a beast, poor or wealthy, beautiful or ugly, it looks after all the same as the wind and the rain and the lightning. It doesn't worry for the mountain's height, the valley's depth or the river's flow, everything is treated as family. Its impartiality is like our breathing, which is vital. Life wouldn't exist without breath, but we never really consider it as such. We take the air around us for granted, except when it's gone. To look up to heaven requires a symbol, something to uplift the spirit of man. To consider the earth below requires the creation of moral laws and commands. This book is about the land and its geography. It only makes sense for it to be about the mountains and the rivers and the things you would find there.

Question: The ape-like creature called the zhuyan, the one with the white head and scarlet paws, when it appears it says: "There will be a major war." It says the same for the fu-xi, the bird that looks like a cock but has a human face, that when it appears there'll be war, too… is it always so? Does war entail massacres?

Answer: Yes, it does, war and wanton death. It can also refer to dictatorship.

Question: There were dictatorships in those times?

Answer: Whenever there're groups of humans, there are classes. Many previous sections mentioned 'all under heaven', 'counties' and 'prefectures'. Well, that means there must've been countries, and therefore, most assuredly, there were class distinctions and dictatorships.

Question: Why's that?

Answer: You've seen the villagers in winter use dogs to hunt rabbits, haven't you? A rabbit runs in fear of its life, trailed by a hundred dogs… well, there's no way for that single rabbit to be divvied up among a hundred hounds and that's because no one's status has been undetermined. Once it is, however, then rules and control are needed.

I couldn't say how long I lived without any kind of status. I'd been working at the Art and Cultural Troupe for what seemed like forever.

As a mountain whisperer, I didn't sing about the living world. No, I sang about the dead, for the dead, for those wandering in-between. It's what I did, it's what I *could* do. But after Deputy Director Xu introduced me to the cultural work of the revolution, and once I became a member of the Party, well, my skills were no longer all that suitable, they didn't fit with the needs of new theatre and I wasn't much good at singing the new songs. There simply wasn't much use for a man like me in this new world. Over a period of nearly twenty years, I hid the truth about my past, covered it up to avoid public mockery and scorn. I kept myself busy handling the logistics of the troupe and other frivolous jobs that required little by way of skill. Even on stage, all I did was help pull the curtains open or closed. In the winter, especially on snowy nights, I wasted my time drinking alone in the local bar, caught up in memories of the past, at least until I was so drunk that I would have no choice but to stumble back to my room. I remember those nights now, the sound of my footsteps in the snow… oh how I hated that sound, those nights. Oh… let me tell you… I'll forever have fond memories of Kuang San. He changed my destiny, and not for the first time… again, Kuang San altered my path.

I remember… at that time we still referred to Qinling's local Party representatives as a prefectural committee, but their status has since changed, they're a municipal committee now, charged with compiling the revolutionary history of the entire area. And to do that, they've enlisted the descendants of the Qinling guerrilla fighters to record their memories. The only problem has been Li Desheng's nephew, Lao Hei's cousin, as well as the relatives of San Hai and Lei Bu. Well, none of them can write anything about anyone other than their own kin, and if that wasn't bad enough, they keep getting their facts mixed up, mistakenly ascribing certain acts to their family heroes. What's more, they make very little mention of Commander Kuang San throughout. In fact, when Kuang San first read their notes, he got incredibly angry and immediately summoned the committee member in charge of the compilation to answer for the historical inaccuracies. Needless to say, he was irate and ended up launching an ashtray across the room. Ultimately he decided to ask Deputy Xu to rewrite the history for him. The only wrinkle in this plan, however, was that Old Xu had earlier on in the same year suffered a stroke and had been left paralysed on one side.

That's when he decided to turn to me: "Say, what's that old mountain whisperer up to these days? He knows what happened, he understands history… get him here now, he can write it for me!"

And that's how I was freed from the work in which I had no skill, and how my social status increased enormously. I was put in charge of compiling history!

The first order of business was to launch new investigations into what to write, which meant we travelled to Santai County and the town of Guofenglou, which was now called the Guofenglou Commune. The Party secretary in charge of the commune was a man by the name of Lao Pi, one of Kuang San's many cousins and who once worked with the commander back when he was the bureau chief for military affairs in Shanyin. It was an odd name, Lao Pi, especially as it meant 'old skin', which was not really the most flattering of names for a new-born. He earned it, apparently, for the way the skin hung about his face, loose and sagging. He looked more like the old men that sat around town than to a child, and, in order to raise him well, his family purposefully chose a name hard on the ears.

Lao Pi had joined the revolution early on, and many knew of him, especially with regard to his search for a proper shave. That is, wherever he was stationed, he'd always try to find the most suitable barber, but because his skin drooped down over his head, even well over his face, shaving the stubble that grew on it was a difficult task, so much so the barber would have to use his hands to pull the skin taut, right up to the cheekbones, before he could put his razor to Lao Pi's patches of facial hair. Lao Pi, of course, didn't really think having flaccid skin was a problem. After all, he would argue, wasn't the skin of a tiger much the same? When the animal tracked over the ground, he would say, it looked very much like it was under cover of some bulky duvet! Having said these words, he would naturally take to sauntering, a slow and deliberate pace with heavy steps. He'd been secretary for the commune for quite a few years by the time I got there, and the tales of his prowess had spread far and wide. The townspeople had taken to saying that he'd come like the wind spirit through Guofenglou.

The wind in Guofenglou blew hard, of course. It was part of the area's identity. In fact, at the beginning of every summer, festivities were held in honour of the wind spirit. It was on the same day that Lao Pi became secretary. The townspeople had all gathered down by the riverbank, banging gongs and drums, and even firing twelve blunderbusses, a ceremony seemingly most fitting for Lao Pi's appointment as Party secretary.

"So," Lao Pi asked, "is everything prepared?"

"Yes," replied the local police chief, "everything's ready."

Seated immediately beside the police chief were two men who now stood up. One was wearing a red shirt and red trousers, and he held a carved wooden knife. The other was dressed completely in black, with ash covering his face. To pay proper respect to the wind spirit required a proper performance, hence the costumes worn by the two men. The one in black represented the offender of heaven who was to be punished and thrown into a pit. The man brandishing the wooden knife and dressed all in red was to be the executioner. He stood behind the wrongdoer and prepared to slide the knife across the back of the other man's neck, which would symbolise the beheading of the criminal. Two decapitated heads, one from a pig and one from a sheep, would afterwards be placed into the pit as symbols of the punishment to come. As the scene was getting ready to be played out, Lao Pi interrupted to ask what he regarded as a most pertinent question.

He spoke first to the man in black: "What village are you from?"

"I'm the local elementary teacher."

"How's it that you have a teacher playing the role of a criminal? Surely there's a dirty landlord somewhere who'd better fit the role... a rightist, a bad element!"

The spectators agreed with their new secretary, but at the same time, they also knew that enemies of the revolution were barred from attending such cultural activities. What's more, there was now no time to go back to the town and get them to come here. Then someone yelled out: "Mu Sheng! Get him here!" Mu Sheng was subsequently pushed forward by the throng of people.

He was a small, skinny man, the son of a counterrevolutionary. A few minutes after the crowd thrust him to the front, he was attired in black playing the role of a ne'er-do-well. Unfortunately, the clothes were rather large for his diminutive frame, forcing him to pull the trousers well up to his chest, and even then he couldn't let them go.

"Alright, alright," yelled the police chief, "we're not performing a comedy!" And he dragged Mu Sheng and pushed him down to his knees beside the pit.

In a stately, dignified manner, Lao Pi walked up to the ceremonial table already prepared. He lit the incense, bowed and began to read the sacrificial words to the wind spirit. When he finished, the wrongdoer's head was to be lopped off, but as he was about to do so, Mu Sheng cried out, slipped off one of his shoes and placed it across his neck.

"Now uncle, oh my, please don't use too much force, alright? Just run the blade across my shoe."

The executioner heeded the man's plea and gently slid the wooden sword over the man's shoe. But he cursed as he did so: "Goddamn fucker!" He thrust the bloody animal heads towards Mu Sheng and told him to fling them in himself.

Holding the gruesome remains tight, Mu Sheng cried out: "These are to be my head?"

The entire crowd roared in laughter. Amid the clamour, Lao Pi spoke, words that everyone claimed to remember ever since: "Take this sacrifice, Wind God. From this summer onwards, we beseech you to stop buffeting the town with your ferocious winds. We pray for a bumper harvest this year. But… there will be another kind of wind this year, the wind of rectification. The rectification of politics will blow through Guofenglou! We shall use class struggle to take care of the big issues, and the smaller ones will be sorted out in the process as well. We shall advance production, put great effort into the next five years and make anew Guofenglou. We'll transform its olden, dilapidated image and raise high the red banner of the revolution!"

Of course, we didn't know any of this until we started our historical investigations. On the day we visited Guofenglou, Lao Pi had earlier on dispatched Mu Sheng down to the river's edge to wait for our arrival and, at first sight, he was to return to the commune offices to tell him we'd come. It didn't work out that way, however. In fact, we arrived just before him, so when Mu Sheng finally appeared huffing and puffing, sweat running down his face and a fresh peach in his hand, the four of us were already standing about. All he could do was hand the fresh peach over to Secretary Lao Pi, a humble recompense.

Unimpressed, Lao Pi flung the newly picked fruit to the ground and kicked the man, saying: "Go, get out of here!"

I rushed to explain that we hadn't passed by the river, but instead came from the county capital, via Chaling Commune and then over the mountain. As I spoke, I noticed Mu Sheng lift his head, wink in my direction and smile briefly. His grin was something to behold, the right corner graced with a deep dimple. This prompted me to look at him more closely.

"So, my dear fellow," I asked, "who might you be?"

"I'm Mu Sheng."

"I beg your pardon, did you say Mu Sheng?"

"Both of his parents were executed, shot," Lao Pi explained. "He was born at that moment, in the pit his mother fell into."

I couldn't help but be a little startled by this titbit of information. "How old are you now?"

"I'm seventeen."

"What… seventeen? How's it you look like a boy of just eight or nine?"

"Um, I guess it's because I'm not that tall… I haven't grown right."

I wanted to ask whether his demeanour had more to do with him being short, or with him just being immature, but Lao Pi was clearly displeased and interrupted our exchange: "It's not your place to say anything, boy!"

Mu Sheng shut his mouth immediately and retreated to the back. Lao Pi shouted after him: "Farther… *farther*!" Mu Sheng complied and squirrelled away behind a nearby tree.

I'd never been in Guofenglou before, and one of the first things I noticed was the absence of any large buildings in town, despite what its name would suggest. To the east, about three *li* away, there were two towering cliffs that slightly resembled man-made structures. A road ran between the two cliffs and into town, but it seemed to carry more wind than traffic. And the wind really did blow, sometimes very fierce indeed. So much so that, when the town's cocks fought for the local hens, their battle-scarred feathers would be whipped into the air, forming great plumes that rushed back and forth through the sky. The cocks weren't the only warriors in Guofenglou. The rams loved to butt heads as well. Sometimes all it took for them to be provoked was for two shepherds to meet on the road into town. The beasts would lower their heads into the wind, take a step back and rush towards the other. The clap they made when the heads smashed together would carry on the wind, echoing throughout the entire town.

The shepherds who guided these willing combatants were quite elderly, but they enjoyed the spectacle to the fullest. Even on those occasions when the wind tore up the sand from the battleground and swirled it around their heads, choking their noses, they didn't seem to mind, but chose to watch the melee to its conclusion. Then, when it was clear that one combatant was beginning to weaken, which usually meant its head began to hang low and blood could be seen, you could hear its owner shout to the wounded creature: "Do you still mean to fight?" Naturally enough, the other shepherd never liked to hear such words, and soon an argument would ensue between the two owners, often resulting in a physical battle. Passers-by would sigh at the scene and reproach the two old men for behaving in such an unbecoming manner.

In truth, Guofenglou wasn't blessed with good *feng shui*. There was a lack of fertile land, and the trees stood well below thirty feet or so. Their trunks and branches were rough and coarse, and should you wish to split one open, dark, brackish water would ooze out. Aware of these conditions, the townspeople had constructed a Daoist temple high up on one of the mountains that surrounded the village. The hope was that it would help in warding off the seemingly evil winds that never ceased to blow. Unfortunately, no monk had been persuaded to take up residence in the temple. For well over ten years the only person to call it home was Lao Pi. And the bell that hung near the temple entrance? Well, when he did ring it, no one heard it, no villager, no beast, not even a mountain echo could be heard in response… no, the only one who'd come would be poor old Mu Sheng, tearing up the mountainside all aflutter, desperate to answer his master's command.

Mu Sheng mightn't be the brightest bulb, but his eyes were certainly large and gleaming. He'd seen so much, but not his father or mother. Almost the only thing the villagers had told him about his father was that he was a metalworker. However, he did learn that, after Liberation, several households in the eastern part of Linggou had quarrelled with the new head of the peasants' association and that his father had pulled a knife and murdered him. Of course, this resulted in all of the households, including his father and mother, being labelled counterrevolutionaries and thus subject to death by firing squad. His father had pleaded for mercy, arguing that he'd been pressured into challenging the commands of the peasants' association head and that he didn't know what they planned to do with the knife. He tried to earn leniency because of his trade, that if he and his wife should be spared, they'd promise to care for the cows and horses belonging to the peasants' association. But his remonstrations were all in vain; they were executed along with the other so-called counterrevolutionaries. Subsequently, baby Mu Sheng fell under the care of his uncle.

Sadly, Mu Sheng's uncle died when the boy was only twelve and he was left orphaned. The villagers showed little in the way of compassion, instead suggesting that should he wish to live among them, he'd need to assume responsibility for his parents' crime: "Tell us boy, are you a cow or a horse? Come on, speak up!"

He obeyed and mooed like a cow. It was so realistic the occupants of the nearby stables echoed in response. The villagers were at first surprised, and then wondered if anyone could teach him to neigh like a horse: "Whaddya say, boy? Should you study how to call like a horse, too?"

"I guess I ought to..."

His docility and good behaviour gradually won the townsfolk over. Even the supposed taint of his parents' wrongdoing began to wane, and more and more people grew concerned for his wellbeing and happiness, if only as the local idiot.

Lao Pi had served once already as a commune secretary and it was this experience that was supposed to help him transform Guofenglou's retrograde image. He'd been transferred especially to manage the turnaround, and when he arrived he lived in the main commune offices. That first night the wind howled, lashing through the trees and causing great swirls of leaves and pollen to blanket the area. There was such a racket that it was hard for anyone to sleep. It was cold, too. Some of his staff decided to relocate into the inner rooms, deeper into the courtyard, but Lao Pi persevered, overturning the main office table to serve as a barrier to the wind and noise.

He didn't fear the cold, and wouldn't use the chamber pot at night. No, he'd get up instead and relieve himself outside, sometimes twice in one night. The outhouse was in a rear corner of the courtyard, constructed out on an overhanging precipice that had allowed them to suspend a solid wooden beam to function as the spine of the structure. People would squat down on it and urinate over the cliff; they'd defecate in the same position as well. The only drawback to such a rickety outhouse was that, in the daytime, should anyone be standing just beyond the courtyard walls, well, they'd have a clear line of sight as to what was going on inside. Indeed, nearly all of Guofenglou could see. Deliberately or not, Lao Pi enjoyed standing in that very spot, especially on those occasions when he'd ring his temple bell. He'd listen to it echo, even if no one else heard it except for Mu Sheng, and then look out over his domain, imagining he was in Beijing atop the Gate of Heavenly Peace. At times, he'd remove his hat and wave it to a fictional crowd.

Lao Pi was an overachiever. He really didn't hold to the idea of when to start work and when to finish, or to weekends when people ought to relax. It was common for him to suddenly think of something in the dead of the night and to ring the commune offices, which he had manned twenty-four hours a day. It didn't matter what time it might be; to his mind, any hour was suitable for calling a meeting. And at each and every meeting he called, he would always begin with a recitation of Marxist-Leninist doctrine, then speak about Mao Zedong Thought, as well as the Party's leadership and the proletarian dictatorship, and then finally he'd get to the business at hand. The first such business was to agree on the best people to deploy and in what positions. Lao Pi had already worked out what he wanted, but he went through the show of debate nonetheless. However, should anyone voice opinions that didn't align with his own, he would never really articulate his own thoughts, but instead pull out a cigarette and proceed to light it. No one knew for sure what it was he smoked, but the stench would cause bystanders to retch and cough while he remained entirely unaffected. This was, evidently, how he displayed his displeasure at what the others were saying. Finally, the meeting would be called to a close and the gathered crowds would disperse, only to be called back a day or two later for another meeting on the same topic. Again they would hear the familiar refrain about Marxism and Leninism, about the Party and the people's dictatorship, and then… continue where they had essentially left off. If agreement was still not forthcoming, or rather, if the people's ideas did not conform with his own, the same performance was enacted all over again. This continued multiple times, until finally agreement about personnel was made, or rather, those gathered accepted Lao Pi's point of view. Thereupon he announced, as though real debate had transpired, that he agreed with them and that they should immediately set about putting the directives into action.

This did not mean meetings were finished, for another was soon called, this time concerning strategic planning. It began with the usual refrain, and by now, these words seemed to roll off the tongue with ease.

But before the discussions, such as they were, could begin, someone in the crowd spoke up: "Secretary, why don't you just decide? Make the decision for us."

"In that case, we shall proceed by democratic centralism," Lao Pi declared. "All decisions will be binding on all of us. Party unity must be upheld."

He went on to announce his strategic decisions and started to distribute cigarettes to those in attendance. Before handing them out, however, he expressed concern about their strength and paused.

"Allow me," he said, as he tucked the cigarette he'd been holding behind his ear. "Our meeting began in earnestness and with great vigour."

A gathered member blurted out: "Mu Sheng, get in here… come and let's hear you moo like a cow!"

On most occasions, Mu Sheng would sit outside the main courtyard, busying himself with whatever odd jobs would occupy his time. This could mean carving at the handle of a shovel with a piece of glass. (He'd smooth the handle of the secretary's shovel to such a fine degree that it no longer pricked the hands of his master.) At other times, he'd be off on the other side of the mountain, enjoying the cool streams that ran down the sloping hills. This time, unfortunately, it seemed Mu Sheng would miss the chance to learn how to mimic the bovine's call.

The workers under Lao Pi would joke at times like these about his seeming dedication to work above all else, and his expectation that those under him did the same: "Secretary, how do you do it? Well, you know, working with you… we fear we'll not even have time to properly take a piss, especially not in these trousers!"

Lao Pi laughed along with them, and the surplus flesh that wrapped round his face trembled in unison.

Lao Pi really was something, let me say. And tales about him spread, about his dark, almost bulging eyes and his apparently double row of teeth (one thinks of a shark). Whenever he visited a neighbouring town, people would actually try to see for themselves his supposedly imposing face, but he would always sport a pair of dark sunglasses and thus disguise his eyes from clear view. They were able to see, however, that he didn't have an inner row of teeth; it was only an impression given by the fact they were unclean, stained and rather filthy looking. The commune cook knew Lao Pi's mouth very well, in fact. He knew that whatever the man ate would end up getting stuck between individual teeth. So regular was this occurrence, the cook had to make sure toothpicks were on hand. Once the county secretary heard this, he actually sent Lao Pi a set of tiger's whiskers. Apparently, he'd been given them while attending the opening of a zoo in the county and thought they might serve Lao Pi better. For his part, Lao Pi accepted the gift with great courtesy and soon after obtained a small bamboo tube to carry them in. Thereafter, once his meal was complete, he'd pull out the bamboo tube and take out a whisker to floss between his teeth. Whoever had been eating nearby would invariably direct their attention to the rather strange performance. But Lao Pi would only allow them to look at the rare sight; they were prohibited from touching the tiger's whiskers.

On this day, a newly minted morning was waking after the downpour of the previous evening, a day that saw the moss-covered rocks welcome the sunshine while the knock, knock, knock of woodpeckers echoed in the air. Lao Pi stirred awake well beyond his normal time. This was most unusual, for he never let himself sleep beyond the rising of the sun. He liked to have the gates open just before the first rays appeared over the horizon. Mu Sheng, too, would be sat just outside, eyes wide and waiting for the morning's orders. But on this day, the alcohol Lao Pi had consumed the night before had claimed his early morning vigour. His main door had remained tightly closed long after the sun had risen, and Mu Sheng, always keen to steal a few winks, had fallen back to sleep in his usual place. When Lao Pi finally awoke and opened the door, his first act was to kick the poor boy.

"Get up… get up you lazy sod!"

Mu Sheng's eyes opened immediately and he began to pound the platform he'd fallen asleep on, berating it for causing him to become drowsy. He spat on his fingers and used the moisture to rub his eyes and ensure that he was truly awake.

"I want to hear you call like a cow," Lao Pi said. "You need to keep practising, you know… grunt like you really mean it."

Mu Sheng obeyed without protest: "Moooooooo!" In response, the woodpecker ceased its assault on a nearby tree and the bovine masses across the area mooed along with him, echoing across the mountains like rolling thunder.

Mu Sheng proceeded to get on with his daily chores, which meant first retrieving the red flag from inside the temple and seeing that it was dutifully raised. But this did not involve raising it near Lao Pi's abode. Instead, he ran off towards the rear of the compound to where a spider-monkey tree stood. The flag was always hung here. According to records, the temple complex, built many hundreds of years ago, was much larger than its current area and once comprised a monastery, a temple arch and a main hall. Once the commune had been established and construction of buildings began to scale up the mountainside, the spider-monkey tree was taken to mark the limit of the temple grounds. In the past, the spider-monkey tree and the alfalfa plant flowered at the same time of year. The flowers themselves were purple in colour, its fruit white. It was a sight that most people in the village enjoyed seeing, and so each and every year they would make the pilgrimage to behold the spider-monkey tree bloom.

To the villagers, the tree also prophesied the season's harvest. Whichever direction it seemed to grow towards and flower plentifully, that area would yield a bumper crop. But over the past three years that Mu Sheng had been hoisting the red flag on its branches, the tree had not borne any fruit. Liu Shaokang, who was from Qipan, told Wang

Yaocheng in private why he thought the tree had ceased to flower. Specifically, it had to do with the five elements and how the red flag symbolised, to the tree at least, an axe and a sickle, and these tools, made of metal, harmed its ability to blossom. At the time, Wang Yaocheng nodded in agreement, but later on he reported the claim to Lao Pi, who slapped the table in response and ordered Lou Shaokang to be brought before him. Afterwards, no one spoke of the spider-monkey tree.

It was Lao Pi's decision to hang the flag, one of his first directives after arriving in Guofenglou. He'd learnt of the practice in Beijing, how the flag was raised each morning over Tiananmen Square. He wanted the same thing for the town, so that when people raised their heads, they'd see the red banner flying overhead. It symbolised the enthusiasm and fervour of the revolution. The spider-monkey tree wasn't the tallest in town, but it had grown nearly straight up, without a bend in its trunk, which was smooth and almost slippery to the touch. It was impossible to climb for all creatures except the red-arsed monkey, which could deftly shimmy up its trunk. The monkey had come from Xigou, reared by the proprietor of the Old Rat Medicines pharmacy. He'd used the monkey to help him hawk his remedies, the creature serving as lure to draw in customers. However, once Lao Pi had assumed the role of secretary, he'd issued orders for all remaining capitalistic practices to cease, and, furthermore, prohibited any villager from leaving the town.

As a result, the monkey was left on its own, before being taught to climb up the spider-monkey tree to hang the red flag. But within a year, the animal had grown ill and so Lao Pi's mind turned to Mu Sheng, the young man he'd first seen during the wind spirit festivities. Having marvelled at his performance as a ne'er-do-well on stage, Lao Pi instructed Mu Sheng to try his luck in climbing the tree. To his surprise, not only was the young boy able to scale its slippery trunk, but he managed it even quicker than the monkey. This was the main reason why the boy had been allowed to remain in the town in the first place.

Holding the red flag, Mu Sheng ran towards the mountaintop. He was quite the runner, even without shoes, since his feet were already heavily callused with several layers of dead skin forming an almost protective cushion on his soles. For most people, scaling a mountain means directing their view upwards and grasping at trees to help propel them up the slope. Mu Sheng looked at what was beneath, his two hands dug into the ground with great ferocity, much like an animal on all fours instead of a man on two. Once he had reached the tree and nimbly hung the flag on its branches, his attention was drawn to the low-level clouds. So much so that he stretched out an arm as though trying to grasp one of them. He was of course unsuccessful, and only ended up taking hold of the wilted branches of a nearby tree.

The branches, however, were not actually dried and lifeless. When he looked closer, he spied a sparkling set of small eyes staring back at him and realised it was a stick insect clinging tightly to the branch. There were numerous species of stick insect inhabiting all corners of Guofenglou. Some bore a striking resemblance to the moss that grew on most rocks. Others looked like the leaves of the most commonly seen tree, right down to the small marks inflicted by some nibbling insect or other, or the discolouration due to invasive bacteria. But this was the first one Mu Sheng had ever seen that looked like a dried and dying branch. Having descended the mountain, his next thought was to show the rare sight to Lao Pi, who he found in the courtyard warming water over a stove in order to wash his scalp.

"Oh… secretary… you're planning to trim your hair, are you?"

"Get rid of that lifeless branch, you fool, and bring me that stool and scissors!"

Mu Sheng quickly put the branch aside and did as he was told. Once Lao Pi was comfortably seated, he began to cut his hair.

"Secretary… that wasn't a dead branch I was carrying, it was a stick insect."

"Oh… you don't say."

"How's it there're so many different stick insects in this region?"

"The work here in Guofenglou is rather… unique… shall we say. The people are just like those blasted insects, always pretending to be something else!"

Mu Sheng was startled by Lao Pi's words and couldn't help but jump. He really didn't understand what the secretary was getting at.

"So," Lao Pi continued, "you like insects, hmm?"

"Well… I don't know… it's just that I've never seen one like it before." To prove he didn't really fancy the creature, he picked up the insect once more and flung it into a corner of the courtyard. A moment of quiet passed between them before Mu Sheng walked over to where he'd tossed the insect and crushed it under his foot.

"Get back to work," said Lao Pi, laughing at the young man. "Cut my hair!"

It wasn't exactly hard to trim the older man's hair, especially since the top of his head lacked a single strand. Every time Mu Sheng carried out this task, he thought to ask the secretary why hair wouldn't grow on the top of his scalp, but he could never work up the courage. He only knew that shaving the secretary's beard was a challenge as the bristles grew so hard and stiff that it really was as though his face possessed the hair that should have been on the top of his head. Nevertheless, he kept at it, pulling the flabby overgenerous skin tight in order to run the razor over it. But this is not to say Mu Sheng was at ease shaving his superior's face. The whole ordeal terrified the young man.

His hair cut, Lao Pi took his seat at the main table, intent on getting to work. In one hand he lit a cigarette, while in the other a ballpoint pen was busy tracing words across a page; once complete, the pen was placed behind his ear. While his superior worked at the table, Mu Sheng rushed to where he had so unceremoniously flung the stick insect. He stared at the crushed bug for what seemed like ages, his head swirling. Finally, he dug a small grave and buried it. It was difficult to pinpoint a reason, but after this incident, Mu Sheng's entire body began to change, and the changes grew increasingly severe, giving rise to no small amount of worry, as well as a great deal of pain.

Lao Pi pounded once on the table, then twice more, his signal for Mu Sheng to attend him.

"Yes, secretary, what do you need me for?"

"I want these papers brought to the village head of Yezhu."

"Ah... yes, yes."

But the first order of business was to dispose of old Lao Pi's hair, which he swept up into a small paper bag and flung upon the roof. After all, the secretary's discarded bristles and hair clippings couldn't just be thrown away.

Once the task was done, Mu Sheng set off for Yezhu, but it didn't take long for him to be asked questions about where he was going:

"Eh… Mu Sheng," said a villager along the way, "what's the secretary got you up to now?"

"Documents… as you can see."

"What kinda documents?"

"Those with a red banner on the top."

Normally, Mu Sheng was quite forthcoming with details on whatever movement Lao Pi had put his mind to, readily sharing details with the locals, who in turn were often able to judge whether or not Lao Pi intended to launch an official investigation. But these documents he was carrying meant something more official, surely involved the county offices of the Party, and thus pointed towards something new. It was inevitable that a cadre-level meeting would be called. On such occasions, it was imperative for them to seize the opportunity and gather up the area's special produce such as eggs, honey, walnuts and persimmons. All of these could be brought to the county capital and sold, legitimately or on the black market. They could even take along hulled rice and trade that for millet or potatoes with communities deeper in the mountains; a *jin* of rice was worth at least three *jin* of corn and thirty *jin* of potatoes. With such trades, they'd have more to eat and their bellies would end up being much fuller; starvation certainly wouldn't be a problem!

Mu Sheng didn't fail to notice the reactions of the villagers whenever he promulgated some new directive written up by Lao Pi. He'd seen the exchanges of rice for corn and potatoes, or the remaining eggs, walnuts and persimmons not sold at the market, but when the townspeople saw him watching them, they'd quickly scurry behind the nearest tree. Mu Sheng would cough, in his usual offhand manner, and then they would reappear, usually to fiercely scold him.

"Mu Sheng, eh, you know why you're called that, right?"

Mu Sheng, however, would never get angry. He knew what they were trying to do. They were more concerned about waylaying him, distracting him by whatever means so that he wouldn't expose them; he'd grown quite used to this type of trickery.

"I'll take some walnuts, I think," he'd say.

And they'd comply, but not without a warning: "No loose tongue, now, alright. Don't go making reports to the secretary!"

"I don't know what you're talking about," he would invariably reply. "I didn't see anything!"

On this occasion, Mu Sheng's mind wandered to the stick insect, and to what Lao Pi had said about the residents of Guofenglou, how they were good at keeping up appearances. He understood what he meant now. These people right here were like that bug… and, in truth, so was he.

Despite the journey to Yezhu, where he handed Lao Pi's official documents to the village head, Mu Sheng did not feel tired and so he thought it best to return without resting. After all, the red flag would need to be lowered once the sun set, and he was the only one who could do it. Unfortunately, Mu Sheng's mind was buzzing. It was as though some wasp or bee was busy pollinating imaginary flowers in his skull. So loud was the buzz that, within half an hour of setting off, he could walk no further. At the same time, he thought he spied a solitary tombstone near the edge of the path, and was taken aback to discover that it was indeed a grave.

The grave actually spurred him on and he continued on his way, reaching the mountain just as the sun was falling. He was right on time to lower the flag. As he shimmied up the tree to collect the flag, he looked for more stick insects, but alas found none. His mind was still swirling, the hum of the imaginary wasp echoed. He began to climb down the tree, the flag held close to his breast.

"Please… let there be nothing wrong with it," he mumbled as he descended.

Unable to wait until he reached the ground, Mu Sheng unfurled the flag. It was untouched, no nicks, no tears, nor any bird droppings. But as he scanned the fabric for damage, he lost his grip and plunged to the ground, slamming his stomach hard onto the ground, leaving a gash across it. He bounced up almost as quickly as he fell and muttered: "Eh… what the hell?"

Confused and puzzled by what had happened, he went in search of Lao Pi, only to discover he was not sitting in his normal place with a tea cup in his hand.

It was the older man's habit to sip tea at the end of the day. He'd boil the leaves in a small iron pot until the liquid was as black as tar, and thick like molasses. To drink tea in any other manner was a terrible waste, according to Lao Pi. He'd also insist on Mu Sheng having tea with him, which the latter loathed; the taste was simply unbearable and stomach-turning. But now, as the day had already fallen dark, Lao Pi was nowhere to be seen, his tea not prepared. Apparently, he was still caught up in the meeting he had called earlier. Mu Sheng then heard a commotion inside, Lao Pi's ire had once again exploded. Something must have happened in Guofenglou, or some new movement, a new struggle was to be initiated. Mu Sheng didn't dare enter the main room. At the same time, he worried Lao Pi would soon call out for him and so he couldn't leave. All he could do was sit and wait, his eyes cast fondly over the mountains that reached up into the blackness of the night. A flock of birds called out, and then soared down the side of the cliffs.

The meeting finally came to a close and the assembled participants filed out of the building to trek back down the hill. The last to leave was Liu Xueren, carrying a small porcelain pot. For each and every meeting called, Liu Xueren would always bring a small pot with him. Filled with hot chilli paste, salted leeks or some other dish, he would give the pot to Lao Pi, but ask nothing in return. Mu Sheng thought to speak to the other man, but Liu Xueren appeared not to notice him. He seemed, in fact, to be lost in thought, like a leaf being carried on the wind, or a cat homing in on its prey. Instead, Mu Sheng directed his attention towards the main office: "Secretary… is everything in order?"

"You're back."

Since the secretary said nothing more, Mu Sheng decided to head down the mountain himself, but as he left, Liu Xueren emerged from his trance and shouted: "I've something to add to the agenda."

He passed the porcelain pot to Mu Sheng and dragged him along. Mu Sheng wanted to ask what had happened, but before he could do so, Liu Xueren scolded him: "What're you dawdling for? Take this down to the river and wait for me there!"

Mu Sheng raced down the hill. He enjoyed running, but at the same time he was careful not to drop the bone china pot. Clutching it close to his chest, he bounded across the canal that connected one of the many rivulets that streaked down the mountain, but to his great surprise, he lost his footing and crashed to the ground, shattering the porcelain in the process. Unsure of what to do, he waited for Liu Xueren as instructed, intent on returning the many shards of porcelain he'd picked up from the remains of the pot.

"Cadre Liu," Mu Sheng began as soon as the other man arrived, "have you ever felt as though a bee were buzzing in your head?"

"What?"

"You know... a buzzing sound... in your head. Does it mean something bad's about to happen?"

"Oh... that's what we call a premonition... a feeling of disaster."

"A disaster... yes, that's the feeling." Mu Sheng slapped his own face.

"Slap it a few more times, I'd say! Hey... where's my pot?"

Mu Sheng handed him the broken shards and explained what had happened. Then he waited for Liu to curse him, and prepared to call out like a cow as per his usual punishment. But Liu didn't scold him, nor did he tell him to moo like a cow. He just looked him up and down, seemingly mulling something over. Finally he shouted: "Open your mouth!"

Mu Sheng misunderstood at first, thinking perhaps that Liu Xueren wished to examine his tongue: "My... my mouth's not quite as big as yours..."

But he complied nonetheless. Liu Xueren then did something entirely unexpected. Instead of checking his tongue, he spat a thick, viscous glob of phlegm into the back of Mu Sheng's mouth. "That's a lesson you won't forget in a hurry!"

Liu Xueren had worked in Guofenglou for seven years, mainly as committee member for the commune. Lao Pi was his superior, as he was for everyone else, but Liu Xueren had no one beneath him, so he brought up the rear. If Lao Pi was the head of the dragon, then Liu was most definitely the tail. However, that didn't stop him from wagging his tongue: "I might be the lowest-ranking cadre, but for every festival, you can't have a dragon's head without the tail!"

On this matter, he was right, and in truth, whenever Lao Pi issued new directives or made new promulgations, Liu Xueren was the only cadre across nearly the entire area to fully carry out the orders. No one else quite possessed his zeal. Indeed, if nothing else, he went through shoes unlike any other member of the commune; it was as though you'd never see him in a pair of new shoes since the soles of the ones he had on his feet were always worn through. He spoke more quickly than anyone else, too. Most people would inhale after a sentence, but he could spill out at least three before needing to take a breath. Once, he joined other comrades in mobilising to work on water conservation in Zhaojiabao. The team leader invited Liu to say a few words before he delivered his own report, and Liu ended up speaking for well over half an hour, and even then he wasn't finished, assuring the comrades he still had five additional points to cover. Once he completed his oratory and it fell to the team leader to speak, all the leader could say was that Liu Xueren had already mentioned everything he'd planned to utter, so there was nothing more to add. Of course, Liu Xueren knew he'd wronged the team leader, so at dinner that evening he decided to raise a glass and toast his commander. He began by relating how much he respected the team leader and how he'd been made incredibly welcome. He also volunteered additional thoughts, noting some minor aspects of the initiative that needed correction, and on and on without end.

Those who stood to toast began to feel an ache in their arms, until finally the team commander interrupted him: "Cadre Liu, it's all there in the glass. Drink."

Liu Xueren felt he'd committed yet another offence, and so he felt obliged to offer a few more words to try and excuse himself. Finally, he stopped.

Naturally enough, these events became a humorous story told more than once, and soon everyone described Liu Xueren's mouth as like a roof tile, one that was thoroughly rotten. But Lao Pi approved of him, and, evidently, his mouth. The only criticism he had was with regard to Liu Xueren's manner of walking. Lao Pi said he was much too hurried, bounding across the road as though he were constantly trying to dodge this or that.

"You flitter about like a sparrow, you know, and let me tell you, that's the sole reason it's remained such a small little bird."

"Well," Liu Xueren would say, "you're already the top dog in Guofenglou. There's certainly no need for another!"

As for Liu Xueren's love of talking, Lao Pi was of the mind that, to be a successful cadre, one had to have a way with words. Shortly afterwards, he had Liu promoted. But he didn't put him in charge of the water services or any other utility, no… Liu was made responsible for the propaganda department.

Liu Xueren considered himself eminently capable of handling this particular job, and so whatever movement was launched by the commune, whatever orders were issued by Lao Pi, he would make sure to visit every town and village to explain and promulgate the new directives. He'd call large meetings and small ones, he'd repeat himself over and over, and he'd use metaphor and simile to get his point across. He'd talk about the need to do things more than once, like an elementary school student who did long lines of numbers and characters, each scribbled in neat rows, one after the other.

In order to engender the correct atmosphere for each new directive, he'd set himself straight to work. First, he'd instruct each town to build a new wall, or at least clean an older one, so that he could properly announce and publicise the new promulgations. This was what they did in the bigger cities, where walls were the main means by which the government announced new rules, movements, campaigns, whatever they wished. Then he'd spend the following months trekking across Qinling, sleeping late and rising early, always with a bucket of red paint nearby. In fact, his trousers became so worn from all that walking, and so spattered with droplets of red ink, that his distinctive passage through the region almost became something they looked forward to, or in some cases dreaded. Indeed, the very sound of his steps on the dusty roads was soon recognised in nearly every village across Qinling.

On one such occasion, in the town of Xiliu, nearly everyone was able to make out Liu Xueren's approach. Mrs Hui, for instance, who was herself an early riser – after all, the chamber pots had to be emptied just after sunrise – heard his familiar shuffle one morning just beyond her courtyard gates. She knew immediately that Liu Xueren had arrived, and that he was busily writing slogans across her compound wall. Naturally, she rushed out to help him.

"How's it look?" Liu Xueren asked the woman.

"Great," Mrs Hui replied, despite the fact she was illiterate. "It's terribly good, so red! If you could write it in white, well, I'd say it'd be even better!"

"I don't think white would be all that eye-catching."

"But you'd be able to see them at night... I bet the wolves wouldn't dare sneak in to steal our pigs!"

Liu Xueren paused a moment, and then continued: "What's your name?"

"Hui Huanghua."

"Go fetch the local branch secretary. Tell him to come here."

The woman did as she was told, and when she returned with the branch secretary, Liu instructed him to call the whole town together for a meeting. He intended to voice criticisms against the woman Hui Huanghua. It was only then that she realised she'd committed an offence, and as a means of self-reprobation, she grabbed a handful of chicken droppings and stuffed them in her mouth, mumbling as she did so that she was a fool for saying what she had.

The second order of business for Liu Xueren in his position as chief propagandist was to make it a requirement that, at the beginning of every meeting called, the assembled crowd was to sing. In advance of issuing this order, Liu busied himself with the tape recorder, learning by heart nearly fifty revolutionary songs. These he would teach to all the villages across the region. Again, this entailed several months of work trekking back and forth. When complete, nearly everyone could sing *Sailing the Seas Depends on the Helmsman, Socialism is Good* and *Sing a Folk Song for the Party to Hear*. Later on, they learnt *Back from Target-Shooting Practice*, which Liu Xueren believed was best suited for singing while the villagers were in the fields or on the way home after a hard day's work. With this thought in mind, he went first to the town of Zhenxijie to teach them the lyrics. After going over things more than ten times, he asked them to sing.

"Alright everyone, I'll start off and you continue... 'As the sun sets, the red clouds fly' – now you!"

In chorus, the townspeople began to sing the song, their mouths open wide enough to swallow a sweet potato whole. Once the first rendition of the song ended, they sang it again and again until the pit in their stomach ached and they began to buckle over.

Liu Xueren finally gave them a moment to pause: "Do you all have something else on your minds?"

"We're singing this song," replied the townsfolk in unison. "What else can we be thinking about?"

"Right! That's right indeed!" Liu Xueren expounded. "In those years of struggle, when the Red Army fought our enemies, well, whenever the battle seemed to be going bad, they'd begin shouting slogans and singing songs to boost their courage and then, in a great spurt of energy, they'd brave the hail of bullets and rush to meet their enemy head-on! We've got peace now, but still… there lingers in each and every one of you, selfish impulses and incorrect, distracting thoughts. Singing these songs will put your minds in order, it'll allow them to soar with the revolution and the building of the New China! Let's sing once more… 'As the sun sets, the red clouds fly' – your turn!"

As the song echoed through the town, Liu Xueren paid attention to each person's mouth, checking to see whether they were really singing or not. One man clearly wasn't joining in, a villager by the name of Zhang Shuiyu.

"Stop!" bellowed Liu Xueren, turning his gaze on Zhang. "Why aren't you singing?"

"My stomach is."

And his gut was indeed singing, just not the words of *Back from Target-Shooting Practice*. Instead, it gurgled and croaked with hunger, and soon almost everyone else heard the same song emanating from their own stomachs, too.

Unsurprisingly, Liu Xueren couldn't contain his anger: "You're hungry, aren't you? When you're working in the fields, well, if you stop to eat while the sun's still up, you'll get no work points for that day… have I come here just to waste my time? Sing… sing and you'll forget your hunger… 'As the sun sets, the red clouds fly' – continue!"

But the choir never reached the same crescendo as it had before. Everyone could see that as the sun disappeared behind the mountains, there wasn't a red cloud in the sky. Only a few crows soared high up above, black as the approaching night.

I don't know how Liu Xueren heard of me, but once he did, he tracked me down.

"You've got experience in cultural work, haven't you?"

"Yes… is there something you need me for?"

Before saying anything further, he clasped my hand tightly, then continued: "I've seen the way you carry yourself, that time you came to Guofenglou. You're unlike anyone else in the town! You've surely had professional training, haven't you… in Peking Opera? You must've played the central character, yes?"

"No," I replied matter-of-factly.

"Then you played one of the common people on stage?"

"No," I replied again.

"Then… you must… yes, yes… you must be a great singer of revolutionary songs. I'd like you to come to our village and teach them how to sing."

"I simply pull the curtains open and close."

Liu Xueren gave a short gasp and asked no more questions about my time in the Art and Cultural Troupe. Instead, his interest turned to the history work I was doing on Qinling's former guerrilla band. I told him Guofenglou had also been an area in which the guerrillas had been active and that there'd been about eight people from the town who had been directly involved. They were all dead now, but there were stories about them, passed down through the townsfolk.

"I've heard a number of those stories myself," Liu Xueren added. "The military campaign in Qipan, for instance… that'd been an especially desperate and bitter battle, more than twenty brave fighters lost their lives, I believe. But Commander Kuang San had been ever so brave… that's what I heard… he killed the local landlord himself… and he crossed the river to kill an additional thirty enemies of the people… including the leader of the local militia."

"Do you know about the apricot trees in Qipan?" I asked. He shook his head and so I told him about them. On either bank of the river, along the edge of a rocky gorge, there was a whole line of apricot trees. Commander Kuang San had planted them, right after that battle… they're rather large now and they bear fruit each and every year. They've also provided wood for building bridges across the river. I could see his eyes darting back and forth as I told him about the trees. Finally, he interrupted my story.

"Are you really speaking the truth," he said, pausing for a moment. "Are those trees real?"

"Yes… they are."

"Was it really Commander Kuang San who planted them?"

"Yes, honestly."

He slapped his head hard, amazed by what I'd told him. "Then we ought to make sure we protect them! We can even use them as a teaching tool for the revolution!"

And he did just that. He made the trees a teaching tool of revolutionary history. I admired his political astuteness, and lamented my own sluggishness. Naturally, he delivered a report to Lao Pi, and added his own personal thoughts on how best to use the trees. Lao Pi's response was even more enthusiastic than his own, and he assured his subordinate that this was something they could definitely do, should do, and that funds ought to be allocated immediately. Lao Pi went on to say he would inform his older cousin so that Commander Kuang San would learn of their intentions. And who knows, they mused, perhaps the commander would even pay a visit to Guofenglou and see for himself. What an honour that would be!

Only three days later, Lao Pi dispatched Liu Xueren to Qipan once more. By now, Qipan had already been declared a focal point of Liu's revolutionary initiatives, but when he went there this time, the first thing he did was scold Feng Xie, a local cadre: "Qipan has such importance to the revolution, and the apricot trees here are a symbol of that. They're truly heroic. Why the hell didn't you tell me of them before?"

And while Liu Xueren had always intended Qipan to become a model town for the entire commune, an emblem to symbolise the work of the revolution, now it also had these heroic trees and so its status would be even higher. They would complete the work of five years in just three with their industriousness. Qipan would be a model for the whole county, and thus the greater honour would be his, along with increased responsibility. Yes, Liu Xueren thought, he'd soon be in charge of Qipan.

It was with all of these musings in mind that Liu Xueren left for the village.

Qipan was located in the northwest corner of the commune's administrative region. The mountains in this area weren't particularly tall, nor did they roll together as many other mountain ranges did. This is not to say they pushed up haphazardly into the sky. In fact, there was a certain order to them akin to the order of a chessboard and its pieces, which, after all, was the meaning behind Qipan's name. The overall area covered by the town was quite large, but most of the soil was reddish clay that would turn to muddy swampland as soon as it rained. And then, when there was no rain, the land would become dry and brittle, cracking under feet into shards. Needless to say, farming was difficult on such infertile land, and life was hard.

Some years ago, the commune authorities convened a meeting to address the issue of autumn harvest shortfalls, and the team leader of Qipan was invited to describe the experiences of his town. He explained how the residents had learnt to cook alfalfa, willow tree leaves and the flowers from the scholar tree. He told them, too, how the leaves from the corn crop could be mixed with sweet potato creepers and black beans to make fried noodles. The bark from the elm tree could also be added to flour to increase production. Finally, oak seeds could be ground into powder and used to make grass jelly and the roots from bracken could be mixed with the slender shoots of grass to make wontons. The most important thing was to have hot chilli; with that, pretty much anything was edible.

Of course, such experiences didn't necessarily go down well with the audience, and other village heads would be quick to laugh at Qipan's expense: "I heard the residents of Qipan must use wooden sticks to clean out their arses in order to take a shit. Could you tell us a little about what kind of stick to use… how coarse or how fine it should be?"

There was one good thing about the land in Qipan, and that was its suitability for growing cotton. No other village was able to produce it, and so most residents would pick the cotton to sell at the local markets. With the money they earned, they'd buy grain and other foodstuffs. Homespun cloth was also taken into the mountains to trade for corn, black beans and potatoes. One winter, the village head's own younger brother had taken some of the cotton into the mountains to trade for a whole cup of buckwheat. And what's more, when he was bartering with one of the mountain villagers, certain residents took a liking to his old-style cotton padded jacket and offered string bean seeds in exchange for it. He agreed, removed his jacket and brought back with him a cup of buckwheat and two thirds of a peck of string bean seeds. He never once thought he'd catch a cold and come down with a fever, and the buckwheat... he never made it back in time to have noodles made out of it. Unfortunately, he died just before returning. Commune documents clearly prohibited all forms of capitalist profiteering. The documents also forbade under-the-table selling and buying. Previously, Qipan had been an impediment to realising these directives, which had been the main reason why Lao Pi had targeted his efforts on the town. It was why he had groomed Feng Xie to assume the post of village head. Qipan had been in need of a makeover.

Feng Xie's previous name was Feng Jiuwa. By the age of three, he still wasn't able to stand up on his own. It wasn't until he was four that he could walk, and then only unsteadily, more a stumbling than anything else. People were heard to wonder whether he'd been born of a crab, given his unusual gait, and hence he was bestowed the name Feng Xie, the same character used to write 'crab'. As time passed, his original name had been all but forgotten, even to himself.

His personal character was perhaps even stranger. After reaching the age of ten, he started trying to get involved in everything. And it was always best to let him get his way, for if he was prevented from doing what he wanted, he'd take to banging his head against the nearest stone wall. He'd do this with great force too, smashing his head against the wall until he'd collapse to the ground and loll about, foaming at the mouth. Of course, his father beat him regularly. But Feng Xie would never dare answer back; instead, he would curse at Lan Cao, his grandmother.

"It's your father who's beat you," she would reply to his curses. "Why the hell are you berating me!"

His retort always cut her to the quick: "Because you didn't give birth to a better man, that's why!"

But for all of this, Feng Xie was a smart boy. When he was a little older, he began to help in the barn with the cows. He was especially adept at weaning the calves from their mother's milk. In the past, the man in charge of the cattle would try rubbing hot peppers on the cow's udders, and when this proved unsuccessful, he'd take to beating the young animals. Feng Xie's approach was entirely different. First, he constructed three smallish strips of wood, and then, using iron wire, he attached the strips to the calves' snouts. When they in turn tried to nuzzle their mother's teats, the wood would prevent them from doing so. The opposite, however, occurred when they put their noses down to eat some grass; the strips would slide forward and they'd have no problem at all. It was an exceptionally clever idea and was soon disseminated to other villages in the region. When word finally reached Lao Pi, he was more than impressed and so when the time came for a change of leadership in Qipan, when things had got so bad something had to be done, the first person he thought of to take on the challenge was Feng Xie.

Lao Pi brought Mu Sheng along with him to see Qipan. As they came upon the fields that lay on the outskirts of the town, Lao Pi stopped abruptly, sat down and pulled out his tobacco.

"Bring Feng Xie here, now!" he shouted at Mu Sheng.

Mu Sheng knew the man's name, but he hadn't met him before. To make matters worse, there was no one about for him to ask and his mind was still buzzing at it had been doing for several days. He couldn't shake the feeling that something bad was going to happen. While these thoughts raced through his mind, a stray dog darted out from a side road, startling him even more. The beast, however, didn't bark; it simply fell on him, biting at his leg. Terrified, but unable to extricate his leg from the animal's maw, Mu Sheng bent forward, picked up a stone and walloped the mangy creature across the nose. The dog released his bite and disappeared back into the alley from where it had come.

Mu Sheng looked down at his leg and saw the tear in his trousers. On the one hand, he was grateful the beast hadn't drawn blood, but this didn't stop him from muttering ruefully that it should've got something more for its trouble: "You ought to have gone for the meat. Look at my trousers… what am I supposed to wear now!"

Tears rolled down his face. He felt wounded despite the fact the animal left him unscathed. But unfortunately, he still had to get Feng Xie: "Feng Xie! Xie! Crab!"

Mu Sheng wandered off in the direction of the local reservoir that was situated in the western part of the town. Once there, he shouted again. This time, he received a response: "Are you trying to wake the devil!"

Mu Sheng looked the man up and down and figured it must be Feng Xie. He wasted no time: "Secretary Lao has summoned you… you're to come with me to the fields just outside town."

Feng Xie had been fishing in the reservoir. His trousers and jacket lay at the water's edge, but he didn't bother to put them back on. He simply stood up in just his wet and soiled underpants and ran off to see Secretary Lao.

"So," began Lao Pi as he saw the man run up, "you're Feng Xie, hmm?"

"Yes, I am."

"You do know who I am, yes? Why aren't you wearing trousers?"

"You summoned me... I thought it best I come right away."

"Alright... at least I know you'll come as soon as you're called!"

Lao Pi instructed Mu Sheng to return to the reservoir and collect the other man's clothes and once he was more properly dressed, the three of them set off. As they approached Feng Xie's home, a goose, which shared the residence with him, rushed out squawking at the Party secretary.

"Don't you know who this is?" shouted Feng Xie. "Get out of here!"

"So you can teach geese as well!" exclaimed Lao Pi.

"It's taken ages," explained Feng Xie. "You know, about three years ago I came across a feral dog, only a pup. I took care of it for about a year and then discovered it was a wolf cub. I had to kill it... its meat was a little sour."

Mu Sheng had been walking behind Feng Xie, but as they moved to step inside, he shifted and sat down on the porch that ran around the outside. Lao Pi strode in without hesitating. A nearly impenetrable darkness covered the room, the curtains all pulled tight. Lao Pi moved to open them.

"Your father and mother aren't in?" he asked.

"They've been dead for three years. There's a picture on the wall."

Lao Pi looked at it. Feng Xie appeared nothing like either of them.

"Are you married?"

"Yes... I am... I got into an argument with her yesterday and... I struck her... she went back to her parents' place after that."

"You hit her?"

"Yeah... I slapped her... on the face."

Lao Pi chuckled. "What do you think of Qipan's village head?"

"Not much."

"Then who do you think would be better suited?"

"I would."

"You!" came Mu Sheng's voice from outside, and as he spoke, the pig in the sty lifted its front legs against the wall and squealed in unison.

"Quiet, you. Just take care of that beast!"

Mu Sheng did as he was told, but as he went, his head began to swirl and buzz again. He worried the animal was in some form of distress, and decided to collect food for its trough. He returned a few moments later with a basket of hay, but before he could feed the pig, the goose ambushed him and nipped at the hay. He was chased by the goose towards the persimmon tree that stood in the corner of the compound. The feathered fowl couldn't climb trees after all. The birds in the tree took flight.

As these developments transpired outside, Lao Pi and Feng Xie continued to talk inside. The rustle of the birds taking flight drew their attention and they both called out: "Were those magpies or crows?"

"Crows!" replied Mu Sheng excitedly.

"Magpies!" countered Feng Xie.

Lao Pi directed a question to his subordinate: "Why'd you say they were crows?"

"Crows are black," Mu Sheng answered, "as those birds were."

"They might've been entirely black, but they were indeed magpies!"

"Did I see wrong?"

Lao Pi laughed again and turned back to Feng Xie: "You want to be village head… hmm… then you'd better watch after your family!"

Feng Xie grabbed hold of his leg. "How's it you know what my heart desires before I've even told you? Liu Shaokang's wife asked if I could help fix her leaking roof since her husband was away. I agreed to replace the tiles and people said I was very magnanimous towards her… but all my wife did was yell at me… how'd you know about this?"

"Do you think I wouldn't know!" Lao Pi countered. "I want you at the commune office this evening!"

Feng Xie did as he was told.

"This morning I tested you. You knew they were crows, but you insisted on calling them magpies. Why?"

"There're a lot of crows in Qipan," began Feng Xie. "Everyone in the village recognises them. But… I think you asked me a trick question, you *wanted* me to say they were magpies, so I did. I went along with you."

"You're something, aren't you! A blasted stick bug like the one Mu Sheng brought along, able to blend in, hmm. I say!"

"I'll be whatever you need me to be!"

After this exchange, Feng Xie was put in charge of Qipan.

Once he was named village head, the first thing Feng Xie did was to move all of his family's belongings out into the main intersection that served as the centre of town. There were large earthen jars filled with wheat and corn, a container of salt, bottles of cooking oil, his bed and bedding, several sets of clothes for winter and summer, and various other household items. Strangely, there was even a bundled-up roll of hair on a prayer mat. Needless to say, the villagers were perplexed by what he was doing.

"What's the point of all of this?" one villager called out.

"It's what Secretary Lao told me to do. To take up the position of village head, I must devote my entire heart to it, everything must be for the public good. These belongings… well, in a few years I'd likely have more and that would be just too much. Hell, I'd be buried in junk, stuff more fit to feed a dog."

"What kinda hair is this?"

"Secretary Lao told me about a Ming general who'd been in charge of protecting a border station… he'd led troops into battle but lost. He had to punish himself for his failure, but he couldn't just kill himself. If he did, there'd be no one to lead the troops, so he stripped himself bare and cut off three chunks of his flesh. This was his punishment. The hair's mine… it's to prove my worth!"

Feng Xie's first directive was to improve the terraced fields in the area. Everyone was required to be in the fields by seven in the morning. Failure to be there on time would mean the reduction of work points. After the first few days, six men had points deducted including a man by the name of Lin. Apparently, he and his wife were in the habit of waking somewhat early, doing the deed as couples are wont to do, and then falling back to sleep for a spell. Once his work points were taken away, however, he swore he'd get revenge on Feng

Xie. His plot began with him sending his wife out in the middle of the night to call on another family, the Yu's.

Miss Yu was a young widow who also once had good relations with Feng Xie. Lin's wife told the other woman she was in great pain, that her stomach hurt enormously, and she wondered if Miss Yu had anything she could take. She performed the same scene for three days in succession, finally arousing the suspicion of the widow Yu.

"How's it every night you come here saying your stomach hurts?"

Lin's wife didn't answer immediately, but instead looked from side to side, wondering if there was anyone else at home. Finally she asked Miss Yu: "Is it just you?"

Miss Yu seemed to glean what the other lady was up to, and a great argument arose between them, loud enough for the neighbours to be stirred from their beds. The next day, Feng Xie heard of the disturbance from the night before and confronted Lin's wife as soon as she returned from the day's work.

"Tell me," said Feng Xie, starting his interrogation, "you've caught him haven't you? Your husband's been cheating on you?"

Lin's wife only lowered her head.

Feng Xie flew into a rage: "Let me tell you, I've chopped off my hair. I know what I must do. Don't tell me I need to speak to the widow, you just need to put it all to one side, just like I only repaired the roof tiles!"

Afterwards, the whole village was terrified of Feng Xie. Missing or showing up late to work became a thing of the past, and within six months, Qipan's terraced fields covered more land than any other village in the commune. Lao Pi arrived before too much more time passed, carrying an embroidered banner and 300 yuan to reward them for their hard work. The money was used to improve the local road, flattening its surface and planting poplar trees along its edges. Soon, other village heads were called to visit Qipan in order to learn from the example they set. Needless to say, it was a great source of pride and happiness for Feng Xie.

But this didn't stop him from asking Lao Pi what some might consider an odd question: "Since you've come here to praise me and what I've been able to achieve, how's about using your hair clippers to cut my hair?"

Evidently, there weren't any clippers in Qipan. They simply used a knife to cut hair and then scrape the blade across the skull until nary a hair was left. Mu Sheng obliged his request and asked him if he'd like the same haircut as Secretary Lao.

Feng Xie's response was not what Mu Sheng expected: "Are you trying to get me into trouble! Just give me a trim, short all over."

To Mu Sheng's dismay, Feng Xie's scalp was not entirely smooth; instead there were dips and bumps all over, which made cutting it difficult. Still, he persevered and cut the hair as short and as level as possible. Once done, Feng Xie looked much more alive, as though his spirit had been revived. Then a particular thought occurred to him: if all the men in Qipan were to receive the same haircut, then everyone throughout the commune would realise they were from Qipan, and thus know of their industriousness. He raised the idea with Lao Pi, suggesting he instruct Mu Sheng to proceed.

Afterwards, a directive was issued: men older than fifty could shave their heads bare. Those under fifty, however, would have to have their hair cut in the same style as their own village head. The directive didn't go off without a hitch, however. One villager, Huo Huo, worried about how he would look with such a haircut. His skull had an unusual shape, more akin to a dog's than a man's. As it happened, Huo Huo also owned a dog, so he got Mu Sheng to first trim the animal's hair in the manner that had been ordered. Mu Sheng consented and, once finished, they held a mirror up for the dog to see itself. Its reaction sealed the deal for Huo Huo: his dog took one look at itself, growled under its breath, and fell to the ground. Huo Huo did not want the same hairstyle.

"Alright," Feng Xie responded, "you don't need to get your hair cut, but neither will you be permitted into the fields to work."

Of course, if Huo Huo didn't work in the fields, he wouldn't earn work points, which, in turn, would mean he wouldn't get any rations either. There was little else to do but have Mu Sheng trim his hair as required. Thereafter, he took to wearing a straw hat whenever he stepped outside.

Since all the men were now sporting the same hairstyle, it made sense for the women to do the same. Soon, women below the age of fifty had uniform, shoulder-length hair. The former village head's daughter-in-law, however, wore her hair in long braids. Marrying into Qipan from another town deep in the mountains, and actually marrying the son of the then village head, she was reluctant to cut her braids that now reached down to her buttocks. Ultimately she relented – she had little choice in truth – but she wouldn't let her braids be thrown away. Instead, she picked them up after they fell to the floor and squirrelled them away in a household chest. From then onwards, she would take them out from time to time and look at them longingly, crying as she did so.

When the other village heads who had come to learn from Qipan's example saw the men and women wearing the same hairstyles, they couldn't help but remark on the sight: "Hey now... is this a village... are they farmers... or are they soldiers?"

Feng Xie was quick to reply: "Yes, I guess you could call them soldiers. After all, Qipan participated directly in the activities of Qinling's most famous guerrilla heroes, and we're their descendants. It makes sense. We just don't have the military attire to wear!"

Once Feng Xie's words spread, other towns lost no time in poking fun at Qipan's boast: "Ha! Descendants of Lao Hei's guerrilla band are they? What, didn't they spend only a couple of days in Qipan? They were able to spread their seed that quickly, huh!"

If only one or two of Qipan's residents went to Guofenglou's central market, they would be laughed at and ridiculed. However, when there were ten or twenty of them, no other village dared to insult them. In fact, they were more than a little terrified, and soon stories spread of Qipan's supposed prowess at Chinese boxing and other martial arts.

It was in this year, just after autumn, that Liu Xueren arrived in Qipan.

Naturally, Liu Xueren's arrival led to placards being made and revolutionary songs being sung. At the first meeting, the local revolutionary history was emphasised. Qipan, in short, was Red, the inheritors of Qinling's most honourable guerrilla history. The village had also protected the apricot trees once planted by Commander Kuang San.

The many mountains that stretched around Qipan were also marked by numerous streams and rivulets. The village itself was on the southern banks of these waterways. Leaving Qipan required a person to walk past the red cliffs, to snake their way through the stone paths that were etched across the mountains like so many lines on an acupuncture chart. Afterwards, one could turn northwards and take the path that wound its way there, a distance of about three *li*. There was also a passage that worked its way from the west of the village and straight down to the water. Here, one could hop across the stepping stones and reach the north bank that way. This was a difficult route, however, for the rocks jutted up unevenly from the water. Some were relatively close to each other while others were much farther apart. As a result, most women and children found the path too challenging, while younger men still needed to take a run up before leaping out onto the stones in the middle of the river.

In that year when the guerrilla band arrived in Qipan, they'd taken the trail that led past the red cliffs. Once in the village, their first order of business was to identify the family with the highest walls around their compound. The higher the wall, the wealthier the family, and thus the greater likelihood they were enemies of the people. The first such family they identified was Yang Shiqun's, whom they subsequently bound and threatened with violence unless they handed over food and money. The guerrillas had stayed in the area for three days when Yang's mother told them that her brother's child was about to celebrate his first month and that she had to attend. They released her, and the old woman summarily informed the county militia of the guerrilla band's presence in Qipan. The village was, of course, encircled and a fierce battle began. Both sides set the village on fire and then all that could be heard was the crackle and smack of gunfire. The conflict raged for most of the day and into the night. After the battle fought in Huangfujie, the clash in Qipan was the next most ferocious. The county militia of the time lost thirty-five men, the Qinling guerrilla forces lost twenty-one. A further nine were seriously injured. As for village bystanders, four lost their lives, the entire Yang family.

With the battle over, Kuang San scaled an apricot tree that stood behind one of the wealthier homes. The apricots were soft but not overripe. They were a golden colour and he reached out and grabbed one. He ate it quickly and then picked another. Two other guerrilla soldiers who were standing below the tree yelled up towards Kuang

San: "All you ever do is eat. Aren't you ever full! Toss us down a few, alright?"

But he didn't oblige, he just kept on eating. The apricots were sour too, forcing him to switch back and forth to either side of his mouth in order to keep on eating. When he'd finally had enough, he answered his comrades below: "Grandads!"

"Grandson!"

Kuang San took hold of an apricot, spied a rock below, and threw the apricot towards it. The fruit exploded on impact, its flesh spilling everywhere. He shouted to the other fighters once more: "Grandads!"

The men below didn't respond this time, but gunfire rang out across the mountains. Kuang San cursed: "What the hell're they doing, fucken knobs. The battle's over!" He swore again at the mountains and shook the tree violently. Apricots fell to the ground, and were quickly gathered up by the men below. The sound of rifle fire grew even more chaotic, and then Kuang San witnessed a group of men burst through Lao Hei's line. Some ran off in the direction of the reservoir that lay behind the trees, while others crouched down beside a nearby stone roller; both groups began to fire.

"The enemies are here!" shouted Kuang San. Unfortunately his mouth was still stuffed with apricot and so his words came out as a jumbled mess. The men seated below the tree failed to understand and so they did nothing. Kuang San shimmied down the tree, grabbed his weapon and ran off in the direction of a nearby alleyway.

The four of them raced past the rich man's home and they could see that, from behind the village, the local militia were arching down the valley, and in among their number was Yang Shiqun's old wife. Kuang San knew immediately she had informed on them. He took aim and fired at the woman but missed his mark. They kept moving and were soon at the main gate to Yang's compound. He could see the entire Yang family in the compound, Yang and his father, his mother was there too, as well as his son. They were scanning the area where the militia had first appeared. Kuang San raised his rifle and fired twice. His comrades fired as well. The bullets tore into flesh and the family members collapsed to the ground, one after the other.

The guerrilla band retreated towards the reservoir. Lao Hei and the others had already made it to the mountain pass. Unluckily for them, the militia had seen fit to dispatch troops down the same route in order to block a potential escape. When Lei Bu spied Kuang San, he shouted: "To the river, the river. Retreat to the rear and fight!"

Kuang San and the other men turned around and headed west, running hard. The path ran directly along the riverbank and would ultimately allow them to come up on the rear flank of the militia. Fortune was not with them, however, for rocks had fallen and obstructed the route. The enemy had spotted them from their vantage point higher up the mountain and began to rain bullets down on them. One of the men fell, a rifle shot ending his fight. Another lost his footing and fell. Kuang San grew increasingly tense.

"Fuck!" Kuang San shouted. "There're no damn trees to even use as a bridge!" Bits of apricot tumbled out of his mouth and he realised he'd still been chewing them. He tossed the remaining apricots in among the stones that littered the riverbank and took several steps back in order to have a sufficient amount of track to make a running leap. He landed near the far bank, but still in the water. Wading through, Kuang San was relentless and finally scurried up the other side. There, in a more promising position, he fired at the militia troops, picking them off one by one. The path clear, Lao Hei and his men escaped Qipan…

At least, this was the story we heard when we visited the village. When I investigated a little further, I discovered the row of apricot trees, their trunks wide and strong, towering up into the sky. They'd been planted evenly, orderly, and they'd grown in the same manner, their branches outstretched and broad, matching the angle of the slope. The location of the trees meant everyone had to pass by them if they wished to reach the other side of the river. It must be said, the trees were a strange sight and I wondered how they could have grown as they did, where they did, especially since they were apricot trees. Of course there was a connection to the battle we'd heard about. Kuang San had, after all, been munching apricots as he fought the enemy. He'd had three or four men with him, and he'd ultimately wiped out the county militia's machine guns. There was no doubting it: Kuang San had been responsible for the apricot trees growing here as they did, of all places.

Liu Xueren had first seen the trees while clambering down the side of the cliff, a rope wrapped tightly around him so that he wouldn't fall. He wouldn't permit anyone else to step on the same land on which the trees grew. He treated them almost reverentially, even unearthing some of their roots in order to lay additional fertiliser. Afterwards, he ordered for the area to be roped off and then had a small pavilion constructed a little way up the cliff. A placard was also nailed up, on which Liu Xueren himself had written the heroic revolutionary story of the apricot trees. The site became another education spot for teaching of the revolution.

Once the apricot grove had been so designated, the commune offices of Guofenglou were sure to disseminate the information, and soon afterwards neighbouring villages were dispatching groups of pilgrims to the site. Lao Pi also requested the county capital to send the official photography team to take pictures of the area; he wanted to send them to Kuang San. The commander himself never visited the trees, but he did telephone the county secretary and asked him to pass on his greetings to his comrades in Qipan. The county secretary was only too eager to convey the greetings, so he immediately set off for Qipan. Unsurprisingly, every other junior secretary across the region visited Qipan as well. The various propaganda offices throughout the commune dispatched people to see the site first-hand, followed by the cultural centres and broadcast stations. As a result, the road into Qipan was widened, and electricity lines were even laid. The village now possessed electric lights and telephones, and loudspeakers were naturally installed, one at the local committee offices, the other hanging on a poplar tree near the reservoir.

Liu Xueren held an important cadre position in the commune, but he was also in charge of public security in Qipan. He worked well with Feng Xie, so much so that Lao Pi took to referring to them as a golden partnership. Together they implemented two new policy initiatives, the first built upon Feng Xie's haircut directive for which Liu Xueren added an additional requirement: uniforms. The plan was to use the funds the county had been awarded and supply the peasants with clothes to wear while working. The attire would be newly made from the canvas cement bags just purchased from the factory. They would be stored in the main offices, ready to be picked up and worn by the local workers in the morning before they went to the fields. Of course, at the end of the day, they'd have to return the uniforms since they would be owned by the commune as a whole.

The second new initiative had to do with lunch. Namely, instead of dividing up the yield of potatoes grown across the expanse of fields, these would all be collected together and then, at noon, they'd be brought along to the fields themselves and served to those working. Each person would receive three potatoes. They could eat them and continue working without wasting the time it took to return to the village and have lunch.

It took approximately a month for these new initiatives to come into full effect, but once they did, all the villagers were ecstatic. In fact, other villages in the area began to look at Qipan quite enviously. This pleased Liu Xueren no end, which in turn made him call even more meetings, just to lord it over the other villages and make them grow even more jealous of what they were doing in Qipan. He'd announce, too, that not only did Qipan provide free haircuts to its inhabitants, it also provided them with clothes and food. In the future, he added, they'll build more houses and more multi-storeyed structures. These would all have electricity and telephones, too. When people awoke in the morning, he assured everyone, they would open their eyes, take a look around and realise communism had truly arrived!

There was one hitch, however: once people put on the new workers' uniforms, they changed. Their backs became stiff, their brains turned to wood. All they knew was that they had to work hard; they couldn't be late, nor could they leave early. They even felt they must relieve themselves as quickly as possible, whether it was a number one or a number two. The people became more like chickens or dogs, or perhaps more akin to mosquitoes, always buzzing around. In the past, when the sun came up and the cocks would crow, there'd be a chorus of one or two, but that was it. Now, however, it was as though the early morning crowing didn't stop. The loudspeaker would blare across the village, Liu Xueren's voice carried on the air, ensuring everyone got up, and quickly too.

Because they were rising earlier and earlier, many took to not washing their faces before heading out. In fact, their eyes would remain closed and they would simply stumble out into the crowd and be carried along with it, like a dog following its own tail. For those a little bit more awake, they'd try to stir their sleepwalking companions.

"Here, take it. It's a hot pepper. It'll wake you up!"

Whether it involved wielding a sickle or fertilising the fields, the work would continue throughout the day. Even when their waists felt as though they would snap as a result of the constant bending over, or when they had the urge to sit and smoke a little, just to relax for a spell, as soon as they sat down, they couldn't help but be swarmed by mosquitoes. So vicious and unrelenting were the insects, the villagers were forced to straighten up and get back to work.

They'd have to work through the morning without a break until the baskets with the potatoes arrived, when the sun was at its highest. A great canvas mat would be spread out on the ground and the potatoes placed in little mounds of three. There'd be a small dish of salt, too, and once everything was set, they would sit around the edges of the canvas mat and eat their lunch.

On one occasion, however, Liu Xueren's voice echoed after they'd eaten just a single mouthful: "Stop!"

Qipan's potatoes were especially delicious, fairly dry and soft, forcing most people to eat by holding the potato in one hand and positioning their other hand just beneath in order to catch whatever fell.

Liu Xueren's voice blared again: "Let's sing, everyone on cue. We'll sing a *Folk Song for the Party to Hear*. It'll help us to relax, but stop eating... if you don't, you'll end up choking. Swallow the food first... alright... remember too, its rhythm isn't the easiest." He paused for a minute, but when he spoke again there was anger in his voice: "Alright, come on everyone, one, two, three – sing!"

The villagers' voices rose and filled the air. All the while, their eyes looked anxiously upon the potatoes, seemingly worried someone would try to nick them, or that their three were smaller than someone else's. It went without saying, of course, that three potatoes were hardly enough to fill a person's belly, let alone enough fuel for the afternoon's work. For many, their stomachs felt as though they were inhabited by ghosts, a forever hungry apparition that would often grab at one's throat, strangling them for more food.

"Water! Did no one bring any water?" was a common refrain. There were usually two containers of water brought along with the potatoes, and after a ladleful, the potatoes in their gullet would be properly mixed. A belch served as confirmation.

Because lunch was less than filling, many workers had taken to eating more at the end of the day. Unfortunately, however, by spring the village's grain reserves had been depleted, and more and more families were reduced to going without. Initially, rice would be supplemented with cornmeal, then radishes would be sliced and turned into a soupy broth. The only problem was, one trip to the bathroom, even just to piss, would result in the person being hungry again. As things got worse, more and more people turned to begging beyond the limits of the village. Regrettably for them, such practices were no longer allowed, and it was considered better to die of starvation than resort to begging for alms. And besides, Qipan could ill afford to lose members of its population and so most took to eating leaves, bark and whatever else they could find.

In fact, people began to look at nearly everything for its potential to be consumed. There was a certain look of ravenousness about many that caused farm animals to jump whenever their eyes fell upon a villager. Pigs would squeal and cows would moo in fright if someone approached, or they would cease all movement and remain quiet. Those who raised piglets privately understood, however, that once the animals reached maturity, they would be given over to the nation, usually in exchange for thirty *jin* of grain. As a result, they couldn't simply eat them. Cows fell under even more complicated regulations since they were considered to be communally owned and to be primarily used as beasts of burden. Chickens and dogs, on the other hand, were considered private, so if a family decided to eat them, they had every right to do so. Of course, this often meant that those who had such animals had to be careful they weren't stolen and eaten by someone else. Consequently, many households took to reinforcing their fences and sheds, even installing locks, to keep their animals under better protection.

As for the village's feline residents, they ran about unmolested; evidently, the locals had thought it improper to eat cats and kittens, primarily because they served a useful purpose of hunting rats and mice. If one happened upon a cat that had just killed a mouse, most would give the cat a whack and take the mouse away from it; after all, mouse flesh was rather tender. There was a negative consequence of this treatment of cats, however: they began to stop hunting vermin in the village and instead shifted their hunting grounds to the fields and the rats and mice that lived there. Qipan's cats were actually quite adept at finding mouse holes, so much so that farmers soon took to following them, sneaking up behind them in an effort to steal their prey. The cats, always one step ahead, would race off once they had a meal and scale a nearby tree, well out of the reach of the farmers below. In response, the villagers would dig up the holes themselves and take whatever grain the mouse had stored away. Sometimes it would be corn, sometimes wheat, sometimes even beans. Such finds, however, were often fought over. On one such occasion, the wife of Wang Laibao, who was known throughout the village for her protruding mouth and considered the ugliest woman around, dug up a particular mouse hole that was filled with nearly three pecks of grain. The discovery caused a fierce argument among the other farmers, which finally resulted in a physical confrontation. As fists and feet were hurled at each other, an elderly lady broke down weeping, only to be cursed at by one of the men: "If you had a mouth like Laibao's wife, well, there's no way I'd have struck you!"

Despite the variety of methods employed to get more food, none were particularly successful. Nevertheless, the villagers still brought whatever they had to eat to the centre of Qipan and there, below the Manchurian catalpa tree, they'd eat. In the past, the residents were said to believe that the tree was at least 300 years old, that it had lived for so long it possessed a unique spirit. They spoke of how it had seen more than eight generations of people come and go. For those who came to eat underneath the tree, it became customary for them to place a morsel of food between the branches as a sort of offering.

Now, despite the lack of food, they continued to offer some to the tree. Instead of a mouthful, however, it would be a grain of rice or a single bean and usually nothing more. This is not to say they no longer respected the tree, for many could still be heard to call out: "Grandfather Tree, please eat!" The ceremony complete, they'd retrieve the small bit of food they'd placed in the tree and swallow it quickly before walking off to read the nearby bulletins that were changed almost daily.

The bulletins invariably proclaimed news about the revolution, its successes and how things were only getting better. The notices also served to promulgate nationwide directives, as well as those initiatives launched at the local level. National decrees always came first, followed by county and municipal pronouncements. Below these statements were enumerated the various punishments for any failure to comply: whoever failed to show up to work, whoever came late, or were lazy, or spent too much time going to the toilet, or whoever indulged in idle talk, would all be penalised and have five work points deducted from their dossiers. One day's work was worth ten points, which could be converted into two *jiao*-worth of money. The loss of five work points thus meant half of their daily allowance would be lost as well.

For most, after reading the bulletins, their faces would turn pale and hard, more akin to iron than flesh. Others would let their feelings show. Usually these were emotions of anger and indignation at what they had read. But they didn't blame Feng Xie, or Liu Xueren. Instead, their curses were levied at what the bulletins meant: "What dirty fuck informed on me, huh!" When such curses were heard, no one dared make eye contact with anyone else. Most would simply plunge their faces into a nearby bowl, licking the bottom if need be, pretending to eat when in fact they had very little or nothing at all. One of them, a man by the name of Cui Bajin, would lick his bowl so rapturously that bystanders would shout at him, reproaching him for the racket he was making and wondering if he might not be a pig in human clothing.

The villagers were remarkably flexible in these matters, it must be noted. Wang Cun's wife, for instance, didn't take much notice of who cursed whom; she'd just bitch at the ants that scurried about, stealing whatever bits of cornmeal gruel might fall from her bowl.

Another villager, an old man who lived in the eastern part of Qipan and was known as Lao Qin, also took to eating his food below the tree, but in most cases it would comprise a few slices of radish steeped in a larger quantity of oil. Whenever anyone looked into his bowl, they'd nearly always exclaim in disgust: "Geez! Ya think you've got enough oil there or what!"

"Eh," Lao Qin would begin his reply, "it's just I've caught a field mouse is all."

"But more than half of it is grease!"

Such an exchange would draw the attention of other people, who out of curiosity couldn't help but come over and see for themselves. The bubbles of grease covered more than half of the surface, and they were clearly derived from the meat of some animal or other, given their distinct globular shape. But the villagers were left wondering about the great amount of grease, and the odour that came with it. It was at that moment that their expressions changed. They recalled stories from five days before, news of two people starving to death in the town of Yanjiamao. It was actually how the deaths were first discovered that was most disturbing, for the authorities soon had to deal with the first case of cannibalism. Apparently, the bodies had been found in a nearby collapsed limestone kiln. One of the bodies had nearly half its flesh carefully sliced off. The victim, unsurprisingly, had been a local beggar; the culprit, it seemed, was a resident, a pockmarked good-for-nothing. The most disturbing feature of the story came when the police went to apprehend the man. They discovered that the family cooking pot that was boiling away was filled with human flesh, the surface covered with the same globular spots of grease they'd seen in Lao Qin's bowl.

Needless to say, the crowd around the tree dispersed as soon as it dawned on them what Lao Qin was probably eating. The rumour concerning his meal soon spread like wildfire. Questions abounded, too. If it was indeed human flesh he was eating, where had it come from? There was a recent birth in the village, and the child had become sick after only four days and died two days later. Its poor little body was deposited in the ravine; could that be what he was eating? When this story reached the young woman in question, she broke into tears, sought out Feng Xie immediately, and claimed Lao Qin had been eating the flesh off the bones of her dead baby. The baby had died in such unfortunate circumstances, too, she wailed. And she'd used a clean quilt to wrap his tiny body, most respectfully, as a means to pray that he'd be reborn, that she'd once again carry him in her belly... but how could that happen now, now that Lao Qin, the monster, the wolf, the dog had eaten him?

Feng Xie took the matter very seriously and assured the young woman he would launch an investigation. The first order of business was to call Lao Qin in for questioning. He did this immediately, and over the course of the evening Lao Qin confessed to finding the baby in the gully. He added, too, that the tiny corpse had already been mauled by a wild dog and there was barely half of the body left. The remaining half he took for himself and boiled it up to eat. Upon hearing the old man's confession Feng Xie became enraged, striking him hard and knocking him to the floor.

"Did you really eat it?"

"Yes."

"Tell me… truthfully… did you really eat it?"

"Yes… yes, I did."

Feng Xie moved closer to the old man, raised his hand again and slapped him hard across the face. "You dirty old fucker… you've tarnished my standing in this place! You ate human flesh, you bastard… do you know what'll happen once this gets out? Did you ever think of that… you ate… you really did!"

"Well," Lao Qin began hesitantly, "I didn't…"

"If you didn't, then where'd the grease come from, huh? Was it placenta or something?"

"Yeah, that's what it was, a placenta… that's what I ate."

It was customary for Guofenglou's residents to take a woman's placenta after birth and bury it beneath the nearest tree. It was supposed to ensure the child's health, that it would grow big and strong just like the tree. On the following day, Feng Xie announced the findings of his investigation.

"Lao Qin hasn't eaten human flesh," Feng Xie proclaimed. "I know he wouldn't try to deceive me… I declare here now he's not eaten the dead child, it was only a placenta that he tried to eat."

Feng Xie paused for a moment, then continued: "Poor old Lao Qin happened to notice a family burying a placenta at the foot of a nearby tree, as is common in Guofenglou. Then, when night came, he sneaked back to the tree and exhumed it… I agree, he shouldn't have done this, but he was desperate… which means you must forgive his transgression, especially since eating placenta was once a widespread means of treating illness… you all know this… the placenta would be dried over fire, then crushed and mixed with water, the mixture then swallowed. You cursed this man… you called him foul and dirty, but is this really the case? No, it isn't… and, truly speaking, who would… who could cook up such meat and eat it? Why, the smell alone would cause even the stoutest stomach to churn, would it not?"

Throughout the difficult and lean times that stretched from February to August, not a single person died of starvation in Qipan, nor did anyone take to wandering the countryside begging for food. At the first autumnal general meeting for the commune, Lao Pi sang the praises of Liu Xueren and Feng Xie.

"The national government, in its wisdom, has once again allocated relief provisions for rural communes. The first recipient will be Qipan, as reward for all of your hard work."

Soon afterwards, the provisions arrived. But they weren't corn, or soybeans. Instead, they were dried radish slices; apparently, the entire yield was to be given to Qipan. Naturally, this got other villages into talking and offering their own opinions as to why Qipan was treated so well. Lao Pi had had his own explanation: Qipan was at the vanguard of the revolution, he said, so their work was to be rewarded! In every other village, inhabitants had died due to hunger; they'd also had people leave to beg wherever they could. As a result, there was really very little they could say to counter Lao Pi's pronouncement. One town in particular, a place called Wangbasi, took Lao Pi's words to heart and decided to change.

Prior to Liberation, Wangbasi had already fallen on hard times. Many of its buildings had collapsed and so all that was left was a traditional three-winged structure. After the repairs, the locals erected a placard across the building's entrance declaring it to be a site of one of the first soviet-style governments in Qinling. In fact, the placard claimed Wangbasi was the first such site, established by Qinling's heroic guerrilla band well before the victory of the revolution. Associated records and whatever else they could find to prove this history were summarily brought to the commune offices, along with a request for Wangbasi to be given special political and economic attention.

Of course, Lao Pi came looking for me as soon as he heard the news, questioning me as to whether it was true or not. I told Lao Pi that I was suspicious. I'd gone to Wangbasi and visited the structure in question, I'd checked the historical records on the guerrilla band and discovered no mention of any soviet. Nor could I remember anything first-hand myself. I never once heard mention of soviet-style governments in Qinling. It wasn't long before Lao Pi ordered me to visit another town. Apparently, the village of Kouqian was also claiming to have discovered a placard and slogans written by Qinling's guerrilla heroes; they too were requesting assistance in protecting such revolutionary heritage and of making the area a tool for teaching about the revolution. During my visit, I was escorted to a collapsed wall, and had the following words pointed out to me: 'Join the guerrillas, down with reactionaries!' The words were there alright, but I could also see they were written only very recently.

Qipan persevered with its vanguard practices. The people still ate communally after the work was complete. The only problem was that there were no longer any potatoes, only the dried radish provisions allocated by the central government. It was said the radishes were grown and then shipped from Xinjiang. They were yellowish in colour, and rather tough, almost muscly. They also had a somewhat odd flavour, and were very pungent. The smell was reminiscent of wet shoes in winter when they were put next to the fire to dry. Most people actually felt terrible stomach pains after eating them, and often burped up a sour liquid as a result. But it didn't seem to matter, at least not to the visitors who came to learn from Qipan. When they saw the apricot trees, saw everyone in matching uniforms, eating together, all they would feel was hatred towards their own towns, regret that they didn't have the same forward-looking leader, or that they hadn't been born in Qipan itself.

In response to the rumbling in their own jurisdictions, the village head of Wangbasi, along with the branch secretary from Kouqian, toured Qipan, intent on seeing again, first hand, the success of the village.

"I guess this really is a village at the vanguard of the revolution," remarked Wangbasi's village head. "We should praise it!"

"What's so good about this place?" asked the branch secretary. "Bullshit is all it is… they're only eating dried, sliced radish… it's all smoke and mirrors… that's what it is! Look over there, huh, there's a couple of old-timers sitting in the sun, their trousers rolled up and everything… you grab one leg and I'll grab the other… then they'll talk."

"What're they even doing?"

"They don't look like they're doing much of anything at all," answered the branch secretary. "Maybe they're watching that fucken hole there…"

"Look... are they suffering from dropsy like almost everyone else?"

As soon as the local residents spied the outsiders, they rolled their trousers down, mumbled to themselves that more men had come to inspect their village, and then they got up and walked away.

The two outsiders continued their tour and soon came upon a toilet. Like nearly everywhere else, it, too, had revolutionary slogans emblazoned across the outer wall. There was no curtain covering the doorway either, and they could see a villager squatting down over the hole inside. He seemed to smile at their intrusion, displaying not an ounce of shame.

"How's it?" began Wangbasi's village head, surprised at the man's reaction. "I mean, how have Feng Xie and Liu Xueren been able to manage the village in this way?" As they strolled closer to the toilet however, they soon realised the man wasn't smiling at them at all; he was doing his utmost to shit, his face screwed in near agony to empty his bowels.

When spring finally arrived, the new yield from the fields came as well. The villagers were once again able to enjoy roasted and boiled potatoes. With renewed energy, they were able to clear the soil and plant an additional ten *mu* of terraced land for Qipan. By the approach of winter, they'd also constructed irrigation canals to better supply and drain the new fields.

Qipan was cold in winter, the coldest region in the entire commune. It was dangerous to even put bare skin to rock for it would stick almost immediately. Most standing water froze within minutes, even the water used for drinking and cooking, washing and bathing. Sturdy wooden sticks were always necessary to break the ice. On the days that followed the winter solstice, the coldest days of the calendar, even the ground froze solid and nothing would survive. People would stay indoors during this period, nestled close to the brazier. The women would usually concentrate on their needlework, mending the family's clothes, knitting new ones. The men would busy themselves weaving their straw shoes and tidying up their cellars. But this winter was unlike previous ones. Instead of the quiet most were accustomed to, now they could all hear the blaring loudspeaker calling them out to meetings. They had to study, listen to Liu Xueren lecture them and sing revolutionary songs, of course.

By spring, divisions between Feng Xie and Liu Xueren began to emerge. As a result, Feng became less inclined to ensure the smooth operation of the many meetings Liu called. He simply didn't see the point in repeatedly lecturing the villagers on the same things, nor did he understand why they had to keep singing the familiar revolutionary songs. Feng didn't understand why a Party cadre had to become so regimental, so unyielding, almost hard-hearted. He looked for an opportunity to voice these growing concerns, but no one in the town would dare stop listening to Liu's pronouncements.

Finally, Feng Xie was able to get Liu alone in the commune office, whereupon a fierce argument broke out between them. As they argued, a slithering sound could be heard in the rafters of the building and they both looked up to see the unwelcome sight of a snake sliding across the roof beam. About three feet in front of the reptile, a rat was itself clinging to the beam, staring back at the predator, unmoving. A second passed and the rodent squealed just before the snake sunk its teeth into it. A moment later, the only sign of the rat was the bulge in the snake's abdomen.

"To control people," said Liu Xueren, resuming his diatribe, "you must make them fear you… but to do this over a long period of time, well then, you need to get your mitts on their hearts. That's how you maintain control."

"So that's your reasoning," Feng Xie said. "That's why you call them to meetings every day, get them to listen to you, sing the revolutionary songs… aren't you turning them into mindless pond frogs, all croaking in unison!"

"It's called indoctrination. Grabbing hold of a single person's finger isn't enough. But taking hold of a thousand, ten thousand, that's a different story…"

Feng Xie shook his head, but Liu Xueren continued: "It's my experiment… ah… it's too bad Mu Sheng doesn't live in Qipan. Alright then… I'll carry out another experiment for you… the previous village head… yes… he has his opinion of you, no doubt… he's also a robust, healthy man. I'll dispatch some men to tell him he's much too undernourished, that he shouldn't be out and about this winter… you watch, I'll make him undernourished for sure."

Liu Xueren did as he promised. Whenever one of his men saw the old village head, they'd remark on his health, wonder if he was sick and ask why he was so seemingly underfed. The former village head would retort by saying there was nothing wrong with him, that he was fine, but the next day, he'd endure the same questions again from one of Liu Xueren's men. This continued for days, the same encounter, the same questions. The old village head's responses changed, however. Now, when he was asked about his health, he'd put his hands to his face and agree: he *was* getting thinner. It took fewer than twenty days for Liu Xueren's experiment to yield tangible results: the previous village head had grown thinner, his body ached and he felt generally unwell. Finally, a doctor was called, medicine was prescribed and imbibed. The experiment was a success.

But Feng Xie didn't seem terribly pleased: "Your mouth's filled with poison!" he shouted at Liu Xueren.

"So is everyone else's," countered Liu.

Feng Xie no longer bothered with the meetings, or with singing the songs. He left all that to Liu Xueren.

For the entire winter, there was no rest for Qipan's residents. In the commune's central courtyard, fires were prepared and lit, the people called, each and every day, to come and study, to sing, to learn about the revolution. They would gather as close to the fires as possible to feel the warmth. Only when the sun fell would the meeting be called to a close. The fires would be put out, the still-glowing embers buried. On the following morning, the process would begin again. The still-hot embers would be uncovered and lit again, new wood would be brought to fuel the nascent flames.

As for the Xu household that had abandoned their dead child, now they had a dog to care for. The animal once belonged to Lao Qin, but after the incident with the placenta, the dog had been given to them as… compensation. That had been Feng Xie's decision. Unfortunately for the woman, she could not forget that her dead baby visited her in her dreams every night, haunting her, snapping at her legs with a half-mauled face. To try to ward off the evil, whenever the family went outdoors they would pull the dog along with them. They even took it to the meetings, and the animal, just like the people, would stand as close to the warm fires as possible. The gathered residents then began to suggest the dog be tied up outside. The dog became a regular participant of the meetings, whether near the fire or tied up at the gate. Soon, it began to bark along with Liu Xueren's words, almost as though it understood what he was saying. Later, it seemed to learn the songs, too, and could be heard howling in chorus with the villagers. At first, no one paid much attention to the beast, but on one occasion, when the gathered villagers ceased singing, the dog continued well after, and as it happened, Mu Sheng had just arrived with missives from Lao Pi. Upon hearing the animal sing, Mu Sheng was obliged to report this to his superior. Not long after, Lao Pi arrived to see for himself.

Qipan's residents had grown increasingly comfortable with all of the new political language. They could also sing a great number of revolutionary songs, but when it came time to launch the movement to eradicate the last vestiges of capitalism, very few were forthcoming about their own actions. No one admitted to exchanging cotton for grain or to using it to buy tofu, eggs, walnuts... nor did anyone inform on anyone else. Meetings had been called, more than a few, but no one volunteered any information. This caused no small amount of consternation for Liu Xueren and Feng Xie.

"Why, I wonder," complained Liu Xueren, "why can't this country manufacture a drug... you know, something that everyone would have to take, and once they did, they'd reveal every little secret they knew? Why?"

Some days later, Liu Xueren returned after a trip to the county capital with several bottles of medicine, and he told Feng Xie to make sure every villager took some. Naturally, Feng Xie wondered what it was, but Liu's response was only that he shouldn't worry about such things. Just tell everyone that it would make them tell the truth. Every person had to take one dose, with water if needed. Upon hearing the instructions, most of the villagers were worried, and behind closed doors they debated and weighed up the pros and cons of coming clean or keeping things secret, for as long as they could at least. The debates, however, didn't last very long, as most soon felt a deep pain in their abdomen that forced them to run to the nearest toilet. After a few excruciating minutes, they all shat out a roundworm, or so they soon discovered having asked their neighbours, ever so quietly, if the same thing had happened to them.

At the next meeting, the gathered villagers still said nothing about supposed capitalistic activities they might have been engaged in. Finally, Feng Xie directed a question towards Liu Xueren: "Just what was it that you made everyone take, hmm? Why did they all end up shitting out a roundworm?"

Annoyed and perturbed, Feng Xie turned to the crowd and waved his hand, dismissing them. At the same time, something strange occurred to Liu Xueren: perhaps he could launch his investigation by asking each of the villagers, one by one, what they had dreamed over the course of the past seven days. That would constitute a form of investigation, wouldn't it? Once he'd spoken to everyone, and made records of all their responses, he could spend nights pondering the significance and meaning of their stories couldn't he? So that's what he did… unfortunately, he couldn't figure anything out, so he came to Guofenglou looking for me.

"Thinking is part of every day," he told me. "Are dreams part of every night, then?"

"Not necessarily," I told him.

"What does water mean in dreams?"

"According to the old stories, water signifies wealth."

"And fire?"

"Prosperity."

"What about dreams in which lice crawl all over you? And stepping in shit, what does that symbolise? How about if you see your dead parents… they've been dead for years… but in your dream your father is walking out the door to make up some herbal remedy… what does that mean? And what about people fighting in their dreams, or wanting to piss but you can't find a toilet, wind blowing over trees, teeth falling out, cats catching mice, people getting married, snowy days, fish in a stream, people borrowing shoes, clothes suddenly torn, digging into stone, someone's intestines hanging on the outside for everyone to see, giving birth to a child without a nose or eyes, eating nails, hailstones falling on a bright, sunny day, a loom that's missing its shuttle…"

He paused and turned to the next page in his notebook. It was empty.

I took advantage of his hesitation to ask my own question: "If you could get Qipan's pigs, dogs, cats and chickens to speak, then no household would have any secrets."

"That… that I can't do."

"Well, then, I can't help you either."

"What do you mean you can't help!"

"Liu Xueren, let me tell you, people are always up to something, but only heaven can know exactly what."

"You're right… well put."

I never would've thought Liu Xueren would take what I said and try to teach it to the villagers. Mu Sheng told me about it. He'd gone to Qipan on Lao Pi's orders and Liu Xueren had told him that my words had been quite inspiring, so much so, in fact, that he made the villagers believe the poplar trees had grown eyes in order to watch everyone. Some, he'd told Mu Sheng, had three or four eyes, others had nearly ten. And to properly frighten the villagers into thinking they were being watched, Liu Xueren went to great pains to convince them the eyes were the eyes of heaven, that while people mightn't see what others were up to, the heavens would! I laughed when Mu Sheng told me this, for I knew the supposed eyes were nothing but knots in the wood, but that didn't take anything away from what they looked like, for it wasn't that great a leap of the imagination to think they were eyes, so similarly were they shaped. Mu Sheng admitted, then, that he hadn't noticed the eyes in the poplars before, but after what I said, he believed they were indeed!

Nevertheless, and in spite of Liu Xueren's efforts, the movement to eradicate the last traces of capitalism in Qipan still met with little success. Exasperated, Feng Xie cried out that perhaps they ought to make an example out of somebody in order to frighten everyone else.

As was usual practice, choosing someone to make an example of meant rounding up a local landlord, or a wealthy capitalist, a counterrevolutionary, a rightist or some other bad element. Unfortunately, there was only a single household in Qipan that fitted the bill, and the sole member of this family was a man who suffered from heart disease and spent his time in bed, his lips a perpetual purplish colour. Before Liberation, this family had already endured the wrath of Kuang San, who had killed the wealthy landlord's nephew, and left them essentially one step away from destitution.

Once Liberation swept through the area, the wealthy family head had died, leaving only the aforementioned sickly heir.

There was, however, a wealthy peasant, a man of seventy-eight years, who wandered through the village on a crippled leg that had become curled up and rigid about ten years previously. There was another family too. Its head was a former teacher at the county middle school. He'd been declared a rightist and thus deported back to his familial home. He kept pretty much to himself, his head always held low to avoid eye contact with the other villagers. No one heard him speak more than a couple of words each day.

These bad elements would most assuredly serve as scapegoats. To move things along, Liu Xueren made a note of each and every person from the village who'd previously made trades involving their rations, who had engaged in buying and selling, and those who had left to ply a handicraft trade elsewhere. Once the names were written down, Feng Xie was instructed to close his eyes and make a mark next to the names on the paper. These names would then be announced, the first being a young married woman by the name of Ma Lichun. She was considered the prettiest young woman around, and got on marvellously well with everyone, neither smiling at other villagers, nor speaking to them. In fact, she also had a connection to Liu Xueren, who had been living in one wing of her family home. As soon as he saw the name Feng Xie had marked, Liu was naturally taken aback.

"Eh? How's it that you've put a mark next to her name?"

Feng Xie also knew that her family wasn't guilty of anything serious, and so he proposed a somewhat suspect solution to their dilemma.

"You see this here coin," he said, pulling it from his pocket. "I'll flip it, and if it's heads, we'll give her a clean slate, and if it's tails, well, she'll have to suffer the consequences." He flipped. It landed tails.

A meeting was subsequently arranged and, as before, no one volunteered to say anything. Feng Xie broke the silence: "Ma Lichun, you're called to speak!"

She stood almost immediately, but the first words out of her mouth were not the ones anyone expected: "There must be an error. I'm no capitalist. I've no tail!"

"Tell me," Feng Xie retorted, "have you ever sold the homespun sashes you always wear around your waist?"

Ma Lichun offered no response to his accusation. She simply broke down and cried.

"There's no point in crying. We won't be swallowing any of that piss here today!"

Ma Lichun gathered herself up and finally offered a defence: "Alright, I did sell them before, but I had a good reason… my mother-in-law… that year she was so ill, it was really serious… and to make matters worse, they'd stopped providing sweet potatoes… and then the potatoes, too… when she was at death's door I only had a few noodles to give her… so I took my sash and sold it. When the village head learnt what I'd done, he deducted a full day's-worth of work points from me. The old village head… what about him, huh!"

The former village head had endured his share of suffering and had been seriously ill himself. In truth, he was a pale imitation of the man he'd once been. But he was still in attendance. When he heard Ma Lichun denounce him as she had, his head deep in a cloud of cigarette smoke, his only response was to say he wasn't the village head: "If you must call me anything, call me Grandad."

"Alright… Grandad, you're the person who authorised my actions. There… satisfied?"

"Yes… I suppose I did."

Ma Lichun smacked her own face before she spoke again: "It was only the one time… and I've already been punished. Am I to carry this crime with me forever? And besides, I'm not the only one in Qipan to have done this. Who'd dare say they haven't, huh?"

Ma Lichun's words had a clear effect on the rest of the gathered villagers. Some squirmed in their seats, some stood up, then sat down again, some thought to speak, others only opened their mouths to yawn. Altogether, there was quite a disturbance caused by Ma Lichun's accusation.

Finally, amid the hubbub, a person who'd been seated, smoking nonchalantly, spoke: "You're like a blind old bitch nipping at whatever she can!"

"Yeah," came other voices in the crowd, "what shit are you on about? Stop trying to drag us down with you. Focus on your own crimes!"

"But," said Ma Lichun, visibly humbled by the response, "I only sold a single sash."

"I've seen her selling eggs at the market too," came another shout from the crowd. "Whole baskets full… covered in grass to hide what she was doing."

"She's also swapped cotton for corn with the villages farther up in the mountains," someone else began, "and when the commune authorities raided the black market… well, she'd been too slow in trying to get away. She'd put her cotton wares down her trousers… they were easy to find. She was on her period then, too. When the cotton was pulled out it was all red."

Other people chimed in: "She'd also stolen wheat before… I saw it myself. I tried to stop her but she wouldn't return the wheat she'd taken. Instead she tried to seduce me, grabbed my hand and placed it on her bosom… but I resisted, I wasn't going to fall for her honey trap."

Ma Lichun protested her innocence: "What vicious lies, slander!" She yelled something else that could not be understood, and then made a run for it, desperate to extricate herself from the situation.

Feng Xie was irate at how things had turned out, and that ire was soon directed at Ma Lichun's husband: "And what the fuck are you doing about all of this! Surely you must've noticed something, huh? All criminals leave some clues! Go and get her, now!"

"But she won't listen to me," said her husband. "She never has…"

"Will someone help this poor sap to get her then," screamed Feng Xie. "Anyone… I don't care!"

In the company of a fellow villager by the name of Liu Shan, Ma Lichun's husband left to bring his wife back. It wasn't long, however, before Liu Shan came running back, shouting as he did so: "Ma Lichun's poisoned herself…"

Ma Lichun had run back home and straight to the portrait of her dead mother-in-law: "Mother… I've lost what little face I had… I'm coming to look for you!"

Frantically, she searched for rope to hang herself, but when that proved fruitless, she saw the vial of poison standing on a cabinet just behind the door to an adjacent room. It was used to kill lice and ought to be enough to do her in. She swallowed the concoction in a single gulp and then collapsed onto a nearby bed. Shortly afterwards, her husband and Liu Shan had arrived. She convulsed and gurgled and the two men saw what she had imbibed. They'd grabbed hold of her, pried her mouth open and rammed a finger down the back of her throat, all in an effort to get her to vomit the poison. Satisfied she'd spewed up what she could, they forced her to drink some starchy water. As she did so, Liu Shan had run back to report on what had happened. Soon after, she was treated at the local clinic, intubated and then subject to an enema. She survived, but was left brain damaged, forever after unable to perform even the simplest of tasks. She'd spend her days in near total stupor, sat down near the main road, a dumb smile on her face. To get her to move, all it took was for someone to shout that Feng Xie was coming. She'd leap to her feet almost immediately and run home, quite hysterically, locking the door behind her and standing behind it, a heavy metal pole in hand.

Feng Xie never once ventured to Ma Lichun's house after these events. He wouldn't even dare to walk by. To Liu Xueren he could only ask if he'd taken things too far, if he had been the cause of what happened to her.

Liu Xueren's response wasn't exactly comforting: "I'm still staying at her house and my conscience is clear. I was given the authority to launch this campaign against capitalist remnants. Who wouldn't congratulate us on what we've accomplished?"

"Ma Lichun was small fry, guilty of a minor offence," Feng Xie said. "But now she's considered a big catch…"

"Well, I certainly won't allow a big fish to escape the net," Liu Xueren said triumphantly. "Do you know… the whole obsession with face was what hindered our investigation, prevented us from exposing enemies of the revolution. No one wanted to call someone else out, not publicly at least… that's why I've changed tack. I've made it possible for people to anonymously inform on each other. Everyone's had to do it, too. I never expected such an approach to be so successful!"

The investigation box used for these anonymous tips was built by Ma Lichun's husband. It was sturdy, made of hardwood, with an opening on top five fingers long and one finger wide. The top, too, could open, so a lock was fastened to it. Once ready, Liu ordered it to be hung on the Manchurian catalpa tree that stood in the centre of the village.

From then on, it became a ritual for Feng Xie and Liu Xueren to open the box at dinnertime. Of course, for those who enjoyed their meals beneath the tree, they couldn't help but see the two men collect whatever had been written and bring it back to their office. No one would say anything while the scene played out, but as soon as they were gone, the villagers would whisper heatedly and anxiously about who had written what about whom.

On one such occasion, Feng Xie, having pulled a piece of paper out of the box and glanced at it, turned to look at the former village head's nephew, a cold smile across his face. Naturally, everyone assumed that someone had informed upon him, had called him out for some crime. On the following day, filled with spite, the young man brought his evening meal to the central square and spoke loudly for everyone to hear.

"Take a good look… I've got something to put in this damn box, too!"

"Ming Tang," called out another villager as the young man placed the paper in the box. "So who're you informing on, eh?"

"Whoever reported on me, well, I'm doing the same to them!"

"But how do you know who it was?"

"Ha ha, I know who it was… I worked it out myself!"

That evening few villagers slept well, each worrying if it had been them Ming Tang had informed upon… each wondering what he might have written… a tit for tat sort of retaliation. Others grew even more fearful of their neighbours, wondering if they would concoct crimes just to deflect attention away from themselves, going on the offensive instead of waiting simply to defend. Over the first few days, there had only been a strip or two of paper, but that number quickly increased. And as it did so, people grew more and more suspicious of each other.

There were about fifty clans in the village, the largest two being the Fengs and the Wangs. It was perhaps unsurprising the two families took to reporting on each other. Remarking on these developments, Feng Xie wondered aloud to his superior how they would ever be able to convene a public meeting again, for it seemed everyone in the entire village was guilty of something: "We can't slice off everyone's tail, can we! To make matters worse, the village has more or less split into two factions… just what're we to do?"

"Well," began Liu Xueren, "I believe things are working out alright. Yes, sure, they've sort of formed two factions, but we can use that… think about it… everyone is taking it all so seriously, which means they'll keep fighting against each other. And as for the both of us, well, such conflict'll only make our work even easier... and more productive, too."

But things didn't go exactly to plan. When they did finally call a meeting to announce things were winding down, that they were readying their report for Lao Pi, the person offered up by the residents of Qipan to be struggled against was Liu Sixue. He had to endure three struggle sessions before he was finally sent to the commune offices for re-education.

This Liu was the son of Liu Shaokang, who had already been sent for re-education due to a report filed by Wang Yaocheng. As a result, the younger Liu harboured an enormous amount of hatred towards the man responsible for getting his father apprehended and was desperate for an excuse to see Wang get his comeuppance. Of course, to do that, he needed some information.

Just as these events were transpiring, Mu Sheng had arrived in Qipan to to give the residents their required haircuts. Liu saw his chance. First, he invited Mu Sheng to his place, and then plied him with food. Once the other man had had his fill, he began his quest for inside information: "So tell me Mu Sheng... I treat you well, don't I?"

"Sure... well enough."

"Then tell me... hmm... has anyone reported on me? Have you seen who it was?"

"Now how would I know about something like that?"

"Oh," came the somewhat surprised response from Liu Sixue, "you're not privy to such details... I didn't know?"

As Mu Sheng ate the cornmeal rolls he'd been given, the buzz that had been plaguing him for far too long returned, causing him to rap on his head as he'd done before.

Liu Sixue continued: "You're here eating my food... don't you think that's deserving of something in exchange? Have a look at the eaves up there, hmm... they leak, do you know... it can be quite awful."

Mu Sheng cast his head upwards and saw the rotting wood, the places where the tiles had come free of the roof: "Sixue, I suggest you take it easy... don't go round trying to stir up anything."

"You're trying to give me advice, a spring chicken trying to tell an old cock what's up!"

Mu Sheng, however, did as was suggested. He climbed up onto the roof and made the necessary repairs. Carefully, precisely. As he did so, he still saw need to remind Liu Sixue of what he had said: "Remember, alright... remember."

Liu Sixue paid no heed to Mu Sheng's advice. In fact, he thought the whole exchange with Mu Sheng was quite funny. Then, in the early hours of that night, he awoke and found himself stealing towards the central square tree. He jimmied a strip of wire into the box and extracted the paper that had been stuffed inside. Taking the paper home, he unfurled it, read it and then stole back into the night to return it. Over the course of the following nights, he repeated his clandestine raiding of the investigation box. When he discovered notes written about him, he'd tear them up immediately. Those written about other villagers were returned, but not before he committed the words to memory. Needless to say, he was quite pleased with himself, assured in the knowledge that nothing written about him would make it to Feng Xie and Liu Xueren.

His demeanour betrayed his overconfidence: "Tell me, Wang Guanglin," he asked a neighbour he saw in the street one day, "do you have any kidney beans?"

"No... I've no kidney beans, but I do have haricots."

"In that case, how's about giving me some haricots?"

"How's about you giving me a grandson then, huh!" came Wang Guanglin's reply.

"Do you know... there's been something I've been wanting to talk to you about. I don't think I will now... just wait for your own misfortune to strike!"

Wang Guanglin thought Liu Sixue's response was rather odd, and it naturally spurred him to inform Feng Xie and Liu Xueren about the exchange. The two cadres already knew something was up in the village, for the notes they'd been collecting at dinnertime were much more wrinkled and scrunched up than before, some even seemed soiled, and so they had grown suspicious someone had been tampering with the box. Wang's report confirmed their suspicions and now they believed they had a suspect. That night, the two men staked out the central square and caught Liu Sixue red handed.

Ultimately, Liu had to endure several struggle sessions before being sent for re-education. The investigation box was also removed from the tree. In all subsequent meetings, the villagers were no longer reluctant to come forward and detail their supposed infractions. The first to do so was Feng Huan. As it happened, three days before the meeting was called, Feng was struck by a severe form of nerve paralysis that caused the right side of his face to contract violently. The best form of treatment was supposedly the application of blood extracted from the local swamp eel, which gave his face an almost deathly look. He admitted in front of everyone his previous capitalist transgressions and that now he wished to chop off that particular tail, to root out all traces of such impulses. To do otherwise would be wrong, but if he proved unsuccessful, then he encouraged his fellow villagers to call him out, to force him to swallow whatever pesticides they had to hand, to truss him and shoot him if necessary. The next person to speak echoed Feng Huan's words, and the third person did the same. One after the other they stood up and professed their strongest desire to root out all capitalist inclinations.

The local rightist was the last to speak. But he didn't parrot what everyone else had said. In fact, his entire demeanour was of someone terrified of saying a single word, fearful that anything he said would be in error. Instead, he wrote a four-line poem on his hand and read that out to the crowd. His performance was repeated at each subsequent meeting. Each poem began with two lines alluding to something wholly unrelated to the debate. The last two were always the same: Sincerely reform one's character and be an upright man, lift high the red flag of the revolution to forge ever onwards!

—

I'll start with the first sentence; you begin with the second.

The third part of *Pathways Through the Western Mountains* begins with Chongwu Mountain. It lies south of the Yellow River, sometimes known as the Great River, with its north face looking towards Mount Zhongsui; its southern face overlooks the Yao Marshes. To the west is another mountain on which, it is said, the Lord of Heaven wrestled with many great beasts; to the east is the Yan Abyss, a deep gorge that cuts into the earth. A unique tree grows on Chongwu Mountain. Its leaves are round, its sepals are white, its flowers are red with dark veins running through them and it produces a citrusy fruit. Eating the fruit is said to increase a man's virility and help him sire many children. An ape-like beast lives on this mountain. Its arms share the same markings found on leopards and tigers, and it is skilled at throwing things. It is known as the jufu. The manman are common on Chongwu Mountain. They look like ducks but have only one wing and one eye. The only way it can take flight is to find a companion manman. Its appearance signals imminent floods for all under heaven.

Three hundred leagues west is Drifting Sands Mountain. Limpid River originates here, flows in a northerly direction and then empties into the River You. The mountain lacks vegetation of any kind, but there is much realgar.

The Inattentive Mountain rises three hundred and seventy leagues farther to the west. To the north, one can see Mount Zhubi, which, in turn, looks out upon Chongyue Mountain. The You Marshes open out to the east and serve as a secret tranche for the Yellow River; great gurgling noises can be heard at its source. Fruit-bearing trees are plentiful here. Their leaves are like those of the jujube tree, while their fruit resembles a peach. When they flower, they have yellow blossoms and red sepals. Consuming the fruit will revive one's strength.

Mishan Mountain is situated four hundred and twenty leagues to the northwest. Cinnabar trees grow in great number near the summit. Their leaves are round, their stems are red, their flowers are yellow and their fruit a deep crimson. The fruit has a syrupy taste and is very filling. The Cinnabar River starts its journey here. It flows in a westerly direction and then empties into Millet Marsh. There is a great deal of white jade on Mishan Mountain. Molten jade can be found in the Cinnabar River. It pushes up from under the riverbed and swirls about. It was said the Yellow Emperor greatly enjoyed consuming this molten jade and would hold elaborate dinners in its honour. When the molten jade cooled, it took on a dark hue. The cinnabar trees on Mishan Mountain draw water from the river and thus drink the molten jade as well. As a result, when the trees reach five years of age, they burst into five different colours, each colour effusing a different fragrance. The Yellow Emperor was so enamoured by the splendiferous blossoms that he had them cut and taken to Bell Mountain; he placed them facing the sun to better marvel at their wondrous colours. Lapis lazuli can also be found on Mishan Mountain. They are of superb quality, firm and sublimely coloured. If lightly polished, they will shine even more and emit an otherworldly radiance. As a result, the spirit-gods of Earth and sky are very fond of consuming these gems; they readily accept them as sacrificial offerings. Gentlemen scholars are keen to wear the lapis lazuli as pendants to ward off calamity. The area between Mishan Mountain and Bell Mountain is mostly marshland and covers a distance of 460 leagues. It is home to fantastic birds, fish and strange creatures.

Four hundred and twenty leagues northwest is Bell Mountain. The son of this mountain deity is called Drum. Drum has the body of a dragon and the face of a human. According to legend, Drum conspired with Qinpi to murder Baojiang on the southern side of Kunlun Mountain. For their transgression against heaven, the Supreme God ordered their execution, which was carried out on the southern side of Bell Mountain below the Yao Precipice. Qinpi transformed into a giant osprey with black feathers, a white head, a red beak and talons that more closely resembled those of a tiger than of a hawk. When he cawed, he sounded like a morning swan. His appearance in the sky portended all-out war. Drum was also transformed into a bird, an ancient jun-bird, that looked like an owl with red feet, a straight beak, yellow feathers and a white head. When he called out, he, too, sounded like a swan. His appearance in the sky foretold imminent and devastating drought.

A hundred and eighty leagues to the west is Mount Taiqi. The River Guan starts here before flowing west to disappear into the Desert of Drifting Sands. The River Guan is home to flying fish, each patterned in dazzling colours. Wings sprout where there should be fins. Brilliantly blue scales run down their sides. Their heads are mostly white and their mouths red. They are said to migrate through the West Sea and swim in the East Sea. They fly after the sun has set and make noises that echo the luan bird. Their flesh tastes both sweet and sour. Consuming it will restore one's sanity. Its appearance heralds abundant harvests in the coming season for all under heaven.

Sophora River Mountain stands three hundred and twenty leagues to the west of Mount Taiqi. The River Qiushi originates on this mountain before flowing north to empty into the River You; luo wasps are especially common near this river. On the upper reaches of

Sophora River Mountain there is gold and jade as well as realgar, treasured stones that bear a resemblance to pearls and are exceedingly rare. Cinnabar can be found in profusion on the south face of this mountain, while gold and silver deposits are abundant on the north face. The Supreme Deity makes his Garden of Peace here, which Yingshao tends. His form is that of a horse with a human face. His torso is marked like a tiger and great wings reach up from his back. It is said Yingshao travels across the Four Seas, subsisting on pomegranates. Sophora River Mountain looks upon Kunlun to the south and is awed by its brilliance and mystical power. To the west of Sophora River Mountain is the Great Marsh where Lord Millet is interred. Jade can be found in abundance on the central slopes of Sophora River Mountain, while on its northern side many great yao trees grow. North of Sophora River Mountain is Mount Zhubi, where the demon, Lilun, resides. In its trees are many goshawks and falcons. East of Sophora River Mountain, the four levels of Mount Constant can be seen. Upon this mountain live the Exhausted Demons, each one confined to their own level. A god, whose form resembles an ox with eight feet, two heads and a horse's tail lives here where the Overflowing River begins. Its waters are clear and flow unhindered. When the god calls out, he sounds like a buzzing beetle. He is an omen of impending war.

Four hundred leagues southwest is Mount Kunlun. It is here where the Supreme Deity built his earthly capital. The god Luwu, whose form is that of a tiger with nine tails, a human head and tiger claws, presides over it. He also administers the nine realms of heaven, the changing of the seasons and the Supreme Deity's garden. The tulou lives here. It is a beast that resembles a goat with four horns on its head. It is said to be a man-eater. The qinyuan also makes its nest here. It is a bird that looks like a bee, but is as large as a mandarin duck. Its sting is deadly to other animals and birds. It can even cause trees to wither and die. Quails called chun live on Kunlun as well. They overlook the Supreme Deity's hundred storehouses. A tree that resembles a pear tree grows on Mount Kunlun. It blossoms yellow before producing a red fruit that tastes similar to a plum. It has no stone. It is known as a sand-pear. It is said the fruit can prevent flooding, and if eaten by humans they will not drown. A plant that looks like a mallow but tastes like spring onions grows in abundance.

Eating it will restore one's strength. The Yellow River originates here. It flows to the south and then to the east before emptying into the Wuda River. The Crimson River begins here as well and flows to the southeast where it merges with the Heaven's Flooded River. The River Vast rises close by to flow south and west into the Unsightly Shoal River. The River Black also originates here to flow west to Bowl Mountain. Many wondrous and strange birds and animals reside in the area.

Joyous-Swim Mountain lies three hundred and seventy leagues to the west of Kunlun. The Peach River starts here before flowing west into Millet Marsh. Copious amounts of white jade can be found amid the muck and the mud. The most waterlogged areas are teeming with a fish that resembles a spotted steed, save for its four feet and penchant for devouring other fish.

Trekking along the riverbanks of the Peach River for 400 leagues, one arrives at the Desert of Drifting Sands. Two hundred leagues beyond this point one reaches Hornet Mountain. The god Long-Ride watches over this particular peak with the Nine Powers of Heaven. He possesses the form of a human, except for a leopard's tail. Jade can be found on Hornet Mountain, while on its lower slopes precious green stones are plentiful. The mountain is devoid of rivers.

Three hundred and fifty leagues west of Hornet Mountain is Jade Mountain. The Queen Mother of the West lives upon its slopes. Her form is that of a human with a tail that looks like a leopard's. When she smiles, one can see her tiger's teeth. She is skilled at whistling and wears a victory crown on her rumpled hair. It is said she metes out catastrophes from heaven and the five cruelties. A dog-like beast lives on Jade Mountain. It is mottled like a leopard and has horns like a great ox. It is known as the jiao and is considered to be quite crafty. It barks like a dog and wherever it appears, the harvest will be bountiful. A reddish pheasant-like bird also resides on Jade Mountain. Known as the qingyu, it feeds exclusively on fish. It is said to be an omen of terrible drought.

Four hundred and eighty leagues to the west is Yellow Emperor Hillock. It is devoid of vegetation, but the River True emanates from here and flows southwards to empty into the River Black. Grains of cinnabar are common in its bed, alongside quantities of realgar.

Three hundred leagues farther west is Store-Rock Mountain. One can reach the Yellow River here through a rocky passage near its base. The Yellow River then flows in a westerly direction. Nothing lives on this mountain, nor is there any vegetation.

Changliu Mountain rises two hundred leagues to the west of Store-Rock Mountain. The White Emperor lives here, although he is also known as Shao Hao. The beasts on Changliu Mountain all have striped tails; the birds have streaked feathers on their heads. There is a great amount of dark jade and other semi-precious stones on Changliu's slopes. In truth, the mountain serves as a palace for the celestial stone clan who are charged with ensuring the sun rises and falls.

Two hundred and eighty leagues farther west is Zhang Mushroom Mountain. No vegetation grows on its slopes but there is an abundance of treasured stones and green jade. Many strange and wondrous creatures live on this mountain. A crimson-coloured feline creature with nine tails and a single horn on its head is known to lurk across Zhang Mushroom Mountain. It is called a zheng and makes a noise like stones being struck together. A bird that bears resemblance to a crane also calls this mountain home. It has a single foot, red streaks through its green feathers and a white beak. It is called the bifang for that is the sound it makes when it sings. Its appearance is a harbinger for strange fires.

Some three hundred leagues to the west is Shade Mountain. The River Mud-Bath starts its journey here, then flows south before emptying into a marsh that has no name due to it being home to so many foreign and unknown plants. Cowrie shells can be found in abundance in the River Mud-Bath. A creature lives here that is a sort of wildcat with a white head. It's known as the heavenly dog and is said to shriek at night. It is also thought to ward off evil forces if eaten or worn around one's belt as a talisman.

Mount Watchful-Tally stands two hundred leagues farther west. It is regularly buffeted by ferocious rainstorms, wind and clouds. On its highest reaches are many palm and wild plum trees, while gold and jade are plentiful on its lower reaches. The god Jiangyi calls this mountain home.

Two hundred and twenty leagues to the west of Mount Watchful-Tally is Three-Dangers Mountain, so-called for its three towering peaks. On this mountain live the three green-birds known to bring food to the Queen Mother of the West. The perimeter of this mountain is at least a hundred leagues. A man-eating creature lives near its summit. It bears resemblance to an ox, but its hair is white, and it has four horns on its head. Its hair grows long so that it looks like straw growing in the fields. It is called the aoyin. A one-headed bird with three torsos also resides on this mountain. It looks similar to an owl and is called the chi.

One hundred leagues on in a westerly direction is Blue-Horse Mountain. Great amounts of jade are found on this peak, but there is an absence of other minerals or stones. The god Old Child resides here. It is said that when she calls out, she sounds like a bell being chimed. On the lower reaches of this mountain are numerous vipers and snakes.

Heavenly Mountain rises three hundred and fifty leagues to the west. Gold, jade and realgar are in abundance. The Eminent River originates here, flows southwest and then disappears into Hot Springs Valley. The god Dijiang dwells on Heavenly Mountain. He is said to wear a yellow sack about his waist that emanates a reddish aura similar to the colour of cinnabar. He is without a face and eyes but has six feet and four wings. He is skilled in song and dance and may in fact be the lord of chaos, Hundun.

Mount You is located two hundred and ninety leagues west of Heavenly Mountain. The god Rushou lives on this mountain. Yingdou jade is plentiful on the highest reaches, while on the southern face jinyu jade is bountiful. Realgar is common of the north face of the mountain. From its summit, one can see clearly to the west where the sun sets. The god Hongguang sits in watch as the sun, a great round globe, dips beneath the horizon.

Travel by water for a hundred leagues to the west and one arrives at Watching-Wings Mountain. No vegetation grows on its slopes, but there are great quantities of gold and jade. A creature called the huan lives on this mountain. It looks like a wildcat, but it possesses only a single eye, and has three tails. Its name derives from its ability to utter all kinds of raucous sounds. It is said to be effective at warding off evil forces, and should you wear some of its flesh about your belt, it will cure jaundice. A bird similar to a crow also inhabits this mountain. It has three heads and six tails and is said to laugh like a man. It is called the yiyu. Wearing its feathers close to the skin will repel nightmares. It is also said to be a talisman against misfortune.

Twenty-three mountains are described in the third part of *Pathways Through the Western Mountains* for a total distance of some 6,744 leagues. The gods inhabiting these mountains all have goat bodies and human faces. A piece of painted jade is to be offered in sacrifice, then buried. Millet and hulled rice are used as the sacrificial grain.

So… anything to ask?

Question: Wow… such a long passage!

Answer: Yes, true, but isn't it a marvellous section, written beautifully and displaying such great literary skill… the rhythm is excellent… a joy to read. The writer ought to have been terribly pleased, wouldn't you say? A total of twenty-three mountains covering 6,744 leagues… such a bountiful landscape stretching over such a great distance. The myriad meteorological features, the origins of so many great rivers, the molten jade consumed by the Yellow Emperor, the places where one can find the mythical grass that can be fermented into a nearly divine liquor, the spirit trees, the multitudinous animals and birds, the beasts that were effective against all forms of disaster, some that caused them. I tell you, this mountain range possessed everything the ancient world had to offer. It was the heart of the past, the capital of the Celestial Emperor himself!

Question: Would this mountain range be the present-day corridor between Qinghai and Xinjiang?

Answer: I suppose you could say that, but to be more accurate, it ought to be called the Western Paradise as it's known in Buddhist scripture.

Question: Western Paradise or the Western Regions… as they were called during the Han dynasty?

Answer: I said Western Paradise and that's what I meant. The text mentions the Queen Mother of the West, after all. According to myth, Mu Kung, the God of the Immortals, reigns over the eastern regions while his counterpart, the Queen Mother of the West, holds sovereignty over the Western Paradise.

Question: Isn't the Qinghai-Xinjiang Plateau desert? How's it that lakes and marshes are found there, as well as all the ferocious animals and spirits?

Answer: Well, according to historical resources, what is now called the Taklamakan Desert was once an inner sea with sixteen kingdoms spotted around its shores. That's where Qinghai gets its name, the blue-green sea, so it makes sense. As for the many mountains in the sea, according to legend these are the bones of the demonic goddess Rakshasa, who was known for always stirring up trouble and causing havoc. To contain her, temples were built on the summits of these mountains… in time, the terrain changed and the seawaters drained leaving only the lakes and marshes mentioned in the text… the place we now call Qinghai Lake.

Question: The passage mentions numerous gods… there's the White Emperor, Shao Hao he's also known as, often said to be the Yellow Emperor's son, deities called Drum, Qinpi, Baojiang, Yingshao, Luwu, Long-Ride… there's also the celestial stone clan, Jiangyi, Old Child, the great god Dijiang, Rushou, Hongguang. Isn't this all just a bit surprising… that there'd be so many gods in one mountain range?

Answer: Well, it is the Western Paradise… it should be filled with numerous deities.

Question: The Celestial Emperor sent all these many gods to

Earth to rule, but why populate the land with so many strange and frightening animals, birds and fish, creatures that eat people or venomous wasps that sting both men and trees and caused them to wither and die? Why cause such terrible floods and disasters… why let the many gods and demigods wage war against each other, like the deity on Sophora River Mountain did, or when Mount Drum and Qinpi murdered Baojiang and were in turn hacked to pieces and left to die on Yao Precipice… only for Qinpi to turn into an actual osprey and Mount Drum into a hill pheasant… and then… then their appearance heralds severe drought… why? I just don't understand… why?

Answer: The Earth must have balance, there must be a symbiosis between yin and yang, harmony and disharmony, life and death. The tension between these is necessary, it is from this tension that the myriad things come forth.

Question: But… there're big creatures and small…

Answer: Have you ever seen one of these so-called 'small creatures' disappear, go extinct? The bigger ones might have more physical strength, but the smaller ones possess their own defences, poison, for instance.

Question: Oh… There's also lots of jade on this mountain range… the Yellow Emperor, it says, enjoyed eating the molten jade. The molten jade also watered the cinnabar trees, and the passage says it can be planted and give birth to precious gemstones… can jade be planted in the ground?

Answer: Everything comes from the earth, so whatever is buried under the ground will sprout.

Question: What about people?

Answer: Well, after someone dies, we do bury them and yet their children and grandchildren live on… right?

Question: Ha ha. What about the Overflowing River, where's that?

Answer: Here.

Question: And these mountains folds?

Answer: They're like the arms of the mountain folded in on itself.

Question: Another question… the Queen Mother of the West loves to howl… does that explain why housewives can be so strict and so talkative?

Answer: Don't talk nonsense, boy. Now repeat after me the most beautiful line from the passage: 'Lapis lazuli can also be found on Mishan Mountain. They are of superb quality, firm and sublimely coloured. If lightly polished, they will shine even more and emit an otherworldly radiance. As a result, the spirit-gods of the Earth and sky are very fond of consuming these gems; they readily accept them as sacrificial offerings. Gentlemen scholars are keen to wear the lapis lazuli as pendants to ward off calamity.'

To Lao Pi's mind, the experiences of Qipan were worth promoting throughout the commune, and, generally, he was satisfied with the work completed by most villages. There were, however, three communities in Dongchuan that caused him to worry, most especially the village of Liuliwa. The residents of this particular settlement were known to be cold and indifferent, ruthless even, and nearly always aggressive towards outsiders. Even the cadre dispatched to manage the village's affairs on behalf of the commune was known to refer to the place as a den of wolves. Nor were things better among the local cadres for they were constantly at each other's throats, disagreeing on nearly everything. As a result, Liuliwa's revolutionary work had made almost no progress.

At the beginning of the new year when troops were demobilised, Lao Pi saw the opportunity to install a returned soldier as the new branch secretary. And to further support his new appointment, he approved fresh regulations that saw Liuliwa take responsibility away from the town of Zhenxijie for the removal of night soil from the secondary commune offices. (The same such services were not necessary for the night soil that built up in the main offices since it was on much higher ground.) This was especially needed due to the layout of the structure, which had a relatively low foundation, and the position of the toilet, which was adjacent to the small river that ran just outside the building. In winter, the river and the night soil reservoir would freeze and all new additions to it would likewise turn to ice shortly after delivery, creating faeces and urine icicles that stood up in the air. Its removal was therefore vital.

To carry out such work, the residents of Liuliwa would come armed with hoes and mattocks and smash the combined filth into more manageable chunks, and then load it into wheelbarrows to be carted away. Should any chunks fall out and break into smaller pieces, there was always someone to pick up the shards and load them into burlap sacks to be carried over the shoulder. Most sacks would be borne by a single man, but for heavier ones, then two men would suffice.

Before this work was officially begun, Lao Pi's newly appointed branch secretary made it known that he needed the older man's oversight and support, notably when it came to ensuring the whole town would be mobilised to work. Lao Pi was only too happy to help and out of the entire village, only one individual didn't show up.

In fact, the man in question had chosen instead to travel to Qingfengyi to purchase rice, a routine he had been carrying out for some time. And, as was generally the case, upon his return to Liuliwa he would sell the rice and make a tidy profit in the process. With this extra money, he'd been living on a much fuller stomach than most of his fellow villagers; he'd been wearing nicer clothes, too. And even more annoyingly, on the days when he wasn't in Qingfengyi, he would be seen strolling about holding a fine wine jar, always ready to crack a one-liner to anyone he saw: "Eat well, friends. Enjoy the spice of life when you can… and do you know what spice I'm referring to, eh?

Well, let me tell you, it isn't some spicy soup or other. No, no, no… it's wine, ha ha, that's what it is!"

Of course, one of the branch secretary's first acts was to attempt to confiscate the man's contraband rice, which proved more difficult than it initially seemed. That is, instead of handing over what he had purchased illegally, the man denounced the branch secretary and accused him of using his new-found power to have at least five of the village's trees felled, which he in turn sold at a discounted price, buying four himself to use as beams for a house extension. The man took his charge to the commune offices, forcing Lao Pi to admonish his handpicked appointment and compel him to pay compensation to the village.

But things didn't end there. The man had further arguments to make, namely that the trees themselves should be returned to the village. Needless to say, Lao Pi found the entire situation quite maddening and finally he instructed Mu Sheng and other commune cadres to guard against letting the man in to make additional complaints. Preventing him from seeing Lao Pi, however, didn't settle the issue. Instead, the man travelled to Qipan and took his axe to one of the heroic, revolutionary apricot trees planted by Kuang San. He didn't flee after committing this flagrant act of violence, however. Instead, he shouted to whoever could hear him that he'd chopped down one of Kuang San's trees.

Unsurprisingly, the officials in Qipan arrested him immediately. They beat him, too, to within an inch of his life. Then he was bound to a stone roller that stood wedged into the ground near the local reservoir. It was only about half the height of a man, thus preventing him from either standing upright or sitting down, to say nothing of stopping him from shouting his curses and accusations. Feng Xie, of course, informed Lao Pi about what had happened, and Lao Pi himself came personally to confront this most troublesome man.

"Ha ha!" the bound man roared with laughter at the sight of the Party secretary. "Finally you've come to see me!"

Feng Xie leapt forward and raised a hand to box the man's ears. Before his hand fell, however, Lao Pi stopped him. To the bound man he said: "You're really something, aren't you! You've certainly got balls… I reckon I've no option but to send you for re-education."

With little delay, the man was transported to a brick kiln factory in

Heilongjiang, ostensibly to learn from manual labour the errors of his ways.

With one of the revolutionary trees damaged by this seemingly mad man, Liu Xueren prostrated himself in front of Lao Pi, slapped his own face and criticised himself for failing in his responsibility to the trees. By way of apology, he went to rub sesame oil into the wounded roots, hoping this would save the tree. Lao Pi also requested… demanded… the villagers double their efforts to protect the trees, to ensure class enemies didn't cause additional damage. It was their responsibility, he stressed, to ensure that not a single additional leaf be harmed.

This situation dealt with, Liuliwa seemed to finally turn the corner, its reorganisation had taken root. Lao Pi himself visited a further four times to demonstrate his clear support for the branch secretary. He would have journeyed to the village more often, but after the last visit he was struck down by a nasty cold and severe fever that prevented him from doing very much of anything for a couple of weeks. Worried about how this might affect his efforts in Liuliwa, the junior cadre was quick to call on Lao Pi and beseech him to come. His presence, according to the younger man, was the only weapon strong enough to drive out any bad elements that still lurked in the village. Such words, however, were in vain as Lao Pi was unable to get himself out of bed, to say nothing of travelling to Liuliwa.

The branch secretary's response to this setback was to build a scarecrow to place at the entrance to the village. On its straw head he pasted a facsimile of Lao Pi's face, and around its neck he hung a placard with the simple message: 'I've come.'

When Mu Sheng arrived some days later to deliver official documents, he couldn't resist wondering aloud to the junior cadre: "So, I can't help but ask… why've you used the Party secretary's image to call out to sparrows?"

"You're a fool," the branch secretary said. "It symbolises his presence in the village… so that even when he's not here, he still is!"

"Ah… in that case, I'll be sure to tell him you've got him stationed here night and day, in wind and rain."

"Well, doesn't the county capital have a statue of Chairman Mao in its central square? You just tell the secretary I see him in the same light as Chairman Mao. He's the chairman of Guofenglou!"

Mu Sheng did as he was told, and informed Lao Pi of the scarecrow created in his image. The Party secretary drew great pleasure from the news, laughing loudly and proclaiming that, once he was better, he'd be sure to see it in person.

"Ah Huang Zhong," he added, "you're one wily little shit!"

Listening to his words, Mu Sheng finally learnt the name of the man who'd been put in charge of Liuliwa: Huang Zhong, one of Liu Bei's Five Tiger Generals from *Romance of the Three Kingdoms*.

The road to Dongchuan went past Bear Cliff, and on top of this craggy precipice stood a towering elm tree. No one knew how it could grow so high up there on nothing but rock, nor how it had become so large, but there it stood, casting a shadow over the entire ledge, a startling presence indeed. In addition to its impressive stature, the tree was home to a single majestic crane.

Feeling much better, Lao Pi had taken Mu Sheng with him on the road to Liuliwa. As in previous journeys through this area, when he arrived at the river that ran below Bear Cliff, Lao Pi felt his body ache, felt in need of a rest. Mu Sheng also felt the urge to rest and directed the older man towards the rocky outcropping so that they could both sit and take a breather. The stone, too, seemed to welcome them into its embrace, almost encouraging them to stay, to give up their journey and simply remain where they were.

"Secretary," began Mu Sheng, "why don't you take your time and have a smoke?"

Lao Pi didn't offer a response but heeded the younger man's suggestion nonetheless, and he lit a cigarette. While his superior enjoyed his tobacco, Mu Sheng picked up a stone and, with as much energy as he could muster, flung it at the solitary elm tree. The stone struck high up in its branches and within seconds the crane squawked and took to the air. It didn't disappear over the horizon, however, but circled above them instead in mesmerising fashion.

Watching the scene unfold, Lao Pi called out to his young subordinate: "So… you haven't got the energy to walk any further, but you can pester a lonely bird!"

"Well," said Mu Sheng, "I'm just making sure the creature properly welcomes you."

In truth, Mu Sheng had an ulterior motive to his actions. He had disturbed the crane as a warning to the village below, a signal to indicate it was safe for them to come out from under the nearby locust trees, should they actually see it circling overhead.

The grove of locust trees was the largest in the entire commune. When they bloomed in spring, the whole of the mountain slope was bathed in white and would soon be populated by an uncountable number of bees, all hard at work. People would be among the trees at this time, too, busily harvesting the flowers. On those occasions when the village authorities seemed to favour a lighter touch to managing the inhabitants, they'd be out picking the fresh blooms during the day. When things were managed more circumspectly, they'd resort to harvesting what they could in the dead of night. After a day's or night's work, a meal of rice and vegetables was prepared, usually quite meagre, and then the blossoms were added; if the person eating the flowers could actually stomach it, going to the toilet would be that much easier.

Unfortunately, the commune had issued a written decree that such extreme harvesting of the locust trees was forbidden, primarily due to the fact that the trees did not bloom every year and were thus being thinned out much too quickly. The authorities went as far as to dispatch a guard to monitor the grove in order to ensure no illegal harvesting was taking place. At first, the man charged with this task was diligent and dutiful, and so the trees went nearly untouched, at least for a time. But his earnestness didn't last, and he was soon prone to looking the other way. He knew, too, what the crane circling above meant, and he would shout out to those busily picking the blossoms from the locust trees. These people, in turn, would scurry out from under the trees and make their way to the adjacent gully and the few maple trees that grew there. Then they'd stoop to grope among the bracken, picking what they could, even though it never amounted to much. The bracken, after all, was old and tired, its leaves striated and weak, barely edible. (In fact, it had to be boiled for a minimum of three days just to reduce the bitterness; only then could it be mixed in with whatever else they found to put in the pot.)

The maple trees shared the land with numerous vines that wound and wended their way through and over everything. It was therefore quite easy to lose one's way. To complicate matters, this swath of mountain trees was also considered part of the county's communal domain, and the man responsible for them was a little, or a lot, off his rocker. In truth, whenever anyone stepped near the trees, he invariably assumed they were attempting to surreptitiously cut them down, and so he'd spare no energy chasing them away, resorting to violence if needed. It was always necessary, therefore, for one to pay attention to the path, and not get lost. To help with this, many villagers took to carrying a wooden sword, often made from the jujube tree, which in turn was only possible when such trees had been struck by lightning and thus had a suitable piece rendered off. (Pieces obtained by other means from the jujube tree were simply unsuitable.)

Consuming the blossoms from the locust trees, as well as the tired old bracken that grew over the roots of the maple trees, was a reasonably effective means to combat hunger. It filled you up at least, but it was also the cause of worms, a rather distressing and certainly unwelcome side effect. To determine whether or not someone suffered from the affliction, the infestation, one only needed to pay attention to the person's complexion, to see if their eyes were puffy, their nose covered with white spots. The only treatment was the hairy agrimony, a wild grass that grew along the riverbank. This had to be picked and then mulched together with sour chinaberries. Once prepared, it had to be spread out over a mint leaf and then pasted over one's navel. Thereafter, the worm would be shat out.

The worms were especially endemic among the young, and when they were expelled their poor little anuses would be rubbed terribly raw. For adults, the process was a little more involved. Once the worm was halfway out, they'd use their foot to make sure the rest of it came along. Stand, they'd say, stand with your foot over one end of the worm and pull the bugger out. A rock was used to splatter it once the person was clear. After he learnt of this practice, Mu Sheng forever felt that the stones surrounding every home in the poor village that stood just under Bear Cliff must be terribly unclean.

Past Bear Cliff, the worst place for seeing proper revolutionary work carried out, besides Liuliwa, was Xiepingzhai. Mu Sheng was unwilling to go directly to this particular village. Whenever Lao Pi had him courier official documents to Xiepingzhai, he'd only ever make it to the mountain pass that functioned as a gate to the village. There he'd wait for a passer-by from Xiepingzhai to entrust with the documents that needed to be given to the village head. He wouldn't actually go into Xiepingzhai for it was the very place where his mother's mother lived, a woman who filled him with fear.

The status of his grandmother's family was certainly not high, but after his mother died, his gran would spend each evening seated near the village's central millstone waiting for her daughter to return. She was ninety-two years old and physically robust, but her mind had started to go. She was easily confused, and refused to believe her daughter was dead. Before, Mu Sheng had been the good grandson. He'd paid visits to his gran, let her embrace him tightly, let her rub her hands over his face. He'd listened to her, too, listened to the same question she asked repeatedly: "Why hasn't your mother come to see me, dear?" Sometimes her voice would be loud and strong, at other times it'd be low and quiet. The question never changed, however. And the exchange would always end up the same way: she'd trail off into mumbling, ultimately forgetting he was even there.

Goujia was another village Mu Sheng was unwilling to visit, even though his aunt lived there. In the main courtyard of his aunt's home stood a large persimmon tree whose bountiful fruit was picked and dried each year. Mu Sheng never got to enjoy the dried fruit, however; he knew she'd prepared them that way to make a little money. All he ever got was the leftover peel. But he never complained. No, his reason for not wanting to visit Goujia was due to the place he would have to walk past in order to reach it, namely Heilongkou.

Heilongkou wasn't a town, or any kind of settlement for that matter. It was simply a place where two rivers merged. In the past, it was home to a large grain mill that had been used communally by the neighbouring villages. More recently, the mill had been torn down and a dam built across the rivers in order to generate electricity. This had failed, however, and so the dam had been transformed into a paper factory. Unfortunately, the operators of the new factory lacked the skills to produce high-quality paper and so all that was made was a coarse, low-quality product. These various initiatives had all been proclaimed by Lao Pi and so, naturally, their failures were a source of great disappointment. Ultimately, he ordered the construction of a kiln on the riverbank, believing that the manufacture of bricks and roof tiles had to be a job the locals could handle.

At the beginning, the neighbouring villages provided the workforce for the kiln and things got off to a good start. Afterwards, however, those in need of re-education – the crimes were myriad – became the primary source of labour. At first, it was former landowners upset with their new lot who were most regularly dispatched to work the kiln. Later, it was those caught voicing counterrevolutionary ideas. These two labour pools, however, were not bottomless, and so soon, those found guilty of capitalist practices – the buying and selling of goods illegally for instance – those judged unreformable, and even those men and women caught out in intimately awkward acts were all sent to work the fires. In fact, the place became Lao Pi's preferred option for dealing with anyone who perpetrated whatever he deemed to be crimes against the revolution. Heilongkou thus became known as a reform through labour camp, not just a kiln built where two rivers merged.

Yan Liben, who had previously been responsible for the commune's arms and munitions, had now been put in charge of the kiln. He wasn't the tallest of men, and his face was usually deathly white. Besides his dark, pronounced eyebrows, there was little about him that seemed imposing. When he walked about the complex, his head was generally held low, his hands clasped behind his back. On those occasions when he wasn't out and about, he would spend his time in his office, usually on the telephone. It was the only telephone in Guofenglou, besides the two in the commune offices, of course. It wasn't the easiest device to use. A crank was necessary to dial the number, and so it generally took half a day to just to make a single call. Afterwards, Yan Liben would return the crank to his pocket, ensuring that he was the only one able to actually use the telephone.

In addition to Yan Liben, there were three team leaders, each assigned a different aspect of the operations. One was in charge of manufacturing processes, another logistics, and finally the third handled the meals. They were all dark-skinned, strapping young men with fierce temperaments. But they all deferred to Yan Liben. Before entering his office, they'd announce their arrival with a shout, and then open the door. Stepping inside, they'd shout once more. Mu Sheng had first witnessed this scene when Lao Pi had ordered him to gift a long red banner to Yan Liben – to be used for educational purposes – but he couldn't understand why these large men acted so meekly in front of their immediate superior. But later, after he and the village head from Laoyingzui had escorted Miao Tianyi to

Heilongkou, he learnt to fear Yan Liben. Ever after, he thought it best to avoid passing by the place.

Miao Tianyi was a man of unique skill in Laoyingzui, perhaps the only one to have gone to middle school and capable of writing quite well. For many generations, the residents of Laoyingzui had the custom of putting up rhyming couplets for the annual Spring Festival activities. The characters would be written in broad, dark strokes, and after Miao Tianyi had graduated from middle school, it was his job to complete. He was also a rather brash and, at times, insolent young man. At the end of the year, he'd set up a table in his main courtyard and lay out his brushes. He would make people queue, and if they didn't arrive with some meat or tofu as payment, they'd have to bring a bundle of onions at least. Needless to say, his mercantile manner had offended a great number of people.

Nearly seven years ago, the village had re-checked the social background of its residents, and Miao's family, once determined to be middle-class peasants, had had their status changed to that of petty landlord. It was a status lower than that of wealthy landowner, and in truth it didn't prevent him from becoming an accountant, but this hadn't stopped Miao Tianyi from writing appeals to have his family background re-evaluated.

Mu Sheng had first come across Miao Tianyi near the commune offices. But not in the manner expected. In fact, the first time he'd seen the man, Miao Tianyi was rummaging through the rubbish piles just behind the main offices. As Mu Sheng watched Miao Tianyi sifting through the mounds of waste, he noticed that he was picking out small bits of paper, smoothing them with his hand, folding them carefully and placing them underneath his hat. It was a surprising scene, one for which Mu Sheng couldn't help but comment: "I've got a problem with oily hair too, you know... how's about giving me some?"

Miao Tianyi's response was not what Mu Sheng expected: "I'm using the paper to write my appeals on, you fool!"

Despite the numerous appeals he wrote, they all proved useless, at least with regard to overturning the commune's decision regarding his family status. However, Lao Pi did find a use for them... in the toilet to wipe his arse. For three years, Miao continued to write appeal after appeal. He'd have persisted into the fourth year if not for the dramatic events that befell Guofenglou, the aftermath of which resulted in him being seized by the authorities.

The event in question began one morning, near the lower-lying offices of the commune. A pile of paper, about twenty pages or so, was found on the banks of the river, prevented from blowing away in the wind by a rock. There was no name on the paper, but each line of text berated the administration of Guofenglou. It cursed them for making all manner of errors, for treating the people unfairly. And to make matters worse, the diatribe ended by cursing the Party and socialism as a whole. Nothing like this had ever happened before in Guofenglou. It was hardly unsurprising that the text was immediately deemed counterrevolutionary. The county offices dispatched more than twenty public investigators, and every household in the commune became subject to intense questioning. If a family member could actually write, they were forced to fill up half a page or more so that it could be compared to the handwriting of the offending document.

After a month of vigorous investigation, however, the culprit had still not been identified, and so attention shifted from handwriting to content. The first claim made by the document related to the issue of arable land in Zhenxijie. Specifically, the text called out the authorities who ordered the removal of graves and tombstones so that new land could be ploughed, especially because the graves removed were those belonging to poor farming families and the formerly rich landowners who had persecuted them. After all, the document asked, wasn't the exhumation and removal of one's ancestors akin to cutting one's self off from the past, from one's own family heritage? The text also criticised the colossal waste of time and energy used in building the hydroelectric dam only to see that reworked into a paper factory that also failed. Wasn't it like a cat that covers its own shit with earth? There's still shit there, right? The rant continued, asking how was it possible to say that the work of the revolution was proceeding apace, that things were getting better, when it was clear that there were more and more people dying of starvation every year? The writer, whoever it was, also cursed the so-called 'heroic' apricot trees in Qipan, the establishment of the soviet government in Bawangsi and the banners posted in Kouqian. The ire expressed in the paper then shifted towards Qinling's former guerrilla band, claiming they were more bandits than heroes of the revolution. Their supposed great battle in Qipan was nothing more than a failure; they'd lost. The claims to history in Bawangsi and Kouqian were fake, inventions of unscrupulous men today.

Given the nature of the content, and in order to reduce the scope of the investigation, it was decided the focus of their inquiry ought to be directed towards men who were most familiar with the events and decisions described. Most recently, the residents of Qipan had informed upon Lao Qin, claiming he'd been cursing at just about everything, shouting out repeatedly that everyone was a motherfucker or worse. Lao Qin's daughter had already been struggled against, so it was perhaps expected he would hold great animosity towards the Party and the project of building a socialist future.

Complying with the inquiry, Feng Xie and Liu Xueren escorted Lao Qin to the Special Investigation team and Lao Pi personally interrogated the man. So frightened was he at being called in, the older man shat his trousers and babbled that he was afraid of his own daughter, that her mind wasn't right, that she was sick in the head, rude and unreasonable at home. She'd even become violent, smashing what few bowls they owned at the least provocation. He'd become so upset with her behaviour that he'd had to find some release. That was why he'd been wandering the village, cursing as loudly as he had. Lao Pi asked him about the contents of the papers they'd found, and his response was that he knew nothing of them.

Lao Pi then shifted tactics: "But the man who did write these words is certainly not the most common of men, now is he?"

The investigation continued like this for some time, ultimately arriving at the conclusion that Miao Tianyi was the most likely suspect. He fitted the profile best, he was cultured, could read and write, and he knew about a great many things. And besides, he'd been writing those blasted appeals for years. The fact they'd been ignored was perhaps the trigger that caused him to write such vile and unfounded criticisms. Or so Lao Pi thought. The only fly in the ointment was that Miao Tianyi admitted nothing. Even after he was detained and tortured, suspended in boiling water, beaten with a stick while being tied up in a sack, he still professed his innocence. Since there was no conclusive evidence, he had to be released. That's how he wound up working in Heilongkou.

On the same day Miao Tianyi was brought for re-education, another man by the name of Zhang Shoucheng, once a teacher at the elementary school, was also being escorted to the reform camp. A resident of the nearby town of Zhenxiaoxue, Zhang's hands had been tightly bound in front of him and it was easy to see he had been crying. In truth, the tears hadn't stopped the entire way to the camp, leaving his face a mess, a mixture of tears and snot hanging from his chin. Zhang's crime was of a physically amorous nature; he'd been caught doing what he shouldn't have been doing with a local girl, apparently more than one. Actually, the sordid business was already well known throughout Guofenglou, and Miao Tianyi felt no sympathy for the man. He decided to pay him no mind, and to consciously try to distance himself, all in the hope of not being directly associated with a man he considered no better than a scoundrel.

Leaning close to Mu Sheng, he actually spoke to this effect: "He's a hooligan… a no-good rascal… surely he knows that… which makes one wonder why's he crying like he is!"

"When they were questioning you, didn't you grovel like he's doing now?" Mu Sheng's response had been quick, pointed.

"I didn't cry, nor did I confess to anything," Miao Tianyi said. "In the palm of my left hand I held Liu Hulan, and in my right… I had Sister Jiang… you know, Jiang Zhuyun… both heroes and martyrs of the revolution. With them in my hands I admitted no wrong, let no tear fall!"

One of the team leaders walked over to Mu Sheng and told him, along with the village head from Laoyingzui, to watch Miao Tianyi for the time being. However, Zhang Shoucheng was guided directly towards Yan Liben's office. From inside he shouted his displeasure: "Day after day they keep sending us people, two more right now… are they trying to kill us or what!"

Mu Sheng and the village head waited in the grounds just beyond Yan Liben's office. Miao Tianyi stood next to them, his hands bound. The other end of the rope was held tightly by the village head. When he got the urge to smoke, the village head got Mu Sheng to reach for his tobacco to make him a cigarette. As he did so, Miao Tianyi spoke:

"How's about releasing my hands so that I can have a cigarette, too... I won't run, I promise."

The village head refused, unwilling to trust him. Instead, he tied the rope around a nearby tree and proceeded to enjoy his smoke. As he did so, a whistle sounded, and soon the area was filled with camp inmates. It appeared as though their day's work was at an end. They were all filthy, their legs covered in mud, their faces black with soot. They formed two lines and listened to the instructions given by the team leader in charge of manufacturing. Miao Tianyi took the opportunity to scan the area all around. Once his eyes fell on an instructional banner held aloft above them, he couldn't help but shout out: "There's a mistake with one of the characters... the sloping stroke there on the bottom, that's characteristic of traditional writing. You don't do that with the simplified version."

"You're here for re-education," said the village head. "Don't go showing off your abilities. You mightn't have been given the counterrevolutionary dunce cap to wear, but let me tell you, the people still have it in their hands and it won't take much for us to put it on your head!" And then he slapped him, right across the side of his head. The blow really hit the mark, causing a slapping echo to ring out in Miao Tianyi's ears.

Mu Sheng turned around, imagining all the men here for re-education had had their ears boxed in similar fashion. This was soon to be confirmed in dramatic fashion. Each man raised his hand and struck the person next to him. They did this in pairs, heavy, dirty hands striking faces. And not just randomly, there was a rhythm to it, one slap leading to another, their pace quickening, faces swelling until blood began to drip from their mouths... their palms turning red, moistened with blood... three red fingerprints, then finally five. Mu was stupefied by what he was seeing, and so, too, was Miao Tianyi.

Finally, the team leader spoke: "Alright... stop, I need to piss."

The men who'd been slapping each other stopped and lowered their faces. Mu Sheng directed his attention towards the roots of the tree, but all he saw were two wild bees in some strange death match of their own. They were large, but twisted together as they were, they resembled more a ball rolling about on the ground. Looking closer, he could see them both tearing at each other's wings. An ant, sensing an opportunity, appeared out of nowhere and ran off with one of the detached wings. Holding it in the air, it looked as though it were bearing a flag as it marched into battle. Mu Sheng picked up a stick and used it to pry the insects apart. One flew off, but the other, minus a wing as well as part of a leg, struggled to move and then, a moment later, it was dead. Mu Sheng's head began to spin again, that familiar buzz returned.

Looking at Miao Tianyi, he said: "Let me untie your hands… OK?"

The other man extended his arms and Mu Sheng released one hand from the rope. The other he left tied to the tree.

"Hey! If you're going to untie one, you have to untie both!"

"One's enough… you've got to take care, you know."

Miao Tianyi spat, but he was too slow, and Mu Sheng dodged out of the way: "Ha! You missed!"

Watching the scene from some distance away, the village head quickly pulled up his trousers and ran back towards his prisoner. He wasted no time boxing poor Miao Tianyi's ears.

From out of Yan Linben's office, Mu Sheng and the village head heard Zhang Shoucheng howl. They had no idea what was happening, but the situation didn't seem to come as a shock to the other inmates, who by this time had ceased hitting each other and had gone instead to the canteen. Unmoved by the continued screams, the men simply sat and wolfed down their meal. Finally, Yan Liben's office door opened. The first person to leave was the principal who was the first to accompany Zhang into the room. He was followed by Yan Liben and one of the team leaders. Zhang Shoucheng exited last. He was completely naked, a steelyard weight suspended from his penis. He proceeded to march around the opening. The weight looked incredibly heavy and as he walked his legs couldn't help but bend outwards.

Greatly disturbed by what he was seeing, Mu Sheng gasped and then quietly directed a question at the village head: "What's the purpose of this… what work is Zhang doing?"

"Well… it was Zhang's prick that he used most. I guess it's only right that it should be the source of his pain, too."

Yan Liben walked towards them, stopped and spoke in a booming voice: "Ah… now you must be Mu Sheng, yes? I've heard you can call like a cow… how's about showing us, hmm!"

Mu Sheng hadn't recently been practising his moo, so he instead explained why they had come: "Me and the village head here... we've brought a man in need of re-education, Miao Tianyi. Here he is... I must go, I've got to lower the flag!" He spun around and ran off. He decided then he'd never go back to Heilongkou.

It wasn't as though Mu Sheng thought fondly of Zhang Shoucheng. In fact, he remembered him as a teacher when he was young. He'd sneaked to just outside the classroom window and spied the goings on, saw how Zhang asked for the students to sit, and how he dealt with unruly children who'd climb onto their desks. He'd break off a piece of chalk and fling it at them. Mu Sheng had laughed the first time he saw this, which led to Zhang discovering him and exacting the same punishment. A piece of chalk had hit him with a bang square on the nose, and shortly afterwards he heard the shout: "Scram!"

Zhang Shoucheng was incredibly strict in how he handled his students, but he couldn't control his urges, and as a result he'd been found guilty of far too many transgressions of a sexual nature. The first time he'd been caught out had been three years ago. The school he worked at had been raising a pig to ultimately slaughter and give to the teachers, each getting a portion of meat. The headmaster had not made this plan public; in truth, it wasn't to be spoken about at all, but that didn't stop Zhang from giving his share to a widow in Zhenzhongjie. The result could be anticipated: word spread of what the teachers and headmaster had done, and soon nearly every family head of the children at their school was at the main gate causing a racket. They accused the school of taking advantage of the children: every Saturday afternoon class involved preparing food for the pig, all so that the teachers could eat it? The headmaster retorted that the pig pen was in fact alongside the teacher's toilet and that was how it had got so large; and naturally enough, they ought to have had the privilege of eating it, now shouldn't they? It was all very unpleasant, and none of the parents really wanted to cause a fuss, but when word reached them of the intimate relationship between Zhang and this widow... Naturally, the headmaster called Zhang to a meeting to discuss the matter, whereupon he confessed to everything, but at the same time he tried to argue he'd been to her place on just four occasions.

"I only meant to ask if you'd sold her the meat… and now you tell me this!"

Zhang broke down into tears. This led to grovelling and assurances that there would be no repeat offences. And to some extent he held true to his word; he never called on this widow again. But it wasn't long before he was discovered having an affair with a female colleague at his own school. The headmaster, desperate to contain the scandal, decided reluctantly to try to deal with the matter internally. Zhang Shoucheng was therefore ordered to write a self-criticism, and then the matter would be considered closed. Six months later, in the middle of autumn, Zhang handed another self-criticism to his headmaster, once more admitting to certain transgressions. Furious at the revelation but still intent on keeping things quiet, Zhang was reassigned to running logistics for the school and forbidden to step into a classroom. Things seemed to be fine for a while, but before winter had got very old, Zhang again knocked on the headmaster's door and handed him a new self-criticism.

"Again… really?" The headmaster was at a loss.

"Well," began Zhang, "just a minor infraction… I'm afraid, however, I won't be able to handle everything myself, I mean, keep things quiet… so I thought it best to report it to you."

"Who's it with this time?"

"Ren Guihua… from Chenjiagou."

The headmaster knew the woman. She was the lead singer for Chenjiagou when the commune held its singing competitions. She was a looker, too.

"Fuck… you say 'just a little'… you've gone and poked the bear you fool! She's married to the military you know… her husband serves!"

"We've… we've only just kissed… busy hands… nothing more…"

"You've not slept with her?"

"No."

"Are you telling me shit, or the truth?"

No matter whether he really believed Zhang or not, things had gone too far, they'd become too serious this time. There was no way he could deal with it himself; he had to report to Lao Pi. Unsurprisingly, the secretary flew into a rage and hurled a tirade of verbal abuse at the headmaster, scolding him for covering things up for as long as he had, and for allowing this current transgression to take place. Did he know the punishment for breaking up a military marriage was an immediate arrest? Things were already complicated enough. Not only was the commune vying for the title of being at the revolutionary vanguard, but it was also having to deal with that inflammatory document and the search for its author.

"And now this!" shouted Lao Pi. "Send him to Heilongkou... make him work the kiln fires!"

The headmaster departed, but before he'd got very far, Mu Sheng came running up to bring him back. Lao Pi had further instructions, which Mu Sheng now relayed: "If anyone asks, tell them Zhang Shoucheng is guilty of philandering. Don't say anything about who it involved. Then... and this is vital... I want you to send an official wire to Ren Guihua's husband... use the commune's name... and tell him his father is seriously ill and that he needs to request time off to return... this isn't as bad as if his wife were present."

It rained heavily the following day, but this didn't stop Lao Pi from instructing Mu Sheng to travel to Chenjiagou to bring Ren Guihua back with him. When she heard the contents of the secretary's missive, she wondered if another singing competition had been called, and then quickly set off to get ready, to comb her hair, powder her face and change her clothes. Mu Sheng returned before her and by the time she finally showed up, he was busy sweeping away the fallen leaves that had accumulated on the steps leading to Lao Pi's office. Worry plagued his heart; he couldn't escape the feeling that the buzzing was about to return. But at the same time, he felt impelled to listen to what was being said inside. He didn't notice he'd swept the leaves into a shape that eerily resembled the face of an old tiger.

The leaves continued to fall, and billowing clouds lowered the sky's ceiling. But strangely, no leaves landed on the porch to Lao Pi's office. The buzzing really did begin again, and when he finally saw Ren Guihua leave the secretary's office, her face was blanched and she seemed terribly out of sorts. Indeed, she even lost her footing and stumbled to the ground, scraping her head in the process. Mu Sheng witnessed her topple over and came rushing over to support her.

"Are you alright?"

"Nothing… it's nothing… I'm fine." Her reply couldn't disguise the distress she was obviously feeling.

Releasing his arm from under hers, Mu Sheng stepped over to the tree that stood in the courtyard to gather up some loose bird feathers. These would serve as a suitable plaster for the wound on her forehead. But by the time he turned around, she had already picked herself up and was walking unsteadily along the path that led away from Lao Pi's office.

—

The first work Miao Tianyi was assigned was the most arduous and gruelling at the camp: the transporting of bricks, by hand, once they were complete. After about a fortnight, he'd lost nearly half his body weight. Nevertheless, and in spite of the difficult nature of the work and regardless of how tired he became, he was sure he could endure it. His problem had to do with the evenings; he simply couldn't sleep the whole night through as he was frequently dragged off to be interrogated about that blasted counterrevolutionary document. The entire performance became so common, he began to wait for them to come and get him with a bizarre sense of expectation. Then, on those days when no one howled for him to come, no matter how long he waited for them, he thought he might be able to get a decent shuteye. This proved not to be the case, however, as halfway through the night the shouts would echo out again.

The interrogation room in which this show was repeated was in the eastern part of the camp. And when they beat him, he couldn't help but scream at the top of his lungs. After a while, even Yan Liben found it so tiresome listening to his constant wailings that he asked the interrogator, the man in charge of re-education, to see if he could make Miao laugh, or at least smile. Ever the creative type, the man devised a strategy and changed his approach. Instead of beating Miao Tianyi, he had him forced to his knees and then tied to a tree. Once securely in place, Miao's shoes were removed, and saltwater was rubbed over the soles of his feet. Unable to free himself, he watched as sheep were led over and then had to endure the sensation of them licking the balls of his feet. Needless to say, Miao no longer shrieked as he had before. Instead he laughed, so hard in fact that he soon lost consciousness.

By the end of that first day, Zhang Shoucheng's penis had swollen so much it looked more like a large white radish than a male appendage. Unable to sit, all he could do was stand and relate his various crimes to his tormentors. Each and every word was scrupulously recorded, and each and every amorous escapade had to be mentioned, down to the smallest detail, no matter how insignificant it may have seemed. The interrogators were especially struck when they learnt the names of Zhang's many romantic partners, of what they looked like – clothed and unclothed – of what they did and in what position. Their reactions ranged from exclaiming that he was indeed a lascivious rascal, to asking him for more and more information.

Indeed, Zhang's adventures were often the subject of their idle talk well into the night, so much so there were even times when they would call him back for further questioning. And while Zhang himself would shout on these occasions that there was nothing more to say, his interrogators remained unconvinced, insisting that there must be. As a result, Zhang began to ad lib, to invent increasingly salacious details, which his interlocutors ate up rapaciously. Of course, a problem did arise: when they asked him to act out the details, he was wholly unable to do so. Still, Zhang Shoucheng's days at the camp ended up being more enjoyable than Miao Tianyi's; he was at least able to bring his captors a degree of titillating pleasure. As a result, he endured lifting bricks for a very short period before he was assigned to the communal kitchen and the fuelling of the cooking fires.

On yet another of his visits to Qipan for a haircut, as he passed by Bear Cliff, Mu Sheng happened to bump into Zhang Shoucheng carrying firewood. His hair had grown long and now covered his ears. His beard, too, enveloped the lower half of his face. Upon seeing him, Mu Sheng instinctively exclaimed: "You've no mouth!"

Zhang peeled back the layers of his beard before speaking: "If it's not a mouth, then what the hell is it, huh?"

"How's it that I only see you out here carrying wood? Where's Miao Tianyi?"

"Ah," explained Zhang, "there's a difference here. I'm guilty of a crime, yes, but my contradiction... yes, that's the word... is of the common people. I might be a philanderer, but I'm not a counter-revolutionary. Tianyi on the other hand… well… his contradiction is much more serious… he's an enemy of the people!" He then asked if Mu Sheng would cut his hair, but he was rebuffed.

A little after a month into his stay at the camp, Zhang Shoucheng became ill. On the day he'd brought a donkey along with him to carry the wood, but before he got very far on the path back to the camp, he felt that particular urge rise in him. He soon unfastened his trousers and pulled out his cock, seemingly intent on buggering the donkey. The beast, however, kept trudging down the path and he was left powerless to follow it. On an adjacent slope, another inmate who had been busily cutting grass witnessed the entire scene unfold. Shocked by what he saw, he set off as hastily as he could to report things to Yan Liben.

In what seemed like mere minutes, a reform meeting was called to struggle against Zhang Shoucheng. Naturally, he denied trying to rape the animal, arguing instead that he simply had to piss, that was why his trousers were open. He added, too, that he'd kept on walking and pissing at the same time, playfully writing words on the mountain with his urine.

The man who had reported him, however, was eminently more trustworthy than a known deviant; after all, not only was he a poor peasant, but he was old as well. Zhang was strung up and beaten savagely with a bamboo pole. The rope he'd been tied with bit into his flesh, and he was struck again and again. The rope balled up, tighter and tighter, and still the bamboo rod tore into his skin. It fell with greater rapidity and strength, his head, his face, nothing was spared. When blood began to run from his eyes like tears, he confessed.

That evening, Zhang's most recent transgression – bestiality – was written up and preparations were made to call the police to escort him away. Looking at the words on the page, the camp authorities thought the crime would cause irreparable damage to the commune's reputation, so the document was corrected and the crime changed to moral turpitude. Even this charge, however, had the potential to cause reputational damage to the commune, if for no other reason than that it was much too vague. Yan Liben also thought it didn't accurately reflect the seriousness of the crime, so finally he made the determination that 'destruction of communal property' be added to the charge; this would clearly indicate the gravity of his wrongdoing.

The charges written up, Yan Liben telephoned Lao Pi and reported the situation, proud of how he had handled it and the crime he assigned to Zhang. While he was doing this, however, something else was happening to Zhang, who had been interred in the interrogation room waiting for the police to arrive. The kitchen had sent down some sweet potato noodles, but due to the beating he had suffered, his mouth was so swollen he couldn't open it to eat. Frustrated and angry, he smashed the noodle bowl and used a shard to slice off his manhood.

A little while later, the kitchen staff returned to collect the dishes, thinking Zhang had by then finished eating, only to discover him in a pool of blood, his penis lying on the floor. Shocked by the scene, the man yelled in horror. The scream was so loud that it reached the ears of Yan Liben, who was still on the phone with Lao Pi.

"Eh?" Yan said into the receiver. "Just a second, please, secretary."

He put the telephone down and marched towards the interrogation room, only to find Zhang already dead, his penis lying next to him. It must have been excruciating, thought Yan Liben. Zhang's crotch was a bloody mess, the flesh torn and ragged; the appendage had to have been sawed off… it was brutal, and blood was everywhere. This would have to be reported to the Party secretary; there was no other recourse.

Lao Pi's response, however, was not what he had expected: "Well, in this case we don't need to report it… put a dunce cap on him and continue the work of re-education."

That very evening Guofenglou was hit with a deluge of rain. It was as though a vast basin of water had been overturned onto the area. The rain was followed by lightning. Mu Sheng wasn't afraid of the downpour, but he was of the electrical charge that twisted through the sky. Each flash was a stark vermillion line running through the clouds, bathing the ground below in a luminescence of scarlet-white. A second later and everything was black again. The thunder would soon follow, a crack of sound that seemed to be trying to rend open the heavens. For Mu Sheng, it sounded as though the thunder was right above his own roof, desperately trying to shatter it to pieces.

On nights like these, Mu Sheng kept his door shut tight, the windows, too. He didn't dare sleep, fearful of what might happen if he did. The locals believed that thunder and lightning was the sign of heaven battling with a fearsome dragon that was trying to escape to gobble up the humans below. Mu Sheng was afraid such a dragon would come for him. When it got really bad, he'd go to his cellar and stay until dawn broke, trembling in fear the whole while.

By morning, the thunder and lightning had stopped, and so too had the wind and rain. And as before, Mu Sheng had to set out towards the mountain to raise the red flag. When he arrived at the familiar tree as he had done so many times before, he scaled it with ease and caught sight of the sun arching over the mountains far to the east. It seemed almost to be toying with him, its colour tender, light, akin to the yellow shell of an egg. It seemed to be acting in deference to the wind, rain and the lightning, that if they said 'come', it would do so, if they said 'leave', it would fall away. He wondered how it was the sun had such a temperament.

His attention shifted away from the sun, and he scanned the branches for more stick insects. But when he looked down, he noticed a white birch tree that had seemingly been uprooted a mere fifty feet away; it had been broken into three uneven pieces. Mu Sheng gasped in surprise, and then quickly climbed down the tree to inspect the birch more closely. The outside of a white birch was always a sight to behold, smooth and impressive, and these characteristics were still apparent. The insides of the tree were a different matter, however, the lightning having scorched the wood, ripping the tree apart. The girth of the trunk, as it turned out, was large enough for him to squeeze in. Safe inside, Mu Sheng decided to stay for a while; he wondered whether his head would begin to buzz. When it didn't, he mumbled to himself, marvelling at the peacefulness of his location.

After another moment passed, perhaps two, Mu Sheng extricated himself from the broken tree and started running down the hill, intent on reporting the fallen birch tree to the Party secretary. Lao Pi, however, just stared at him, the dark spots in his eyes betraying a lack of interest in what Mu Sheng was telling him. Before letting him finish, Lao Pi interrupted his 'report' to instruct him to make all haste to Chenjiagou and bring Ren Guihua back with him; the quicker, the better.

Mu Sheng had already turned and was half way out the door when

Lao Pi extended himself over his desk to call out: "So the lightning tore down a tree?"

"Yes, a white birch."

"Fuck… why couldn't it have done the same to Zhang Shoucheng!"

When Mu Sheng arrived in Chenjiagou and walked up to Ren Guihua's home, he saw her standing on the porch, combing her hair. It was the only place where she could comb its entire length, the rooms beyond the door being much too small and confining. Upon hearing Mu Sheng's directive that she was to report to the commune offices, the comb dropped from her hand and fell to the ground. She was considerably flustered by the ominous summons, her heart raced. Trying to reclaim some semblance of calm, she sat down, her hair piling up behind her on the porch. Mu Sheng interrupted her attempted repose and told her that Lao Pi wanted her immediately; any delay would be met with a fierce haranguing. Ren Guihua mumbled a response under her breath, and then proceeded to put her hair in a braid and wash her face. Mu Sheng berated her for her vanity; she wasn't being asked to attend the county magistrate. Resigned to his insistence, the two of them left in haste to return to the secretary's office.

Once they arrived at the outer courtyard, Ren Guihua collapsed to the ground: "My heart is beating out of my chest!"

Mu Sheng paid her no mind and instead knocked on the office door. A moment later, Lao Pi emerged to see Ren Guihua on her knees.

"You," she panted, "you called for me?"

"Why were you so slow in coming? I've got this for you… are you going to take it?"

Surprised, Ren Guihua blurted out: "Yes, yes, I'll take it… how much is there?"

"What did you say?"

"Well… I know all about what happened to Zhang Shoucheng."

"How do you know about that?" Lao Pi shouted, feigning anger.

"Mu Sheng told me on the way back here."

Lao Pi lifted his foot and levelled it at Mu Sheng, striking him hard. Ignoring his subordinate's explanation, he continued to address Ren Guihua: "I said you need to take this!"

"Take what?"

"This! Your husband has telephoned for you!"

Ren Guihua gulped as though something was stuck in her throat. Struggling, she finally stood and walked into Lao Pi's office. Taking hold of the receiver, she heard her husband's voice on the other end.

The telephone conversation concluded, Ren Guihua left the office and went straight to speak to Lao Pi: "I've finished."

"What did he have to say?" asked Lao Pi, quick and to the point.

"He told me he was taking leave, that he'd be here in three days."

"We're doing this to protect you," Lao Pi added. "You should know what you've done, yes?"

"I do..."

A few days later, everyone in the commune offices had heard about the telephone call between Ren Guihua and her husband. The story was that when she grabbed the receiver, she gasped and panted "hello, hello" several times before her husband answered. But the first words out of his mouth were to ask if she were indeed his wife.

"Can't you hear me?" she asked. "Is it a bad connection?"

"It's been a long time you know... I just need a rest."

"My place is quite far from the commune, you know... will that be alright?"

"More than alright... I've asked for leave... I'll be home in three days."

"Eh... you're coming home? But... I'll be busy three days from now... how am I supposed to come and greet you?"

"You don't need to... just do yourself up, take a bath and wait for me to come."

The more the story spread among the cadres, the funnier it became. Lao Pi wasn't especially happy about the rumours going around, preferring people to keep their mouths shut, but it had got out and he wanted to know who had said what first. Naturally, he questioned Mu Sheng, who answered that he had told the office director that Ren had spoken to her husband over the phone, but he didn't say more than that.

"I swear," Mu Sheng added, "that if I spoke a word more, my mouth would fill with shit and I'd let the dragon come and grab me!" For three days running he swore the same oath to Lao Pi, who finally relented and took him for his word, accepting that it wasn't him who had started the rumours.

"But you're still looking at me like a suspect..."

"I've just got big eyes... can I help the way they look!"

The tension in Mu Sheng's face ebbed, and he felt more relaxed. He even thought to call out like a cow, something he knew Lao Pi greatly enjoyed.

Once the work compiling the history of Qinling's guerrilla band came to an end, I was intent on leaving Guofenglou. I remember that morning. The sky was clear but for a single white cloud wafting across the sky, large and billowy like a bundle of soft cotton. I'd gone to take my leave of Lao Pi, who was busy convening a meeting for all of the nearby village and town cadres. Mu Sheng was there as well, but not participating in the clamorous debate. No, he was sat outside in his usual place, under the tree that stood near the main building, just beyond the din coming from inside. One hand was clasped hard over his mouth, something that made me laugh.

"I suppose you reckon you're Lao Pi's secretary, huh!"

As I spoke these words, however, I noticed Mu Sheng wasn't just holding his hand over his mouth, he was in fact grabbing at it. His other hand then broke into action and pinched and poked at his lips and teeth inside. Soon a stream of blood rolled down his chin.

"What the hell're you doing, boy?" I yelled.

Mu Sheng looked up at me, eyes wet with tears: "I'm trying to learn my mouth right!"

"Why? Has it betrayed you too often?"

"It spews nothing right."

"Why? What's it said?"

"But if I told you what it said, wouldn't that mean I'm saying something wrong again?"

His mouth was beginning to swell. He started sobbing, too.

The meeting inside came to a close and once Lao Pi realised I had been waiting for him, he sternly reprimanded Mu Sheng for failing to tell him I'd arrived. In his defence, Mu Sheng tried to say I'd not told him who I'd come to see, but his voice was garbled and much of what he said was unclear. I explained to Lao Pi that Mu Sheng had been trying to punish his mouth for what it had supposedly said wrong in the past. His response was predictably unsympathetic: "That's what he ought to be doing! Punish it some more, I say!" He then ushered me into his office and offered me some tea.

He began to gush about the accomplishments of Guofenglou, of how the commune had been at the revolutionary vanguard for the past five years and how it had been held up as a model for others to follow. Other individuals had also been praised for their achievements, he told me. Three cadres, in fact, had been nominated for a special award, but he had won it. He was due to pick up his award tomorrow and wondered if I might stay until he returned. He hoped I might include his achievement in my narrative, make him part of the guerrilla band's history, as it were. I congratulated him, of course, and promised I'd wait for him. Grasping my shoulder firmly, he didn't actually thank me.

"Good, good, that's how it should be. You wouldn't want me to have even more regrets, would you!"

"Regrets… you have regrets?"

"Naturally I have regrets… after all… Commander Kuang San's not come to see the apricot trees!"

Lao Pi rambled on… he wanted me to wait until after he'd received the award and then we'd go to the apricot trees together to have our picture taken. He asked if I could relay a message to Kuang San, tell him how everyone in Guofenglou longed to see him, hoped he would return to his old haunt and pay them a visit. I responded by telling Lao Pi I wasn't sure if I'd see the commander, but that if I did, I would certainly pass on the message. Lao Pi continued his soliloquy. The trees had brought good fortune to the commune, despite Kuang San not seeing them in person. He then came to his main point, the issue he'd raised in the meeting that had just concluded: the trees had to be given a birthday. He spoke of when he was young, of how people had their birthdays and so, too, did the trees and flowers. The second of March was the birthday for orchids, 4 April for lotuses, 8 August for the sweet osmanthus, so it only made sense for the apricot trees to have a birthday, too! And since the commander's birthday was 29 April, Lao Pi went on, that seemed to be the ideal date for the trees. Naturally, it would have to be properly celebrated. What's more, Lao Pi enthused, it was almost 29 April, which meant he'd already requested each village to begin rehearsing for the song competition he'd planned. I just had to stay, he said, it was going to be quite the show!

On the following day, Lao Pi set off for the provincial offices to receive his award. Liu Xueren and the other cadres organised a proper send-off, banging gongs and beating drums. The gongs and drums weren't all that loud, it must be said; they were, after all, used more for local festivities and not really for political functions, but their rhythmic sounds took me back to those days when I crisscrossed the entire area singing my folk songs, songs of mourning. It had been so long since I'd done so, so long since I even held a drum. It was really quite stirring. I said as much to one of the nearby drummers, and then asked if I could relieve him for a spell. He complied, and soon I was playing familiar melodies, to the astonishment of the crowd. Lao Pi even halted his steps.

"How's it you still remember such music?"

"I guess... since I learnt them when I was a child, they've stayed with me."

"Excellent, excellent... you should teach them, pass them on."

I returned the drum to the young man, and he quickly rejoined the procession following Lao Pi out of the village.

"Just look," Lao Pi shouted, "who could ask for more devout villagers!" He bowed and told the drummers to return to the village, his eyes moist.

After seeing Lao Pi off, Liu Xueren and Feng Xie decided to go to the kiln at Heilongkou. While their visit may have been unexpected, Yan Liben insisted on them staying so that they could dine together. They were to have lamb for their meal. It was one of the same sheep that had been used to 'punish' Miao Tianyi. Since enjoying meat was rather exceptional in the times they lived in, Liu Xueren and Feng Xie readily accepted the invitation. They didn't eat at the normal hour, however, but waited until well past midnight, until the workers, those enduring reform through labour, as well as the other administrative staff, were comfortably asleep. The three leaders then dragged the animal into the main office as quietly as they could, bound its mouth tightly so that it wouldn't make a sound when the blade fell, and proceeded to stew the freshly slaughtered meat. There were three bowls for each of them, and it didn't take long for the meal to be devoured.

Liu Xueren, now sated, was the first to speak after they'd finished eating: "It's a shame our secretary wasn't here to enjoy this."

"I thought of him... while I was eating my first bowl," Yan Liben said. "It ought to have been for him... I suppose I ate it in his name..."

"We really should've had him here... he's liable to criticise us if he finds out... he's never had stewed lamb, either. Once he returns from getting this award, we have to make sure he's properly welcomed back, we have to make this up to him... a celebratory general assembly... all in his honour."

"That goes without saying," agreed Yan Liben, "but is that enough?"

Feng Xie now chimed in: "I could make something out of silk, a crimson red flower. We just need to buy the cloth... we could then drape it over his shoulders..."

"I'll present him with a new banner, carved into wood," said Yan Liben. "We could raise it up just as the meeting starts."

Liu Xueren and Feng Xie nodded their agreement. A wooden placard would be ideal, it would stand the test of time much better. Even after the secretary retired, it could be hung over the door to his home, a testament to his achievements, a lasting sign of his honour and glory. The only question was: what kind of wood would be best?

"Leave this with me," Feng Xie said with confidence. "Qipan has more than its fair share of suitable wood, carpenters, too."

"Sure, sure," said Liu Xueren. "We've got the wood, but using our local carpenters... that makes me a little uneasy... we ought to get someone from the county capital to do it. And while we're at it, what should we have written?"

Yan Liben was first to come up with a suggestion: "The secretary always preaches about absolute loyalty and dedication to the Party... he takes himself as the model of such devotion. You write well, Liu... how about some words to that effect? I mean, that sounds good, right?"

Liu Xueren demurred. His skill with a brush, he insisted, was nowhere near good enough for such an important gift: "No, not me... the man you need is... is Miao Tianyi."

"What!" baulked Feng Xie. "How... how could we get him, of all people, to write it!"

"Ha ha," interjected Yan Liben. "This particular job… I'll take care of it… you just get everything else ready."

On the following day, Liu Xueren had laid out the ink, the brushes and the stone. Before long, Yan Liben arrived with Miao Tianyi in tow. He was instructed to write a certain four characters, ones they had decided upon that would highlight the secretary's devotion to the Party. That was all they said. Miao Tianyi was not to be told why they were getting him to write such words, fearing his potential for insolence, his resistance to reform. Unsurprisingly, Miao wouldn't just do as he was instructed. His first complaint had to do with the paper, and so he requested Mu Sheng be sent for more. Then the brush was unsuitable: it was too small and had to be changed. After this, there was an issue with the ink: it was much too thick and needed to be prepared again. This he did himself. He then asked for a cigarette as this would help him write more exquisitely; if he didn't get one, he assured them, the calligraphy would lack the necessary vitality. Tobacco was supplied and he gestured to Mu Sheng to light it for him. Once his conditions were satisfied, Miao Tianyi wrote the characters across the paper. He finished with a flourish and turned to Mu Sheng to ask for water.

By this time, and with the work completed, Yan Liben had run out of patience. His foot shot out and connected squarely with Miao Tianyi's rump. His irate voice came shortly after: "Get this… this person back to the factory… now!"

The wooden placard and the characters Miao Tianyi had written were sent to the county capital to be engraved. A few days later, Feng Xie and Liu Xueren procured a cart and travelled to the capital to collect the gift. Once they'd paid for it, they had five yuan left, which they used to buy two boxes of biscuits. By the afternoon, they were back in the commune buildings, the office cadres having already decorated the meeting grounds for their arrival. They had even raised a gable above the chairman's seat. Naturally, Mu Sheng was there, busy at work, perched on a ladder nailing the gable together and attaching hooks to the placard. Once it was lifted into place, they had to make sure it was level and suitably imposing. Satisfied with how things looked, the placard was taken down and transported up the hill to Lao Pi's personal office. This would be its true hanging space, so it had to look good there as well. Mu Sheng was ordered to take hold of one side of the placard; Feng Xie and Liu Xueren would both take the other side.

"I… I… I don't think I'll be able to lift it on my own," said a nervous Mu Sheng.

"What nonsense!" retorted Liu Xueren. "Of course you will. Now lift!"

Without saying anything further, Mu Sheng took hold of one end and lifted; Liu and Feng had the other end. Before they ascended five steps on the way to Lao Pi's office, Mu Sheng fell to his knees with a thud.

"You dickless little shit!" Feng Xie cursed.

Mu Sheng's response was rather unexpected: "You two take it, and I'll moo like a cow instead."

Finally, having reached the office overlooking the lower compound, Mu Sheng calculated the dimensions of the placard so that the wooden pegs could be inserted in the proper place. Once more, the placard was heaved high and secured above the entrance to Lao Pi's office. Sitting down, Feng Xie and Liu Xueren enjoyed the biscuits they had brought back with them.

"What're you eating?" asked Mu Sheng.

"Biscuits."

"I bettcha they're good, huh?"

"Taste is one thing, but they're bloody dry… go back down the hill and fetch us something to drink." There was impatience in Feng Xie's voice.

Mu Sheng went off to get water. On the way back, he was tempted to spit into the pitcher he was carrying, but he didn't. Instead he cursed them, hoping they'd choke on their biscuits, or drown themselves in the water he now carried. A moment later, he handed over the water and watched as the two men continued to eat the biscuits and drink the water. Feng Xie stared at Mu Sheng as he devoured the biscuits and gulped the water, but the younger man kept his eyes trained on the sky above and away from those of his superiors.

"What the hell are you doing?" Feng Xie's voice dripped with venom.

"Counting birds…"

"Would you like some?" Liu Xueren asked.

"No… that's alright."

"Really? Then I guess that's all the more for us."

"Well, perhaps I could…"

"You little fuck… you clearly want some of these biscuits, but you don't have the balls to say whether you really do or not!" Liu Xueren's words were full of derision, but still he passed the younger man three biscuits.

Mu Sheng wolfed down the first biscuit in just two bites, but he took his time with the remaining two, nibbling them slowly. Then, with his mouth still full, he grabbed at the water, sloshing it over his face, before craning his neck like a gull to swallow the biscuits down. Originally, Feng Xie and Liu Xueren had planned to enjoy the biscuits for themselves. They figured they could eat them all. It never occurred to them that they would only get through about half of what they'd bought.

"Would you like any more?" asked Liu Xueren.

"Alright."

"You've seen the cart we used to bring the placard back from the county capital?" Liu Xueren continued. "We borrowed it from the kiln factory… you return it, and we'll give you some more."

"Sure!" With this quick reply, Mu Sheng gulped down the remaining biscuits.

"Well… will you look at that… grown a set of balls after all, hey… you fucker… you've eaten more than me!"

Mu Sheng laughed, seemingly rooted to the spot, and his neck arched again: "Give us a moment, OK… I'll return the cart in a little bit."

Later in the day, as Mu Sheng returned the cart, he discovered three new workers had arrived at the tile factory, one from Chenjiagou, another from Xiajing and the last from Liulinwan. Apparently, the men had been arguing with the village head in Qipan, saying they wanted to cut down the apricot trees. Given the supposed importance of the apricots, the village head had them arrested and sent to Yan Liben for re-education. On this occasion, Yan did not take his usual course of action of holing himself up in his office and speaking on the telephone; instead, he chose to stroll along the elevated bank near the river, hands clasped behind his back, his mind seemingly mulling over some problem.

A moment passed and Yan stepped down. He'd come to a decision: it would be necessary to make a show of strength. A heavy rope was dipped in river water, then wound tightly around the three men, binding them as though they were chained together. One of the men remained silent, another began to breathe somewhat heavily, while the last squealed like a stuck pig, at least for a little while before he fell silent.

"Come on piggy," came an anonymous shout, "have you lost your voice? You'd best find it again! Here now… get the air pump used for the cart wheels… shove it up his arse and blow away, ha ha!"

Mu Sheng didn't dare to stay and watch. He simply placed the cart against a nearby wall and departed. By the time he returned to the compound, the sky had already gone dark. He'd run most of the way back and was now painfully thirsty, so much so that he waded into the nearby stream to get himself a drink.

The office manager happened to see the unusual scene unfolding and shouted out to Mu Sheng: "What the hell are you doing?"

"I'm just getting a bit of water before I go and take down the flag."

"But it's already dark… what's the point of lowering the flag now?"

"It's my job… mine, it's what I have to do." He lifted himself out of the stream and ran off in the direction of the mountain and the tree that supported the flag.

By the time he reached the foot of the mountain, his stomach was bloated, extended far beyond normal, almost as though his innards were ready to burst through. It hurt terribly, but still he scrambled up the tree and untied the red flag. Glancing above, he could see the sky filled with stars. Another meteor shower, he wondered, before reaching out his hand as if to catch them. In his current condition, this was a mistake and before he knew it, he'd lost his grip and plummeted from the tree, head first towards the hard ground that lay below. The rocks below weren't exactly big, but they were sharp and had little trouble piercing his skull.

The cry he let loose when he fell was loud and reverberated across the land. A flock of birds took to the air in fright. Unfortunately for Mu Sheng, however, nobody was around; no one would know he'd fallen. Mu Sheng didn't realise himself that the rocks below the tree had bitten into his scalp; all he felt was dizziness. He mistook the red that began to blur his vision for the flag he thought he'd already lowered. Then he looked to the sky again and reached out his hands, naively trying to grasp the falling stars. Blood gushed from the awful wound on his head and he reclined a little more against the tree. Shortly after midnight, he grew silent and then stopped breathing.

Having returned from receiving the award for his accomplishments, Lao Pi was feted by a grand ceremony organised by Liu and Feng. Each village had cadres in attendance who all beat drums and gongs in Lao Pi's honour. Firecrackers were lit and a red sash made of silk was draped round his shoulders.

Liu Xueren was the first to speak: "Secretary, your face is practically glowing, a bright red hue. You look ever so vigorous!"

Lao Pi beamed at the praise Liu had showered him with, using words generally reserved for the Great Helmsman, Chairman Mao. He feigned humility: "Oh... it's just that it's so hot, I'm sweating terribly..."

The wooden placard was now taken out and deftly hung above the central chair, Lao Pi's chair. Once it was put in place, Lao Pi began his speech. The pitch of his voice was high, higher than it had ever been before, almost a vibrato: "Comrades, fellow villagers, whatever honours I've received belong to the whole of Guofenglou, each and every one of you, the entire commune..."

A sudden and resounding thump rang through the air, interrupting his speech. It hadn't come from the drums and gongs the cadres had been beating, but rather from the placard that was formerly hanging behind him. All the attendees directed their eyes to where it lay, cracked in two and splayed on the ground. The crowd gasped and Lao Pi turned his head around. He made no sound, but it was clear to see that the rosy, proud look his face bore not a moment ago had gone.

Before another second had passed, Feng Xie and Liu Xueren, the office manager and Yan Liben, rushed forward to inspect what had happened. To their dismay, they discovered the wooden pegs had cracked.

"How's this?" said Yan Liben. "The pegs are broken... who's... who's responsible for putting them there in the first place?"

As was his habit, Lao Pi shouted as if in response to Yan Liben's question: "Mu Sheng! Mu Sheng!" But unlike on previous occasions, Mu Sheng did not come running up.

Liu Xueren looked around, wondering where the younger man was as he'd not seen him yet today, even if he only noticed his absence now: "Mu Sheng? Mu Sheng!"

In fact, no one in the crowd had seen him either.

Growing increasingly annoyed, Lao Pi directed his attention to his private office up on the hill, assuming Mu Sheng was there, but the place was empty. Farther up the hill, he saw that the red flag was not fluttering in the breeze. There was no way he could continue his speech, but he remained fixed in the chairman's seat. All he could do was consider what had happened, wonder why the flag had not been raised.

Liu Xueren broke the silence: "Fuck! Curse that no-good bastard!" Mu Sheng, in his mind, was to blame for the debacle, he'd been the one who'd nailed the pegs into the beam, he must have done it wrong and now he'd fled. That was the only explanation for why the flag had not been raised. Turning to Yan Liben and the office manager, he instructed them to prepare tea for Secretary Lao, and then he set about restoring order to the meeting. It had to continue at all costs, Lao Pi had to be properly celebrated. At the same time, Feng and Liu excused themselves and set off for the mountain.

The scene they came upon was quite unexpected. Mu Sheng had been dead for what seemed like days. His mouth was agape, the red flag was clutched to his breast; the cold temperature had ensured his body remained rigid. There appeared to be leaves scattered across the flag, but when they reached down to grab hold of the flag, they realised they weren't leaves, but stick insects crawling all over.

Lao Pi arrived not long after the meeting had come to a close. He looked at the scene in front of him and determined immediately Mu Sheng hadn't committed suicide to avoid punishment; the poor fool had simply fallen, cracking his head on the stones that were scattered about at the foot of the tree.

"Oh, Mu Sheng… you died before your time!" Lao Pi's eyes welled up and he turned away, refusing to linger over the corpse of his faithful assistant. As he began the walk down the mountain, he shouted over his shoulder: "He was an orphan. Bury him there."

Workers were called to do the digging, but no one removed the stone that had cut so deeply into his scalp. And no one cleaned the blood that had poured down his face, either. He wasn't given clean clothes to be buried in, nor did anyone burn hell money as an offering to the dead; no incense sticks were lit. All they did was dig a grave, seemingly intent on dumping him into it. As they worked, however, Feng Xie's eyes were drawn to the hollow tree that lay a little farther down the mountain. He interrupted the solemn work to say Mu Sheng deserved a coffin at least. Everyone agreed, and Mu Sheng's poor corpse was soon wedged into the dead tree. Mud sealed its open top and bottom. Afterwards, the makeshift coffin was rolled into the grave and covered with earth.

As they walked back down the mountain, the cattle roaming here and there across the various ditches and fields mooed nonstop, long cries and short, a dirge for the dead Mu Sheng.

I left Guofenglou a day or so later. Naturally, Lao Pi was there to send me off. He looked tired, I remember, like he hadn't slept. The skin about his face seemed even saggier than usual, and he was unshaven. Nevertheless, in spite of his condition, he made sure I was given a proper goodbye. Feng Xie was there, so too were Liu Xueren and Yan Liben. The junior cadres were also there, ready to ring their bells and beat their drums. I noticed then how long Feng's hair had grown, Liu's too, as well as the other cadres from Qipan… their hair was so long, in fact, that you couldn't even see their ears… A brief, ceremonial statement was made and then the gongs and drums began to echo. We walked, all of us, down the hill from Lao Pi's office… I took a drum from one of the men… as I'd done before… and began drumming myself… then I felt like singing… for myself… and for poor old Mu Sheng.

One, two, three, four, five,
Metal, wood, water, fire, earth…
The moon is full but one day out of thirty,
The bagua define reality, the earth its cardinal directions…
Clouds waft through the air,
Water trundles on in waves.

"Eh… you're singing a funeral elegy," said Lao Pi, breaking my rhythm.

"Once… this was what I did… I was a mountain whisperer… I sang songs all across this region."

"Really?"

I continued singing:

Nine, eight, seven, six, five, four, three...
The ancient world lies far off in the past.
All is darkness, no sky, no earth, no mountains...
No wind, no clouds, no lakes of crystal clear water...
This is the record of bedlam,
Of chaos...
When, may I ask, will there be a crack for the light of heaven and
  Earth to shine through?
In the beginning there was the primordial universe,
The Taiji...
Yin and yang emerges from the supreme ultimate,
The Four Guardian Beasts from yin and yang...
The Beasts beget the bagua...
I sing now of Pangu's reckless splitting of Earth from heaven,
So much has been forgotten...

Lao Pi interrupted me again, but I paid him no heed this time and kept on singing…

Into this temporary forgetfulness,
The singer beseeched the heavens...
First to the five elements,
Second to the sun and the moon and the stars in the sky,
Third to the Jade Emperor,
Fourth to the Dragon King of the Four Seas,
Fifth to Chenghuangye, god of counties, cities and towns,
Sixth to the Duke of Thunder and the Mother of Lightning,
Seventh to the God of Wealth and the God of the Kitchen,
Eighth to the mountain guardians wielding their vajras,
Ninth to filial piety and one's ancestors,
And the last request to Yama and his home in hell.

I sang for the many deities that inhabited the land, and for the deceased to find their way into heaven. By the time I reached the valley floor, Lao Pi was nowhere to be seen, nor were Feng Xie, Liu Xueren and Yan Liben. As we reached the stream, the remaining cadres departed as well. The only people left were those I was in charge of, the men who'd helped me compile the history of Qinling's guerrilla band. As well as the drummer whose drum I had borrowed. I stopped singing and turned to ask the young man if there was a shadow behind me. He answered that there was, and I told him it wasn't mine, but rather Mu Sheng's. I remember his face blanched when I told him that… and then he began to stomp on the shadow with all his might… I intervened, got him to stop, and told him to return. I wondered why he hadn't already… and that's when he told me I still had his drum.

Two days later, I arrived in the county capital. While I was no longer the team leader for compiling the history of Qinling's guerrilla band, I wasn't permitted to return to my previous post in the Art and Cultural Troupe. This was because of Lao Pi and his report to the central authorities about me. In truth, it didn't bother me much. I mean, it wasn't as though I'd always been doing that sort of work…

It was Deputy Director Xu who summoned me. He was sitting in a wheelchair and as he spoke, there was a noticeable lisp. He asked if I'd like to head to the countryside, to become a peasant… a farmer. I told him I'd like to return to Zhengyangzhen… and he agreed… although when I finally returned, no one in the village knew who I was. I remember going up to one household to ask for some water… the young lady of the house said their family's pickled vegetable broth would better quench my thirst, and she proceeded to fetch me a bowl. On returning with the mixture, she asked me where I was from… I said I'd just been travelling on the road, that I was passing through. Where was I going, she asked. I told her wherever my feet wished to take me. Would you like something to eat, she asked… and then from out of the kitchen I remember hearing another voice shout… it asked me if I was the mountain whisperer…. Before waiting for my reply, the disembodied voice answered its own question in the affirmative… I peered a little further into the house and spied an old man sitting near the kitchen stove… I looked at him and nodded… he seemed to know me, recognise me… but to me, he was a stranger. Then he told me he'd seen me once before, when he was just a boy… now he was old… and paralysed… bedridden. He asked how it was that I was still alive… I laughed by way of reply, then told him I hadn't yet been punished enough… Yama wouldn't let me die… and continue to live I did… it must've been tens of years. I stayed in Zhengyangzhen, but I never sang funeral dirges again… not really by choice, mind you. I mean, it wasn't as though people stopped having children, or that they stopped dying… no, it was just that no family ever came to ask me to sing… times, I guess, were changing.

THE FOURTH TALE

Question:

Sometimes I see 'Great River' and other times I see 'Yellow River', are they one and the same? Is that why the others are referred to simply as running water... is the Yellow River really the only great river?

Answer:

Well, the word by itself refers to huge channels of running water, the largest imaginable.

Question:

So why doesn't the text call it the Yellow River? Was it because... at that time... it wasn't yet filled with the yellow earth we see today?

Answer:

Correct... when Pathways *was written, the banks of the Yellow River were still lined with trees, great majestic trees.*

THE FOURTH TALE

I'll read the first sentence, you follow.

The fourth part of *Pathways Through the Western Mountains* begins with Moon-Dark Mountain. Paper mulberry trees grow in abundance upon its highest slopes. The soil is generally free of stones. Cogon grass and sedge cover the lower reaches of the mountain. A river bearing the same name as the mountain rises here to flow west into the River Luo. Mount Lao is only fifty leagues to the north. Gromwell grows on its slopes. The River Ruo flows from here in a westerly direction into the River Luo. Fifty leagues to the west is Bagu Mountain. This is where the Er He River originates before flowing west into the Luo. Gromwell is common on the slopes of Bagu Mountain, and there are many precious stones around.

One hundred and seventy leagues north is Shen Mountain. On its upper reaches paper mulberry trees proliferate, as do toothed oak and red apricot trees. Lower down the mountain, holm oak and oak trees dominate. Deposits of gold and jade litter the south face of Shen Mountain, making them easy to find. The River Ou emerges here to flow east into the Yellow River.

Bird Mountain stands two hundred leagues to the north of Shen Mountain. Near its base, silk mulberry trees grow in great number.

On its northern slopes iron is common, while on its southern slopes are great deposits of jade. The Disgraceful River starts on Bird Mountain and flows east where it merges with the Yellow River.

A hundred and twenty leagues to the north is Upper-Shen Mountain. Unlike Shen Mountain, there are many stones upon its slopes, but hardly any vegetation. On the lower reaches of the mountain are numerous hazel and thorn trees. White deer is the most common creature on Upper-Shen Mountain. Danghu birds nest in great numbers. They resemble a pheasant but fly with their throat feathers. Consuming their flesh is said to be good for the eyes. The Boiling River gurgles up here and flows in an easterly direction towards the Yellow River.

Mount Zhuci rises a hundred and eighty leagues farther north. A river with the same name emerges here to flow east into the Yellow River. Trees cover its slopes, but there are no grasses or shrubs. Birds and four-legged beasts are absent, but there are numerous snakes and vipers.

Another hundred and eighty leagues to the north is Wailing Mountain. Many lacquer and palm trees cover its slopes. White iris, medicinal herbs, and xiao and xiong grasses can be found in abundance. Soapstone is also common. The Duan River emerges here and flows east before being swallowed up by the Yellow River.

Two hundred and twenty leagues farther to the north is Jar Mountain. Its northern side is heavy with iron deposits while its southern side contains copper. White wolves and white tigers call this mountain home. White pheasants and white kingfishers live alongside the wolves and tigers. The River Life originates on this peak and then flows eastwards into the Yellow River.

White-Crow Mountain rises two hundred and fifty leagues to the west of Jar Mountain. On its peak you can find a great many pine and cypress trees. Lower down its slopes, chestnut-leaf oak and sandalwood trees grow in abundance. Yak and antelope graze up and down White-Crow Mountain. Owls nest in its trees. The Luo River first rises on its southern slope before turning east to disappear into the River Wei. The River Ga works its way out of the rocks on the north face of White-Crow Mountain, then flows east into the River Life.

Three hundred leagues to the north and west is First-Shen

Mountain. It rises so high into the sky that it is nearly always covered in snow. Therefore, there is no vegetation on this mountain. It is here where the River Shen begins. It flows under the snow before emerging at the foot of the mountain. White jade is said to be plentiful, but it's mostly hidden.

A relatively short trek fifty-five leagues to the west is Mount Jinggu. This is where the Jing River begins. It flows to the southeast and into the Wei. Deposits of white gold and white jade are plentiful.

Unyielding Mountain stands a hundred and twenty leagues farther west. Lacquer trees grow on its slopes, and there is much tufu jade. The Unyielding River rises here as well to flow north into the Wei. Chui-spirits are said to reside in great numbers on this mountain. Their form is that of a beast with only a single foot and a single hand, but their face is that of a human. Their call is more of a chant, and there are some who liken them to chimei goblins.

The lower peaks of Unyielding Mountain stretch a further two hundred leagues to the west to give birth to the Luo River. It flows north before emptying into the Yellow River. A creature that looks like a beaver is a common sight here. Its body is that of a large, watery rat, while its head is more like a turtle's. It is known to bark like a dog.

Heroic-Shoes Mountain lies three hundred and fifty leagues to the west of the lower peaks of Unyielding Mountain. Near its summit are numerous lacquer trees. Much gold and jade can be found closer to the base. The creatures that live here, both birds and beasts, are white. It is the origin of the Meandering River, which flows north into the Hill-Ram River. Turtle-back fish are plentiful. Their head is like a snake, six feet sprout from their abdomen, and they have the ears of a horse. Eating their flesh wards off blindness. They are also said to be a talisman against evil forces.

Three hundred leagues farther west is Middle-Bend Mountain. On its southern face there is much jade, while on its northern face there is a great deal of realgar, white jade and gold. A white-bodied horse-like creature can be found on this mountain. Its tail is dark, a horn like that of a unicorn marks its forehead, and it has the teeth and claws of a tiger. When it neighs, it sounds like the beating of a drum. It is often called the bo and is said to prey on tigers and leopards. If tamed, it can make an excellent war horse. There is a tree that resembles a plum tree, but its leaves are rounder. It produces a reddish fruit that is as large as a papaya. It is known as the huai. The fruit has a reputation to increase one's strength.

Mount Gui is two hundred and sixty leagues farther west. An ox-like animal dwells on this mountain. It has hedgehog bristles over most of its body and is called the qiongqi. It is said to howl like a dog and be a man-eater. The Misty River starts here before flowing south into the River Yang. Yellowish cowrie shells can be found in great abundance in the river, along with a fish called the ying. It is said that this fish bears the wings of a bird and sounds like a mandarin duck. They are an omen of a disastrous flood.

The Mountain Upon Which Bird and Rat Share a Cave is two hundred and twenty leagues west of Mount Gui. White tigers roam in great numbers on these slopes and white jade is plentiful. The Wei River originates here and flows east into the Yellow River. A fish known as the sao swims freely. It bears resemblance to a sturgeon and is said to herald the arrival of a great military force in the area. Another river begins its journey here as well and is known to often breach its banks. It flows into the Han River that lies to the west. Many rubi fish swim in this river. These flat fish resemble an overturned cooking pan. Their head looks like a bird's, while they have the body and tail of a fish. They gurgle under the water and remind one of chiming stones. It is said they give birth to pearls and jade.

Three hundred and sixty leagues to the southwest stands Mount Yanzi. Near its peak are many cinnabar trees that bear leaves that look like those on a paper mulberry tree. Their fruit is as large as a gourd with red calyxes with black markings. Consuming this fruit is said to be a cure for jaundice. Its skin and flesh are also known to insulate against fire. Many tortoises roam on the southern face of this mountain. Jade deposits are common on its north side. Sweet Potato River originates on Mount Yanzi and then flows west into the sea. The riverbed is littered with whetstones, both coarse and fine. A beast that has a horse's body, the wings of a bird, a human's face and the tail of a snake resides on this mountain. It is said to greatly enjoy carrying humans on its back. It is known as the shushi. An owl-like bird can also be seen on Mount Yanzi. It has a human's face, the frame of a monkey and a dog's tail. It has no name and is only distinguished by its call. It is an omen of terrible drought.

Nineteen peaks are included in the final section of *Pathways Through the Western Mountains* covering a distance of more than 3,680 leagues. A single white chicken should be used to sacrifice to the gods that live among these peaks. Glutinous rice is also to be given. Attendees must sit on white reed mats. Altogether, there are seventy-seven mountains in the west, covering some 17,517 leagues.

Any questions?

Question: Sometimes I see 'Great River' and other times I see 'Yellow River', are they one and the same? Is that why the others are referred to simply as running water… is the Yellow River really the only great river?

Answer: Well, the word by itself refers to huge channels of running water, the largest imaginable.

Question: So why is it that in places it's called 'Great', and in others it's called 'Yellow'? Was it because… at that time… it wasn't yet filled with the yellow earth we see today, or at least not as much?

Answer: Correct… when *Pathways* was written, the banks of the Yellow River were still lined with trees, great majestic trees. As the environment changed, well, the many small rivers that the text mentions have either disappeared, or their routes have changed, and in some cases their names, too. That's not to say they're gone completely, no, they're still there… but even so, they don't necessarily have the same amount of yellow silt as the present-day Yellow River. I mean, should their colour turn that familiar yellow, well, their name would change. The larger the river, the more probable it is that mud and sand will mix together.

Question: When the text states that several of these mountains have no plants, no trees, only stones… what kind of stones is the book talking about?

Answer: Very large ones, massive ones that could easily crush a person.

Question: The passage talks about different stones and minerals on the mountains… what are these?

Answer: Ah, they're like soft stones or rocks.

Question: Rocks can be soft?

Answer: All that is living is soft, all that is dead is hard. These minerals, well, perhaps they were first like lava, or they formed out of lava, then, after they hardened, well, I imagine they would look much like the loess dolls we find quite frequently around here.

Question: Well, there are a lot of those loess dolls around here, that's for sure!

Answer: Well, sand is what's left when there's no water, like the earth dying of thirst… I suppose you could say the loess dolls are like the corpses of the rivers.

Question: What spirits is the book talking about?

Answer: Ah… it's talking about malicious spirits, ghosts, demons.

Question: Ghosts, demons, malicious spirits? What's the difference between them?

Answer: Some animals possess certain human characteristics, they're sort of like half beast, half man. Those are the creatures we call mountain spirits, sometimes demons, or ghosts. We don't like seeing these creatures. Most humans consider them to be abominations, which is why we've so often tried to vanquish them, kill them off. Those that we couldn't, well, we have had to take a different approach: we worship them. It's sort of like using both the carrot and the stick... so I guess you could say that a spirit is one of those beasts, demons, what have you, that we worship, whereas the demon demons, well, they're the ones we were successful in driving away.

Question: Much of what is described on this mountain range is the same as on the other mountains, there's very little difference... but the farther west the text takes us, the greater the number of strange beasts, birds, snakes and fish it talks about... why's that?

Answer: In the past, the farther west one went, the fewer humans they would encounter. But now... well, how many people do you know who have seen these strange, monstrous animals... how many have even heard about them? The only creatures you find on the mountains these days that are strange and monstrous are people... the longer they're up here, the more beast-like they become. It's just like those who live near the sea... the longer they're there, the more fish-like they become. In truth, it's very hard to distinguish the people from the animals.

Question: The passage says most of the animals on Upper-Shen Mountain are white deer, and on Jar Mountain there are white wolves, white tigers, as well as white pheasants and white hill pheasants... I'm not sure what the difference is, but... and then on Heroic-Shoes Mountain the birds and animals are all white, too. The Mountain Upon Which Bird and Rat Share a Cave also has white tigers... and white jade... but anyway, my question is... are all the animals on this mountain range white?

Answer: Didn't the passage also talk about snow in summer and winter? The environment changes of its own free will… thus everything in it must adapt.

Question: But the text says when sacrificing to the deities of these mountains one has to use white chickens and white rushes… for the seating mats. The same is true for the first southern mountain range, the first western one, the second one too… but… but those mountains don't have snow through the entire year, do they?

Answer: In those days, as a person travelled farther west they would encounter more and more snow, and greater numbers of deities, spirits and demons… ancient people used white to appease these gods and ghosts… later on, even the Western Paradise in Buddhist scripture became known for its whiteness… bliss and extreme happiness were also represented by the colour white… whereas the human world took on the colour of black, darkness began to symbolise bitterness, the hardship of living.

Question: Hmm… so why is it that when people die today their family and friends wear white?

Answer: There's a saying: when people die, the gods come to collect their souls… this you know. But did you also know that those gods fear fire. Now the living, the family of the deceased for instance, well, they radiate an intense light, it's almost as though they're ablaze… and the gods fear this… so, naturally, a filial family dons a white hat and white clothes to mask their living glow… it's a way to welcome the gods come to collect their loved one's soul, and to ensure that it's safely carried to the Western Paradise. The ancient people mentioned in *Pathways,* well, they're like the first people… the first to figure this out… and their way of thinking has been passed on ever since… it's become part of the collective consciousness… part of our culture… understand?

Question: Er... I suppose so... I think I can understand that...

Answer: Well... let's see... say what I've told you in your own words.

Question: OK... in the ancient past, people used things that were white to sacrifice to the many gods and deities that walked the land. Later, people used white to represent cleanliness, pureness. The ancients paid worship to the mountains, and later, the emperors of each and every dynasty did the same... for example, people in the past believed they could communicate with the gods through pieces of jade, which is why jade is prized so much today, it's why people put it in jewellery and wear it on their person. Another example... in the far-off past, when people saw red, they believed it symbolised the coming of war and its disastrous consequences... and today, red symbolises power, revolution. Oh... I've got another one... the ancients distinguished between yin and yang... they knew what grasses and herbs to pick for making medicine.

There were more than 2,320 types of medicinal herbs in Qinling. In the county of Shanyin, it was possible to find bellflowers, forsythias, milk vetch roots, gold thread, psyllium and something colloquially known as tongue fern due to its striking resemblance to that part of the body. Santai was recognised as the home of honeysuckle, cornel dogwood, red peonies, barrenwort, false daisies and motherwort. In Lingning County, one could find liquorice root, thorowax, cangzhu, the stem of a black sunflower-like plant, crow-dipper, magnolia trees and their medicinal bark, rhubarb, tuckahoe, an edible fungus that grew on trees, selaginella and purple violets.

The most well-known of these herbs was the fructuscorni that grew in Shuangfeng Prefecture. It was the most valuable, too. In the Republican period it was said that a single tree was worth at least one head of cattle, an enormous amount for the time. The herb itself grew in the deep forests that covered Mount Dayu, the same mountain that was the origin of the river that flowed uphill through Qinling. If a person were to trace the river back up the mountain in the direction of the dragon basin from where it began, they'd notice there were at least eight steep-sided valleys throughout the mountain range and in each of them they'd find a plethora of medicinal herbs and plants.

The third valley, the one that etched its way east, was the longest. Starting high on the mountain it wound its way past Mount Dayu and reached down into faraway Hubei Province, all the way to the small town of Donggou. The opening of the valley was the location of the village of Danggui. It was here that female ginseng could be found, the only place, in truth, where it grew. But it was plentiful since the people who lived here had cultivated it for generations. The village's name was a direct reference to the ginseng they grew, *danggui* being a local name for the plant. As the village matured over the years, more and more people began to arrive, each carrying baskets to pick the ginseng, each intending to sell it in Huilongwan, the regional capital. Business had become so brisk, in fact, that on the road back to Huilongwan, outsiders ended up establishing shops, eight in total and all peddling the female ginseng.

Medicinal herbs and plants became the main source of income for the villagers, both the picking and selling of them to the shops that lined the road to Huilongwan. But despite its expertise in herbal medicine, for generations Danggui suffered from a particular malady; at least, the men did, for the disease left the women untouched. The men weren't born with it, however. Up until the age of seven or eight, they were the same as any other boy anywhere else, but that never lasted. Soon, before the age of nine, they'd experience swelling around their joints, especially in their legs. It would get so bad that they would soon be bedridden, unable to stand for even brief periods of time. Needless to say, this would terrify the parents, especially as there seemed to be no cure. All they could do was massage their poor children's legs, crying all the while for the swelling to subside and for their boys to grow as normal.

This situation generally lasted for a number of days until finally the swelling would subside. By this time their boys' legs seemed to have merged together, their thighs growing into calves and vice versa. Where their knees once were, there was now a hollow, an inexplicable gap that would grow wider and wider as the children grew older and older. Their legs became curved and bent, in most cases quite seriously, and still this strange hole in the middle would continue to yawn. This in turn caused the parents to fret even more, and they could often be heard wondering whether or not their child had been leaping off cliffs in their dreams, risking life and limb, if only subconsciously. In fact, the children did have dreams of climbing and leaping off cliffs when they had been of normal stature, but by the time they reached a little over four feet tall, such dreams would cease. Whatever the case may be, the affliction took its toll and for generation after generation, the men of Danggui never grew much beyond four foot five inches, eventually earning the name of 'halfling' or 'dwarf' by those who ran the shops on the road to Huilongwan. Unsurprisingly, their condition led outsiders to ask question after question whenever they showed up in their shops.

"So tell me," the exchange would often start, "would you be able to traverse… in a single day… a road that was, say, forty *li* or more?"

"Sure, we could if we set off when the cock crowed."

"Shit! That early…"

Other questions would follow.

"Now… I'd like to ask… well… after you get up… do you spend some time massaging your legs. Could you still walk if you didn't... at least a little?"

"We do… yes… we do rub our legs. After all, everyone has their morning habits, like you getting up and boiling water to make tea."

As one might expect, drinking tea in the morning was a popular custom. It was actually quite common for people to boil up the tea from the day before, jabbing the old leaves with a pair of chopsticks in order to release what taste remained; the result was usually a strong and almost barky flavour and for many, such tea was the only thing that enabled them to truly wake up.

"Why don't the women in Danggui worry about contracting this… affliction?"

"If they did worry about it, well, tell me, who'd till the land?"

"Ah yes, I suppose so, but… well, that means the women are the heads of the family, yes… I mean, that's rather unusual…"

"What're you talking about? How can a woman lead a family… no… no… you've got that wrong. Here, let me tell you… I guess it's like a grindstone, it has a top and a bottom, yes, and that's what makes it a proper grindstone, I mean, it takes two things to rub together... hmm."

This response would generally result in great fits of laughter, followed by further banter: "Well now, aren't you describing an argument between a husband and wife... and doesn't that usually end up with a man wishing to raise his hand and the woman running off to her bedroom? But, well now, a man such as you... you wouldn't really be able to get up in bed to sort things out now, would you? I guess you'd just have to swear and ask the bitch to lift you up... ha ha!"

Listening to this kind of thing, they'd finally realise the outsiders were belittling them, and they refused to answer any more questions. Instead, they'd keep their money in their hands, shake their heads and depart, mumbling under their breath as they did so: "Hmph, next time I'll come with Xi Sheng!"

Xi Sheng was a fellow villager, but unlike the rest of them, he was famous. His family, in truth, had earned a certain prestige nearly three generations ago. And no, no one at all had the balls to bully him or his family.

The three generations of renown enjoyed by Xi Sheng's family, according to the villagers, was due to the favourable feng shui of their family home. Situated in one of the deeper depressions that seemed to be carved into the valley walls, the village overlooked tapering slopes that fell to the valley floors, while the western ridge towered high up behind it. Farther up the ridge lay the village's primary water source, a spring that bubbled up from deep in the mountain to flow downhill into Danggui. The stream meandered haphazardly down the valley sides, branching out into two like a pair of trouser legs. Xi Sheng's family home was nestled near the source of the spring, upon a relatively flat piece of land nearly overlooking the village below. The plain extended for quite a distance and was the only area where wheat could be grown. The crop for this year, however, had already been harvested and so the field appeared a tattered mess, wheat husks mixed in among small stone shards that had been broken off as a result of the many stone rollers that had been used. All that stood in the field was a small and very old rubber tree, valued for its medicinal properties. Xi Sheng would stroll out to the tree every morning to rub his bare arms against its trunk, then his spine and finally his knees. Once finished, he'd have no need to massage his legs like every other male in the village. His morning ritual didn't stop there, however, as he would next take an old rag and clean a wooden board that was fixed above the main door; emblazoned upon it were the words 'Martyr of the revolution'. He'd carried out this ritual with such dedication that the character for 'revolution' was now hardly visible, despite the fact that the placard itself seemed to have a bright, brilliant coat of paint. When the sun shone upon it, the board would shimmer and become highly visible throughout the village.

Xi Sheng's grandfather was the martyr so honoured; an honour Danggui didn't hesitate to celebrate.

The villagers still revelled in telling the story of Xi Sheng's grandfather. It always started in that year. Qinling's famous guerrilla band had been active in the nearby area, they'd ambushed two county militia platoons near Ganjialiang, but then they'd been surrounded by the Kuomintang. Apparently, the Kuomintang had an enormous force and were ready to exterminate all trace of the band, when, unbeknownst to their commanders, the guerrillas escaped via a secret mountain pass. The story went on to say that the guerrilla band arrived in Huilongwan, stayed just a day and then soldiered off to Danggui. Here they stayed for much longer, and it was here that Xi Sheng's grandfather asked to join the revolution.

Things didn't go all that smoothly, however, since Lao Hei, the band's leader, had refused him due to his diminutive stature. He had even doubted whether Xi Sheng's grandfather could carry a rifle without it scraping across the ground. Undeterred, Xi Sheng's grandfather told the commander how well he could run and set off to demonstrate. Unfortunately, his bow legs meant he couldn't run all that fast, to say nothing of how comical he looked with his buttocks protruding at the top of his tiny legs. Needless to say, he was unsuccessful in changing Lao Hei's mind.

Still, he was unrelenting in his desire to join the guerrilla band, and so he went in search of Li Desheng. On finding him, he clamped his arms around the taller man's legs and wouldn't let go, beseeching him all the while to allow him to enlist. Li Desheng acquiesced, partly to get him to release his leg, and partly to see what he could actually contribute to their activities. It was decided that he wouldn't engage in any of the fighting, but he could deliver messages; after all, who would pay much attention to a halfling scurrying underfoot when so much else was going on? That's how his revolutionary story started.

It wasn't long before everyone started calling him 'uncle' for his willingness to carry out mundane tasks. Initially he was sent to Huilongwan to buy supplies, and at the same time, Lei Bu was dispatched to another valley to source food for the troops. Xi Sheng's grandfather was sent back and forth, delivering regular communiqués and ensuring all the soldiers were equally well informed despite the distance between them. He performed his responsibilities exceptionally well, thereby earning the respect of his comrades. But he was also given to bouts of silliness. The first such instance was when he once more pestered Li Desheng for a rifle. Needless to say, Li refused; after all, he'd not got any taller, and so, to remedy the situation, Xi Sheng's grandfather resorted to carving a pistol out of wood. Strikingly similar to the actual weapon Li Desheng carried under his belt, next to the red bandana marking his revolutionary allegiance, Xi Sheng's grandfather attached a similar piece of red cloth to his 'pistol' to show his loyalty to the cause. (It made more sense, he surmised, to tie the red bandana there instead of looping it around his belt and having it drag on the ground.)

Regrettably for Xi Sheng's grandfather, the wooden pistol would lead directly to his death. And unsurprisingly, it happened while he was on the road, busy relaying messages between guerrilla groups. On this particular mission, his straw sandals came apart and at nearly the same time, two herb collectors came upon him. Instead of asking for assistance, Xi Sheng's grandfather chose to hold them up with his fake pistol and force them to hand over their shoes. They complied, but after Xi Sheng's grandfather left them shoeless, they continued on, finally coming to a small shop selling roof tiles. There they reported the incident to the local militia, who in turn dispatched troops to apprehend the shoe bandit, Xi Sheng's grandfather. At first, he was fortunate for he spotted the troops searching for him and was able to hide behind a clump of tall grass. Now, if Xi Sheng's grandfather was a man of normal stature, everything would have turned out alright, he'd have gone unnoticed. However, his small frame and protruding arse worked against him, for he was easily recognised by the soldiers sent after him. They were merciless. Instead of actually arresting him, they strode up to the clump of tall grass and thrust their bayonets into it.

The blades pierced his buttocks like a spit through a pork roast – Xi Sheng's grandfather was dead.

Forty years later, the custom of singing mourning songs was revived throughout most of Qinling, and I soon returned to my old profession in Zhengyangzhen. Now, of course, there isn't a specific sort of place, no ceremonial location as it were, for me to sing these songs, and so before the year was out I found myself in Huilongwan. None of my many and varied experiences could lead me to imagine that Huilongwan's main thoroughfare would become the biggest and most diverse of shopping centres. All sorts of shops and stalls were now selling a huge assortment of things; in the intervening years it had clearly prospered. I remember staying there for quite a while, but still, in all that time, I'd never heard the tale of Xi Sheng's grandfather, which I found a real shame... I wondered, too, how it was that nobody had told me about him, especially when I had been compiling and writing down the history of Qinling's guerrilla band. Li Desheng, Lao Hei, Kuang San, these were the heroes, without question, but there were more troops like Xi Sheng's grandfather, common soldiers fighting for the cause.

I took it upon myself, then, to include his tale in one of my songs, telling of how he was first denied entry into the guerrilla band since Lao Hei deemed his unmistakable arse to be too much of a target. I sang of how he was undeterred by this setback and ultimately welcomed into the band by Li Desheng who tasked him with being a courier. My song then turned to his demise, the unfortunate encounter with the militia, his protruding arse, the grass and his unsuccessful attempt to hide, his death by bayonet, his sacrifice for the Party, for the revolution. Each time I was asked to sing a mourning song, I was sure to add at the end this refrain about Xi Sheng's grandfather. It didn't take long for the residents of Huilongwan to learn the story, the words; soon they'd sing it with me. Needless to say, Xi Sheng and his father were incredibly grateful, especially his dad... he actually came into the town to seek me out... showed up in front of my home directly opposite the Guandi Temple... he wanted to give me a shadow play set, and I remember telling him thanks, but no thanks... but he insisted. Finally, I acquiesced and ended up putting on shadow plays to accompany my old tunes.

Not only did Xi Sheng's father suffer from dwarfism like all the other men in Danggui, but he was bald as well. His distinct appearance led to him being given the nickname Tortoise, but in Shuangfeng he was best known for being the most amazing shadow play puppeteer ever seen.

Shuangfeng came under the supervision of Kujiao County, one of Qinling's many administrative units. For what seemed like forever, shadow puppetry had been popular among the population. During the Qing dynasty, puppet troupes were celebrated, esteemed even, and there were generally a dozen or more operating in the area. In the chaos of the Republican era, however, things changed and the popularity of shadow plays started to wane. Some troupes managed to survive for a while, but most fell into bankruptcy within three to five years of being established. Less successful troupes might put on only a single show before disbanding. For a long time, theatre troupes were like family. Shows would be performed in one village and then packed up in the play boxes before they moved off to another. Each and every performer in the area was a celebrity in their own right, and all of them belonged to the Sanyi Troupe, the most well-known and respected theatre company in the region and an integral part of Shaanxi's theatrical tradition.

The year their travelling troupe came to Huilongwan was the same year Xi Sheng's grandfather had his unfortunate, and fatal, encounter with the local militia. In fact, the day the performers arrived in town along with their equipment pulled in donkey carriages was the same day the militia put Xi Sheng's grandfather's corpse on display, right in front of the Guandi Temple. This was a sign of what would happen to those who opposed the Kuomintang forces. The shows ran for three days, and the corpse was exhibited for the same length of time. On the fourth day, a smallish man arrived, bald despite his youth and with legs bowed like the dead man. He had a handsome face, however, and his eyes flared a sense of purpose. He had come to collect the body.

He sat down next to the dead man, leaning his back against the deceased's chest. Then he pulled out a rope and tied it around them both. Once secure, he attempted to stand, which took several goes before he was successful. The head of the dead man lolled back and forth, before finally settling on the bald man's shoulder, giving him the appearance of a man with two heads. The scene was witnessed by the lead actor of the theatre troupe who hurried over with a cloth in his hand. This he wrapped gently round the deceased man's head.

"Who are you?" asked the actor.

"I'm his son," replied the young man.

"Why haven't you brought a rooster with you... you know, to protect your father's spirit."

"I've already asked others for menstrual blood – it's in my pocket." The actor reached into the young man's pocket and pulled out the small vial. He opened it and poured a drop onto another piece of cloth he had with him, and then rubbed the blood on the other man's hairless scalp.

Three more days passed and the theatre troupe was preparing to leave Huilongwan. On the day of departure, the young man returned expressing a wish to join them. He was not welcomed in, however, as most were suspicious of his family background, assuming – correctly – that his dead father had been a guerrilla fighter, a member of the band supposedly terrorising the countryside. But the lead actor spoke in his defence.

"Whatever his father may have been, he's his own man," he said. "And besides, did you see his legs?" The actor paused for a moment before continuing: "When I saw him tie that rope around his father, I marvelled at his skill with knots. He also carried his dad home... how many *li* was that... hmm? He's a good young man... filial... someone, I think, who has potential."

The words worked, and young Tortoise was accepted into the troupe. Not long after, at the behest of the actor who spoke so favourably of him, he began learning shadow puppetry.

The work of a shadow puppeteer, as is commonly known, takes place behind a screen. In front stands an actor who provides the vocals and moves the story. The key for the puppeteer is to perform the actions in tandem with the narrative. This was what Tortoise studied and after three years, by the time he was nineteen, he had already become famous for his skill and technique. Indeed, it was a marvel to watch him work. Not only was he able to deftly manoeuvre the puppets into grasping swords and flying through the clouds in ferocious combat, but he could also have them mimic more sorrowful poses such as weeping when the play turned tragic. To see them behind the screen sobbing and convulsing like in real life was something to behold.

Four years passed, and Tortoise's fame continued to grow, putting the troupe in rather high demand. In the nearby town of Damingping, a wealthy landowner who was preparing a big celebration to mark his grandson's first month sent word that he would like to hire the Sanyi Troupe to perform. Considering the payment they were likely to receive, the company accepted and set off without delay, the actors travelling at the front of the procession, Tortoise at the rear. In truth, due to his particular infirmity, Tortoise did little walking and instead sat upon the back of one of the company donkeys. As the troupe tramped along, with the donkey obediently carrying Tortoise at the back, they passed a river. Tortoise was struck by the freshly blooming peach blossoms that reached out over the water. They were as brilliant as the sun and so amazed Tortoise that he couldn't help but call out happily and sing a few lines from one of his favourite arias.

Farther up the stream, a young woman was out washing her clothes when she heard Tortoise's voice pierce the air. She looked up, her eyes boring into the small man seated upon a donkey.

As she stared, another voice called out: "Kai Hua, Kai Hua, don't you just love Tortoise's skill with shadow puppets. Ask him where he's performing this evening… come on, ask!"

Instead of replying, Kai Hua cursed: "What the hell are you talking about? Who loves his shows?"

"Alright, alright, I misspoke, you don't love watching his performances… you just love watching him!"

"A dwarf… what's to love about looking at him!"

That evening a stage was set up in Damingping, much as it had always been. Just beyond the stage a rather large gathering of men and women were stretched out, their chests on the ground, their heads arching upwards in anticipation of the show. Later in the evening, when the performance was over, Tortoise peered out from behind the screen and scanned the crowd. As he did so, his eyes met the young woman called Kai Hua; it seemed as though she'd been looking for him, too. He smiled and she smiled back at him. Their eyes were aflame, igniting passions neither had expected.

The after-show party was to be held at the house of the wealthy landowner who had invited them in the first place. They were to eat together, but Tortoise demurred and excused himself, saying he needed to take care of some business back near where the stage had been set up. There waiting for him was Kai Hua.

"I thought you said you didn't like dwarfs?"

"If that were true, would I be here waiting for you?"

"Ah... true... well, let me tell you, I mightn't be able to walk that well, but I can do everything else."

"I bet you can!"

Tortoise embraced her, tilted his head to search for her mouth and kissed her passionately. From then on, they would be lovers.

Kai Hua had actually been a child bride, promised to marry the son of the family she'd been adopted into. The marriage had already been consummated, at least partially, but since her husband suffered from an undiagnosed illness and was unable to fully complete the act of consummation, Tortoise convinced her to seek a divorce. It wasn't easy, but eventually Kai Hua was successful in leaving her husband. The only problem was her mother, who vehemently opposed her desire to marry Tortoise; she was fearful of the prospects if she did, namely, bearing a son who would be crippled and short like every other man from Danggui. Love lost, Tortoise later married a woman from his home village; Kai Hua ended up with a hunchbacked man.

Liberation occurred some years later, and not long after Tortoise found himself performing in a nearby valley. By coincidence, the town he was in was the same one Kai Hua had married into. He soon learnt her hunchbacked husband had died three years before, and she was now the widowed mother of a small girl. They had both longed to see the other, and now that they were together again, it didn't take long for them to fall single-mindedly into a heap; Kai Hua worked at the town mill, and Tortoise took her there on the floor. Their reunion soon turned to embarrassment, however, for Kai Hua's daughter stumbled in on them in the act.

In mock terror, Kai Hua yelled to her daughter: "Quick, help me... he's trying to hurt me!"

Her daughter rushed forward, intent on grabbing the man's hair, but Tortoise had none to grab. She yanked on his ears instead.

"Not the ears," her mother shouted once she realised what her daughter was doing. "You'll tear them off."

"So what? He'll still have his fat arse."

Separated, the two adults put their clothes back on. Later, Kai Hua asked Tortoise if he would take on the role of adoptive father for her daughter, and he agreed. Now that the two families were bound together, every month or so after, Tortoise would visit his adopted daughter and bring gifts of cotton candy, fried doughboys or other sweets; he bought gifts for Kai Hua, too, from printed cloth to pomade for her hair. In return, she stitched his clothes, his shoes and his socks.

Xi Sheng, Tortoise's son with his wife, was like his father. By the age of seven, he became bow-legged and fated to be a halfling. They didn't worry about this, it was part of life in Danggui, but they were concerned about the boy's crop of hair and whether or not he'd be bald like his dad. So anxious were they that when he was only five or six they began using knotweed to wash his hair, and then, every three to five days, they'd massage crushed garlic into his scalp. As a result, Xi Sheng's hair grew long and lush.

Over time, Xi Sheng gradually came to learn of his father's romantic affair, but he never breathed a word of it to anyone. That mess belonged to his mother, and he wished to stay out of it. His father wanted him to study shadow puppetry just as he did, but Xi Sheng had no desire to do so; his passion lay in singing folk songs. Tortoise therefore thought about having him sing the opening chorus for the shadow plays he performed. He could stand behind the curtain and prepare the audience for the upcoming show. Xi Sheng refused this as well.

Then one day, as it turned dark, he quietly picked up a hoe and a basket and headed off for the hills to harvest ginseng. The ginseng he exchanged for cash, and with the money he decided to surprise his mother by buying her a new comb and headscarf. Xi Sheng told his mother he wasn't yet done, and he asked her to wear the headscarf so that he might sing a tune for her. She obliged, and Xi Sheng began to sing. He would periodically repeat these performances to his mother's delight, but whenever his father happened to return before he had finished, he would always stop abruptly, choosing not to sing when his father was home.

After a while, Tortoise was no longer surprised by his son's behaviour, and so he cared little that he would stop singing each time he returned. He was now seventy, Kai Hua had died and he no longer performed his shadow plays. His aged body had made it impossible to repeat the actions he once managed so easily. Half of his former troupe had died already, and no one wished to learn the shadow puppetry he had spent his life performing. The likelihood of his craft dying with him caused a pang of guilt, and so, with great difficulty, he set out on the road again to try to drum up interest. But in every town, village and hamlet he visited, he was treated coldly, his performances failing to draw an audience, the young more inclined to head off to the city to find employment; any kind of work seemed better than learning a dying folk tradition.

Tortoise's final years were miserable. His family life was a shambles and whenever he thought of his father, he grew even more resentful of the way the authorities treated him. They ought to do more to take care of the children of revolutionary martyrs, he often thought. He took to writing letters to the regional government offices, then the county. He requested assistance, financial and non-financial, for his old age. For years he sent these letters, and for years he received no response. This only enraged him further, resulting in him taking offence to anything and everything. On those occasions when he fed the local pigs, he'd invariably end up punching and hitting them in the most violent manner. At dinner, he'd get angry for no apparent reason and begin throwing the dishes around. Even speaking to his son would cause him to fly into a rage; he'd rarely get past a sentence or two before he'd start cursing and spouting all kinds of vitriol.

To the villagers, this was all a sign. It was commonly said that a warm and soft temperament changed over time, making someone who was once easy to be around the most difficult companion. This also foreboded something else.

"Xi Sheng," a villager told him, "I'm afraid to say it, but I reckon your dad is leaving soon."

"Leaving for where?"

"He's… he's hard to be around now, isn't he?" the villager continued. "His temper explodes at the least provocation. He's grown… heartless, you could say… so much so he's making all of you hate him. When he dies, you probably won't even feel all that sad, but…"

The villager trailed off and Xi Sheng ceased listening. He didn't believe what the other man was saying. But a month later, Tortoise, his father, was dead. He was rather delirious in his final days, rambling on in garbled speech, incomprehensible to Xi Sheng and his mother. The two of them struggled mightily during those last days, vainly trying to understand what he was babbling about.

"I think your father wants a drink," his mother said on one occasion.

Xi Sheng obliged, but his father only tipped the liquid onto the floor.

"Perhaps he wants to see a shadow play?" she wondered.

Xi Sheng rummaged through their house and finally pulled out his play box. His father, however, turned towards the wall and mumbled: "Kai Hua…"

His voice was clear when he spoke these words. Xi Sheng heard them distinctly. He looked at his mother, trying to guess her response; he wondered if she knew the significance of what he was saying. But all she said was that his father was gone. Xi Sheng turned his eyes to his prostrate father and realised he was no longer speaking, nor breathing. He was dead, and there was a smile on his face.

Xi Sheng's mother shed no tears for her dead husband. Her first and only words were that he had left her, and then she began to make preparations for someone to dig a grave for him and construct a coffin. The day of his departure had been clear, but by late afternoon, the sound of thunder began to roll down from the mountains. The carpenter hired to build the coffin grumbled as he worked in the courtyard: "Whatever you do, please don't rain… I could finish the coffin inside, but there's no way a grave can be dug in the rain."

The rain, despite several concerted attempts, never did come. Lightning, however, streaked across the evening sky. Xi Sheng's mother was busy in the kitchen, intending to cook for the carpenter, but the stove would only smoulder and billow smoke, it wouldn't catch a flame, and so she resorted to blowing on the embers to try to get them to alight. As she bent low and blew into the stove, a loud crash was heard outside. A gleaming bolt of white light, a veritable fireball, burst into the kitchen from outside and struck her dead, just like her husband.

In the span of just a few hours, a single household experienced two deaths, something that had never happened before in Danggui, or in Huilongwan. The village immediately fell into gossiping about what had transpired. Despite not liking his wife much when he was alive, they surmised, it seems Tortoise didn't want her to keep on living after he was gone. Some wondered if it wasn't Xi Sheng's mother who wanted to accompany her husband into the afterlife, to prevent him from finding Kai Hua in the nether world and spending eternity with her. Xi Sheng listened to the gossip, heard every word, but he responded to none of it. He simply requested the grave diggers dig a pit large enough for the two of them, and that the carpenter build a two-chamber coffin.

His parents were laid out in their coffins for five days while the workers worked. That's when he invited me to sing. Altogether I knew the words to more than two hundred funeral dirges, and I sang all of them at least once, beginning to end; and then I started again. On the fourth day when I took a break for lunch, a string of firecrackers burst into flames outside, creating a racket that echoed off the courtyard walls. Carried along with the popping and cracking of the firecrackers was the sharp sound of a person weeping. I remember a voice calling out, assuming it must be someone coming to pay their respects. I could only wonder who that might be. Then I saw a young woman walk into the courtyard, crying out for her father. She seemed to be really struggling, almost paralysed, her body so wracked with grief she was nearly unable to stand. She stumbled towards the altar where the bodies lay in their coffins. Evidently, she was Tortoise's adopted daughter from Damingping. A few of the other villagers recognised her too, and quickly rushed to support her, consoling her over the death of Tortoise.

"Qiao Qiao," they called to her, "he's dead, he's not coming back. Don't take it so hard… it's part of life."

She remained there next to the bodies, crying and babbling through her tears. She knew she'd arrived too late, she wouldn't be able to see her father's face again. She was alone now, she mumbled, with no one left to love her as he had; nor was there anyone left to whom she could show her filial devotion. She cried and cried, lost consciousness, overwhelmed by grief, and then she woke and cried some more. Finally, I recall, someone came and got her, took her to one of the back rooms so that she could rest… at least a little. Xi Sheng even brought her some water to drink. It was after he'd given her the water that he came to speak to me… he wanted my opinion, advice. I asked him about what, and he told me that Qiao Qiao had brought the bones of her dead mother with her… she wanted to bury them with his father's body. I had never heard of anything like this before, so I told him, in all honesty, I wasn't sure what was best. He told me not to share it with anyone else, to which I of course agreed. Then I added that perhaps this was what his father had wanted in the first place… that perhaps she hadn't just come by this idea by chance, but that he – his father, her adoptive father – had told her to do it. Xi Sheng was conflicted, unsurprisingly… if he allowed Qiao Qiao to place her mother's bones with his father's, well, that might be doing right by his father, but it certainly wouldn't be doing right by his mother. I asked him if he thought his mother knew of the affair… he wasn't sure, but figured she had an inkling.

The following morning, the bodies were laid into the coffin. Xi Sheng placed ritual white flowers in their casket, as well as a lycoperdon, a greyish puff mushroom, and a ceremonial mat meant to symbolise the extension of life into the afterworld. Before the lid was closed, he placed the small, wrapped bundle that Qiao Qiao had brought. Once sealed, I went to relieve myself before the full funeral began. I was surprised to see Xi Sheng follow me in to the bathroom and before I could do what I had gone to do, he dumped a small something into the toilet. I asked him what it was. In a low voice he told me it was the ashes Qiao Qiao had brought… unbeknownst to her, he'd switched things around… he said, after all, his responsibility was to *his* family… not hers.

That night I sang of the vicissitudes of life… how we take things for granted… like the summer trees stripped bare by autumn winds… or the boat that's not properly moored and is soon carried off by the river and the breeze. I continued to sing… comparing life to the monkey that races up and down the pole just to tease unsuspecting bystanders… to the cock that likes nothing better than to fight, to nip and snap at the head of its enemy until blood flows… to the farmer who diligently plants and harvests his crop even though the size of the yield depends on the weather… to the silkworm that dies having wrapped itself in its own silk prison. We don't pay attention to life, I sang. When it's time to go, we leave, whether as a commoner or a prince. It is worse for those we leave behind: wives, children, family and friends... no one will tell you the reason why... willing or unwilling, we all lose it in the end... we take that road.

After I sang in mourning for Tortoise, I never returned to Danggui. One reason was it was rather far to travel between Huilongwan and the village nestled high up on the valley walls. No matter what time I might set off in the morning, it would mean spending a night there. That wasn't necessarily a problem, I suppose, but the beds in Danggui were all too small and their quilts too short so that I could never get a good night's sleep. The second reason I never went back to Danggui was that I was much too busy in Huilongwan as so many people died over a relatively short period of time... and I was the only funeral singer. I was simply too, too busy.

I kept up residence in the building that stood opposite the Guandi Temple, which allowed me to see that memorial arch whenever I happened to look out of my window. On those occasions when the sun was shining brightly, the arch took on the appearance of some refined palace hall, its ceramic glaze and greenish tiles glittered brilliantly, highlighting the inscription on top. I enjoyed staring at it, not for the words themselves – four large characters that read 'Righteousness is derived from tolerance' – but rather for the black swallow's nest that lay behind. The other inhabitants of the street looked at the creature (and me, it seemed) as though it was a crow, an owl or a bat, ugly and inauspicious, but I saw the small bird in a different light. It was man's great companion, living in and among the nooks and crannies of our buildings, and yet it always maintained a safe distance from us. In a certain way, I felt as though I myself was a black swallow, living in the same type of mud and straw nest as the bird itself. I would always whistle a playful greeting to it whenever I stepped outside... and it seemed that on every occasion I did this, I'd get a response... but not from the bird, rather from Lao Yu.

Lao Yu was the new member of the secretariat who had been dispatched to Huilongwan. His name suggested he was old, but in fact he wasn't; it was simply a sign of respect shown by the villagers... he was, after all, a Party cadre.

"Hello there... mountain whisperer!" His greeting always suggested a familiarity with his interlocutor, even if no familiarity actually existed. "Say now… you've got rather dark circles round your eyes, haven't you?"

"Yes… I suppose I do," I replied. "I didn't sleep all that well last night… the wind kept me up."

"Perhaps it was a retinue of ghostly spirits wailing outside your door, asking you to sing for them? Wouldn't that have been grand… a sign of a healthy business, for sure!"

"What're you talking about? Business? I don't sing those mourning songs any more… those spirits that can't pass the Bridge of Helplessness, well then, they'll scatter in every which direction… say… as a cadre… isn't it your job to maintain the peace?"

"No, it's not… and I'm not here to talk about that… I've come to ask you to travel to Mount Cockscomb. There was an explosion there… some old men died… last month, three of them… things are still not fully under control… five more men died yesterday. Perhaps this is all due to spirits who've lost their way, you know, anger, wild ghosts searching for bodies to possess!"

This was the first time since I'd come to Huilongwan that I had had dealings with another government cadre. And that afternoon I left for Mount Cockscomb… I would sing for the five dead men. This was also the start of my close relationship with Lao Yu.

Mount Cockscomb lay on the southern bank of the river, just eight *li* from Huilongwan. It was home to a gold mine. That evening I sang in the town of Hengjian, which sat at the foot of Mount Cockscomb. The five men who had perished had been setting explosives high up in the mountain. Apparently, they'd lit the fuse, scurried off to a safe distance to wait, and then, when no explosion followed, they went to investigate. The moment they got back to where the explosives had been laid… boom! The blast didn't separate their heads from their bodies, but they did lose their four limbs.

I never thought for a moment that even more people would end up dying, but that's what happened. First there was the accident at the brick-making factory. Because of the increasing demand for construction materials, the village of Shangwan decided to extend their factory operations. To do this, they began to excavate more and more earth from the side of the mountain. Eventually, they'd removed so much that the area where they'd been digging collapsed, injuring three and killing four. The Gong family lost a daughter when a bulldozer tipped over and crushed her underneath. In two nearby towns, the men of Qijiacun ended up getting into a dust-up about gold with the men from Xiawancun… three were killed in the confrontation and eighteen were arrested.

There were about eight small villages scattered around Mount Cockscomb, and each one now had vacant rooms due to the number of deaths. Therefore, Lao Yu advised me to move more permanently to the area, and so I eventually relocated to Qijiacun. I didn't realise it at the time, but I would never return to my home opposite the Guandi Temple. In a way, it had all seemed like a dream… my room… the window… the memorial arch… the swallow… but whatever it was, it was gone and within a few short years, Qijiacun became my operational base, so to speak. The area around Mount Cockscomb was transformed, too: the large-scale relocation of numerous small villages, the acquisition of farmland from local growers, the plan to establish economic development zones… things were definitely changing.

In the past, people had come to Mount Cockscomb for the gold… you would always see them panning for gold near the foot of the mountain in one of the many streams that ran down it. But when the survey teams arrived from the provincial capital and ascertained there was more gold actually up in the mountain itself, not in its rivers below, the village government issued new policy directives to attract outside investment and encourage development. Not long after, the regional county government became involved in the local village development, therefore bringing to bear the full power of the upper levels of government on moving things ever forward… the plan was to transform Huilongwan into the gold capital of Qinling.

From then on, from morning until night, the sound of explosions echoed across Mount Cockscomb. Joining in the cacophony was the noise of heavy machinery, and nearly every accent to be found in Qinling itself, for people from all over the region flocked to Mount Cockscomb. A common refrain soon heard from the mouths of everyone who had come, and kept coming, summed up the excitement: "Throughout the day before it grows old, let's all make sure we dig for gold!"

Needless to say, all this development led to a building boom. The central street in Huilongwan was growing at a rapid pace and new shops selling nearly everything under the sun seemed to pop up daily, welcomed each time by the pop and crackle of so many lines of firecrackers. And there were all types of people there, too. It was as though the main street had taken up the call for development as heartily and with as great a force as the miners who now piled into Mount Cockscomb.

Indeed, the place was becoming quite rich. Soon there were little cars whizzing down the streets, more and more people dressed in Western-style clothes, alcohol and drunkenness, too, seen much more regularly, as were gorgeously dressed women hanging off the arms of the nouveau riche. There were also more people losing their lives in the pursuit of wealth. It was often the case that before I even finished singing songs for one wealthy family, another would be knocking on my door to request the same. It was on one of these days that I bumped into Lao Yu again. He greeted me in the same manner, and asked me if what he had said before was wrong… I responded by telling him that there were rather too many dying too quickly… and he shouted exaltedly that I must indeed be making quite a bit of cash… and that perhaps I could give him some! Before I could answer, however, he laughed loudly and said he was speaking only in jest, he'd rather not have any money that'd come from singing for the dead… better for me, he insisted, to treat him to a drink!

It turned out that Lao Yu had more than his fair share of free time as he often called on me for a drink. Each time he came, he'd grab a bottle, sometimes two, from a shop not too far from where I lived… and each time it came to settling the bill, he'd look at me and then the shopkeeper and say that I'd be picking up the tab! He was really quite something, I must say…

Now this store that he kept buying the alcohol from… well… two weeks after his last visit… I think that's when it was… it fell into a bit of trouble. It happened in the middle of the night when a frantic knock on the door woke the shopkeeper. Not knowing what the ruckus was about, he opened the store front to see two young men outside. Apparently they were desperate to buy booze, cigarettes and instant noodles… they wanted a whole sack's worth. Now, the shopkeeper asked them why they wanted so much, and the two young men shot back that there was no need to worry about them not having enough money to pay for anything... they clearly had more than enough, as they flicked out a huge wad of cash. The following morning the shopkeeper took his fresh bundle of money and went off to buy more stock for his store, and this was when he discovered that the money the young men had given him was all counterfeit... he'd been swindled, and there was nothing he could do about it. A day later, the shop changed hands.

Lao Yu introduced me to the new shop owner, but he never explained why its ownership had changed. Later that evening, he lit firecrackers to celebrate the new... reopening... of the shop. It was a rather large firecracker, too... well, more firework than firecracker... the small pouch of explosive actually ripped apart the greased paper windows of the place I was staying in.

The opening celebration complete, Lao Yu came over to my place once again to have a drink, and we fell into conversation straight away.

"Are there," he began, "are there really ghosts that haunt this world?"

"If there weren't, why would I be singing for the dead?"

He continued to drink and his face and eyes became increasingly flushed. "So where are they... can you show them to me?"

"Well, those ghosts that are truly dead, you can't see them, those that haven't yet departed this world – the sort of living ghosts you find in Huilongwan – they're the ones that can trip you up, make you stumble. That's how you know they're there..."

"Living ghosts?"

"What else would you call those spirits that cause a racket and haunt the living?"

"You mean... those are living ghosts? But you do the same, don't you, trouble follows you around, follows me, too... and in Huilongwan these days, shit, tell me who's *not* causing trouble?"

"Then I guess we must all be living ghosts."

That night... we had both drunk plenty... and before long, Lao Yu started asking me where I came from, about who I was and how long I'd been in Huilongwan. I didn't tell him the whole truth of course... and before long he took to talking about himself, bragging about his own personal experiences, talking nonsense, mostly. I did learn a little though... for instance he told me how his father was a bigwig in the county, a regional director… and that he was nephew to Commander Kuang San's wife's younger brother… and on top of that, the wife's younger brother was also a deputy director in the National Development and Reform Commission. Lao Yu was now nearly inebriated… but I remember he paused for a moment, and then looked at me with piercing eyes.

"You know, I've got certain qualifications. There are conditions that'll allow me to progress in government… you get what I'm saying… mountain whisperer… I bet you could sing a mourning song about that, now couldn't you!"

"I believe you," I told him. "You've got a bright future ahead for sure!" As I said these words, he rolled off the table and slumped to the floor, quiet and unmoving.

Learning of Lao Yu's background made my mind wander to Xi Sheng. If he could pass the application his dead father had written on to Lao Yu, then perhaps it could find its way further up the chain of command, possibly even to Commander Kuang San… and who knows what after that? They might in fact officially include his father as the son of a martyr. But I was far too busy… I never made it back to Danggui… and this particular issue… well, it just dragged on.

One evening, I found myself in a particularly filial home. The deceased was a hawker of sesame-seed flatbread. Before the gold mine had opened, he used to spend his days on the main street doing brisk business, but once he learnt of the number of miners, he decided he'd do even better business up there, and so he piled his flatbread into a basket and marched off in the direction of the mine. Unfortunately for him, as he began his ascent, the miners farther up had just finished laying their explosives… when boom! Rocks were thrown into the air. Now, the larger pieces were nearly incinerated, but there were still stones the size of chicken eggs that were propelled high into the sky, and it was these pieces that now rained down on the poor man, one of which bored into his skull and killed him instantly. A tragedy indeed…

Now, while I was at their home enjoying some tea in the courtyard before I was due to sing, we were surprised by the sudden parting of the dark, foreboding clouds that had been blanketing the sky. Indeed, the clouds split so evenly they appeared to be marking a wide passage into heaven. I turned to the family, and suggested they take this as a sign for me to begin my singing... I added, too, that heaven was responding in kindness to the violent death their father had suffered. But, unfortunately, their daughter's husband's family lived nearly eighty *li* away, and since they were bringing the deceased's grandchildren, we had to wait. It took until the cock to crow for their oldest daughter's family to arrive. The lanterns that hung round the courtyard were all lit... and I strode purposefully to the crossroads near their main gate to burn the hell money and begin my song.

Things were seemingly going fine, but then trouble arose. At the same time as I was about to start, a wedding procession filled with villagers from a nearby town, quite a few in fact, began to march past right where I was standing... a wedding and a funeral had crashed into one another.

According to custom, whoever went first was deemed to be most auspicious, but neither party would let the other go. A great argument broke out, and before long, a crowd of bystanders and onlookers congregated as well. For me, well, I appreciated my position and the need for me to not get involved, so I took a few steps back and simply waited for a resolution. As I stood there, I noticed what appeared to be a small child trying to squirrel into the mass of people. Unsuccessful at that, he manoeuvred towards the rear of the crowd and began leaping up and down, vainly trying... it seemed... to peer into the crowd. Again unsuccessful, he climbed on top of a millstone that stood nearby... but instead of surveying the group of arguing people as though he was looking for someone, he now began to spit at them as a whole. His phlegm didn't carry all that far and instead landed squarely on one of the bystanders, which, predictably, resulted in a less than favourable reaction.

"You little fucker... just where the hell are you trying to aim!" bellowed the man as he wiped spit from his head.

Moving deftly, the child, as he still appeared, bounded off the millstone and it was at that moment I recognised who it actually was... not a child at all, but a dwarf... Xi Sheng.

I remember yelling out to him, getting his attention before I dragged him over to the side and out of sight of the angry man whom he'd spat on. I asked him why he was here but he wouldn't answer my question… there was a look of discomfort on his face… and then he turned towards the crowd once more and cried out: "Where the hell else should I spit, huh?"

He abruptly turned back to me, straightened his clothes, and said he must be off, he had to buy some medicine from the chemist on the main street… and then get back home. He'd just been distracted by the funeral and he thought – correctly – I might be there and wished to say hello. But when he saw there was a wedding going on as well, that was… he stopped his explanation and spat towards the marriage party once again… then shouted for them to be visited only by misfortune. Needless to say, I was rather stunned by his actions.

"Aren't you worried it's unlucky to come and watch a funeral?" I asked him.

"No, not at all, there's nothing unlucky about it. The dead take their poverty with them, their disease and their hurt, too. I reserve my hatred for weddings… coming upon one by accident, that's an ill omen… a wedding's what'll steal my happiness."

Looking at him, I remembered Lao Yu and what he had told me of his background… how it might help Xi Sheng… and so I mentioned the local cadre, offered to introduce them, and suggested how he might be able to send his father's application to the higher-ups.

"Are you for real?" Xi Sheng responded, his voice betraying his excitement. "You're not shitting me, are you?"

"Now why would I do that?" I answered, somewhat testily.

Evidently convinced of my sincerity, the young man fell to the ground and kowtowed before me. "Heavens," he shouted, "how's it I've met such a person of high standing!"

Xi Sheng didn't return to Danggui that evening. Instead, he accompanied me as I finally did get to sing the mourning song. It was after midnight before we returned to my own home, but we didn't get to sleep; we spent the night talking until the sun rose again. I knew Huilongwan had particular evening customs associated with marriage… they'd been introduced when the Tatars had ruled the area ages ago. The Tatars were a ruthless, tyrannical tribe… under their dominion, each and every new marriage had to uphold Tatar traditions, which stipulated the first wife was to be the most esteemed and receive the most attention, a large dowry had to be paid to the incoming wife's family, and while multiple wives were permitted, the first one and her children were always to be considered the most legitimate in terms of hereditary rights. As a result of these impositions, many Han Chinese took to secretly marrying in the evenings so as to avoid the new prescriptions on matrimony… the tradition had been passed down ever since.

I knew Xi Sheng and Qiao Qiao were together. There were three photo frames on top of his wardrobe. One contained a picture of Tortoise, his father, on the left was his mother, and on the right was Qiao Qiao. It was unfortunate they had no photo of Xi Sheng's grandfather… the revolutionary martyr… but such was often the case… in fact, they had no memento of him, not even a slip of paper.

I also knew they were still making a living by picking medicinal herbs, but that it was becoming increasingly difficult to find the plants that were once so common… on nearly every mountain and slope, they'd been picked clean… as a result, Xi Sheng had had to travel to a forest more than thirty *li* away to collect a sufficient quantity of herbs for them to make the money they needed. Normally a trip lasted between three and five days… but even on some of those trips, he came back empty-handed.

As he related all of this to me, he paused for a moment before complaining: "A horse that doesn't eat wild grass will never grow fit, but why does that mean I can't find even the smallest amount to make just a little cash!"

"If I introduce you to Lao Yu," I said, smiling, "well, who knows, the authorities might end up helping you, and then you'll have more money than you know what to do with."

"How… how much do you reckon I might get?"

"Well, from what I've heard, those Red Comrades still living are fully supported by the state," I said. "But you and your dad… you've received no benefit whatsoever… I'd say the first lump sum ought to be eighty to a hundred thousand, wouldn't you?"

"If that money really comes our way… I'll make sure Qiao Qiao makes you the finest set of clothes possible!"

As noon approached, I led Xi Sheng to see Lao Yu. Of course, he had a wash before we left to see the secretary, especially since he hadn't slept the night before. He also stuffed cardboard in his shoes to give him a little more height, but I suggested he just needed to relax, the cardboard wasn't necessary. He responded by saying the extra height gave him more confidence, but I was not totally convinced. I drew upon the example of his grandfather and father… the former had been a guerrilla fighter, the latter had found a lover… surely he ought to grow up and not worry about things like the height of a person. I guess he agreed since he removed the cardboard.

I was surprised at Lao Yu's response after we met him in the government offices. His enthusiasm for Xi Sheng's plight was unexpected: "Your father was a member of Qinling's guerrilla forces? That means you're a direct descendant of a revolutionary hero!"

Xi Sheng shared in the excitement, answering every question Lao Yu posed, unable even to sit down. Finally, Lao Yu offered him a seat, saying that when he was sitting, no one would be able to see his true height… he'd be like everyone else. Xi Sheng suggested he should return to Danggui later that afternoon and look for the application his father had written before his death; he could then return and give it to Lao Yu. Again to my surprise, Lao Yu assured him it wasn't necessary, he'd personally write a report detailing Xi Sheng's situation.

"That means you'll be using your position in the municipal government to make my case," Xi Sheng said. "But shouldn't Danggui also stamp such a report to give their support, too?"

"There are layers and layers of procedure to go through, you're right, but why would I go backwards? I'll write this report and give it to my father and get him to see if there's an opportunity to pass it along to Commander Kuang San. After that, well, you'll only need the commander to look at it carefully, say a single sentence, and then each and every problem will just disappear."

Xi Sheng's eyes grew red again as he continued to speak: "How… how will… how can I thank you! I… I can sing you a song." And with that, he opened his mouth wide and began to sing:

Peering from atop this mountain,
I see another peak reaching higher into the sky,
I see the faithful sister collecting firewood,
Yao-hao, yao-hao, yah…
I see the faithful sister collecting firewood.
Here, let me help you, I tell her, I'll carry this wood for you…
Here let me help you, I tell her, I'll carry your well bucket, too…
Oh do not let a faithful sister be burdened so.

Peering from atop this mountain,
I see another peak standing lower down.
I see a melodious laughing thrush, too,
Yao-hao, yao-hao, yah...
The bird spies the man and takes to the air so high,
The faithful sister spies a man and lowers her head,
Her words she keeps deep in her heart.

Xi Sheng's teeth were entirely yellow, but he sang with great skill, his song was unique. Lao Yu and I were floored; we never expected this from him.

Clapping his hands, Lao Yu turned to speak to me: "Say... you ought to take him as your apprentice, don't you think?"

"This is the first I've heard him sing, too," I said, turning to Xi Sheng. "Where, how did you learn this song?"

"Secretary Yu has shown me great kindness, but I've nothing with me to give in return... if I were a woman, I'd let you have me, defile me. I can't thank you enough. All I could do was sing that tune."

His words were rough, but they were also heartfelt. Lao Yu and I could do nothing but laugh. "And you sang very well indeed!" we said in unison.

We took our leave of Lao Yu, and as we walked outside, Xi Sheng turned to me and said: "I've not embarrassed you, have I? I've not made you lose face?"

"Not at all," I replied.

"You know... what Secretary Yu said about me becoming your apprentice, I'd never thought of that before, but I think it's a great idea. Will you let me? I could travel with you and learn your craft."

"But I sing songs of mourning... your song was a love song... how could I take you on as my apprentice? It's better you keep doing what you're doing. Gathering medicinal herbs and plants makes much more sense."

I refused his request, I couldn't take him on. He never brought it up again, but that didn't mean he stopped coming to see me. In fact, he'd pay me a visit every couple of days, wondering especially if I had heard any news from Lao Yu. I told him I hadn't, I wasn't sure if the report had been sent or not. After several visits and no news, Xi Sheng grew suspicious; he wondered if Lao Yu had written it, or if he'd given it to his father, or even if his family actually did have a close connection with Commander Kuang San. Each time I saw him, I could see the tension in his face, the heaviness of his heart… what could I do but press Lao Yu for a response… but no reply came. When I did finally see Lao Yu, there was a slight look of embarrassment on his face as he said he wanted me to go to Danggui, and that he intended to replace the worn sign that hung above Xi Sheng's door marking him as the descendant of a revolutionary martyr.

Xi Sheng had really married Qiao Qiao, and looking at her again, I could see she'd put on weight, which in truth made her more attractive. The makeup she wore accentuated her looks even more. It wasn't overdone, just enough to bring out her features. The house was clean and tidy, too. The only surprising thing was the red papercuts she'd pasted on the greased paper windows. They were lively scenes taken from famous tales such as *Oath of the Peach Garden*, which came from the longer classic *Romance of the Three Kingdoms*. There were characters from *Journey to the West*, notably Sun Wukong, the Monkey King, and scenes from other well-known stories such as *The Trial of Su San*, a Peking Opera, and the characters involved in the story about the heartless and unfaithful Chen Shimei, taken from *Judge Bao's Cases*. There were also lots of flying animals, fish, insects and flowers. It was really quite something.

"These papercuts are quite impressive. Where did you buy them?" I asked.

"I cut them out myself," answered Qiao Qiao.

"Such a pretty face, and such skill, too. How's that possible?" asked Lao Yu excitedly.

"Yes," added Xi Sheng, "her hands are really skilful, but I can't say the same about her mouth. She's tried to learn my songs, but even after nine or ten goes, she still can't manage it!"

"Rather picky, aren't you?" replied Lao Yu. "Would *you* be able to cut so finely!"

"I reckon I could learn!" Xi Sheng reached into a storage chest and pulled out a roll of red paper, separated a sheet and began to fold it. "How about the characters for good fortune and long life?"

Without waiting for an answer, he set to cutting out the words, pausing periodically to sing as he did so. It was another love song, a tragic sort of ditty, again about some unknown young woman, the hardships she endures at the hands of family. As before, he sung beautifully.

Once he finished, Qiao Qiao asked him: "Those are just words, how about figures?"

He picked up the scissors and began again, this time deftly manoeuvring them to create more than just words. The first item was a silver and gold ingot, the second the hat worn by an imperial official, the third shape, a mask, large in the forehead and with a beard that would hang nearly to one's belt.

"You're fortunate to be a halfling," I marvelled. "Otherwise your skill would belittle everyone around!"

That evening, Xi Sheng sang three more songs for Lao Yu, and he produced three more wonderful papercuts. After he was finished, he told us he would serve us dumplings for dinner, but that first he must go and buy some tofu and other ingredients, including citron daylilies for extra flavour. He also called in on a neighbour to borrow some hot peppers and vinegar. He made sure, too, to tell everyone he met that the regional secretary was paying him a visit. This, of course, had not happened to anyone in Danggui before, a member of the regional government had never deigned to visit such a small place, to say nothing of actually having a meal in the village. As a result, several locals decided to drop by, just to see if it were true or not. In fact, so many people came along that there was a veritable crowd gathering outside Xi Sheng's door, all straining to catch a glimpse of Lao Yu, seated, as he was, on a floor mat enjoying some tea. At first, Lao Yu had waved them away, but when they quickly returned, he changed tactics and invited them to come in. Those with the most courage accepted the invitation and stepped inside, and before long, Xi Sheng's not-so-large home was packed with people, a whole crowd of dwarfs, some old, some young. Needless to say, Xi Sheng was immensely pleased and his face showed it. His chest puffed out a little more, and I swear he even looked taller.

After the visit, Xi Sheng made sure the footprints left by Lao Yu in the courtyard remained untouched. Qiao Qiao was forbidden to sweep them clean, so two weeks later when a powerful wind swept through the area, picking up the sand and throwing it everywhere, including over the prints, Xi Sheng's ire was so raised that he cursed against the heavens.

In an effort to placate him, Qiao Qiao wondered why it was necessary to keep the footprints for as long as they had: "Husband, there's something I must say, it's been on my mind. Lao Yu paid us a visit, yes, this is true, but I don't think you can count on the report he promised being sent. His visit, I think, was a way to console us in advance."

Xi Sheng ruminated for a moment on what Qiao Qiao had said, before replying: "But the mountain whisperer said it, and even if we can't count on it being sent, his visit has certainly helped to firm my resolve. Didn't Liu Nainiu come by and speak to you last night?"

"No, we spoke of nothing."

"What about Yao Baicheng?"

"We fought and argued terribly last year. Do you think he'd come here?"

"Well… Yao Baicheng took the initiative, you know, and came to speak to me. He told me his son worked at the granary in the regional capital, then he asked when I might be able to bring him to see Lao Yu. Liu Nainiu has been thinking about submitting a request to extend his home, but he's been sitting on his hands for six months, not sure what to do. He came to tell me about this, and then asked about my connections with the regional government, asked if I could put a kind word in for him…"

Qiao Qiao listened to her husband, her eyes never leaving his face. "Is all of this true?" she asked.

"Yes, it is."

"Off to the stream with you, go get some water. You can't see what's right under your nose. You sure as hell can get pissed off about things beyond your control!"

Early one morning, Qiao Qiao stepped down from bed, only to see mice scampering across the floor. She shrieked and cursed about how she didn't sleep well the night before, how she supposedly heard a noise outside on the roof and thought it was a thief. Xi Sheng had already got up and was busy outside with his morning ritual, rubbing his bare arms, his spine and his legs against the squat rubber tree that stood lonely in the field. As his ritual progressed, he was startled to realise his scalp had grown flaky, and he wondered if this was not a sign of something more ominous.

At the same moment, Qiao Qiao yelled out to him: "I've got something to say to you!"

"Then say it."

"I need to buy a cat."

"Do think I've got taller?"

Qiao Qiao stared at him blankly for a moment: "Maybe that dirt on your unshaven face has!"

Xi Sheng stopped rubbing his legs and back against the tree, and instead decided to hurl his whole body at it. The more he did so, the greater the force he impacted into the tree. He was wondering whether meeting Lao Yu really had changed his fortunes.

"Do you mean to say there're too many mice?" he asked his wife.

By now, Qiao Qiao was paying him no attention, busy instead with emptying the chamber pot from the night before.

"You know… more mice around the place is a good thing. It means we've got brighter days ahead."

In the end, Xi Sheng wouldn't allow Qiao Qiao to get a cat. Instead they travelled off together to collect herbs. The forest was three to four days away, so before they departed, Xi Sheng remembered to leave some crumbs and bits of maize out around the place. He was afraid, after all, that the mice might go hungry.

Qiao Qiao carried a bamboo basket on her back as she trudged along the mountain paths towards the forest. Inside the basket she'd packed their tent, an aluminium pot and some maize; there was also a spade, a knife and a hook. Xi Sheng didn't carry anything, but instead waved his arms happily as he kept a quick pace. Even so, he was quite unable to overtake her, no matter how fast he pumped his legs, and this caused him no small amount of consternation.

"Are you trying to run me into the grave, is that it?"

She halted her steps and waited for him to catch up. Then, as he walked up beside her, she put her arms around him and lifted him up onto a small stone wall that had been built into the mountain.

"Wolves don't just attack in the night, you know," she said. "We ought to keep on the pass so we can cover as much distance as possible, and then put up the tent when it gets dark. Otherwise, we'll end up on the dinner plate for sure!"

"Ha ha," chuckled Xi Sheng. "Well, if a wolf does appear, it'll go after the plumpest prize first!"

"Maybe so, but a dwarf is much easier to swallow!" Qiao Qiao stomped off, soon walking on much farther ahead.

The work in the forest was tiresome and unproductive, at least with regard to the amount of ginseng they were able to dig up. Qiao Qiao ended up finding more thorowax than anything else, but she was pleased because this was her usual haul.

Xi Sheng, however, was particularly upset: "How is it that this is all we've found once again!" He looked up at a bird perched in a nearby tree. "Let's make a bet," he shouted at the bird, "if you fly off, then I'll find a basketful of ginseng!"

The bird squawked and took to the air. Before it ascended higher into the sky, it released its bowels and a streaky white stream of shit poured down over Xi Sheng's shoulder. Qiao Qiao laughed.

But on the evening of the third day, Xi Sheng discovered an enormous batch of ginseng, a unique batch, as it happened, colloquially known as *qinseng*.

That afternoon, the two of them had gone their separate ways. Qiao Qiao failed to find any ginseng and returned before her husband with a basket of honeysuckle instead. Alone in the tent, she began to prepare dinner. She had already finished cooking their meal and the forest was growing dark by the time her husband got back. He was empty-handed and looking dishevelled, his jacket ripped and torn, missing its lower half.

Despite his appearance, the first words out of his mouth were: "I found a whole batch of *qinseng*!"

"Were you attacked by a leopard? What the hell happened to your clothes!"

"A whole batch, I tell you!"

"Come here… come here and let me look at you."

As Xi Sheng moved closer to his wife, she rapped his head with her chopsticks: "Are you dreaming or something? Eat your dinner!"

"But I really did, I found a whole batch!"

Qiao Qiao knew such ginseng could be found in the forest, but it was said to be a precious root for the immortals, not something you could hope to find, and if you tried, you'd never be successful. She looked at her husband; he didn't appear to be lying.

"Show me. Take me to where you found it."

Xi Sheng took her hand and led her out of the tent. They walked in the direction of a gully that stretched over the edge of the mountain. It was covered in vines, twisting and winding every which way. Rocks and stones made the passage even more difficult, especially for Xi Sheng. Seeing him struggle, Qiao Qiao lifted him on her back and continued on. Finally they crested a ridge and came upon the patch of *qinseng*, just as Xi Sheng had said. Qiao Qiao, who could barely contain her excitement, let her husband fall roughly from her back, and began to scavenge frantically at the ground. Xi Sheng, from where he hit the ground, shouted out to his wife in great seriousness, exhorting her to stop what she was doing, the *qinseng* was too precious to be simply ripped from the ground. Moreover, it couldn't be picked if it was raining or merely cloudy. He then went quiet, his footsteps gentle and careful. It seemed as though he was intent on not disturbing the *qinseng*, afraid that if they did, it would crumple and burrow itself away into the ground. Xi Sheng reached up towards his wife's head and untied the red shawl she had been wearing. Carefully, he placed it over the *qinseng* and looked at Qiao Qiao. "I've told you to stay where you are. Now don't you dare run!"

They left the *qinseng* where it was and returned to their tent where they belatedly ate their meal. Xi Sheng was the first to speak: "I told you I had to do something to change our fortunes, but how did that lead me to finding that batch of *qinseng*? You ought to admire me for what I've done!"

"Sure, I'm impressed."

Xi Sheng pulled himself close to her, a lustful look in his eyes. Qiao Qiao didn't protest, she gave into his desire. He moved his mouth close to her ear and spoke: "Give me a child, won't you?"

"You'll blame me if your seed doesn't take?"

"Discovering that *qinseng* is a good omen. I'll get you pregnant this time for sure."

His desire sated, Xi Sheng rolled off his wife and began to sing. He tried to teach her as well, but after a dozen or so attempts to get her to remember the words, he gave up; she was hopeless.

On the morning of the fourth day, they decided to pick the *qinseng*. First, they found two tree branches to make a sort of frame, and these they placed in the ground around the *qinseng* leaves. Qiao Qiao's red shawl was then placed over them, and they began to dig approximately three feet away. It was painstaking work, so much so that they barely breathed, frightened by almost every movement of their hands. They dug for the entire afternoon, eventually pulling up a quantity of earth the size of a large basket; they had removed the whole batch. It was an impressive amount of *qinseng*, eerily shaped like a human being, with a head, arms and legs.

"Male or female," Qiao Qiao thought aloud, and then turned to her husband. "If it's male, our child will be a boy. If it's female, we'll have a daughter."

Xi Sheng inspected the *qinseng* some more but couldn't find distinctive male characteristics hanging between what could be considered its legs. His mind began to drift and he wondered if he'd been successful in getting his wife pregnant. He kept these thoughts to himself, however, choosing not to shatter the mood. Placing the *qinseng* in their bag, Xi Sheng marvelled at the sheer volume they had picked: "Today *was* a good day!"

Upon their return to Danggui, news of their amazing find spread quickly throughout the village, eventually reaching the ears of Lao Yu. He decided to pay them a visit once more, this time to offer to buy the entire batch off them. Xi Sheng was inclined to sell the *qinseng* to Lao Yu at a discount, but Lao Yu would hear nothing of it. He was determined to pay a fair price out of respect for Xi Sheng's father. This was how it had to be: just as his father had respected the deputy director of the local administration, who, in turn, showed respect to Commander Kuang San.

"Oh," Xi Sheng mumbled, before blurting out: "I must go to the toilet."

A few moments later, Lao Yu heard Xi Sheng yell out to Qiao Qiao to bring him some toilet paper. Her response was not what Lao Yu expected to hear: "Can't you use dirt?"

Lao Yu laughed at the exchange, and pulled some paper out of his pocket to give to Qiao Qiao. "Take him this," he said.

Qiao Qiao obeyed and walked off towards the toilet. She was surprised by Xi Sheng wanting to talk to her, what with him sitting down on the toilet with his trousers around his ankles. He was insistent that they had to talk, albeit quietly, without Lao Yu hearing. As she listened to him mumble on, an expression of displeasure grew of her face until finally she spun around and marched off towards the kitchen. Xi Sheng pulled up his trousers and returned to where the secretary was waiting. With great determination in his eyes, he told Lao Yu he couldn't accept any money for the *qinseng*. Lao Yu had shown him such great kindness, and even though the *qinseng* was probably worth more than a hundred thousand yuan, he was intent on giving it all to Lao Yu.

"So," Lao Yu started, "you go to the toilet and then decide not to take any payment, huh?"

"What's money, after all? And besides, whether I'm being foolish or not, I'm still no piece of shit!" Xi Sheng's voice did not waver as he spoke.

"You truly have a heroic spirit, don't you. But I can't leave you with nothing but bitterness to chew on." Using the authority of his position, he wrote up a note authorising the payment of fifty thousand yuan to Xi Sheng, and then forced him to sign and stamp it with his name chop.

With their new-found wealth and excitement in their hearts, Xi Sheng and his wife headed off to the main street determined to add to their household possessions. Afterwards, they enjoyed a meal of buckwheat noodles at a local shop, which is where Qiao Qiao's eyes were drawn to something she'd not expected to see.

"Say... over there in the corner, at the barbecue, the two men sat drinking and eating... isn't that Shuang Quan and Ping Shun?"

Glancing over, Xi Sheng dismissed the idea: "I heard the two of them had become junkmen. Surely it can't be them if they're wearing such fancy Western clothes!"

"I think it really is though..."

Hearing the certainty in her voice, Xi Sheng turned again and looked at the two men more closely. A second later he gasped, loud enough for the men to hear. They looked up from their food and stared at Xi Sheng, and then looked away as though they didn't recognise him. Perturbed at their apparent dismissal of him, Xi Sheng stood up and marched over to them.

"Look here, you two fuckers with your Western clothes. I guess I should take you to be businessmen, huh?"

Shuang Quan spoke first: "Oh, Xi Sheng… I didn't recognise you… here, try some… have a kebab." He held up some of the grilled meat for Xi Sheng to accept.

"Shift over… you ought to let me sit down." He laid his hand onto Ping Shun's shoulder to nudge him to one side.

The other man recoiled from Xi Sheng's hand and shouted: "Don't lay your filthy hands on me!"

Stunned, Xi Sheng said nothing more. He didn't sit down, he didn't accept the kebab. Instead, he turned and stomped off towards Qiao Qiao.

"Who the fuck do they think they are? They were paupers not long ago… and now look at them! I guess I need to get a suit myself."

Xi Sheng and Qiao Qiao had already purchased the most necessary items with the money they'd been given, and the remainder Qiao Qiao wanted to put in the bank. Xi Sheng, however, had different plans. The first thing they had to do was to buy themselves some Western clothes and shoes. The only problem was Xi Sheng's feet were abnormally large and somewhat malformed, meaning it would be a challenge to find a pair of shoes that would fit him properly. As a result, they settled on buying just a pair for Qiao Qiao.

Dressed in their new clothes, they strolled back to the barbecue restaurant with the express purpose of showing Shuang Quan and Ping Shun their changed appearance. The two men, however, were nowhere to be seen.

"Pity… they won't be able to see us like this."

"Oh hell, just what're you playing at!"

Xi Sheng couldn't refrain from chuckling: "Come on, let's order some barbecue. Fifty kebabs should do!"

Together they devoured more meat than they had in ages, and once they were finished, they decided to return home. On the way back, he couldn't help but notice how his wife's arse swayed back and forth as she walked in those new leather shoes, two soft cheeks twisting up and down.

"I'm a lucky man to have married you!"

"And without me you'd be nothing. You know that, yeah?"

The people of Danggui were poor. Most of them didn't even have the basic household goods to live on their own; in many cases, they'd even borrow chopsticks from one another, or baskets, or every such little thing. But once they saw Xi Sheng in his new Western clothes, more and more villagers wanted to be close to him, to seek him out whenever they needed to borrow something. Some even offered their sons as future husbands for the daughters he and Qiao Qiao might have one day. And whenever one of the villagers got into a mess, whatever it was, they'd come to ask if they could borrow his suit, just for the supposed prestige and power it would give. Of course, Xi Sheng never once agreed to lend anyone his clothes, and before long they all started to call him stingy.

Xi Sheng's usual response did little to change their minds: "Then let me borrow your wife for a spell!" As a result, and because of the suit, Xi Sheng earned the animosity of many of his fellow villagers. Rumour and salacious gossip spread about the couple, and most wished them misfortune. They might have money and be living the good life, but they would never have a child, no heir to care for them when the money inevitably ran out.

The more he listened to such talk, the more bitter he became. Eventually, the two of them began spending more and more time in the forest, dogged in their pursuit of harvesting more *qinseng*, and consequently making more money. Xi Sheng's aim was clear: he wanted the villagers to eat their words, to choke on them in fact.

But the work was not easy. While in the forest, Xi Sheng would spend the entire day vainly searching for new batches of *qinseng*, often returning to their tent quite late, exhausted and empty-handed. To make matters even more challenging, each night he crawled back into the tent he'd take one look at Qiao Qiao and shout: "Let's make a baby!"

He'd then fall onto her, quickly remove her clothes and… get to work. At the same time, he'd keep thinking about the next day, that he would find ginseng, even pieces that appeared to have long 'middle legs' hanging down. Unfortunately, they failed to find new growths of ginseng, despite the many days they'd spent in the forest.

At the beginning of winter, they heard news about one of their neighbours, a family by the name of Hui who lived not far below the plain on which their own house stood. The husband had developed cancer, and it was expected that by summer he would be too far gone.

As winter turned to spring, however, he began to show gradual signs of improvement. No longer bedridden as he'd been during the winter, now he would get up and about, and whenever he bumped into fellow villagers, he'd roll up his shirt to expose his stomach and begin massaging the lump that was there.

"Feel for yourself," he would often say. "It's much softer than it was."

At around the same time, his wife discovered a tumour on the persimmon tree that stood near their house. Startled by her discovery, the man's wife grew increasingly anxious. It was a bad sign for both her husband and the persimmon tree to grow tumours. Finally, she decided to cut the strange growth from the tree, never imagining it would have any effect on her husband. But it seemingly did, for his tumour grew hard, and began to increase in size. By the time winter came again, her husband was dead. The villagers, ever fond of gossip, believed the persimmon tree had been serving as surrogate for the husband's cancer, and once his wife had cut it out, the cancer attacked her husband with a vengeance. Whatever the truth of these seemingly fanciful assumptions, the effect they had on Xi Sheng was enormous. In fact, they made him wonder if the reason he and his wife had remained childless was due to their repeated harvesting and selling of the prized *qinseng*… or at least their attempts to do so. In any case, his heart experienced such turmoil that he soon resolved never to return to the forest.

Naturally, this meant trying to find normal growths of ginseng elsewhere in the valley, a job much easier said than done. Before long, Xi Sheng was at his wits' end about what to do. His heart was also heavy, as though a great weight was pushing down on it. To add to his discontent, during the winter twenty or more villagers followed in the footsteps of Shuang Quan and Ping Shun and had become junkmen, scouring the streets of the regional capital and making good money in the process. The whole town of Danggui knew, too, that one of the members of this junkman posse was a dwarf, meaning he'd come from their own town.

"So, husband, are we going or not?"

"No, we're not!"

"Why?"

In his mind, Xi Sheng believed the time wasn't right, that the bridge they'd need to take to get into the capital would be full of other people doing the same, and the bridge itself was very near to collapse.

"I'll sell my songs first."

"You're going to do what now?"

"The mountain whisperer makes a living from singing funeral songs. I ought to be able to do the same but singing love songs instead. Come on, we can work together, you can sell your papercuts."

Astonished by this turn, Qiao Qiao attempted to dissuade him from trying to live off his singing. However, she was unsuccessful, and Xi Sheng began to spend his days learning songs, more than thirty in total. Perhaps even more bizarre was that once he'd finished learning the new songs, he still travelled to the regional capital in search of Shuang Quan and Ping Shun. He had a proposal to make: he wanted to join their team, but not as a junkman as such. No, his plan was for them to continue to work as they had, while he would accompany them and sing.

Unfortunately for Xi Sheng, something had happened to Shuang Quan and Ping Shun before he could pitch the idea.

Shuang Quan and Ping Shun were among the first men from Danggui to go and find employment in the regional capital. With no qualifications or skills, they started off by doing whatever menial work they could find. One of their earliest positions was waiting tables, but because most customers felt uncomfortable in the presence of the two dwarfish men, they were soon dismissed. Their next job was as bouncers for a local bar, but when the patrons saw their diminutive size, they laughed. Dismissed once again, the two men found themselves sitting on the main street, dejected and at a loss as to what to do. Naturally, they cursed their parents; after all, a dwarf father couldn't help but have a dwarf son, so why bother having children at all, unless it was to purposefully make their lives difficult.

Afterwards, as more and more outsiders arrived in town, the two men began to realise there were different ways to make money. They were drawn in particular to a group of men who would sneak into the night and up Mount Cockscomb to steal the ore that had been mined, and then they would return to the city to sell it on the black market. Once introductions were made, Shuang Quan and Ping Shun began to participate in the illegal and clandestine business. Unfortunately for them, no one had told them about the guards who were now stationed around the mines to stop this very activity. Soon discovered, the other gang members were able to run away into the darkness, but given their distinctive disadvantage – their short legs were barely able to carry them back through the main gate, in spite of how hard they tried – the two men from Danggui were apprehended. To add to the ignominy of being captured, their captors tied them up in a burlap bag and proceeded to beat them with sticks. Eventually, neither could stand the abuse any more, and so they screamed to be released. Tumbling out onto the ground, they kowtowed to the guards and begged for mercy; they were, after all, cripples and wasn't life already bitter enough? Whether it was out of mercy or some other reason, the guards stopped beating them, but they still took the two men's shoes and flung them down the mountainside. Barefoot, Shuang Quan and Ping Shun had little recourse but return to the city. By the time they climbed back down Mount Cockscomb, their feet were a bloody, pulpy mess. Their only bit of good fortune was when they encountered a junkman who offered them worn shoes. At first, the shoes didn't quite do the job of protecting their feet, but after a little bit of ingenuity, and a bit of rope, they were able to tie the new footwear around their swollen and sore feet. This was the beginning of a great friendship.

The junkman who'd shown them such kindness was called Chen Laoba. The combination of a small chin and an incredibly long set of incisors gave his face a sort of inverted hook-like appearance. His first words to the two men, after he'd given them the shoes, was that they ought to become junkmen like he was, providing they could handle a little hard work and didn't mind the filth. In fact, he assured them, being a junkman was the surest way to stand on an equal footing, or at least their own footing, with all the outsiders now flocking into Huilongwan. If their luck was good, they could even make up to fifty yuan a day; and if it wasn't, they should have no trouble making at least a tenner, which would be enough to prevent them from starving.

Both Shuang Quan and Ping Shun replied in unison: "You mean there's even more shit to swallow? More than we have already endured? What is it... the dirty and fly-infested places we'll be working will be even filthier than a public toilet?"

They spent the evening in Chen Laoba's ramshackle hut, and then on the following morning, and every one after that, they'd get up and head off separately to find what junk they could. Soon they learnt there were five particular places that would pay them decent money for the rubbish they collected, and that there were twenty or thirty junkmen working the streets of the capital. Chen Laoba, who had been at this kind of work for a while, had a cart to pull behind him; this was something they lacked, and so a hemp rucksack had to do. Whenever they came upon a pile of rubbish, the first order of business was to sift through it in order to find plastic bottles. If they happened upon a public toilet, they'd go in and clean up the used tissues. Then, as the day closed, they would return to Chen's hut, crawl under their blankets and start counting money.

"So," Chen Laoba said as he kicked one of their blankets, "how much did you make today?"

"Forty-three yuan," Shuang Quan replied.

"Thirty-one for me."

"Who directed you down this path?"

"You did, we haven't forgotten."

"Then get up, I feel like a watermelon!"

The two men did as they were told and strolled off towards the main street. They came back with a bottle of mineral water. "Fucking shit... the damn watermelons weren't ripe enough, we had the bastard storekeeper cut a few open and they were all unripe... so... out of respect to you, we bought you this mineral water. It tastes really sweet!"

Chen Laoba looked them over for a moment, before he reached inside his jacket and pulled out a bottle of sorghum wine. "Fuck, you dwarfs are pretty dense, aren't you! You actually thought I wanted watermelon... that I wanted you to buy it for me... fuck... do you know how much cash I made today?"

"A hundred?"

"More like a thousand five hundred!"

Both men's mouths fell open, amazed at the amount he'd made in just one day.

Later, when Shuang Quan and Ping Shun were alone, they still hadn't got over the news: "How the hell did he make fifteen hundred in a day? What else did he sell… his own arsehole!"

"He's bullshitting us," Ping Shun offered. "If he was really making that much in a day, fuck, every boss along the main street would choose to be a junkman, too!"

Eight days later, the provincial capital's police showed up and arrested Chen Laoba. Shuang Quan and Ping Shun discovered that while he was collecting rubbish, he was also helping himself to construction tools and anything else not nailed down. His most recent heist was a forty metre-long electrical cable.

With Chen's incarceration, the shabby, makeshift hut now became their home. As for Chen's belongings, they were divided equally between them: the household items, the tools of the trade, even the recyclables he hadn't yet sold, including some paper and plastics. And both of them now had Western suits to wear. Their new-found position – and apparent wealth – eventually resulted in more villagers coming from Danggui in search of their assistance. Together, Shuang Quan and Ping Shun would parcel out districts for the newcomers to scavenge through. They also organised groups of Danggui villagers to serve as defence units against junkmen coming from elsewhere. Before long, they were veritable junk lords over entire swathes of the city. And like lords, they would hold audiences with inexperienced junk collectors from Danggui, telling them where they could best go, what streets were worth scavenging through, as well as what items to take and what to leave behind. They even gave instructions regarding who were the easiest to rob, and where they could snatch the most prized pieces. And while the city had nearly always put up banners exhorting the population to guard against fires and thieves, the townsfolk added another: protect against dwarfs.

Spring arrived. And again Shuang Quan found himself in close proximity to the local constabulary, but not because he'd been arrested for a crime. He visited the police station this morning to report that Ping Shun had been missing for nearly a day. Apparently, he'd gone out the previous morning as usual, but had still not returned. At first, before going to the police, Shuang Quan assumed his partner had simply returned alone to Danggui, but after telephoning the village, he learnt Ping Shun wasn't there either, so his mind turned to darker possibilities: perhaps he'd got into an accident? The police instructed

Shuang Quan to file a formal report, but later that afternoon they found a corpse hidden in the reeds that grew along the river. The victim's skull had been caved in and his eyes dug out, leaving two gaping black holes. It was Ping Shun.

At first, the police were stunned by the discovery. Ping Shun was a junkman, and a dwarf, so that ruled out a crime of passion, and a murder for money. What's more, he had no known enemies; there didn't seem to be anyone who held specific animosity towards the dead halfling. An investigation was launched, but after several leads ended up nowhere, they weren't especially hopeful of finding the killer. Then, suddenly, the police cracked the case: the murderer was Shuang Quan.

Not once had Ping Shun returned to Danggui to give his old family back home some of the money he had earned from scavenging. Nor had he put any of the money in the bank. In fact, whatever he didn't spend was tucked away in the same bag that held his underpants. He'd kept this secret, too, not even telling Shuang Quan. No one knew, or at least that's what Ping Shun believed.

However, on one particular day, Shuang Quan, who had been out doing his usual rounds, suddenly felt lightheaded and decided to return home early to sleep. Later that evening, when Ping Shun returned, hungry and in need of something to eat, he tried to wake his partner so that they might get something to eat together. But Shuang Quan wouldn't stir, and so Ping Shun reluctantly let him be, assuming he must be deeply asleep. His mind then turned to the money he'd made that day, and since Shuang Quan was presumably sound asleep, he figured he might as well take the opportunity to put his money in his usual hiding place, namely his bag of underwear. As he proceeded to hide his hard-earned cash, he wasn't aware that Shuang Quan had turned over and at that very moment had opened his eyes. Unbeknownst to Ping Shun, Shuang Quan had witnessed everything. Fearing discovery, however, Shuang Quan quickly closed his eyes and pretended to still be fast asleep. But his mind was racing: Ping Shun had been hoarding so much money, he thought, and yet he still played at being poor, the dirty fucker. Then he recalled all the times they'd gone out to eat and how he always ended up footing the bill. Again Shuang Quan cursed his friend. That night, the seed was planted for him to rob his partner.

The following evening, the two of them were sitting down to eat. Each had made his own food. Ping Shun had prepared cornmeal porridge, but since he lacked vegetables to add, he simply dashed some salt into the gruel and slurped it down rather quickly. Shuang Quan, on the other hand, had made noodles, and once he had dished up his own, he offered a bowl to his friend.

"Here," he said, "you should have some."

"Brother," Ping Shun responded with true, heartfelt emotion, "you're really too kind. Tomorrow morning I'll treat you to some kebabs, alright?"

"Er… I'm not really a fan of the kebabs you make. Sorry…"

"Then I'll fry you up a dish of peanuts!" He paused and lifted the bowl of noodles up to his face. "Ah, if only the noodles had some hot peppers…"

"I've got some." Shuang Quan reached into the cupboard to pull out a packet of peppers, but when he turned around he had a steel pipe in his hands instead. In one quick movement the pipe bit into Ping Shun's head, cracking his skull instantly. Ping Shun's eyes stared at his friend, but no words came out of his mouth, and then he toppled to the ground. Shuang Quan dropped the pipe and reached over to his dead friend, rummaging through his pockets. Then he dug out the underwear bag holding the rest of his former partner's money. He began to count it, scrunching up his nose at the rancid smell of it: 21,240 yuan.

"You don't even have as much as I've put away."

He counted it again. As he did so, a strange gurgle escaped Ping Shun's blood-covered mouth, and his legs twitched. He wasn't dead. Shuang Quan put the money down and extended his hands around Ping Shun's neck, choking his friend until his legs went still. He felt under Ping Shun's nose; there was no breath, he was dead for sure. Dragging the corpse out of their dilapidated hut, he stuffed it into one of the many hemp rucksacks that lay around their place, and waited for night to fall before he would dispose of it. As he turned to head back inside, Shuang Quan suddenly remembered something Chen Laoba had told them. In the past, ancient people believed a victim's eyes held the image of their killer, the last thing they saw, so he grabbed a pair of chopsticks and gouged out his former friend's eyes.

"Don't blame me, Chen Laoba told us about this."

The police didn't crack the case on the basis of whatever image might have remained on Ping Shun's eyes, but they did prove beyond doubt that Shuang Quan was the killer. There was no trial, but rather a swift execution. Just before the shot was fired to end his life, Shuang Quan uttered these last words: "Ping Shun said he'd fry up some peanuts for me, he really wanted me to eat them."

After his death, the only male left in Shuang Quan's family was his old father. He did not come to collect the corpse of his son.

The dwarf junkmen soon departed the regional capital and returned to Danggui to resume tilling the land and cultivating ginseng. It was bitterly hard work, as it had always been, but in the past it hadn't really seemed that way. Now, however, was different. They'd spent time away, had experienced a life quite unlike the one they'd had in the village; for those returned villagers, things were harder than ever before. Ever since Huilongwan had established its mining sector, there had been a widening gulf between those with money and those without. Fearing this would eventually lead to all sorts of problems, the regional government implemented new plans to pull the tiny, remote villages out of poverty, too. Equality was the goal. Given the growing intimacy between Lao Yu and Xi Sheng, Danggui was included in these efforts.

Lao Yu's first order of business upon arriving in Danggui once more, was to eradicate any remaining trace of Shuang Quan and Ping Shun. Their homes were roped off and quicklime was scattered over the land. Dog blood was painted on their courtyard gates to ward off any lingering evil influence. Finally, a boulder was positioned on the path into the community, on which Lao Yu wrote the following slogan, in red, naturally enough: 'Extreme sorrow turns to joy.'

His second order of business was to replace the village head and appoint Xi Sheng in his place. At first, Xi Sheng resisted the title, but Lao Yu insisted: "The old village head was just that, *old*. That's why this incident with Shuang Quan and Ping Shun was allowed to happen. He was unable to stop the rot."

"But who's to say I haven't been contaminated by it as well!"

"Well… it's good if you have. Every great man must be at least touched by evil in order to be successful. Besides, I'll support you all the way, you needn't fear anything."

"It's not anything else that I fear. I'm only afraid of you."

Once Xi Sheng was in place as village head, Lao Yu announced his five-year plan. The main objective was to transform the economic base of Danggui. Aside from the production of essential foodstuffs that would continue, Danggui was to be remade on an industrial scale; it would become the agricultural base of operations for all of Huilongwan. To realise this plan, Lao Yu was relocated to the town. His wife went as well, to help with the planning and design.

The first time Xi Sheng saw Lao Yu's wife, he noticed the leather shoes she was wearing, as well as her smart blue-and-white top.

"See," he later told his wife, "Secretary Yu's wife wears essentially the same clothes as you, but she works for the County Commercial Bureau."

"I'd like to work for the county government, too, but my deadbeat husband hasn't put in a single word for me!"

Xi Sheng just stared at her without opening his mouth.

"Tell me, I've heard what Lao Yu wants to do – transform Danggui – but just what does that mean?"

"What, you don't understand? Eh... you haven't got the brains for it! Well then, let me tell you. Soon, Danggui will be producing every agricultural product you can think of, and all of it on a massive scale. We'll raise pigs and chickens, we'll have large vegetable plots that'll grow cabbages, radishes, leeks, cucumbers, aubergines, courgettes, onions, garlic, you name it. We'll produce tofu, too, there'll be beansprouts and big machines to make all sorts of noodles... we'll have persimmons and walnuts... everything."

"Oh... you certainly know a lot now, don't you!"

"I know I'm going to be busy... you'd be just better off making sure you have three meals ready for me each day."

"Go on, get out... you wanna eat, huh? Then go pick some damn garlic sprouts!"

Xi Sheng departed, intent on getting some garlic, but before he'd got very far, he bumped into Lao Yu who wanted him to look at something. He forgot all about the garlic sprouts.

Lao Yu wanted Xi Sheng to look at a draft of the report he was writing for the authorities in the regional capital. The notebook he'd written it in was impressive, luxurious even, for its cover was leather and it was nearly two fingers thick. He wrote in it daily, chronicling everything that transpired. Opening the notebook, he flipped through the many pages to land on the ones containing his draft report, and then he handed it to Xi Sheng for him to read.

"I think it's fine," Xi Sheng said after a few moments, "but I have a question… you've nearly filled this entire notebook… what've you been writing about?"

"I record everything."

Lao Yu thumbed through the pages again, showing Xi Sheng its contents; he really did include everything. His notebook recorded the exact population of Danggui, as well as the names of the heads of each household. There were even notes on which families had hardy young men, which had proper daughters, which family was better at rearing animals, which was better in the fields, and even which families could be allied together. There were notes and sketches concerning how best to implement the engineering project he envisioned for Danggui, from repairing a particular path, to rebuilding the town's reservoir, to rerouting the flow of the streams down the mountain. Lao Yu had written notes on how to build the necessary drainage pipes, and even what trees to plant near the town entrance.

Production targets were also listed. Lao Yu envisaged Danggui supplying Huilongwan with two out of every five chickens eaten, one of every five eggs, three of every five servings of vegetables. They were also to have a monopoly over the production of tofu and beansprouts. Needless to say, as Xi Sheng looked through the many pages of information, he couldn't help but feel a little overcome.

"I must say… you really are invested in transforming Danggui!"

"That's why I'm here. I wouldn't've come if it'd been small beer. No, I'm here because I've planned great things for this place."

Xi Sheng continued to flip through the pages, finally coming upon something that caused him to pause. Lao Yu had also made note of his own personal objectives: in three years, he planned to be promoted from town secretary to mayor; three years after that, he intended to take a position in the county government, then three years later promoted to one of the city administrative centres, then to the provincial government three years after that.

"Your plan for Danggui, well, it's good, fine… but… this all seems like promising a cake that'll never be delivered!"

"What… what the hell are you saying?"

"Do you really believe Danggui can be transformed in just three years?"

"Three years… no, that's why we have five."

"Five years? But in your notebook you say you want to be mayor of the regional capital in three years…"

Lao Yu rapped Xi Sheng's head with his pen: "You really are a fool aren't you, you fucken dwarf! If I'm mayor in three years, won't that be even better for Danggui?"

The report was submitted and subsequently approved, and holding that power, Lao Yu used all the resources at his disposal to make it happen. The first task was to obtain funding and additional support staff from the county. During the first year, the agricultural yield of grain staples was below target as much of the available arable land had been converted into vegetable plots. To exacerbate the situation, most of the pork, chicken and tofu produced, along with the vegetables and other local specialities, were transported for sale in the market. While revenues had increased, many of the residents began to change their minds on what was happening in the village.

As a result of these difficulties, Lao Yu and Xi Sheng travelled to Shanyin as it had early on transformed its previously subsistence agricultural sector into something much more industrial and large scale. The amount of fresh produce they grew was enormous; their pigs were ready for market in only six months; chickens were full grown in just two months. They learnt a great deal from the experience of Shanyin, and upon their return, orders were placed in the city for agricultural pesticides and other chemicals to increase production, along with artificial colourants and growth hormones for livestock feed. Yields increased accordingly and over a much shorter period of time. The shape and colour of the agricultural produce was perfect, and a single *jin* of soybeans could be used to make three times as much tofu as before. The beansprouts were bigger and plumper than ever before, and the yield was three times as much. The greatest impact of these new techniques, however, was found in their livestock. The new feed resulted in pigs growing so fat, so quickly, that their bellies scraped on the ground; as for the chickens, that was even more impressive as some ended up growing four wings instead of the normal two.

Xi Sheng became the specialist when it came to using the fertiliser, pesticides and growth hormones in the livestock feed. In fact, his house became the distribution centre; everyone purchased what they needed from him. By the end of the second year of Lao Yu's five-year plan, Danggui's agricultural produce was famous throughout Huilongwan. There were three shops on the main thoroughfare, and five more on the new main street that had sprung up near the foot of Mount Cockscomb. The income revenue for Danggui now equalled that of Huilongwan, which of course meant numerous visitors from other county administrative teams, all there to see for themselves the great success of the village. The first of these important cadres to call was none other than Lao Yu's father, who was naturally excited by what his son had accomplished. Truly a beautiful and rich area of land, he was heard to say, confirming what others had said already. Then he proclaimed that he himself would spend his retirement years in Danggui.

As the year came to a close, Lao Yu was promoted to deputy mayor of Huilongwan, slightly ahead of his own schedule. Despite the new position, however, he was determined to maintain his presence in Danggui, formally requesting special arrangements that would allow him to essentially serve the Party in two locations. After some discussion, the Party committee secretary of Huilongwan agreed. Lao Yu could spend half his time in Huilongwan, the other half in Danggui. Pleased at their decision, Lao Yu was further incentivised to succeed. While the village might now be famous across the entire county, for Lao Yu, this was just the start; the main aim was to ensure the name of Danggui was soon on the lips of every resident in all of the major cities. His unique arrangement didn't go unnoticed.

"Off to Danggui again, are you?"

"Yes... we've just acquired an automatic livestock feeder. I need to make sure it's properly installed. After all, there're mostly halflings working there."

"But surely their wives could all lift them up!"

Lao Yu understood the subtext: "Do you think my mouth's as dirty as yours?"

"Then are you saying you're just going for the sake of wasting money?"

"You fellows really are something!"

In this mind, he couldn't help but think these... colleagues... had become far too accustomed to earning a little praise; they didn't realise his ambitions were much grander. Everyone in Danggui had become wealthy, while the village as a whole had a healthy amount of cash in reserve. But strangely enough, these weren't the things Lao Yu coveted. All he wanted was a good drink, a chance to improve his capacity for alcohol, a quiet night, every night... a session at Xi Sheng's, that was all.

They always drank at Xi Sheng's place. At first, the men who went there were those Xi Sheng needed to win over as the new head of the village. Later on, as the drinking became more frequent, and as the booze flowed more easily, the relationships between the men became closer and closer. Before long, the other men would take to inviting themselves over for a drink rather than Xi Sheng himself telling them to come.

On those evenings when they would be entertaining guests, Qiao Qiao would be sure to clean herself up and make herself pretty. Then she'd be at the door welcoming the guests in the warmest manner possible. When they came alone, she'd tease them by asking them why they hadn't brought someone else with them, a younger brother or sister. Qiao Qiao couldn't drink, but she loved to talk! When the men brought their wives, they didn't come in order to drink themselves, but rather to keep an eye on their husbands, to make sure they didn't overdo it, and if that didn't work, they would at least be there to carry them home. Qiao Qiao would drag these women off to the kitchen to help her with the snacks, slices of dried red and white radish, a plate of roasted peanuts, dried meat, and fried eggs with garlic and chives. Their conversations would often revolve around the same thing.

"I think the men have really grown accustomed to coming over for drinks. It certainly makes your house lively!"

"The more the merrier, that's what Xi Sheng thinks. Show

everyone a good time!" As she spoke, a loud crack echoed over the din. "Mayor Yu… you've come!"

Of course he had. He rarely missed a session. Whenever anyone else came, they'd always knock on the door and wait to be welcomed in. Lao Yu, on the other hand, would simply kick the door and step inside, not waiting to be formally received. On this particular night, he didn't come empty-handed.

"Oh my," exclaimed Qiao Qiao, "you've brought sausages for us to enjoy!" She took hold of them and continued: "You know I've got some already. Where'd you get these?"

"What do you mean, you've had sausages all this time? Why've you never laid them out before!"

Qiao Qiao laughed along with him, and gestured for him to remove his hat so she could hang it up properly: "Oh, and to answer your question, I've never dished out sausages before as I never wanted you to get more drunk than you already were… are soon to be! Ha ha, I mean, too much drink and you'll be stumbling all over the place. You wouldn't want to get hurt… I wouldn't want you, too… and too much drink'll do that to you, you know?"

"Well," chortled Lao Yu, "tumbling over, hurting myself… all worth it, I say! Give us a drink!"

Jesting aside, Qiao Qiao was actually referring to three nights earlier when Lao Yu had been over and had drunk too much. On his way back to his doss house for the night, he had stumbled and fallen over, walloping his head on the ground. He'd have remained laid out that way, too, if it hadn't been for some unruly kids who'd been making a racket outside and which had caused a man who lived nearby to come out and shout at them. After he'd chased the boys away, he heard a low gurgling sound and discovered it was Mayor Yu. He'd actually carried him home, which was especially fortunate. As for the rather large bump this drunken adventure had left on his forehead, it swelled, naturally, and that was why he'd taken to wearing a hat: to cover the wound and hide his shame.

Like so many other drinking parties, this one also went on late into the night, despite the fact most said they'd only have a bottle or two when Xi Sheng began to bring the alcohol out. Bullshit, that's what that was. After two bottles, the men would relax, their tongues would loosen and so would their inhibitions. Glass after glass would soon find their way to their mouths. And if there was any danger of running out of drink, someone always offered to go home and fetch some more. Needless to say, the booze flowed.

As for the wives, they made no effort to stop their husbands. In truth, they didn't care what they got up to as they were usually deep in conversations of their own. Seated out in the courtyard, they could go on as long as the men. However, the courtyard did have its drawbacks, for it seemed as though visitors were always coming to call on Qiao Qiao asking for this or that. Someone might be soaking beansprouts and then they'd discover they didn't have enough of some ingredient or other and they'd come all in a rush to try to buy some. Qiao Qiao would sell it to them, usually, but always less than the amount asked. Someone else would come, and while they might compliment Qiao Qiao on the effectiveness of the growth hormones in the livestock feed, they'd moan about the price being too high, and then they'd ask for some other type of chemical compound, something they could substitute for the hormones.

They would never come empty-handed, but always bring a gift with them, a box of persimmons or a small bag of walnuts, always something. Qiao Qiao, however, was ruthless. She wouldn't accept persimmons; she had her own after all, as she would tell them, or she would complain that they sprinkled flour over them instead of sugar and they weren't suitably sweet. Then she'd explain a little about the growth hormones themselves, how they were factory-produced and that she had no idea which chemicals were used. Of course she couldn't tell them about any possible substitute. And besides, she would add, making their own substitute might save them a little money, but in the long run they'd lose out because the pigs wouldn't grow the way they wanted. Often these arguments were met with a complaint about how much money Qiao Qiao and Xi Sheng were making selling the hormones in the first place, but she would only ever answer by saying she didn't make them herself. Then they'd grumble about how Qiao Qiao was at least distributing them, or how they'd heard that in the city the hormones were cheaper by a third. Qiao Qiao would counter that she didn't really enjoy what she was doing, but her husband was the village head and she had to make some money after all, didn't she? This was generally met with a complaint about the incessant parties, the money needed to buy the drink, and a plea for her to sell them the stuff a little bit cheaper than usual. At these moments, Qiao Qiao's ruthless streak would shine through again and she told them she couldn't reduce the price, that they either buy it or not, and if they didn't, well then, they were welcome to pop inside and have a drink or two. Of course, they'd never take up her offer of the drink; they'd mumble under their breath instead and buy the hormones they needed before leaving in a sulk.

Naturally, once Xi Sheng had sunk a few, he wanted to sing. His wide repertoire included tunes such as *The Spring Onion that Grows Opposite My Door* and *A View of Flowers*, but that didn't stop his audience calling out for him to sing *Ten Lovely Maidens*. One evening, in response to such a request, a cocksure Xi Sheng shouted to his wife that he would sing and do the papercuts in which she herself was so skilled. Qiao Qiao's only thought was he must have drunk a lot, but she didn't share this with anyone, nor did she call out to her husband or bring him any paper. Xi Sheng didn't wait for her in any case, as she could hear he'd already begun singing. The song was long, too long. And they'd all drunk too much. By the time he'd reached the seventh maiden, people were already standing up to stumble off to the toilet, in some cases run.

Lao Yu was one of the men who'd stood up and staggered off, but after quite a bit of time, he'd still not returned. Noticing his absence, Qiao Qiao yelled out to him, wondering if he'd collapsed again, this time in the toilet. Then he suddenly appeared, using the wall as though it were a walking aid, and professing he was fine, he'd only had a few bottles and certainly wouldn't be falling down this time. But he didn't rejoin the men still drinking. Instead, he stumbled into a side room and before long his gurgled, intoxicated snoring could be heard.

All the while, Xi Sheng was calling out for Mayor Yu, for his leader, but since the men in the room were as inebriated as he was, they didn't really understand what he was up to. To their ears, he was simply shouting and nothing more. Partly to get him to shut up, the women outside responded by shouting back that the mayor had passed out in a side room, to which Xi Sheng laughed and praised his boss; it was a good thing, after all, for a person to pass out rather than to keep on drinking! Xi Sheng now yelled out to Qiao Qiao, suggesting she get a bucket for him and place it beside the bed; Lao Yu was bound to puke. Qiao Qiao brought the bucket into the side room for Mayor Yu. A second later she yelled out for one of the wives to come. There was Lao Yu, collapsed on the bed, shoes still on, his head lolled to one side like that of a gutted pig. There was shit all over his shoes, which he in turn had spread all over the sheets. A pig indeed, rolling in its own muck.

Xi Sheng never once got drunk, never once threw up the many, many bottles he'd drunk. So capable was he of handling alcohol that he was even sober enough to escort some of his drinking companions to the door and then return to sit with Qiao Qiao as she calculated the night's profit. Note after note she counted, different amounts each time, her thumb moistened with saliva to separate the money. He always asked her the same question: how much had they made? She'd wave the cash in front of him and ask if he fancied anything to eat, he'd been drinking all night... how about a bowl of noodles perhaps?

As is often the case, new-found wealth brought a boom in construction. The inhabitants of Danggui, increasingly aware of the need to look the part of an up-and-coming place, set about renovating their old homes. In most cases, this actually meant destroying their previous abodes and building entirely new ones fashioned out of concrete. In Huilongwan, the houses there had long been of a certain size, often with five cross-beams and four rafters making up the roof, or at least four and three, and always with ornamental eaves. The best houses were designed so that the main central and decorated support beam and roof tiles were arranged precisely down to the upturned eaves. For extra strength, these houses often had bricks to reinforce the load-bearing walls, not just concrete, and large wooden beams inserted into the front and side walls, both for support and for appearance. By contrast, Danggui's old houses were primitive, more like small three-room shacks cobbled together with mud, earth and planks of whatever wood they could find. The roofs were often flat and constructed with suspect materials, old pieces of trees plastered together with whatever was around. Some had actual roof tiles, but most had only thatched roofs, barely able to keep out the rain. Considering the state most of these houses were in, they wouldn't be missed.

Xi Sheng had been the first to remake his house, and the other villagers had followed after him. Of course, he had learnt the technique from examining the homes in Huilongwan, and these skills were passed on to his fellow villagers. The new structures, built as they were with concrete, allowed for the addition of an upper floor, so naturally Xi Sheng's new home had a second level. In Huilongwan, most doors were fashioned out of metal, and so too was Xi Sheng's. They also had glass in their windows, not greased paper; again, Xi Sheng followed suit. Lao Yu assisted in the transformation of the village, using some of its reserves to buy ceramic tiles to be affixed to the newly built houses. As a result, when the sun shone, the town sparkled, lighting up the entire valley in a dazzling display of colour. So reflective were the tiles, in fact, that when the moon was full and clear in the night sky, Danggui blazed a brilliant white.

Lao Yu, of course, invited many members of the senior leadership to come and see what he had achieved in Danggui. After the viewing was complete, he would manoeuvre the men back to his place for some water, despite the fact he still lived in the old cadre building that had not been remade. Naturally they were a little shocked at this, some complaining that he lived in squalor. Lao Yu responded by saying that when the structure was first built, even though that was now long ago, it was considered modern; if nothing else, he would often add, keeping the building intact would show clearly the transformation the village had undergone (under his leadership, no less).

Needless to say, Lao Yu left quite an impression on those he had invited. Xi Sheng, however, couldn't help feel a pang of dismay at Lao Yu's insistence to remain in the old structure. He felt it impacted negatively on the reputation of the village; made them all lose face, in fact. To deal with the problem, Xi Sheng began to solicit opinions from other villagers about whether to construct a new home for him. Most agreed they should, but not on the site of the old structure. Somewhere different, somewhere better was needed, somewhere with more space as they had to build it bigger. The idea was for it to be Lao Yu's *home*, a place where he could properly entertain the bigwigs.

Xi Sheng was the first to suggest his land was the best; after all, everyone seemed to accept the fact its feng shui carried the greatest power. He would even give up part of it at no cost, a magnanimous gesture to their dear leader. At first, Xi Sheng offered the rear part of his land, but it was decided that that was too small, and besides it was perhaps too close to the neighbours who, it turned out, were not in favour of having a new structure built so close to them. In fact, when the plan was brought up, they were adamantly against having Lao Yu's new home encroach on what they considered their own open space. To add to their argument, they rightly claimed that Xi Sheng would be equally unwilling if the situations were reversed. In truth, when Xi Sheng had rebuilt his own home he had nearly crossed the line into his neighbour's land, and a terrible argument had ensued. It was clear hurt feelings persisted, and so Xi Sheng's rebuttal brought up Lao Yu's name, and the argument in favour of the structure they planned to build was for him to greet important officials. The land, he added, wasn't something he wanted, so why did they seem to care so much? Finally, the town paid Xi Sheng's neighbour five thousand yuan to agree to the new build. And of course Xi Sheng had to be paid the same amount; that was only fair.

Four months later, the structure was complete, a three-storey property, the highest in Danggui. Lao Yu moved in shortly afterwards. From then on, all meetings were held in the new building, and any senior leader invited to the village was greeted and welcomed there. Standing on the balcony, Lao Yu could see far off into the mountains, the trees and the clouds that encircled the peaks. Looking down, he could see Qiao Qiao carrying out her daily chores, washing clothes or watering the Japanese roses they'd planted. The roses, in truth, were quite the sight. Their vines grew voraciously, crawling and stretching everywhere, creeping up and around the door frames, blooming bright red flowers that emanated a red hue over Xi Sheng's porch. Lao Yu often called out to Qiao Qiao on occasions like these, teasing her as to whether she'd made good use of her time in the kitchen, or had she simply been wasting the day away outside watering flowers. Qiao Qiao would raise her head and reply in equal good humour, shouting back that if he wanted to have a little something special, she'd better get to it. She looked even prettier when she smiled, and Lao Yu would answer in the affirmative, to which she'd respond by saying she'd shout for him when she was done. Qiao Qiao meant what she said, too, and soon the chimney would be billowing smoke. A moment later the smell of food would carry on the air, all the way to the balcony on which Lao Yu stood.

But this period of stability didn't last. On the day Lao Yu asked the county leadership committee to refurbish and expand Danggui's electrical-carrying capacity, to install new poles and lines – Xi Sheng even purchased a telephone for the village, conveniently placed in his own home – something happened in Huilongwan. It was as though a hurricane had punched through the small crack in the door, tearing up everything inside and making such a mess it would take quite a while to clean up.

—

It started with the man who had tried to give Qiao Qiao candied persimmon in exchange for the growth hormone used in the livestock feed. Besides raising pigs and tending fields, the family of the man also sold persimmons. There was only one place in all of Danggui that had persimmon trees. And like the men of the village, the trees never grew that tall. The fruit the trees yielded, however, was plentiful, even if the persimmons were more flat than round. Their unique shape gave them their nickname: peak-less kepis. The fruit would only ripen towards the beginning of winter, but they never became sweet; instead they possessed a rough, pulpy texture and offered very little taste at all. In the past, the villagers generally waited until spring to harvest the fruit, and then they would be mulched and mixed in with wheat and bran to make chow mein. Later on, the noodle dish grew out of favour and the persimmons were picked, dried, rolled in icing sugar and sold as a sweet.

This particular house became quite famous for producing the candied persimmon, so much so they regularly sold out in the market, quite quickly, too. To make the sweets they sold, they would first purchase all the persimmons that grew in the village; sometimes they would even travel to other towns to buy the persimmons there. Once they'd bought a sufficient amount, they'd lay them out to dry. There was nothing out of the ordinary with any of this. Later, however, in order to maintain the peak-less kepi shape and keep sales flowing, corners had to be cut. The persimmons were still soaked in sweet syrup, but instead of rolling them in icing sugar, simple white flour was used instead. The look was the same, the taste less so.

The villagers knew the family were making fake candied

persimmon, and whenever the man gifted some to his neighbours, they would never eat them. Then, one day, while at the market, a pregnant lady had a craving for dried persimmon. She ended up buying a whole *jin* of the fruit, and ate them in nearly a single mouthful. That evening, her stomach was distended and she was in great pain. This carried on through the night, resulting, ultimately, in a miscarriage. Overcome with grief and anger at the tragedy, her family were resolved to find out what had caused it. This brought them to the market where they caused quite a stir outside the local chemist; they brandished receipts showing what medicines they'd purchased and demanded compensation of twenty thousand yuan.

Once this story got out, more and more people began to reflect on their own experiences: beansprouts from Danggui usually resulted in diarrhoea, while tomatoes, cucumbers and garlic chives caused dizziness. The more people thought about it, the more they came up with instances where the food had affected them adversely. The furore grew until finally the county dispatched investigators from the Food and Drug Administration and the Industry and Commerce Bureau to look into what was happening. Soon after their arrival, they discovered the four-winged chickens, some even with three legs, the third one often protruding from the fowl's arse. In the pig pen, they learnt the animals were growing to a weight of two hundred *jin* in only eight months, so fat that the animals could no longer stand. Upon examining the feed, the investigators discovered that not only were they loaded with growth hormones, but the feed also included oral contraceptives to stop the beasts from breeding and depressants to keep them lethargic. The vegetable fields were no better, where they found thirty times the recommended covering of pesticides.

As the investigators explored the village and its seemingly questionable practices, they noticed some men squatting beside their doors using old toothbrushes to rub clean piles of soft, greenish walnut kernels.

The sight only raised more questions: "Just what are you doing here?"

"Cleaning… to sell…"

"You can sell them even though they're that colour?"

"Ah… we'll douse them in formaldehyde first, that'll whiten them up before we sell them."

The investigators kicked at the pile of walnuts and then showed their ID cards. The surprised local villager didn't try to make excuses: "Hey now… why've you shown up without informing Xi Sheng what you were planning to do?"

The investigators said nothing further, but turned and headed off to speak to Xi Sheng. At the same time as they began walking towards his home, Xi Sheng was having the telephone installed. When he saw them cresting the hill, his first thought was that the county government had dispatched officials to oversee the new developments and what they had invested in. Wishing to have a proper welcome for the esteemed visitors, he turned around and called out to the man who had been helping him with the installation: "Say now… you see those men coming? I want you to take them on a tour of the village, make sure you show them everything… oh, and be as welcoming as you can!"

"Should I have them over to my place for dinner then?" asked the pockmarked man.

"Sure, sure… just go."

The man raced over towards the guests intent on ensuring their visit was a good one. After the requisite greetings, he invited them to eat at his place. This didn't receive the response he had been expecting.

"You'd eat the produce you grow here?" said one of the investigators, a rising note of anger in his voice. "I don't somehow think we'll take you up on that offer… we'd rather not fall ill, you know."

The pockmarked villager laughed before replying: "Well, the village head has asked me to show you around, to treat you well… so I'll feed you with what I grow in my own personal plot… not the stuff we sell."

"You've got your own personal plot… used only by your family?"

"Of course we do. We've got our own pigs and chickens, too. It's no problem, you can rest assured that what you're eating is safe."

At that moment, the villager whose pile of walnuts had been kicked by the investigators came running up, shouting for Xi Sheng: "Xi Sheng! What're you playing at? Do you have some grudge against me or what? Why didn't you tell me government investigators were coming!"

As he stepped into the courtyard, he saw the very same

investigators he was now complaining about. They had encircled Xi Sheng's man and seemed to be interrogating him. Without saying anything else, he spun around and beat a hasty retreat. On his way out, his eyes fell on Xi Sheng, but he didn't open his mouth; he simply waved and started to walk away.

"What the hell were you hollering for?" Xi Sheng shouted as he caught up with the man. He told him of his encounter with the investigators and Xi Sheng stood dumbstruck. A moment later he groaned: "We're done for. We're ruined." Then, instead of walking the rest of the way home, he grabbed the man and pulled him away, leaving together. He was intent on never going home again (even if he did).

Once the investigation was completed, the true scale and severity of the problems emerged. The village was immediately ordered to cease the production, sale and distribution of goods. They were also prohibited from attending the markets in Huilongwan. The village as a whole quickly collapsed, and those responsible were at a loss as to what to do.

"What now?" was the first question Lao Yu asked Xi Sheng.

"Whaddya mean? We're ruined… there's no 'what now'!"

"The sky might've fallen in, but that means someone must lift it back up!"

"Well… you're the tall one, not me."

"But I'm not a local…"

"So I'm gonna take the rap for everything?"

"I've already tried to smooth things over with the men in charge, those connected to what we've been doing here… they'll protect you too."

"How… how'll they protect me?"

"Well… the first thing you need to do is step down as village head… they need to be seen to be taking away your position."

Xi Sheng's face blanched, and his head hung low for what seemed like forever. Finally he responded: "You gave me this hat to wear… you bloody well take it."

With Xi Sheng removed as village head, Lao Yu had to appoint a new one. The telephone he'd only recently installed was just as quickly ripped out and reinstalled in the home of the new village head. He no longer invited people over for his once famous drinking parties, nor did anyone show up at his door with a bottle in hand. Lao Yu also provided guidance for the new head in drawing up what would be the new development plan for Danggui.

Lao Yu continued to go out onto his balcony, staring at his surroundings.

"Qiao Qiao, how's Xi Sheng?"

Qiao Qiao had been outside sweeping the veranda. A powerful wind the night before had made a mess of things, and there were rose vines and petals scattered all over the place. She waited a while before responding: "He's asleep."

"It's nearly noon and he's still in bed! Say now... what're you planning to make for lunch?"

"Pancakes... would you like some?"

"Sure... but make them spicy!"

Before she had even finished preparing lunch, Lao Yu showed up at their door with a bottle of spirits in his hand. By the look of things, Xi Sheng had just woken up, but he no longer went out to the rubber tree as he did before. Perhaps he didn't need to massage his back or legs against the tree, or else he just couldn't be bothered. Instead, he sat on the doorstep and rubbed his knees with his hands. Lao Yu said that he'd worked out a new means by which Danggui could grow its economic base once again. But Xi Sheng displayed little interest.

"I've stepped down... remember... why tell me?"

"You're still the descendant of revolutionary heroes... and you're still the richest and most capable man in the whole village!"

"Bullshit! The village might be better off, you got your promotion. And what did I get... fuck all... that's what!"

"As long as you have me here... well... you shouldn't worry about turning things around, OK?"

Together they discussed Lao Yu's plan and as they did so, Xi Sheng's mood began to lift. Before long, the bottle was finished and on the following morning, Xi Sheng set off early for Mount Cockscomb, dressed in his best Western suit.

There were nearly a hundred different mine owners on Mount Cockscomb. Some were small time and ran only a single mine shaft, while others had three or four. There were even a few who had controlling interests in ten shafts. If good fortune was on their side, it would only take a little bit of digging before they found the valuable minerals that would make them rich. For those who didn't have the Midas touch, they might work through several shafts with only holes in the ground to show for all of their work. For some who went broke, they ended up hanging themselves, or throwing themselves off the nearest cliff. Others, however, were cleverer in that they'd scout around to see who was striking it rich, who had the best veins, and then they'd angle their own digs in that direction. Of course, this usually resulted in open conflict and an ever-increasing body count. To date, a dozen men had lost their lives to such hostilities while a further twenty had been injured or crippled; another forty or fifty had been imprisoned. The man Xi Sheng had learnt about was a fairly well-off proprietor by the name of Yan. Lao Yu had provided some of the finance for his first exploratory dig, and now he had made introductions for Xi Sheng. After all, Lao Yu had told him, if he no longer wished to show his face in Danggui, then he ought to get rich elsewhere – so why not Mount Cockscomb?

Yan was from Qingfengyi in Shanyin. He'd come to Mount Cockscomb at the start of the boom and had opened six mine shafts in total, all of which had yielded enormous amounts of precious ores and minerals, making Yan a very rich man. As a consequence, Xi Sheng's arrival was not met with warm words and open arms, but rather with a scowl.

"So," he said after first seeing Xi Sheng, "Lao Yu says you're a capable fellow, hmm?

"I've got brains, yeah." Xi Sheng's response was confident, cocksure.

"Is that so?"

"I can see you're carrying report forms, right? Show me them now, and I'll remember everything I see."

Yan handed over the forms and allowed Xi Sheng to scan through them. Once finished, he tested the dwarf. Xi Sheng was able to rhyme off every number he'd seen, so that all Yan could do was acknowledge his ability: "I guess you do have brains… but be that as it may, I didn't invite you here to be my bloody secretary! Lao Yu told me your grandfather fought with Qinling's guerrilla band, is that right?"

"Yeah, he did. He was a guard for Commander Kuang San." This was a lie, naturally, but Yan didn't seem to notice, or he didn't care.

"Lao Yu might've given you an introduction, but let me tell you something – in those days Qinling's guerrillas stayed for a while in *my* family home… do you understand what I'm saying? I'm going to make you a guard too… just like your grandpappy… do you hear? I want you to go to the eastern edge of my property and stand watch over the ore I've had dug up… can you handle that?"

Xi Sheng was disappointed. He hadn't planned on being simply a guard. He mumbled words to that effect under his breath, but he hoped Yan had not heard him clearly.

"You're not keen?"

"No, no, not that at all… I'll do whatever you want me to…"

"It's a twenty-four-hour position, you hear? You've got to be there, always. You're not to wander off or mess around, understand?"

"Heh, my legs wouldn't let me even if I wanted to… and besides, where the hell would I run to?"

Yan laughed before continuing: "You're damn right, there's nowhere to run to, but shit me… you won't be able to chase down a thief should one appear either!"

"Give me a mobile then… I'll ring you should anything happen."

"You want me to give you a wife, too!" He tossed a large bronze gong at Xi Sheng. If anything happened, he had to pound it as hard as he could and then someone would come.

Xi Sheng trundled off up the northern mountain slope until he reached the far eastern depot where the ore in question had been piled up. After three days of standing guard, he felt the job wasn't all that bad, perhaps the easiest bit of work that could be found anywhere in this world. In the morning, he had a porch on which to sun himself, to clip his fingernails, and when it was time to eat, he'd make himself some *mashizi*, a Shaanxi delicacy that comprised small roundish doughboys in a spicy vegetable broth. He'd make sure the doughboys were all about the same size, too, by shaping them in the inside of his conical straw hat to form perfect little balls.

But after three days of nothing to do and no one to talk to, Xi Sheng began to feel a little restless. So he resorted to singing, whereupon the gong Yan had given him seemed to be rather handy. That was until he clanged it for the first time, as within moments three men came bounding down the slope thinking there were thieves about. Soon realising this was not the case and that Xi Sheng was merely using it as a musical instrument, they proceeded to give him a tongue lashing. Afterwards, Xi Sheng left the gong hanging up in his shack and refrained from singing. Instead, he would squat on his porch and wait expectantly, impatiently, for a vehicle, any vehicle, to climb up the mountainside and pay him a visit.

When people did show up to cart off a quantity of ore, they always arrived with some company documentation or other, which Xi Sheng would examine carefully and then he'd help them take the specific ores they wanted. The amounts loaded were measured in tonnage, which meant it took time for the work to be completed. It was during these moments that Xi Sheng would try to strike up a conversation with the drivers, asking them where they'd come from, how they were, how long they'd been driving, if their old fathers were still robust, and so on. The replies were usually short: yes, my old man is fine, etc. Xi Sheng would then ask if they had children, if they were well-behaved, that sort of thing. Yes, came the answers, they had kids, and yes, they were all well-behaved...

"So... what about your wife, she's not come with you, has she?"

Questions like this, however, often drew strange looks from the drivers and they would sometimes wonder if Xi Sheng wasn't a bit off his head. Fearing he might be, they'd hasten the loading so as to get away as quickly as possible. On these occasions, Xi Sheng was prone to become irate, insulted that his interlocutors seemed to be in a hurry to get away. He'd even make some of the drivers unload what they'd already put in their vehicle. Sometimes the drivers would comply, sometimes they wouldn't. Of course, Xi Sheng had never raised his fist to anyone before, so when the drivers seemed disinclined to follow his instructions, he'd lie down on the ground in front of their vehicles and prevent them from leaving.

"You'll have to run me over to get out of here! Go on, do it, crush me!" This became his common refrain in such situations. And it worked, too. The drivers, at first refusing to heed his commands, would unload the ore they'd already picked up.

"You're one crazy dwarf bastard, let me tell you!" was the typical response.

"You wanna really see something... then let me clang my gong!" Xi

Sheng would then laugh and everything would be alright between him and the driver once more.

The driver might then proffer a cigarette, but Xi Sheng would rarely smoke it; instead he'd place it neatly behind his ear, presumably saving it for later.

It would now be time for the drivers to ask questions of their own: "So tell me… what kinda salary do you make? How much does your boss pay you in a month?"

"How much do you get for a load of ore?" Xi Sheng would respond by way of another question.

"I reckon this job of yours is alright… just sit around and make money," the driver would continue.

"What's good about it, huh? I haven't seen my missus for two months."

"You've got a wife?"

"What the hell does that mean!" Xi Sheng would then regale them about his village, how the men might be short but not one of them was a bare stick; and what's more, every wife was a metre six at least.

"Hey now… I'm impressed!"

Pleased with their response, Xi Sheng never failed to add his further two cents: "Let me tell you, a woman might get by on a pretty face, but a man has to use his brains!"

"Well now… with no woman around, I reckon your brains'll end up doing you in."

This statement usually cut to the quick, and Xi Sheng could feel his heart ache. He wouldn't acknowledge it openly, however, but respond cryptically instead: "Winter never leaves, summer never sticks, between February and August tomorrow never comes, it's summer now…"

The next time this truck arrived for a load of ore, Xi Sheng was surprised to see a woman accompanying the driver, a young woman. Her nose was somewhat flat, but her lips were rather plump and welcoming, and covered with red lipstick, they looked like fine cuts of fresh meat ready to be devoured raw. Before introductions were made, before they even alighted from the vehicle, the driver had given the young woman specific instructions: "Make sure you take good care of him… he's like a brother to me."

Once out of the truck, the young woman strolled into Xi Sheng's shack. She called him 'big brother' in such a way that Xi Sheng was shocked by her forwardness: "What... what the hell're you doing? What... what is this?"

The driver answered: "I've got some work to do down the mountainside. I'll be about an hour." Then he turned and left without another word.

Xi Sheng had heard the mines were crawling with whores, and he'd thought of trying one out for himself. He was curious about what sort of woman became a prostitute, but now such a woman was actually in his shack, he didn't know what to say, much less what to do. He was flustered, not daring to return inside, nor even look in the direction of the woman. To his further dismay, the prostitute didn't wait for him to come back, or for him to make up his mind. She strode outside confidently, sure of her work, and straight away grabbed at his trousers.

"Oh my," she said, surprised at what her hand had fallen on. "This doesn't really compare, does it!"

Xi Sheng was dumbstruck and everything after was a blur. He didn't know if he had removed his trousers, or if she had, but there he was, naked, with a prostitute stripping in front of him. She turned her back on him, showing her curved, bare bottom, but Xi Sheng reached out to turn her around, he wanted to see her face. The prostitute, however, demurred, and instead tossed her crumpled clothes over his head. He realised then she didn't want to look at him, couldn't bear to see his eyes, his squat face. And as soon as these thoughts came into his mind, his physical desire for the whore was gone; his virility deserted him.

The hour passed and the driver returned. His first words were naturally about how it had gone, but Xi Sheng remained quiet; he couldn't... wouldn't... admit he'd failed to get off. Averting his eyes, he simply asked if he had to pay.

"Heh," laughed the driver, "can business happen without the exchange of money?"

"How much?"

"Three hundred."

"But... I didn't do anything with her." Xi Sheng's voice was low and barely disguised his embarrassment.

"You didn't... or you couldn't?"

"Eh? Let me tell you, at home I fucked my wife nearly every day! Don't go talking about couldn't..."

"You were too nervous then... ha... your loss. You still have to pay!"

"Then," said Xi Sheng, his voice hushed once more, "you... go... go and load your truck... if I've gotta pay, I might as well get what I'm paying for."

On this occasion, Xi Sheng didn't care how much ore the driver loaded onto his truck; it didn't matter, he had... other things to do. Afterwards, the driver brought prostitutes twice more, but each time Xi Sheng felt a pang of regret, embarrassment it seemed, whenever he paid for the services provided. The driver, unsurprisingly, felt no moral qualms whatsoever: "Why're you embarrassed... it's just business. How about this... next time, say you get papers requiring you to load three tonnes into my truck... you give me three and a half and then I won't need to take any of your cash."

"I knew this would happen... I'm a bad man, aren't I..."

"What're you talking about... the ore isn't even yours... and besides, it's not like your boss is doing you any favours. Tell me... he's making millions, yeah, and what do you get? You get a fucken pittance..."

This put Xi Sheng's heart more at ease, and they shook hands on their... mutual understanding: he would see that an extra half tonne was loaded onto the driver's truck without being recorded, and the driver, in return, would keep bringing girls. It seemed like an amicable and beneficial agreement, until Xi Sheng realised that half a tonne of ore, once sold on the black market, earned the driver more than he was getting in prostitutes. Consequently, they made a new arrangement: Xi Sheng would keep getting the whores, as well as a third of the profits.

They carried on like this for about two months, but as the number of visits with prostitutes increased, Xi Sheng began to feel increasingly guilty; he wasn't doing right by Qiao Qiao, he thought. Eventually, he decided to request a leave of absence to return to Danggui.

On the evening he finally returned to Danggui, the first thing that struck Xi Sheng was that every house but his had their porch lights on. He asked Qiao Qiao why she hadn't turned them on, but her response was simply that the bulbs were broken and she hadn't yet had the chance to replace them. Unsatisfied with this answer, Xi Sheng instructed his wife to go and buy new bulbs immediately.

With his wife off to the store, Xi Sheng spent some time outside on his doorstep, staring up at the sign that still hung over the door: 'Family of a revolutionary martyr'. At the home of the new village head, the sounds of a bustling drinking party could be heard, and this further weighed on Xi Sheng's heart. He didn't want to go inside, but nor did he want to just stand on the porch. Finally, he turned, sauntered sadly over to the stone washboard where his wife used to do the laundry, and plopped down.

"Why's it taken so long to turn things around?" he shouted to no one in particular. "Are you trying to get rid of me?"

A little while later, Qiao Qiao returned. As she approached the courtyard gate, Xi Sheng noticed her steps were hurried and urgent; it was as though she were chasing some dog, or being chased by it. Then, suddenly, Lao Yu's voice could be heard: "You look so pretty tonight, come on... let's have a drink!"

"Xi Sheng's back..."

"He's what?"

"He's back... he's come to clean his clothes."

"Oh... then let's get him to come and have a drink with us too!"

"No... he won't. I know it..."

"I suppose you're right... he won't... he can't... alright, then, I'll tell you what: you stay, but tell him I'll come see him tomorrow."

Xi Sheng heard the exchange but said nothing; nor did he make any effort to stand up and greet his... friend. He waited patiently, quietly, for Qiao Qiao to enter the courtyard before speaking: "So... you can drink, now, huh?"

"Everyone in the village attends the parties. If I didn't go... well... that would just cause problems."

Xi Sheng refrained from saying anything else. He simply stood up, took the bulbs from his wife and proceeded to replace the broken lights. Having done this, he went inside and closed the door behind. He wanted to sleep.

Qiao Qiao remained outside for a little while, but then followed her husband inside. He was already splayed out on the bed as she entered, but she was adamant that he had to strip down before he could sleep. She spoke matter-of-factly, his clothes had to be washed in hot, scalding water; she didn't want him to bring fleas into the bed. Xi Sheng obeyed, and soon Qiao Qiao was boiling water to wash his clothes. She told him to wash his filthy feet, too. After all, how could he crawl under the covers like that? Again, Xi Sheng complied and washed his feet. He washed his crotch, too. Qiao Qiao, however, chose not to notice him, and instead carried out her nightly chores. First she prepared the pig feed for the morning, then made sure the chicken coop was locked, and finally checked on the rice containers to see if they were properly closed.

"You really know how to keep yourself occupied, don't you!" Xi Sheng's words dripped with anger.

"Drop dead you prick!" Qiao Qiao's words dripped with much of the same anger.

Xi Sheng stayed for a few days, and during that time he took to watering the plants occasionally, as well as spreading fertiliser. He also repaired part of the collapsed wall encircling the pig pen. He even helped Qiao Qiao cook the meals and wash the bedding. His help with the washing was especially timely as it was difficult for a single person to properly spread the bedding out to dry. At first, Qiao Qiao chose not to say anything about his changed behaviour, his helpfulness around the house. But when he took hold of the bedding and struggled to hang it up to dry, his actions brought a smile to her face.

"Why're you smiling... you can't do it yourself?"

"No... not that. I just bumped into Lan Shen... she said you were a changed man."

"Did she say I've changed for the worse, or for the better?"

"For... the better. She said you looked like you really love your wife!"

"You didn't tell her I bet... didn't say that I was making three hundred yuan a day while I was gone!"

"Where is it then... where's the money?"

"I'm not bullshitting you!" Xi Sheng then lowered his voice and urged Qiao Qiao to do the same. "Tonight... let's have a party... like before... invite everyone. Whoever can come, get them to come."

For the next three nights, they drank and partied, almost like before. But then, on the day he was set to head back to Mount Cockscomb, resigned to the fact that this was now his life, Xi Sheng heard news that Lao Yu's father was about to arrive in the village. This news immediately got Xi Sheng to thinking; he had to stay, this might be his only chance. With these thoughts in mind, he took up a spot on the porch of Lao Yu's home and waited for the older Party man to come. His intention was plain, he was going to invite Lao Yu's father to his house for dinner. Originally, of course, the plan had been for the older man to dine with the new village head, but Xi Sheng cut this plan off, aided by the fact the village head hadn't been there waiting for Lao Yu's father as he had. Seizing the moment, Xi Sheng pounced and quickly escorted the senior Party member to his home. To add insult to injury, he didn't even send word to the village head, nor did he invite him along.

That evening, Xi Sheng was the centre of the party. He was drunk and talkative, barely letting anyone else get a word in edgeways. So much so his wife even told him about it, urged him to slow down. Xi Sheng's response was to show incredulity. He wasn't drunk, he proclaimed, and even if he was, had he said anything inappropriate?

"What did I say, huh? I just said… uncle. I know everyone else calls you director… but I'll call you 'uncle', OK? Yes… OK… you said before… Danggui… its mountains, its streams, its air… that it was all perfect… that you'd like to retire here… and now you are here… yes. Ha ha… well… I wanna welcome you… my wife, too… she welcomes you… the whole damn village does! We'll… I mean the everyone here… we'll look after you, OK? You just tell us what to do… give us guidance… and then… and then I'm sure Danggui will soar again… because of you! "

He burped and then went on: "Now tell me, wife, did I say anything wrong? Am I drunk?" He burped again before continuing: "Bring us some more, another bottle. I'm fine… another toast… come on, another toast to our uncle here!"

The meal went well into the night. Xi Sheng was inebriated. So, too, was Lao Yu's father. The two men sat next to each other, sharing drink after drink. Lao Yu's father even took Xi Sheng's hand in his own and wouldn't let go.

"You're a good'un, Xi Sheng," said the older man, shaking his hand vigorously, "a good'un. I like you my boy… I really do!" He shook Xi Sheng's hand some more, and then the two of them vomited together.

Today we begin *Pathways of the Northern Mountains*. As before, I will start and you follow.

The first peak of *Pathways Through the Northern Mountains* is Lonely-Fox Mountain. Ji trees grow in abundance on its slopes, as well as many flowering plants. The Feng River emanates from here and moves in a westerly direction towards the River You. Mauve-coloured pebbles line its bed, along with deposits of aragonite.

The Entreating Mountain stands two hundred and fifty leagues farther north. On its highest reaches, there is much copper, on its lower reaches, jade. Nothing grows on this mountain. The River Slippery begins here and flows west into the Zhubi River. It contains many slippery fish with crimson backs that resemble eels. When in large schools, they make a clamorous noise, akin to that of the parasol tree. Consuming them will treat tumorous growths. Slender hippopotamuses that look more like horses also call this river home. They have stripes on their legs and ox tails. They are said to shout.

Three hundred leagues to the north is Mount Belt. Jade is plentiful at its peak, while a darker variety is prominent nearer the base. The huanshu lives here. It is a horse-like creature that has a horn on its head that is excellent for grinding. It is reputed to prevent fires. The yiyu also lives on Mount Belt. This bird looks like a crow, but is multicoloured. It is said to be hermaphroditic. Eating its flesh will cure carbuncles. The River Peng begins here and flows west into Mallow Lake River. It is home to numerous shuyu, a fish that resembles a chicken, apart from its crimson down, three tails, six feet and four heads. It is said to caw like a magpie, and that if you consume it, you'll no longer feel depressed.

Watchtower Mountain rises four hundred leagues to the north. A river with the same name begins here and then flows west into the Yellow River. The heluo fish is commonly found in its waters. It has one head and ten bodies and is said to bark like a hound. Eating it will reduce the size of tumours. A beast that bears similarities to a porcupine lives on this mountain. It has reddish bristles and is prone to squealing. It bears the name menghuai and is said to ward off evil enchantments. There is little vegetation, but a great deal of realgar.

Three hundred and fifty leagues to the north is The Mountain That Dribbled. The River Raucous emerges on this mountain and journeys west into the Yellow River. Mudfish gather in great numbers in the Raucous. They resemble a magpie, except for their ten scale-tipped wings. They also sound like a magpie and are said to be able to prevent fires. Eating this fish will cure one of jaundice. On the higher reaches of this mountain are many pine and cypress trees. Palm trees and oak dominate nearer the base. Antelopes range here, while owls nest in the trees.

Guo Mountain stands three hundred and eighty leagues to the north. At its peak, there are many lacquer trees. Paulownia and bamboo grow together nearer the foot. Deposits of jade are numerous on the south of the mountain, while on the north there are large deposits of iron. The Yi River begins here and flows west into the Yellow River. Heavy-footed camels are common on this mountain. The yu bird, which looks like a flying rat, is common as well. It caws like a ram and is said to be an effective defence against melee weapons.

The tail of Guo Mountain is four hundred leagues to the south of its peak. Jade is plentiful on its highest reaches, but there is little else. Fish River emanates from here to flow west into the Yellow River. Cowrie shells can be found in great abundance.

Some two hundred leagues to the north is Fragrant-Cinnabar Mountain. Juniper trees are common on the peak, and so too are ailanthus plants. Wild garlic and shallots grow in great number as well. Fine cinnabar, as the name of the mountain suggests, is plentiful. The Fragrant River originates here and runs west into Wild Plum River. The only creature to live here resembles a rat, but it has the head of a rabbit and the body of an elk. It barks like a rabid dog and can fly with its tail. It is known as the ershu. Eating its flesh can reduce abdominal swelling and serve as an inoculant against myriad poisons.

Stoneman Mountain rises two hundred and eighty leagues to the north of Fragrant-Cinnabar Mountain. Its peak is devoid of vegetation, but there is plenty of jasper and green jade. The Limpid River rises high up on this mountain and travels west into the Yellow River. A white-bodied, leopard-like creature resides here. It has stripes on its head and cries 'mengji, mengji', which is the name it has been given. This animal is rarely seen, however.

A hundred and ten leagues to the north is Boundary Mountain. Spring onions, mallow, wild garlic, and peach and plum trees are plentiful on its slopes. The Bar River originates here and flows into You Marsh. An ape-like beast with markings across its torso calls this mountain home. It is said to be good at guffawing, but whenever it sees a human it feigns sleep, so one cannot be quite sure if the creature does indeed laugh. It is called the youyan.

Two hundred leagues to the north stands Creeping Vines Mountain. Its peak is barren. A creature lives here that resembles an ape, but it has a lion's mane, the tail of an ox, and stripes on its legs. Instead of feet, it has horse's hooves. Upon seeing humans, it calls out its name, 'zuzi'. Flocks of birds nest here, but they only fly in pairs. They are called the jiao, and both male and female have the plumage of a female pheasant. Consuming their flesh is said to restore mental stability.

A hundred and eighty leagues north is Leaflet Mountain. Its peak is devoid of vegetation, but there is a beast that lives here. It bears a resemblance to a leopard, but its tail is much longer, and it has the head of a human. Its ears are those of an ox and it has but a single eye. It is called the zhujian and seems to constantly howl in anger. When it stalks along the mountain it holds its tail in its jowls, but when it is seated it coils it like a snake. A bird called the baiye also nests on this mountain. It has the form of a pheasant and has intricate markings on its head, along with white wings and feet that are a yellowish hue. Consuming its flesh will relieve a sore throat. It is also said to be a remedy for idiocy. The Chestnut-Oak originates here before flowing into the Bar River.

Anointment Mountain stands three hundred and twenty leagues to the north of Leaflet Mountain. Near its peak ailanthus and mulberry grow in abundance, whereas upon its lower slopes there is mostly sandstone. An ox-like beast stalks this mountain. Its tail is white, and when it neighs it sounds like a human. It is called the nafu. A type of pheasant resides on this mountain as well. It has a human face, but on seeing an actual man, it cannot help but jump high into the sky. When it sings, it calls its name: 'songsi'. The Jianghan River begins here and flows west into You Marsh. Loadstones are common in its bed.

Two hundred leagues to the north is Marquis Pan Mountain. Pine and juniper trees grow in great numbers near the peak; hazelnut and thorn trees grow closer to its base. Jade is readily found on its southern slopes. On the northern slopes, there is much iron. An ox-like creature called the maoniu lives on this mountain. Its limbs each have four joints, and they are all hairy. The Boundary River begins here. It flows in a southerly direction to empty into Chestnut-Oak Marsh.

Smaller Unity Mountain stands two hundred and thirty leagues farther to the north. It is devoid of vegetation and is snow-covered the year through.

Larger Unity Mountain is two hundred and eighty leagues north of its smaller sibling. It, too, is devoid of vegetation, but it is not covered in snow. Near its base one can easily find deposits of jade. The four faces of the mountain are too steep to climb. A long snake lives here. It has pig bristles on its back, and a rattle on its tail that sounds like a watchman's clapper.

Three hundred and twenty leagues farther north is Dying-Lord Mountain. On its highest reaches there are many palm and wild plum trees, while on the lower reaches there is much gromwell. A river bearing the same name as the peak flows from here west into the Great Marsh. It appears again on the northeastern side of Mount Kunlun. It is widely known that this is the origin of the Yellow River. Red salmon swim in this river, while rhinoceroses and yaks roam its banks. There are also a great number of turtledoves.

Lesser Unity Mountain rises two hundred leagues to the north of Dying-Lord Mountain. Its slopes are devoid of vegetation, but there is much jade to be found. A creature bearing the form of an ox lives here. Known as the yayu, its body is red, and it has a human face, and horse's feet. It is said to sound like a human baby. It is a man-eater. The River Dun rises here before flowing east into the Wild Goose Gate River. Many peipei fish swim in these waters, but their meat is poisonous to humans.

Mount Penal-Code stands two hundred leagues to the north of Lesser Unity Mountain. This is the source of the River Huai, after which it flows north into Grand Lake. Zao fish live in abundance here. They look similar to a carp but with chicken feet growing out from their bellies. Consuming their flesh is said to reduce the size of tumours. A creature called the shanhui lives on this mountain. It bears the form of a dog but has a human face. It is skilled at throwing things, and when it sees a human it falls into fits of laughter. It moves swiftly like the wind. Its appearance heralds impending storms for all under heaven.

Two hundred leagues farther north is Mount Northern-Peak. Hardwood trees bearing oranges and jujubes grow in abundance. An ox-like creature lives here. It has four horns above a face that has four human eyes, and sow's ears. It honks like a goose, is called the zhuhuai and is said to be a man-eater. This is the source of the Zhuhuai River, which later flows into the Raucous River. Zhi fish swim in great numbers here. They have a fish's body, but a dog's head. They coo like a human baby. Consuming their flesh is said to ward off dementia.

Turbid Night Mountain rises a hundred and eighty leagues north of Mount Northern-Peak. No vegetation grows on its slopes, but there is much copper and jade. The Raucous River emerges here to flow west into the sea. A snake with a single head but two bodies resides in this area. Called the feiyi, it is a harbinger of imminent and severe drought.

Lonely North Mountain stands a mere fifty leagues away. No grass grows on this mountain, but spring onions and wild garlic are plentiful.

Brown Bear Mountain is a hundred leagues farther north. This mountain is devoid of vegetation, but many wild horses roam here.

Fresh North Mountain is one hundred and eighty leagues to the north of Brown Bear Mountain. Wild horses range in great numbers, too. The River Fresh emerges here to flow northwest into the Shoal River.

Many wild horses can also be found on Dike Mountain, which lies a hundred and seventy leagues to the north. A creature called the yao lives on this mountain. It resembles a leopard and has markings on its head. Dike Mountain is the source of the River Dike, which flows east and empties into the Great Lake. It is heavily populated with dragon-turtles.

Twenty-five mountains are described in *Pathways Through the Northern Mountains*. A distance of more than 5,490 leagues is traversed. The gods that live here all have the face of a human and the body of a snake. A rooster and a pig must be slain and buried as the offering, along with a jade sceptre. No grain offering is needed. The northern tribes prefer uncooked meat.

Surely you have questions…

Question: What does the text say about the bird… the yiyu? It's both…

Answer: Both male and female, yes.

Question: What's jaundice?

Answer: It's when your skin and the whites of your eyes turn yellow… it's usually a sign of something more serious.

Question: Are there different types of camels or are they all much the same?

Answer: Much the same, except some have two humps, others have one.

Question: What kind of markings are on the forehead of the mengji?

Answer: The text doesn't say…

Question: How can an animal 'sound like a parasol tree'?

Answer: Ah… it doesn't mean it sounds like a tree, but rather like the musical instrument that is made from the tree. The wood from the parasol tree is often used to make stringed instruments like the pipa. In this case, the passage is referring to two-stringed instruments sounding in perfect harmony.

Question: This mountain range has fish that look like chickens, but the passage also says they have crimson down, three tails, six feet, four heads… and they sound like a magpie. There're also the so-called 'heluo fish' that have one head and ten bodies… they bark like a dog… then this animal, the menghuai, it's like a porcupine but it has crimson bristles… and the mudfish that looks like a magpie… but with ten wings… there's also the yu bird that has a rat body on top of its bird wings… its squawk is like a ram… and the… the ershu, that's what it was called, it has the head of a hare but the body of an elk… it howls like a dog, too… and the… what was it called… the zuzi… it's like an ape but it has an ox's tail and horse's hooves… there's also some creature called the zhujian, which looks like a leopard but its tail is much longer and it has a human head, ox ears and one eye… then the zao fish that look more like carp, but they have chicken feet… and the… the zhuhuai… an animal that resembles an ox but it has four horns, human eyes and pig ears… lady pig ears… and finally the zhi fish… the fish with a dog's head that's cries like a human baby... there's more, too, but… but… why're these animals… so many of them… why're they all so strange and peculiar? And how's it they're all on this mountain range?

Answer: That's right, the mountains to the west are filled with many spirits, much jade, and a great number of impressive and auspicious trees, but the northern range, well, there're certainly stranger and more fantastic creatures. This, of course, has much to do with the type of climate and the terrain of the mountains in the north. As I've told you before, if you remember, the environment and climate in which one lives determines everything from how a person looks, to their accent, their character, culture, everything. Let's take Shaanxi Province, for instance. To the north there's the loess plateau, to the south you have the Qinling mountain range, in the middle there's the Guanzhong Plain. For the people who live on the loess plateau to the north, and for those who live in the Qinling region to the south, folk songs are still popular to this day; the communities in the Guanzhong Plain, however, don't have many folk songs, but they do have opera. This suggests the civilisation of the Guanzhong area developed earlier than other parts of Shaanxi. But – and did you notice this – the fish with the crimson backs that you find here can cure warts and disease if you eat them, as well as carbuncles, gangrene. The shuyu, too, cures depression if you consume it. The menghuai can help a person avoid misfortune, and the huanshu creature guards against fire. The camels are effective against military incursions, and the ershu neutralises poison. There's more, too, of course... All of this demonstrates that ancient people knew how to use the ancient animals they shared the world with to deal with numerous maladies. This also brings us to another line of thought. Ancient people didn't assume ugliness meant evilness. In fact, the opposite was true: that which was ugly generally warded off and protected one against the malevolence in the world. This perspective eventually led to the formulation of a system of images, the Heavenly Lord, Yama, the god of death, the Kitchen God, the Earth Land, Zhong Kui, the vanquisher of evil spirits, Judge Bao, and so many others. Nowadays, the parents around here enjoy naming their children after all sorts of terrible things, awful names of lowly character... they think this will allow them to rear their children well. It's like the old saying, perhaps this is where it comes from, you can't judge a book by its cover. Of course, calling someone ugly doesn't usually mean they're ugly, it's more they're strange, fantastic.

Question: I've another question about the animals... the yao has markings on its head, the mengji has markings on its head, too. So does the ape-like creature called the youyan, it has markings as well, the same as the zuzi. Why do these animals have... markings... decoration like this?

Answer: Perhaps their mothers are responsible for that? What's interesting, though, is the passage states that nearly each and every one of these beasts possesses human qualities, like the youyan that laughs like a man, but then goes to sleep when it sees one. There's also the mengji that's good at crouching, the zuzi that calls out to people whenever it sees them and the hippopotamus that shouts like a man. These descriptions are all written from the point of view of us, people, and since we like pretty, beautiful things... we may consider these creatures beautiful. Ha ha, perhaps the animals were trying to please people in the past, maybe that's still true to this day... like the butterfly, the golden pheasant, the panda, peacock and zebra, even the tiger, the leopard and snake...

Question: Ha ha...

Answer: I'm the one allowed to laugh, not you! Any other questions?

Question: The passage contains a lot of information about what items had to be used when making sacrifices to the mountain spirits, and how the sacrifices were to be performed, but during the sacrifices... well, did the people who lived in the northern mountains... did they not cook their food?

Answer: Maybe they feared fire... there were a lot of animals in the area, animals are afraid of fire, too. Perhaps... during the sacrifices, there were many proscriptions, many taboos... you know, this is where festivals and holidays come from. Even now, on holidays, we have to pay close attention to what we eat and what we're not allowed to eat, isn't that right?

Question: The passage also talks about how many of the animals had human features, looked like us or sounded like us, or in some cases both... could we say this shows how people were gradually becoming more dominant over the world, that the creatures in the mountains were growing closer and closer to us, that their welfare was becoming more dependent on us... domestication... or was it an attempt for them to become us?

Answer: These ideas are not the thoughts of wild animals. You're still thinking like a human.

Question: But surely the animals should be thinking this way.

Answer: Not only is this human thinking, but it's the way humans think today, more so than ever. People today are far too inclined to think this way, and what's more it's this type of thinking that's causing us to get sick, it's rotting our brains. Let me tell you something: pure beauty exists, its radiance can be found in the infinitude of its natural, inherent qualities. Trees don't know the Ten Commandments, small birds don't read The Bible, only mankind creates these sorts of problems for himself, only mankind condemns his natural instincts. That's why we're always at each other's throats, that's why there's so much insanity in the world.

Question: Are these your words?

Answer: No, no, it's a famous philosophical quote.

With his father now living in Danggui, Lao Yu carried himself in a much more respectable and filial manner; most of the villagers did likewise. His father had moved into the upper floor, and his presence was felt across the town, so much so that at nearly every meal, villagers would come one after the other to invite him to eat. The old man, however, generally refused the invitations. They were improper, or inconvenient, or he could make the meals himself, which meant the food would always be to his taste. Other, similar excuses were offered. Undeterred by his refusals, the villagers instead installed a stove so he could better prepare his own meals, and furnished him with the pots and pans and dishes he would need. They also sent, nearly every day, portions of rice and noodles, meat and eggs, and various vegetables, too. The villagers demonstrated such care for the elderly man that they thought to install a security door in order to allow him to enjoy the same sense of safety he had had before, whether that was in the county capital or along the main streets of Huilongwan. Iron bars were even fitted over the windows.

In spite of his father's presence, however, Lao Yu still loved his drink, which meant he continued to attend the parties the village head held at his home. Each time he went, he was also sure to call on Qiao Qiao, who would join him and his father, usually with an arm under the old man to help him walk. Lao Yu's father couldn't handle the booze like his son; a *jin* or so, and that would be enough. But he did love to chat, and once he got started, he couldn't stop. This generally led to him shouting out to Qiao Qiao for some food; his favourite was turtle soup.

His love for turtle soup was something he had picked up before retirement. Wherever he toured the countryside on official business, which usually meant he was investigating local work practices, his assistants would be sure to telephone ahead so that several bowls of turtle soup would be ready for when he arrived. Before long, he grew to expect them as a natural part of his trips. When he first arrived in Danggui, none of the locals knew of his particular tastes, so when he went to purchase some turtle, he discovered that no one in the village had even tried one before. As a result, a local was dispatched and financed to bring some turtle back. Afterwards, the villagers knew they had to think of some way to have turtles available. Unfortunately, the mountain stream had none, so that meant either buying the reptile from the market, or sending someone all the way down the valley floor and the uphill-flowing river that cut through Qinling. But how could they let Lao Yu's dad pay? An alternative method to get hold of turtles had to be devised. Might some family or other be given a small subsistence payment to procure them, or perhaps they could be provided with new living arrangements? Or maybe, just maybe, they could choose to officially recognise one of those children who had been born in violation of the one-child policy because, supposedly, their elder sibling was ill? That child could then be tasked with obtaining the turtles? Whatever plan they came up with, they had to get Lao Yu's approval. And if he gave them the green light, they could proceed. While all this was being discussed, however, an official delivery arrived carrying a sizeable number of turtles. Lao Yu's father received them happily and then in one of the rooms on the ground floor of the structure he shared with his son, a pool was constructed to properly care for them; it was a veritable vivarium.

Lao Yu's father was very precise about how he ate the succulent turtle meat. The creatures had to be soaked in crystal clean water for three days, one at a time. Afterwards, the reptile would be placed in a pot of cold water and then boiled slowly over a small flame. Once the water reached the desired temperature and began to bubble, the turtle would extend its head and gasp its last few breaths. A pinch of monosodium glutamate would be sprinkled in, along with a slightly larger pinch of five-spice powder. Some cooking wine, vinegar and sesame oil would be added and the cover placed on top until the creature was cooked all the way through. Lao Yu's father was meticulous; this was the only way to make turtle soup.

Whatever else he cooked, he went about it in much the same way as anyone else, but there was an art to preparing turtle meat. There were other methods, too. It could be steamed in a soupy broth, sautéed or included in a bowl of *mashizi*, the doughboy soup enjoyed by many across Shaanxi. On some occasions, he would invite Qiao Qiao over to enjoy the turtle dish together, and then he would tell her all about fine cuisine. A gourmet cook, he told her, was always careful about what he put into his mouth; he wouldn't eat just anything, except for pork, which was the only exception. That meant whatever dish he enjoyed was one he could make himself, even though the flavour and the taste might never be identical. Each time he enjoyed turtle meat, he had to have a soup to go with it, not just the broth the turtle was cooked in, but a noodle soup as a necessary accompaniment to the main dish. The noodles, however, could never be the first bowl from the pot, always the second. The result of this idiosyncrasy meant Qiao Qiao ate the first bowl of noodles, which she was generally happy to do.

That winter, the village head's mother passed away, and I was invited to sing. I was there for two days, and after I finished, Qiao Qiao wanted me to pay her a visit, too. She actually asked if I would play the role of fortune teller and use the trigrams to determine whether or not Xi Sheng had a woman on the side. She then told me how he hadn't been back for a month, but that even the last time he'd come he'd been so much skinnier than ever before... and he'd been having horrible dreams, spending the nights seemingly talking to ghosts, something he'd never done before. I was useless at such divination, however, and tried to tell her so. In return she accused me of being unwilling, that I was deliberately refusing her request… after all, she said, how could it be that a man who communed with this world and the next couldn't read fortunes?

She did introduce me to Lao Yu's father, though, and I told him how I'd met Commander Kuang San so many years ago. At first, he wouldn't believe me, and then he asked me my age. I didn't want to tell him, of course, so I deflected the question and just started talking about the commander. I assumed, correctly, that he'd heard many of the same stories, but at the same time I figured he didn't know all the small details… I remember he had a very distracted and blank look on his face when I was telling the stories. That's when Qiao Qiao interrupted to say she was amazed at what I knew, claiming, exaggeratedly, that I must know everything about… all under heaven… that was the phrase she used. Then she said I must be some divine entity… which meant, of course, that I must be able to tell her fortune… clever girl, I thought. Before she could say more, Lao Yu's father took his turn to interrupt and shouted that I must've seen so much of the history of Qinling, of its famous guerrilla band… and then he asked me if I could divine using the trigrams… unlike Qiao Qiao, however, all he wanted to know was whether he was going to get any turtles that morning.

I remember getting a bit angry at this, and then I said, perhaps in a louder voice than usual, that he'd had none, but that soon a bill would come… a moment later a man arrived holding three turtles. He'd got them from the market, he said, and he heard there was always someone in Danggui who would take them off his hands. Lao Yu's father was ecstatic at this turn of events… each turtle cost ten yuan, if I remember correctly. Qiao Qiao was apparently going to pay for him, but he told her not to, he'd get the money himself. As for the turtles, well, he said they were of very good quality, they'd come from the wild… and were older, too… hence their yellowish shells… evidently this was a good sign… I don't know.

Oddly enough, he let the turtles crawl around on the floor, and I can still recall the sound their claws made as they scratched across the concrete… it was like the echo of a copper gong being clanged. I remember, too, that he kicked at two of them, purposefully flipping them over… I could see their tiny claws pointing at the ceiling… then I heard him challenge me... after all, I'd said he'd have no turtles today, but now... well... what were these pitiful little creatures squirming on the floor, their claws flailing about in a vain effort to flip themselves back over? I smiled and told him they were the bill I was referring to... he picked up one of the animals and poked his finger hard into its soft underbelly, then with his thumb and index finger he held hard onto the rear part of the turtle's carapace. The creature stopped moving instantly, and Lao Yu's father chuckled before adding that perhaps they'd just come for his thirty yuan... and then he laughed some more... even a bowl of tofu in the county capital now cost forty yuan!

—

Xi Sheng's position had not changed. He was still tasked with guarding the ore belonging to Yan, still engaged in the illegal skimming of the pile, still fast friends with the driver who'd come to collect the ore, and bring the prostitutes in return. He'd grown quite accustomed to the routine, the camaraderie with the driver, the liaisons with whores, it was what it was. On one day when the truck never arrived, however, Xi Sheng sat in his small shack feeling quite ill at ease. What's more, his crotch was no longer feeling all that comfortable; in fact, it was increasingly itchy and he could no longer ignore the hot, burning sensation that seemed to emanate from between his legs. Upon closer inspection, he discovered a red rash all around his penis that reached half way down each leg. The rash burnt, and there were small blisters that oozed a yellowish puss. Needless to say, he grew worried and assumed the worse: he must've contracted that interminable disease that made one go blind. His isolation only exacerbated the worry he was feeling, so he abandoned his post and trundled off down the mountain in search of... something. As he reached the valley floor, he saw an advertisement on an electricity pole that promised treatment for sexually transmitted diseases. The more he stared at the ad, the more he felt he had indeed contracted syphilis. He tore off a slip that included the telephone number and address of the clinic, and returned to his hovel to wallow in sorrow.

The following day, the driver returned, another lady in tow. Unlike before, however, Xi Sheng was less welcoming and did not invite her inside his humble shack.

"Hey… what're you at? She's a virgin, I have to get her broken in… I brought her for you to do me this favour, and this is how you respond!"

"I'm not in the mood… I've had enough of whores."

"Fuck… you try to do a good turn for someone and this is the thanks you get?"

"I," Xi Sheng's voice was low, "I'm not… feeling well. Do you get what I'm saying?"

The driver told Xi Sheng to pull his trousers down, he wanted to see for himself: "Fuck me, that's nasty. But hey, don't go to that travelling doctor that works these parts, I'll go to the hospital and get you something for it. There's a shot you can take, but I'm afraid once you do take it, well, there'll be no action for a while, a few days at least… but you'll be alright after that."

He turned and gestured to the woman he'd brought with him, urging Xi Sheng once more to pop her cherry. Xi Sheng, however, refused. "Come on, brother… she's here for you." Without another word, Xi Sheng stormed out of his shack and made his way awkwardly over to a small depression that sat a little to the right of where he lived. He squatted down and emptied his bowels.

As he crouched, another guard from a nearby mine shaft strolled across the path in his direction. Displaying no embarrassment at the position he found Xi Sheng in, he simply shouted a greeting: "Hello there, little man! That time, eh? Well, let me give you some advice – make sure your cock doesn't touch the ground, you wouldn't want an earthworm to take advantage and crawl right up into it… it'll swell up like a balloon if that happens."

Xi Sheng said nothing, but he did manoeuvre some stones under his feet, and then with his hands he removed the earth immediately in front of him.

"Ah… in truth," the other man continued, "I don't think you've got much to worry about, given how small your pecker is…"

Xi Sheng grunted, and then ignored the other man.

The next time the driver arrived, he had three vials of medicine for Xi Sheng's ailment. But the first question Xi Sheng asked him was whether or not the drugs would kill earthworms.

"If an earthworm had crawled up your cock," the driver said curtly, "it'd be all swollen. It's not." He then told him to sit still and show him the back of his hand; he'd stick the needle in there. Oddly, however, the needle wouldn't pierce the skin, not even after several attempts. Visibly annoyed, the driver gave up on that hand and told him to give him the other one.

Xi Sheng didn't fear pain, he wasn't bothered about the difficulty of actually injecting him with the medicine. His greater concern was with its effectiveness: "Will this really work?"

"I've done this twice before, to Party cadres no less, men much more important than you… whaddya think, your life's as precious as theirs?" The injections finished, the driver once again loaded his truck, taking the extra half tonne as usual. Then he departed.

Five days later, there was clear improvement. His crotch no longer itched, nor did it burn. But the whole experience had given him a shock and he made a pledge to himself not to use whores again. He stopped the driver from taking his skim, too. Unsurprisingly, this did not go down well.

"What the fuck are you playing at?" said the driver. "How… how could you? I've a mind to tell everyone you've got dick rot!"

"Fine, go ahead, tell whoever you want," Xi Sheng retorted. "I'll be sure to tell them you've been skimming from the top, too!" He pulled out a notebook in which he'd carefully recorded each instance of the driver taking an extra half tonne. The driver grabbed at the notebook, but Xi Sheng was too quick and pulled it away. He wouldn't turn it over for anything. The driver grew enraged and pounced on the much smaller Xi Sheng, pinning him to the ground and punching him. Xi Sheng didn't hit back, but rather stuffed the notebook between his legs and rolled up into a small ball. Blood soon trickled down the back of his head, but he wouldn't surrender the notebook.

In the end, the driver never told anyone about Xi Sheng's brush with syphilis, nor did Xi Sheng inform on his illegal loading activities. But the driver never returned to Xi Sheng's depot; instead he began loading his truck elsewhere, perhaps under similar arrangements to the one he'd had with Xi Sheng. As a result, the amount of ore Xi Sheng stood watch over grew and grew, which in turn attracted even seedier elements, notably thieves who would try to raid the depot in the evenings. During the day, Xi Sheng wouldn't dare let his guard down, but as he gazed out across the mountains, the trees, the fields, the land rolling up and down, he couldn't help but notice people tramping along, baskets tied to their backs, or sacks slung over their shoulders, much as he used to do. He would sit and stare in their direction. He worried he'd be forgotten, and so on these occasions he'd stretch his neck and begin to sing.

On winter evenings, as the wind blew, it would get too cold to remain seated outside singing so he would take to walking along the battlements, as it were, guarding the pile of ore, a rope always in his hand, and the gong tied to the end of it. One ring and men would come running.

He spent two weeks in this sort of routine. But then the rain seemed to join him, drenching the area for days and nights on end, forcing him to remain inside his small, rundown shed. When it finally stopped and he was able to venture outside again, the first thing he noticed was the gaping hole he discovered at the southern end of the ore pile. There were footprints all over the ground; the depot had been robbed.

Xi Sheng, however, didn't ring his gong; he didn't dare to. Instead, he picked up his shovel and turned over the earth, erasing the footprints before anyone else could see them. At the same time, his eyes drifted down the slope of the mountain where he saw a small group of people carrying rolled-up seating mats. Someone was crying, for the sobs carried on the wind, intermittently punctuated with moments of silence before the wail would again reach his ears. He couldn't understand why the person was crying, but it was clear the sobs were heartfelt.

Before another moment passed, three other men appeared, each carrying a straw basket on their backs. He knew they were thieves, the glint in their faces made it plain enough, but he didn't ring the gong to sound the alarm. Rather, he sang. Whether his song was meant as a deterrent or not, it seemed to have no effect on the men as they continued their ascent.

"Hey there," Xi Sheng yelled once they were close enough, "what're you guys stomping up the mountainside for?"

"We're coming to get some ore."

"Ya… brave fuckers aren't you? Here to nick ore from my depot in the middle of the day! If I ring this here, I'll have help in no time and you pricks won't be able to get away!"

"Go ahead, ring it… let's see if anyone'll come to help you."

Their audacity struck Xi Sheng hard. His anger surged and he clanged the gong. Unlike before, however, no one came to assist him. The men then gave him an explanation: the torrential rain had collapsed eight mine shafts on the southern slope of Mount Cockscomb, while on the north there were mudslides, which in turn had buried the main administrative office at the foot of the mountain; twelve people had died.

"That's why those people were crying?"

"Don't you know what's happened to your partner?"

"Who the hell's my partner?"

"Ersheng's your partner… you damn fool!"

So that was his name, Xi Sheng thought. The driver had never actually told him before: "He's not my partner, he's never shown his face here."

"Oh… is that so now? Well, I guess he'll never come now as the fucker's dead!"

Xi Sheng tried to hide his surprise, and simply asked what had happened. They told him he was one of the men in the building who had been buried in mud. It was in the night, he'd stepped outside to take a piss right at the same time as the mudslide came washing down the mountain. He probably could've got away, the men told him, but he turned and ran back inside in a vain effort to wake up everyone else. There'd been no time for that, however, as the building was gone a second later.

Xi Sheng fell to the ground as the men finished their story, no longer able to hide the impact that the news had on him: "Ersheng… Ersheng!"

The men paid no more mind to the dwarf crumpled on the ground. Laying their baskets down, they began to load them with the ore, shovelful after shovelful, finally removing about ten cubic feet. As they worked, they commented on the colour of the gold and other minerals. And when their baskets were filled, they left. Through it all, Xi Sheng sat on the ground, distraught, unable to even stand.

Xi Sheng spent the remainder of the day inside his shack, curled up into a little ball. He didn't eat, nor did he have anything to drink. That night, he finally uncurled himself and started scanning through his notebook. Coming upon the pages where he'd recorded Ersheng's visits and the amounts he'd taken, Xi Sheng decided to destroy the evidence. Putting fire to the notebook, he was surprised how insatiably the flames consumed the book. It was as though he'd had a fan in his hand and was waving it over the fire. When the book was little more than ash, a wind swept through the depot and lifted them into the sky. It looked like black butterflies taking to the air, forever drifting on the wind. That night, he set off for Danggui.

He never returned to Mount Cockscomb, not even to pick up his salary. Later, he pleaded with Lao Yu to ring the mine owner and ask on his behalf for the wage he was owed. Lao Yu responded by saying the owner had already telephoned him; apparently he was enraged by Xi Sheng's departure, especially without notice, and he wanted him to return immediately. Four days later, however, the owner's mine was struck by a massive explosion that killed three people. Wishing to cover up the truth about what had happened, the owner never reported the disaster; it would have remained that way if not for an anonymous tip-off to the authorities. The owner ended up having to spend an enormous amount of money bribing officials to keep things quiet. He also had to pay off the victims' families to compensate for their loss. When everything seemed to be smoothed over, the owner's losses had become so great he had to shut down the mine. His remaining three mine shafts were soon transferred to new owners.

Naturally, Lao Yu relayed the news to Xi Sheng, informing him the owner no longer needed him to return. Lao Yu's demeanour was overly sympathetic, as if he was trying to console Xi Sheng for some loss or other. He added that his own losses in this endeavour were huge as well, all due to the poor management of Xi Sheng's former boss. Xi Sheng understood he would never be receiving any salary for the work he'd done, but he didn't say a word. He simply sighed, as though he were acknowledging Lao Yu's disappointment at an investment turned sour.

That night, while he was in bed next to Qiao Qiao, he pulled her close and told her everything… almost everything. And when he was finished, he told her he could no longer be apart from her, he'd been away for so long already and he knew how important she was. She was his wife; without her, he feared he would go bad. Qiao Qiao was incredulous at first, before she asked him point blank if he'd had a woman on the side.

"Where could I find a woman as good as you? What's more, let me tell you, the only thing a man will find looking for a woman in the places I've been is disease, nothing more, nothing less!"

Although he'd spent a fair bit of time at the quarry high up on Mount Cockscomb, now that he had returned to Danggui, old feelings of sullenness about his lost position as village head resurfaced. He couldn't help but feel Danggui had prospered under his leadership, and that things were no longer as good. Predictably, he began to formulate schemes that would see him reinstated. But this was easier said than done. In truth, he'd no idea what to do, and so he spent hours on end propped up against the wash stone in the courtyard, massaging his stunted legs. The more he rubbed them, however, the more frustrated he grew, until finally he would ball up his fist and begin pummelling his malformed legs.

At times, Qiao Qiao would keep him company; Lao Yu's father as well. But before long, his wife started to complain and nag at him, wondering why he was continually torturing himself about his lost position, about something he couldn't really change, or at least couldn't figure out how to change. Lao Yu's father would carp at him as well.

"You love tormenting yourself, don't you? That's why heaven makes it so easy for you. But you know… just sitting here and doing nothing or sitting here and torturing yourself, well, neither will change anything."

Listening to the older man's words, a sense of calm came over Xi Sheng. He could finally move forward and get on with his life. Every day afterwards, he would tromp off over the hills in search of medicinal herbs and plants, just as he'd done so long ago. He no longer went in search of ginseng, for there was almost none left to find, but there were other plants to be picked. One was an inferior version of ginseng that was usually referred to as the poor man's root. Coltsfoot could also be harvested, along with thorowax and schisandra, more commonly known as magnolia vine, despite it not being of the magnolia genus. In the evenings he would return and spread out the roots and plants he'd picked to dry in the setting sun. The courtyard was transformed into a veritable apothecary with only a small path to the front door remaining uncovered. The evenings were still the time for drinks and partying at the village head's home, and Lao Yu would invariably try to drag both Xi Sheng and Qiao Qiao along. Xi Sheng, however, would decline the invitation, professing he had a cold or some other ailment that meant he couldn't drink. He'd watch them depart together from the porch, before spending the rest of the night chopping up the dried medicines he'd picked during the day.

At the end of the month, Xi Sheng put on his straw sandals once more, hoisted a basket over his shoulder and was preparing to head off to scavenge for more herbs and medicines. Before he left, Lao Yu had spied him making preparations and yelled out to ask him where he was heading: "Off to the mountains, or the forest?"

"The price for cypress seeds is rising, so it's a good time to start harvesting them."

"A price rise, hey, how high do you think it'll go? You know what they say – grass won't grow unless it's eaten by a horse!"

Qiao Qiao chimed in as well, directing her reply to Lao Yu: "Your father's words already did the trick. What's the point in adding fuel to the flames?"

"Perhaps… but my father said those words as a retiree. A young man like your husband, well, he needs ambition… he needs to toss and turn in his sleep, he needs to strive forward… that's the only way!"

"Where does a horse graze?" Xi Sheng interrupted.

"Eh… that's what I want to hear… big things are on the horizon, my boy, big things!"

The big thing Lao Yu was talking about had been the appointment of the young brother of Commander Kuang San's wife to the position of head of the provincial forestry department. Once in post, his first order of business was the compilation of a dossier outlining, in minute detail, the province's natural resources and the terrain where they could be found. Local almanacs and geography books had been borrowed from the many libraries that dotted the region, and these in turn had been read voraciously by the new departmental head. It was while studying these materials that he learnt of the historical presence of tigers in Qinling. As he mused over the potential significance of this information, the Party secretary of the County Committee filed a report urging the government to take extra measures to protect the region from forest fires. This further stimulated his interest in Qinling's natural resources.

"Tell me," he asked the younger man, "are there still tigers in the area?"

The secretary hesitated. He wasn't a local and really had no idea, in spite of the fact he'd been stationed in Qinling for nearly six years. Finally he offered a response, unhelpful though it was: "I… sir… I don't know… I haven't heard anything about tigers in Qinling..."

"If there are, that would really be something… something wondrous. We could implement policy, get funding to establish a protected area… a natural reserve… endless possibilities."

Those words had hung in the air without either of the men saying anything further. But they had had their effect. Soon after, the secretary took the initiative and called a meeting of all village and town heads across the area. The pressing issue to be discussed was clear: were there still tigers in Qinling and if so, where might they be? Those discussions went back and forth for ages until finally a consensus was reached: the most likely location for tigers was in the forests surrounding Huilongwan. The task fell to Lao Yu to find out for sure.

"Hey, Xi Sheng… while you're out, look for tigers for me, will you!"

"Look for… what? Tigers? Is that why you were talking about grazing horses!"

"If you find some… well, Danggui will be included in the natural reserve… and let me tell you, we won't be talking about what to eat or drink, we'll be talking about how much!"

Xi Sheng remained unsure: "Aren't you just talking nonsense, sending me on a fool's errand? There aren't any tigers in the hills… even from the time my dad was a child, there was no talk of tigers near Huilongwan, let alone Danggui!"

"Just because your old man didn't hear about any tigers doesn't prove there weren't any."

Lao Yu directed his next question to Xi Sheng's wife: "Qiao Qiao, you've made papercuts of tigers… tell me, how'd you know what they looked like?"

"My mum taught me… and she learnt it from her mum… but I never heard them once say they'd seen a tiger."

"Well… for them to know how to cut paper in the shape of a tiger means someone must've seen one! You remember where you found all that *qinseng*… that was a huge forest… now tell me… don't you think tigers could've been there?"

"Rats! That's all I bloody well saw!" said Qiao Qiao, always quick with her tongue.

"Well," Lao Yu continued, "if you lack the ambition, if you're not willing to be proactive, I guess I'll just have to find someone else, someone who'll actually look for the tigers for me. The county is offering a reward you know… one million yuan…"

"Has the county government lost its mind?"

"Alright, fine, go and get your cypress seeds…"

Lao Yu began to stroll away. As he did so, he noticed the rose vines that hung from the roof were blossoming. He turned to Qiao Qiao: "You ought to clip them… the flowers are beautiful… perhaps you could put a few in bottles for me."

Xi Sheng was still seated, seemingly lost in thought. Then he noticed Qiao Qiao cut the roses, and it was as though something snapped. He stood up and walked over to where Lao Yu was on the porch.

"How much is that reward again?"

"You only need to find them."

"What if it takes years?"

"Then it takes years."

"What if I don't find them, will the county, the town, whoever… will I get some compensation for the time lost?"

"You'll find them… I'm sure of it."

Not long after, Lao Yu furnished Xi Sheng with a camera and explicit instructions: as soon as he saw a tiger in the forest, he was to take a picture. Only a photo would prove tigers lived in the area, and if Xi Sheng came back with such a picture, he'd confirm authenticity and send it to the county government which would in turn pay out the reward. The county would also send word to the provincial forestry department that there were tigers in Qinling, and thus it ought to be designated as a special reserve.

Xi Sheng took some time to familiarise himself with the workings of the camera, and so too did Qiao Qiao. Together, they would take pictures of the rubber tree that once featured prominently in Xi Sheng's morning ritual. They also snapped the revolutionary placard that hung above their door, and pictures of each other. Finally, they caught a dog in the act of chasing one of their chickens, and the two of them beating the animal for doing so; before long, the entire reel of film was gone.

Having gained experience in using the camera, Xi Sheng and Qiao Qiao travelled to Huilongwan to buy sturdy rubber boots that could shield them from the rain, as well as a flashlight and lighter, along with some more photographic film. When they were buying the film, they also paid for the camera shop to develop the roll they'd already used. They were astonished by the images they'd captured.

"Hey! You see this… you look like a dog!"

Qiao Qiao laughed as Xi Sheng grabbed the photo from her. It was true, the image of him included the dog, but you could only see his head; the dog's body was blocking his own.

"What're you talking about, that's no dog… it's a tiger!"

"Isn't it too skinny to be a tiger?"

"You've never heard how people say a falcon at rest looks like it's sleeping, and a tiger running looks like it's ill? It's a tiger… and a sign, it foretells that I'll find a tiger in the hills!" Xi Sheng called loudly, seemingly assured in the belief it was his destiny to find the tigers Lao Yu wanted him to find.

"And do you know what… I was born in the year of the tiger… how can I fail!"

"Alright, alright," said Qiao Qiao, "it's not a dog, it's a tiger… you're a reincarnated tiger… sure, sure, sure."

Husband and wife set off for the forest, eating and sleeping outside, enduring no small amount of pain, discomfort and suffering. Their first trip lasted twenty days and the second a month. After their third and fourth excursions, six months had passed. Still, despite the amount of time spent in the wilderness, they'd not seen any tigers or even any prints. They did, however, discover three clusters of *lingzhi* mushrooms clinging hard to the rocky cliffs.

Lao Yu took two of the *lingzhi* mushrooms Xi Sheng and Qiao Qiao returned with, telling them he was going to speak to the county committee secretary to draw up their expenditures invoice. The mushrooms would serve two functions: one, an introductory gift since he'd not met the secretary in person before, and two, a means by which Xi Sheng could be paid for the hard work they'd done, despite not finding any evidence of tigers. When they had first been sent on this task, Lao Yu had spoken of an allowance, a bursary of some form or other… he'd talked of payment… but there'd been no news on that front.

Shortly after Lao Yu left, Xi Sheng and Qiao Qiao discussed what to do with the remaining mushroom, whether they should keep it for themselves, try to sell it or do something else. Eventually, the decision was made to gift it to Lao Yu's father, this in spite of the fact they'd not heard anything about getting paid. For all his unfilled promises, Xi Sheng still believed in Lao Yu, had put his faith in the man; it was the least they could do. With the third mushroom held close to his chest as though it was some prized asset, together they set off to walk over to Lao Yu's home, a short while after Lao Yu himself had departed. As they came upon the building, however, they heard two men deep in conversation inside. They paused for a moment, not to eavesdrop necessarily, although this is exactly what they did.

"Father, I want you to write the letter. You have to get them to visit Danggui again. I know… certain things have happened, there's no denying that, but I'm doing my utmost to keep things as they are… and if we really do locate tigers in the area, they'll be sure to inform the minister in charge of the forestry department. It'd be in their best interests to do so in any case!"

"You bring the secretary those mushrooms, tell them they're from me, and then report on the work taking place in Huilongwan. Tell them you've been here… working tirelessly… for eight years already… he'll understand that."

Xi Sheng didn't want to hear any more. Quietly, he shifted his feet, put his arm around Qiao Qiao and pulled her away. They had to leave without being discovered. Once back on their porch, Xi Sheng was adamant about what he was going to do with the last mushroom.

"We're keeping it, I'm not giving it to the old man."

"Why?" Qiao Qiao didn't understand.

"Lao Yu wants to give the mushrooms to the county secretary… but not from us, he's not even going to mention us, he's going to take the credit all for himself. We looked everywhere for tigers and didn't find any… it was a bloody waste of time and effort."

Xi Sheng and Qiao Qiao didn't go back into the woods to look for tigers. Instead, they went to the nearer of the mountain slopes to gather thorowax, honeysuckle and whatever else they could find. They also prepared the land to plant crops. The days bled into each other, but neither seemed to notice. That is until one night when, well after midnight, Xi Sheng awoke and cried out to his wife: "Am I dreaming?"

"What?" she called out groggily. But then she slowly came round and grew annoyed: "What else would you be doing while asleep, digging dirt?"

"A dream… yes, a dream… I dreamed I was still looking for tigers… we were still looking… and then… as we tramped through the forest… you shouted 'Tiger!' and there it was. I saw it too… and then I smiled and laughed… its teeth were *so* white!"

"Go back to sleep, it was just a dream. We have to get up early tomorrow, you know… the fields need to be fertilised… someone's gotta spread the shit!"

"Could my dream be a… a premonition?"

"Dreams are usually the opposite! Now go to sleep."

But two days later, just after midnight, Lao Yu appeared and was knocking at their door. In his hand, he held three photos. At first, Xi Sheng resisted the urge to get up, but the knocking persisted and so he finally stumbled out of bed and opened the door. No words were exchanged between the two men; Lao Yu simply pushed the three photos towards him, evidently wanting him to look at them before either said anything. To Xi Sheng's surprise, each photo showed a tiger, each from a different angle.

"Where were these taken?"

"It's the tiger you found."

Xi Sheng was stunned, unsure how to respond. After a moment's silence, words coalesced in his mind: "The tiger I found?"

"In the forest, where else? It's just you haven't actually seen them yet… in the effort to… expedite the process of having Danggui and Huilongwan declared a nature reserve, I took the liberty of 'preparing' these photos… you just need to say these are indeed your photos and you took them while out in the forest."

"That's all… that's all there is to it?"

"You were tasked with photographing a tiger, of getting proof they were in the area. You weren't supposed to capture one, so who can say these pictures aren't proof, what can they use to say these aren't real?"

"So… they're fake. How'd you make them?"

"No need to ask... I can see you don't understand what I've been telling you."

"*I*... took these photos?"

"Yes, you... and I'm here to return them to you."

By this time, Qiao Qiao had joined the men on the porch. Lao Yu now turned to her: "Qiao Qiao, you need to remember this too, you need to remember where they were taken, when and how." The three continued to talk until the sun came up.

With the morning sun already shining over the mountains, Xi Sheng and Qiao Qiao once more found themselves trundling off to the forest. They returned ten days later claiming they had 'proof'.

"Are there really tigers in the woods?" came a question from an excited villager.

"The proof's right here in this camera." Xi Sheng's voice was confident, sure, despite the lie he was telling.

The hubbub continued for a while before they went to see Lao Yu. Once he'd heard the 'news', he ordered the bells to be rung in celebration. Then the camera was taken into Huilongwan so the film could be developed. Three days later, the 'proof' was proudly displayed on the village notice board and in the county capital. Even the regional television station sent a crew to broadcast the news.

That same evening, Lao Yu telephoned the village from the county capital and told them all to head to his home to watch the television. It was a moment of great pride for the village, but when the programme was over, Xi Sheng and Qiao Qiao departed without saying much. Instead, they went home where Xi Sheng asked his wife to make him some dumplings. She complied, but he ended up eating too many and spent the night tossing and turning, his stomach bloated, preventing him from falling asleep. It wasn't until the sun rose that he finally dropped off, sleeping until after noon. Rubbing and massaging his legs, he called out to his wife while still sitting in bed.

"Qiao Qiao, go and see if it's going to rain, will you? My legs are killing me... there's gotta be rain coming."

Qiao Qiao stepped outside and looked up at the sky. A moment later she returned and shouted back to Xi Sheng: "It does look like rain... the clouds are hanging quite low and there aren't any pockets of blue."

Suddenly, a booming clang echoed through the air.

"Ha! I betcha that's the village head making that racket... he's come to curry our favour no doubt!"

"But the village doesn't have a horn," Qiao Qiao said. "I'm sure I heard a horn amid the clamour."

At the same moment, a child came bounding through their courtyard gate to announce that Lao Yu had come and brought the brass band from Huilongwan; there were also quite a few people carrying video cameras. Qiao Qiao raced towards the gate to see for herself. It was as the child had said: Lao Yu, leading a contingent of people, was drawing close to their home. An instant later, they were calling for Xi Sheng to come out dressed in his best Western suit.

"We're here to congratulate you of course. Now, if we give you the opportunity to say a few words... do you know what you'd like to say?"

"Yes, I think so."

"Make sure you don't misspeak," Qiao Qiao warned. She went into the kitchen to fetch Xi Sheng something to drink, before telling him not to be nervous, to take his time, to think before speaking.

The courtyard was filled with people who'd come to congratulate Xi Sheng. The band continued its musical praise while the television crew busied themselves, filming the entire scene. The newspaper reporters nearly fought over themselves to get Xi Sheng's attention. The questions were all the same: how did he find the tiger, how did he take those three photos? Xi Sheng spun his tale. They'd been searching for even the smallest trace of tigers for eight months; they'd gone through nearly all of their savings; it felt as though they'd been moving heaven and Earth in their search; and then, finally, as they'd trekked deeper and deeper into the mountains, passed over a narrow ridge and down into a small valley not much bigger than a pit, they discovered the animal there. It was some distance away, lying in a tangled growth of forsythia with a recent kill in its jaws, perhaps a pheasant, Xi Sheng couldn't be sure. But it was focused on its meal so Xi Sheng was able to crawl a little closer to it. Then, to make sure he got the clearest shot possible, he removed his shoes and shimmied up a nearby Japanese blue oak, drawing a further three metres closer to the beast as it devoured its prey. That's when he took the picture. Xi Sheng wasn't sure, but the sound might have startled the creature and it looked up in his direction. He quickly climbed back down the tree and hid in the grasses that grew there, not daring to move. He didn't want to risk taking any more photos, fearful the unavoidable clicking sound would draw the animal towards him. He was on his stomach for a good five minutes or more, and throughout that time he could hear the tiger's breathing. It was loud, he told them, but when he lifted his head to see where it was, he saw that it was walking away. That's when he got the two other pictures. He would've taken another shot, but it was out of sight before he could do so.

Xi Sheng's story was engrossing; he had his audience hanging on his every word. His actions to go along with the tale only enraptured them even more. He crouched in front of them, sprang up and then back down again, prostrating himself on the ground as though he were a tiger stalking its dinner. When he stood up, he was covered in dust and dirt, and Qiao Qiao moved forward to brush it off; he was, after all, wearing his good suit. But he yelled at her to stop, and again fell to the ground, rolling around before jumping up yet again. That's how the animal moved, he told them. Could he really see it tearing into the pheasant? Yes, he could. One set of claws had impaled the pheasant's flesh and it was this that held it in place. The tiger didn't seem to savour its meal, it just plunged its gaping maw into it, eating everything, bones and all. All that remained were some feathers. When it had finished, it lifted its heavy form off the ground and stalked away. It kept its head low, its gait lazy, sated. Its fur seemed almost fluffy as though it were just draped over its skeleton. Its massive jaw hung a little open, its fine ivory-coloured teeth laid bare. The edges of its mouth were wrinkled in a sort of mischievous grin. It gave the animal a bearing that suggested it had accomplished everything it had set out to do that day. It was, he assured them, an awesome sight.

This was the end of his story, but as he finished, he made sure to pull Qiao Qiao over close to him and in front of his audience: "We did this together, discovered it together. She actually heard the tiger first. Without her, well, I wouldn't have even made it up the mountain, to say nothing about finding the tiger."

Qiao Qiao didn't offer anything more, she just smiled slightly, evidently pleased with the acknowledgement her husband had given her.

News of the discovery of tigers in Qinling spread quickly and widely, if for no other reason than that there were supposedly so few of the animals left in the wild. But now, in China, where most people thought they'd long since disappeared, they'd been captured on camera! Needless to say, it was exciting for the whole nation. The further the news spread, the more reporters arrived in Danggui, coming from way down in the south, from the farthest northern reaches, from everywhere. And they were all requesting interviews. Xi Sheng spun his tale again and again, and the reporters lapped it up over and over. But still people came, all asking him to tell his miraculous story of how the tiger had been captured on film. On one particularly day, the reporters came one after the other, and before long Xi Sheng's voice began to betray him. He grew hoarse and found it difficult to carry on. But he did nonetheless, so important was it for him to tell everyone who would listen how he and his wife made the great discovery.

Husband and wife no longer had time to trek across the fields and mountains to collect the medicinal herbs that once served as their primary source of income. Nor did they have time to tend the crops they'd planted before Lao Yu showed up with those pictures. They barely even had time to sleep and eat, so busy were they in entertaining reporters. Eventually, Xi Sheng began to loathe the attention, and took to shutting his door, not daring to step outside and into the limelight once more. But this didn't stop those who were now camping out around his home. When he chose not to address the crowds, they took to knocking on his door, and calling out to him. They didn't use his name, but instead simply shouted: "Tiger, Tiger, if you won't consent to an interview, how's about a picture instead? We'll give you five yuan for a single photo together with us!" The promise of money drew Xi Sheng outside, if only for the picture to be taken. After a day or two of only taking pictures, another reporter seized the initiative and offered money for an interview, too. Qiao Qiao was soon in charge of collecting the fees.

Finally, they had a quiet evening after a day filled with interviews and photos. Qiao Qiao took advantage of the lull in their schedule and started to count the money they had made that day.

"So... how much did we make?" Xi Sheng's voice was noticeably hoarse, but he was keen to learn how much they'd earned.

"I've counted 325 yuan..."

"Not bad for a day's work. If we can make 325 yuan in a day, then over ten we'd have 3,250 yuan. If there're thirty days in a month, twelve months in a year, shit, I'll be a real boss for sure!"

He reached into the bamboo steamer that sat on the counter and pulled out a steamed bun, despite it being cold. He also grabbed a handful of spring onions and proceeded to eat, a mouthful of spring onions followed by a mouthful of steamed bread. When they'd been out in the forest, his jaw had begun to hurt, on both the left and right sides, and soon he realised he had two problem teeth. Upon their return, the teeth were removed and the result was that he now had to chew with his mouth nearly wide open. Like a cow mulching grass, Xi Sheng's chin and mouth would shift back and forth as he worked on the food he was eating.

"Qiao Qiao, tell me... don't I look like a tiger when I'm eating?"

"Er... I'll just say there's no one around to steal your food, so don't choke on it, alright."

His bread finished, Qiao Qiao told him to go outside and make sure the chicken coop was closed. Then she instructed him to cover the scraps of food that remained on the chopping board in order to prevent the mice from getting at them. His next night-time chore was to collect the chamber pots from the toilet and bring them inside to be placed at the foot of their bed. Xi Sheng wasn't particularly fond of these chores, indeed he was a little reluctant to do them. When he began to scuff his shoes against the ground in subdued protest, Qiao Qiao had had enough: "What're you, huh, an old man pushing seventy, having to drag your feet?"

"Well, a tiger's stride is neither rushed nor languorous."

"Hmph, you really think you look like a tiger?"

"I've seen one after all, we both have!"

Later that evening, once his chores were complete, he returned inside and sat down next to his wife: "Tell me... have I seen a tiger or haven't I?"

"You know you haven't." Her response lacked any emotion.

"How's that possible? I have seen one, I'm sure of it!"

"Alright, fine, whatever, you've seen a tiger. Oh, here… scratch my back, will you? I've got an itch I can't reach."

Xi Sheng obliged and set to work on his wife's itch. At the same time, he mumbled to himself over and over that he'd seen a tiger.

—

Lao Yu no longer spent much time in Danggui. In truth, he was in the county capital nearly every day. Whether or not this contributed to him getting the stipend for Xi Sheng or not, it was difficult to say, but he did manage to provide him with 10,000 yuan, and apparently the confirmation of a reward of one million yuan for discovering the tiger. More important than all of this, however, was that the provincial forestry ministry had already signed off on the paperwork declaring the region as a natural reserve. Everything seemed to be going swimmingly, and he often stole a moment or two to think there was really nothing he couldn't accomplish. Unfortunately, within days more news came from Danggui: a devastating fire had hit the village and his father had been its victim.

Before the fire, life in Danggui had carried on much as it had, except for the fact that from nearly the same moment Xi Sheng had begun to prosper again, the nightly drinking parties resumed at his home. One of the first things calculated was how much booze could be purchased with the 10,000 yuan he'd been given. They also gave thought to the impending reward they would receive, and how best to spend it. Discussions, always over drink, ranged from home extensions – a third storey might be handy – to purchasing a car, which could prove to be even more useful. With no decision in sight, however, Xi Sheng fixed his mind on purchasing a mobile phone, which was at least something everyone could agree upon. Of course, the phone would need a leather case, one that he could attach to a leather belt for easy access; something, too, he could wear to bed so the phone would always be on his person. As the talking dragged on, it had an effect on Qiao Qiao, too. She already wore leather shoes, had a leather jacket and trousers, but she fancied more, and, as it happened, had recently heard leather mattresses were becoming all the rage. As a result, the discussions degenerated into people nattering on about this and that, like a busy chicken coop with all the hens clucking at the same time. It seemed everyone had an opinion on how best to spend the money Xi Sheng was to receive, until finally Xi Sheng himself had to put his foot down.

"Hey now," Xi Sheng said, his voice carrying over the din. "Don't all of you get so worked up about the million yuan, don't be so green with envy. You should all start preparing for the fact that Danggui will soon be named a nature reserve, which means we'll need hotels. You'd all be better off converting your own places into restaurants and bedsits, or perhaps small shops selling local specialities."

The partygoers listened while he spoke and their admiration for him grew by the minute. He was always able to think of the bigger picture, always able to scheme and work out stuff that looked beyond small, short-term gains. For the increasingly inebriated crowd, he couldn't be considered anything but the true leader of the reform efforts in Danggui! He was the example they all should follow.

They continued to talk, the boisterousness of the party growing in tandem with the amount people were drinking. Some fell into an intoxicated mess, reduced to babbling fools waiting for their wives to escort them home. But as those men were led outside, their eyes, and those of their less inebriated wives, were drawn to a great glow that made the night almost seem as though it were day. One of them turned round and shouted back into Xi Sheng's house, alerting the partygoers to what was happening outside.

"Who's lighting a fire... at this hour? What're they roasting?"

Qiao Qiao was the first to respond to the alarm, stepping out onto her porch to see the northern reaches of their plot of land bathed in an iridescent crimson radiance. She asked a question to no one in particular: "Is tomorrow the third anniversary of Defa's wife's death?"

The man she was referring to was one of their neighbours. Three years before, tragedy had struck his home and he'd lost his wife. It would be customary for the town to pay its respects on the anniversary, as they had done each year before, but, Qiao Qiao soon thought, if the following day was to be the memorial service, why hadn't they been told to come along to his place tonight to offer their respects and perform the necessary sacrifice? But this thought left her as quickly as it had come, for she suddenly realised it was not Defa's house at all, but Lao Yu's home. Looking more closely, she saw, too, that the fire was engulfing the top floor, dancing across the balcony like a ravenous ghost gleefully consuming the poor soul inside. At this point she yelled, loud enough for everyone to hear.

The drunken crowd, startled by the ferociousness in Qiao Qiao's voice, stood up and raced outside. A second later, and in spite of their intoxication, they scrambled across the field to help put out the fire. Unfortunately, they were a little too late as the fire already burnt hot, tearing at the house with an insatiable appetite. To make the situation worse, the iron door was closed shut, and the windows were all barred. No matter how much they tried, no matter how much they banged and pounded against the door and windows, they wouldn't open. The fire tore at the house, spitting flames through the windows, scorching the closest bystanders. By this time, the entire village was awake and helping to bring water to douse the fire as best they could. Some were even throwing earth onto the conflagration, in an attempt to smother the inferno. They worked all through the night, and finally by morning the blaze had weakened. The villagers were then able to push the iron door open, which had burnt so hot it had become warped and its frame no longer blocked their access. That's when they found Lao Yu's father. He was at the back of the structure, his head protruding between the bars in the window, his torso and legs burnt to a cinder. They were sure it was him; his face was essentially intact, frozen in a death stare, his mouth agape as though he had howled nonstop while the fire consumed his flesh.

Lao Yu hurried back as soon as he heard the news. Once his father had moved to Danggui, he'd said repeatedly that he wanted to remain in the village, wanted to be buried there as well when the time came. But the building he'd called home for the time he spent in Danggui was entirely scorched; there was no place for a memorial, nowhere to hang his picture. While Lao Yu struggled over what to do, Xi Sheng offered a solution by claiming that if it weren't for the old director, the village wouldn't have benefitted from Lao Yu's presence, and if Lao Yu hadn't come, then he'd be a nobody too. It seemed only proper, therefore, for the memorial to be in his home. He would repurpose one of the rooms in his home to be the memorial hall, and the coffin could be buried just outside. As he said these words, the old man's face looked out impassively on them, its mouth still agape in some horrific death mask. Qiao Qiao stepped forward and placed a cloth over it, covering the poor man's face as a sign of respect. Lao Yu informed the authorities of his father's death, and men from across the county and up into the provincial offices came to offer their condolences.

Since the memorial services were to take place over a number of days, Xi Sheng went to Huilongwan looking for me. He wanted me to sing.

And so, well, I found myself back in Danggui, despite thinking I never would. Normally this meant I'd be there for three days and nights, but on this occasion, after I finished the first night's singing, I told them I was leaving the next day. This was because on that following morning there were already far too many reporters congregating outside, all wishing to speak with Xi Sheng, and, well, the memorial hall was in the same place... I just couldn't do it, I told them. I remember Xi Sheng not being too concerned about this, however. In fact, if I recall properly, that morning he went out to the rubber tree to greet his... fan club, I suppose you could call it, and told them the interview fee for the day had doubled due to the funeral ceremony taking place.

That's when something unexpected happened. That is, once the audience was settled in and the interview could start, I remember Xi Sheng being taken aback by the first question they asked: Did you really see a tiger? Were those photos really taken by you?

Needless to say, Xi Sheng got angry right away. What the hell were they getting at, I recall him saying, to which they responded that doubt had been thrown on the photos after they broadcasted the story, someone claimed they were doctored, fake, composite images put together to make it look like tigers inhabited the area around Danggui. Xi Sheng didn't really understand what they were talking about... composite pictures... but that didn't appease him and I remember him shouting that he had in fact seen the tiger, that he'd discovered it. It looked as though he was about to lose it, before he called out to Lao Yu and got him to come over and address the reporters too. Before Lao Yu actually spoke, however, Xi Sheng filled him in on what they were saying, that the photos were fake... and then he asked Lao Yu the same question he'd been asked: were they doctored images, was that even possible? Lao Yu didn't get the chance to answer for he was dragged to one side by a Party committee member, someone in the propaganda bureau, I think, who told Lao Yu the question was rather serious, really serious, in fact. He also told him that newspapers across the country were all feverishly speculating on the pictures' veracity...

I remember Lao Yu was temporarily nonplussed, unable to muster any response before finally asking if the committee member knew whether or not the higher-ups had heard about this. Of course they had, came the cadre's answer, and they were all rather stressed out, he added... that's why he was there, he'd been ordered to accompany the reporters and to investigate the matter. He was also going to get Xi Sheng to take them into the wood, to the spot where he'd snapped the photographs... Lao Yu then reiterated Xi Sheng's words, the tiger was real, before adding, however, that he hadn't actually seen it, he'd not been out in the forest after all. The cadre didn't seem all that impressed with his response, I remember. Lao Yu was the mayor, he said, which meant he was ultimately in charge of all of this... then he told him to take care of the situation with the media.

Lao Yu did step back in front of them, told them he was the Party representative for the area, the one in charge, as the cadre had just told him, and then he confirmed that Qinling did indeed have tigers. He paused for a moment after saying that... letting his words sink in, I suppose. Then he asked the assembled crowd that if outsiders were suspicious, what could he do to alleviate those concerns? He paused again for a moment, then turned to Xi Sheng and asked him if the tiger was real... of course, Xi Sheng responded emphatically that it was real... then Lao Yu added that Xi Sheng came from a line of revolutionary heroes, that his peasant background was beyond reproach, and that everyone should pay attention to these facts.

After he finished, I saw him pull Xi Sheng to one side, evidently wanting to speak to him in private... but, well, you know what reporters are like, they wouldn't give up that easily and so they tried to tag along. Lao Yu and Xi Sheng had managed to duck back inside, and when they returned to face the mob that was chasing them, they were dressed in mourning clothes... Qiao Qiao was with them, too... they looked at the reporters and told them someone in the family had died and they should show respect to them, and to the dead as well. The reporters were therefore barred from encroaching any further... but they didn't leave... not until other local villagers showed up shouting and yelling at them. Indeed, it quickly turned into a great shouting match... a mass of people all trying to out-yell everyone else. Naturally, I couldn't continue to sing... it was all such a mess. The only thing I could do was take advantage of the ruckus and slip away.

The issue did not go away, nor did the tide of public opinion change: they wanted proof, they wanted the photos to be verified. Ultimately, the county government was forced to accede to public demand. The pictures were formally scrutinised and despite Xi Sheng's protestations that they were genuine, forensic specialists determined they were in fact doctored. Consequently, the whole story about finding tigers in Qinling was officially declared a fraud, a great swindling of the nation. A tribunal was called and Lao Yu brought to testify. He admitted to fabricating the photos, to getting Xi Sheng to lie on his behalf and to creating a negative effect on society. He was, moreover, willing to submit to whatever punishment the authorities deemed sufficient.

Lao Yu didn't have to wait long for sentencing. He was given an official and internal Party censure, none of which would be made public. As for Xi Sheng, his case was different. He was not a Party member, so they couldn't censure him as they did Lao Yu. He was, moreover, a peasant. And while he maintained the veracity of the photos even after they were proved to be false, the legal system had no means by which to actually punish him. The only determination that could be made was that Xi Sheng had been blinded by greed, that he was a liar, but beyond that, there was nothing they could do. Therefore the matter was closed, if unsatisfactorily.

Xi Sheng's name became a curse. His reputation among the villagers of Danggui was ruined. Whenever he found himself in the market, people would stare and point at him and call him the fake tiger, the paper tiger. The comments enraged Xi Sheng. He quarrelled constantly with everyone, pushed and shoved until they came to blows and he returned home bloodied and bruised, his clothes, his Western suits, torn and ripped. Qiao Qiao had to endure her own form of punishment, namely, listening to Xi Sheng grumble and curse his lot.

"I did see a damned tiger," he would continue to say. "Everybody says I lied... that it was all a hoax..."

"You didn't deceive them," Qiao Qiao would retort. "No... you deceived yourself, you bloody fool!"

"I lied to myself?" Xi Sheng wouldn't say anything more; he'd just amble off into their bedroom and fall into bed. He'd spend the next few hours mulling things over, torturing himself and wondering what was real and what was not, had he seen a tiger or was it all a lie... finally the truth would crystallise in front of him, he would sob the rest of the night away.

He did this for three days, never getting out of bed the entire time. On that third day, Lao Yu came to see him.

"Xi Sheng," he said, his voice sympathetic, understanding. "It's nothing, you're alright. If I haven't been toppled, then you certainly can't be toppled either."

"Hmph, I'm already finished."

"If that were true, would I be here, would I be looking for our next opportunity?" Lao Yu's voice was confident, self-assured. "And once I succeed... again... I'll lift you up with me, you know that. Give me three to five years and I'll have remade my whole image, yours too!"

Lao Yu continued, telling Xi Sheng about his plans for the development of Danggui. They'd focus their efforts on natural herbs and medicines, its economic possibilities would revitalise the village. There were, however, issues that had to be worked out. One, the villagers didn't really want to see him around, so he'd been contemplating whether or not it would be best for a local to lead this new enterprise. Two, there was the question of cataloguing the types of medicinal herbs that grew on the mountainside, and in what quantities. Three, how could he get the county and city medicinal herbs market to investigate and research the plants in the area, and determine the means by which they could be farmed in more easily accessible fields instead of constantly having to be picked from up in the mountains, which was not only work-intensive, but also more dependent on the weather and the natural terrain, meaning there was no way to ensure a stable crop. Unfortunately, no one in Danggui seemed willing to take on this new initiative. What's more, Lao Yu complained, he wasn't even getting support from the village head, who, despite his orders for him to call a meeting, had continually put it off. After relaying all of this to Xi Sheng, Lao Yu again went to see the village head.

"So... are you in or not?" he asked with a noticeable sound of irritation in his voice. "Will you actually do something for Danggui, or are you just going to sit on your hands?"

"For many generations," the village head began, "the residents of Danggui have harvested the natural herbs that grow in the mountains, but they've never seen ginseng, or any other herb for that matter, grown in a field... is such a thing even possible?"

"Have you ever seen an atomic bomb? Just because you haven't, it doesn't mean they don't exist. If you're not on board, then the town won't be either! I need your support."

"I suppose Xi Sheng is on your side. Tell me, do you wipe his arse for him, too?"

Despite his outward intransigence, the village head did call the village meeting. During the proceedings, Lao Yu outlined how, ten years ago, Santai had been successful in cultivating ginseng in its fields. In fact, they'd been so successful that they were now far out-producing Qinning and other areas. So it was clear, Lao Yu argued, that if they failed to realise this plan, failed to cultivate medicinal roots and herbs, they'd miss out on earning great profit. What's more, if they prevaricated, if they held off on making a decision, they'd only end up postponing the arrival of the enormous amount of money they could make from such an initiative. They had to show confidence, Lao Yu proclaimed, and seize the opportunity before it passed them by; this was their chance to get rich – they couldn't just let it slide by, could they?

Lao Yu's powers of persuasion worked. The villagers agreed. After all, to get rich was glorious. The only hitch was that it would take at least a year to sow a ginseng field properly and to tend the plants as they grew. A year, cried out some of the villagers! And what would happen if the crop failed? What would they eat if they planted nothing else, what would they drink? Then finally someone yelled out that this was a task that Xi Sheng was best suited for, he had the land and the time to waste if it all went to pot!

Soon after, Lao Yu invited an expert from Santai to visit the village. Xi Sheng was to use his ten *mu* of land to nurture the young plants, but to ensure they would grow, advice was needed. Xi Sheng had already begun to prepare the land. Between the last week of May and the first week of June, he'd ploughed the field, turned over the soil, and then used old growth, which he burnt, as a fertiliser base. The land was now ready to be planted. During the middle two weeks of June, the seeds were spread and gently covered with soil. On top of the soil, a layer of dried grass was added. Twenty days later, small sprouts of the ginseng plants were edging up through the earth, odd little things, but bright and vibrant in their own way. Before the first frosts came, the small sprouts had grown into seedlings, which were now tied together into small bunches and covered with fresh earth that had been piled up near the outer courtyard wall. Scaffolding was then erected and a sort of canopy was laid over the entire crop. It wasn't sealed completely since they needed wind to blow through, but they also needed shade as the plants wouldn't grow in direct sunlight.

By November, the winter freeze was nearly upon them and so the still smallish crop had to be exhumed, roots and all, and replanted in an earthen cellar. They built this just beyond Xi Sheng's courtyard wall. For each layer of virgin soil they dug up, they'd replant one layer of seedlings. Eventually, the layers would fill the entire cellar, right up to its opening, which was then covered with dried grass and straw, a sort of insulation.

The other villagers grew curious about Xi Sheng's progress, and wanted to see the rather odd crop he'd been tending to so devotedly for the better part of a year. Xi Sheng's appearance had deteriorated. He was filthy from head to toe, covered with mud and bits of grass and straw. In truth, given his diminutive size, he looked the part of some tired and worn-out monkey that had been spending its days scavenging in the dirt for whatever food it could find.

The expert who'd come to inspect the field had the family name of Lei. Upon his arrival, Qiao Qiao played the good host. She offered him a cigarette, a cup of tea, and even took to calling him Brother Lei. Staring at the crowd that had come to see him, Xi Sheng couldn't help but toast his hard work.

"Have a look, everyone. Can you all see, these seedlings here are the ones I've been taking care of for so long. I reckon you all ought to start doing the same, the sooner the better! The land here… its texture… well, it's proved to be ideal for growing ginseng… sort of… my land seems to be somewhat infertile, but that's been dealt with by a little extra elbow grease and some peasant night soil! Ha ha!"

Xi Sheng's words had the effect Lao Yu had hoped for, at least on some of the villagers, who straight away began to prepare their own plots of land. Other villagers, however, just shook their heads, unwilling to see the value in what Xi Sheng was doing.

"Still unconvinced, huh?" said Lao Yu, not mincing his words.

"With my old lady, well, I just can't!"

"What does that mean?"

"Qiao Qiao's so capable when it comes to waiting on the expert who's visited..."

"What rubbish are you getting at? You're talking out of your arse!"

Lao Yu subsequently dispatched the expert to every home in Danggui, advising and directing them on how to prepare their fields, how much fertiliser to use, and so on. It took the better part of two weeks' hard work, but it was a success overall. When the next planting season came round after the winter, the villagers all came to Xi Sheng's house to buy the small sprouts to begin their own plantations. They were not cheap, however, so naturally the villagers complained: Xi Sheng's heart was cold, too ruthless, he made them spend so much of their money, they had little left to buy anything else. Xi Sheng didn't seem to care.

"You don't like the fact these sprouts are expensive, but I'm the one who cared for them, cultivated them... and what's more, none of you offered to share the burden. If I had failed, I'd be fucked, not you, so why should I sell them cheap? If you're willing to cough up, then do so. Otherwise, piss off!"

Hearing of this exchange, Lao Yu chose to intervene and force Xi Sheng to reduce his prices, but at the same time, he tried to persuade the other farmers of the value of what they were planning to do: "You think you're a little hard up now, sure, it's costly to get something started, but afterwards, when people begin buying your ginseng and you start making money hand over fist, I'm sure you'll look back on this and say it was worth it." The words worked, the villagers ceased grumbling and bought the fresh sprouts.

With the new plants in the ground, the expert from Santai explained how the fields would need weeding three times, the first around the beginning of summer in late May, then again in the latter part of June, and finally about a month after that, towards the end of July. They also had to protect the crop from blight and insects, so when the land was being prepared, they had to make sure they used some form of pesticide, a phosphorus sulphide compound was perhaps best. Then, when they were actually putting the plants into the ground, it was advisable to sprinkle some additional fertiliser in the depression dug to sit the plant, an alkyl compound would do. Finally, when hoeing the field, a fungicide such as carbendazim ought to be sprayed to control plant diseases. By now, the villagers had grown used to using all manner of chemicals to enhance the growth of their crops, but still the instructions given by the expert stirred questions among the farmers.

"Just what are all of these chemicals we're supposed to use?" asked one of the villagers. "We used various fertilisers in the past, things with all kinds of strange names and we know what happened... and now you're saying we need to start spreading and spraying our fields again. Won't history repeat itself?"

"Ah, that may be true," said the expert, ready with an answer, "but you're not growing vegetables and the like, not this time. All of these chemicals are simply to prevent the ginseng from getting diseased and perishing, a sort of root rot that can destroy whole fields of ginseng... just ask Xi Sheng about it, he's used it already."

In due course, harvest time arrived, and the villagers were struck by the changed situation. Before, when they'd simply harvested whatever ginseng they could find in the hills, often selling a handful of roots and not much more, now they had whole piles, enough to fill most courtyards when laid out. The next step was to process the crop and classify the roots according to the way they'd grown and matured, which would, in turn, determine how they were marketed. *Maogui,* for instance, seemed to lack both a head and a tail and was more uniformly tubular. *Tongdi,* another ginseng classification, had a fragrance similar to a pine tree and had fewer blemishes than *maogui,* as though it had been picked almost clean out of the ground. In truth, the entire crop was in pristine condition compared with what grew wild on the mountains. There were essentially no traces of fungal or bacteriological growth, and little sign of insect infestation. On the whole, each of the roots in these two lower classifications was about fourteen centimetres in length; in each *jin,* there would be about thirty-five roots. After the *maogui* and *tongdi* ginseng were sorted out, they would then focus on the remainder, what they considered to be of superior quality and thus more valuable. *Changxin* were identified out of the *tongdi* crop, and then *xianggui* were picked from the batch of *changxin*. These latter two types were more root-like, they had a coarser feel and a more off-white colour, but they were fresher, there were no dry patches and no signs of insects even taking a small nibble.

It wasn't long before the chemists and medicinal herb shops in Huilongwan were inundated with Danggui dwarfs all selling ginseng. And soon after, there were even more entrepreneurial people from Huilongwan who would drive their cars or pedal their bicycles up to Danggui in order to purchase the ginseng from its source. Advertisements began appearing everywhere, on electricity poles, on shop walls and even government buildings. They all in turn claimed the myriad benefits of Danggui ginseng; it was good for menstrual pains, headaches, tinnitus, contusions and sprains, carbuncles, gangrene, swelling, more general aches and pains, abdominal tenderness, dry skin and constipation.

Everyone in the village was benefitting from the sweet taste of their new ginseng product, and the area they were using to cultivate the crop continued to expand. Xi Sheng's name was once again heralded throughout the village. Not only was he responsible for growing and caring for the ginseng when it was still in its infancy, and for selling the young crop to the villagers, he also no longer needed to travel to the market in Huilongwan to sell his mature crop and make some money. Indeed, Xi Sheng took the initiative and opened up his own shop in the market so he could sell his product wholesale and cut out the middle man altogether. Within the span of a few years, Xi Sheng had become the richest man in Huilongwan.

Xi Sheng now had many more Western suits, which he would wear in one after the other. He also bought a car that he used for commuting back and forth between Danggui and Huilongwan, as well as the county capital. He'd learnt how to drive very quickly and now when he drove, he held himself incredibly upright and rigid, his eyes always focused ahead. To look at him would make his passengers nervous, but nothing ever happened, his driving record was spotless. This was not to say he'd never been stopped by the police – he had – but this was because of his short stature which made it seem as though no one was actually driving the car when it passed by, or that it was being driven automatically.

Lao Yu had also done well, eventually being promoted to the

position of deputy head commissioner for the county. Given his new status, he didn't return to Danggui, but that's not to say he had nothing to do with his partners there. In truth, he assisted Xi Sheng in buying a commercial property in the capital, after which Xi Sheng would spend more and more time there, hardly returning to Danggui himself. On those occasions when Lao Yu entertained guests, he was sure to invite Xi Sheng, who'd always attend, no matter what he might have been doing. Of course, Xi Sheng's presence nearly always entailed copious amounts of alcohol being consumed, with Xi Sheng often supplying the entertainment by singing his ballads and love songs and performing his shadow puppet theatre. The tab was nearly always footed by Xi Sheng, too, a sign of respect towards those supposedly more influential than he was.

Qiao Qiao remained in Danggui in charge of the ginseng crop and the purchasing of pesticides.

That winter, Xi Sheng had been invited to the provincial capital for a meeting, the subject of which was how to get rich. Xi Sheng was to be considered the model. For convenience's sake, and to make the travel easier for his halfling partner, Lao Yu requested Qiao Qiao accompany him. For some time now, things between husband and wife weren't all that amicable. When in the county capital, they would never walk side by side as husband and wife; instead, Xi Sheng would take his own path and Qiao Qiao would do the same, or rather, she was told not to walk next to him. Now in the main seat of provincial power, Qiao Qiao expected this habit to continue, so on their first day in the city, she made sure to measure her pace and always remain some distance behind her husband, carrying his bag like a dutiful servant.

"Come on wife, catch up!"

Xi Sheng's words surprised Qiao Qiao so she didn't reply straight away. After a short pause, she offered a response: "But I thought I wasn't permitted to walk next to you?"

"I used to worry before that people would laugh at us if we did, but now's different, I want you to… after all, look, I'm short and I'm ugly, but look at my beautiful *and* tall wife!"

Later on, during the meeting in which he was to be rewarded for his entrepreneurial successes, when the host called out his name to come forward and receive his award, he stood up and turned to Qiao Qiao instead of just walking up onto the stage.

"Wife... let's go... together."

"But... you're the one who's won the award, not me."

"Then at least escort me to the stage."

The host called his name again, but as so many times before in so many different situations, Xi Sheng was not easy to see. The man called again: "Comrade Xi, please, your award is waiting. Where are you, Comrade Xi?"

Put out at not being noticed, Xi Sheng responded in a loud voice: "I'm here!"

"Please stand up."

"I already have!"

All eyes turned in the direction of his voice, which was easy enough to hear, and saw a sight none of them expected. There was almost total silence among the crowd for there, striding to the stage, was a short, ugly dwarf accompanied by a tall, handsome woman. At the foot of the stage, while the audience still looked on in amazement, this short little man was unable to climb the steps, so Qiao Qiao put her arms around him tenderly, and lifted him up. A great roar of laughter rang out, and then above the noise Xi Sheng's voice could be heard.

"This is my wife!"

The laughter turned to applause that echoed throughout the hall.

Five years later, business was still booming for Xi Sheng and he was making more money than ever. A new steel frame stood at the entrance to the city, catching the sunlight and sparkling in multiple colours. Emblazoned on the top were the words 'Ginseng capital'. There were still advertisements everywhere, but these had been updated and now proudly displayed Xi Sheng's image, seated so that no one could really see how tall, or short, he was. The range of medicinal uses for Danggui's ginseng had expanded, too, so that they now claimed it was good for treating almost any ailment or affliction. The advertisements were not entirely free of graffiti, however, but not all of it was negative: someone had written across

Xi Sheng's face on one particular advertisement that he was a model worker (which Xi Sheng took to be a positive comment, whether it was or not). Soon after, another phrase began to appear, but in this case, it seemed to be more of a challenge: How's it this doesn't treat Kashin-Beck disease?

Over this same five-year period, Mount Cockscomb's flourishing mines and its quarry had shuttered their gates. This was simply due to the fact that the ores and minerals that were once so plentiful in the mountain had been exhausted, which resulted in abandoned structures and mine shafts across the mountain face, as well as collapsed cliffs and gouged-out slopes. In short, it was a ruined mountain, a desolate landscape. Even the waterways that once flowed down its surface were dead; the small amount of water in them couldn't be considered much more than a stinking bog. The miners had long since disappeared, soon followed by the executives in their offices. Left in the rubble were the work sheds, the shops, the hotels and restaurants that once served the community.

Of course, the local authorities weren't content to let the mountain remain a wasteland, and so they published redevelopment plans and petitioned each level of government in the area, all the way up to the provincial committees, for the allocation of funds to help in this endeavour. At the same time as they attempted to secure the necessary money, they also sent envoys to solicit the assistance of Xi Sheng in establishing the same type of ginseng cultivation that had proved so successful for Danggui. Since Xi Sheng was considered the expert, he was hired to apply this expertise for the redevelopment of Mount Cockscomb.

Xi Sheng considered these days to be the highlight of his life. He spent his time being ferried back and forth between town, village and hamlet, sharing his knowledge of ginseng cultivation. At each place he was warmly received and treated as though he were a king. Fine food was always prepared, from fragrant dishes to spicier fare, and everyone referred to him as the Big Boss. He took all this quite seriously, too, and went over in the greatest detail how to plant the seeds, prepare the earth, and even how to properly fertilise the land and spray pesticides. Then he took care to explain how to best harvest the crop when it was ready, and how to separate the ginseng into the various classifications. Once he'd gone through all of this, he turned his attention to instructing the numerous households how best to market their crop.

His oral skills were already quite advanced, and he could probably recite the same information over and over again from memory, but to enthral your audience, you need to put on a performance. Xi Sheng was especially good at this. He would stand on a stage and wave a notebook in front of the crowd as he spoke, proclaiming he'd prepared copious notes to share with them, to teach them what he had already learnt. The audience would be quite unaware that the notebook was empty, not a single word written in it.

On one such visit, Lao Yu had arranged for the county television station to film the event, to present it as a documentary outlining the methods for cultivating ginseng by an expert in the field. Of course, Xi Sheng was the star of the show, the camera lens constantly fixed on his performance.

That evening, when the film crew had departed and the two men were alone again, enjoying a meal at the residence set up to house them, Xi Sheng directed the conversation to something that had weighed on his heart for many, many years. Namely, he wanted to know if Lao Yu's father had actually submitted that application on behalf of Xi Sheng's own father. Of course, Xi Sheng wasn't probing into this issue out of avarice, since he had no need for government money, and certainly not charity, but he couldn't help but wonder and think about the possibility of him meeting Commander Kuang San in person, and then, should the matter come up…

Lao Yu was startled by Xi Sheng's question, and responded accordingly: "You'd… you'd like to meet Commander Kuang San… what on earth for?"

"It's just… given my current status… well, I think now I'm of a stature, pardon the pun, to meet him!"

"I must say, you're even more ambitious than me!"

Lao Yu was not in a position to arrange a meeting with such a senior figure, he didn't even know where Commander Kuang San and his family lived. Nevertheless, Lao Yu did promise Xi Sheng one thing: if the opportunity ever arose, he'd certainly try. Xi Sheng just had to be patient.

And so Xi Sheng waited. Nobody would have guessed, however, that he was waiting for disease to strike.

An epidemic had tracked its way across Qinling once before. It happened the same year China's 'Christian General', Feng Yuxiang, revolted and chased the last emperor of the Qing out of the Forbidden City. The scourge was eventually identified as cholera, and it swept through the region, causing diarrhoea so severe most people were barely even able to pull up their trousers, to say nothing of having to run to the toilet. Invariably, they were caught short and ended up shitting in their pants. A yellow stream of faeces would drain down their legs as their bodies were destroyed inside. Within seven days, they'd be dead.

In the eastern part of Qinling, nearly every county was affected. In many instances, entire towns and villages were decimated, leaving nothing but ghosts. In the north of Qinling, it was yet more severe, with whole counties losing half or more of their population. Rough figures calculated afterwards showed the death toll in certain counties as 420 households destroyed; in other counties, at least fifteen villages were wiped out of existence, leaving not a single survivor, not even livestock or a family dog.

The story of this pestilence was shared generation after generation by those who survived so that the fear of such a calamity happening again was enough to set hearts racing with terror. So when a new epidemic hit Qinling, the fear of it spread like wildfire, consuming nearly all rational thought. Questions were asked: where had it originated and what was it exactly? Apparently, it had come from the south, that's where it had started, finally making its way to Beijing. From the national capital it extended its tendrils throughout the country, leaving no place untouched. The first symptoms were akin to catching a cold: a headache, blocked nose, fever, joint pain and incessant coughing. Once the infection made its way into the lungs, death would follow shortly. The people in Qinling took to cursing the southerners, then Beijingers, all asking the same question: how the hell had it spread to Qinling? And then they'd offer their own answer: it had spread all across China, it was inevitable that Qinling would be affected. Needless to say, anxiety travelled as quickly as the affliction, leaving most befuddled and unsure what to do.

When news of the epidemic first reached Xi Sheng's ears, he refused to believe it, thinking it must simply be rumour, so he carried on as normal. As it happened, a merchant from Hubei had travelled to

Danggui to buy three tonnes of *tongdi* ginseng, but when the order was to be fulfilled, the merchant displayed his dissatisfaction with the packaging. Always attentive to his customers' concerns, Xi Sheng ordered the ginseng to be repacked. As this was being carried out, two men sent by Lao Yu to fetch him arrived, and Xi Sheng soon found himself seated across from his old friend and partner.

"Dream well last night?" were the first words out of Lao Yu's mouth.

"I'm busy day and night. I don't have time to sleep, let alone dream."

"Eh... you little fucken dwarf... always sharp with your tongue, and no time to even dream... and here I got my guts all twisted up worrying about whether or not I've done right by you!"

Xi Sheng smiled, but said nothing. Lao Yu went on to tell him about the forestry minister, who was, in fact, no longer in the position; evidently he'd been promoted to vice-chair of the provincial People's Political Consultative Committee. What's more, Lao Yu told him, he'd been tasked by the new vice-chair to select representatives to be sent to the provincial legislative committee, and as fortune would have it, Commander Kuang San was currently recuperating in the provincial capital and so there was an opportunity to pay him a formal visit. Once he was finished, Lao Yu stared at Xi Sheng, whose face still held the smile from just a moment ago. Waiting for his former partner to stop smiling, Lao Yu held his tongue before saying anything further.

"So," he began, once Xi Sheng had stopped smiling, "whaddya think, huh, quite the good luck, I'd say. It's like I'm repaying some major loan you extended to me in a previous life! Now then... get yourself cleaned up, go for a haircut, take a shower, and then tomorrow we're off to the capital."

Xi Sheng nodded in agreement, understanding the instructions clearly. But before departing Lao Yu's office, he turned and said: "I've heard... rumours... nearly everywhere, they all say some epidemic has hit the area... they're just rumours, right?"

"I'm afraid not," Lao Yu said in a voice that was now solemn. "They're true."

"If that's the case, then why're we going to the capital?"

"Meteors fall every day from the heavens, but have they ever taken aim at you? If you want to pay Commander Kuang San a visit, he's not going to be there forever, and he sure as hell won't be waiting for you!"

The night before they left for the provincial capital, Xi Sheng couldn't get to sleep; he was far too excited about the prospect of meeting Commander Kuang San. As a result, he spent the night changing into many different suits, trying in vain to find one that was sufficiently comfortable and smart. Finally, unable to make the decision himself, he telephoned Qiao Qiao who suggested he wear his white suit, which would allow him to look especially striking, clean and well groomed. Xi Sheng also asked his wife about what he should say, but she answered with a question of her own: wasn't he already a famous orator, to which Xi Sheng demurred and said he was all right, at least in front of villagers like himself. However, meeting Commander Kuang San was an entirely different matter. Qiao Qiao suggested that he talk about his grandfather, a man the commander should remember; that way, she told him, the commander could take the lead in the conversation and he'd just have to answer questions. Xi Sheng was persuaded by her reasoning and seemed to relax, until he realised there wasn't much time before the new day dawned and then he grew even more worried than before. He wished she were going with him, and so Qiao Qiao told him just to think of her when he was there, and then everything would be fine. Xi Sheng chuckled; she knew just what to say, and then he hung up.

A second later, however, Xi Sheng's telephone rang. Qiao Qiao wanted to know what gifts he'd prepared to give to the deputy vice-chair and to the commander. She suggested he take as much as he could, local produce would be best, walnuts, dried persimmon, traditional honey. Xi Sheng laughed again and told her he wasn't visiting some county boss or village mayor; the only gift he could give was money in a red envelope. Qiao Qiao acknowledged her husband's experience in these matters, but then suggested he ought to cut out some figures to add to the envelopes, and perhaps even sing a couple of songs when he saw them. She was right, Xi Sheng told her. He thanked her, he'd almost forgotten.

When they arrived in the provincial capital, the vice-chair was the first person to visit, and he had already heard that Lao Yu was bringing a successful local businessman with him. When the knock finally came on his office door and Lao Yu stepped inside, he was at first surprised to see him arrive alone.

"The businessman then, has he not come?"

"Oh no, he's here." Lao Yu answered, gesturing in Xi Sheng's direction.

The vice-chair shifted in his seat and tilted his head downwards, following Lao Yu's hand. That was when he saw Xi Sheng, the dwarf standing erect alongside Lao Yu.

Waving them forward and offering the sofa for them to sit on, the vice-chair initiated the conversation: "So… you must be Mr Xi Sheng, the pharmaceutical magnate… well, for Chinese medicine at least, yes?"

Xi Sheng hurriedly stood back up: "Excuse me sir… but my family name's not Xi, it's Gou."

"Eh… is that so? Well, no matter, Gou's rather hard on the ears, so I'll stick with Mr Xi."

"If the vice-chair wishes to call you Mr Xi," Lao Yu interjected, "then that's what we'll call you!"

Xi Sheng then relayed his company's successes and current quarterly dividends. By all accounts, the business was doing very well, very well indeed.

"Tell me," said the vice-chair, directing his attention to Lao Yu, "that business with the tiger… wasn't a dwarf responsible for that fiasco? And now you're here accompanied by…"

"They're one and the same," said Lao Yu. "Xi Sheng here is the same person who claimed to have seen a tiger."

The colour of the vice-chair's face turned almost immediately, and then he broke out in raucous laughter: "So it *is* him! Ha ha! Do you know how much fuss you caused for the Forestry Ministry! I say! Fortunately for you, you were just trying to improve your family's prospects, looking to make a quick buck, that's the mistake you were guilty of, and, well… aren't we all trying to do that… ha! Ah… it's nothing, is it… and besides, you've shown since then to be a capable man… just look at your business acumen… everyone looks a little better once they've got money to spread around!"

Xi Sheng had been a little startled and worried at first, wondering why Lao Yu had seemingly sold him out so quickly, but these words by the vice-chair set him at ease. He wiped the sweat from his brow and offered a cigarette to the vice-chair. The other man declined, he didn't smoke. Before anyone else said anything, Xi Sheng blurted out that the tiger was real. Lao Yu stared at him in disbelief, shifted back on the sofa and didn't say another word.

They met Commander Kuang San in the Hot Springs Convalescent Home in the southern part of the provincial capital. They didn't set out until after their evening dinner, and when they arrived the commander was soaking in a hot bath, forcing them to wait outside a little longer before they could meet him. They were also told of Kuang San's advanced years, which they already knew, and his failing health, which they had expected since they were in a convalescent home. Consequently, they wouldn't be given much time. They were offered strong, steeped tea while they waited, which gave the three men the opportunity to discuss how best to address the aged hero of the revolution.

Being perhaps the least familiar with such formalities, it was Xi Sheng who initiated the conversation: "How should I best address the commander… surely I can't call him 'grandfather' as his assistant does can I?"

"Well, I believe you can," the vice-chair said. "The commander has been retired for quite some time now, and he doesn't really enjoy being called by his former titles."

Xi Sheng nodded, accepting the explanation, and then excused himself so he could nip to the toilet. He returned some moments later, but before another ten minutes passed, he again excused himself.

"What's the matter with you?" asked Lao Yu. "Have you got the runs or something?"

"No, nothing like that… I just feel this need to piss, but then when I do, only a little comes out."

"You're nervous… that's why… just stay here and take a few deep breaths."

Xi Sheng went along with the suggestion, standing erect and breathing in and out as deeply as he could. An hour later, the door to Commander Kuang San's private room opened and a security official appeared. He was dark-skinned with a broad face, and his eyes bored into them as though searching for possible threats. Xi Sheng smiled, but the security guard's face remained impassive. Xi Sheng couldn't help but stare, the man's arms seemed to be more substantial and bulging than his own crumpled old legs.

A few moments later, a female assistant wheeled the former

commander out to greet them, but Xi Sheng and Lao Yu didn't at first notice, so transfixed were they by the imposing security guard who was still sizing them up. The vice-chair, familiar with such situations, did see the commander being wheeled out and immediately stood up to greet him, offering first a formal hello before asking quietly after his health. Lao Yu and Xi Sheng then became aware of what was happening and quickly stood up. They took a few hurried steps forward before greeting the commander in unison.

"Grandfather! How do you do?"

Xi Sheng looked the old man up and down. He really was old, ancient even. His legs were short and shrivelled with age and bore a striking resemblance to a pair of stockings filled with shelled walnuts. His hair was still thick, but completely white. His mouth was partially open as though he could no longer close it firmly, and when he spoke only his lips moved.

"So... who's come to visit me?" His voice was raspy, but still full of confidence.

"Grandfather," Lao Yu answered quickly. "Xi Sheng and I have come to see you."

"And who might you be?"

"I'm the deputy county commissioner for Qinning." Waving his hand in the direction of Xi Sheng, he continued: "And this is Xi Sheng, from Danggui, a small village near Huilongwan."

"And what's wrong with you, huh?" said the commander, shifting his attention to Xi Sheng. "Why're you so short?"

"Every man in Danggui suffers the same fate. We're all short."

The commander gestured for the men to sit down, and they complied. His mouth remained a little open, but he didn't say anything further. The vice-chair, who had stayed silent while Kuang San asked his questions of Lao Yu and Xi Sheng, now made the proper introductions. They were both from Qinling, a former revolutionary stronghold during the tumultuous events of the early twentieth century, as the commander knew well, and they both longed to see him. In fact, he added, the citizens throughout Qinling all thought very fondly of the commander. They all wished him the best, too.

The vice-chair was continuing to ramble on when Kuang San abruptly interrupted him: "I heard those apricot trees I planted bore a great number of fruit this year... is that true?"

The vice-chair had no idea what the commander was talking about, he'd heard nothing about apricot trees, and so he looked plaintively at Lao Yu and Xi Sheng, hoping they could answer the older man's query. Unfortunately, neither of them had heard anything about the trees.

Not willing the silence to drag on, Xi Sheng intervened: "Eh… I believe they did, yes. Grandfather, I've just told you I'm from Danggui, but I'd like to add… well… you know your guerrilla band spent some time in Danggui oh so many years ago, a local there, my grandfather, he joined your band… do you perhaps remember him… everyone used to call him 'Uncle'."

"Uncle? Ah… yes… Uncle… I remember him… he was as short as you, wasn't he…"

"That's right, yes."

Kuang San's face brightened as the memories flooded back: "So he was your grandfather, eh? I tell you… he was a devil that one, ghostly powers… did you know he didn't carry a gun… he always wanted one… wanted mine in fact… but Lao Hei and Li Desheng, they wouldn't have… so I helped him carve out a wooden one. He was bow-legged you know… of course you do… but I tell you what, he could run deceptively fast… and I didn't know many braver than him. He gave his life, you know, as a runner, a courier… it was me who went and collected his body… miserable tragedy that was."

He paused the story and unclasped his hands, then wrapped them tight around the wheels of his chair. It appeared as if he was about to try to stand. He didn't, however, and his assistant leapt to support him. Semi-suspended above the chair, he coughed hard, his chest wracked with convulsions.

"After my grandfather sacrificed himself," Xi Sheng continued, "my grandmother and father fled the area to escape the famine, and later on my dad learnt how to perform shadow plays. He was…"

"Don't say any more," the vice-chair interjected. "Bringing up all these old memories is a little too much for the commander… it gets him too excited… talk about something else."

Xi Sheng shifted the conversation to his business successes. As he went through the details, he kept a close eye on the commander and slowly, little by little, the older man relaxed and colour came back to his face after the fit of coughing. He didn't speak, however, only his mouth hung slightly open as before.

"Xi Sheng," Lao Yu suggested, "why don't you sing a song. It's been ages, I imagine, since the commander has heard a song from Qinling."

"A wonderful idea," said Xi Sheng, standing up and preparing himself.

"He can sing?" asked the vice-chair as he leaned in close to Lao Yu.

"Oh yes, he's really quite something, too. It'll make the commander happy, I'm sure."

Xi Sheng began his tune, a song about his grandfather, his desire to join the guerrillas, how at first he was not welcomed, then how he became a courier and finally how he died at the hands of the then local militia; his sacrifice for the revolution and for the Party. Kuang San listened intently and when it was finished, he clapped excitedly.

"Excellent, excellent… you sing wonderfully. I remember that time, Lao Hei didn't want your grandfather… didn't think he could cope…" The old man fell into another coughing fit.

"Why are you singing about the past, about the guerrillas?" said the vice-chair, visibly upset. "I've told you already… ah… sing something else."

"How about a ballad then? A folk song from the mountains?"

They agreed and again Xi Sheng raised his voice to sing. It was a song about love and hardship, of the difficulties of life in the mountains, especially for women. Once he finished, their clapping was even more boisterous than before, and he grew increasingly pleased.

"How about another… a ballad, too…"

He sang the first verse, then the second and the third, and as he did he removed from his pocket some red paper. He swayed as he sung, moving closer to Kuang San as he did so. With his other free hand, he pulled out his scissors for cutting paper, but just as he did so, the guard, who'd never moved very far away, leapt to action, moved in and delivered a kick straight into Xi Sheng's chest. There was a great snap and Xi Sheng flew into the wall opposite, and then crumpled to the floor. It all happened so suddenly that everyone was stunned. The vice-chair looked aghast, frozen in shock. Lao Yu was similarly horrified. By the time they collected themselves, the female assistant had wheeled Kuang San back into his private room and shut the door behind her. The guard was standing over Xi Sheng, gripping hard onto his clothes and shouting viciously at the prone little man.

"What the hell were you trying to do?" His voice dripped with anger and animosity.

Lao Yu realised, then, what had happened and tried to offer an explanation: "Xi Sheng is the descendant of a revolutionary, a model for our times. When he sings, he's also able to cut out these wonderful forms in red paper… it's part of his performance… he was trying to show that to the commander…"

The guard said nothing further. He merely released Xi Sheng and stomped off towards the inner room. Xi Sheng remained on the floor, unable to get up.

"It's all just a misunderstanding… come on… get up," said Lao Yu, trying to console his wounded friend. Xi Sheng's face had blanched; snot and tears dripped onto the floor.

It was evening when Xi Sheng returned to the county seat. Once there, he went straight to the apartment he owned and didn't re-emerge for nearly two weeks. He didn't attend to his company affairs, nor did he go to market. His mobile was turned off and he wouldn't communicate with anyone. He also vowed never to sing again.

During that fortnight he spent in seclusion, the epidemic that had started in the south and had gone through Beijing was now tearing its way through the rest of the country at even greater speed than before. Treatment centres had been set up everywhere, and a strict isolation regimen established to separate those who had contracted the disease from those who hadn't. In train stations, bus stations, ports, every transportation hub, disease-testing centres were erected to monitor the people coming and going. In an attempt to stem the rise in infection rates, the provincial government required anyone coming from Beijing, Shanghai or Guangzhou to register with the local authorities upon arrival. They would then be subject to isolation procedures for the purpose of monitoring them, taking their temperature and drawing blood to be tested for signs of infection. The county seat in turn enacted the same strict measures, requiring anyone coming from the provincial capital or other large cities to register and be subjected to the same rigorous tests. The market in Huilongwan even implemented checkpoints and stipulated that all visitors needed to register and be checked for symptoms of the epidemic. So seriously were they taking the epidemic that isolation and monitoring were set for ten days, after which, if there were no signs of illness, they would be released, but still subject to monitoring. Danggui, however, never followed suit. They didn't require newcomers to register. All they did was set up local patrols that worked shifts around the clock. Each patrolman was equipped with a police baton and their task was simple enough: strangers or those villagers who'd been away were not permitted to enter the village. Even stray cats and dogs would be beaten away for fear they might transmit the disease.

Qiao Qiao had received no word from her husband, and so she was left to assume he was still in the provincial capital. Unfortunately, the more she watched the television news and learnt of the increasing death rate and numbers of people seeking treatment, the more she grew worried for Xi Sheng. Since Xi Sheng hadn't been answering his phone, Qiao Qiao tried Lao Yu instead, soon learning that the two of them had left the capital some time ago. Naturally she asked why Xi Sheng's phone was switched off, and Lao Yu could tell there was growing anger in her voice. She was worried and blaming both Xi Sheng and Lao Yu for the lack of communication. Understanding how she was feeling, Lao Yu offered an excuse for his friend, saying that since Xi Sheng was an important businessman in the area, and the boss of a pharmaceutical company, if only traditional medicine, he'd been tasked by the county government to procure indigowoad root, which had been shown to be effective at preventing infection. Of course, the procurement of this plant didn't end his work; he also had to ensure that it was properly processed into doses that could be given individually, and as a result he was no doubt so busy that he hadn't been able to get in touch with her. Once he'd finished fabricating this lie, Lao Yu hung up and tried Xi Sheng's mobile. It was still turned off, so he felt compelled to find out just what the devil his friend was doing.

Arriving at his place, he had to pound the door for some time before Xi Sheng finally opened it. But the man he saw was not the same as before. His hair was a mess, matted, long and unwashed for what looked like weeks. A scraggly beard covered his face, and his cheeks were drawn and sunken. He appeared even shorter than before.

"What the hell have you been doing... why'd you shut your phone off? It's been two weeks..."

"I haven't been outside for all that time..."

"Fuck... looking at you like this... don't you think you resemble a ghost... a ghoul!"

"Yes... a ghost, a ghoul... a dishonoured spirit!" Xi Sheng's voice was a howl, bringing truth to the way he looked.

Lao Yu began to realise what was wrong. Xi Sheng was still troubled, tormented by what had happened under the boot of Kuang San's bodyguard. He tried to console his friend: "Why're you still so worked up about that? It was nothing, a misunderstanding... he was just carrying out his duty... he didn't know what you were doing. Put yourself in his shoes... shit, a dog's bite won't kill you, will it! Come on, come with me, there's work to be done, it's all hands on deck to deal with this epidemic... you need to get your company to procure indigowoad root... hiding out here won't do you any good... come on, don't you still want to be the model businessman!" Refusing to take 'no' for an answer, Lao Yu dragged his friend out the front door.

After three days of intensive work, Xi Sheng was able to get his company to acquire three tonnes of the root for processing. With this task seemingly well in hand, he phoned his wife and explained what he had been doing. The county capital was under great threat and the situation was dire and getting worse every day. The theatres had all been closed, the markets and shopping centres, too. Even most restaurants had shut. Disinfectant was being sprayed all across the city and everyone, without exception, was wearing face masks if they had to go out; most chose not to. No one even shook hands any more. As for himself, he was fine, thankfully. The company's contribution to the tackling of the disease was the procurement of three tonnes of indigowoad root. Despite his assurances, however, Qiao Qiao was still upset and ill at ease. She was pleased he was able to contribute to the fight against the sickness, but now that he'd done that, he should come home, and quickly. After all, she added, there aren't many people in Danggui so the chances of the disease spreading were unlikely. And the weather was much better, much cleaner. He mulled it over, and then agreed; he would return.

That night, when everyone had already gone to sleep, Xi Sheng quietly and surreptitiously left the city. He knew Huilongwan was interrogating outsiders who showed up in the town, and even though he was easily recognised by most, he worried that the men questioning new arrivals might not know who he was, which would in turn cause no small amount of trouble and nuisance. Since he was so familiar with the town's layout, and to avoid such a possible annoyance, he decided to avoid the main road into town, but instead chose the small mountain paths he'd once tramped over to bypass it altogether. On the following morning, a little before lunch, he was already near Danggui; just two more streams to cross and he would be there.

Normally, when travellers walking these pathways grew hungry or thirsty, they'd drink from the small streams and sit down and eat whatever cake or provisions they'd brought with them. Xi Sheng now did the same, and as he sat, he massaged his warped and malformed legs as he had done so many times before. They were already aching, and painful to the touch. But he still had some distance to traverse, so after a moment he lifted himself up and continued on to Danggui.

As he drew close to the village, he noticed his nephew's wife seated on the millstone that stood at the town's entrance. He called out to her almost immediately.

"Xiao Mai! Xiao Mai!"

The young woman was startled by someone calling out her name, but instead of replying as one normally would, she shouted something that took Xi Sheng completely by surprise: "Disease! The disease's come!"

Almost immediately, a posse of young men rushed out from the nearby building, each one holding a club.

Terrified at this reception, Xi Sheng shouted "It's me!" but it seemed to do little good.

"We know who you are… where's it you've come from, the big city or the county capital?"

"From the county capital."

"How're things there?"

"There've been ten cases and five deaths." As he spoke, he tried to move a little ahead, and kicked at some of the stones that littered the path. He was about to tell them about indigowoad root when seven or eight of the clubs swung in front of him to bar his way.

"I'm not sick, I haven't contracted the disease. Why're you stopping me from going home?"

"Who's determined you're not sick, where's your proof? You've come from an affected area, who's to say you're not affected, too? Why've you come, huh, what're you here for?"

"But I'm from here… are you trying to tell me I can't go home? Tell me, which one of your families have I not made rich, and now you're treating me like this?"

"You might've brought riches to us in the past, but now you're only bringing disease! You're not allowed in, at least not without going through some form of quarantine so we know you're not sick… ten days… yeah, you need to stay down in that cellar, just over there, for ten days so we can make sure there's nothing wrong with you."

"Why you no-good fuckers, I'm coming in!"

Xi Sheng pushed at the young men barring his way, and in return their clubs fell hard, knocking him to the ground. Prostrate before them, he tilted his head and spat at the men standing around him, hitting one by the name of Hei Shuan.

Enraged, Hei Shuan yelled out: "That dirty bastard is trying to make me sick!" He turned and ran back inside to wash his face. Then he grabbed some dirt and rubbed it hard against his skin, trying desperately to wipe away any traces of Xi Sheng's saliva.

"He's definitely sick," the rest of the crowd spoke in unison, looking down on Xi Sheng crumpled on the ground. "He's come here to spread the disease, to make us share in his fate!" Lifting their clubs again, they began to pummel Xi Sheng without mercy.

Taking stock of the escalating situation, Xi Sheng twisted his body and emerged briefly out of the crowd. He tried to flee, but the men gave chase and tackled him once again to the ground, seemingly intent on satisfying their rage.

It didn't take long for word of this incident to reach Qiao Qiao, and she rushed over to help her husband. Frightened and with tears streaming down her face, she pulled and pleaded with the young men to stop. The village head also made an appearance, and Qiao Qiao implored him to do something as well.

The village head, however, defended the actions of the crowd: "This is all in the best interests of Danggui. We've got to ensure the town is safe from infection."

"But what's wrong with him... look at him... tell me, what's the problem? You know who he is, what he's done for the village... how can you say he's unsafe?"

The village head remained quiet for a moment, before shouting at the crowd to stop beating poor old Xi Sheng. The young men refused, however, and Hei Shuan, who was at the front of the mob, could be heard yelling out with all his might that Xi Sheng had given him the disease, had in effect killed him, and so he was going to make sure Xi Sheng died first.

Xi Sheng had little chance to fight back, so he tried to get away once more, running up on top of the embankments that encircled their fields. Hei Shuan pursued him, seemingly lost to an uncontrollable fury. But the farther up they scaled the embankment, the narrower it got, too. Xi Sheng's pace was slow and it would only be a moment or so before Hei Shuan's club was within reach of him. His only option was to spin around and bound back down the slope. Whether it was the speed at which he trundled down the hill, or his age, unfortunately for Xi Sheng, he fell and fractured his leg.

Qiao Qiao ran over to her husband, determined to pick him up and bring him home, but still they prevented her from returning inside the village limits with Xi Sheng, wounded or not. To resolve the situation, the village head called a meeting in which it was decided that Xi Sheng could enter the village, but he was barred from going anywhere else; in effect, he was to be quarantined at home. The decision made, Qiao Qiao returned to her husband, who had been forced to wait on the outskirts of the village, despite his broken leg. Carefully, she picked him up and hoisted him onto her back. As she strode along the familiar paths, Xi Sheng cursed the entire time. The villagers were all blind fools, idiots, small minded, the lot of them. Qiao Qiao urged him to stop his rant, but her entreaty fell on deaf ears. Xi Sheng was now as enraged as the mob had been when they attacked him.

Finally, Qiao Qiao resorted to threatening her husband: "Go on, keep cursing them and I'll let you down right here. I'm from Danggui as well, you know! It's your home, too... so who're you cursing? Yourself?"

He stopped bad mouthing the village, and turned to crying: "I'm not sick! I'm not..."

In truth, Xi Sheng hadn't contracted the disease that was ravaging the country, but three days later, the village head was bedridden and unable to get up. His temperature rose and not long after he couldn't even be stirred awake. Most of the villagers suspected Xi Sheng had brought the contagion with him, but neither he nor his wife showed any symptoms, and even Hei Shuan, who'd come in direct contact with Xi Sheng's saliva, was also asymptomatic. Eventually there was a grudging acceptance that Xi Sheng hadn't brought the sickness to Danggui, and so they began to wonder if the village head had not picked it up from somewhere else.

Soon after, stories began to circulate. A week before, a number of villagers had apparently seen the village head's dog mating with some bitch from outside in one of the many glens that ran down the mountain. The bitch didn't belong to anyone in Danggui, and so wanton conjecture led them to wonder if it was an infected stray that had passed the disease on, first to the village head's dog and then onto its master. In response, patrols were stepped up and the exclusion rules became even stricter. Not only were all outsiders prevented from entering the village, but any beast that accidentally roamed outside, whether it was a cow, a donkey, pig, dog or chicken, would be beaten to death. The residents also attempted to confiscate the village head's dog, despite protestations from the man's wife who tried to stop them by saying their pet had not been wandering, nor was it sick, for if it had contracted the illness, why hadn't it already perished? The beast, sensing the peril of the situation, scurried away from the clutches of the men and up onto part of the collapsed courtyard wall. It then leapt over to the lowest part of the roof, and off and away from Danggui. A day later, the village head died.

His death hit Danggui hard, partly because they feared how quickly he'd succumbed to the illness and how that may in turn presage the virus running rampant through the rest of the village. At the same time, they of course wanted to assist in the funeral preparations, the construction of a memorial, the coffin and the burial. The body lay in state for three days, and they thought they ought to invite me to come and sing, but the only person who actually knew me was Xi Sheng, and they had already done so poorly by him that they were too embarrassed to ask him to come and find me. And besides, they thought, I had been living in Huilongwan and they feared sending anyone to come to the market town to find me, worried about the possibility of further contagion, to say nothing of having me come and potentially bringing the disease with me. As a result, no dirges were sung for the village head; the dead man's only accompaniment was his wife's crying, which lasted the same three days he lay in state.

On the day of the burial, besides the young men who continued to patrol the village perimeter, everyone was at the funeral with some serving as pallbearers. In other places, four pallbearers were involved in carrying the coffin, in others, eight. For Danggui and its dwarfish residents, however, different measures had to be put in place. First, a long vertical bar was tied across the length of the coffin, and then six more horizontal bars ran the width; consequently, it took up to sixteen men to carry the coffin. But in the case of the village head's funeral, there were only four to five men on each side, with two at the back and two in front. Thus the coffin tilted back and forward, swaying in a sort of deathly rhythm as the men stumbled and tripped their way to the burial site. By the halfway point, most of the men were drenched in sweat and required their wives to march along with them so as to wipe their brows. More than once the women were heard to yell out about the amount of sweat draining down their husbands' faces.

"Heavens, you're going to sweat yourselves dry!"

"We're growing light-headed, too."

Once they reached the village head's final resting place and were able to put the coffin down, the pallbearers collapsed onto the ground, not daring to move any further, and hoping at the same time the wind would turn and provide them some respite. The sweat still poured down their faces, however, soaking their clothes that had begun to stick uncomfortably to their dwarf frames. They looked like they'd just stepped out of the water.

"Tired?" one of the other villagers asked as he wiped a pallbearer's forehead and sat down next to him. "But why do I feel as tired as you?"

The question went unanswered, but it hung in the air. Then, as agreed, the pallbearers were to be carried home and the man who'd just sat down next to one of them reached his arms around the other man and strained to pick him up. Once positioned on his back, however, he couldn't help but call out: "You're running a fever, shit! You're hot enough to burn me."

The pallbearers were taken home and each one was nearly delirious by the time they got back. Soon after, their breathing grew laboured and most fell unconscious. By the following morning, three of the men had died. The people panicked, certain that the village head had contracted the disease that had been plaguing the towns and cities, and now it had arrived here. To make matters worse, everyone had attended the funeral and so now they all believed they were infected. The village was plunged into chaos, most cursing the heavens for what had supposedly befallen them.

Xi Sheng and Qiao Qiao had not stepped outside for what seemed like ages. It's not that they didn't want to – they'd thought about it – but they were prevented from doing so; the villagers had barred their gate, sealing them inside as part of their quarantine measures. That said, they could still hear the cries coming from the village, growing in volume daily.

"So many bad things have come back with me, haven't they," Xi Sheng grumbled to himself. "Perhaps I did bring the affliction with me."

Qiao Qiao put a finger up to close her husband's mouth, and spoke in a low voice: "What nonsense are you saying? You're not sick, you haven't died… nor have I… so how could you be responsible for what's happened?"

They resolved to move beyond the walls in order to find out what was going on. First, they attempted to remove the metal bar that had shut them in, but no matter how hard Xi Sheng bashed at it, the door wouldn't budge. Qiao Qiao grabbed a ladder and climbed over the courtyard wall. A moment later she'd unlocked the door from the outside, and then hoisted Xi Sheng onto her back and together they went into the village.

The first thing they noticed was that the patrols had ceased, although Hei Shuan could still be found roaming around. Upon seeing them he shouted out: "Xi Sheng, I mistakenly blamed you, I'm sorry. You were never ill to begin with!"

"It's me who should thank you… if I hadn't broken my leg, who's to say I wouldn't have contracted the disease, too? All of this has happened… has anyone called the government in Huilongwan?"

"I'm not sure," Hei Shuan replied. "I reckon no one's thought of it."

"Then bloody well go and do it, get on the blower and call Huilongwan!"

Xi Sheng searched his pockets for his phone, but realised he didn't have it with him. Qiao Qiao had forgotten to bring hers as well. That's when they noticed where they were: the village head's house was just down the lane and it had a phone. They walked over and opened the door without knocking, only to find the village head's wife gasping her last breath, her daughter-in-law standing next to her dying body, weeping profusely.

"Eh… she's… she's gone." Xi Sheng's voice was heavy.

Qiao Qiao picked up her husband and returned home. Once there, Xi Sheng used his mobile to call Huilongwan and report on the calamitous conditions Danggui was enduring – the disease had arrived and already claimed four to five lives, dozens more were suffering symptoms; he reckoned the entire village was infected. The person who answered the phone, however, had no idea what was going on. In truth, the man on the other end couldn't help but grow a little perturbed at listening to Xi Sheng's frantic voice. The receiver was passed to the mayor who listened solemnly to Xi Sheng's report, and he said they were aware of the situation but there was nothing they could do. Undeterred, Xi Sheng hung up and rang the county capital. He was determined to get them to dispatch the medical emergency services to ferry the sick back to the county hospital. While they waited for the ambulances to arrive, the villagers who had already succumbed to the disease had to be buried quickly; and the graves had to be deep, at least a dozen feet or more, and lime had to be spread over the corpses before they were finally covered over.

Given the situation, and the need for the villagers to understand what was happening and what they had to do, Xi Sheng was intent on taking the lead. Of course, he would no longer allow Qiao Qiao to carry him throughout the town, that would be too embarrassing, and so instead he bound his broken leg with a wooden splint, grabbed another piece of wood to use as a makeshift walking stick, and then went door to door urging the residents of Danggui not to panic. He told them the authorities in Huilongwan, and in the county capital, were sending doctors and emergency vehicles. What they had to do before outside help arrived was to bury their dead as swiftly as possible, using their own courtyards if necessary, so long as they buried them deep.

The only issue was how they were going to bury their dead, since the survivors were too exhausted to actually do the digging. To make matters worse, by the time evening fell, the emergency crews were nowhere to be seen. This remained the case three days later; there was still no sign of help. Three more had died by then, and even the strapping young man who had formerly attacked Xi Sheng so viciously fell ill himself. The dead had gone unburied, and as a result the corpses had begun to grow fetid, blanketing the village in a rancid odour that welcomed only swarms of flies.

The rapid deterioration of the situation caused even greater worry for Xi Sheng, and soon he began to curse the villagers as he had so many times in the past. A meeting was finally arranged, but only eighteen residents were called to attend. Xi Sheng instructed the men to investigate each and every household, looking for victims of the epidemic. Once the rounds were complete, a communal grave was dug, and even though it was hardly large enough to hold the entire number of corpses, the bodies were still deposited in the pit, covered with lime and then soil. In instances where the entire household had perished, their homes were torched and when the fires had burnt out, the ruins were covered as well.

Once they'd completed their work, the eighteen men were covered in soot and ash. Their faces were dark and their hair singed, creating the impression of walking ghosts prowling the village. They'd actually just finished torching three homes and were again near the pit they'd dug close to the entrance to the village. That's when they heard the sound of someone crying out from behind them. It was an ear-shattering howl, but as quickly as it had begun, it ended. That's when they saw Xi Sheng, a heap upon the ground. He'd gone to nearly every house and courtyard, had spun his head around frantically at the devastation, and then when he'd directed his attention to the village gates and saw no sign of outside help, no emergency vehicles, no doctors, he had collapsed, reduced to mumbling and cursing to himself: "Those motherfuckers... bastards... all of them... why haven't they come?"

As it happened, immediately after Xi Sheng had informed Huilongwan, the authorities there had reported the situation to the county government, which, in turn, called an emergency committee meeting to discuss possible measures. The first thing the county government discussed was whether to file a report with the provincial government; the second was when to contact Huilongwan again. It so happened that the county hospitals were already inundated with patients suffering from the contagion, and so there was no way they could dispatch any of their medics to deal with the situation in Danggui. The only solution, they thought, was for Huilongwan to organise the remaining villagers to gather up the sick and dying and to transport them by the fastest means possible to the county hospitals. This was relayed to Huilongwan, and the authorities there telephoned Danggui to make the arrangements.

When the call came, the only person left to answer it was the village head's daughter-in-law, who after receiving the information, raced off to tell Xi Sheng. By the time she reached him, he was already crumpled on the ground and forced to crawl, the splint gone.

"Uncle, uncle… are you alright?" came the young woman's plaintive cries.

"Am I alright? I'm covered with poison, why should I fear the virus, use poison to kill poison, I say… nothing wrong at all!"

"The town's been fortunate to have you, uncle…"

"Fortunate to have me… I'll say they are… three lifetimes over they benefitted from my family… but here I am… saving them again!"

The young woman helped him return to the village head's home, and then he took the call from the authorities in Huilongwan: "You need to get all of the villagers suffering from the disease to the county hospital. It's the only way they can receive treatment."

"Really," said Xi Sheng, his voice betraying his exasperation and anger, "just how the hell am I supposed to get them there? They're all dying… there'll never be time… and those who haven't yet perished can barely stand any more. So who's going to bring them?"

He hung up the phone, his rage boiling over. Turning to the daughter-in-law, he told her she had to carry him back to where the men had just burnt one of the villager's homes, but she refused. He cursed her and shouted that she must fetch Qiao Qiao. She complied with this command, and his wife showed up not long after the young woman had gone to get her. Before collecting her husband, however, Qiao Qiao ordered the few remaining children, some already orphaned, others soon to be, to make their way to the former home of Lao Yu's father. The place had stood vacant for many years, so it was likely to be the safest place for the children to wait things out. She then ran off to get Xi Sheng, carrying him quickly to the burnt-out homes.

When they came upon the still-burning inferno, they could see the roof had already caved in and the men who had started the fire were busy pushing against the exterior walls, forcing them to fall inwards, burying the dead inside.

"Eh… such a tragedy." It was clear by the sound of his voice that Xi Sheng was greatly affected by developments. "Do you know… it was only this past spring that they'd renovated this place." His grip around his wife loosened and he began to fall.

"Put your arms around my neck," she said quickly before he slipped away completely from her.

"I'm so… tired… you don't suppose…"

"Don't say it!"

Xi Sheng spat and coughed, then turned his head to the sky and spat some more. "Take me… take me over to the village entrance… I want to see those houses again."

"Alight, sure… let's go." She twisted and manoeuvred, pulling her husband back up onto her shoulders, and then took off running. She didn't, however, bring him to where he wanted to go, but returned home instead.

After listening to Xi Sheng's vitriol on the telephone, the mayor of Huilongwan relayed it all to the county government, emphasising, as Xi Sheng did, the seriousness of the situation in Danggui. On this occasion, the county representative he spoke to was none other than Lao Yu, who called for a car to set off immediately for the place he'd once called home. He brought two doctors along with him, as well as two large containers of disinfectant.

But as the car neared the village, all he could see was smoke and ash hanging low over everything. He was shocked by the sight, and straight away telephoned the government in Huilongwan. They were told to muster troops and blockade the village of Danggui; nothing was to be allowed out, not a single resident, nor even an animal. Donning a biohazard suit, Lao Yu and the two doctors walked into the village searching for patients.

In the first three houses Lao Yu visited he found only death. The next house had flames just starting to eat away at its roof; the seven after that one were already torched. From their courtyard gates, he could see the ruined homes, great piles of rubble, earth and lime. In some he could see the limbs of the recently deceased; in others, dogs sniffed about and whined at the passing of their masters. As he reached the far end of the village and wandered in behind one of the alleyways, he came upon a millstone with four men sat upon it. At the threshold of the five nearest houses, not yet burnt, a further seven men lay slumped against each other. They were all breathing, but none looked very much alive. When they saw Lao Yu, all they could do was cry; they had no energy to say anything. His eyes then shifted to Xi Sheng's home, which stood a little farther on. There, near the rubber tree, he spied Qiao Qiao, unmoving, as expressionless as bone china.

"Qiao Qiao," Lao Yu yelled, "Qiao Qiao!"

There was no response.

Racing over to her, he yelled again: "Where's Xi Sheng? Where is he?"

Again she remained silent. Her only reply was to look in the direction of the house. Lao Yu followed her eyes and then stumbled towards the building, seemingly aware of what he would find: there on the bed lay his friend, already dead.

Lao Yu was filled with grief over the death of Xi Sheng, of the disaster that had befallen Danggui. After making his report to the county government, he requested they send the emergency services at once; those still alive needed to be transported away. He also asked that a disinfectant crew be dispatched together with emergency personnel; they had to make sure the virus wouldn't spread beyond Danggui. After he had completed his report, he asked the doctors to identify those most seriously ill so that they could be brought to the county hospital in the vehicle he had come in. Those villagers not yet displaying symptoms were told to hole up in his father's old house. Their objective now was to isolate the healthy; it was too late for the sick. Once they were out of the way, Lao Yu ordered the disinfectant he'd brought to be sprayed everywhere; any animal spotted was to be killed, no exceptions.

Danggui soon became known as a ghost village, the hardest hit in all of Qinling. What few survivors remained were relocated and subjected to quarantine procedures in Huilongwan. Then, after a period of ten days under observation, the first villager was released: Qiao Qiao. Two weeks later another forty residents were allowed to depart the quarantine centre, but twenty new cases were also discovered, each of whom was removed and transferred to the county hospital. A month later, the remaining twenty-eight residents of Danggui were released. None of them, however, returned to Danggui… at least, that's what I heard… apparently they chose instead to make arrangements to move into the abandoned structures at the foot of Mount Cockscomb.

Six months later, maybe a little longer, the devastating plague finally ran its course. In its aftermath, reporters descended on nearly every area of the country to collect first-hand accounts of what had happened. When they arrived in Huilongwan, the government decided Qiao Qiao would be a most suitable interviewee, if for no other reason than that she had proven herself to be the healthiest person in Danggui. She was also the most knowledgeable about what had really transpired… and, like her dead husband, she was an excellent orator.

She told me later that the interview requests soon came one after the other, and the more she told the story, the more she grew tired of it and the more annoyed she became… That's how she came to knock at my door… she was looking for a bit of peace and quiet… I couldn't blame her. In truth, it was nice having her around… we even got to talking about the village, although not in the same way as the interviewers had.

"So tell me, Qiao Qiao, do you think you'll ever return to Danggui?"

"Even if I wanted to, where would I live? There's no one else there, the place is mostly ruined, burnt and destroyed buildings… I think I'd rather forget the whole village."

"Do you think you can… forget it, I mean?"

"I… no… I don't think so… even though I want to. In those quiet moments… you know, in the evenings, when I'm just sitting… I can always hear a sorta… what… I don't know… but it sounds almost like Xi Sheng calling out to me… it also kinda sounds like the wind…

blowing as it always did through Danggui. I know what it's telling me too... Xi Sheng... and the other villagers... they're not at peace... that's the other reason I've come to you, yes, I want to escape from all those damned reporters, but I also want to ask if you can help me..."

"But how?"

"I want to ask... I... would you sing for them?"

I was startled by her request, I admit it. I'd been singing for more than a hundred years, but I'd never sung for an entire village. What's more, I thought to myself, I'd never sung for those already long since dead, I'd only ever sung at funerals before... when the dead were being lowered into the ground. But she persisted.

"Please... you must... Xi Sheng... the other villagers... they were never even buried properly... that's why they're haunting my memories... they're lost and lonely ghosts, trapped. If you were to sing for them, that would put them at ease... allow them to rest... and then I could slowly forget..."

What could I do? I had to promise her I would try... and as I did so, I also felt something... like my own premonition of the future... this would perhaps be my last ceremony.

The day Qiao Qiao and I travelled to Danggui it rained... a fine sort of mist that soaked into the ash and dust that had accumulated over the village since it had been abandoned. The result was a slippery sheen that covered everything, forcing us to choose carefully where we stepped. So many of the buildings had fallen under the torch... so many had collapsed... and so many people remained buried under the rubble. No effort had been made to bury them again... all that had been done was for fresh earth to be piled on top and then lime and disinfectant mixed in... layer upon layer... creating an odd, misshapen sort of funeral mound... grass had even started to grow upon the haphazard graves, a rough, coarse grass that appeared to push violently up through the earth... it was a charred sort of grass, a dark solid green that seemed to be enflamed... on three or four of the graves there were even small flowers growing, each one a bright, blood red.

Qiao Qiao walked a little in front of me and I heard her call out the names of dead villagers: Zhongmin, Fushe, Sanxi, Erhu, Shanchun, Wulei, Laifeng, Yinling, Jianfen, Shuanghuan, Shicheng, Uncle Dequan, Grandad Men, Auntie Jian, Sister Sao... she kept wailing as she walked through the village, finally arriving at her former home. She went silent before a laboured cry welled up inside her and she called the name of her husband... Xi Sheng! The deathly quiet village... the fine rain... her cry now echoed off the mountains, reverberating through the air.

"Qiao Qiao... Qiao Qiao..."

I remember calling her name like that... and finally she stopped... but she didn't move afterwards... it was as though she was rooted into the ground like a great tree... but petrified.

"What should I sing?"

A moment passed before she said anything: "Sing whatever..."

"Alright... let me start..."

I started a rhythm on my drum and sang. It was a song I'd sung before... calling on the heavens, on the Lord Yama... the bitterness of life and death... and so on. As the words flowed, I turned to look at Qiao Qiao... she was walking over the rubble, picking up roof tiles, wash basins, charred wicker baskets... bowls and dishes and worn pots and pans... she was collecting whatever her feet stumbled over and the clang soon added to the cadence of my singing... she'd hold what she picked up... clang, clang, clang... and throw it to one side, only to find something else and... clang, clang, clang...

I stopped for a moment to tell her she had a musical ear... she simply told me to keep singing... so I did.

This time my song was about me... my craft... my words... how I sang for the dead, for monsters and spirits, for Pangu, the first living being, and for the chaos that preceded him, for life and for death, for rich and poor, for the revolution and for reform, for people and for heaven's will... then I stopped, for I had forgotten the words.

"Sing!" Qiao Qiao shouted at me... but I couldn't remember the words... I told her to remove a book from my rucksack and she obliged without further protest. It was my songbook... but I let her read its contents.

"There're so many songs... so many words..."

"I can sing over three hundred tunes, you know, but right now... I don't know why... my mind is a blank. This has never happened to me before... suggest something... just read the first line and I'll take it from there."

Qiao Qiao tapped on the page that was open and began to read the lines… it only took the first two or three words for me to sing the rest… the opening tunes were Shaanxi elegies and folk songs… then I sang about more recent events… about Xi Sheng's grandfather joining the guerrilla fighters… finally I moved on to more popular ditties like *Singing a Mountain Song for the Party, Looking Towards the Sky, The East is Red* and *Walking into a New Era*… the words didn't flow as easily with these newer tunes, and I was often off key… so I returned to what I knew best, Qinqiang Opera… an age-old tradition in Qinling.

We started our performance near the rubber tree that was somehow still standing in her old courtyard, and from there we wandered out through the village, crisscrossing its old paths and alleyways, singing as we went, once, twice… until the sky grew dark and the sun set. We sat down to enjoy a breather, along with some food and drink. Once finished, we sang again… all three hundred melodies in my songbook… I remembered the lyrics, all of them, even the words to the newer songs and the Qinqiang Operas I'd sung… over and over again we sang, for three days and nights. By the end, my legs would no longer move, my throat would no longer allow any sound to escape, my drum, too, had broken, its skin torn from the constant beating. We knelt at the entrance to the village and kowtowed… on the morning of the fourth day, we left.

As we prepared to depart, satisfied Danggui's residents had been left at peace, I lifted my head once more to stare at the mountainside. To my surprise I saw someone farther up… he had a dark padded bed sheet wrapped around his shoulders and he was bounding down the hill… he was running so fast it almost seemed as though he were actually flying… it looked like Xi Sheng… I rubbed my eyes, then narrowed them and looked again… it was not a man after all but the shadow of a cloud drifting quickly overhead.

"Xi Sheng!" cried Qiao Qiao next to me.

Evidently she'd seen the same thing… I tried to head her off, then to console her… it was only a cloud crossing the heavens, I told her, it was its shadow that flitted down the mountain: "I assure you, Qiao Qiao, he's been reborn… he's returned from the bardo a man once again."

This was the last time I ever sang mourning songs. I don't think I could have sung any more, even if I'd wanted to… I'd forgotten all the words… age… that's what it was… I knew I was old… knew, too, that I had to return home… the only problem was I didn't know where home was…

Winter came and a westerly wind came with it… it blew for months, nonstop, and I let it carry me where it willed… first through Qinning and onto Santai, from Santai I arrived in Shanyin… and finally to Ziwuzhen… that's where the wind ceased to blow… my cave was still there… I strolled inside, ready to spend my last days where my story had begun.

EPILOGUE

I'LL READ THE FIRST SENTENCE, you continue with the second.

The River Fen lies east of the Yellow River and it is here where the first mountain in the second part of *Pathways Through the Northern Mountain* is described. It bears the name Guancen Mountain. There are many plants, grasses and shrubs near the summit, but no trees. Further down the mountain, considerable quantities of jade can be found.

Lesser Yang Mountain rises two hundred and fifty leagues to the west of Guancen. On its peak there is an abundance of jade, while nearer its base deposits of crimson silver are common. The Aching River originates here before flowing east into the River Fen. The waters of the Aching River run a reddish brown.

Fifty leagues to the north is the Mountain of Harmonious Counties. Its peak is covered in jade, while its foot contains a lot of copper. Large elk roam across this mountain. Long-tailed, white-feathered pheasants nest in great numbers. The Jin River emanates from here and flows southeast into the River Fen. Many sawbelly fish with reddish scales and pointed heads like those of a swordfish swim in the Jin. They are said to howl. If this fish is eaten, you will not notice its foul smell.

Mount Huqi stands two hundred leagues to the north of the Mountain of Harmonious Counties. It is devoid of vegetation but there is much green jade. The Victorious River runs from here in a northeasterly direction until it empties into the River Fen. Green-grey jade lines the bed of the Victorious River.

Three hundred and fifty leagues to the north is the Mountain of White Sands. As its name attests, this mountain is heavy with sand. Its base is more than 300 leagues in circumference. No vegetation can be found on this mountain, nor do any birds or beasts make it their home. The Yaito Tuna River rises on its peak but courses under the sand. There is an abundance of white jade.

Ershi Mountain lies four hundred leagues to the north. It lacks vegetation and there is no water.

Three hundred and eighty leagues north of Ershi Mountain is Mount Mad. It too is devoid of vegetation and is snow-covered the year through. Mount Mad River emerges here to flow west into the Shallow River. There is a great quantity of precious jade in its bed.

Three hundred and fifty leagues north of Mount Mad is Zhuyu Mountain. Copper and jade deposits are common at a high altitude, while pine and juniper trees grow in great number nearer its base. A river bearing the same name as the mountain rises here to flow east into the Tail-Banner River.

Honest-Head Mountain stands three hundred and fifty leagues to the north. Near its peak there is much gold and jade, but there is no vegetation. The Tail-Banner River begins here and then flows east into Imprint Marsh. Along the banks of the river, many bo-horses congregate. Their bodies are white, they have a single horn on their heads and ox-like tails. When they neigh, they sound like a human calling out. They are said to be able to walk upon water and are an omen of good tidings.

Gouwu Mountain rises three hundred and fifty leagues to the north of Honest-Head. Jade deposits are common nearer its peak. Copper can be found in abundance near its base. A creature that resembles a goat lives on this mountain. It has a human face, eyes behind its armpits, a tiger's maw and human hands. It cries like a baby and is reputed to eat men. It is known as the paoxiao and is often said to be kin to the taotie, one of the mythical four evil creatures of the world.

Three hundred leagues to the north is North Raucous Mountain. Its slopes are devoid of rocks and stones, but there is much green jade on its southern face. More common jade can be found on its north face. A tiger-like creature with a white body, a canine head, a horse's tail and pig bristles lives on the mountain. It is called the dugu. A bird with the body of a crow and the face of a human nests here. It is called the banmao. It is a nocturnal creature. Eating its flesh will cure one of heatstroke. The River Rainflood starts its journey here and flows east into Marshy Hillock.

Bridge-Channel Mountain rises three hundred and fifty leagues to the north. It is devoid of vegetation, but there is much gold and jade. This is the source of the Withered River before it journeys east into the Wild Goose Gate River. Many juji live on this mountain. They resemble a hedgehog with reddish fur, but they sound like a small pig. A bird resembling Kuafu the Arrogant can be found here. It has four wings, a single eye and the tail of a dog. It is called a din and sounds like a magpie. Eating its flesh will relieve abdominal pains, especially constipation and diarrhoea.

Guguan Mountain lies four hundred leagues to the north of Bridge-Channel Mountain. It is devoid of vegetation and covered in snow throughout the four seasons.

Mount Huguan rises three hundred and eighty leagues north of Guguan Mountain. Common jade and green jade are plentiful on both its southern and northern faces. Wild horses range in great numbers. The Huguan River originates here before flowing into the sea. Many tao eels swim its waters. A tree resembling the willow grows on this mountain. Red markings vein its trunk.

Trekking north along rivers that stretch for more than 500 leagues and through desert sands that cover nearly 300 leagues, you will eventually arrive at Huan Mountain. Its peak is rich in gold and jade. There are three mulberry trees on this mountain. They stand hundreds of feet high, but have no branches. A hundred fruit-bearing trees also grow on Huan Mountain. Many strange vipers curl about their roots.

Three hundred leagues farther north is the last mountain of this range. It is called Honest-Inscription Mountain. There is no vegetation here, but an abundance of gold and jade.

Altogether, seventeen mountains are described in the second part of *Pathways Through the Northern Mountains*. Beginning with Guancen Mountain and ending at Honest-Inscription Mountain, 5,690 leagues are traversed. The gods that live here have the body of a snake and a human face. A cock and a pig must be used in sacrificing to these deities. Once slain, hurl them at the mountain with a ceremonial jade plate and a rectangular piece of jade. No grains should be offered.

What questions today?

Question: The passage talks about sawbelly fish and that if you eat them you won't smell… what does this mean?

Answer: Ah… it's talking about the unpleasant smells that our bodies exude occasionally… like sweaty armpits.

Question: What's heatstroke?

Answer: The same as sunstroke.

Question: What kind of bellyache is the passage referring to?

Answer: Diarrhoea…

Question: That bird that looks like Kuafu… is that the same Kuafu… you know… the giant who supposedly chased the sun?

Answer: You know that story?

Question: Yes… Kuafu chased the sun from east to west… as he did so, he grew thirsty and ended up drinking the Yellow River dry… he drank the Wei River, too, and then drained the northern marshes… but that was still not enough, and he died of thirst… then, where he died, well, a large grove of peach trees grew. That's that story. But in this passage it says the bird, the din looks like Kuafu… so was Kuafu a wild beast?

Answer: Yes, he was.

Question: If that's true… then why would an animal want to chase the sun?

Answer: Ahem…

The boy wanted to ask more questions, but he stopped, suddenly, as a cough gurgled up from behind them. It sounded as though a blocked pipe had finally burst open in a violent gush of water, or as though stones had been hurled into a mine shaft, only to crash into the water that evidently had flooded the deepest recesses of the mine. The student thought it had first come from his teacher, that he was upbraiding him again for some indiscretion, or he was castigating him for some error. He stared at his teacher, unable to offer a reply, but then realised the murmuring and cough were not coming from him at all.

"Did you hear that noise?" the student asked.

Apparently the teacher hadn't, and in truth, he seemed a little annoyed at the question, demonstrating his anger by walloping the boy over the head with his book and shouting: "Concentrate!"

At the same moment, from deeper in the cave, a gust of wind swirled around them, enveloping the shallower part of the cave in a white mist similar to a cloud. It hung leisurely for a while, and then escaped out of the entrance. Both teacher and student were stunned and stared at each other, unsure of what to do or say, and then their attention shifted to outside. The mass of air was growing larger and larger, and stretching towards the south and beginning to move off. The student gasped and turned around hurriedly to look into the inner recesses of the cave. The mountain whisperer was still lying prone on his bed, his eyes closed, his face still looking miserable and forlorn, but there was also a happiness about his face, the crinkle of a smile, perhaps. At the same time, a certain aroma arose and his torso began to shrink, followed by his limbs, his neck. The mountain whisperer lifted his shortened and still retracting arms to feel under his nose, to touch his mouth, but he could no longer detect any breath emanating from them.

This was how the mountain whisperer died.

The teacher wanted to continue the lessons from *Pathways of Mountains and Seas,* but there was no way to carry on: "Oh... we've completed four days of lessons. The remainder of the text includes *Pathways of the Southern Mountains, Pathways of the Central Mountains,* then four chapters on the regions beyond the seas, another four on the regions within the seas, and finally four chapters on the great wildernesses in all the cardinal directions. Next time... we'll look at *Pathways of the Inner Seas.*"

After the mountain whisperer died, it was decided he would be buried in the cave he called home. In truth, however, he wasn't buried at all, not in the traditional sense. The shepherd and his son simply filled in the entrance to the cave with stones and boulders, whatever they could find, sealing the corpse inside. The student, not entirely satisfied with these burial arrangements, wanted his father to have a placard prepared and then hung over the former cave opening. The shepherd and his son obliged and located different types of old mountain wood to see which would be best for carving. The next issue was to decide what to write. The student turned to his teacher, asking him if he would write something to memorialise the old man. The teacher, however, was embarrassed and felt somewhat awkward at the request. The only thing he could think of was a statement of fact, that the mountain whisperer had spent these many years singing the dead off into the next world; wherever death visited, he followed soon after... but how was it that he'd lived so long, sung funeral dirges for so many, many years? That wouldn't do, not as a memorial. The teacher thought some more, racking his brains for words that would suitably memorialise the mountain whisperer. Perhaps a phrase drawn from literature, something about how he had lived his life sending the dead onto the bardo and what lay next. The problem was he had died without there being anyone to sing for him. The teacher was stumped.

"Then what should we write?" came the student's melancholic cry.

The teacher fell deeper into thought, mulling over how best to commemorate such an extraordinary life. Finally he struck on what he believed was best: This man sang mourning songs for a hundred years and more; in the end, he sang his own death.

That night, after the placard had been placed, a deluge of water issued from the cave, a torrential current that flowed down into the river that runs uphill through Qinling.

AFTERWORD

Youthfulness brings with it a certain vitality, similar to what I imagine a wild hare possesses as it spends its days bounding across the countryside, either in search of food, fleeing some ferocious predator, or perhaps just racing as it is wont to do, carefree and happy. It doesn't seem to know tiredness, nor feel the ache in its bones, no matter how hard it might run. At least, that's what I imagine. I'm past sixty now and I feel a heaviness that once wasn't there. I feel it especially when I go for mountain walks. The trail stretches out, winding its way through the mountains until I come to the halfway point and see the sign urging rest. I obey as though it were a command. And then I smoke. Naturally.

My daughter keeps telling me to stop; she chides me for smoking even more now I'm older. But I've smoked for forty years, probably a whole field's-worth of tobacco, so I don't know if I could stop. And maybe I shouldn't. In the ancient past, it was often the tribesman most adept at keeping the fires burning who was considered to be the most reliable, the most trustworthy in the whole tribe. Fire was life. Now… if that was the case, then perhaps I too have kept the faith, I've kept the fire burning, after all.

I know I'm old. I know, too, that with age comes a longing for the past, a chance to relive memories. To think of what was. These memories, of course, don't come easily, they pass by like trees on the roadside, more a blur, a fleeting shape, almost intangible. But they are there, the trees, if only visible through the smoke… the smoke giving them form itself.

This book, which in Chinese was published as *Laosheng*, meaning 'old life', emerged from these wispy trees; it curled its way up through the smoke.

My birth certificate lists my home, my *hukou*, as the village of Dongjie in Dihua Township, Danfeng County, Shaanxi, but in truth I was born in the town of Jinpen, about twenty-five *li* from Dongjie. As country villages go, Jinpen wasn't all that small. In 1952, it was home to a PLA garrison, which had been formed out of the guerrilla bands that had been active in southern Shaanxi prior to the Revolution. The platoon commander was my maternal uncle, and they were stationed in what used to be the home of a former landlord by the name of Li. My mother's sister had invited her – and her sizeable stomach – to live with her in the army compound. Nineteen days later, in heavy rain that seemed to pour from the heavens with a vengeance, I was born.

In those days, Dihua was gripped with fervour for land reform, and I learnt much later that my family received quite a bit of land. My uncle, my father's eldest brother, was a political activist, quite an enthusiastic one at that, and it wasn't long before he was recruited to be a Party cadre in the town. As a result, my childhood years were filled with stories about the activities of Shaanxi's guerrilla troops before the Revolution, and the early efforts at land reform when I was very small.

When I was thirteen, I finished elementary schooling. The plan was for me to travel some fifteen *li* away to attend middle school, but before I could, the Cultural Revolution erupted and I had little choice but to drop out and start farming with the rest of my family. Two factions emerged in Dihua, both committed to the Cultural Revolution, but each often in conflict with the other. I witnessed these conflicts first-hand: those arguing that reason (*wendou*) should be used to further the revolution, and others advocating coercive, physical violence (*wudou*). Later, my father, who was a teacher, was accused of being a counterrevolutionary. Therefore I became known as a child of one of the five enemies of the people – landlords, rich peasants, counterrevolutionaries, bad elements and rightists. I learnt then of the hypocrisy of the world. And, moreover, I experienced what it meant for simple farmers to live under the dictatorship of the proletariat, the strictness by which they would be forcibly reformed and become unified in thought and action.

Afterwards, by chance, I was presented with the opportunity to travel to Xi'an, and then to work, and write. For more than ten years I spent time in the region's highest mountains, walking through its deepest valleys. And then that was over. The Reform and Opening-Up period began. It was unlike anything that had come before; it was as though the heavens had been turned upside down. And I went with the ups and downs until I arrived here, an old man.

This is my past, my life of sixty years, my fate. However, I often think about how I ended up with this life, this destiny. From one mountain to the next, there's a path that stretches behind me, but when I stop for a moment under the sun and look back at what has brought me here, all I can see, or rather all that's left, is the shadow of my footprints; I can't really see from where I've come. Perhaps that's by design, my shadow is just my tail, busily wiping clean any and all traces of my passage through this world; or might we say that fate leaves no trace whatsoever? If that were true, then it wouldn't matter if the road was real or imaginary, it would still be a road, a path we've travelled. My only concern, then, would be whether or not I walked it. That is, did I even come by any such road, real or imagined?

Three years ago, I returned to Dihua, on the eve of the lunar New Year. I visited my ancestors' graves and lit a lantern to remember them. This is an important custom in the countryside, and if lanterns aren't lit for some graves, it means there is no one left in the family to light them. I remember kneeling down in front of them, lighting a candle, and then the darkness that hung around me grew even denser. It seemed as though the only light in the entire world was the one emanating from the small candle I held. But… my grandfather's visage, my grandmother's too, as well as the forms of my father and mother, they were all so clear! There in the darkness, I could see them.

We always curse the darkness and blame it for obscuring the world in front of us, for preventing us from seeing things clearly. In the distant past, the world and everything in it was whole; it was just that we lacked the eyes to see it. On that evening I came to realise something: it's common to speak of life and death as being *somewhere*. We have heaven, we have hell, but that night, I understood both life and death inhabit the *same* place. We should acknowledge and appreciate that we come from *somewhere* – a place – that's where our first breath comes from, from there we draw our lives. And when death comes to call, it is to *somewhere* we escape to and that becomes our grave, our resting place. Everything comes from this *somewhere* and the many vagaries of life happen in its vicinity, special things, too, we're born here and then when we die, we cross over to the other side, or we're born on the other side and cross over here… to somewhere… and in such cases, it means our first breath comes from the other side… and we float to here… are reborn here… we leave the bardo and return to it, only to be born again, over and over. The place where my ancestors are buried isn't all that far from the town. It's on the slope of a mountain, one used for grazing cattle. It's not only my family that's buried on this slope, but numerous others as well. The mountain is important to my family and many others, to my hometown it's sacred. You could also say that it is from this Oxhead Mountain that we're born, and it is to it that we return. It's a sort of acupuncture point, I suppose, a place where *qi* emanates, clear and yet opaque, auspicious and yet fiendish. Can you imagine how many lives have come barrelling out of it, the many sounds and colours into this world?

From Dihua I returned to Xi'an and for a long time I remained silent, uncommunicative, often shut up in my study doing very little, except for smoking. And there, in those clouds of tobacco that blanketed my study and swirled about my head, I recalled the past decades, time seemed to flutter by, unstable, fleeting, surging in great waves of reminisce… the changes wrought on society over the past hundred years, the wars, the chaos, the droughts and famines, revolution, political movements upon movements, then the reforms and to a time of relative plenty, of safety, of people living *as* people. Then my thoughts drifted to my grandfather and what he had done with his life. I wondered how he had lived, and how his son had come into this world, my father and his life, and the lives of the many townspeople from the place we called home. My thoughts turned… churned… and brought me to the present, to my life and my future, to my children and grandchildren and the lives they lived… the lives they would live in the days to come, would this be what brings glory, honour and respect to life, or would it bring shame and sin? There had been so many changes, the vicissitudes of life lived, the ebb and flow, without end, so much came to me, especially when I closed my eyes, then everything seemed to unwind in front of me, even those things I didn't wish to think about… my mind raced from things I had spoken of many times before, to things I didn't want to talk about. To think of something is to be able to talk about it, and much of this stuff I'd written in my books, but for those things I'd not thought of before, had not spoken about before, I was sixty now… a not insignificant moment in one's life… and I thought, how could I not have thought and spoken of these things before now!

All of this… this is what *The Mountain Whisperer* was for, that was its intent.

When I began this book, the words flowed easily from my hand; I was in my element. In those early days, I never once thought that I would become so bogged down, so sluggish as though some unseen agent was plotting against me, preventing me from finishing. Three times I put my pen down, unable to continue. I strained and tortured myself trying to find a means by which local history could return to literature, how narrative could grow in the spaces between words. The story I wanted to tell needed a certain form of elasticity, a certain flavour, but it was proving difficult to get what was in my mind down on the page in front of me. During this struggle, I found myself thumbing through *Pathways Through the Mountains and Seas*, an old favourite I'd been returning to more and more frequently these past few years. Now, it is also true that *Pathways* is fixated on geography, on numerous mountain ranges, on rivers flowing into other waterways, on the flora and fauna that supposedly populated these multiple and varied terrains; but looked at from a different perspective, one can see the book is about the entirety of China itself. The mountains and rivers the book describes still exist, it's just that, perhaps, the ancient world was inhabited by many more fantastical creatures, amazing and terrifying in all their beauty, nestled among equally fantastical trees and mountains. Or perhaps the fantasy has not left us altogether. After all, there is still much of wonder in nature; the animals, birds, fish, insects, flowers and trees can still make us gasp in surprise.

There are many myths in *Pathways Through the Mountains and Seas*; you could say it was a time of myths. Or perhaps the book is being truthful, who's to say? As for the stories we tell today, might later generations look back on our tales and regard them as rather simple, basic? While reading *Pathways*, I took many trips to Qinling. The best aspect of Xi'an is its proximity to Qinling. An hour's drive gets one into the mountains, and the mountains themselves are as deep as the sea. Across the many ridges one can see numerous, small thatched cottages, places that would take the better part of a day to reach, perhaps longer. There are about a thousand men residing in the mountains, devoting themselves to spiritual endeavours. Qinling attracts them, you see, it always has, perhaps always will.

On one trip, I called on such a man. He'd been living in a mountain cave for more than five years, and while he didn't refuse my visit, he wasn't altogether welcoming, either. In fact, it was more that he ignored me as though I were some small, wild creature skittering about, or a wisp of cloud blowing through on the wind. I remember he sat at the entrance to his cave, unmoving, his eyes transfixed on the far-off horizon, on the countless number of mountains and peaks strewn disorderly towards the edge of the Earth. I asked him if he was looking out to the setting sun, but he said he wasn't, it was the river he was looking at. I was surprised at his answer, and responded with another question: "But alongside the rivers and deep down in the valleys, your eyes are directed towards the tops of the mountains. How can you see anything else?" He told me then that all the rivers began there, high up in the mountains. Once again, his answer stunned me, and when I returned home later that day, I took brush to paper and started painting.

Each time I write a new novel, I paint a wall scroll, accompanied by calligraphy, as a way to further stimulate my mind, to encourage myself as it were. On this occasion, the title of the painting I produced was 'Traversing the Mountains and Streams'. The rivers in my picture didn't flow through valleys as I had often painted before. No, in this work they gushed forth violently from the mountain peaks, just as the old hermit had told me.

Not long after, I found myself in Qinling again. This time I paid a visit to another old man who lived in the area, someone whom I knew well, a family relative. He told me a great deal about the hermit, about how he was incredibly well known throughout the region. In the six or seven hamlets that dotted the hills, he was held in particularly high regard, accorded a certain prestige and respect. He was also famed these past dozen years or so for his services on both happy and sad occasions. In fact, so valued was his skill at handling such affairs, that even though his legs had more or less failed him and it had become increasingly difficult to trek up and down the mountains, this didn't stop feuding families from sending men to come and collect him in a sedan chair so that he could preside over the dispute and seek a resolution.

When I next saw him, I asked how he'd earned such respect among the villagers, how he'd acquired such a reputation for rectitude. He simply replied that he'd only said what was just and right. His answer prompted another question from me: How could he so easily see what was just and right? His answer stuck with me: A man lacking in selfish bias cannot be wrong, even if he were to commit a mistake. At this point, I recognised this man as my teacher. After all, weren't the stories I wrote my own particular experience of being? About good moral conduct? Not long after, I picked up my pen again and continued with *The Mountain Whisperer*. It was the fourth start, but unlike the previous ones that ended up with me putting down my pen, I didn't encounter any more writer's block. Three months later, the manuscript was complete.

Four stories constitute *The Mountain Whisperer*, each of them focusing on a different period in the past. Interspersed within the stories are sections taken from *Pathways Through the Mountains and Seas*, which records the history of the mountains and waterways, as I mentioned above. *The Mountain Whisperer* does much the same; it records the history I had seen, heard about and experienced first-hand. The former book begins by describing first the hills, and then the rivers. *The Mountain Whisperer* starts with certain towns and the vagaries of history in which the locals are enmeshed. *Pathways* limns geography, my book describes people.

From one perspective, it could be said that literature is a form of memory, which means it's intimately connected to our lived experiences. Should an author, say, wish to write in a highly realistic way, then special care needs to be taken to ensure that connection to lived experiences is as accurate as possible. However, memory doesn't always work that way; in truth, it's more likely that it pits me against you, my memories failing to mesh with yours. When literature narrativises memory, it is representing life, and this representation must determine how things are written. In *The Mountain Whisperer*, I grapple with the connections between people and society, people and the physical world around them, people and people, which are all very complicated and entangled relationships; some are pure and warm, others are confused and filled with bitterness, and even more are riddled with cruelty, bloodiness, ugliness and great absurdity.

I know this all seems very remote, or at least something that is gradually growing distant. It's in our character to easily forget the bad when good circumstances are visited on us. Wealth can make people think less of the times when they had to grasp at straws, at anything and everything just to keep going, but over these past many decades, this is how we've lived, this is how we've come to be here, this is our background. We've grown from bitter soil into bitter vegetables. *The Mountain Whisperer* consciously grapples with these things, with the circumstances of the nation, the world and the people who reside in it.

It's not important for me to look upon history with a certain form of jocularity, although this type of narration and the means by which it presents the real does have the habit of returning in different guises, intentional or not. In the recent past when famine struck, elm bark and corn husks were used as meat substitutes; they looked like meat, too, but were they really? The vegetarian restaurants you now find in most temples don't sell real vegetarian fare, or at least, that is one way of looking at it for they often use tofu and radishes and mould them into chicken strips with a pork-like flavour, so while Buddhism pays particular attention to not destroying what lives – that is, they don't wish to kill with their hands – you could say that in their hearts they are committing murder, and isn't that perhaps even more against the law? When writing reality, an author needs to be sincere, but nowadays that is often done by means of mirthful banter, or ridiculing the real and adorning their stories with a decorated reality, which means sincerely arriving at a real representation of life is increasingly difficult. To truly confront the real, we need to be genuine, and that genuineness situates us in what is real.

What an author writes will always be different from other writers; we each take our own paths to build the worlds we present in the form of a narrative. Like building a fire, the more wood is added to the blaze, the higher the flames. But the deeper the water flows, the more tranquil its surface. Flames lick and burn, they consume fuel voraciously. People and wild beasts can be seen clearly in the flames, and upon close inspection the ripples in the sea can suggest the true depth of the water, but it is only the boatman who really knows what to look for.

I once saw the paintings of Qi Baishi in Beijing. At first, people sneered at his whimsical approach and considered it much inferior to his contemporaries, but many years later, tastes changed and his true talent was recognised. This, in turn, led many to imitate him, but these imitators struggled with their approach: should they employ a more freehand style in what traditional aesthetics refers to as the *xieyi*, or should they use the *gongbi* style, which is more realistic, more controlled? To this dilemma, Qi Baishi had an answer: imitation had to be "somewhere between similarity and dissimilarity". Now, if this were possible, who might be able to achieve it? Where was this in-betweenness he speaks of? Perhaps only Qi Baishi could truly grasp this facet of what he had said. Another artist from an earlier era, Bada Shanren, once said that painting the real, or the five elements of metal, wood, water, fire and earth, or trying to surpass these elements and paint the fantastical, the division between the metaphysical and the natural world was just a point situated in a circle. But then, where is this circle and where is the point within it? Knowledge of this is what differentiates great art from that which is not. Gazing at a mountain is to see the mountain, and the same holds true for gazing at a river. But the opposite is also true: the mountain and the river are not what one sees, and yet they still are. The reasoning behind this only becomes apparent with age and experience; these are the two things life is brewed in.

This is why the Chinese edition is called *Laosheng*, or perhaps it's because the central character lives such a long life, or maybe I've simply borrowed a character from opera, or it's a eulogy, or a curse. Age is a thief, but not death. That is, time loathes those who hang on for far too long. From another point of view, there is the old truism which says the older people are the less they enjoy idle gossip, rumours and lies. In each story in this novel, there is a character whose name possesses the word *lao*, which means 'old'. The word for 'life', *sheng*, is also used in each story to name a central character. This was deliberate on my part. As we live, as the days pass, the sun rises to meet the Buddha, it sets to meet the devil. Wind blows until it's tired, flowers bloom and then close, these are the times we live in, we're a product of these times, which is to say the trials and tribulations we endure, the muddy paths we traverse, this is what life is.

My old hometown, Dihua, is on the southern slopes of Qinling. The sky is very blue there, and at the same time, there are often white, billowy clouds that hang in the air, like great balls drifting through the sky, or handfuls of cotton freshly picked. There are many valleys there, too, and rivers run through most of them. The water is so clean that it's perfectly safe to drink. But the greatest, deepest impression my hometown has made on me, the thing I find most difficult to imagine, are the many roads and paths that now crisscross the region, some narrow, others empty, they stretch chaotically through the mountains like a rope winding its way around nature. At times, you can't help but wonder who might've cast a net over the area, or who was holding onto the end of the rope, or its beginning, who it was that was dragging you, pulling you through the hills and valleys. As the mountain paths are revealed, so too is the character of Commander Kuang San in *The Mountain Whisperer*.

The commander is a long-lived character in the book, his later years being spent enjoying wealth and splendour, a very high position indeed. But it is the mountain whisperer who is even longer-lived than Kuang San. In Qinling I saw so many ancient trees, the cassias with large, yellowish leaves that draped down their trunks like finely woven baskets, as well as gingko trees with trunks so wide it would take four men to wrap their arms around them. I also saw the people who lived in the mountains, often busily rebuilding homes and there within their compounds planting many saplings. There are times when life can surprise and amaze you, and there are other times when it is cruel and vile. The mountain whisperer is like a spectre wafting across Qinling, decades upon decades, winding his way through the affairs of this world without obvious reason, without clear intent or form, solitarily observing the lives as lived but never delving in too deeply, never becoming too involved. Then, finally, death visits him. Everyone dies, and so too does every age. We see the world rise to great heights and then we see it fall. The mountain whisperer sang songs of mourning, and those same songs welcomed him into the netherworld.

After finishing *The Mountain Whisperer* in the winter of 2013, I locked it away in a desk drawer for six months. I didn't seek to have it published, nor would I let anyone read it. I smoked, and the clouds of burning tobacco wafted around my head. I didn't know what to think of the book I'd written. Were there parts that I simply had to write, other parts I should've left alone, or were there still parts I hadn't yet included? What can be remembered is what's etched in one's mind, and one shouldn't easily tamper with these things. But should you write these things down on the page, it does come with a certain feeling of relief, as well as a feeling of anguish. Reflecting on *The Mountain Whisperer* engulfed in my smoke-filled room, opaque within the haze, it is both about the past revolution, and also my farewell to it. The land is suffused with faeces, but its foul odour is not carried on the wind. The faeces, moreover, serves to nourish the land, enriching and enhancing the farmers' yields. On this planet we call home, there is no mother to curse and complain about the difficulties of childbirth. They do not begrudge the excruciating pain of bringing a child into this world; rather they see it as a blessing, a great fortune.

Therefore, on 21 March 2014, according to the Gregorian calendar, what would have been the twenty-first of the second month on our old Chinese calendar, I celebrated my birthday. *The Mountain Whisperer* was my birthday present. I completed this afterword on the same day.

GLOSSARY

dan
unit of weight, equivalent to one hundred *jin*

feng shui
literally, wind and water, energy forces intended to harmonise individuals with their surrounding environment

jin
unit of weight, also known as *catty,* equivalent to about half a kilogram

kang
bed built of mud bricks

li
unit of distance, about half a kilometre

lingzhi
a kind of mushroom valued for its medicinal properties

mu
unit of area, ten *mu* equals about 1.6 acres

qi
also written *ch'i,* vital energy, life force

yuan
unit of currency

ABOUT THE AUTHOR

Born in 1952, Jia Pingwa stands with Mo Yan and Yu Hua as one of the biggest names in contemporary Chinese literature. He has a huge following on the Chinese mainland, as well as in Hong Kong and Taiwan. His fiction focuses on the lives of common people, particularly in his home province of Shaanxi, and is well-known for being unafraid to explore the realm of the sexual. His bestseller *Ruined City* was banned for many years for that same reason, and pirated copies sold on the street for several thousand yuan apiece. The novel was finally unbanned in 2009, one year after Jia won the Mao Dun Award for his 2005 novel *Shaanxi Opera*. Over recent years, a steady stream of his works have been published in English translation.

ABOUT THE TRANSLATOR

Christopher Payne has co-translated the award-winning novels *Decoded* and *In the Dark* by Mai Jia, and along with his frequent collaborator, Olivia Milburn, he's also brought Jiang Zilong's magnum opus, *Empires of Dust*, to an English-language audience. Christopher holds a PhD in Chinese literature from the School of Oriental and African Studies at the University of London, and he has spent more than a decade teaching at postsecondary institutions, most notably Sungkyunkwan University in Seoul, South Korea, and the University of Manchester in the UK. In 2020 he took up a position at the University of Toronto, where he has continued to champion Chinese literature in the English-speaking world.

ABOUT **SINO**IST BOOKS

We hope you enjoyed Jia Pingwa's allegorical story of a funeral singer who gives a deathbed account of rebellion and revolution in the countryside of Shaanxi.

SINOIST BOOKS brings the best of Chinese fiction to English-speaking readers. We aim to create a greater understanding of Chinese culture and society, and provide an outlet for the ideas and creativity of the country's most talented authors.

To let us know what you thought of this book, or to learn more about the diverse range of exciting Chinese fiction in translation we publish, find us online. If you're as passionate about Chinese literature as we are, then we'd love to hear your thoughts!

sinoistbooks.com
@sinoistbooks